The Pillars of the House; Or, Under Wode, Under Rode, Volume II

by Charlotte M. Yonge

Copyright © 6/22/2015
Jefferson Publication

ISBN-13: 978-1514658369

Printed in the United States of America

Contents

CHAPTER XXIV.

FAMILY GHOOLS.

'Know ye that Love is a careless child,
And forgets promise past?
He is blind—he is deaf where he list,
And in faith never fast.'
Raleigh.

Captain Harewood was gone. There was a good deal of truth in Wilmet's plea that much pain might have been saved if she had been allowed to abide by her first answer; but by this time she would not have saved it.

She was a brave woman, and never sought indulgence; and all she accepted was the spending his last Saturday and Sunday at his home with him; and even on this she durst not venture without taking Alda, and exposing the dear untidy household to her disdain; but that October Sunday walk by the river was worth it all—worth infinitely more than the July walk; and they both declared it gave them strength.

Wilmet returned in time for Monday's school, nor did she give in all the week; but she looked whiter and whiter, and on Saturday morning turned so faint while dressing, that Alda in a great fright called in Sibby; and the unprecedented event occurred of her spending two whole days in bed. She only begged to be let alone; and after this space of quiet came down again fully recovered, only, as Geraldine daily felt, softer, gentler, tenderer, less severely strict, and moreover a less hard mistress to her own beauty.

Meantime Alda grew increasingly restless and drooping as the autumn advanced. The confined rooms and monotonous life really affected health accustomed to variety, change, and luxury; nor could idleness, disappointment, or ill-humour be wholesome diet. Listless and weary, she dropped all semblance of occupation, except novel reading; and there she perversely set her mind on whatever Froggatt and Underwood wished to keep out of their library. If Ferdinand did come down for a Sunday, they both looked at the end of it as if they had been worrying one another to death; if he did not come down, she was affronted and miserable. Her restlessness was increased by the fact that people were returning to their winter-quarters in London, and it was to be inferred that the Thomas Underwoods might soon be there; but Marilda had not the art of letter-writing, and though she had several times sent a few warm-hearted lines, encouraging Alda's correspondence, this had dropped soon after the yearly migration to Spa; and no more was known of the family movements till there was a letter from Edgar to Cherry. He was a very uncertain correspondent—always delightful, affectionate, and amusing, when he did write, but often not doing so for weeks together; and nothing had been heard of him since he had as usual gone abroad in the middle of the summer.

He now wrote from Spa, in amazement at the accumulation of family events which Marilda had poured upon him, and especially desirous to know how *any* captain of any service had ventured upon accosting W.W. He could not recover the loss it had been not to witness the siege and the surrender! For himself, Cherry gathered that he had begun, as he had led her to suppose he would, with the Channel Isles; but whether he had seen Alice she could not make out; and he had then made his way, wandering and sketching in old Continental towns, as he had done last year. He always declared that it answered; he could dispose of his sketches when he came home, and could likewise write clever bright descriptions, that could usually command tolerable remuneration. This time, however, he had been nearly reduced to the condition of George Primrose, and had made his way to join the family caravan at Spa, by way of getting helped home.

There he was hailed with delight, for Mr. Underwood was very unwell and irritable, prejudiced against German doctors, yet not choosing to have advice from England, and not fit for a journey without some effective person to rule him and his wife; for resolute as Marilda could be, the passionateness of one parent, and the fat flabby helplessness of the other, had overcome her powers of management at such a distance from home. It was Edgar's private belief that 'the poor old boy had had some kind of stroke;' but he had recommended the homeward journey, and under his escort it was to be immediately undertaken. A few days more, and tidings came that it had been successfully accomplished. Mr. Underwood had grown better at every stage, and now scouted the notion of a doctor; Alda's letters of inquiry were joyously answered and her spirits sank.

One afternoon, however, a moon face beamed upon Felix, and a hearty voice exclaimed, 'How d'ye do? This is a surprise, ain't it? My father is come down on business, so I made him bring me. I don't like Alda's account of herself.'

'I'll take you to her,' said Felix, who decidedly disapproved of private greetings in the present locality; so as soon as she had dealt with her fly, he conducted her upstairs. Her father had gone to Mr. Bruce, and would come for her. Alda was alone in the drawing-room, but she sprang to her feet in ecstacy; and the two cousins were soon clinging together, and devouring one another with kisses. Felix asked where Cherry was.

'Oh! for pity's sake, Felix, do let us have a little time to ourselves!' said Alda; 'I'll call Cherry by the time she has done with Stella.'

Felix had come to trust nothing concerning Geraldine to Alda; so he shut the door, and found Cherry in her own room, overlooking Stella's copy to the sound of Theodore's accordion, all three in warm jackets. Six months ago he would have made an authoritative remonstrance. Now he had learnt that cold and exile were more tolerable than Alda's displeasure.

Stella leapt up, connecting Cousin Marilda's name with the choicest presents; but Cherry was quite willing to withhold herself. It was eight years since she had seen Marilda, and she was conscious of more repulsion than attraction. She was still debating between civility and consideration for the tête-à-tête, when Wilmet, for whom Felix had sent, came for her, with cheeks glowing from Marilda's energetic kisses and congratulations.

There certainly was a treading on the delicate tips of the feelings. 'O Geraldine, I am glad to see you getting about so well! You are a courageous girl.' Then to Stella: 'You little darling duck! Here is a box of goodies for you and the other poor little dear.—Where is he? You'll let me see him.—What, Lance! I've not seen you since I found you up a tree!'

The cousinly cordiality was pleasant, and her patronage was not coarse, like her mother's; but there was a certain excess of frankness that made them feel like sensitive-plants, when she examined Wilmet how often she heard from India, and how the Harewoods treated her— when she wanted to know exactly how matters stood between the Pursuivant and Tribune, whether Mr. Smith were to blame, why Lance had gone into the business, and—worse than all—what was the measure of Theodore's intellect.

It was all meant in kindness and sympathy, but it was very trying to each victim in turn; and the lookers-on found it as impossible to lead it away as to divert the rush from a pump. When Felix was about to return to his work, Marilda jumped up, exclaiming, 'Felix, I must speak to you;' and when she had him alone in the drawing-room, she began, 'Felix, I must take Alda home. We can't get on without her; and she looks very poorly, and all that nonsense is blown over.'

'You know she is still engaged.'

'Oh yes; but no one will think of that unless it is brought forward, and that she promises not to do.'

'I believe it will be best,' he answered. 'Our life is not suited to her, and she is neither well nor happy; but it is very kind of you.'

'Kind to ourselves. If Wilmet had married at once we should never have got her back at all, and we want her sadly. I can help my father in some ways, but I can't amuse him as she can. You don't mind?'

'Certainly not, if Mr. and Mrs. Underwood wish it,' said Felix, wondering how Alda made herself either amusing or useful; 'I suppose it is all right, and that they know how it stands.'

'Of course they do. They will only be too glad to have her; and though it is better to say nothing about it just yet, very likely it may end in his coming into our house, and being what Edgar might have been. How well he has behaved!'

'So has some one else,' thought Felix, as he saw her glistening eye; but he only answered, 'He is an excellent fellow.'

'Another thing, Felix. This engagement of Edgar's—is it in earnest?'

'Yes!' emphatically said Felix; 'I trust so.'

'You! I should have thought nothing could be more foolish. Is she such a nice girl, then?'

He had had time to recollect himself, and answered in his set manner, 'She is all that could be wished; and though of course there is a certain imprudence in the engagement, I can only wish to see Edgar persevere honourably in what he has undertaken.'

'But wouldn't it be great misery?'

'It might be,' said Felix; 'but it is not going to happen yet. Of course, no one could have wished it to begin; but having begun, he ought to go on.'

'Of course! I hate shilly-shally. My father would not believe there was anything in it. But you are right, Felix; it has done Edgar good. Somehow there's more purpose in him; and I believe he has worked more steadily this season. I am so glad you say she is a nice girl.'

And Felix went down to his work happier than he had been for nearly a year. What loss to himself equalled the gain of such a report of Edgar?

Marilda insisted on being shown every corner of the house, and was evidently full of enjoyment, like a child let loose from school, talking at random, so as to draw on herself more than one remonstrance from Alda, who had perfectly recovered her good-humour, and was absolutely gracious to Cherry.

About four o'clock came Thomas Underwood, embracing Alda like another daughter. 'My poor child, you are not looking well.'

'Not at all, papa,' said Marilda. 'We will take her home, and set her up again.'

'Ay, we will!' said her father. 'It has been a pretty muddle altogether; but there—we'll say no more about it. You'll come home, and be a wise girl.'

'O Uncle, how kind you are!' cried Alda.

Wilmet and Cherry looked at each other in amaze. What might this mean? How could Alda bear to be received back on such terms? But they could say nothing; indeed, they were scarcely seen till the greeting to Alda was over. Then, however, he made up for it by hearty kisses, for which they were not prepared; and Wilmet coloured crimson as she was again congratulated and rallied on her slyness in making the most of her time at Minsterham.

The illness at Spa had told upon Thomas Underwood. He was still under fifty, but an elderly look and manner had come on him; he walked feebly, and seemed to look to his daughter to help him out with purposes and recollections; while towards Alda there was an almost imploring tenderness, as if she had carried away with her a good deal of the enjoyment of his life, which he hoped to bring back again with her. He did not even seem to like leaving her for the evening to pack up, but wanted her to come out to Centry Park, and caught eagerly at Marilda's proposal that Felix should come and spend the evening there. It was as if they were both afraid of their own dullness in the great uninhabited house; and no doubt they would have caught at an invitation to share the family meal. Alda and Wilmet, for different reasons, sat in dread of Felix, in the reckless hospitality of the male heart, making such an offer; and in very truth, he was only withheld by certain authoritatively deprecating glances from those housewifely eyes.

And let it be observed that Wilmet was right. She could not have fed Mr. Underwood as would have suited him on such short notice, without a great deal more expense and personal exertion than would have been becoming; and to his eyes, their ordinary fare would have seemed ostentation of neediness.

Needy was exactly what the Underwoods had never been. It was not merely the effect of conscience and of resolution, but of Wilmet's more than ordinary power of method and adjustment, which had kept them from ever being behindhand, or in difficulties requiring external aid; and it was this that had won them already respect that hardly belonged to their years.

Thomas Underwood really respected Felix, as one who had never asked assistance from him, yet who had not declined what was offered in a friendly kinsman-like manner; and besides, had more than once asserted—modestly indeed, but still asserted—an independent will and way of his own, and shown that he was capable of carrying it out. It was five years since Mr. Underwood's prediction that he would find the attempt keeping house for such a family an utter failure, and would have to fall back on help he had not deserved: and here he was, without having made one demand, a partner in the business, and with so small a fraction of the family apparent, that there was no air of oppression, no complaint, even though Thomas himself had returned on his hands both those of whom he had meant to relieve him.

No wonder, then, that without intending it, his manner to Felix was not that of patron, but of equal—of kinsman to kinsman, not of rich man to struggling youth. And Felix, as he sat in the great handsome dining-room, could not help being amused at all the state that had followed one man and his daughter for one dinner in their own house: the courses, and the silver, and the perplexing family of wine-glasses beside every plate, and all with the Underwood rood and its motto shining on him—whether on the servant's buttons, on the panels of the oak-wainscotted hall, and the very china from which he ate his dinner.

Nothing interested Mr. Underwood more than the account of the visit to Vale Leston; and warming up under the influence of dinner, he talked much of the old times there, and with much disparagement of the two present Fulberts; but Felix was startled to find that he regarded himself as next in the succession.

'If you could only have gone into the Church, Felix, I could have given you the Vicarage. Or is not one of your brothers to be a parson?'

'Yes, Sir—Clement,' said Felix, smiling, but feeling a sense of injury that revealed to him how much more he must be reckoning on the chances than he had supposed himself to be doing. As Alda said, wealth flowed to wealth; and a little attention from Thomas to his cousins would easily turn the scale.

At any rate, poverty did not suit Alda. She was a different creature now that her exile was coming to an end.

'It had been like Portsmouth to Fanny Price,' said Geraldine, not greatly flattered by the overflow of benevolence, which Wilmet accepted as the token of real affection.

What would she do about Ferdinand? Wilmet ventured to ask.

'He certainly must not call,' said Alda; 'that would never do; but with Edgar's help it will be manageable enough. It will do the gentleman no harm to have a few difficulties in his way. I don't want him to feel his coming such a favour.'

So Alda went; and must it be owned, if there was more peace in the house, there was also a certain flatness after the incessant excitements of the former part of the year. At least so Geraldine felt, and hated herself for feeling, when the numbers had come down to 'the peace establishment,' and she had no companions but Stella and Theodore through the greater part of the day. She had been recommended to walk, when the weather permitted, for half an hour every day; and whenever it was possible, Felix contrived that he or Lance should be her companion; but as the days shortened, and it became less easy to contrive this, the constitutional turns up and down the narrow garden were more dispiriting than sitting occupied upstairs, especially when she viewed this distaste as frightful unthankfulness; and even when one of the brothers took her out in the street, or to the 'People's Park,' though she was happy with them, the wearisome sameness and dull ugliness of the town oppressed and wearied her; and to be taken out by Wilmet on a Saturday was more wearing still. Each brother was her devoted cavalier; but Wilmet, though kind and considerate, made airing Cherry a secondary object; and to be set upon a high chair in a shop, to see Wilmet bargain, was what she did not love. She might have admired to see Wilmet's perfect knowledge of articles and their value, and the manifest esteem in which that experience was held by the respectable tradesmen, who did not scruple to tell her that they had thought 'this will just suit Miss Underwood;' while her scorn and indignation at an encounter with a Cheap Jack were something rich. But though Cherry could describe such an expedition with humour that threw Felix and Lance into a convulsion of merriment, it was very wearisome to her; and the more she knew it ought to be instructive, the more it depressed her, and made her feel, as never before, the straitness of the family means. She longed wearily at times for the sight of something beautiful. Edgar's descriptions came back on her with an almost sick longing. She had made much progress in drawing, but the want of criticism, instruction, or models, made her feel baffled; and when her brothers and sisters admired most, she was most dissatisfied. Edgar's criticism alone was worth anything to her æsthetic sense, and gave her real assistance; and his not coming home was a great loss to her art, as well as to her affection and intellect. Those windows that he opened to her of all lovely scenes and forms in nature or art, his brilliant stories of artist society and foreign manners, could not but be greatly missed as she lived her monotonous life, not without intellectual interest, for that came to her through the help she was able to render to Felix in his newspaper work, and the books she reviewed or discussed with him; but it was not the living interest of actual communication at secondhand with that outer world, which looked so full of beauty, and of all that was bright and charming; and then poor little Cherry applied to herself all the warnings about not loving the world.

Her aspiring compositions and her studies in drawing she almost laid aside in a fit of hopeless disgust, and she applied herself to what was less improving, but more immediately profitable. She and Lance took to the manufacture of Christmas cards, she taking the sentiment and he the comedy; and what they produced by their joint efforts were pretty and clever enough to bring in an amount of pocket-money that was very agreeable to those who otherwise would have had no claim to any.

The chief outer interest was, as usual, parish affairs. Mr. Bevan was too ill to come home; but Mr. Mowbray Smith's resignation was accepted, and he was to go at the beginning of the new year, while his successor was reported to be elderly and wise.

Another interest, that was not at all bad for Cherry, was stirred up by her brothers. There was an interminable family belonging to one of the printers, who died, leaving them in circumstances that somewhat parodied those of the Underwoods themselves; and in which the example as well as the counsel of the young master was no doubt a great incentive and assistance to the pillars of the still humbler house. There was a perennial supply of 'little Lightfoots,' to fill the office elegantly termed printer's devil; and the existing imp being taken young from school, Felix had his education on his conscience, and asked Cherry to give him lessons after hours. She was at first desperately afraid of the boy, and only accepted the work when she found that if she did not, Felix would impose it on himself; but by-and-by she became enough interested, and enjoyed enough devotion from her pupil, to make the time she daily expended upon him not far from one of the pleasures of her life.

So came on a winter of unusual bitterness; and the holidays filled the house, bringing Bernard back under an entirely new phase. At Stoneborough he had discovered that it was some distinction to be an Underwood of Vale Leston, and his accession of dignity was enormous. He regarded the Nareses from a monstrous elevation; and thus infinitely scandalized Angela, who had a great hatred of pretension, and whose laughter threatened to dissolve their mutual alliance, offensive and defensive. Their janglings were a novelty, and not a pleasant one; and one bitter afternoon, when a sore throat had made Felix come up early from the shop, Cherry quite rejoiced that Bernard was reported to be reading downstairs.

And there sat Felix by the fire, with Theodore at his feet, humming in rivalry of the big kettle, which had just been brought in, and was soon followed by Lance, whistling as he came upstairs.

'Look here!' and Angela, who, for her bane at Brompton, had her full share of the family talent for caricature, showed him a likeness of Bernard strutting down the High Street, turning his back on certain figures in the distance; and beneath was written—

'There was a young Bear of Stoneborough,
Who thought his gentility thorough;
To his townsfolk he said,
"Snobs! I'll cut them all dead,"
This high-bred young Bear of Stoneborough.'

'Capital, Angel!' said Lance; 'but don't show it to him; he's a horrid Bear to poke fun at.'

'Oh, but he does get into such jolly rages!'

'It is beyond being jolly,' said Lance. 'I did this once too often last holidays; and I don't think he has got over it yet, though I promised never to do it again.'

'The more reason I should,' said Angela, laughing saucily in his face, though both spoke under their breath.

'No,' said Lance. 'Consider! He is absurdly stuck up; but anything to disgust him with the Nareses is good.'

'I see no harm in Jem Nares,' said democratic Angela. 'I'll not have him cut! give me my picture.'

'No, I promised he should not be done again.'

'Promise for yourself another time.'

She snatched, and there was a sparring match. Lance held off with one hand, and with the other dashed her drawing into the fire, where it fell on the top of some black coals; and as he relaxed his grasp, she sprang to rescue it. Felix looked up in time to see the kettle toppling over. He flung Theodore out of the way of the boiling stream that rushed from lid and spout as the whole descended on the hearth, amid cries from Angela and Theodore that brought all the others together; nor could the little one be pacified, even though Wilmet ascertained that he had only been touched by one boiling drop.

'But Felix!' exclaimed Lance; and they all turned.

'Never mind,' he said, but with more of a contraction of the lips than a smile; 'only my neck and arm. Here, Lance, help me;' presenting the end of his sleeve, and setting his teeth.

The hasty vigorous pull, made in ignorance on both sides, removed the coat; but Felix gave something between a gasp and a cry, tried to totter to a chair, and was caught by Clement as he fainted away; so much to the terror of Lance, that in three minutes' space he had broken in on Mr. Rugg's dinner with a peremptory summons. By the time he crept into the room behind the doctor, he saw Felix on the sofa, white as a sheet, with closed eyes and drawn brow, Clement standing ready with a roll of wadding, and Wilmet, having more gently removed the shirtsleeve, regarding the injury with some perplexity, increased by the tearful Sibby's voluble counsels.

She welcomed the arrival with the anxious inquiry, 'O Mr. Rugg! I am so glad! Should the cotton touch where the skin is broken?—Here—inside his elbow and hand.'

'Broken! You have been tearing off the clothes, instead of cutting them! I thought you knew better, Miss Underwood.'

'It was my own doing,' murmured Felix, so faintly, that Mr. Rugg, with his usual roughness, scolded at his not having had some brandy at once, and then at there being none nearer than the Fortinbras Arms, whence Clement brought some in about the time that a grand butler would have taken to produce it. Felix choked at it like a child, but it brought back his strength; and Wilmet and Clement were assistants too handy to give much occasion for scolding. The shoulder and chest had suffered likewise, though partly protected by the flannel shirt.

On the patient asking how soon he might hope for the use of his arm, the gruff answer was, 'Not so soon as if you had not begun by tearing it to pieces. I can't tell. Depends on general health. May be three weeks, may be six, may be three months, before you get these places healed, if you trifle with them. Now I'll stay and see you in bed, with this arm properly settled.'

This was real kindness for a man in the middle of his dinner; and Felix stood up, finding himself more shaken than he had expected, and commanded by acclamation to betake himself to Mr. Froggatt's bedroom. He chose, however, first to go into the next room, where Cherry had sunk down, trembling and overcome, and so hysterical that her utmost powers had been taxed to prevent herself from disturbing those who could be useful.

'Here I am, all alive!' he said in a cheerful tone, that somehow had no solidity in it, and which she could hardly bear. 'Why, Cherry, you poor little thing! you have come by the worst of it!'

'Don't, Felix! Isn't it dreadful pain?'

'Not now; I scarcely feel it. Never mind, Cherry; I'm all right now, only you will have to write those little fingers nearly off.'

'Oh! Felix, if Wilmet had been gone!'

'She wouldn't be looking Gorgons at me now. Where's Angel?'

Angel had been seized by Robina, and forcibly withheld from flying out after the doctor; and when assured that Lance was gone, she had dashed upstairs, and hidden herself in bed, so that Felix was obliged to go to sleep without seeing her. Remonstrate as he would, he was not allowed to get up the next morning. Mr. Rugg, who came very early, assured him that the speed of his recovery greatly depended on perfect stillness at first, and told him that he would feel the injury if he tried to move; and Wilmet would not do anything but rejoice that he was compelled to submit to discipline that was so good for the cold, a much more real subject of anxiety.

'I must not grumble,' he sighed, as the doctor shut the door; 'but I did not reckon on such a stupid disaster when I got two boys to look after everything.'

'People will not mind for a few days.'

'I hope not. Tell Lance to send Lamb up to me as soon as he comes in. And would Clem walk over to Marshlands? or the Froggery will be in great commotion.'

'Perhaps Robina will go too; and they always like to have her.'

'And Angel? Poor child! I wish she would come.'

'I'll send her. I want you to talk to her. She is such a perplexity.'

'*This* was no fault of hers!' exclaimed Felix.

'I don't know that. Lance takes it on himself, and says it was just a squabble; but that is sure to have been her fault.'

'I shall not go into that,' said Felix.

'It does seem a chance of making an impression, if you would try,' said Wilmet. 'Sibby says she was crying half the night, (you know she has to sleep in the nursery,) and you might get at her now. I don't know what to do with her.'

He looked up, astonished at this avowal, from her who had hitherto queened it so easily.

'Look at this letter,' she proceeded. 'I have been keeping it till you had time to think about it.'

He sighed, feeling, like many another head of the house, that time was swept away from home responsibilities, and indeed, that great girls needed a more experienced guide. The letter was the school character, speaking most highly of Robina, who had quite reconquered esteem. If she had not so much of any one talent as some of the others, she had excellent capacity, and studied in a business-like way, as one learning a profession; so that she had won her promotion into the first ranks, among elder girls.

But Angela was one of those who will not or cannot do anything tolerably except what they like; and she had only two tastes—for music and fun—except perhaps for churches. She was a puzzle to every one, by her eagerness for devout observances, and the very little good they seemed to do her, even by outrageous irreverence when the spirit of mischief was roused. Teachers detested her, but she was the idol of half the school. All unclaimed misdeeds were laid to her share; and in recklessness or generosity, she never troubled herself to disavow them, even when not her own. She was popularly believed to learn nothing but music, and even in that to use talent to save pains; and she had a lead-like affinity to the bottom of her class, yet in the final examination she had surpassed far more diligent girls.

Felix read, and puzzled himself, and did not refuse obedience when Wilmet insisted that he should 'talk to Angela;' though he was only too well aware that reproof was that paternal duty to which he was least adequate. First, however, he had time to despatch Robina and Clement on their mission to his partner, whose winter rheumatics had set in—to receive young Lamb, laden with a pile of letters and papers, and lastly, to be cooed over and stroked by Theodore, who curled himself up at his feet in that perfect serenity that his presence always infused.

At last Angela came in on tip-toe, looking immensely tall and lank, with Clement's propensity for longitudinal growth, and the same infantine smallness of feature, and much less brilliant colouring than the others; but while his hair was as closely cropped as if he were just out of a cell, hers was as long and as unmanageable as herself; and she had moreover the beautiful large-pupilled, darkly-lashed, mischievous blue eyes that belonged to Edgar, only now their lids were swollen, and all the colour in her face centred in two great red patches beneath them—a scarlet garibaldi over a very old brown skirt, half-way up a long pair of grey legs, seeming to make the whole object more deplorable.

'You poor Angel!' exclaimed Felix, his heart more than ever melted; 'you look as if you had been crying all night. Why don't you come and give me a kiss?'

'I'll—I'll do anything you please, Felix, but I had rather not.'

'But I do please! I want you,' said he, holding out his hand; so that she was forced to come, touch his cheek with her lips, and submit to a far heartier kiss. 'You are as cold as ice,' he added, trying to capture the blue, chilly, long, sausage-like fingers, and warm them in his grasp.

'No, don't! it will only make my chilblains rage. Let me go, now you've forgiven me for your own comfort.'

'Forgiven you for my own comfort! I don't want to forgive you—'

'Oh—h!' and the eyes disappeared, and the face puckered in unutterable woe.

'I haven't anything to forgive you, Angel.'

'Oh, that's worse! when I've hurt you so terribly!'

'*You* didn't; you never meant it. Of course I never blamed you.'

'Then,' said Angel, trying to get away her other hand, 'why did you send for me to row me, for I don't call that forgiving.'

'I heard you were unhappy.'

'And did you think it would make me any happier to see you lying there frowning with pain?' broke out Angela, with an angry sob.

'If I frowned, it was not with pain, but because I don't know what to make of you.'

'I don't want to be made anything of!' she said pettishly. 'Wilmet told me you wanted to talk to me. I suppose that meant she ordered you! So now you've done it, let me go.'

'My dear Angel, don't you see that I am just as anxious about you as Wilmet can be? and when there is plainly something amiss—'

'Oh, it's old Ful and Fen's character of me, then?'

'It is, Angela. Perhaps it does seem taking an unfair advantage of you to catch you now; but you see I so seldom get a chance of a talk with any one; and I must do the best I can for you, you poor little ones, who, I'm afraid, haven't even the faintest recollection of our father and mother to help you.'

'I remember mamma, but after she was ill,' said Angela, probably trying not to be softened. 'But I don't think that has much to do with it. You and Wilmet mind us as much, or more, than most people's born parents. Yes, Wilmet worrits twice as much as any rational mother does.'

'That's the very thing, Angel; parents can do the thing without worrying.'

'No, I didn't say you did,' said Angela; 'you never did till this minute, and now you are *druv* to it;' and she regarded him with a certain fellow-feeling so comical, that she nearly made him laugh, though he felt sad enough.

'Have I neglected you then, Angel?'

'Oh no; I think you do just as well as most fathers. You keep us all going,' said Angela, considering; 'and you look after us and set us a good example, as people say; and isn't that all that fathers have to do?'

'My poor little sister! you just show that I cannot be really like a father to you.'

'Would a father *do* all the scolding?' asked Angela in an odd voice.

'If we still had our own, you would be coming to him to help you, and telling him freely what it is that makes things go wrong with you.'

'I'm sure,' answered the girl, 'I'd just as soon tell you, Felix, if I only knew; but there's only one thing that would do me any good, I believe.'

'And that?'

'If I could only be a Trappist.'

'A what?'

'A Trappist, or one of those *Sepolte* nuns, that never see anybody, and can't talk to their relations. Oh! I wish I was old enough to turn Roman Catholic! and then wouldn't I go and cut off this horrible hair, that is the plague and torment of my life, and never be naughty again!'

'Which do you want to be rid of most—your hair or your relations?' asked Felix, half diverted, half dismayed and wholly at a loss.

But Angela had passed the boundary of earnest now, and went on more from the heart. 'If I could but be in a real strict nunnery, it would be so nice! It would always be church. Oh! if church could but last always!'

He was more puzzled than ever at the intent yearning look that had changed the face. 'You could not keep up. It would lose effect,' he said.

'I don't know. Lots of girls much better than I—Bobbie herself—don't like long services, and get tired, but I don't. I'm safe then; I'm happy altogether. I seem to get wings inside—I could go on singing for ever. I don't want to be bad; but the instant I go out, I can't live without fun; and so they think me a horrid false hypocrite—but I'm not! Only unless I get shut up somewhere, I don't know what will become of me.'

'You must try to make your life out of church suit your life in church,' said Felix, much puzzled how to answer.

'I would, only I can't be half-and-half, and wishy-washy.'

'I don't understand.'

'Don't you? Why, if I have fun, I like to have it real fun. I can't be always drawing it mild! It is no real fun if one is to be always thinking about who will be vexed, and what's lady-like, and all that stuff!'

'But that's what life in this world is made of.'

'I know it is; so I hate life in this world, unless one could just have no conscience at all;' then, as she caught his anxious eye, she went on, trying to rattle, but with tears in her voice, and submitting to let him warm her hands all the time, 'Felix, you'd better let me go into a Sisterhood. It is the only chance for me! Thinking about being a horrid governess makes me wicked. When I'm good I do long for a

Sisterhood; and when I'm bad I want to get some great rich duke to marry me, and let me have no end of horses, and go to the races and the opera—and I don't suppose he will ever come. And I sup*pose* you are all too dull and tiresome to let me get to be a public singer! No, don't tell me to put it out of my head, for it is what I should like best—best of all!'

'Better than the duke?'

'Oh yes! for I think he would be in the way—Felix! *do* let me be a Sister! You see it is the only chance.'

'I can't, Angel; they would not accept a Sister at your age.'

'Then let me think about it *really*, Felix. Promise that it may be when I am old enough.'

'It is impossible to promise that; but I do not think I am likely to hinder you, if you then wish it, and it seems right.'

'I wish you would promise me. Look here, Felix,' and the eyes assumed a deep yearning expression; 'I always did think that if I had a dedication, like Clement, I could be as good as he is. But I don't think anything else would put the duke or the opera out of my head.'

'My dear Angel,' and Felix's eyes grew soft too, 'I could not wish anything better for you than to be such another as Sister Constance, but I do not know how you could be dedicated. Even Clement is not; he could change his mind before he is three-and-twenty. It all depends on how he goes on.'

'And if I go on well, will you let me look to it?'

'As far as may be right.'

'Only then what is the use of my going to this school, if I am not to turn governess? It only makes me worse.'

'No, Angela. It would not be right to stop your education. You must have the means of maintaining yourself. It would be against my duty to hinder that. And remember—some Sisterhoods require an endowment. You would not wish to be a burthen. You may have to work to raise means for admission; and if you are set to teach, you will need all you are learning now.'

'May I think I am preparing?'

'Yes.'

'I will, I will—I mean, I will try,' said Angela. 'O Felix! I do like you now I find you don't want me to be respectable. No, don't say something grave and prosy, for I *do* like you now; and never mind about not being one's father, for I don't believe anybody could be better to me.' And she put her face down to his and kissed him as she used when she was a baby girl; then ran away on thinking she heard some one coming.

'So,' thought Felix, as he raised himself on his sound elbow, 'the upshot of it is that I don't want her to be respectable! I hope to goodness she won't take to being like Tina—though I don't know why I should either! Poor child! I'll write to Audley about her when I can. And here comes the dear little Cherry for her hard day's work.'

With his dictation and superintendence, Geraldine was quite equal to the Pursuivant's Friday requirements; and altogether this day of rest and leisure was welcome. The sisters were much less anxious about the sore throat than if it had been in the shop! and indeed it was nearly well, and no obstacle to his being talked to and amused, to the general enjoyment, in the rare pleasure of having him at their mercy. In the afternoon came a message—'The Miss Pearsons' love, and if she could leave Mr. Underwood, would Miss Underwood step up?' Such messages were not infrequent, and this was supposed to spring from a desire to know the particulars of the accident; so that on her return Wilmet was greeted with the inquiry whether she was considered responsible for the tea-kettle's misbehaviour, since she had been kept in so long.

'No,' said Wilmet, gravely. 'Run away, little ones!'

Stella alone accepted the epithet; but Wilmet was too much absorbed in her tidings to look about in the fire-lit twilight for further victims.

'The Miss Pearsons are very much troubled by their letters from St Heliers,' she said. 'Alice Knevett is actually married.'

'To Edgar?' Angela sprang up with a bound. 'Oh, what fun!'

'No, indeed,' Wilmet replied in her most repressive tone. 'It is to a Frenchman of the name of Tanneguy, in the wine trade.'

'The abominable girl!' cried Angela at the top of her indignant voice. 'A Frenchman! I'll never believe in any one again.'

'Yes, Angela,' said Wilmet; 'it is a lesson, indeed, of what tricks and subterfuges—'

'Never mind that, Mettie,' disrespectfully broke in Cherry, who had quietly moved a curtain so as to cast a shade over Felix's face. 'Tell us about it. Who writes?'

Wilmet told that Major Knevett, in a storm of fury, had written to the aunts that the whole affair had been so secretly conducted, that neither he nor his wife had guessed at it until his daughter's sudden disappearance, only sending home a letter to announce her marriage to M. Achille Tanneguy, with whom she had embarked for Havre, and given an address at Pau, where her husband was concerned in a wine agency. Major Knevett had then found out that she had been in the constant habit of meeting this Tanneguy in the garden of their next neighbour, which joined to their own; and that she had entirely eluded the vigilance of 'her second mother,' who had, however, never ceased to warn and watch her; but nothing had been capable of curing her of the coquetry and intrigue, with which in his passion he accused Bexley of inspiring her.

'Too true.' The words were breathed on the back of a sigh suppressed with difficulty.

'Nonsense, Felix,' said Wilmet; 'It was in her before, or she could not have so carried it on here. I am sure it had gone on at her horrible school!'

'What has she done about Edgar?' asked Clement.

'The aunts doubt whether she has done anything.—Children, you ought to be getting ready for tea;' then when Robin and Angel had obeyed this very broad hint—'I would not say so before them, but they believe that there is a sort of excuse in the unhappiness of her home.'

'Of course,' said an almost grateful voice from the pillow.

'Ever since Edgar was there in the summer,' said Wilmet, 'she has been doubly watched and teased and scolded. Nothing she could do was right. The aunts heard from her last a fortnight ago, very miserable, and entreating them to believe that whatever might happen, she was driven to it by the unbearable wretchedness of home.'

'Do you call that an excuse, Wilmet?' exclaimed Clement. 'Is the privilege of suffering to be made an excuse for treachery?'

'Much Clement knows of the privilege of suffering,' said Felix, low and quietly; but Geraldine detected so much of that privilege in his voice, that she longed to clear the room for him; but though she rose to set the example, and laid her hand on Clement's arm, there was no preventing his testimony from being delivered.

'Personally I do not know it; but I do not understand Wilmet's lowering her standard to excuse disobedience and unfaithfulness.'

'Come along, Clem,' entreated Geraldine; 'it is all most sad and grievous, but the more we say about it the worse we make it;' and she succeeded in dragging him out without a defensive reply from Wilmet.

Presently she was sought out by Wilmet herself, to say, 'Cherry, do you know, there's Felix looking as pale as when he fainted yesterday.'

She could believe it; but she only ventured to ask, 'Did he say anything?'

'No, only to answer "No," when I asked if I hurt him as I was *doing* his arm. Cherry, can you tell me, or do you know—does this touch him for himself?'

Cherry could only look up with eyes swimming.

'How blind I have been! Oh! if I had not come and told it so abruptly, before every one!'

'Perhaps he liked the unconsciousness better!'

'Were you in his confidence, or is it guess?'

'Guessing at first; but we had a very few words about it when he came home from consulting Dr. Lee last summer.'

'Then it was that wretched child that hurt his health?'

'So we thought. Dr. Lee asked him if there was not something on his mind.'

'The little wretch! Oh! if I had never asked her here! she has done more harm than she is worth!'

'He had got quite well,' said Cherry; 'and now he has his cough back again. O Mettie!'

'No,' said Wilmet, 'it is not *that* cough. It is only a chance cold; it is nearly gone. Besides, it cannot be the same as her first treason to him must have been.'

'That's true,' said Cherry, mournfully.

'After all,' said Wilmet, 'it *is* a happy escape for both our boys, if they can but feel it, poor fellows—but oh! to have been so deceived. And how ignorant one is—even living in the same house!' And Wilmet had a hearty fit of crying.

'And Edgar!' sighed Cherry.

'You must write. They all come to you, Cherry,' she added wistfully. 'You shall sit with dear Felix this evening, and I will keep the others away.'

This ordinance was carried out, but with no result as to conversation; for Felix's distress took the form of great tenderness as to the manner in which the blow was to fall upon Edgar. Nothing would satisfy him but Geraldine's writing immediately, under his own eye. Of course he ascribed all his own feelings to his brother; and though Cherry doubted, and could have written much better as from herself, she could but patiently write and re-write, when poor Felix found—as he did with everything that cost him consideration—that he was falling into his leading-article style; while all the time she saw him becoming more excited and flushed, till at last Wilmet came in, put an end to it, and sent her to bed, almost brokenhearted for both brothers, and struggling against her own hatred to the mischievous little witch who had played with their hearts.

She took care that the letter should go by the earliest post, partly to ensure Edgar's getting it without the Sunday's delay, but still more that it might not be within Felix's power to recall for two whole days. He just inquired after it, and finding it was gone, said no more. He was not so anxious to get up as the day before; his arm had come to a more painful stage, and he had had a feverish sleepless night; so that he looked so worn and depressed, that Mr. Rugg concluded that he had been imprudent, and scolded him accordingly.

When Geraldine came in to put the finishing strokes to the Pursuivant, she found him so silent and dreamy, that she did nearly the whole on her own responsibility; till at last he suddenly roused himself, begged her pardon, and gave his whole mind to the dictation of the political summary; then became dreamy again, and presently fell into a long sound sleep, after which he looked, even to the anxious eyes of his sisters, much better, and began to talk of getting up for the evening.

At about five o'clock, just as Wilmet was laying his things ready for him, the door was opened, and there entered first a perfume of tobacco, the next a lively voice—'What, Blunderbore, lying in state in Froggy's four-poster! Whom have you been getting into hot water with? Is there much the matter?' he added in a lower tone, as Wilmet kissed him.

'Not much,' said Felix; 'it is nothing but a scald in a disabling place on my arm.'

'The tea-kettle ought to know its friends better. I met Jem Bruce and heard of it, so I ran down to see how much of you was boiled. I looked into the shop, but Master Lance was too important to vouchsafe me a word. Are you sure it is only your arm, old fellow? you look baddish.'

'I'm well enough,' said Felix, shifting his head into the shadow of the curtain; and Wilmet, perceiving that he wished to have it out at once, left them together. 'Edgar, do you know?' said Felix, earnestly.

'I scent a crisis in the air, and am doubting whether the Pursuivant is up a tree, or Wilmet's engineer turned out no go.'

'You have not had Cherry's letter?'

11

'No. Don't torment yourself to beat about the bush. I'd stand anything rather than see you look like that.'

'Have you heard from Jersey?'

'Oh! It is that, is it? I believe it has lasted twelve calendar months, and that is as much as is reasonable to expect. Little humbugging puss! What has she taken up with?'

'Had you no idea that she had fallen in with—with a Frenchman?'

'The beggar! How far has it gone? or is it only a report from the old cats of aunts?'

'It is too certain.'

'Well, what is it? I suppose she hardly commissioned you to give me my *congé*?'

'I fear that she commissioned no one. Harsh treatment seems to have driven her to desperation. She was married privately, and has written from France to announce it.'

Edgar gave a long whistle, then turned round and laid his hand on his brother's, saying with a short laugh, 'Cool and easy! Well, it was pretty sport; and this conclusion is unique for simplicity and saving of trouble. Dear old Fee, here's that pulse of yours going like a young lady's in a field with a mad bull. Have you been working yourself up all day to expect me to hang myself, or shoot the frog-eater? Didn't I always tell you that only the ancient chivalry of the Pursuivant could take the affair *au grand sérieux?*'

'Very well,' said Felix in a somewhat smothered voice, 'it is your affair, and I must accept modern customs. I am glad you understood one another so well.'

'Spoken with grave irony worthy of the heavy father, your laudable model. Dear old chap, you'll be better now.'

There was something strange in the half-reverent, half-pitying tone of the tall powerful young man, as, with a sneer on his curling lip, but a tear in his softened eye, he stooped, pushed back the fair hair, and kissed the face which in its wistfulness looked younger than his own (having moreover the hirsuteness of only two days instead of two years).

Felix fulfilled his intention of getting up, though he went no farther than his own fire-side, where soon after tea he was joined by Clement, looking very serious, and armed with Bible, Prayer-book, and copy-book. He was to take Felix's Sunday class the next day; but whereas he had done so for the two months of the Ewmouth visit in the summer, there seemed no special necessity for a consultation, which in fact proved to be a rehearsal of the morrow's lesson, with various instructions to Felix himself, on what Clement called 'Church Teaching,' in oblivion that the simple truths of religion are as much Church teaching as the distinctive doctrines of his own set.

As vehement laughter pealed across the passage, Felix ventured to suggest that something was going on there.

'Yes,' said Clement; 'they were beginning some game, but I distrust Edgar's wit.'

'I don't think holding aloof always good.'

'When one's presence is a stimulus to irreverence?'

'Because you present yourself as a butt, instead of laughing with him, and giving things a turn.'

'Impossible, where one feels deeply.'

Felix believed it was impossible in the present case, and resigned himself, though pricking up his ears at the ripples of mirth and the shrieks of ecstatic uncontrollable laughter that reached his ear; until at last Lance burst in, laughing so that he could hardly stand upright, and bringing a paper in his hand for Felix's benefit.

It had been the game of adjectives, and Edgar, the conductor, had audaciously made its framework the Pursuivant's report of the valedictory sermon that Mr. Mowbray Smith was to preach on the morrow. It was a most comical combination, so well had Edgar's outline hit off the editor's desire to make the best of it, coupled with personalities that neither Mr. Smith would have preached nor he reported unless they had been in the palace of truth; the whole rendered the more grotesque by the hap-hazard adjectives that seasoned the discourse, sometimes deliciously inapposite, sometimes fantastically appropriate. An audience had stolen behind Lance to taste its sweets a second time; and the drollery, the *vraisemblance*, and touches of malice, quite choked him as he read, and overpowered Felix with mirth, all the more at the shocked countenance that Clement preserved throughout, while in the background there was a renewed chuckling, roaring, and rolling, at the more brilliant sallies.

The whole family had been viewing Edgar with more or less of awe, pity, and curiosity, as an injured hero, but had been beguiled into the maddest mirth, though as much disgusted with themselves for giggling as with him for making them giggle. Wilmet herself had succumbed, and Cherry had been in an almost hysterical transport of laughter, till her jaws ached, and her eyes were weak; and she was so exhausted that she could hardly crawl into Felix's room to wish him good-night, and then scarcely durst speak to him lest she should burst into tears; while as to the younger ones, it was altogether delightful to them at the moment, and they regarded the transactions of February as a dream.

When they met the next morning, Edgar professed that he could not venture on sitting under Mr. Smith's actual sermon, but should go to Minsterham, to pay his respects to Wilmet's future relations, if there were a feasible train.

'Yes,' said Clement, 'there's one in twenty minutes, which brings one in time for the Cathedral.'

'Dr. Wilmet is engrossed with a distinguished patient. Eh? Come along then, Lance; I must have some one to present me.'

Lance gave a joyful leap; but Wilmet interposed, 'Indeed, Lance, it is hardly safe. Remember how bad your head was after Christmas Day.'

'It's my own head, and I may do as I like with it!'

'That's just what you can't now. If you were knocked up to-morrow—as you certainly would be, between the railroad and the organ—'

'That would be what you *may* call a fix,' observed Edgar. 'Knocked up between a railway and an organ! What a position!'

'It is quite true, Edgar,' said Wilmet, the more severely for the laughter of Lance and Angel. 'Lance knows very well that one of his headaches perfectly disables him. Felix would not be content to leave Mr. Lamb alone in the shop; and all the good of these three days would be undone.'

'Oh—h! it was a pillar of the state I was asking?' said Edgar. 'Is your head really so ticklish, Lance?' as the boy made a gesture of disgust.

'Don't persuade him, Edgar. He ought not to do it,' said Wilmet, in her blunt authoritative way.

Lance kicked the heel of his boot against the floor, and said, 'Don't I pity Jack Harewood, that's all!'

'Well, a couple of ducks instead of a goose—Bob and Angel, you've no heads.—Come! I'm too modest to face the Librarian alone, much less the red-headed daughters.'

The two girls eagerly looked at their sister.

'"Gorgons and hydras and chimæras dire!"' ejaculated Edgar. 'If I were you, W.W., I'd get up a little more charitably disposed towards my brother on a Sunday morning!'

'It is Angela's wildness that I am afraid of,' said Wilmet.

'She sha'n't go near a tea-kettle,' said Edgar. 'Put on your hats, chick-a-biddies, if you wish to catch the Cathedral.'

'May we? O Wilmet, pray!' entreated Robina.

'I will see what Felix says.'

'A graceful form of shifting the obloquy of the negative,' muttered Edgar, as Wilmet disappeared.

'Felix will decide as he thinks good,' said Robina with dignity.

'As *she* thinks good, you mean,' said Edgar. 'Well, I wonder how you all contrive to stand it. I couldn't, I know, even for a quiet life.'

'You've not been broken in, you see,' said Lance, trying to answer with nonchalance.

'No, I only see a specimen occasionally. What has she been doing to you this morning, that has spoilt your appetite, and brought you under her thumb?'

'Don't, Edgar!' burst out Lance, starting up and running away.

'No, Edgar,' said Geraldine; 'it is not kind. It *is* hard enough for him as it is, and it is all for Felix's sake.'

Luckily, Clement had the wisdom not to speak, and therefore Cherry obtained a more reasonable answer.

'Well, that is a plea, Cherry; but it does rile me to see a fellow like that dragooned over, and thrown away, to bolster up a wretched little business such as this. It's a mistake, depend upon it, to let the demon of present necessity engulf another of the best of us. My squibs are conscientious, I assure you.'

'I don't care for her!' exclaimed Bernard: 'I'll go with you whenever you please, Edgar!'

'Well, Wilmet, under what decent mask do you veil your stony heart?' asked Edgar, as she re-entered.

'Felix sees no reason against their going,' said Wilmet, rather gloomily. 'Only, Edgar, pray don't encourage Angela to get into one of her states. You don't know what they are.'

For Felix had decided it against her. 'Yes, let them go. I don't believe he can bear to face any one in the town, and the charge of them will be a safe-guard.'

'But Angela?'

'My dear, the worst that can happen with her is that she should be a little boisterous with the Harewoods;' and as Wilmet showed that the prospect was unpleasing, 'that is better than what he could do alone, or with Lance.'

'Yes, I was resolved to stop Lance. I don't know whether to tell you, but I think you ought to know.'

'What?' asked Felix anxiously,

'Last night at half-past eleven—just when I had finished your hand—I smelt smoke. So I went down to see what was on fire and—'

'You found Edgar smoking in the kitchen.'

'If it had been only Edgar, I should not have minded, but it was Lance too. I do think you ought to give him a warning, Felix, for they would do nothing but laugh at me. Edgar would only go into transports about my hair, and say how long it was. I don't think I was ever so nearly in a passion in my life! If he is teaching Lance those ways—'

'He is not Lance's first instructor in smoke,' said Felix; 'I believe your own Harewoods were that, Mettie.'

'Now you are laughing too, Felix! I don't know how you can. It seems to me that it is all up with us if Edgar is to lead away Lance; and Lance was not up this morning for Church—the first time I have known him miss.'

'Well,' said Felix, rather hastily, 'it is of no use pulling reins too tight. Don't keep those poor children waiting, or you'll make them all too late.'

Wilmet had to obey, with the fretted sense that she had not been met as she expected, and that her alarms were injudiciously made light of; and Geraldine meantime tried to explain Edgar's bitter mischief as pain of heart; but it grieved her, whatever it was, and her spirits sank the more for the physical exhaustion of yesterday's violent laughter. But Edgar, looking in to see whether the little girls were ready, and finding her alone, leaning against the window disconsolately, came up, and putting his arm round her, said, 'So I scandalize you, Gerald? I can't give my carcase to be battened on by the ghouls, were they best family ghouls in the world.'

'Edgar!'

'Besides, you know all this was diligently fostered by old Blunderbore's duteous intermeddling; and as it was not my fault that I furnished a spectacle for gods and men *then*, I *will* not now.'

'Only, Edgar, if you *do* care for Felix, do not, pray do not spoil his comfort in Lance!'

13

'If I don't, nature will, Cherry. That boy is not the stuff to make a journeyman stationer, at Wilmet's orders. Oh! if you could but have seen her, when she surprised us with our pipes last night! I couldn't get her to stand still, or she would have been a perfect study for Antigone. She is a magnificent creature with her hair down!—Ha! little kids, we must scamper for it for the train!'

And off he went, leaving Geraldine not much less unhappy for his apology. The long day alone with Felix was a better consolation. She could not leave the house in such cold as the present; and Felix was dressed as soon as breakfast was over, and came into the drawing-room, where after their home service, and when he had proved his freedom from cough by reading a grand sermon of Newman's, his reserve gave way in the Sunday calm, and he asked, 'Did Edgar say anything to you, Chérie?'

She repeated the saying about the ghools, as it was evidently meant for circulation among those respectable parties.

Felix smiled, and said, 'I thought so,' and told in return Edgar's defiant reception of the tidings.

'I don't think,' said Cherry, 'that I was ever more uncomfortable than through his fun. It felt like laughing-gas; it forced one on, and yet it was so unreal. He wants to treat it on the hawk-gone-down-the-wind principle.'

'It is the gallant and the wise one, Cherry. So you ought to admire it more than you seem to do.'

'It cannot be wise if it be not true. That is, if it ever went deep with him.'

'He never meant it to go deep,' said Felix; 'but the very extravagance of his defiance makes me afraid it took stronger hold than he knew, and that the shock may be very bad for him.'

'But she—' and Cherry stopped, afraid to vex him by speaking of Alice's incapacity to raise a character.

He calmly finished. 'She was not all we thought her. True, poor child; but an attachment worthily and steadily maintained, as for all his nonsense this has been, must be well for a man; and a disruption of this kind must be a breaking-up—whether he treat it lightly or no—of foundations such as one who seems to have little besides can ill afford to stand.'

It was the first time that the secret anxiety had been openly named, and Cherry clasped her hands.

'That is my chief anxiety,' resumed Felix. 'Otherwise the end of this matter is of course an advantage.'

'If she could use him so, she was not worth constancy,' said Cherry.

'No!' It was a decided No, though it was followed by 'As they had made her. Poor child! She was full of sweet womanly gifts, and might have been made everything excellent; but Edgar estimated her more truly than I did. There was always a certain spirit of intrigue, and want of substance, or she could never have so treated him.'

'Entirely unfeeling.'

'Or rather, too light to appreciate feeling otherwise than as a tribute to herself, or to dwell on the absent,' said Felix sadly. 'I now believe that she was conscious of—of my liking. Indeed, I am sure of it; I only tried to hope otherwise, though it was easy to forgive her preference for one so much more attractive. There was no harm in that. But as things stood with him, to throw him over without a word shows an essential want of comprehension of what was due to others.'

'She might at least have written through her aunts.'

'With a right sense of honour she would; but I believe she had no education in such things. Poor little thing! I hope the Frenchman will do well by her.'

'Felix dear, may I ask you—this is not the pain that it was before?'

'No' said Felix, looking steadily at her, with his chin on his hand. 'No, certainly not. I was greatly shocked and upset at first, but not personally; though of course I must always feel towards her as I never can for any other woman;' then, at Cherry's start, 'I mean that the woman who fills one's life with a certain glory and radiance of—possibility, never can be the same as others to one, even though it lasted ever so short a time, and was ever so great a mistake. But that does not mean wishing to begin it over again.'

'Not with her.'

'It is absurd to make auguries or protests,' said Felix quietly; 'but from a boy I knew well that that sort of thing could hardly be for me, and I am content to have returned to that conviction. Even ending, as it has done, the year of—of—perhaps fools' paradise was well worth having, but I hope it will serve me for life. If I can keep faithful to what I once thought Alice, it will be best for all of us. So don't be anxious about me, my Whiteheart. The trouble of last winter was over long ago, and the zest and spirit of life came back with strength and work. I am quite as happy now as I was before—happier, I think.'

'Then this need not make you ill,' breathed Cherry, aware that she was saying something foolish. Indeed, Felix laughed a little.

'Hardly,' he said playfully. 'Remember, Cherry, what a predicament I was in—obliged to act the heavy father, as Edgar calls it, when I was so much concerned myself, and with him telling me I was a fool for my pains, as I believe I was. Besides, it was a good honest cold I caught at Brompton, in a very sharp east wind. If you insist on going any further, you will become a family ghool, Cherry.' She was obliged to laugh; and he continued, 'No, don't be anxious. This was an opportune scald. I should have found the day's work severe, if I had not had time to face this thoroughly. Such a quiet day last spring would have been worth a quart of cod-liver oil later.'

Therewith the pattering of many feet resounded on the frost-bound street; and the church-goers returned, averring that Mr. Smith's sermon had been like enough to Edgar's to render it difficult to keep their countenances, and to make them rejoice in Angela's absence. Of this Felix might judge for himself, for not long after the preacher himself arrived, offering the MS. for an abstract for the paper, all unconscious of the second-sight that had reported it already.

There he lingered, trying to talk, as if he wanted to say something that would not come out; and at last he was only driven from the field by the return of Edgar and the girls, who came in open-mouthed and eager out of the cold.

Edgar had had a great deal of fun with Mrs. Harewood, and had on his side fascinated all the family; so that Robina confided to Lance that she thought Grace Harewood ought to be warned, for Edgar went on with her like 'You know what.'

'Make yourself easy,' said Lance; 'Grace and Lucy know all about that better than any girl in Minsterham. What did old Bill say? and what anthem did you have?'

Felix and Geraldine spent the Evening Service hour in very different fashion from the morning; for Edgar was their companion, and took the opportunity of making the remonstrance he had threatened about Lance and his prospects. He had never been *fine* in Alda's way, and had not her feelings about losing caste; but whereas his politics were diametrically opposed to those of the Pursuivant, he thought Felix ranging himself, according to his essential Blunderbore nature, on the side of the old giants destined to destruction, and wasting talent and substance on a hopeless and thankless cause; but he knew his brother to be past remonstrance, and to be perfectly well aware that this was the losing side. Only Edgar entered a strong protest against Lance being, as he said, sacrificed just to make Wilmet's pot boil, and bolster up the old Pursuivant a little longer.

'You can't be more averse to it than I,' said Felix. 'If he could only go back to his work, he might yet get to the University.'

'Pshaw! that's not what I meant. He is not the stuff; you were the only one of us that had the making of a scholar. Now Lance has got just the taste and the talent that were baulked in my case by old Tom's sticking me down to hides and tallow, when I ought to have been cultivating them.'

'There's this difference,' said Geraldine; 'Cousin Thomas stuck you, but Lance sticks himself.'

'Under moral compulsion, eh?'

'The compulsion was on me,' said Felix. 'I was really afraid to deny him; the idleness, and the fretting over it, were doing his head so much harm.'

'That's all very well. No harm done; but to let him go on here in the stodge is a bit of short-sightedness I can't understand. He'll never be happy in it; and you'd better let him go before it is too late.'

'Go? but how, and where? His health is not fit for study, and his voice ought to rest for another year.'

Then Edgar explained his own plan. Lance had already considerable musical knowledge, and ability such that his way in the musical world would be secure. Amateur as he was himself, Edgar had such a footing there that he could secure an introduction for his brother, who while learning would be able to maintain himself; and either by violin or voice, if not by original composition, win name, fame, and fortune, in a few years. A manager of high reputation Edgar mentioned as likely to accept and train the boy; and he added that for his own part he would watch over the little fellow; and he added, with a look in his eyes that went to Felix's heart, 'And nothing would do me so much good *now* as the charge of him.'

'That I *do* believe, Edgar,' said Felix warmly; 'but it would be throwing the helve after the hatchet in a way you can't expect of a heavy father.'

'Exactly what I knew you would say. You veil it a little more; but we poor Bohemians don't meet with much more charity from you than from our stately sister. Reprobates all—eh?'

'Living a life of temptation enough to make me choose no one to be drawn into it that I can prevent. Have you been talking to Lance about it?'

'Well, it rose out of last night's talk to him. Not that he gave in to it. He's loyal to you to the back-bone, and all importance too with the charge of the shop. Besides, that cathedral—it's a sort of mother's milk to him, not out of his mouth.'

'That's a good hearing!' said Felix, with a rather defiant smile.

'But it won't last,' said Edgar; 'the drudgery and sameness will tell; and you'd better give in with a good grace in time, Blunderbore.'

'You've been persuading him,' said Cherry reproachfully.

'Well, Cherry, I'm not in the habit of confounding virtue with dulness; and when the little chap talked to me of the musical doings I had been after, I felt the sin and shame of getting a nightingale to make a barn-door fowl of.'

'I can only tell you,' said Felix, with more annoyance than he usually betrayed, 'that if you took your nightingale to the din of London, and the excitement of a concert, you'd have him with inflammation on the brain before the week was out. Why, I sent him over to see his doctor at Minsterham, and he says it would be murder to send him back to his books and the choir for this next quarter at least; and if cathedral music will not do for him, judge if London concerts would!'

'And did you think I wanted to carry off your deputy right hand while your own is hung up in a bag, you jealous old giant? Why, I proposed to devote myself to the Pursuivant to-morrow!'

'Thank you; I am afraid it would be taken for the Tribune.'

'As if I couldn't hit off the complacent, gentlemanly, stick-in-the-mud style for squiredom! I'll write you a leader—on what shall it be, municipalities, or the smut in wheat?—that you shall not know from your own.'

To wish Edgar away was impossible, and yet how feel willing that Lance should be under such influence? Withal there was the difficulty of showing Wilmet that to fret Lance with restrictions was a dangerous thing at such a moment. She would yield to Felix's desire that she would not interfere with that orgie over the kitchen fire—which he regarded all the time with as much dread as herself—but she thought his concession weak: and Lance himself was perilously like Edgar in all his bright pleasant qualities, talents, and tastes, so that the two had an enjoyment in one another's company that it was painful to regard with anxiety.

CHAPTER XXV.

DON GIOVANNI.

'Towered cities please us then,
And the busy hum of men.
* * * * * * * * * * *
And ever against eating cares
Lap me in soft Lydian airs.
* * * * * * * * * * *
With wanton heed, and giddy cunning,
The melting voice through mazes running.'
Milton.

The Monday brought business instead of sentiment. Not only was the Pursuivant to be provided for, but Felix had on his mind the year's accounts. No one had ever had Froggatt and Underwood's Christmas bill later than the second week in January—and no one should. Besides, he was very anxious to balance his books this critical year, and was unwilling to employ a professional accountant for what, as far as head went, he could do perfectly well. His willing helpers began to perceive what they had never realized before—his practised power of quickness and accuracy. The Pursuivant was quite work enough for Cherry, even if she could have borne the strain of application to accounts; Lancelot was needed in the shop; and Wilmet and Clement found themselves whirled on beyond their power of speed. Robina proved the most efficient helper; for arithmetic had been so well taught by Miss Fennimore, that she understood with less trouble to herself and Felix than any of the rest. They laughed to find that five had been about what he usually did singly; and that he had all the time been the main-spring of them all—referee to Lance and Cherry, arranging for the others in pencil with his left hand, breaking off to direct one, verify for another, explain to the third, and often distracting them by whistling to Theodore, amusing Stella, or gossiping with Edgar—all with ease and without hurry, as if it came naturally to him. 'Julius Caesar was nothing to him!' laughed Geraldine, as she perceived the ability and power that she had never ascribed to him before, because he had not Edgar's brilliance. As to Edgar, though he had been trained for a merchant's clerk, he professed to have forgotten all his training: he would only proffer help to the editorial business, and there put out Cherry's arrangements more than he helped her; and finding every one much too busy to loiter, he took his departure early on Tuesday morning, leaving an unsatisfactory sense that he had not been comforted nor made welcome enough—a sense of regret and yet of relief.

The result of the balance was that the Pursuivant was a less profitable investment than hitherto, but by no means a loss; while the Tribune seemed to have reached a present level of circulation, where it might rest till some further excitement. There would henceforth be a hand-to-hand struggle; but the Pursuivant still held its own. And as to the private budget, the household *had* pulled through without exceeding their income, when all the demands of the year were answered. Moreover, Fulbert had been appointed to a well-paid office, and had sent home twenty-five pounds, begging that Lance might have the preference in the disposal; and the whole family were very proud of this, the first substantial help that had been sent in by any of the brothers—Lance proudest of all, perhaps, though he declared that it was no good to him, and begged that it might clear Bernard's first year.

Lance had said nothing all this time of Edgar's invitations, and no one was sure whether that unscrupulous person had made them to him in person or not, till one dismal foggy afternoon at the end of the week. Felix, though still helpless as to his hand and arm, had resumed his place down-stairs; and Cherry was sitting in the window, to get light to pursue her work of unpicking a dove-coloured French merino dress, a legacy of Alda's, which was to be dyed and made up again for Angela. It was a business that she disliked—it always seemed to bring the sense of grinding to her mind—and this particular dress seemed to carry in every fold the remembrance of some jar between the wearer and herself; nor was she exhilarated by the accompaniment, for Robina was dutifully puzzling out on the worn old piano a long difficult sonatina—a sort of holiday task, which lay heavy on the child's mind, and seemed to Cherry a mere labyrinth of confused sounds. The dull day, the dull work, and weary clash up to the place where Robina never failed to stumble, and then go back to the beginning with no better success, wore Cherry's spirits. She began to feel as if this were like her life—all mist, all toil, all din, everything fair and lovely closed up from her, nothing left but the yearning knowledge that it existed, and that everybody could enjoy it except herself—she, who felt such capacity for making the most of it. The sense of imprisoned tedium grew so strong at last, that she was ready to cry out to stop the only thing she could stop, when she was sensible that a very different hand was on the keys—no confused or uncertain touch, but the harmony was being read off, and the stammering spelling work was exchanged for clear, true, feeling discourse. She needed not to look round to know that Lance was standing behind Robina; but presently he came to a dull discordant note, and broke off with a growl of disgust, 'What, another gone!'

'Didn't you know that?'

'No; I can't bear to touch the wretched old thing, it makes me sick!'

'I wish we could learn to tune it.'

'Poulter did show me once, but it's no good. It is just as makeshift and disgusting as all the rest of it!'

'You've got a head-ache, Lance.'

'No, I haven't. Felix has been at me, too.'

'What! he sent you up?'

'Ay;' and as Robina sat down on a low stool, he threw himself on the floor, with his head on her lap, delivering himself of a howling yawn.

'Why did he send you up?' as she stroked his hair back from his temples.

'Oh, it has been an intolerable bother! All the samples of writing-paper have somehow been and gone and got into the wrong drawers, and Mr. Underwood has been in no end of a state of mind—quite ferocious; and Lamb and I have been sorting and struggling to get 'em right, till at last I didn't know fancy pink from widow's deepest affliction; and Felix, by way of the most cutting thing he could do to me, orders me up-stairs!'

'I am so sorry! It must have been Lamb's doing.'

'No: he's much too sober-sided. It was mine, I'm sure, one day when I was hating it all a little worse than usual.'

'Hating it all! O Lance! I thought you got on so well!'

'A nice sort of getting on! I know when it was. There were those two Miss Bayneses—out at Upham—came in with some fad about note-paper, made a monstrous fuss; but they are very pretty—something like that girl at Stoneborough. So I wrote up to Scott's—took no end of trouble. Scott had to cut it on purpose—wouldn't do less than a ream—and after all, when it came down, my young ladies just take one quire of it, turn everything over again, never say one word of thanks, but stand chattering away to an ape of a cousin that came in with them. I was in such a wax, that I believe I jumbled up the paper when they'd gone, and tumbled it all over again; and it has never got the better of it, though I always meant to set it to rights.'

'Well, I think it served you right, if you only did it because they were pretty!'

'It wasn't altogether that; but I knew they would say nothing was to be had when Mr. Underwood wasn't there. That's the way of it; one's just a bit of a machine for getting things!'

'You knew that before, when you took the work.'

'Yes; but somehow I did not know it would be so disgusting. I don't suppose that girl at Stoneborough would look at me over the counter now. No, and I don't know that she ought, either; only people might have a civil "Thank you" to throw at one. I'm an ass, that's all! Only one hates having no one to speak to!'

'It is different from the Harewoods.'

'Don't talk about that!'

'But, Lance, I thought you liked it all. You said you did when I came home; and when Felix was laid up, you were everything, and did so well. I thought you would have been pleased.'

'Yes; I saw the whole stupidity and botheration of the thing. It has got to be work instead of play—I suppose that's it.'

'But, Lance, does it follow that you must go on with it all your life, because you are helping Felix through this winter?'

'While the accounts look like this, I don't see how he is to pay a stuck-up shopman. No, it is all stuff and nonsense! I didn't think Edgar's talk would have upset me like this.'

'What? his talk about operas, and concerts, and pictures—?'

'And the spirit and the fun that are always going there. That must be life! One's eyes and ears do seem given one for something there! Do you know Bob, he wants me to come up and live with him, and get an engagement as a pianist, and learn the violin?'

'O, Lance! but Felix and Wilmet would never consent!'

'No, and they didn't ought to. No, I could never,' and he spoke low, but Cherry heard his clear voice distinctly, 'give the stage what was taught me for that other purpose. If I can't be what I want, I must do this common work for my living, and not make a market of my music. I can *give* that freely to the Church—that is if I ever get my voice again.'

'That's right, dear Lancey,' said Robina, looking down at the face on her knees; 'you could not really like that odd life Edgar leads.'

'Like it? Much you know about it, Bob. It does make everything else seem as dull as ditch-water!'

'Not always.'

'Not when I can get it out of my head. Only I do wish things wouldn't be so stupid here. It's just like a horse in a mill seeing a fine thorough-bred come and kick up his heels at him in a meadow. I say, Bob, let's go and get a turn at the organ—you can blow for me; it will get the maggots out of my brain best.'

'Oh yes, dear Lance, only—'

'Only what?'

'If you didn't much mind those horrible notes, could you just show me the sense of that thing? I must learn before I go back to school; and Angel hates it so, I did it when she was out.'

Lance made an ineffable grimace; but having undertaken to act music-master, he first played the piece as exquisitely as the cracked piano would allow, and then scolded poor Robin within an inch of her life at every blunder, for her utter lack of taste, vituperating the stupidity of those who threw good music away upon her.

She took it all as an honour and a kindness, though she cried out for a respite long before she had come up to his rather unreasonable requirements; and reminding him that it would soon be too dark for his designs on the church organ, she went to get ready; and the two were not seen again till after dark, when the patient Robina came in very cold, but there was a bright peacefulness on Lance's face, as if he had played away his repinings.

Felix explained the having sent him away by saying that the strain of the days when he had been in charge had told on him, for he had grown so confused and distressed in the endeavour to remedy the mistakes that had been made, that it had been needful for every reason to send him away from the scene of action. No doubt the responsibility, and the resistance to Edgar's invitations had been a considerable pressure on his mind; but whatever his longings might be, he said no more about them, and continued to be the sunshine of the house—so bright, frank, and open that no one would have guessed at the deep reserves within.

It was about a month later that one evening he darted into the room, exclaiming, 'I *say*, who do you think is here? Why, Renville, Edgar's boss!'

'Nothing the matter, I hope?' cried Cherry.

'Oh no, nothing; only Tom Underwood has sent him down to see about some picture at Centry, and so he dropped in, and Felix has asked him to spend the evening.'

'The evening!' Wilmet started up.

'Hark! there they are on the stairs!'

The introduction was deferred, for Felix shut him into Mr. Froggatt's room, and then came himself to say, 'I couldn't but ask him; I hope it is not *very* troublesome?'

'N—no—oh, no,' said Wilmet 'Only—Lance, should you mind just running down to Prothero's to get some rashers; and let me see—eggs, if he has any he can recommend, and not above sixpence for seven?'

'Little Lightfoot is there,' said Felix, who even in his shoe-cleaning days would not have liked such a commission.

'He has no sense,' returned Wilmet; 'and I can't spare one of the maids. You don't mind, Lance?'

'Not a whistle. Only how is my sense to act, if Prothero's conscience won't warrant his eggs?'

Wilmet's answer was lost in the clank of coppers, as she left the room with her willing *aide-de-camp*, and neither of them was seen again for the next half hour, during which time Felix had introduced the neat dapper little Mr. Renville to his sister Geraldine and little Stella; and a conversation had begun which entertained Cherry extremely—it was so like a breath from that wonderful world of art in which Edgar lived; and meantime the painter's quick eye was evidently taking stock of the drawings on the walls, and feasting on little Stella's childish beauty, though he was too polite to make remarks. There had been only just time for Felix and Cherry to look at each other, wondering what their house-keeper designed, when the door between the rooms was opened by Lance, with a face as red as a boiled lobster: and behind the tea-tray appeared Wilmet's head, likewise considerable heightened in complexion, though not so unbecomingly. Nor had they roasted themselves for nothing. Lance looked and winked with conscious pride at the poached eggs, frizzled contorted rashers, and crisp toast, wherein he had had his share of glory; and Wilmet's pile of scones in their snowy napkin divided the honours of the feast with the rissoles, previously provided for the brothers, who since Felix's health had become matter of thought, had come to make their principal meal in the leisure of the evening, when that notable housewife of theirs could provide for them.

Certainly, Mr. Renville's own Nuremburg haus-frau could not have turned out a neater little impromptu supper than Wilmet had done; though she had decidedly objected to Lance's concealment of the uncouth forms of the butter with fern-leaves from the garden, and had flatly refused to let him station either a pot of jonquils or a glass of snowdrops in the middle of the table. 'Eating, was eating, and flowers were flowers,' she said; which sentiment somehow tickled Lance so much, that choking added to the redness of his visage, as, while buttering the muffins, he tried to exercise some sculpture on the ill-shaped lump.

To a Londoner, however, all country fare was fresh, pure, and delicious, more especially when dispensed by one who, for all her disdain of the poetry of life, could not but be in herself a satisfaction to the artist's eye. He could not help a little start of amazement; and as he paused while Cherry made her slow way into the other room, he could not refrain from whispering to Felix that he had always thought the portraits Edgar brought from home a little too ideal, but that he perceived that they did not do justice to the reality; and Felix, with a little curl of his mouth, and rub of his hands, asked whether Mr. Renville had seen his other twin sister. 'Yes; she was extremely handsome, but somehow her style did not explain that classical beauty in the same manner.'

To look at Wilmet and Stella, and to talk to Felix and Geraldine, was no despicable pleasure. Felix's powers of conversation were a good deal cultivated by the clients of the reading-room, who had always gossiped with Mr. Froggatt as now with him; and Geraldine had native wit and liveliness, that were sure to flash out whenever the first chill of shyness was taken off, as it easily was when her brother was there to take the lead.

But Cherry was not prepared for that proposal of Felix's that she should show her drawings to the guest. Poor man, he must be so much used to the sight of young-lady drawings; and of late Cherry had been in the depths of despair about hers, with all their defects, that she knew not how to remedy, glaring full upon her. She would have protested, but Lance had handed out the portfolio; and fluttering, nervous, eager, she must conquer her silly sense of being 'all in a twitter.'

Those two or three fanciful groups—his 'Ah, very pretty!' was just courteous and almost weary. But then came an endeavour to produce Lance as the faithful little acolyte in the Silver Store. Mr. Renville looked at that much more attentively, smiled as he nodded at her model, and praised the accuracy of the drawing of the hand. From that moment his manner of looking was altogether different. He criticised so hard that Wilmet was in pain, and thought poor Cherry would be annihilated; but Cherry, on the other hand, was drinking in every word, asking questions, explaining difficulties, and Mr. Renville evidently extremely interested, seeing and hearing nothing but the sketches and the lame girl.

'Who had been her teacher?'

'Edgar.'

'No one else? Only your brother?' in great surprise. 'I don't know when I have seen such accuracy even in the school of art.'

'Edgar is so particular about that.'

'Well, if I could only get him to learn his own lesson!'

'I have so little to copy,' said Cherry. 'I have nothing to distract me.'

It was little enough; a few second-hand studies of his; a cast that Felix had given her off an Italian boy's board, which came opportunely on her birthday; and her living models when she could catch them, generally surreptitiously. But upon her small materials she had worked perseveringly, going back to the same subject whenever she gained a new light, profiting by every hint, till the result was an evident amazement to the artist; and as he emphatically said, pointing to an outline caught from John Harewood as he was reading last summer, 'This is not talent, it is genius! You ought to give yourself advantages, Miss Underwood.'

Cherry smiled rather sadly. 'It is quite enough that Edgar should have them,' she said.

'Ah! if he would only take half the pains with his drawing that he seems to have inculcated upon you!'

It was a disappointment. She had much rather have heard Edgar's genius praised than her own, which, be it what it might, she had come to believe must, for want of cultivation, be limited to the supply of Christmas cards and unsatisfactory illuminations.

But when the sisters had gone to bed, Mr. Renville had much more to say. He had sought Felix out a good deal for the purpose of talking over Edgar, He said that the young man's talent was of a graceful, fantastic, ingenious description, such as with application would be available for prosperity if not for eminence; but application Edgar had never perseveringly given, since he had first found himself surpassed in the higher efforts of art. His powers were too versatile for his own good, and he dabbled in everything that was *not* his proper occupation—concerts, amateur theatricals, periodical literature and journalism, comic sketches. His doings were not all wholly unremunerative; but though he viewed them as mines of wealth, they were really lures into a shifty uncertain life, and distractions from steady consistent labour. His fine voice, his brilliant wit, and engaging manner, made him a star in the lively society on the outskirts of art; and he was expensive, careless, and irregular in his hours to a degree that sorely tried the good man, a precisian in his domestic customs. He and his little German wife, however, loved the lad, as everybody did love him who came under the influence of his sunshiny grace and sweetness of temper—the unselfish manner inherited from one whose unselfishness was real; and used as they were to the freedom of artist life, their allowances were liberal; but of late there had been a recklessness and want of purpose about his ways which both grieved and alarmed them: he was more unsettled than ever, seemed to have lost all interest in his studies at the Academy, was getting into a set that had degenerated from permissible eccentricity into something very like lawlessness, and even while an undesirable inmate, had vexed his kind friend and master by proposing to remove from under his roof, and set up with a chosen comrade of his own.

Committed to his charge, as Edgar Underwood had been by the elder brother, the kind little artist felt it his duty not to let him go without an intimation to his family, though well aware that a father could have little control in such a case, how much less a brother only by two years the elder?

All that Felix could hope was, that since this state of dreary recklessness was so evidently the effect of disappointment, it might pass with the force of the shock. He himself had experiences of the irksomeness of the dull round of ordinary occupation when the heart was rent by a sudden shock; and though he had forced himself on under the load that had so nearly crushed him, he could perfectly understand the less chastened, more impetuous nature, under less pressure of necessity, breaking into aberrations under a far more astounding blow of desertion. So he hoped. But what could he do? He knew but too well the cool manner in which Edgar turned over his remonstrances as those of the would-be heavy father. He could only thank Mr. Renville, promise to write to Edgar, and entreat him not to remove from the roof which was so great a safeguard against the worst forms of temptation, advise him perhaps to study abroad for a time to pacify the restlessness of his disappointment—at any rate, if he could do nothing else, not let the brother whom he still loved best of all drift away without feeling that there were those who grieved and strove for him.

It was not only of Edgar that Mr. Renville spoke, however. He was so much impressed with Geraldine's drawings, that he argued that she should have a quarter's study in the South Kensington Museum, undertaking, as one of the masters, to facilitate her coming and going, so that she should not be involved in any scrambles, and declaring that she only needed a few opportunities of study to render her talent really excellent and profitable.

Felix declared her going to be simply impossible; but either Mr. Renville or Edgar did not let the matter rest there, for a warm invitation arrived from the family in Kensington Palace Gardens, backed by many promises of tender care from Marilda. It seemed to be absolutely throwing away opportunities for Cherry to refuse to avail herself of such an opening; and though she was in exceeding trepidation, she had enough of the sacred fire to long to perfect her art, justified by the wish to render it substantially beneficial. And then Felix could not help thinking that the presence of his favourite sister might be a wholesome check to Edgar in one direction, and incentive in another, at this critical time, and this was no small weight in his balance. While Cherry, on the one hand, dreaded going out into the world with the nervous dismay of an invalid, who had never been anywhere but to St. Faith's; and on the other, felt this opportunity for herself almost an injustice to Lance, with all his yearnings.

She was to go immediately after Easter; and whether by Edgar's suggestion or not, Marilda imperiously begged that Lance might bring her up to London, and stay as long as he could be spared. It was impossible to give him longer than from Saturday till the last train on Monday, for Felix had reporting business on hand, and must be out on Tuesday, and did not perhaps regret that things had so settled themselves.

Lance's overflowing enjoyment somewhat solaced Geraldine's alarm on the way up; he was so careful of her, and so proud of the charge; and after his wistful glance at Minsterham, the novelty was so delightful to him. His journey with John Harewood reckoned for nothing, for he had then been far too unwell to look about, and it had besides been on a different line; but now everything was wonderful, and his exclamations almost embarrassed Cherry, she thought they must so astonish their fellow-travellers. Even the hideousness of the suburbs seemed to fascinate him—there was something in the sense of the multitude that filled him with excitement. 'It is getting to the heart, Cherry,' he said, 'where the circulation is quickest.'

'Into the world—the vortex, I should call it,' returned Cherry thinking of drops being attracted by the eddy, and sucked into the whirlpool; but Lance was gone wild at the glimpse of a huge gasometer, and did not heed.

Edgar's dainty beard and moustache were the first things that met their eyes upon the platform; his strong arms helped Cherry out, and in a wonderfully short time seated her beside Alda in a great luxurious carriage.

To her disappointment, however, the two back seats remained vacant.

'No, no,' said Edgar, his white teeth gleaming in a smile; 'we must make the most of our time, Lancey boy. What do you say to walking by Westminster—then we'll get something to eat—and you shall know what Don Giovanni is like before you are many hours older, my boy?'

Cherry's last view of Lance was with a look of dancing ecstasy all over his person.

'Don Giovanni is the opera, isn't it?' she said in bewilderment.

'Of course; what did you think?'

'But I thought that was dreadfully dear.'

'Oh! Edgar can always get tickets for anything. You must not bring out Wilmet's frugalities here, Cherry. Dear old Wilmet, how does she bear this long waiting?'

Alda was really interested in home tidings, and pleased to point out matters of interest, so that Cherry was fairly happy, till the awe of the great handsome house, alone in its gravelled garden, fell on her.

But when once up the stately stone steps, she was kindly, solicitously, welcomed by Marilda and her mother. The reception-rooms (as Mrs. Underwood called them) were all on the ground floor; and Cherry had only to mount one easy flight of broad steps to reach the former school-room, with two little bed-rooms opening into it—one assigned to her, the other to Marilda's old nurse, who had been kept on with little or nothing to do, and was delighted to devote herself to the lame young lady.

She took charge of Geraldine's toilette for the late dinner, so tremendous to the imagination used to the little back-room at home, but which turned out after all more tedious than formidable. In truth, Cherry was very tired, and Alda quite kindly advised her to go to bed. She wanted to sit up and wait for her brothers, but was laughed at, and finally was deposited in her very pretty pink bed, where, however, the strangeness of all things allowed her very little sleep. Quiet as the place was, she thought something seemed to be going on all night; and at some semi-light hour in the morning she bounded up as if at a shot, for there really was a step, and a knock, and her door opening.

'Cherry, are you awake?'

'O Lance! what is the matter?'

'Matter! nothing—only I'm going out to look about me, and I thought I'd leave word with you and see how you were.'

'Out! Why, didn't I hear the clock strike five?'

'Ay. Have you been awake?'

'A good deal. Have you?'

'As if anybody could sleep after that! I've gone it all over and over. I see there's a piano in this outer room. I'll just show you.'

'O Lance!—*now*—and Sunday!'

'I forgot. But it is so awful, Cherry: it made one feel more than a hundred sermons;' and the far-away look came into his eyes; as in rapid words he sketched the story, described the scenes, dwelt with passionate fervour on the music, all with an intensity of feeling resulting in a great sense of awe. His excitement seemed to her so great that she begged him to go back to bed for the hours that yet remained before breakfast.

'I couldn't, I tell you, Cherry.'

'But you'll have *such* a head-ache.'

'Time enough for that when I get home. I don't know what to do with myself, I tell you; I must get into a church somewhere, or I can't bear it.'

'You'll lose your way.'

'I've got the map of London. If I can I shall get to St. Matthew's; and so I thought I had better tell you, in case I wasn't back to breakfast. Edgar showed me your room.'

'Is Edgar sleeping here?'

'No; he went to Renville's when he'd put me in. I'll be back anyway by the time Robin and Angel come, but I can't stay quiet. Nobody ever gave me any notion what this place is. It makes one feel I don't know how, only just to see the people—streaming, streaming, streaming, just like a river! And then that wonderful—most wonderful music!'

The boy was gone, and Cherry felt as if his fate were sealed—the drop gone to join the other drops, and to swirl away!

Edgar was rather amazed and disconcerted, when on coming in about ten o'clock he found that he had vanished. He had meant to take him to any ecclesiastical wonder that he wished; but he laughed at Cherry's fears of the boy losing himself. 'He is a born gamin,' he said—'takes to London streets as a native element. But Felix is right, he must not have too much of it. I was heartily glad when it was over last night, and durst not keep him for the ballet, though I much wanted to see what he would say to it; but he was worked up to such a pitch I didn't know what would come next, and I'm sure his remarks taught me more about Don Giovanni than ever I saw before. He was in such a state when he came out that I hardly knew what to do with him. I should have given him a glass of ale but he wouldn't hear of that, so I could only let him have his will—a great cup of coffee—and send him to bed. I knew he wouldn't sleep.'

Lance *did* appear at the moment of luncheon, when Robina and Angela arrived to spend the rest of the day. He had not reached St Matthew's; but he had found a church open early for a grand choral Celebration, and this not being customary at Minsterham, had been almost overwhelming to a nature like his. It had lasted so long, that the bell rang for matins before the congregation had left the church; and Lance had stayed on, and heard a service far exceeding in warmth and splendour that of his sober old cathedral, and such a soul-stirring sermon as was utterly unlike the steady-going discourses of his canons.

He had never even missed his breakfast, and yet seemed not to care for the meal before him, though he ate what was put on his plate; and he had that look of being all brow, eyes, and nose, that had often recurred ever since his illness; but he would not allow that he was tired; and so far from being able to sit still, wanted his little sisters to walk with him in Kensington Gardens, and Robina being a discreet person, and knowing her way, there was no reason against this; and off they went, all three supremely happy, and Cherry feeling a certain hopefulness that Robina's steady good sense would be a counterpoise to other influences and excitements. But Lance had not come to any state for sober sense. Under the trees of Kensington Gardens, the influence of the brilliant spring beauty, and the gay cheerful vivacity of the holiday crowd, still acted on his eager self; and he used his sisters as audience for all his impressions as to Don Giovanni, till he had driven Angela almost as wild as himself with his vivid descriptions—and to be sure, he treated it as a sort of religious exercise. Indeed, the sensation he seemed chiefly to have carried off with him, was that London had been maligned; he had always supposed it to be a Vanity

Fair, where one's religion would be in extreme peril; and behold, he had found religion there like everything else—more quickening, more inspiriting, more exquisitely beautiful and satisfying in its ministrations, than anything that he could have conceived! Nor did the late Evening Service with which his day finished—with all its accessories of light and music, and another sermon from a celebrated preacher—lessen this impression, which made St Oswald's by comparison so utterly flat, dead, and unprofitable.

Robina could not help saying to Cherry, with that old-womanish air of wisdom that belonged to her sometimes, 'I do wish we hadn't taken Lance to such a nice church. He knows less what London really is now than he did before.'

Dear little Robin! as if she knew what London *really* was! And Cherry was too anxious an elder sister to give her much comfort, except by saying, 'It is fair that he should know the truth of what is to be found there, Bobbie. You see he is only getting good out of it in his own mind.'

'Yes, that's true; only he will make himself ill.'

This had come to be Edgar's fear as well as Cherry's, when they found that Lance had slept quite as little the second night as the first, though he brought down those great lustrous blue eyes of his quite as wide open and full of zest in the morning. It made Edgar cautious in his choice of sights for the Monday; but one so long habituated to London, and regarding with contempt its stock lions, could not estimate what they were to a lad at once so susceptible and so unsophisticated, and his diversion at Lance's raptures passed into anxiety, not unmingled with tedium, and almost disdain, at anything so very countrified; but his real care and good nature never flagged till he had safely, and to his positive relief, seen his little brother off for Bexley by the five o'clock train, to work off his intoxication at home, among his proper guardians.

'I am sure,' he said to Geraldine, 'if I had had any notion that his brain had continued so ticklish, I would never have had him on my hands. The difference between lionizing him and old Blunderbore! why it was—not exactly fire and water, but Ariel and Gonzalo. Shut the two up in the same shop! It is ridiculous! No, no, Lance must vegetate down there till his brains have cooled down from that unlucky stroke; but after that, you'll see, nothing will keep him down in Felix's hole; 'tisn't in the nature of things that he should be buried there. I've given him the violin I got at Liège, so he won't be quite wasting his time.'

There was rest—at least, for the present—in Edgar's acquiescence in Lance's vegetation, except so far as it gave food for present anxiety, by showing how the boy's excitability had alarmed him; and Cherry anxiously watched for reports from home. Felix and she herself were the chief letter-writers in the family, and he kept her daily supplied with tidings. His first account—written at intervals at the reporter's table at Minsterham—bore that Lance had come all right, and seemed to have enjoyed himself much. So he had kept up for one day; but on the third came the inevitable tidings, 'Poor Lance is in bed, with headache in its worst shape. Wilmet has been obliged to stay at home to attend to him. It must have been coming on yesterday, for he seems to have talked more than enough, and made more blunders than can be remedied in a day. I suppose Edgar would have laughed if I had cautioned him; but I would about as soon have put the boy to stand on the Equator as have taken him to that opera.'

The days of pleasure seemed to have a heavy price; it was not till Saturday that Felix reported Lance as in his place as usual, but still looking ill, quiet, and subdued. 'I am afraid,' proceeded the letter, 'that it has been a very fascinating glimpse he has had of Edgar's way of life, and that F. and U.'s house is more against the grain to him. I doubt whether it be suited to him; but the other course seems over-perilous. I wonder whether fathers have the power of insight and judgment that I need so much. However, for the present, health speaks plainly that home is the only place for him; and I can with a free conscience enjoy his bright face and service of good will. To have you and him both out of the way *was* severe; but if it were not for his good, it is for yours.'

Yes, Geraldine trusted it was for her good. When Thomas Underwood went to the City in the morning she was always set down at the Renvilles', whence the transit to the Museum was so short, that she could make it either with her brother's arm or the master's. It was not thought fit for her to work all day, so Mrs. Sturt (the old nurse) always came to meet and take her home to luncheon; after which she either went out with Mrs. Underwood and Marilda, or was carried about by her brother, in which case her conveyance was always defrayed at the door with so little knowledge on her part, that Edgar accused her of supposing Cousin Thomas to keep innumerable very seedy equipages always in waiting on her steps.

It was great enjoyment—real instruction of the best sort in that which was most congenial to her, putting the crown on her long lonely perseverance, and giving a daily sense of progress and achievement, was delightful. She had no notion of rivalry; but when she perceived that she was excelling, that commendation almost always attended her attempts, and that in any competition she always came near the mark and was sometimes foremost, she was conscious of a startling sense of triumph; and Edgar was full of exultation. If his own studies at the Royal Academy had been fulfilling all his golden dreams, he could not have been half so uplifted as he was by Cherry's chances of a medal; while, if he had only acted on a quarter of the sensible advice he gave her, he would already have been far advanced in his profession.

If he had been imprudent in Lancelot's case, he showed much tender good judgment in his selection on Cherry's behalf of exhibitions and rehearsals—never overdoing her, and using all his grace and dexterity to obviate her fatigue and prevent embarrassments from her lameness, till she began to take courage and feel at ease.

Alda never went with them. She said Cherry's pace would be the death of her, and she knew it all by heart. Yet, go where they would, there generally appeared, soon after four o'clock, a tall, handsome, black-moustached figure, seldom uttering more than 'Good-morning!' and 'All well at home?' and then content to stalk beside them, perfectly indifferent to their object, but always ready to give an arm to Cherry, or to find a cab.

'Dogged by Montezuma's ghost!' Edgar would mutter when the inevitable black head came towering into view; and even Cherry sometimes felt the silent haunting rather a bore. Edgar and Ferdinand were both good company alone, but together she knew not what to do with them; since her sole common subject of interest to Ferdinand, church details, provoked Edgar's sarcasm; and though Edgar had enough to say on a thousand other points, Fernan was totally silent on all, except horses, of which on her side she knew nothing. Nevertheless, for very pity, he was always allowed to know their designs; and Cherry delivered messages between him and Alda, and marvelled at her never finding it possible to avail herself of such chances of meeting.

21

Indeed, it puzzled Cherry why Ferdinand should be banished from the house, since Marilda took pains to mark her friendly feeling towards him as Alda's betrothed; and the resentment of her parents appeared to be inactive; but Alda declared that any advance on his side would provoke great wrath, and that open intercourse was impossible; and it could only be supposed that she was the best judge.

However, to Cherry herself, Alda was far kinder than at home—perhaps because her own ground was too secure to leave room for jealousy; and she viewed her sister as guest rather than rival. During the first shyness and awe, she was a kind helper, full of tact, which parried the rather obtrusive patronage of her so-called aunt; she provided books, quietly ameliorated matters of dress, and threw in judicious hints and encouragements, so that Cherry's warm heart beat gratefully, and she thought she had never known how nice Alda could be in her proper element.

As to Marilda, she was thoroughly good-natured, perhaps rather teasing, and tyrannical as to what she thought for Cherry's good, and very careful that she should not be neglected; but there did not seem to be much in common between them, they never could get on in a *tête à tête*; and Cherry, who had heard vast statements from her brothers about Marilda's original forms of goodness, was disappointed to find her life so entirely that of a common-place young lady. She was clumsy, over-dressed, and of a coarse complexion; and though she sometimes said odd things, they were remarkable not for wit but for frankness. It seemed as though the world had been too much for Marilda's better self, and as if she were becoming the purse-proud heiress who fancied wealth could atone for want of refinement or of delicacy towards people's feelings.

It was with the master of the house that Cherry got on best. At first he treated her like a frail china cup that a touch might break, but gradually he discovered in her resemblances to all manner of past Underwoods, talked to her about her parents in their youth, expressed endless wonder how 'that lad Felix made it out,' and by-and-by found that a few questions about the day's doings would draw forth a delightfully fresh, simple, and amusing narrative, given with animated lips, and eyes that charmed him. He became very fond of little Geraldine, and accepted her as his special evening companion when his wife took the other two girls into society. She could talk, read the paper, or play at cribbage; and was so much pleased to be of use, that she became as much at ease and therefore as amusing as with old Froggy himself.

She had been assured of exemption from parties, but she found that the sumptuous luncheon was a popular institution, and that radiant ladies, lounging men, riding parties brought home by Alda, and stout matrons on a cruise of morning calls, were always dropping in. It was diverting to sit quietly by and listen to the characteristic confidences of the city dames, to the dashing nonsense of the girls, and the languid affectations of the young men; and capital material was furnished for the long letters that amused the breakfast-table at home—journals, half full of beautiful description, half full of fun and drollery. Those gay dames and demoiselles little thought what a pair of keen grey eyes were watching them, as they passed, almost unheeded, the little sober-hued person whom they never fairly understood to be the sister of the beautiful Alda.

Of the school establishment at Brompton Cherry saw something. She was invited to drink tea there, for the sake of talking over Angela; the two heads of the establishment being very glad to get an elder sister to discuss that puzzling personage with. Of Robina, since the catastrophe eighteen months ago, they had nothing but good to say; she had really lived it down, so far as to have proved that if she had erred, it was only in judgment; but with Angela they still knew not what to do.

She had come back subdued and with better impulses, and these had carried her on up to Easter, giving such satisfaction to the Vicar, that he had sanctioned her Confirmation; but immediately after the holidays, the wild spirit had broken out again. She neither learnt nor tried to learn, attended to nothing but music, and showed up exercises and dictation flagrantly ill-spelt, and not unfrequently making fun of the whole subject. As a reward for her weeks of propriety, she had been promoted to the German class; but she had openly declared that she hated German, and saw no use in it, and she would not attempt anything but an occasional caricature of pronunciation. Everybody liked her—even those whom she most disrespectfully provoked; and she was like a kind of tame monkey to the school, turning her very punishments into absurdity. She would lighten solitary confinement by fantastically decorating the chairs and tables. If shut up in the dark, her clear shrill voice would convulse all the household with Lance's whole repertory of comic songs, the favourite being Thackeray's 'Little Billee,' which she always sang as if she expected to be rescued by the sight of 'Admiral Nelson, K.C.B.,' if not made 'Captain of a Seventy-three!' and even impositions she always managed to make ludicrous, by comments, translations, or illustrations, bringing them up with a certain irresistible innocence and simplicity of countenance. What was to be done? No, they did not want her to be taken away; she was a bright dear girl, with a great deal of good in her—very warm-hearted, and certainly devout; and Miss Fennimore confessed that she should be very sorry to part with her, or to confess herself beaten in the struggle. 'Your name is Geraldine?' she asked, suddenly; 'are you Irish?'

'My grandmother was.'

'That accounts for it!'

'She must have absorbed all the Irish nature in the family, then,' said Cherry, laughing.

'Perhaps. But it throws a light on it. I don't know which is the most curious subject, national or family character.'

Of course Cherry was set to talk to Angela—an operation that she hated almost as much as Felix did; and the result of which attempt was this, 'Now don't—don't, Cherry!'—hugging her round the neck; 'you never were made for scolding, and it is no use spoiling your own pleasure and mine! Leave it to Wilmet; she does it with dignity, you know!'

'But, Angel, I do really want to understand why you are so set against German?'

'It's a nasty crack-jaw language, that all the infidels write their books in.'

'I only wish they did!' murmured Cherry.

'And it's the Protestant language, too; and that's *worse*,' persisted Angela. 'No, I won't learn it on principle.'

'I thought principle was to do what one was told.'

'That depends. Now, German will never be of use to me; I'm not going to be a governess, and I sha'n't qualify myself for it!'

'Yes, Angel, I know what you mean; but isn't obedience the qualification you must learn—if you are to come to the other thing?'

'I shall learn it fast enough when the time comes. Don't you know, Cherry, a republic is much better preparation for despotism than one of your shilly-shally rational limited monarchies?'

'That may be true,' said Cherry; 'but you know I think the rational loyalty the most wholesome training.'

'Yes, I know. Family life suits you; but I must have the—the real religious life or none. I don't like secularity.'

'O Angel, you are much worse with these fine words that deceive you, when you are really and truly only a naughty idle child!'

'That's true, Cherry; and yet it is not true,' said Angela, thoughtfully. 'I am a naughty idle child, and yet I am more.'

'How is it—after this Confirmation and all?'

'Ah!' said Angel, frankly. 'I thought it would have done me good and made me different; but instead there's just one anticipation gone, and nothing to look to.'

'Not your own possible future?' (Cherry knew of it, though not Wilmet.)

'That's such a dreadful way off! No, if you all *will* keep me in the world, I must have my fun! Come, Cherry, don't look so horribly vexed! I'll tell you what, if you'll cheer up, I won't have another flare-up with old Fen as long as you are here to be bullied about it!'

And she kept her word so faithfully, that the two ladies thought that charming little elder sister had had a great effect upon their troublesome charge.

CHAPTER XXVI.

TRANSMUTATION.

'Affection follows Fortune's wheels,
And soon is shaken from her heels;
For, following beauty or estate,
Her loving soon is turned to hate.'
Sir Walter Raleigh.

'Do you remember,' wrote Cherry, 'poor Fernan's old rival in the Life Guards, Sir Adrian Vanderkist? I have seen him! He descended upon us at luncheon-time in all his glory; and Mrs. Underwood was like Eve entertaining the Angel. I hope that is not profane! it is only Paradise Lost. I don't comprehend her delight, for he is only the grandson of a man who made a great fortune by inventing some metal to look like silver. Though he must have been Dutch, this youth is not the conventional Dutchman in seven knickerbockers perched on a barrel, but is small and insignificant, in spite of his magnificent get-up. Never did Fernan, in his most bejewelled days, equal that studious exquisiteness; and I could pity the baronet for having had a rival with black moustaches that curl of their own accord; but pity evaporates when I find that he has got Brown Murad, and hear Mrs. Underwood's gratitude for his promise of tickets for somebody's concert. I wonder whether he is thinking about Marilda?

'April 15th. Two great events begin to loom. One is our *soirée musicale*, for which the cards are actually being written; and Edgar and Alda are debating the programme. I am to have a quiet corner out of sight, and use my eyes and ears. How I wish you and Lance could send up yours!

'The other is a great function at St. Matthew's, on the opening of the new infant-schools, on Whit Tuesday. Clement is coming down for it; and Robin, Angel, and I are to go with Cousin Tom to his office, where Clem will meet and take charge of us. It certainly is a fine thing to come to London, and see the world; though the nicest part of the world to me is that odd little room of Mrs. Renville's where people are so entertaining, and one catches glimpses of great luminaries in their moments of unbending and good nature.......

'May 3rd. Where shall I begin the story of our *soirée*? I will pass over the misery of serving as a *corpus vile*, for Alda and Mrs. Sturt to try experiments on with scraps of head-gear and jewellery, and merely state that I had the white alpaca with blue velvet edges, and blue beads round my head and neck; and then they did not *very much* mind the sight of me; and Edgar even said I looked a tidy little thing enough. He and Marilda disposed of me in a nice little nook in the recess of a window, more than half hidden by a curtain, and capital for seeing and hearing, nearly as good as my old perch in the organ gallery. Alda looked beautiful—such lovely rosy clouds of soft gauziness, and wreaths of wild roses! She has put an end to the habit of dressing like Marilda, to their mutual benefit; but, oh, if I could see old W.W. in such garb! Doesn't she look disgusted? But who knows what John may put her into?

'Oh, the things people wear! (then followed some pen-and-ink outlines,) and the colours and the festoonings! I trust that in some stratum of society somewhere there is more notion of the beautiful. If the world is all like this, I can't tell why it should be so dangerous; for, as far as I can see, it consists in conjugating the verb *to bore*.

'However, there was the music, and that was compensation. (A critical account ensued then.) *Private.* Poor Edgar was quite upset when one of the ladies varied from the programme by singing Alice's favourite old "Sands of Dee." I saw him frowning and biting the end of his moustache, as if he could hardly bear it; but, as you may guess, he was the more funny and lively when he came to me, teasing me about that Sir Adrian, whom he calls a specimen of the transmutation of metals—Dutch slime made shiny, and threatening me with who or what would be transmuted next; but I think Marilda has more principle.

'Afterwards I had a great treat, for Edgar spied Mr. Grinstead, whom we had never expected, though he had a card, as he does not care for music; and Cousin Tom only knows him through having bought his lovely group of Una and the Lion. I had met him at the Renvilles'; and

Edgar brought him to my corner, where he leant against the window-shutter, and talked most pleasantly, only he would go on all through the songs; but one could excuse a great deal to a man who knew Thorwaldsen, and has seen Canova; and he told me so much that I wanted to hear, that it was a perfect feast. When he found I had never seen the Leonardo at Morecombe House, he caught Mrs. Underwood, and arranged to take us there at four o'clock on Wednesday. Fancy seeing a Leonardo! and with him to explain it! Mrs. Underwood was quite in a rapture, because she wants to see a cabinet that Lady Morecombe gave £150 for; but I thought it very nasty of Sir Adrian to say that he knew Lord Morecombe very well, and could take her there any day, to which Alda answered that she hated show houses.'

(Enclosed from Edgar.)

'The fact is, that the Cherry is a brilliant success. She is our one native genius for conversation; and I will say for the Pursuivant that it has kept her up to the day. At Renville's she is the life of everything; and even here the ocean of dullness cannot so entirely asphyxiate her but that she sparkles up through it; and luckily Alda has not so perceived it as to begin the extinguishing process—indeed, she has affairs of her own to look to. As to Grinstead—it is a case of captivation. Don't be afraid, or the reverse: he is a confirmed old bachelor, bald and spectacled. Renville showed him her sketch of his Una, and he said nothing had ever so hit off the soul. He met her at their house; and she, not knowing who he was, was not encumbered with any awe of greatness, but chattered like her own little self, till he was taken with her freshness and cleverness, came here on purpose to meet her, and is to show her the Morecombe gallery. A fine chance! Altogether, the little maid has so many feathers in her cap, that she wouldn't know where to stick them, if—poor little dear!—she ever found them out, and didn't think every attention pure pity to her lame foot.'

The next was the day of the festival at St. Matthew's. Mr. Underwood graciously consented to use a carriage large enough to transport Cherry and both her little sisters to his office, at the door of which there appeared, however, not Clement, but Ferdinand Travis. The organist had been suddenly taken ill, and Clement was supplying his place; so Ferdinand, whose firm had taken a Whitsun holiday, was the substitute, in the vain hope that Alda would have been of the party.

'No,' said Angela; 'they are going to ride. And, O Fernan! I am sure I saw Brown Murad com—'

There she stopped short, either aghast at a sort of spasm that crossed Ferdinand's countenance, or diverted by the full current of life in Holborn; and he, recovering, began to point out whatever could interest Cherry. He had a great deal to tell about St. Matthew's, where he knew his way as well as Clement himself, and piloted his charge in good time to the very place their brother had indicated for them.

The service was most beautiful, and full of life; and then ensued a procession to, and benediction of, the new school and nursery for the little ones. Afterwards came the new experience of luncheon for the large motley party in the refectory of the clergy-house—new at least to Cherry, for her sisters were not unfamiliar there; Robina had a dear friend's little brother among the choristers, and Angela was chattering to a curate or two. Clement was happy in meeting with old comrades; and Cherry was glad that she was saved from being a burthen by Ferdinand's devotion, and quite accepted his assurance that it was a great delight to him.

Then followed a feast for the school-children and the aged; but the atmosphere soon became too much for Cherry, and she thankfully accepted Ferdinand's proposal of showing her the church in detail. It was only on the other side of the quadrangle; and there was a great charm in the lofty, cool, quiet building, where she could dwell thoroughly on every decoration, permanent or temporary, and in full sympathy with her companion, who went so fully and deeply into all these subjects, as to lead her on, and open new meanings to her. At last they sat down in a sort of cloister that ran round the court, to wait for the rest.

'Do you know,' said Geraldine, 'this place gives me a sense of life and vigour. Our own seems to me, in comparison, a sort of sleeping, or rather a mechanically acting, body, wanting a spirit and soul to be breathed into it and make it effective.'

'You have never told me about your new curate,' said Ferdinand; and indeed, by tacit consent, they had avoided the subject in Edgar's presence.

'Mr. Flowerdew? Oh, he is very good, very gentle, and kind; but he is a depressed elderly man, with all the energy disappointed and worn out of him. His wife is dead; and he has two or three children, out, settled, and fighting their way; and there he is alone, still an assistant curate, tumbled about in secondary positions too long to care for any more than just doing his duty without any life or spring.'

'Do you see much of him?' said Ferdinand, surprised by this intimate knowledge.

'Yes. He makes the sick his special care, and he thinks me one; so he comes sometimes, and sits half an hour when I am painting, without saying a word. I think it is cheerful for him, in his way,' said Cherry, with a merry laugh. 'And he is very musical; so the boys like that. But do you know, Ferdinand, when I look at him, I do feel thankful that my own dear father had not the long weary wear and tear to change him. That man is older than he would be even now.'

'Of course it must be good,' said Ferdinand. 'And is there no chance of Mr. Bevan coming back?'

'He wants another summer at the baths. The absence of the head paralyses everything so. I always feel, when I go back from St. Faith's, as if we had the framework, and of course the real essentials; but we have to do all the work of bringing it home to ourselves.'

'I know what you mean,' said Ferdinand; 'though Bexley must be more to me than any other place, this one is the great help and compensation to me. How I wish Alda were near it!'

'Has she ever been here?'

'Once or twice; but only under its shadow does one enter into the real life. Some day perhaps—'

Geraldine could not imagine the day of Alda's entering into the real life of St. Matthew's; but she could only say, 'Of course there is a vast difference between only coming as an outsider, and being one of the congregation.'

'Immense; though I never found it out till I came to live here; and so it would be with her. After all, were she but near, or I could see her freely, I should enjoy my present life very much.'

'I'll tell you what I should do in your place,' said Cherry. 'I would go straight to Mr. Underwood, and ask his leave to visit her; and I don't believe he would make any objection.'

'No. Alda forbids that,' he answered, decidedly; 'and she can be the only judge.' Cherry felt small. But presently he added, 'I wish I could be rid of the doubt whether the present state of things is not burdensome to her. Perhaps I ought to to have freed her at once; I could have worked for her without binding her.'

'Nothing but affection really binds,' said Cherry, in some difficulty for her answer.

'No; I might have trusted to that, but I thought the release would cost her as much as myself; and she was at home then!' and he suppressed a heavy sigh.

'She said it would be easier to meet you in London,' said Cherry; 'but I don't think it is.'

'And absence leaves room for imaginations,' he said. 'And I have nothing tangible to set against what I hear—ay, and see.'

'What?' the word was out of Cherry's mouth before she could check it.

'You can cast it out of my mind, perhaps,' he said. 'Do you ever see a fellow of the name of Vanderkist?'

Cherry could not help starting. And his black brows bent, and his face became stern, so that she was fain to cry, 'Oh, but it's Marilda!'

'Impossible!' he said, with what she thought a terrible smile at her simplicity. 'I tell you, I saw his first look at her—at my Alda!' Some ruthless Spanish ancestor must have looked out of the deep glow of his eyes, as he added, 'I hear he has betted that she, as well as whatever I used to prize, shall be his before the end of the season.'

'Let him!' said Cherry, proudly. 'Alda can't help that. She can't hinder his coming to the house.'

'I know,' he said. 'Do not suppose that I doubt her. I trust her entirely; but I am foolish enough to long for the assurance that there is no cause for the rumour that she encourages him.'

Under such eyes of dark fire, it was well that Cherry could sincerely answer, 'Oh no! Every one does come round her; but she does not let him do so a bit more than other people.'

'You entirely believe that I may dismiss this as a base groundless suspicion?'

'I do!' she said, with all her heart. 'We all know that Alda is used to admiration; it comes to her as naturally as pity and help to me, and makes no impression on her. Mrs. Underwood likes to have him as a fashionable guest, that's all. Oh, Alda could never be so wicked!'

'You are right, Geraldine. Thank you,' he said, just as Clement and the younger ones came in search of them, with Fred Somers, erst fellow-chorister, now fellow-Cantab—a little wiry merry fellow, the very antipodes to his bosom friend.

All wanted to stay for seven o'clock Evensong; but Robina was clear that it was impossible, since the ladies were dispersing, and they had no invitation to the clergy-house. Angela wildly asked if Clement could not take them to the Tower, or St Paul's; Cherry could sit in a seat while they went round.

'Sit in a seat!' cried Robina. 'She is tired already. Clement, do go and call a cab.'

'Could you not go to Mrs. Kedge's, Cherry?' asked Clement. 'I want you to hear our Pentecost Hymns.'

'Come to my rooms,' said Ferdinand. 'They are much nearer; and you shall have tea and everything in no time.'

'Like greased lightning!' returned Angel, who always talked what she supposed to be Yankee to Ferdinand. 'Oh, what fun! Do come, Cherry!'

'Do come,' repeated Ferdinand, eagerly; 'it is only round the corner, no crossing, and no stairs; and you shall have a good rest—much better than jingling away in a cab.'

'Thank you;' and Cherry looked inquiringly at Robina, whose discretion she viewed as little short of Wilmet's. 'Would Miss Fulmort approve?'

'Yes,' said that wise little bird; 'we need only be in by ten. You had much better, Cherry. You are quite as good as a brother—aren't you, Fernan?'

In ten minutes more, Mr. Travis's landlady was aghast at the procession pouring into her quiet ground-floor; while, after insisting on Cherry's installation on a dingy lumpy bumpy sofa, their host might be overheard giving orders for a sumptuous tea, though not exactly with the genius of Wilmet or Lance.

He had cast his anxieties to the winds, and had never shown himself so lively or so much at ease. To all it was a delightful frolic. Mr. Somers was full of fun, and even Clement was gay—perhaps because Whittingtonia had become a sort of native element to him, or else because the oddity of the thing overcame him; and Angela was in an ecstatic state, scarcely kept within bounds by her morning's promise to be *very* good.

Those dingy bachelor's rooms, close upon the street, and redolent of tobacco to the utmost degree, could seldom have re-echoed with such girlish fun as while Angela roamed about, saucily remarking on the pipes and smoking equipments—relics, not disused, of the Life Guard days. So likewise was the beautiful little chased silver tea-pot, which was committed to Robin's management. Indeed, there was a large proportion of plate, massive and remarkable.

'Mexican taste,' said Ferdinand, handing a curious sugar-basin. 'It belonged to my grandmother, and was turned over to me when I set up for myself.'

'What's this on it? said Angel. 'I declare, 'tis the caldron the Mexicans boiled people's hearts in.'

'For shame, Angel!' said Robin; 'the Aztecs were not cannibals.'

'I beg your pardon, Bobbie; I know we read about Cortes seeing them cutting out people's hearts on their temples like the tower of Babel, because I thought of Fernan.'

'Hush!' said Cherry, seeing that the horrid subject was displeasing. 'There's nothing witty in talking of horrors. Besides, is not this the Spanish olla?'

'I believe it is,' answered Ferdinand. 'It is the Mendez bearing, and as the Travises can boast of none, I followed my spoons.'

'With the dish,' said Mr. Somers; a joke that in their present mood set them laughing.

'Nothing can be more suited to the circumstances,' said Cherry, 'as the olla is the emblem of hospitality.'

'What are the three things up above?' asked Angel; 'turnips going to be stewed?'

'Santiago's cockle-shells, the token of pilgrimage,' said Ferdinand. 'That's the best part of the coat.'

'Some day I'll work you a banner-screen, Fernan,' said Robina; 'but that will be when you impale our Underwood rood.'

'And the pilgrim is brought to the cross,' said Angela, in one of her grave moments of fanciful imagery.

The echo of her words, however, struck Cherry as conveying an innuendo that the child did not mean. Crosses could hardly be wanting to one who had Alda for his wife; but happily no one else seemed to perceive it; and they drifted on from grave to gay, and gay back to grave, till it was time to return to the festival Evensong.

Clement and his friends had to hurry away to the station directly after. He would have put his three sisters into a cab, and sent it home with them; but Ferdinand insisted on squeezing his long limbs into durance and escorting them, to the tune of Angel's chatter and the clatter of the windows. Cherry was the first set down; and she went straight to the drawing-room, ready for interest and sympathy.

'How late you are!' said Alda.

'How did you come?' asked Marilda.

'In a cab. It is gone on with the little girls. We stayed for evening service. The lights were so beautiful!'

'Just what boys and girls run after,' said Mr. Underwood. 'I like my opera to be an opera, and my church to be a church.'

'Yes,' said Mrs. Underwood, 'staying out so late, and in the city. I don't half like such doings.'

'What could you have done between services?' added Alda. 'Were you at the clergy-house all day?'

'Of course they were,' said Mr. Underwood. 'Trust a curate to take care of a pretty girl. High or low, they are all alike.'

'No,' said Cherry, in blushing indignation; 'we had tea at Mr. Travis's.'

'Indeed!' said Alda.

And Cherry knew the tone but too well; and under this plentiful shower of cold water, perceiving her own fatigue, bade good night. She was kindly bidden to send Nurse for wine, tea, or whatever she needed; but she was still conscious of displeasure.

In the morning she was weary and dispirited, and for the first time felt that there was no one to remark, as Felix or Wilmet would have done, that she was flagging. Failing this, she prepared as usual to go to her class; but before starting she encountered Mrs. Underwood.

'Geraldine,' said that lady, majestically, 'you are a talented young person; but—you must excuse me—I cannot have such independence under my roof. It is not *comifo*. Bless me, don't tremble so; I don't mean anything. You meant no harm; only you should have come home, you know, when your brother wasn't there.'

'But he was!' gasped Geraldine, colouring.

'Why, wasn't it that young man Travis met you?'

'He met us, for Clement was hindered; but Clement was there, and was with us all the time.'

'H'm! That ought to have been explained. Why didn't you tell your sister? She is quite distressed.'

A summons from Mr. Underwood obliged Cherry to hurry away, her heart throbbing, her head whirling, and no comfort but hard squeezing the ivory back of Lord Gerald; and when she reached Mr. Renville's, her hand was trembling so, that she could not have drawn a line if the good haus-frau had not dosed her with the strong coffee, which in true German fashion was always ready. Then the absorbing interest of her art revived her; and she returned home, cheered, and believing that the misunderstanding was cleared up.

Indeed, Mrs. Underwood was as good-natured as ever; and Alda was chiefly employed in rejecting all the solicitations to accompany the party to Morecombe House, and rebutting the remonstrances on the incivility to Mr. Grinstead; to which Marilda had yielded, but grumbling loudly at the bore of seeing pictures and taking no pains to conceal that she was cross and angry with Cherry for having brought it upon her.

Poor Cherry! Of the few parties of pleasure of her life, this was that which most reminded her of the old woman of Servia! After having Marilda's glum face opposite through the drive, she was indeed most kindly welcomed by Mr. Grinstead; but how could she enjoy the attention that was so great a kindness and honour, when every pause before a picture was a manifest injury to her companions?

Mrs. Underwood indeed had occupation in peeping under holland covers, estimating the value of carpets and curtains, and admiring the gilt frames; but this did not hold out as long as the examination of each favourite picture in detail; and what was worse, Marilda plumped herself down in the first chair in each room, and sat poking the floor with her parasol, the model of glum discontent. How could the mind be free for the Madonna's celestial calm, or the smiling verisimilitude of portraiture? how respond or linger, when the very language of art was mere uninteresting jargon to impatient captives, who thought her comprehension mere affectation? While to all other discomforts must be added the sense of missing one of the best opportunities of her life, and of ill responding to a gracious act of condescension.

She came home tired to death, and with a bad headache, that no one took the trouble to remark; and she dressed for dinner with a sense that it mattered to no one how she felt.

Just as she was ready, Marilda came gravely in, sitting down in preparation, Cherry felt, for something dreadful; but even her imagination failed to depict the fact.

'Geraldine,' was the beginning, 'Alda wishes you to hear that she has put an end to the engagement.'

Cherry absolutely screamed, 'Oh, oh, don't let her do that! It would be so dreadful!'

Marilda looked severe. 'I don't suppose you thought what it was coming to.'

'O! I have often been sorry to see things, but it seemed so atrocious to think so.'

'Then you must have known you were doing wrong.'

'What—how—what have I done? I don't know what you mean!'

'Indeed! It is of no use to look frightened and innocent. Perhaps you did not mean anything; but when it grew so marked, Alda could not but feel it.'

'What? Does Alda mean *that?*' cried Cherry, starting up, scarlet with horror.

'Now I see you understand. She is terribly hurt. She excuses it, for she says you have been so petted all your life, that you don't know the right bounds.'

'And can you really think this of me?' moaned she.

'It is just like every one when they have the chance—no one ever means it,' said Marilda.

'Oh!' cried Cherry, as a fresh horror came across her, 'but if Alda thinks ever so horridly of me, how can she doubt him? Oh, stop her, stop her! Let me only tell her how he talked of her yesterday! His whole soul is full of her. Oh, stop her, Marilda, do!'

'It is of no use,' said Marilda; 'she has sent her letter. She was resolved to do nothing hastily, so she went this morning and saw the little girls.'

'Oh, oh!' broke in Cherry, with another cry of pain. 'Those poor children have not been brought into trouble again?'

'No; it was no doing of theirs; but when she perceived the exclusive attention that—when she found,' hesitated Marilda, forgetting her lesson, 'how you had been sitting in the cloister—in short, how it had all gone on—she said it was the finishing stroke.'

'Oh!' a sigh or groan, as if stabbed; then with spirit, 'but why wasn't she there herself? He only took me for want of her! He only speaks to me because I am her sister. He was so unhappy—I was trying to cheer him.'

'So you might think; but that's the way those things run on. There's the gong!'

Cherry rose, but felt that sitting at table would end in faintness, and Marilda went away in doubt, between pity and displeasure, whether at contrition or affectation.

No sooner was the door shut, and Cherry alone, than a terrible hysterical agony came on. There was personal sense of humiliation—passionate anger, despair, for Ferdinand's sake—miserable loneliness and desertion. She felt as if she were in a house full of enemies; and had absolute difficulty in restraining screams for Felix to come and take her home. The physical need of Wilmet or Sibby, to succour and soothe her agitation and exhaustion, soon became so great as to overpower the mental distress; but she would not call or ring; and when Mrs. Sturt came, the kind woman made as if the headache accounted for all.

She reported that Miss Alda likewise had gone to her room with a headache; and Cherry saw no one but Mrs. Underwood, who looked in to offer impossible remedies, and be civilly but stiffly compassionate.

The stifled hysteria was much worse for Geraldine than free tears. She had a weary night of wretched dream fancies, haunted by Ferdinand's sombre face, convulsed with rage, and tormented by the belief that she had done something so frightful as to put her out of the pale of humanity; nor was it till long after daylight that she could so collect her ideas as to certify herself that if she had done wrong, it had at least been unwittingly; but even then she was in a misery of shame, and of the most intense longing for her brother or sister to defend and comfort her.

She managed to rise and dress; but she was far too unwell to attempt the classes for the day. Alda spoke coldly; and she crept away, to lie on the sofa in the old school-room, trusting that before post-time her hand might grow steady enough to write an entreaty to be taken home, and longing—oh! longing more every hour for Edgar, and still he did not come! Marilda looked in, began to believe her really ill, grew compassionate, asked how she treated such attacks, deemed her penitent, and began to soothe her as if she was a naughty baby. Then, in desperation, Cherry ventured to ask what had been heard of him—Mr. Travis. He had been at the door—he had taken no refusal—had forced an interview—he was gone. Alda was in her own room, bolted in. Marilda had not seen her since.

Cherry shook from head to foot, and quivered with suppressed strangling sobs, as the shame of such a requital for the sacrifice of Ferdinand's whole career agonised her at one moment, and at another she was terrified at the possible effect on that fervid nature.

Oh, that long, long piteous day! She never did write—never even felt as if she could sit up to guide a pen. At last Alda came in, with a strange awe-struck paleness about her face, as if she had gone through something terrible; and in a tone that sounded unnatural, said, 'Come, Cherry, don't give way so. I didn't mean to accuse you. People don't always know what they are doing. I am thankful on my own account.'

Cherry had longed for a kind word; but this sort of pardon was like Alda's taking the advantage of her when Felix was not there to protect her. Not naturally meek, she was too much shaken to control a voice that sounded more like temper than sorrow. 'You have no right to accuse me at all, as if I were a traitor!'

'Not a deliberate traitor, my dear,' said Alda, in a voice of candour; 'certainly not; but you don't know the advantage helplessness and cleverness give over us poor beauties who show our best at first. I blame no one for using their natural weapons.'

'Don't, Alda!' cried Cherry, with the sharpness of keen offence. 'You may keep that speech for those you got it up for!'

'Well, if you are in such a mood as that, nobody can talk to you,' said Alda, going away, and leaving her to a worse paroxysm of misery than before, and an inexpressible sense of desolation, passing into an almost frantic craving for Edgar, to make him take her home.

Marilda gave a little relief by telling her that he was sent for; but after long expectation, word came that he was not at home, nor did his landlady know when he would return.

By this time it was too late to send a letter; and Cherry began to feel ashamed of having so given way, and to think of exerting herself to recover, if only to be in a condition to go home when Edgar should be found; so she made an effort to remember the remedies with which she was wont to be passively dosed by Wilmet, went to bed, and tried hard to put herself to sleep. Though it was long before she effectually succeeded, she was much calmer in the morning, deeply wounded indeed, but trying to accept the imputation that her habit of expecting aid might have led her into what had given umbrage to Alda, and that self immolation might yet heal the misunderstanding, and the desire to plead with Alda seemed to brace her nerves; but Alda was not attainable. She only just came in, in her habit, while Mrs. Sturt was dressing Cherry, and said that she had such a headache, that she must take a country ride; and Cherry, who felt as if she had been under a stampede of wild horses, could only just crawl to the sofa, and lie there; while the whole family were in such wholesome dread of that dumb hysteria, that they were as tender as they knew how to be, and abstained from all reference to the previous day.

The afternoon had come on the weary, home-sick, exhausted spirit, when a springy step came along the corridor, a light airy rap struck the door, and a tall, lithe, yet strong form, and a pair of kind smiling eyes, brought the sense of love and guardianship that the spoilt child of home had been pining for. She had yesterday meant to cry out to him,' O Edgar, take me home!' but she did not speak, only looked up, glad and relieved.

'Why, Cherry,' as he kissed her hot brow, and caressingly held her limp cold hand, 'it seems to be the family fashion to suffer by proxy for these little catastrophes. Who is to take to his or her bed when some Indian spinster hooks W.W.'s engineer?'

'Hush, Edgar! Have you seen *him?*'

'Have not I?'

'Ah, I knew you must be with him, when they could not find you!'

'Me? No; I had enough of it the night before! I had had too narrow an escape of getting my neck wrung for declining to act as go-between, to subject myself to the same again, and went off with some fellows to Richmond—only came back an hour ago.'

'O, Edgar! if you had but tried—'

'Take my advice, Cherry. Never put your foot into a boiling cauldron! Besides, don't you know perfectly well that never was there a worse matched pair? St. Anthony and Venus attired by the Graces; and very little more attire could he give her. If dear old Blunderbore had had a grain of common sense he would have told them so a year ago; and I should have thought even you could have seen it to be a happy release.'

'I see you don't know the cause—'

'Visible enough to the naked eye!' And Edgar, in imitation of Theodore, hummed 'Mynheer van Dunck.'

'For shame, Edgar! Oh no! it is only what could be mended if you would but show her that I—that he—that he only was kind to me for her sake. If she would only hear what he was saying to me! but she won't! Just set it straight; and then, please—please take me home.'

'Well,' said Edgar, as he gathered the drift of her broken phrases, spoken with her face hidden on his shoulder, 'this is as nasty, spiteful a trick as Alda ever played! He said she put it on some motive of jealousy—and she always was a jealous toad; but I never guessed at this! Never mind, Chérie. She only wanted a pretext, and you came first to hand. I'll let her know what I think of it—and Polly too!'

'But, indeed, I don't think I was guarded enough.'

'Of course you don't. You and Tina think yourselves the most heavenly-minded when you can accuse yourselves of anything utterly ridiculous.'

'It was what she heard from Robin and Angel.'

'The marplots of the family—little minxes!' said Edgar, with a bitterness she was sorry to have provoked. 'No,' he added, 'not marplots in this case. I see it all as plain as a pikestaff! Felix having shown his usual refreshing innocence by leaving Alda in this predicament, she had to get out of it as best she could; so she trumps up this charge between Robin's prudery and Angel's chatter; nor would I have blamed her a bit if she had only flourished it in his eyes; but to poison Marilda with it, and annihilate you—I can't forgive that!'

'Oh, but she believes it.'

'If she gets up a little delusion—a slight screen to the Mynheer—she ought to keep it to herself.'

'I shall try to write it all properly to her when I get home.'

'Home! You aren't going to be ill?'

'No; but I can't stay after all this—to be looked on in this way.'

'I'll settle that.'

'You can't expose Alda.'

'I shall expose her no more than I have done fifty times before. Don't be afraid. We understand one another—Polly, Alda, and I.'

'Don't defend me! I had so much rather go back.'

'Of course; but you need not be a little goose. You did not come here for pleasure, but business. And is this great genius to be stifled because Alda talks a little unjustifiable nonsense?'

'Do you think Felix and Wilmet would tell me to stay?'

'Wilmet certainly would. Felix might be tempted to take his baby home to rock; but even he has sense enough to tell you that the only way to deal with such things is to brazen them out.'

'I haven't got any brass.'

'Then you must get some. Seriously, Cherry, it would be very silly to go flying home, throwing up all your opportunities, and the very thing to give some *vraisemblance* to Alda's accusation. If I had only been here yesterday, I'd have choked it in the throat of her, and hindered you from caring a straw; but I didn't want to meet Travis in his exies.'

'I wish you would really tell me about him—poor dear Fernan!'

'Take care! That looks suspicious. Well, poor fellow! the Mexican is strong in him. *Grattez lui* ever so slightly. Well for Mynheer that he is not out with him on a prairie, with a revolver! But, whereas Audley and Felix caught him in time to make a spoon out of a bowie-knife, I don't expect much to happen, beyond my distraction from his acting caged panther in my room till two o'clock that night!'

'He came here and saw her yesterday. Have you seen him since?'

No; Edgar had kept out of the way, and would not talk of him; but stood over his sister, wishing to soothe and relieve the little thing, for whom he cared more than for all the lovers put together, and whose wan exhausted looks, visible suffering, and nervous shudders he could not bear to see. 'I wish you weren't too big for rocking, Baby,' he said. And then he sat down to the piano, playing and singing a low soft lullaby, which at last brought quiet sleep to the refreshment of the harassed mind and weary frame.

The hum of conversation in an undertone at length gradually roused her.

'The long and short of it is, that she was tired of it.'

'But she wouldn't have invented such a story.'

'I never said she invented it! She's not so stupid but that she can put a gloss on a thing; and you *know* she hates to have a civil word said to any one but herself—particularly to that poor little dear.'

'Then it wasn't right to let him be always running after her.'

'Stuff! They'd been cronies ever since he was first caught; in fact, she was one of the tame elephants that licked him into shape, long before he set eyes on either of you. No stuff about it at all; they are just like brother and sister. The poor child would no more be capable of such a thing than that lay figure of hers—hasn't it in her; and for you to go and bully her!'

'Well,' in a half-puzzled, half-angered tone, 'that's what Alda says. She declares she only told me, and never meant me to speak to *her* about the cause.'

'She wanted to play off the injured heroine; and you—not being up to such delicate subtilties, walked off to speak your mind. Eh!'

'I thought I ought.'

'You put your great thumb on a poor little May-fly, just as if it had been a tortoise!'

'I'm sure I had no notion she would be so unhappy; all girls do such things; and most are proud of it. I was only disappointed to find her like the rest; but I'd no notion she would cry herself ill.'

Here Geraldine's senses became sufficiently clear to make her aware that she was the topic, and ought to rouse herself, no longer to let the discussion mingle with her dreams. With some effort she opened her eyes, and saw Edgar astride on the music-stool, and Marilda leaning on the mantel-shelf.

'I'm awake,' she drowsily said.

'To the battle over your prostrate body,' said Edgar. 'Go to sleep again, little one. Polly is very sorry, and won't do so no more.'

'She didn't say so, Edgar,' said Cherry; 'and if I had really done so, she ought to have been a great deal more angry with me.'

'Well, Geraldine,' said Marilda, 'I believe, whatever you did, you didn't know it; and I know I was hard on you. My father and mother don't know anything about it—only that it is off—'

'And that they rightly ascribe to Alda's good sense,' said Edgar.

This much relieved Cherry, who had thought it impossible to remain where she was, viewed as a traitor to her own sister. It wounded her, indeed, that Marilda should merely condone the offence, instead of acquitting her; but when she recollected the probability that Marilda had suffered the like treatment from Alda, who was nevertheless loved so heartily, it began to dawn upon her that there was a disposition to view the offence as common, natural, and light, rather than not excuse the offender. She despised her cousin for lowering the standard to suit a favourite, and was sure she should never be comfortable again till she got home; but she was reasonable enough to perceive the force of what Edgar had shown her—as to the folly of forsaking her studies, and abandoning the advantages offered to her; and his kindness had much cheered her; so she said no more about going home, and resumed her former habits, though feeling that Marilda's patronizing cordiality was gone, and that Alda was simply cold and indifferent.

She felt especially unwilling to face the two little girls, who seemed to have acted as false witnesses against her; but an imploring note from Robina besought her to call; and on arriving in the parlour, where interviews were allowed, she was greeted with, 'O Cherry, is it true? and was that why Alda came here?'

Then she found that they had heard from home of the rupture of the engagement; and that they had immediately connected it with Alda's extraordinary visit of the week previous.

'She came to bring us a cake,' said Robin; 'but as she never did so before, I thought something was at the bottom of it, and that she just wanted to hear more about Ferdinand and his lodgings.'

'And,' added Angel, who, if less sensible, was far before Robina in a certain irregular precocity, 'I thought I'd get a rise out of her, and chaff her a little. She used to be so savage last year, whenever Fernan treated you with common humanity.'

'O Angel, how could you!'

'You don't mean that it did the harm! Bobbie said so; but I didn't think Alda could be so silly as to think it in earnest, Cherry.'

'Angel, you have been playing with edge-tools.'

'Cherry, tell me what you mean!' Angela pounced on both her arms, as if to shake it out of her.

'Never do such a thing again, Angel. You cannot tell what you may be doing.'

'Well, if any one could be so stupid! So dense, as not to see it was fun! Now, Robin—'

'I think,' said the practical Robin, 'that all you can do, is to write down a full confession that you meant to tease Alda.'

'Yes, yes, yes,' cried Angela, with less shame than Cherry would have thought possible, 'I will! I will! and then they'll make it up. Who would have thought Alda could have been so easily taken in? But how shall I do it unknownst to the harpies?'

Cherry offered a pencil, and a bit of her drawing-block. She made no suggestion, thinking that the more characteristic the confession was, the more it would prove its authenticity. Angela retired into a window, and wrote, in her queer unformed hand:

I, Angela Margaret Underwood, hereby confess that whatever I told Alda, my sister, about Geraldine and F.T., was all cram; and if I did it too well, I'm very sorry for it. F.T. didn't take a bit more notice of Cherry than of Robin and me; and of course he cannot marry the three of us: and of course it was all right, for Clement was there. Ask him.

Witness my hand,
ANGELA MARGARET UNDERWOOD.

Then she called, 'Come and witness it, Robin.'

'Nonsense,' said Robina; and coming to look, she exclaimed, 'you have made it simply ridiculous. This will do no good!—See, Cherry.'

But Cherry would not have it altered, and merely bade Robina write her testimony.

This took much longer, though the produce was much briefer. It was only—

MY DEAR ALDA,

Angela was only talking nonsense the other day. If I had not thought so, I would have told you.

Your affectionate sister,
ROBINA B. UNDERWOOD.

'You've made a letter of it!' exclaimed Angela. 'I thought it was to be a last will and—no, a dying speech and confession; which is it? Well, if that does not set it all straight, I can't tell what will!'

Cherry was a good deal perplexed by the testimony now she had obtained it. She thought the matter over on her return, and ended by seeking Marilda; and with much excuse for Angela, putting it into her hands to show to Alda. She felt it due to herself to make sure that Marilda saw it, such as it was.

Marilda undertook that Alda should see it. Geraldine watched and waited. There was no apology to herself. At that she did not wonder. Was there any note of recall sounded to Ferdinand? Was Alda proud? or was she in very truth indifferent, and unwilling to give up her excuse for a quarrel? or had she really relented, and apologized in secret?

It was strange to know so little, and venture so much less with her own sister than could Marilda, whom, in their present stiff reserve, Cherry durst not question.

CHAPTER XXVII.

DON OR MYNHEER?

'Hear the truth—
A lame girl's truth, whom no one ever praised
For being patient.'
George Eliot.

One morning, after a private interview with Alda, Mr. Underwood entered the drawing-room, hilariously announcing that Alda was a lucky girl this time, for now she had a man in no fear of his relations.

Geraldine was glad of the need of getting into the carriage directly, and that her transit to Mr. Renville's was too brief for any answer to be needed to her companion's warm satisfaction. Affairs of this sort had come so thickly upon the family in the course of the last eighteen months, that she did not feel the excitement of novelty; and she wished so little to dwell on the present, that at the museum, the absorbing interest of her life-study drove out the immediate recollection of the stranger life-study she had left.

There could be no question as to the veritable cause of Alda's conduct to Ferdinand; but Cherry was too much ashamed of it to rejoice in her own justification, scarcely even hoping that Marilda would perceive it.

Most likely Alda would have preferred staving off the crisis a little longer—at least till those keen eyes were out of sight—but she had now to do with a man whose will it was not easy to parry, and whom delay and coyness might have driven off altogether. Cherry did not see her till they met at luncheon; and there was Sir Adrian, who promoted the little lame girl to a shake of the hand. Alda looked gracious and unusually handsome, being, in fact, relieved from a state of fretting uneasiness; Mrs. Underwood was beaming with triumph; Marilda—again there is no word for it but—glum!

There was a rose show at the Botanic Gardens; but Cherry had declined it, and Marilda immovably refused to go. After they had seen the other two ladies set off, resplendent under Sir Adrian's escort, Marilda announced her intention of driving, as she often did, to the City, to fetch her father home, and, more cordially than of late, offered a seat to Cherry, if she did not mind waiting.

The City to Cherry's ears meant Ferdinand, whom she would not face for worlds; but she told herself that it was not like Bexley, where every one who went to the bank was sure to be presently seen at Froggatt's, and she would not reject this advance from her cousin.

Indeed, Marilda wanted to talk, and freely told all she had been hearing. The baronetcy was in the third generation, having been conferred on the original transmuter, a Lord Mayor, with whom his son had toiled for the larger half of his days, and comparatively late had bought an estate, and married a lady of quality. He had not long survived, and his widow had remarried. Of her nothing more was known; but her son was so entirely his own master, that her opposition was not likely to be dangerous. Sir Adrian had the reputation of great wealth; and though he partook of the usual amusements of young men, there was no reason to suppose that he did so to an extent that he could not afford. Altogether, it was a brilliant conquest; but 'How one does hate it all!' concluded Marilda.

This was all the amends Cherry received for the reproach that had so keenly wounded her. Probably Marilda had really dismissed the charge; but hers was not a fine-grained mind, used to self-examination or analysis; and she acted on a momentary impression, without much regard to the past or to consistency. Her affections were deep and strong; but partly from circumstances they were like those of a dog, depending rather on contact than esteem. She had accepted Edgar and Alda as brother and sister, and whatever they did, stood by them with all her might; nor did she ever so much as realize that Alda had been wrong, and she herself misled. She would rather believe it the way of the world, and part of the nature of things, than open her mind to blame Alda.

Besides, the sense of not understanding Cherry, and the recollection of the effect produced on her by words apparently quite inadequate, the seeing her power of talking to and amusing gentlemen with whom she herself had not an idea in common, Edgar's tender fervent pride in her, and Alda's half-contemptuous acknowledgment of her ability—all this contributed to give Marilda a certain shyness, awe, and constraint, that sometimes looked cold, and sometimes cross, and puzzled Cherry, who never dreamt of being formidable.

When they reached the house of business, Marilda went to her father's room, for since his illness she often helped him to wind up his correspondence; and Cherry sat in the carriage, her attention divided between a book and the busy traffic of the street.

Presently she saw a tall lean figure in black, with a deeply-cut sallow face set in grey whiskers. She knew it for the Vicar of St Matthew's; and he, after bowing and passing, turned, and coming to the window, said, 'Will you kindly tell me the right address to Mr. Audley, in Australia? Clement left it with me, but I have mislaid it.'

'The Rev. C.S. Audley, Carrigaboola, Albertstown, West Australia.' And as he repeated it with thanks, she could not restrain herself from stretching out a hand in entreaty, and saying, 'Oh! pray, pray tell me! How is he? Mr. Travis?'

'Your eldest brother's letter has done him a great deal of good.'

'Please tell me about him,' implored Cherry, colouring. 'We have known him for so long before. How does he bear it?'

Mr. Fulmort let himself into the carriage, and sat down by her, saying, 'He is bearing it as you could most wish.'

'I longed to know. I feared it would be very terrible. His is not an English nature.'

'It has been a great struggle. That first night he never went home at all, but wandered about till daylight. I found him at five in the morning, sunk down on his knees in our porch, with his head against the church door, in a sort of exhausted doze.'

'Oh, well that he knew the way!' sighed Cherry. 'No one ever was so cruelly treated!' she added with frowning vehemence. 'And then?'

'I took him to my rooms, and made him rest, and I went to Brown's and excused his non-attendance. By the time he went to your sister he had quite mastered himself.'

'He must. She never told about it; but we are sure she was quite overawed.'

'He came back quite calm, with a certain air of secrecy, and has gone on with a sort of stern quietness ever since,' said the Vicar, lowering his voice. 'Only on Sunday—he is one of our collectors at the Offertory—he brought up his alms-bag bursting with bracelets and rings, and things of that sort.'

'Poor Fernan! how like him to do it in that way!'

'I think it relieved him. He is perfectly free of bitterness towards your sister—allows no flaw in her; but he is striving hard not to retain animosity against your uncle.'

'It is deserved by no one but her!' exclaimed Cherry; 'and there's worse to come. I don't know whether I ought to mention it; but it will be better for it to come to him from you.'

'*It* is true, then?' said Mr. Fulmort, understanding her directly. 'My sister told me it was reported.'

'It was only settled yesterday evening. I am afraid *this* is worse for him than if it had been any one else.'

'So am I. It seems to be the crisis of a long emulation. I begged Aston—my brother-in-law—to ascertain what was thought about it in the corps; and he said that though poor Travis had never got on well with the other men, there was a general feeling that he was not handsomely treated.'

'That wretched man betted—'

Mr. Fulmort kindly but decidedly checked her. 'You had better not dwell on such reports. Things for which we are not responsible must be made the best of when they bring us new connections. Our friend is not unprepared, and I will take care he does not hear this casually.'

'Thank you—oh! thank you! Give him my—' she caught herself up and blushed—'my very best remembrances; and tell him,' she added, carried away in spite of herself, 'that he must always be like one of ourselves.'

'It will be a great comfort to him. Nothing can exceed his affection and gratitude to your family—indeed he said, with tears in his eyes, that to your brothers he "owes his very self also." I hope nothing will disturb that friendship.'

'What will he do? Set about some great work somewhere?'

Mr. Fulmort smiled sadly. 'It is not safe to rush into great works to allay disappointment,' he said. 'I think he is wiser to keep steadily to his occupation, at least for the present; but he is giving his whole leisure to his district and the evening classes. I am glad to have met you. Good-bye.'

It was lucky that Cherry had plenty of time to subside before the return of Marilda and her father. The latter was much exalted by the explanation he had had with Sir Adrian and his man of business. The rent-roll was all that could be desired, and so were the proposed settlements; nor was there any fear on the score of the family. The lawyer privately told Mr. Underwood that the mother, Lady Mary Murray, was a most gentle lady, without a spark of pride, and very anxious to see her son married.

Nor did her letter belie this assurance. She expressed gladness that her son's choice should be a clergyman's daughter, and warmly invited Alda to come and visit her at the Rectory, and make herself at home among the new brothers and sisters there.

It was gathered—partly from Sir Adrian, partly from gossip—that Lady Mary, a scantily-portioned maiden, had been too timid and docile to withstand the parental will, which devoted her to the wealthy old baronet; but in her widowhood she had followed the inclination that had been pooh-poohed by her family in her girlhood. As a country clergyman's wife, her homely quiet existence had less and less influence over her son; and there was no danger of Alda finding in her an imperious mother-in-law, though, except as a connecting link, she would be valueless as an introduction. She was absolutely foolish enough to be romantically delighted at her son's marrying for love; and Geraldine fell in love with her on the spot, on reading her letter—one of the very few which Alda showed, for in general she kept her correspondence to herself. She avoided Cherry, and only talked to Marilda of externals.

Nothing was to be definitively arranged till Felix had come to London, and given his approval to the draught of the settlements, of which he and Mr. Murray were to be trustees. He was so much grieved and ashamed, that much urging from Wilmet was needed to convince him that he ought not to leave the whole to Tom Underwood; but as a counterpoise there was Cherry to see—and oh! joy of joys! to fetch home. So he consented to go up on a Saturday afternoon, and return on Tuesday; and thus it was, that one evening in July Cherry was gathered into his arms, murmuring 'Felicissimo mio, what an age it is since I have had you!'

Good-natured Mrs. Underwood had made it a family party, including Robina and Angela, the worthy dame having little notion how slightly they appreciated the honour, nor how curiosity, and love of Felix and a holiday, contended with very tumultuous and angry sensations. That Alda had never taken the smallest notice of Angela's confession, did not render her cold kiss the pleasanter, nor the circle less awful as the party sat round, awaiting the arrival of Sir Adrian. There they were, nine uncomfortable people, sitting on gilded blue damask chairs, too few and too far apart for a comfortable whisper; the two youngest very conscious of their best white frocks; the two eldest—the one in a flurry of anxiety and suspense, the other in a fret of impatience and testiness; and Marilda—having announced her opinion that Sir Adrian would shirk it, and not come at all—in a state of glumness. Edgar, however—an exception both to the discomfort and the seat—threw himself into the breach with the story of the mysterious disappearance of a nun, (Cherry suspected it of being *ben trovato* for the nonce,) and when that was worn out, and the master of the house insisted on ringing for dinner, and the mistress was almost in tears at his hunger and temper, and her own fear of rudeness, while Marilda only declared that it was no more than the due of tardiness, it was Edgar alone who had strength of mind to declare that patience ought to end, and to pull the bell.

The guest arrived with the dinner, looking so sulky about the eyes, that Cherry suspected him of having delayed while pitying himself for the ante-nuptial infliction of this party. However, he proved to have some justification, for a little stiffness of movement in giving his arm to Mrs. Underwood elicited that he had bruised his shoulder in a fall; and that good lady, pursuing the subject with less tact than solicitude, drew from him that he had been mounting at his banker's door, when his horse shied, and got its head away from the groom, but was caught at once by a clerk sort of fellow. A showy brute, with an uncertain temper. He should get rid of it.

Angela had been nudging Edgar all the time, to make him ask what horse it was; and as he turned a deaf ear, her voice erected itself with the shrill pert sound that is the misfortune of girlhood—'Was it Brown Murad?'

Sir Adrian had to look to find out where the voice came from before he answered in the affirmative.

'Then he isn't a brute at all!' said the same voice, with great decision. 'He is as gentle as a lamb, and will eat bread out of your hand if you know how to use him properly!'

Her cheeks were crimson, and she was greatly displeased that Edgar and Geraldine should both begin talking of other things with all their might.

Sir Adrian had more of the art of conversation than poor Ferdinand; and as politics came up, Edgar declared himself to have become a voluntary victim to unanimity between the three contracting powers, who had harmoniously joined in rending his carcase. He left them, nearly as soon as the ladies did, to discuss the business part of the affair, and came to the aid of Cherry and Robina, who were vainly trying to convince Angela of the inexpedience of her outbreak, and obtaining in return the sentiment, 'I don't care what he does to Alda. It is her choice, but not poor dear Brown Murad's, that he has got such a master!'

'You have done your best to make him fare worse.'

'Now, Edgar, you only want to frighten me.'

'No. If Vanderkist does not entirely forget the pertness of an *enfant terrible*, it will just add another sting to his dislike of the poor beast.'

Angela fairly burst into tears, and ran away to the school-room, whence she returned with a bearing so magnanimous and desperate, that Cherry and Robina dreaded lest she should be meditating an apology and an appeal on behalf of the horse; so that they were much relieved when the carriage came to take the young ladies home, before the consultation in the dining-room broke up. Even then Angel did not wholly abstain, but when Alda gave her mechanical kiss, she said, 'Alda, please don't let Sir Adrian be unkind to that poor dear horse!'

'Silly child! What fancies you take into your head!' said Alda, laughing, with a good-humoured superiority such as she had not shown at home. 'You need not fear but that whatever belongs to him is made happy.'

Angela returned an unfeigned look of astonishment, and exclaimed, 'After all, I do believe you are really in love with him!'

'Angel,' said Edgar, putting his hand on her shoulder, 'I called you an *enfant terrible* just now; but you are too big for that indulgence, unless you mean to be equally hateful to friend and foe.'

Angela shook off his hand, and tossed her head disrespectfully, but went off in silence. Sir Adrian only came upstairs to say he had promised to look in on Lady Somebody; and Alda bade good night as soon as he was gone. She had evidently nothing to say to Felix that night, nor the next morning, though he waited about after breakfast to give her the opportunity; accompanied the family to their very dry church; and then, announcing his intention of repairing to St Matthew's, was seen no more—not even at dinner-time, when his absence was somewhat resented by his hosts, and vexed Cherry a good deal.

However, he appeared before ten o'clock, made an apology about his unexpected detention, and when the family circle broke up obeyed Cherry's wistful look, and followed her to her room.

'Was it about Fernan?' she asked.

'The clerk sort of fellow who stopped the horse?'

'It did cross me, but I thought it too good to be true. How was it?'

'He had been sent on some business to the bank, and was almost at the door when Sir Adrian came out. The groom may have been holding the horse carelessly. Sir Adrian spoke angrily; the horse started, got his head free, and reared, throwing him down with his foot in the stirrup, so that he would have been dragged if Fernan had not got hold of the bridle, and his voice quieted poor Brown Murad in a moment.'

'Dear good fellow! I hope Sir Adrian did not punish him.'

'He is too valuable for that, I hope; but Sir Adrian did not spare abuse to man or beast, and threw a thank-you to Ferdinand as if he did not recognise him. Most likely we should never have heard of the adventure if it had not jarred the weak place in poor Fernan's back. He did not find it out at first, and stayed at his work the rest of the day; but it has been getting worse ever since, and I found him on the sofa, lengthened out with a chair.'

'That most horrible of sofas—all bars and bumps! Poor Fernan!'

'He only told me he had got a sprain in catching a rearing horse; and then I leapt to the conclusion, and made him tell me. He says he has hurt himself in the same way before, and that the Life Guards' surgeon told him there was nothing for it but rest.'

'Rest, indeed! like St. Lawrence's gridiron—all but the fire! What did you do for him?'

'Wished for Wilmet, and remembered Lance's telling me that I was of no use to myself nor any one else.'

'Fancy Lance saying that! But you didn't really do nothing?'

'Luckily Edgar came in search of me, and showed what resource is. He had up the landlady, and as usual captivated her. She produced a mattress, and Edgar routed out some air-cushions that Fernan had used before, and they made him much more comfortable, I want to take him home, but he does not think he can bear the journey.'

'No,' said Cherry; 'and he would be always in the way of hearing about *this;* but it is dreadful to have him laid up in that dismal hole.'

'I ran round to the clergy-house, and they will look after him as much as they can.'

'How is he looking?'

'As if he had not slept all night, but otherwise I believe this has done him good; I fancy he never knew what the first impulse of the ferocious old Mexican might be.'

'Did he say anything?'

'No, but the Vicar did. He has had a terrible time; but I hope the worst is over. We read the Evening Service together; and he looked so full of peace, that I thought of the contrast with that Christmas morning when he opened his heart about the fire. There was all the difference between blind feeling after truth and holding it in the hand.'

'Was Edgar with you then?' asked Cherry, eagerly.

'No, he came later.'

'You Blunderbore!' said Cherry, rallying her playfulness to hide the extinction of that moment's hope; 'how like the good Christian who gave the wounded man the sermon first and the raspberry-vinegar after!'

'Come with me to-morrow, and give him the raspberry-vinegar then, Cherry.'

'Nay,' said Cherry, feeling this impossible, but withholding the reason; 'I am as bad—just as much demoralized by a Wilmet—and should be no good.'

'The sight of you would be ever so much good. You needn't be shy. You went with Clem.'

'Once too often,' faltered Cherry.

'Eh? Why W.W. said not a word against it!'

'I would go with all my heart, Felix,' said Cherry, earnestly, 'but that I am afraid Alda gave him the—the same reason she did to Marilda.'

'What do you mean? You are all one blush! You can't mean that she pretended jealousy?'

'I never meant you to know,' said Cherry. 'O Felix! nothing ever was so dreadful! Marilda thought it so bad of me. I did so long for you!'

'You should have sent for me. I never thought of exposing you to such an insult.'

'I tried to write, but my hand was too shaky; and then Edgar came, and was so very dear! He said Alda only laid hold of this as a plea for getting out of the affair; and you see he was right. Don't be vexed, Felix; it is all over now, and I hope it has made me more of a woman and less of a baby; but after this, I could not go to him.'

'No. I declare I can forgive Alda anything rather than this!'

'She does not know what she is saying when she is in an ill-used mood—especially of me. Indeed, I believe I ought to have been more guarded. Shall you tell her about the horse?'

'Certainly not.'

'And are you letting this go on without speaking to her?'

'I have written twice.'

'She never told me. What did you say?'

'A prose—I fear in the leader and heavy father style—which probably she never read; and the answers were civil enough, but meant that she would please herself.'

'You really do not mean to say anything?'

'If she asks my opinion, I must; but she does not. I am not here to give my consent to the marriage, but to see fair play in the settlements.'

'Do you think that right?'

'Remember, we know nothing against him, except his conduct to Fernan.'

'We know he has not much religion.'

'Cherry, I should put that objection forward decisively if she were a younger one, for whom I am bound to judge; but she is only a year younger than I am, and has seen more of the world. She must know more about his principles than I can, and be able to judge whether she chooses to trust to them. No argument of mine would make any difference to her; and I have not the right to thrust in objections unasked.'

'O Felix!'

'What?'

'Is not that rather "Am I my brother's keeper?"'

'I hope not. You see, the sort of fatherly relation I bear to you all has never existed towards her. She was given quite away; and where I do not suppose even a father's remonstrance would avail, I do not feel called upon to alienate her further by uplifting my testimony unsought.'

'No, it would hardly do her good; but it would clear your own conscience.'

'It might bring dissension and harsh judgment on my conscience. Nothing can be most conscientious that is not most for another's good; and I do not think forcing an additional opposition or remonstrance, on mere grounds of my own estimate of him, would be useful. You observe, too, that our cool manner of treating this brilliant match is token enough of our sentiments.'

'Then you won't go to the wedding?'

'Not if I can help it; and I don't think my company is desired. Remember,' as he still saw her dissatisfied, 'it is not the same thing to be an overt scamp as to be what you and I do not think a religious man.'

With a sudden impulse Cherry burst out laughing. 'If the great Sir Adrian could only see what the little country bookseller thinks of his alliance?'

'Don't let pride peep out at the holes in our cloaks,' said Felix, kissing her.

She could not refuse herself the satisfaction of letting Marilda hear the real history of the accident; but she could extract nothing but 'Indeed.'

Altogether, Marilda disappointed Cherry. She went so entirely along with the stream, only now and then remorselessly giving way to a tremendous fit of crossness towards every one except her father, never seeming scandalized by any doing of Alda's, and snubbing Cherry if she showed any sort of disapprobation.

Felix stole the first hour of his busy day for Ferdinand, and then was distressed to leave him outstretched in his dull, close, noisy den, ill adapted for the daylight hours of anything but blue-bottle flies; though neither heat nor idleness was quite so trying to him as they would have been to an Underwood. He had a cigar and newspaper; but when books were proposed to him, allowed that reading bored him. When Felix shifted the cushions, however, under them was a deep devotional mystical work; and colouring a little, he owned that nothing interested him but reading and slowly digesting fragments of this kind. And Felix felt that it would be unreasonable to regret the snapping of the tie that bound him to Alda.

After some hours of business in the City, Felix came back, but was amazed to hear that Mr. Travis was gone. The landlady seemingly rather hurt at the slur on her attentions, said that an elderly lady had come and taken him away, leaving an address. This led Felix into Finsbury Square, where he was started to see waiting at the door a big carriage, the panels and blinkers displaying the Underwood rood. On his asking for Mr. Travis, a neat young maid took him to a downstairs room, where Ferdinand was lying on a large sofa, accepting luncheon from a big stout housekeeper-looking body, and—Marilda Underwood, her bonnet off, as if quite at home!

'Felix!—Granny, have you never seen Felix Underwood!'

Mrs. Kedge turned round and held out her hand. 'I've never seen Mr. Felix Hunderwood,' she said; 'but there's no gentleman I 'olds in 'igher respect.—Sit down Mr. Felix, and take your bit of noonchine.—Mary, give him some weal.—I could have had some soup if I'd known I was to be so honoured; but I am a plain body, and likes a cut from the servants' dinner—and so does Mary, for a change. So,' before he could insert his civil reply, 'Vell, we've brought off your friend; I 'ope you think him in good 'ands.'

'The kindest hands,' said Felix; though, as good Mrs. Kedge discoursed on hopodeldoc and winegar as sovereign for a sprain, he began to think the change a doubtful good, and was glad Ferdinand seemed chiefly sensible of the motherly care of the old lady.

Marilda offered her cousin a seat in the carriage, when after the meal she set forth to take her father home, there to hold conference with Mr. Murray and the lawyer.

'This is your doing,' he said, gratefully, as they drove off. 'How very kind!'

'Grandmamma always liked him,' said Marilda. 'He is so respectful, and he plays backgammon.'

'It is much better for him than that doleful room, which was only made endurable by its being near his friends the curates.'

'They will come to him there. Granny does not mind. She used to think they starved Clement; but of late they have come to be great friends with her, and come to her for rag, or broth, or hospital tickets.'

'Does she go to their church?'

'Oh no, she wouldn't to save her life—she thinks it quite shocking; and there are two young merry ones who have regular quarrels with her, teasing and making fun, and she scolding them, but so fond of them, giving them quite large sums for their charities. She really delights in them.'

Marilda spoke far more freely to Felix than she ever could to Cherry, but still she steered clear of Alda and her affairs. Only she did ask him earnestly to avert all additional care and anxiety from her father in arranging for the settlements, and above all to hinder any question over which he could become excited. Then, as he promised to do all in his power, she asked him what he thought of her father's health and looks. He could truly say that he thought he was much better since last autumn, and she looked cheered; but the few words she whispered made it known to him that she was all this time living in a watchful state of continual anxiety—being in truth the only person, except perhaps Edgar, who really understood what last year's attack had been, or the dangers of another. If her mother and Alda knew, they did not realize; and he could perceive both the burthen, and the manner in which it rendered her almost passive, except in obviating discussion or alarm.

Of the former there was no danger at the conference. Mr. Murray was just as anxious as Mr. Underwood and Felix could be, that the five thousand pounds that had been promised to Alda should be settled upon herself and the younger children, together with a fair proportion charged upon the estate. He was a pleasing person, a perfect gentleman, of mildly cordial manners, accepting his new connections with courtesy and kindness. He was evidently charmed with Alda, whom he wanted to take home with him to be introduced to Lady Mary, before returning to choose her outfit. This was to be completed by the end of the month, that the honeymoon might interfere as little as possible with the moon fatal to partridges.

Felix was right. His presence was not desired. The father's part naturally belonged to Thomas Underwood; and though an invitation was not wanting, Alda did not remonstrate when Felix spoke of the assize week requiring him to be at Minsterham, and of Charles Froggatt having come home in such a broken state of health, that his father's presence in Bexley could never be depended upon. She had no desire to display the full dozen *geschwister;* but to Cherry she qualified things a little: 'I suppose as Felix will not come, one of you will stay with him?'

'Of course I shall! You know I'm wedded!' And she merrily held Lord Gerald's ivory visage close to her own.

'I knew you would shrink from it. And those two children at Brompton—it will be the middle of their holidays, and it will not be worth while having them; besides, it would be encroaching, as Uncle Tom gives all those dresses—and one never knows what that Angel might do.'

'Never,' said Cherry, in full acquiescence, and sure of the same from Wilmet.

'But Wilmet and Stella must come. One of the little Murrays will pair with Stella; and I want Adrian to see her. You will not feel slighted, Cherry; I know you had rather not.'

'Much rather not,' said Cherry, for Alda was really speaking considerately. Indeed, Alda was taking such a leap out of the same sphere, that she could afford to be gracious to 'the little deformed one,' as Sir Adrian most inappropriately termed Geraldine. She graciously accepted for a wedding-present an intended portrait of Stella, and rejoiced heartily at Cherry's prize for the life-study.

Never had Cherry, however, been happier than in getting home, away from constraint, away from fine houses, away from half-comprehended people, back to free affection and mutual understanding.

'One's own cobweb for ever! The black caterpillar is crawling home again to the dear old nettle!' she cried.

'But you are not sorry to have gone,' said Felix.

'If only to get back again.'

'But they were kind.'

'I don't want people to be kind; I want them to be one with me.'

'My dear! you did not seem unhappy. We thought you enjoyed yourself.'

'I did. I was only unhappy once. I liked things very much and shall more, now I have time. It was such a bustle and whirl; and I felt so obliged to make the most of it, that it seemed to wear my senses. Don't you see, it was like snatching at flowers; and now I can sit down to make up my nosegay, and see what I have gained.'

Cherry almost expected Wilmet to decline, in her hatred of finery and her general dissatisfaction; but Wilmet's love of Alda was too strong for her not to long to be with her at such a crisis of her life, and she was eager to accept the invitation, without fearing that the effects of her absence would be as direful as in the previous year.

The party at home were not by any means disconsolate. Felix was very busy, for Charles Froggatt had come home, a repentant prodigal, and slowly sinking under the disease that had carried off his more worthy brothers; and the father could seldom persuade himself to leave him for long together, and besides, needed cheering and comfort from his young friends. But Lance and young Lamb were working well and helpfully; and William Harewood spent almost as much time at Bexley as his brother had done.

He had passed his examination with flying colours, and had previously matriculated at Oxford; and thus being emancipated from the choir, which had kept him close at home, he seemed to think it liberty to be always at Bexley. As a Harewood, Wilmet let him do as he would—sleep in the barrack, and be like one of their own boys; and Lance's neighbourhood seemed to be all he wanted, though little of Lance's company was to be had, except in walking to see him bathe in early morning, and in long walks after seven in the evening—and for these the long July days gave ample verge. Robina, Angel, and Bernard often benefited by these expeditions into the dewy fields, redolent of hay, and came home to that delightful twilight that seems as if it would never be darkness.

Bill professed perfect content in the day hours. He was a voracious reader, and would remain for hours in the reading-room intent on some pursuit; and what perhaps was a still greater attraction, he could talk, and find listeners.

Cherry only now understood what Lance had always maintained—that that shock-headed boy was full of thought, poetry, and ability. He had shed his school-boy slough; and he had moreover adopted the Underwoods, and for the first time learnt what an appreciative woman could be.

His poem of this year was so good, that Lance and Robin thought Felix shockingly blind because he refused to put it bodily into the Pursuivant, though allowing that it was much better than anything that would appear instead; and short pieces that the lad was continually striking off were only too good for the poet's corner, where, however, they gave an infinity of pleasure and satisfaction to two households at least. The poet—March Hare, as he signed himself—was an odd mixture of his father's scholarly tastes with his mother's harum-scarum forgetfulness; and the consequence was such abstraction at one moment, such slap-dash action at another, that he was a continual good-natured laughing-stock. To talk and read to Cherry seemed to be one of his great objects in life. He began it with Robina; but gradually Cherry, partly as critic and sub-editor of the Pursuivant, partly on her own merits, became the recipient of ten thousand visions, reflections, aspirations, that were crowding upon the young spirit, while she tried to follow, understand, and answer, with a sense that her powers were being stretched, and her eyes opened into new regions.

And then, if a stranger appeared, he sank into the red-headed lout; or if he had a message or commission, he treated it senselessly. Lance used to send Bernard up—as he said, to see him into the right train; and in the home party in the evening, his wit and drollery were the cause of inexhaustible mirth—Willie, as Robin and Angela agreed, was better fun than all the weddings, and even all the sights that London could give. Sometimes they were weary with laughing at him, sometimes with the lift he gave their minds; for even Angel understood and followed, and was more susceptible than her elders gave her credit for; and certainly she had never been so good as she was this summer, though it was still a flighty odd sort of goodness.

And all this time there was not a word between him and Robin of that evening walk. Whether he thought of it or not she knew not; but with her the recollection had a strength that the moment had not had. It seemed to be growing up with her. It was a memory that went deeper—far deeper than was good for her, poor child, since there was no surface chatter to carry it off; but the maidenliness of fifteen shrank with a sort of horror and dismay from the bare consciousness that she had allowed herself to think that those words of his could be serious, even while they had formed in her a fixed purpose of striving for him; and every mark of kindness or of preference assumed a value unspeakable and beyond her years, while her whole self was so entirely the good, plodding, sensible, simple child, that no one detected the romance beneath. Did the object of it, himself?

Meantime Wilmet had found Alda much gratified by her reception at the Rectory, though confessing that she was glad that it was not in her immediate neighbourhood. Lady Mary Murray belonged to a severe school of religious opinions, and was antagonistic to gaiety and ornament, both secular and ecclesiastic. What effect they and Clement might have mutually had upon each other was not proved, for he had found a pupil, and was far away; but as Alda herself owned, Wilmet would have been the daughter-in-law to suit them.

Wilmet and Marilda were very congenial in their housewifely tastes and absence of romance, and above all, in a warm and resolutely blind love for Alda, never discussing the past, and occupied upon the trousseau, without an *arrière pensée*.

Sir Adrian was civil to Wilmet, but he never would acknowledge the resemblance between the twin-sisters; and as Wilmet wore no earrings, and kept her hair in the simple style that John Harewood had once pronounced perfect, he had only once been confused between them, and then was so annoyed, that Edgar said he was like a virtuoso, who having secured some unique specimen, finds the charm of possession injured by the existence of a duplicate.

Even in the Murray family there might be those who questioned whether the beauty were equal. Either the smooth folds and plaits of the rich brown hair pleased a homely taste better than fanciful varieties, or housewifery and early hours were better preservatives than London seasons; or maybe the stately sweetness of the original mould was better and more congenially maintained in the life of the true 'loaf-giver or lady' of the laborious thrifty home than in the luxurious dependence of the alien house, and the schemes, disappointments, and successes of the late campaign.

At any rate, at three-and-twenty the twins were less alike than of old; and if Alda had the advantage in the graces of art and society, Wilmet had a purity of bloom and nobleness of countenance that she could not equal. If Wilmet were silent, and by no means so entertaining as Geraldine, her little companion thoroughly compensated for any deficiencies. Every one was taken by surprise by Stella's beauty, after the three intermediate sisters, who had little pretensions to anything remarkable in that line. The child was of the same small delicate frame as Cherry and Lance; in fact, much what Cherry might have been with more health and less genius to change those delicately-moulded features and countenance. The colouring of the blue eyes and silken hair was rather deeper than the prevailing tint, and the complexion was of the most exquisite rosy fairness and delicacy, giving a sense of the most delicate porcelain—the movements and gestures perfectly graceful, and the innocent chatter delightful, from its eagerness and simplicity. She was in every one's eyes an extraordinarily lovely and engaging child; and she could have reigned supreme over the whole house if she had ever perceived her power, or emancipated herself from her loyal submission to 'Sister.'

Many a time did Wilmet's restrictions vex her hosts, and call forth Edgar's epithets of dragon and Medusa. Luckily the child was of the faithful spirit that honestly trusts its lawful authorities, fears forbidden sweets, and feels full compensation in the pleasure of obedience. One day, when a refusal to take her to the theatre had caused great indignation, Sir Adrian, who was by no means insensible to her charms, enlivened an idle moment by trying to excite her to rebel.

'I would not stand it, Stella—not I! Tell her stars have no business to be hidden.'

'It's no use,' said Stella. 'Sister says when once she says No, it is for always.'

'How very dreadful! She must be cured as soon as possible!'

Stella looked greatly perplexed; and Edgar, the only other person present, looked on in great amusement.

'Let us organise a combination,' continued Sir Adrian. 'What should we come to, if women were allowed to keep to a single No?'

'Which would be the greatest sufferers?' muttered Edgar.

'It would be very nasty if Sister didn't,' said Stella, understanding him verbally more nearly than he had expected.

'Indeed!' said Sir Adrian.

'Yes. One would never know when to make up one's mind.'

'One's mind! You little china fairy, have you got the mind of a midge?'

'Yes, *I* have!' said Stella, with an emphasis that Edgar at least understood as an allusion to the difference between herself and Theodore; and a little in fear of what might come next, he said, 'Mind enough to assert her woman's privilege, though how she may come to like to be bound by it is another thing.'

'Look here, little one,' continued Sir Adrian, 'we'll not let Sister alone till she comes round, and then I'll put you in my pocket and take you.'

'No, thank you,' said Stella, retreating.

'I thought you wanted to see the fairies?'

'I did; but Sister knows best.'

'Come, now; I'd give something to know where, in her secret soul, this little thing would like to send all the sisters that know best?'

'To the Neilgherry Hills,' said Stella, with surprising promptness; 'that's where Captain Jack is!'

'A capital location!' cried the baronet, laughing triumphantly. 'Well done, little one! Send her off—and then we'll have pine-apple ice, and smart frocks, and go to as many plays as we please! You know what it means to have the cat away.'

'That was what Bernard said when Wilmet was away, and Alda at home,' said Stella; 'but it was very miserable. It was the very horridest portion in the whole course of our lives!'

'Long may it so continue, Stella,' said Edgar. 'You'll get no change out of her, Vanderkist.'

'It's an odd little piece of goods. I can't make out if it is a child at all,' said Sir Adrian. 'I can't believe it is more than drilling.—Now, my little beauty—no one will tell—walls can't hear—honour bright—which are you for in your heart of hearts—Sister Wilmet and propriety, or Alda and—liberty?'

Edgar listened curiously; but Stella had that good genius of tact and courtesy that sometimes inspires children; and she made answer, 'Wilmet is my own dear sister, and I am very glad it is Alda that you have got.'

'Well said, you little ingenious morsel!' cried Edgar, laughing with delight, and catching her up in his arms. 'What does nature design this little being for, Adrian? To marry a great diplomat?'

'To do execution of some sort, I should say,' returned Sir Adrian; 'unless such alarming discretion cancels the effect of those eyes. Never saw a pair more meant to make hearts ache,' and he sauntered out of the room.

'Why, what now, you star of courtesy? has he kindled the spark of vanity at last, that you are craning over to the big pier-glass—eh?' said Edgar, with his little sister still in his arms.

'I only want to see what he means that is so horrid in my eyes,' said Stella; 'please show me, Edgar. How can they hurt people so?'

'It's a way they have, Stella,' he gravely answered, 'when they are clear, and blue, and big-pupilled, and have great long black lashes.' And he looked with proud pleasure at the reflection of the sweet little puzzled face beside his own brown beard.

'But your eyes are just like that, Edgar; and so are everybody's, aren't they? Why do you laugh, Edgar? I wish I could go home, for I don't understand any of you.'

'So much the better, Sister would say. I declare, I must risk it, and see the effect. I say, Stella, don't you know that you're a little beauty, that they are all raving about? There!'

'Oh yes,' said Stella composedly; 'I know people always do like things for being little, and young, and pretty. And then they don't see Tedo, and he is so much prettier than me, you know.'

'You impracticable child! What! have you no shade of a notion that it is a fine thing to have such a phiz as that one? Did you never thank your stars that you weren't as ugly as Martha?'

'Do you worship the stars, Edgar? For I heard Clem say you were very little better than a heathen; and I suppose worshipping the stars is better than worshipping idols.'

'Is that malice, or simplicity—eh? Never mind my creed. You are my sister at this moment, and are to answer me truly. Do you know that you are a beauty? and are you glad of it?'

'I shouldn't like to be ugly,' said Stella; 'not so ugly that I couldn't bear to look at myself. But if I was, they wouldn't leave off being kind to me at home.'

'Nor abroad either,' said Edgar, kissing her. 'You've got the tongue that is nearly equal to the eyes, my Stella.'

Stella's simplicity might soon have been put in the way of further trials, for there was a serious proposal of adopting her in Alda's room, and promises of excellent education and an ample provision: and when Felix's decided though grateful refusal arrived, Mr. and Mrs. Underwood spoke angrily of his folly, as selfish, and almost undutiful to his father, who had freely trusted them with the two elders; but Edgar cut this short. 'No, no, my dear good governor. That won't do; Felix knows that if my father could have seen the results, he would ten times rather have let us fight it out in the Irish cabin at home.'

'I am sure,' exclaimed Mrs. Underwood, 'we have done everything for you, Edgar! It is enough to cure one of offering to do anything for any one!'

'Just what I say,' was Edgar's grave response; but he added, with his natural sweetness, 'Not but that I believe, in the common herd, we should have been, if anything, worse than we are now. We brought the bad drop with us. You did not infuse it.'

'Speak for yourself, Edgar,' said Marilda, rushing to the defence, as usual.

So the family was only represented by two sisters and one brother at the wedding, which was solemnized by Mr. Murray at the parish church, and was a regular common-place smart affair, with carriages, favours, and crowds of spectators in much excitement to catch a sight of the beautiful bride.

Murrays mustered in force, and Mrs. Underwood's felicity was complete; for the titled uncle was so glad to see his Sister Mary happy about her son, that he came in full state, and made a very gratifying speech all about nothing. While Wilmet thought of her own soldier on the Neilgherry hills, and felt how widely her path and that of her twin-sister must diverge. And Mr. Underwood enjoyed the compliments to the 'more than father,' and congratulated himself on having truly done well by poor Edward's child.

'I only wish he were here to see her!' he cried with an effusion of almost tearful delight, as he handed Lady Vanderkist to her carriage.

CHAPTER XXVIII.

STARS GRATIS.

'Back to the cell, and mean employ,
Resume the craftsman and the boy.'
Browning.

Three months later there was another family gathering, but it was for Thomas Underwood's funeral.

It had come very suddenly. Spa had been given up in favour of Brighton; and there what had seemed a slight casual ailment had been followed by a recurrence of the disease, and a stroke came on which terminated life in a few hours.

Mrs. Underwood was prostrated; but Marilda managed everything, with the help of Spooner, the confidential clerk. She wrote to Felix that he was joint executor with herself, and that as her father had wished to be buried at Centry, he should give orders. Edgar had gone abroad, and no one knew where to write to him.

The chosen burial-place was quite in accordance with poor Mr. Underwood's desire to restore the family. Every year he had made an effort to reside there, and been as regularly frustrated by his wife's predilection for German baths, and dislike to the Bexley neighbourhood. Hers had been the dominion of a noisy tongue, and of ready tears and reclamations, but, poor woman, she was quite passive between the two stronger spirits of her mother and her daughter, who brought her down to Centry the day before the funeral. Mrs. Kedge led her away at once to her room; but Marilda stood in the hall, excited, yet business-like, discussing arrangements with Felix, in that prompt, lucid, all-considering manner that sometimes springs out of the pressure of a great affliction, settling every detail with eager peremptoriness—as, for instance, finding that Felix had intended his brothers only to meet the procession in the grave-yard, she vehemently stipulated that they should come to the house, and be transported in carriages like the rest. Her mother would not go, and would be left with Mrs. Kedge; but she herself was resolved on being present, with Felix for her supporter.

'You will like to have Wilmet with you?' he asked.

'I thought Wilmet would have been here now,' she said, as if disappointed.

'Alda is coming by the five o'clock train; and she thought you had rather be together.'

'But you will stay?' she earnestly entreated.

Alda arrived, weeping so much that she had to be taken upstairs at once. The occupation and excitement were perhaps good for Marilda, who was in a restless tearless state, only eager to be doing something for some one. She sat at the head of the dinner-table, Mr. Spooner at the foot; but the conversation was chiefly due to the instinctive habits of good breeding belonging to Sir Adrian, whose 'go through with it' air was not unlike what he had worn at his wedding.

When the ladies went away, he inquired what was known about the will; but Felix knew nothing, and if Mr. Spooner knew, he would not say. Thereupon Sir Adrian became silent, and asked the way to the smoking-room, whither Mr. Spooner deemed it needful to follow, while Felix repaired to the drawing-room.

He thought it empty; but Alda's head looked round the tall back of an easy-chair.

'Felix, is it you? I was nearly asleep.'

'Are you tired?'

'Yes, rather. It is such a shock—and my poor aunt's grief! It is so frightful to see a large person give way; it makes me quite ill. Where's Adrian?—smoking?'

'Yes.'

'That's man's way of getting out of trouble. If poor Marilda could smoke, she would not be half so restless and wretched. She has been up and down here four or five times in ten minutes. It wears one out!'

'She will be calmer when the bustle is over.'

'She tells me that you are executor with her.'

'I am afraid so.'

'Afraid! why?'

'Of the complication of business of which I have no experience, and that must be thoroughly looked into.'

'Now, for my part,' said Lady Vanderkist, 'I should have expected you to be gratified at such a mark of confidence.'

'So I am, Alda. It is not want of gratitude; it is only that I wish I were better qualified.'

'You understand business.'

'Understanding my own business shows me how little I know of other people's.'

'It would not be other people's, if you take this as it is meant. There can be no doubt that he meant to pave the way. Don't look so senseless and uncompromising, Felix; you must have heard Edgar say so!'

The colour glowed into Felix's face as he answered, 'You have not been so silly as to take Edgar's nonsense in earnest?'

'It is absurd in you to pretend simplicity,' said Alda, sitting upright, and looking at him earnestly. 'Here is such an opportunity as you may never have again. This arrangement must have been made on purpose to remove all scruples.'

'Nay, Alda,' interrupted Felix, in a tone of regret and shame at the subject and the time. 'If there were no objection, this arrangement would be the greatest in itself,' and as she looked at him incredulously, 'don't you see that he has set me to do a brother's part to her? anything to interfere with that would be both unfair and cruel.'

'She knows nothing of such ridiculous refinements as you work yourselves up to. Besides no one wishes you to do anything at once; only you ought to have it in your mind, and might be making way all the time.—Felix,' as she saw his face and gesture, 'you don't mean that you are so absurdly fastidious. I call that quite wrong—in your position, too—and when she is the dearest best-hearted girl in the world!' added Alda, with more genuine feeling.

'True, Alda; I esteem her goodness and generosity too highly to treat her with the disrespect and insincerity such a course would imply.'

'Nonsense! as if it would not be the greatest kindness to save her from fortune-hunters!'

Felix smiled. 'What should I be myself?' he said. 'I must speak plainly, to put this out of your head. Nothing else would lead me to this, and in me it would be especially abominable, because I am the only man in the family able to be of any use to her; and besides, I am not only poor, and in a lower grade, but I have so many dependent upon me.—Don't you see?'

'I only see that you are obstinate and unreasonable, throwing away all my pains to guard her for you!'

Felix could not but laugh a little ironically as he said, 'Thank you.'

'You think it mere fancy,' said Lady Vanderkist, nettled into proving her words by an exposure of herself; 'but she would have had that young Travis two years ago, if I had not managed to give him a hint before he got involved.'

'Alda!' He started up, and stood over her, speaking low, but with pain and horror inconceivable. 'Alda, if you had not told me this, I should not have believed it. I do not believe you now.'

Alda had the grace to colour violently under the force of his indignation. 'Well, well,' she said, 'of course it was not only that. No one out of a novel would be so disinterested without a little bit of infatuation besides; but it is of no use recollecting these things now, when they are gone by.'

This was so incontrovertible that Felix made no answer, and was glad that Marilda returned, trying to work off her restlessness by ringing all the possibilities of Edgar's seeing the announcement in the 'Times,' and coming home.

Felix was still too much stunned to reply freely, and took his leave as soon as possible. He walked home, finding no solace for his dismay at the usage of Ferdinand, save in plans which his better sense knew to be impracticable for bringing Ferdinand and Marilda together; but the match which might have been easily accomplished as a veritable *mariage de convenance*, could not be contemplated by an almost penniless clerk. Moreover, the heart had been given away, and Felix could not believe that it would be possible to turn to Marilda from one of his own graceful sisters. Even though the essential vulgarity of Alda's nature had been so painfully evident, the delicate contour of her face, her refined intonation and pronunciation, and elegance of appearance and manner, returned on him in contrast with poor Marilda's heavy uncouthness, and the shock she inflicted on his taste by plain speaking—worse in manner, if better in matter.

On his return home, he found that Edgar had arrived, having travelled day and night ever since the tidings had met his eye. He was very much tired, and genuinely grieved and overcome, too much even to battle with the manifestation of his feelings. Always affectionate, he mourned for one who had, as he said, been far kinder to him than he deserved, and though often angered with him, had pardoned and overlooked his offences with the partiality of a father. That their final farewell had been one of sharp remonstrance on the one hand, and of gay defiant coolness on the other, added poignancy to his regret; and there was so much more of actual self-reproach than usually came from his tongue, that a gleam of hope glanced through the minds of Felix and Cherry that this shock might be the beginning of better things.

They certainly had never seen him so subdued as when he set out for Centry the next morning with his brothers and Wilmet; and the meeting with Marilda was like that of an orphan brother and sister. With all her esteem and confidence for Felix, her affection for Edgar was a much warmer and more instinctive feeling; and the sight of him brought her tears freely and heartily, while she told him the history of her father's last hours, and his gentle warmth of manner soothed and comforted her.

He was sent for to her mother's dressing-room; and when he left it only to join the funeral party, he looked pale, shaken, and overwhelmed by grief he had shared as well as witnessed. The position of son of the house seemed his right. It was he who led Marilda to the carriage, and handed in first her, then Wilmet followed. Felix was just about to step in, when another person thrust forward, and had his hand on the door, when Edgar said, 'I believe my brother comes with us,' and 'Come Felix,' was hastily murmured from under Marilda's veil. He obeyed, and met a shrug and scowl of displeasure and amazement; but nothing could be thought of except poor Marilda's choking sobs under her veil.

It is one curious effect of good breeding, that while in one class publicity seems to stifle the expression of grief, in another it enhances it; and when Marilda's excitement had once dissolved in tears, her agitation became so excessive, that her cousins watched her anxiously, Wilmet attempting all that salts and kind pressures of the hand could do, and the brothers supporting her, when she clung to Edgar's arm, as if resting her whole weight on him, when the movement to the church began.

It was one of the regular conventional, and therefore most oppressive of funerals, with a great array of pall-bearers, friends from London, and a train of persons with whom Thomas Underwood had been associated; and after all was over, most of them came to a great cold luncheon, which was to occupy them till the next train.

There they trooped, a black multitude, into the dreary big dining-room; and Felix, knowing nobody, and unwilling to take the lead, was much relieved when Edgar returned from taking Marilda upstairs and went round with greetings and replies to every one. When he came to the gentleman who would have entered the carriage, he said, 'Good morning, Fulbert. Here—my eldest brother.'

Felix held out his hand, but met an ungracious bend. 'You muster strong here,' were the words, chiefly addressed to Edgar.

'I am sorry not to show you any more of us,' said Edgar, with a spice of malice; 'the others have walked home.'

Then Felix made some courteous inquiry for the elder Fulbert, and was answered in the coldest and haughtiest of tones, and the Vicar of Vale Leston turned away. In this company, all in mourning, he would not have been taken for a clergyman, chiefly from a sort of free-and-easy air about his dress, and his unclerical cast of countenance, which was wearied, bored and supercilious.

'Take the other end of the table,' indicated Edgar; but Felix would have abstained, had not Mr. Harford summoned him by a look; and another scowl from the Reverend Fulbert was the consequence.

Before long that gentleman was examining the lawyer as to when the will was to be read; and hearing in return that so few were concerned that there was to be no public opening. Did Miss Underwood know that he—Fulbert—was here?—Yes, certainly.—He should like to see her and her mother. Mr. Harford applied to Edgar, who undertook to ascertain whether they would wish it.

'What can it be for?' said Marilda, who was sitting between the twin sisters, calm, though spent with weeping, and unusually gentle.

'To warn you against us,' said Edgar. 'He is ready every moment to insult Felix; but if you can bear it, you had better face him, or he will say we beset you, and let no one have access to you.'

'That would be better than his teasing her,' said Wilmet.

'No, I don't mind whom I see now,' said Marilda. 'I must stand alone. Send him to me in the library, Edgar.'

This left Wilmet for the first time alone with Alda, longing to enter fully into her sister's new life, and hearing that Ironbeam Park was delightful; beautiful house, splendid drawing-rooms, beautiful grounds, sheet of water, swans, deer, good neighbourhood, people calling, dinner invitations without number, guests who had had to be put off. There was a little attempt at complaint at being overwhelmed by the welcome, but pleasure and exultation were visible enough; only it seemed to Wilmet that there was more of the splendour and less of the Adrian, than she would have expected. Marilda soon came back.

'Well, was it as Edgar said?' asked Alda.

'He offers his wife to come and stay with me.'

'I dare say!'

'I shouldn't wonder if he meant to be kind!'

'Now, Marilda, you aren't going to let yourself be talked over!' cried Alda.

'He is my relation,' said Marilda, bluffly, in a tone that showed she meant to be mistress of her own actions. 'I came back to say that there are things to be done. There are Felix and Edgar walking in the garden; I want them in the library.'

She was going to ring to have them summoned; but Wilmet undertook to fetch them, going through an ante-room with a glass door; which she was just unfastening, when she heard a voice behind her—'Holloa, where are you going now?' She perceived her brother-in-law, lounging on a sofa with a newspaper.

'I am looking for my brothers.'

'I say, haven't I told you that I'll not have you eternally running after that concern?'

She faced about, and looked full at him with her grave eyes, and neck held like a stag's.

'I beg your pardon,' he stammered. 'This confounded mourning makes everybody alike.'

She did not wait to hear more, but was gone as soon as the bolt had yielded.

The Tartar had shown himself without a scratch. Were these his domestic manners to his three months' bride?

She said nothing to her brothers, but brought them to the library, where Marilda was awaiting them, with the lawyer, Harford, and the manager, Spooner, to settle about the will.

Alda's five thousand pounds had been made over to her at her marriage, so that she was not mentioned. A large share in the mercantile house already belonged to Mrs. Underwood, and to her was bequeathed the lease of the Kensington house, with the furniture; but Centry Park was absolutely left to Mary Alda, the daughter, with all the property in the funds, or embarked in the business, coupled with a request that in case of her marriage she should carry with her the name and arms of Underwood. Among the legacies were fifteen hundred pounds to Felix Chester Underwood, and one thousand pounds apiece to Thomas Edgar, Theodore Benjamin, and Stella Eudora—Felix and Mr. Harford trustees for these last, with liberty to use the interest for their benefit, or let it accumulate, as might be best.

No one made any remark; and the lawyer was beginning to tell the two executors what immediate steps they must take, when Edgar rose, saying, 'I suppose I'm not wanted!'

Marilda jumped up. 'Edgar, you ain't vexed! Poor Papa thought the executorship might take time, trouble, and expense, that ought to be made up for.'

'Now, Polly,' said Edgar, with his sweet candid smile, 'you are not thinking me grudging dear old Fee anything man could give him! I only wish he had mine. He'd do some good with it;' and he fondly laid his hand on the shoulder of Felix, who, not being used, like him, to view Harford and Spooner as tame cats, had rather have had this more in private.

'You'll leave it in our hands, and let us make the most of it for you, Edgar,' said warm-hearted Marilda; 'that Pampas railway is never less than seven per cent., you know.'

'All very well, Poll, if the item could be suppressed when the will is blazoned abroad. It is not ingratitude, dear old girl. It is more than I deserve or expected, and will give me a hoist.'

'I hope—' began Marilda eagerly.

'Never mind me. The best part of it is that nest-egg for those babies.'

'It is indeed,' said Felix; 'I cannot express how thankful I am, especially for poor Theodore's sake.'

'It will not do much in the funds,' said Marilda, gratified; 'but leave it in our hands, and little Stella shall have quite a fortune. You will judge of our security when you look into our books.'

Marilda's habit of identifying herself with the firm had begun half in play years ago; and in fact, the house now chiefly consisted of herself, her mother, and grandmother, with Spooner, who had shares enough to give him a personal interest in the transactions.

'You do not mean to go on with the business?' asked Felix.

'Why not? I have worked at it, and like it much better than the piano or bead-work—and I can, can't I, Mr. Spooner?'

'We all know your competence, Miss Underwood. I would not wish for a more sagacious head, if—'

'Yes, if,' said Marilda more sadly; 'but you see, Felix, you may trust me. Let me keep your own and the twins, for you.'

'For the twins, I do not know how the law stands. Mr. Harford will tell me; but for myself, it may make a great difference to have this capital just now,' said Felix, who had already perceived what it might do for him.

Charles Froggatt had been dead about a month, and with him his father had lost all personal hope or interest in the business, and the few times he had come into the town, had shrunk from meetings even with old friends, and crept upstairs to talk to Geraldine. He wished to retire, and he would have liked to have put Felix Underwood, who had for nearly nine years been as a dutiful son, into a son's place; but he had relations to whom he must do justice, and he was unwilling to bring in a new partner, who might, as a moneyed man, lord it over Felix; while if he left things in their present condition till his death, the succession would pass to a family whom he knew to be uncongenial. All this had been discussed, but without seeing any way out of the difficulty, until in this legacy Felix saw the means of making himself master of the house and stock, and thus would obtain a footing as a citizen, by which he could profit as he gained in age and standing. The available income of the family would hardly be increased, since the absolute possession of the house involved expenses that had hitherto been paid over his head; but the security and independence were worth more than the pounds, shillings and pence that might otherwise have been brought in. The certain provision for the helpless Theodore also made Felix more free. The lawyer, his fellow trustee, greatly to Wilmet's satisfaction, would not allow the sum in trust to be invested in anything but government security, and as nothing was needed at present for the child, the interest might there accumulate in case of need.

Edgar showed himself much subdued by the change in the household. He never spoke plainly about his doings, and direct questions drove him to his retreat in the ludicrous. However, it could be inferred that in the recklessness induced by Alice Knevett's desertion, he had gone far enough to alarm himself, and behold some abyss of exposure and disgrace whence the legacy would retrieve him, and that he was resolved to pull up and begin upon a different course.

He talked eagerly and edifyingly of setting about a picture for exhibition, the proceeds of which might take him to Italy, to begin a course of study at Rome, where he might make a home for Cherry to come and work with him; and they built up a *Château en Espagne*, the more fervently in proportion to Cherry's want of faith therein. Hours were spent in devising and sketching subjects for *the* picture, or rather pictures, for Mr. Renville was very anxious that Geraldine should make a venture in water-colours, such as might at least make her known as a possible illustrator. Edgar's eye and advice were very useful to her; and she decided on one ideal subject—the faithful little acolyte, who while the priest slept on the cold morning,

> 'Turned and sought the choir,
> Touched the Altar tapers
> With a flake of fire.'

And likewise the sketches of Stella in different attitudes, which she had made with a view to Alda's picture, were worth working at with her utmost power.

For Edgar's own part, he had resolved on a scene which Cherry thought wild and impracticable, till he had dashed in his sketch of Brynhild asleep in the circle of fire, with Sigurd about to break through. There was something so bright and fiery, so expressive and powerful, in the hastily-designed and partly-coloured *ébauche* that Cherry gazed at it like something of weird and magical beauty, only longing for her master to see it, and own Edgar's genius.

Brynhild's model was Wilmet, who, much against the grain, was induced to let down all her mass of hair, and let Edgar pose her on the sofa squab with bare arms. In his mischief, however, he produced a counter pen-and-ink outline of Marilda in the same position, with all the pointed flames labelled with the names of various stocks and securities; while Sigurd's helmet disclosed Felix, armed with the Pursuivant, and hesitating to plunge in. He might with equal propriety have drawn himself, his sister Alda thought, for on failing with Felix, she had actually whispered the same hint to him, but was met with the reply, 'Oh no, I am not bad enough for that.'

She was spending a week longer at Centry, that Sir Adrian might massacre the pheasants, which, however, he considered to be so disgracefully preserved, that he spent much time and eloquence in explaining to Miss Underwood how she might render her game a source of profit.

One November day, the last of the Vanderkists' stay at Centry, when the sisters had been sent for in the afternoon, and he and Lance were to follow for the evening, Felix, returning into his office, was amazed to see a figure standing at the fire.

'Ferdinand! what good wind brings you here?'

'I am come to say good-bye.'

'What? Mr. Brown sends you out to America?'

'No, it is on my own account. His correspondent at Oswego has telegraphed to him to find me, and let me know of my uncle's death.'

'Death!'

'Yes, I know no particulars.'

'And are you his heir?'

'That I do not know. Probably. I cannot bring myself to care.'

'How much is it?'

'Brown knows of fifty thousand in stock that he can lay his hand upon; but there must be more than as much again afloat in the States, in goodness knows what speculations, and I shall have to deal with it all!'

'It is well you have had an apprenticeship. The Life Guardsman would have known less about it. When do you start?'

'I go back to town by the mail train to-night, to Liverpool to-morrow. I could not go without telling you; and when I tried to write, I felt I must see you and this place again. But you are going out.'

'We were, but we shall be glad to get off.'

'To Centry? Is she there?'

'Yes. Going early to-morrow.'

Before Ferdinand had done more than stare into the fire, Lance opened the door. 'Mr. Flowerdew wants—Holloa! Fernan dropped from the skies!'

'Is Mr Flowerdew there?' said Felix, about to pass him.

'No; he only wants you to write up to Novello's.—Do you hear, Fernan? we are to have *such* a concert in the town hall, for a real good organ. Edgar will bring down no end of stars for it. You'll come down for it?'

'Fernan will be in the utmost parts of America by that time, Lance.'

'Look here, Lance,' said Fernan—that dark sad countenance lighting as it sometimes did—'just you wait a fortnight, and I can all but promise you—'

'An organ by Atlantic cable, eh?' said Felix, laughing. 'Look at Lance, Fernan; he'd hardly thank you. It is the concert they want; the organ is the excuse.'

'Now, Felix, you are as much set on the concert as I am. He is to sing, "Return, blest days,"' rattled on Lance, too eager on his own hobby to draw the inference as to Fernan's fortunes; 'and Mr. Miles has promised to come himself with all our own fellows; and so we can have the sacred part something respectable. It is a horrid pity you can't come!'

'He will be better employed, Lance; he believes he is come into his fortune.'

'And if so, Felix, nothing can hinder me from my greatest possible pleasure, the giving this organ to St Oswald's—the church of my baptism.'

'Well, Fernan, the bear is not caught yet, remember; but when it is, I'm not the man to hinder you from making up the deficit I strongly anticipate after this same concert of ours.'

'Felix! A hundred and sixty reserved seats at a guinea, and—'

Felix put up his hands to his ears. 'Meantime, Lance, find little Lightfoot, and tell him to get ready to take a note into the country.'

Ferdinand of course rose up, insisting on starting by the five o'clock train, but was withheld while Felix wrote a note to Marilda, in which he communicated the tidings, leaving it to her and to Wilmet to inform Lady Vanderkist.

The note was delivered in the expectant time before dinner, when Marilda, without any preliminary but 'Bless me! what does Felix write to me for?' read—

MY DEAR COUSIN,

You must have the kindness to excuse Lance and myself from joining your party to-night. We are unexpectedly prevented by the arrival of Mr. Travis, who has come down to take leave, having been telegraphed for to Oswego on his uncle's death. He must go back by to-night's mail train; and perhaps you would kindly send my sisters home a little earlier, as I think they would wish to see him.

Your affectionate cousin
F.C. UNDERWOOD.

'His uncle dead without a will! If we had but known!' said Mrs. Underwood, unguardedly.

'Insolvent, depend on it,' growled Sir Adrian, fitting on the consequence so that Cherry felt an uncontrollable impulse to giggle, and was glad to be sunk in the depths of a huge chair.

She was startled by Alda's answering rather fretfully, 'I don't see why—he was very rich.'

'The more reason. It is always the way with those Yankees.'

Mrs. Underwood took on herself to defend the solidity of the Travis interest as an article of her husband's belief; Wilmet and Cherry longed to change the conversation, but neither knew how; and it was Sir Adrian who found a fresh subject at last, on which the others willingly rode off.

They begged to have the carriage ordered at nine, and bade good-bye to Lady Vanderkist, who had good taste enough not to make another remark after the first into which she had been betrayed.

Marilda, however, did. 'Tell him I hope it is all right, and that I congratulate him with all my heart,' she said; and she looked as if she could have said more.

Perhaps Wilmet and Cherry were not sorry that Stella's being seated between them prevented discussion on the difference patience and constancy might have made. Wilmet, with her love for her sister, and recollection of that conjugal interpellation, might regret; while Geraldine, less prejudiced, felt that Ferdinand could hardly be pitied for the test that had spared him a wife with whom he could have so little in common; but both felt the contrast when they were met by Ferdinand, whose countenance, though not intellectual, was singularly noble, and full of a grand melancholy sweetness according with the regular outline and dark olive colouring, while the gentleness of his tone was not the conventional politeness of society, but somewhat of the old Spaniard enhanced by Christian grace.

For all that had come and gone, they were more comfortable with him now than when he had been Alda's exclusive property, and what was wanting in love had been made up in jealousy; but he was very low and sad; he had not come to the point of ceasing to regret Alda, and his native inertness shrank from the trouble and turmoil before him, when he had nothing to make riches valuable to him, and could not bear to be wrenched from the shadow of St. Matthew's, and tossed he knew not where in the West, among strangers and worse than strangers. But after all, the home party were soon caring most of all about their concert.

The St Oswald's Choral Society did in fact give a concert every year, but in a very quiet way, aiming only at covering their own expenses, and seeking for no extraneous aid; but this was to be an affair on a very different scale. It had grown up no one knew how, under the influence of Mr. Flowerdew, and of two Miss Birkets, daughters of a gentleman who lived out of the town but in the parish. They were enthusiastic young ladies, about thirty years old, who had been enough at Minsterham to have known 'little Underwood' in his glory there, and to take him up with all their might when they found him with renovated powers in the choral society.

He was 'little Underwood' still, and perhaps would always be so, for in spite of the start of growth he had so eagerly hailed, he would never be tall, but the slenderness of his bones, hands, feet, and general frame, made him look neatly and well made; and he was what every one called, very gentleman-like in appearance. His face had not the beauty of some of the others, the colouring was pale, and there was nothing to catch the eye, till it lighted up into mirth or sweetness; and his manners, from their perfect simplicity and absence of self-consciousness, were always engaging. He was either a cypher, or else he had an inexpressible charm about him. When his violin-playing powers were discovered, the ladies made a point of getting up a piece on the piano in which he was to accompany them, and a prodigious quantity of practice it took. Lance had to walk over to them at least two afternoons in a week. Felix looked on it as patronage, and could not think how he could bear it; but Lance was too simple to perceive patronizing—a petticoat was always a petticoat to him, and a little lingering chatter in their drawing-room was his delight, a few friendly words over the counter enslaved him.

Those holidays came, as Felix well knew, much too often; and if he tried to keep the balance true by tenders of the like liberty to Ernest Lamb, Lance proved to have left his head behind him, and made mistakes, or still worse was guilty of neglects. When called to account, partly from pre-occupation, partly from easiness of temper, he really seemed incapable of taking a reproof, or understanding the enormity of his errors. Had these been the days of Redstone, there must have been an explosion; but young Lamb was one of those whom Lance unconsciously fascinated, and being used to sparing him in the early days when he was scarcely more than a convalescent, the good plodding lad took it for granted that the unmusical should set the musical free, toiled quietly after him to rectify his mistakes, was absolutely amazed when Mr. Underwood apologized to him for the unequal weight resting on his honest shoulders, and was by far the most shocked and distressed when at last the value of some careless piece of damage was imposed as a fine. Indeed, Lance viewed this as expiation, troubled his head no more about the matter, and was in far too transcendent a state to perceive that he was Felix's daily worry, provocation, and disappointment.

There was the hope that it would be only for a time, and that it would blow over the sooner that nothing was heard of Edgar or his stars. Lance was indeed so radiantly happy, that it was only when he was doing something very provoking indeed that it was possible to be displeased with him, and not even to Geraldine would Felix whisper the heart-sickening misgivings that came over him when he found himself experiencing exactly what Kedge and Underwood had gone through from Edgar.

The concert was to be just within the Christmas vacations, so that the performers would include Clement, and the audience Robina and Angela, besides William Harewood, who was to bring his sisters over. It was delicious to hear Lance's demands upon Wilmet, in his ecstasy at being once more with his own beloved Minsterham choir. And Wilmet's soft spot was Minsterham, as the rogue knew.

'Train comes in at five eleven. I say, Mettie, our fellows must come here before they go to tune up.'

'My dear Lance, there are five-and-thirty of them at least! It is quite impossible! Why they couldn't sit down!'

Lance whistled. 'I must have little Graeme, Mettie, the little chap has never been here.'

'Poor little Dick! Well I don't mind him.'

'And if he comes, he must bring little George Lee—he's only seven, and not fit to knock about with men and all.'

'Very well.'

'No more is his fellow—that mite of a Bennett that is come instead of Harewood. His brother was an uncommon good friend to me when I was a little squeaking treble.'

Wilmet swallowed the mite of a Bennett.

'And Poulter! You remember Poulter, surely, Wilmet.'

'Who used to come twice a day to ask after you. Yes, we must have him.'

'Then there's Oliver—our big bass! Oh! you must remember old Oliver with that grizzly beard, coming in and carrying me out like a baby the first day I went into the avenue.'

'That good-natured old man—only I should think he would be happier among his friends.'

'And Mr. Miles—'

'Really, Lance, I don't think Mr. Miles would wish to come.'

'Oh, you're afraid Jack will be jealous!—You know, Cherry, Miles was almost caught, he had the slyest little flirtation with Mettie when they thought I was asleep or delirious or something—'

'Delirious indeed to think so,' interrupted Wilmet indignantly; but Lance went on unheeding,

'And if the engineer hadn't been the sharpest, who knows if she wouldn't have got permanent lodgings in the organ gallery? and now you see she thinks poor Miles's heart is in such a state that she can't venture to let him come!'

'Ah!' said Cherry, gravely taking up the cue, and much amused at Wilmet's indignant blushes and innocent amazement. 'I've always understood that things go very deep with those sort of misogynists, when once they begin.'

'Now, Cherry, I didn't expect such nonsense in you!' exclaimed Wilmet. 'Mr. Miles is extremely welcome—just as any of Lance's friends are.'

'There, Lance,' laughed Cherry, 'there goes the wedge! Dick Graeme was the small end, then came the two little trebles, then the two basses, and now Mr. Miles himself and any of your friends. And I imagine all the five-and-thirty are your particular friends.'

'Why, all that are coming—except Rooke and Higgins, and they always were disgusting little cads, only one couldn't leave them out by themselves, as they would be eating dirt some way and getting not fit to sing; Rooke's got my part now—I always used to be the lady when there was any spooning going on out of an opera! and if we don't take them in hand they'll go and stuff themselves with pastry, and wash it down with cherry brandy, and won't be good for anything.'

'But there must be some senior to keep them in order.'

'Oh! there's Black, but he will go to his cousin's in Long Street, and Charlie Harris, but he was next to me. If any one comes, Charlie must.'

'My dear, how many are there to come?'

'Well! four of the little chaps will be away for the holidays, and it is only six of the lay-vicars that ever do come out, and two of them have friends here, so it is only two more of them besides Mr. Miles, and but five more boys. Really, Wilmet, I know Mr. Miles and the Precentor would be for ever obliged, there's nothing they hate so much for us as knocking about hotels, and that's why we hardly ever went to any but private concerts.'

'Well, every one was so very kind last year, we do owe some return. I will see what Felix thinks.'

Felix, so far as he had time to think at all, was sure to be on the hospitable side, so that ended by a provision of cold meat and tea and coffee on the back-room table, and permission to Lance to bring in and feed whomsoever he pleased. After the concert, a regular supper was provided in the school for all the performers, and Wilmet was released from all concern except with stray womankind who might want shelter till the mail train.

The excitement went on increasing. To use Lance's expression, the tickets went off like wild-fire; Marilda took a large allowance for her servants and dependants.

The type of the programmes was all set up, and Lance had proudly carried the proof round the house, when a note arrived from Edgar.

'Prebels consent to come and give three National Magyar airs, expenses being paid. Engage rooms for them at the F.A. I trust this is in time to draw. I shall come down with them.'

T.E.U.

Here were the stars, after all! Lance crushed up his proof and played at ball with it in his ecstasy; and Felix—for all the trouble it gave him—was carried along and not much less delighted, as he sent Clement up to Mr. Flowerdew with the intelligence.

The brother and sister M. Stanislas and Mlle. Zoraya Prebel were not exactly in the first ranks of public singers, but were rated highly, and their fame, when making the round of the provinces with a company who performed varieties of characteristic national music, had been quite enough to fire the souls of Bexley with ardour; nor did Felix murmur, although he had to stay away from the final choral society's rehearsal to provide for the programmes and hand-bills, without which the attraction of Mlle. Zoraya would remain unknown to the public. Time to put it into the Pursuivant would have made all the difference!

But on that last supreme day, the excitement was such, that anybody was willing to do anything. Felix could do little but explain to people where their seats would be on the map of the town hall spread on the counter, and answer their questions about the Zoraya; Wilmet was over head and ears on her preparations for her entertainment, and would have been unable to get any help in laying out her table but Cherry's if Marilda had not come in to see what was going on, thrown herself into the business with zeal and promptitude, sent back to Centry for a supply of flowers, knives and forks, and done the work of half a dozen parlour-maids. Stella was obediently keeping Theodore out of mischief; and the other two girls were, with Bill Harewood, assisting a select party in decorating the town hall with evergreens; and Clement, who had to his dismay found a whole part made over to him by a young Bruce, who had an inopportune cold, was practising hard at the old piano (which, by-the-by, Lance had learned to tune); Mr. Flowerdew and the manager were catching the doubtful and putting them through their performances; and little Lightfoot was only preserved by his natural stolidity from utter distraction among the hundred different ways he was ordered at once. As for Lance, he tried to help every one, was too excited to keep at anything, and was usually scolded off from whatever he attempted till at last he shut himself up in the barrack with his violin, and practised till he was so desperate at the sense of his failures, that when Bill Harewood came in search of him, he was, as he mildly expressed it, hesitating whether to hang himself like Dirk Hatteraick on the beam.

'Well, come down, here's Miles as savage as a bear with a sore head—vows that he was very near turning back again when he saw your rose-coloured placard of the Zoraya at the station.'

'If he's sulky, that is a go!' exclaimed Lance, with a look of consternation, utterly overpowering his stage fright. 'Do you remember his putting us all out at the Deanery, because Miss Evans affronted him?'

'Well do I remember it! He boxed my ears for it so that they sung for a week!'

And the two ex-choristers went down, feeling much as when an anthem had gone wrong. The room was pretty well filled with their old comrades, but Lance only went from one to the other quietly shaking hands, and quaking for the future as he heard the organist thundering away to Wilmet and Cherry.

He hated singing women some degrees more than the rest of their sex, and above all Italian singing women, who never appreciated Handel. Cherry ventured to suggest that the lady was not Italian, but, if anything, Hungarian.

'Madam,' he answered in Johnsonian wrath, 'she is cosmopolitan, that is to say a half breed or quarter breed of everything, with neither home, nation, nor faith!'

'Do you know anything against her?' gravely asked Wilmet, with a view to the possible contingency of being desired to call upon her.

'I know enough in knowing her to be a second-rate *prima donna*. Faugh! Now and then comes a first-rate one who can't help it, and is as meek and simple as you might be; but when this sort of woman comes down as a favour, I know what that means! Who is to pay the debt you'll have?'

'They come for their expenses.'

He held up his hands. 'I'd ten times rather she came at a hundred guineas a night! Then you'd know what to be at! Whose doing is it?'

'My brother Edgar's.'

'Then I hope he is prepared to pay for it. That is, if she comes at all. You'll have a telegram to say she has a cold, and who is to announce it to an indignant audience?'

'I think you had better, Mr. Miles,' said Cherry daringly, 'for you will congratulate them upon it.'

'Isn't his face a caution?' whispered Bill to Lance. 'He never got such sauce before.'

'He likes it,' returned Lance, triumphantly rubbing his hands. 'Cherry could come over Pluto himself!'

And in effect, the lively gracious tongue of the one sister, and the calm beauty of the other, were producing a wonderful placability and good-humour; the lads who were feeding by relays in the back room ventured to talk and laugh above their breath, and the only fear was of a relapse when Marilda's carriage, with Mr. and Mrs. Spooner in it, called for Cherry, and the fascination had to be removed.

Lance was as much delighted to walk down with the choir, though he sorely missed his cap and gown, as was Will to go, as he said, like a gentleman, the only one except little Bernard available to escort the ladies. Robin was quite content, as he took to himself all the honour and glory of representing his brother, and giving an arm to the belle of the room, as he persisted in declaring Wilmet, though to well accustomed Bexley eyes, she was much more likely to appear as the school teacher.

They were a merry little snug party, those four sisters behind, with the three Harewoods; only Wilmet was rather scandalised by the titter of Grace and Lucy in their delight at being relieved from Mr. Miles's presence; and their excitement about Edgar, whom they viewed as the most beautiful vision that had ever dawned on them. Vain were Wilmet's endeavours to keep them in order by stern repressions of her own comparatively unoffending sisters, who had little attention to spare for nonsense, since Robina's whole soul was set on Lance's enjoying and distinguishing himself, and Angela was in an absolutely painful state of tension with expectation and anxiety for the star's appearance and Mr. Miles's temper.

Presently, after long waiting, there was a look of sensation and eagerness, and Felix, who had been detained to the last moment, came edging himself through the lines of chairs, his whiskers in their best curl, and his hair shining, to exchange a word with his outermost sister, who chanced to be Robin.

'All right, if the train is not late. Edgar has telegraphed. Is Cherry comfortable? I couldn't get away before. There's not a ticket left.'

Happy those that caught the whisper as Felix made his way up the lane, and was admitted through the orchestra; but there was still delay enough to allow some impatient stamping of feet to begin before the revolution in the programme could be settled which was to give these erratic meteors time to appear. Then at last came the overture, and the concert took its course. There was no doubt that Mr. Miles was accompanying in his best style; Angela was soon far too blissful for personal anxieties; but it was a great comfort to the sisters to be secure that all was right, when not only the three brothers—of whom they had seen and heard their share in the sacred part—but Edgar came forward. Any sisters might be proud of four such brothers—so bright, so straight, so strong and fair; Edgar, with his fine robust figure and silky beard, giving them altogether a distinguished look and character, though Clement's head was a little the highest, and Lance's voice was the sweetest and most remarkable in power and expression; but all were in wonderful accord and harmony. Any other audience would have encored the performance as something rare and exquisite; but the Underwood brothers and their glees were rather stock pieces at Bexley, and people wanted something new.

Lance's performance with the Miss Birkets was very correct, but not of the style calculated to produce any very lively sentiments among the uninitiated audience, who were on the tip-toe of expectation of the lady whose arrival had been notified in whispers, and hardly fully appreciating the best that either their own powers or the Minsterham choir could produce. The first part went by without her; and in the interval came hope in the shape of Lance, who made an incursion to ask his sisters how they liked it, and to impart that the Zoraya was safe come, but was supposed to be dressing. 'Mr. Miles said she would be dressing till midnight, and would be less worth hearing then than a decently trained choir-boy. But he's not sulky, after all; yet,' added Lance, with a look of brightness in his face, 'fancy his telling Fee that I played that remarkably well just now—truth and taste, he said—the old villain—only that the ladies would spoil my time if I didn't take care. And there's a sallow-faced fellow come down with Mademoiselle, who said it wasn't bad either!'

No wonder Lance was exalted; and he required equal admiration for all his favourites, until he had to hurry back again.

A little of what seemed to the excited commonplace—then came the event of the evening. The glistening silken lady, with a flashing emerald spray in her dark hair, lustrous eyes of a colour respecting which no two persons in the room agreed, and a face of brilliant beauty, was led bowing forward, and her notes, birdlike, fresh, and clear, rang through the room, her brother accompanying her. It was a strong clear voice, and the language and air being alike new, entranced every one; the applause was vehement, the encoring almost passionate; but the lady would not be encored, she gave them two songs alone, one with her brother, accompanied this time by Lance's 'sallow-faced fellow;' and though she smiled and curtsied graciously, was not to be induced to repeat herself.

It seemed to Robina as if the lady herself and the whole public had taken a great deal of trouble for a very brief matter; but she found it was rank treason to say so, when at the conclusion of the whole, those faithful brothers hurried down each to pick up a sister and bestow her safely at home before repairing to the Fortinbras Arms for the great supper to the Minsterham choir. The Bexley public had been favoured beyond all desert or reason; the newness of the airs had been a perfect revelation to Lance's ears, and he was very angry with Clement for being disappointed, and repeating Mr. Miles's judgment that there was lack both of science in the singing and of sweetness in the voice.

Altogether the evening had been a great success; every one was delighted with every one else, and the supper was not the least charming part, preceded as it was by Lance's bringing the little seven years old choir boy, half asleep, ready to cry and quite worn out, and putting him under Wilmet's care. He had half his night's rest out on the sofa before he was picked up in the kindly arms of the big bass and carried off to the mail train. Lance seemed much disposed to go with them by mistake; indeed, he was only withheld from accompanying them to the station by Felix reminding him rather sharply that someone must be kept sitting up for him.

It was over, and the morning began with Felix standing straight up in the office, master now rather than brother, and gravely saying, 'Now, Lance, that this excitement is at an end, I shall expect attention and punctuality, and shall excuse no more neglects. Take this invoice, and overlook the unpacking of those goods.'

'Yes, sir.' Lance wriggled his shoulders feeling intensely weary of such tasks; and as he stood, paper in hand, still he partly whistled, partly hummed the Hungarian air, till the foreman came out of the printing-house, saying, 'Mr. Lancelot, I should be much obliged if you would desist. It distracts the young men.'

Of course Lance bothered the young men, but desisted whenever he recollected it, and then inly bemoaned the having passed a light-house of anticipation, and having before him only a dreary irksome twilight waste.

Edgar had not been seen that morning, except to leave word that he meant to breakfast with his friends at the Fortinbras Arms; but at the dinner hour he looked into the office, and saying, 'You are at liberty, Lance, I want you,' carried him off, Felix knew not why nor where, and had no time to ask, even when Lance came back, and this was not till past two, with the shop overflowing, and customers waiting to be attended to. It was one of those times when gossipry was rife, and the master had to stand talking, talking, while his assistants had more than enough on their hands with the real purchasers, a division of labour that usually came naturally, but to which Lance was evidently not conforming himself as usual; and at last Felix heard him absolutely denying that certain blotting-blocks ever had been, would, or could be made, and had to turn hastily to the rescue and undertake that they should be forthcoming by the next week. Also two orders proved to have been left not entered, and therefore not attended to, and Felix was thoroughly roused into vexation and anger. As soon as the last hurried customers had come and gone, while Stubbs and Lightfoot were closing the shutters, he again summoned Lance with, 'This will not do, Lance. Your ignorance and laziness are not to be the limit of people's wants, and I will not have my customers neglected. I have had patience with you all through this business, and that good fellow Lamb has shown forbearance that amazes me, but it must go on no longer. Things cannot be done by halves. Either you must turn over a new leaf, and give your mind to the business, or you must give it up, and look out for some other employment.'

'You wish me to give it up?' mumbled Lance, in a voice that sounded sullen.

'You are going the way to make me do so.'

'You don't want me? Very well.'

'Stay, Lance,' said Felix, whose reproofs had never before been received by Lance in this manner, 'I wish you to understand. You offered your services under a generous impulse last year, when I was overdone and perplexed; but I doubted then if it were not a mistake. You had come to be very valuable, more so than any mere hireling could be, and I am very thankful to you; but if you are to be like what you have been for a month past, you are doing some harm to the business and a great deal to yourself; and you had better choose some line that you can be hearty in.'

'Could you afford it, Felix?'

'I must afford it! Such work as yours has been of late is the most expensive of all. Eh!' rather startled; 'have you anything in your head?'

'I hardly know.'

A message came in at the moment, and by the time Felix had answered it, Lance had vanished, rather to his vexation and uneasiness. He went up to supper, the first family meeting where there had been time to talk over the humours of the day before. Edgar was full of fun; and the report Cherry had been writing for the Pursuivant was read aloud in the family conclave, and freely canvassed, but Lance, though he put in a word or two here and there, was much quieter than usual; and when all the others moved back into the drawing-room, he touched Robina's arm, and kept her with him in the dark room.

'What should you say, Bob, if I got out of it all?' was his first word.

'Out of it all!'

'Ay. Felix thinks me no loss, and I've got a chance.'

'Oh!' a long interrogative not well pleased sound it was, not answered at once; and Robina added, 'Does Mr. Miles want an assistant?'

"Tisn't that sort. You saw the gentleman that came down with Edgar and the Hungarians?'

'Yes, his name is Allen, he is manager of the National Minstrelsy,' Edgar said.

'Just so. He has got a lease of a concert-room in town, and he would give me five pounds a week to sing two nights a week through the season!'

'Lance!' Robina could only stand breathless.

'I'll tell you all about it. You know Edgar came and called me just at dinner-time.'

'I know, and Felix got no dinner at all except a sandwich that Wilmet sent down.'

'Well, that was his own fault. However, there they were at the Fortinbras Arms, in the best blue room, just come down to breakfast.'

'Who? The Hungarians?'

'Yes. Mr. Allen and M. Prebel were waiting for the lady, to ring and have the hot things up. What a stunner she is, to be sure! the finest woman I ever saw in my life, and such pretty ways when she can't find an English word, I should think a queen must be just like her.'

'Yes, if she is waited for in that way. Did you get anything to eat, then, Lance?'

'Didn't we, though? Why, they had asked us to breakfast; and such a breakfast I never set eyes on—devilled kidneys, and pie with truffles in it, and pine-apple jam—and wine! They asked for wines that Reid the waiter had never heard of—nor, it is my belief, Mr. Jones either.'

'But is this all to come out of their expenses that are paid for them?'

'You're getting like W.W., I declare, Bobbie. I never thought of that; but I'll go up to Reid, and find out the worth of my own share, and wipe that out. Well, they were uncommonly kind and civil. Edgar's quite at home with them, you know; talks French like a house on fire, or German—I don't know which it was, but she made it sound as pretty as could be, and I should soon pick it up. I had no notion what they were at, but Edgar said she wanted to hear me sing that song of Sullivan's again, and I could not help doing it; and then she smiled and bowed and thanked, and Mr. Allen made remarks, about my wanting lightness and style, said it came of singing too much cathedral music.'

'O Lance, wasn't that like the Little Master saying Montjoie St. Denis?'

'Nonsense! He's no more like the Little Master than you are; Edgar says he's as respectable as Old Time, and has got a little mouse of a wife as good as gold. But he does want a high tenor to sing his English ballads, and he'll give me this, with chances to sing at private concerts, and opportunities of getting lessons on the violin. Think of that, you solemn bird, you.'

'Where would you live?'

'With Edgar. Then I could make up the difference to Fee; and what I could save, with Edgar's picture, will take us to Italy. And there I could get finished up first-rate.'

'You've not settled it so?'

'Why, no. The first thing that struck me was that it was awfully cool by Felix, to say all this without notice to him, and I told them as much; but then they said they didn't want to inconvenience Felix, and wouldn't want me till March.'

'Just as if you were his servant.'

'In that light, so I am.'

'You don't really think of doing it, Lance?'

'I don't mean one thing or the other yet, Robin! Here's Felix one side telling us that he's very much obliged to me, but I am worse than no use at all; and Edgar and this Allen on the other, saying that here's the line that I am cut out for.'

'But Felix can only mean when you are gone mad after the concert.'

'And who is to help getting mad, when their life is all dulness and botheration? Edgar told me it would be so—and now Felix himself declares it was a mistake my ever working here.'

'Felix must have been terribly displeased, to say so.'

'I believe he was indeed! but I couldn't help it. How can one mind foolscap and satin wove, and all the rest of it, when there are such glorious things beyond?'

'O Lance, I never heard you say "couldn't help it" before!'

'Now, Robin, say in three words. Do you want me to be a mere counter-jumper all my life?'

'O Lance—don't.'

'There, you see what you really feel about it. Now—without coming to such a point as Sims Reeves, or Joachim, or—' (and Lance's face was full of infinite possibility), 'I could with the most ordinary luck get up high enough to have a handsome maintenance; and at any rate, I should live with what is life to me—have time to study the science—be a composer, maybe—and get into a society that is not all inferior. I hate the isolation we live in here—not a real lady out of one's own family to be friendly with one.'

'But I don't think ladies are so with musical people.'

'Maybe not, but they are a strong, cultivated, refined society of their own, able to take care of themselves. What now, Robin, can't you speak? What is it now?'

'I was only thinking of what you said last time Edgar asked you.'

'I hadn't seen London then, I knew nothing about it. The very Sundays there are different things from what they are in this deadly lively place.'

'That's as you make them. Besides, that makes no difference as to that other thing you said.'

'What?' (A little crossly.)

'About the cathedral and the stage,' whispered Robina, hanging her head.

'One doesn't want all that one ever said when one was a high-flown ass to be thrown in one's teeth,' said Lance, angrily.

'Oh!' but otherwise Robina held her tongue.

Presently Lance began again persuasively. 'You see this is only training, after all, Bobbie; I may take to sacred music, oratorios or anything else, when once I have got thoroughly taught; and I can only do that by living on my own voice. I must lay by enough to take me to Italy, and when I have learnt there, then I can turn to anything.'

'Do you think you ever would lay by?'

That was rather a cutting question, for Lance, though never in debt, never could keep a sixpence in his pocket.

'I could if I had a real object.'

'Only I don't think it would wholly depend on yourself,' said sensible Robina. 'I suppose they don't pay by the week; and then if the concern should not answer?'

'That's sheer impossibility. There isn't a safer man in London than Allen. It is a much more profitable investment than old Pur.'

'Then if you lived with Edgar, you don't know how much you might have to go shares for.'

Thereupon Lance broke out into absolute anger against Robina for her unkindness to Edgar, talking much of the want of charity of people who lived at home, and thought everything beyond their ken must be wicked. She ventured to ask what Felix thought of it, and was told in return that Felix was not only not his father, but though the best fellow in the world, had no more knowledge of it than a child in petticoats. It was for the good of Felix, and everyone else, that they should not all hang about at home in the stodge and mire.

How long this might have gone on there is no saying, but Felix's voice was heard calling to them in preparation for evening prayers. When Robina heard Lance's voice rise in all its sweetness in the Evening Hymn, her heart was so full of yearning pain and disappointment, that she could hardly hold back her tears till she could kneel and hide her face in her hands.

She had this comfort. She did not understand from Lance that he had accepted, and he certainly did not join Edgar that night in the kitchen, but, saying he was tired out, he went at once to bed.

On Saturday she had not one private moment with him, but on the other hand, neither she hoped had Edgar; for the work both of the press and of the shop happened to be unusually heavy, and neither he nor Felix had a moment to spare; and Edgar spent the evening with some friends in the town.

Sunday afternoon, the family hour for walks and talks, poured with rain, and thereby was favourable to letters to Fulbert. Indeed, Angela's commencement of some sacred music was stopped, by the general voice entreating her to wait till the letters were finished. Lance, who never wrote to anybody but Fulbert, had resumed the practice ever since he had received an affectionate letter called forth by his illness, and was now busy with his little blotty portfolio; while Robina, having no Sunday correspondent, was half reading, half watching Stella explaining pictures to Theodore.

Presently Lance stretched across, and silently put a sheet of note-paper into her lap, hushing her by a sign. It had been begun in his best hand, and it must be confessed that that hand was at present a scratchy one, and there were various erasures.

DEAR SIR,

I have done my best to consider your kind and flattering proposal, and have come to the conclusion that for the present it will be better for me to continue where I am. There will thus be no need to apply to my eldest brother.

With my respectful thanks,
Yours faithfully,
LANCELOT O. UNDERWOOD.

Robina made a little pantomime of clapping her hands, for which Lance did not appear to thank her, but still in dumb show required her judgment on the choice of several words. She mutely marked her preference, and he returned to his place and copied it. Still he had not addressed the letter. He put it into his pocket, with a significant smile at his sister. Evening came, late service, supper; still it was in his pocket till the moment of bed-time, and then it was that Robina saw him linger with Edgar, and went to her room with a heart full of trembling prayer.

'Edgar,' as his brother arrived in the kitchen, and prepared his pipe, 'how shall I address this?'

'Eh! you needn't be in too great a haste. We had better break it to poor old Blunderbore first.'

'There's no breaking in the case. I'm not going.'

'Ah! I knew how it would be when you began running about to all the womankind in the house.'

'I've not spoken to a soul but Bobbie,' said Lance rather hotly, as Edgar laughed.

'Then one was enough to do your business?'

'I only spoke to her to clear my own mind.'

'Ay, to get someone to contemplate Hercules between Vice and Virtue; but it won't do, my boy. Little Allen is as virtuous as Felix himself, and the choice is simply between the thing you can do and the thing you can't.'

'I can do my duty here,' said Lance bluntly.

'You've tried, my boy; you made a gallant effort, and I let you alone while you had a head to be spared, but 'tis no good trying to force the course of the stream, and you had better break loose, before you get too old for the real thing that you are made for.'

'No, Edgar, I've thought it over, and found out how things stand. Here will Felix begin now to have more on his hands, and can manage to shell out less than ever while he had Froggy to fall back on. Now, not only is my nominal salary much less than he could offer a stranger, but half of it goes back into the housekeeping, while I'm *done for* at home, and I don't see how he could meet the difference just now.'

'Whew! that's the blind way you all go on, putting the present before the future. If Felix had a grain of spirit, he would revolt at preying on your flesh and blood. Flesh and blood—why, its genius and spirit crushed up in this hole!'

'It is no more than all of us have done by him, ever since he was of my size.'

'But it is so short-sighted, Lance. You could make it up to him so soon. Five pounds for certain the week—and possibilities, remember. You'll lodge with me—that's nothing; and for the rest, you'll soon live as we do—like the birds of the air.'

'I couldn't make it up to him, and save for Italy; besides I should be earning nothing there.'

'But I should! Copying is a certain trade. Come now, Lance, you've taken some panic. Tell me what is at the bottom of it! Have they been warning you against us wicked Bohemians?'

'They? Nonsense!'

'*She*, then?'

'It is nothing at all that Robina said.'

'Come, make a clean breast. What lies at the bottom of this absurd rejection of the best offer you'll ever have in your life?'

Edgar took the pipe out of his mouth, that the smoke might not obscure his view of the young face whose brow was resting on an arm leant on the mantel-piece, and the eyes far away. 'What's the bugbear? and I'll clear it up.'

'No bugbear.'

'You don't trust me. Eh? Is that it? Have they told you I mean to prey on your innocence?'

'No, indeed, Edgar!'

'Are you afraid of the great and wicked world? I thought you'd more spirit than that; and I've always told you, you might run after as many churches as you chose. I'd never hinder you. Come, have it out, Lance, you think me a corrupter of your artless youth?'

'No!'

'Come, out with it. What has turned you?'

The answer came at last in his low clear voice, speaking more into the fire than to Edgar, the eyes still fixed and far away—'"And here we offer and present unto Thee ourselves, our souls and bodies, to be a reasonable, holy, and lively sacrifice."'

'What do you mean? what's that?' said Edgar, half startled, half angry.

'It comes after the Holy Communion,' said Lance, quite as much shocked by the novelty with which the familiar sound struck on his brother's ears.

'Oh! a pious utterance that only a *tête exaltée* takes literally.'

'I should not join in it if I didn't mean it,' muttered Lance, in the most brief matter-of-fact way.

'Then why aren't you living barefoot on bread and water in a hermitage?'

'Because that's not my duty. It would not be reasonable.'

'There's great force in that word,' began Edgar, with a little scoff in his tone, but altering it into one of more earnestness. 'Now, Lance, I want to understand your point of view. How does that formula hinder you?'

'Because,' said Lance, much against his will, 'it wouldn't be making my soul and body a reasonable sacrifice, to turn the training I had for God's praise into singing love songs to get money and fame.'

'Why do you assume that beauty and delight of any sort is not just as pleasing to God as your chants and anthems?'

'No. One is offered to Him, the other is mere entertainment.'

'So is the first to most folks. Now, you boy, honestly, do you mean that it is not much of a muchness with sacred and profane, so far as motive goes?'

'It is what I am always trying that it should be,' said Lance.

'Only trying?'

'Only trying.'

'And you consider yourself to be this sacrifice, this victim, by singing in a surplice for ladies to whisper about, instead of getting trained to interpret—nay, what I do say! maybe, compose—the grandest human music. You've got it in you, my boy.'

'You may say what you please,' said Lance, turning away to the fire.

'I don't want to vex you, boy, I only want to make it out. I see the *sacrifice*.'

'It was my own fault for saying a word about it to you,' muttered Lance.

'But I don't see the sense of it,' proceeded Edgar, 'or what it is but your own fancy that puts the one thing up in the heights, the other down in the depths.'

'You must know that,' said Lance, 'the fever and transport that comes of one kind of music has nothing good in it.'

'That's the question.'

'I know it has not for me.'

'And has the other?'

'Of course it has! Besides, I don't do it for myself. Come, Edgar, tell me how to direct that letter, and let me go.'

'You may leave it till I go to town.'

'That would not be fair. He will want to look out for someone else. Tell me!'

'Not I! I'm not going to let you make a fool of yourself in a fit of religious excitement.'

Lance smiled. 'Much excitement in a cold dark church in a wet morning, with not twenty people there.'

'That's as you work yourself up. Here, sit down and take the other pipe.'

'I can't; I can hardly stand yours, my head is raging!'

'Oh! that accounts for it! Go off to bed, and wake in week-day senses.'

'I wish you'd let me have done with it,' sighed Lance; but Edgar shook his head with, 'All for your good, my dear fellow!'

'If Balak's messengers *will* stay the night, it is not my doing,' said Lance to himself, as he wearily mounted the stairs to his sleepless bed in the barrack; for though his headaches had become much less frequent and disabling, still his constitution was so sensitive, that a course of disturbed nights always followed any excitement; and thus the morrow found him dull and confused enough to render his attempts at diligence so far from successful, that he was more than once sharply called to order; and Felix came in at dinner-time, exclaiming, 'I can't think what's the matter with that boy. He seems as if he would never do any good again!'

'*Précisément!*' muttered Edgar. 'You had better give him up with a good grace, as I told you before.'

49

And being at the moment alone in the room with Felix and Geraldine, he not only detailed his plans for Lance, but eagerly counselled Felix to invest at least half Thomas Underwood's legacy in the National Minstrelsy.

'Really!' said Felix, in a tone of irony, 'this is nearly coming to the old plan of setting up a family circus! Then it is this that has so entirely unsettled him?'

'That the old must pass away is not sufficiently appreciated here.'

Then Edgar appealed to Cherry for the charms of artist society, and the confutation of the delusions respecting it held by Philistines at home, a conversation only interrupted by the arrival of dinner, and the rest of the population.

Felix as usual had to go down after a few mouthfuls; Edgar followed him to say on the stairs, 'I've one piece of advice to give. Remember that you are an old Philistine giant, and act with due humility.'

'Is he set upon it?'

'I cannot say heart and soul, for heart and what he thinks soul are pulling opposite ways. I say, Felix, you should take into consideration the effect on me. I haven't sat still to listen to so much piety since my father's time; it is a caution to see a little chap so simply literal.'

Felix could wait no longer. He found Lance alone in the office, resting his head on his desk. 'You'll be in time for dinner, Lance!'

'Thank you, I'd rather not. Send Stubbs home.'

'Head-ache?'

'Not much now!'

'I'm sorry I was sharp with you this morning, Lance. You should have told me!'

'It was not worth while, but I did mean to have done better to-day, Felix!'

'I believe you did. If you think it will set you to rights, I would let you off this afternoon.'

'No, thank you; it is getting better.'

Felix looked at him a moment or two, then said, 'Edgar tells me he has been talking to you.'

'Yes. I hope you have given him a settler, Felix.'

'Have you?'

'I tried, but he would not take it. He thought it was only Sunday.'

'Only Sunday!'

'That made me sure it would not do.'

'You are quite right, Lance. So far as it depends on me, I should have done all in my power to keep you from what cannot but be a life of much temptation, and I am thankful that you have decided it for yourself. You are really content to stay here with me?'

'Content—well, not just now; but I shall be again when all the remains of the bear-fight have subsided,' said Lance. 'I ought and I must, and that's enough.'

With which words he ran out as some one was heard entering the shop; and Felix stood for a few moments over the fire, musing on the brave way in which his young brother had met the enticement, and on the danger into which his own reproofs, however well-merited, had driven him.

Lance's other occupation that evening did not make him better pleased with Edgar's friends. Wilmet had decreed—and he had submitted half ruefully, half-merrily—that what remained of his salary after his contribution to the house expenses, should be guarded by her for his wardrobe, only half-a-crown a week being put into his own hands; and as this always managed to disappear without much to show for it, she viewed it as quite enough for waste; and indeed, out of what was in her keeping she had managed to provide him with a watch.

With his Monday half-crown, and sixpence besides, he repaired to the Fortinbras Arms to pay for his share of the notable breakfast; but he found some demur; Mr. Jones was aghast at his own bill, and really unwilling to send it in. The private supper, the next day's breakfast, and all that the party had called for, amounted to what would make a terrible hole in the receipts of the concert.

As to Lance's paying the fifth part of the *déjeûner*, the landlord thought it was impossible, and though his three shillings might perhaps represent the cost of what he had individually consumed, to offer or accept that was not according to rules. Mr. Jones would gladly have made this bill his subscription to the organ, if he could but have afforded the loss; but this, as he told Lance, he could not do. He listened, however, with a smile of some pity, when Lance assured him that his own and his brother's shares should be made up; and Lance picked out the charge, and carried it off to Edgar.

There again he met with no success. Edgar laughed at him, and told him he did not know the privileges of the artiste; and when Lance waxed hot, and declared that if the concert paid the expenses of the two stars themselves, it was a wicked exaction to make it defray the expenses of either Mr. Allen or their guests, he was answered coolly that expensive articles must be taken on their own terms, and that spoiling the Philistines was always fair.

'Then don't you mean to pay, Edgar?'

Edgar gave his foreign shrug, and made a gesture of incapability. He was vexed with Lance, and at no pains to soften matters.

'Now,' said Lance, with a sort of grave simplicity, 'I understand what living like birds of the air means.'

Lance went back to Mr. Jones, and told him that the two-fifths of the breakfast should be paid. And in twelve weeks it was done, But by this specimen it may be guessed that the new organ was not exactly purchased by the concert.

CHAPTER XXIX.

BRYNHILD.

> 'Oft with anxious straining eyes
> We watch the coming of some joy long hoped for;
> And now 'tis near. But at its side a dark
> And stealthy thing, that we should fly like death
> Did we but see it, is advancing on us,
> Yes, step by step with those of its bright compeer.'
> *King Henry II., a Drama.*
> (*Quoted in Helps' Casimir Maremma.*)

'Which is to have the precedence, Alda's child or ours?'

'Alda's child is not likely to be ready for inspection as early as ours.'

'Oh! I thought you would vote it treason to babydom not to begin with Lowndes Square.'

'My maternal feelings draw me the other way, you see.'

'You won't confess it to Wilmet!'

'It is of no use to go to Alda before twelve,' put in Marilda. 'Cherry had better go to the Royal Academy before it gets full.'

It was May, and the catalogue of the Royal Academy bore—

```
No. 260.----Brynhild. . . . . . . . . . . T.E. Underwood.

                {The Lesson          }
No. 601.----Four studies, {Hearing a Story     }   Geraldine
                {With the Kitten      }   Underwood.
                {Listening to Music  }

No. 615.----The Faithful Acolyte . . . Geraldine Underwood.
```

and a good way further on, among the water-colours,

> 'But abruptly turning,
> Hied he to the choir,
> Touched the Altar tapers
> With a flake of fire.'
> (*The Three Crowns.*)

So, these having been accepted, Geraldine had come up to town to see them in their place. The undertaking was far less formidable than it had been a year ago, for Cherry was now much more at home with her cousins.

She understood Marilda better now, and reproached herself for having taken for worldliness what was really acquiescence rather than cause any disturbance in the family such as could worry her father, of whose state she had been aware all that last summer. Cherry respected her now, though they had little in common. Marilda had become too much acclimatized to London to like country life. She made some awkward attempts at squiress duty, but was far more in her element in her office, where she took on herself to attend to business so vigorously, that no one would have known there had been any change but by the initials. Felix had been of much use to her, and had certainly gained a good deal in consideration by the manifest reliance placed on him; and his position among the citizens of Bexley was now a fixed and settled thing.

Mrs. Underwood, in the inertness of grief, did not move from Centry until she was carried up to town by her strong desire to preside at Lady Vanderkist's confinement. She was, however, disappointed, for Lady Mary undertook the care of her daughter-in-law; but she made up for it as well as she could by permitting all the assiduities from the good lady that Alda would endure, and being herself extremely friendly and good-natured.

The first proposal had been that Cherry should go up with them and see the pictures on the private day, but the east wind and flying threats of rheumatism had prevented this, till Marilda, running down to inspect her works at Centry, carried her off, undertaking, with better knowledge than before, that she should be well cared for.

So here was the carriage at the door, and Edgar come to escort her to the realization of the almost incredible fact that she, as well as himself, was an artist and exhibitor. She had heard favourable opinions, but none the less did her heart palpitate with far more of distress than of exultation as at a strange presumptuous unnatural position—she, who, while striving to be satisfied with faithfully doing her best, had so much wished for success as to make it a continual prayer, that the works of their hands might be prospered upon both, and to feel it an effort honestly to add the clause, 'If it be thy will—if Thou see it good for us.'

She had not seen Edgar's picture, nor himself since the concert, and there had been some breaths of rumour which took form in the saying that the absence of the family from Kensington Palace Gardens had been a sad thing for him.

However that might be, he was as much at his 'Chérie's' service as ever, though with something of the forced manner she had known in him at moments of crisis, and which betrayed much anxiety. He repeated to her many times on the way that Brynhild had been unfairly dealt with in the hanging, and related anecdotes of injustice suffered by whoever did not belong to favoured cliques, all which made her uneasy. Of hers he said little. She knew that water-colours at the Royal Academy exhibition received little notice, but had obediently followed some crotchet of Mr. Renville's which had taken her thither. Trafalgar Square was then still the locality, and when the steps had been surmounted, and they stood between the two doors leading to the water-colours, it was straight on that they went, for the sight of Brynhild was the triumph and delight that Geraldine had figured to herself for months past.

It was, as she already knew, in the second room, rather below the privileged line; and at this early hour, the numbers of visitors were so scanty that she could see the cocoon shaped glow of yellow flame across the room.

'Oh! there she is! She is smaller than I thought.'

'Just what Polly said. All ladies go in for 'igh hart on the Zam zummin scale.'

She must have hurt his feelings, she saw, or he would not have compared her criticism with Marilda's; and as she felt that he was watching her countenance as he led her forward and lodged her opposite. From eager expectation her look became constrained, as it shot through her that this was not the Brynhild of the sketch and of her imagination. She was disappointed!

'Well, what?' asked Edgar impatiently, reading the countenance in spite of all endeavours.

'How like Marilda!'

'What, Brynhild, the toad! So she would be. I suppose the caricature demoralized me, and the family features are the same.'

'And Sigurd is Ferdinand.'

'Nature created him for a model.'

It was not the likeness to Marilda which gave Cherry the sense of unfulfilled expectation and dissatisfaction. The lofty expression, the deep awe, the weird cloud-land grandeur that she had connected either with the sketch or her memory of it, had passed away from the finished oil-painting; and when she had called it small, it was not because it was cabinet sized, but because it was wanting in the sense of majesty that can be conveyed in a gem as well as in a colossus. What was to have been a wild scene of terror in the world of mists *would* look extravagant, and neither the pose of Brynhild's limbs nor the position of Sigurd's sword, approved themselves to her eye as correct drawing.

Brother and sister were both far too acute, and too well used to read each other's looks and tones, for fencing or disguise to be possible.

'You don't like it.'

'O Edgar!' much distressed, 'indeed there is a great deal very beautiful, but somehow I had imagined it different.'

'Oh, if you came with a preconceived notion.'

'Perhaps that's it,' said Cherry, peeping through her eye-lashes, as long ago at the great Achilles, and making them a sieve to divest the image before her of all that her eye would condemn in spite of herself.

'I see a great deal of beauty, but somehow I thought the whole would have been more finished,' she said.

'Not possible. A rude half developed myth is not in keeping with the precision of a miniature. Besides, the finish of Sigurd's armour throws back the vague beyond.'

Her feeling had been that the Pre-Raphaelitism of the hauberk was too like worsted stockings, and not in keeping with the Turneresque whirl of flame and smoke around the sleeping Valkyr; but the disloyalty of not admiring Edgar's picture was impossible to her loving spirit; she listened and looked through her eye-lashes, till though Brynhild's limbs were to her unassisted sense almost as uncomfortable as those of Achilles had been, he imparted a glamour, so that she thought she beheld it as it ought to have been, and believed it to be so great and deep a work of art that study alone could appreciate it.

'Yes, I see—I see it now—I could not before—but that is all the better!'

The room was filling and they were jostled by a group diligently working their way with their catalogue from No. 1 to No. 1200.

'What's that glaring red and yellow thing?'

'260, Brynhild. Who was she, Flo?'

'Don't you know, Mamma? That French queen who was torn to pieces by wild horses.'

'I don't see any horses. She is all on fire.'

'I suppose she was burnt afterwards. And that's the king who did it.'

'What a horrid picture!'

'There's the intelligent public one works for,' said Edgar. 'Come and try your luck.'

He paused, however, to show her the difference a foot's elevation would have made to his painting; and she, with a mind more at leisure from itself, waited not only to sympathize but to be fascinated with the loveliness or power of more than one picture past which he would have hurried her, with murmurs at the R.A. who had secured the best situation.

Here they were in the water-colour room, obliged to wait, to penetrate the throng round the lesser ones, which were so close together that there was no distinct appropriation of the remarks.

'What a dear little thing!' 'Is it all the same child?' 'It can't be portrait, she is so pretty.'

Edgar smiled at her, and she whispered, with great inconsistency, 'No, it can't be that. Besides, childish prettiness always pleases more people than anything high and ideal.'

She tried to turn to the Acolyte, and two or three gentlemen yielded place to the lame girl. 'Geraldine Underwood,' said one, making her start, till she saw he was reading from his catalogue. 'I don't remember her name before.'

'No, and there's so much power as well as good drawing and expression, that I should not have thought it a woman's work.'

This, the most ambitioned praise a woman can receive, made her indeed Cherry-red, and Edgar's beaming glance of congratulation was most delightful.

Certainly, whatever his faults, among them was neither jealousy nor want of affectionateness; and Cherry's success gave him unqualified pleasure, both agreeing in the belief that she was on a level with the public taste, while he soared too high beyond it.

Her paintings had a strength of colouring unusual in inexperienced artists, perhaps owing to the depth of hue she had grown accustomed to when painting for her old woman, and thus they asserted themselves, and were not killed by their neighbours, but rather, as Edgar said, committed slaughter all round.

Yet 'The Acolyte' was on the whole a dark picture: the Church was in a brown dim shade, within which, however, its perspective vaultings, arches, and tracery, were perfectly drawn, knowing where they were going and what they meant, yet not obtruded; and the Altar hangings, richly patterned in olive green and brown gold, were kept back in spite of all their detail, throwing out the 'flake of fire' and the glitter reflected on the gold ornaments, which had been drawn with due deference to Clement's minute information, while in the fragment of the east window just seen above, glittered a few jewels of stained glass touched by the rising sun, and to which the subdued colouring of the rest gave wonderful glory; and the server himself was so tinted with grey that even his white dress did not glare, while his face was the face of Lance, as it had been a few years back, boyish and mirthful through all its dutiful reverence. Of course it was not new to Edgar, but he owned that he was always struck by it whenever he came that way; and Cherry heaved a little sigh of parental pride and delight as she owned that her little 'server' did look better than she had expected.

Then Edgar elbowed her to what was called at home her 'Constellation,' where she had caught Stella's sweet little head four times over—in the seriousness of lesson-learning, with eager parted smiling lips with which she listened to a story, with her tender caressing expression towards the kitten she was nursing, and with the rapt dreamy gaze that her brother's music would bring over her countenance. All had the merit of being caught—in the first sketch—entirely without consciousness on Stella's part; and though she had been nailed to the positions afterwards, it had been possible to preserve the unstudied expression that was one great charm of the drawings, much more sketchy and suggestive than was their companion.

It was not easy to maintain a stand before the frame that held the four, for people must have told one another of it, and squeezed their way to it; till the poor little artist, growing nervous at the press, was grasping her brother tight to make him take her away. Just then there was a kind eager greeting, 'Good morning; I am delighted to meet you here. You must allow me to congratulate you.'

It was Mr. Grinstead, too considerate to utter a name that would instantly have brought all eyes upon the little lame girl, whom the gazers were almost sweeping away. He was full of that gracious fatherly kindness that elderly men were prone to show her, and solicitously asked where she was staying, and whether he might call upon her; and then, taking advantage of an interval of people, he brought her again in front of her pictures. With him on Lord Gerald's side of her, and Edgar on the other, she felt safe enough to enter into his kind critique, so discriminating as to gratify, improve, and stimulate her far more than if it had been all compliment. By the time this was over, Cherry could stand no longer, and it was time for her visit to her sister, so the sculptor did Ferdinand's old part by taking care of her while Edgar hunted up their cousin's brougham.

'O Edgar, aren't you coming?'

'Well! I can't say the Mynheer's *ménage* likes me better than I like it.'

'Oh, Eddie, dear, *do*. How shall I ever get in among all those dreadful strange servants?'

'What, the crack exhibitor, whose pictures transcend woman's genius, afraid of a flunky or two!'

Nevertheless, he let her pull him into the carriage, laughing, and demanding whether she could not have opposed coachman and footman to their congeners; but he recollected the stair-case, and was all the more amenable that in her he had the only perfectly willing auditor of all his whys and wherefores of all Brynhild's characteristics, all his hopes of purchasers and plans built upon her, and (now that Brynhild was out of sight) the most profound believer in her beauties and sublimities.

The arrival was impressive. The vista of liveries, flowers, and marble, was so alarming, that Cherry could hardly have found courage to make her way through them with no support but Lord Gerald's; but when she entered the drawing-room the grandeur was instantly mitigated by the plainly attired, gentle, motherly lady who came forward to greet her with a kiss. 'So you are Geraldine, the only sister I have never seen. Alda will be delighted.'

Lady Mary Murray must have been rather surprised by the sight of 'the little deformed one,' with her sweet pensive face of sunshine and shade, and the small slender form, as shapely as that of her sister, though leaning a little forward when walking. So kind was she, that Cherry felt that she could quite spare Edgar when he made his retreat, and never observed that he was not pressed to stay to see Alda, who had a dress-maker with her, and would send down when ready.

This gave Cherry time to become at home with Lady Mary, and to receive some gratifying compliments upon her Constellation, united with a little caution on the danger of making the little girl vain. 'I hope not,' said Cherry much in earnest; 'indeed, I think Edgar and I are mere terrors to all our pretty ones, we tease them so with sitting.'

'The little boy in a surplice is another brother, I think I heard.'

'Yes, my brother Lance. He is gone into the business now. He was in the Cathedral choir at Minsterham.'

'Oh! I understood that it was a portrait of the one who was in the St. Matthew's brotherhood, in his ornaments.'

'Oh no. That was Clement; and I am sure neither of them wore anything like that! I made out the ornaments from a book.'

'I am glad to hear it,' said Lady Mary, a little less cordially; and when Cherry, recollecting her views, proceeded to lead away by speaking of Brynhild, it was to be met with a kind smile and avowal that Mr. Underwood's picture was not so easy to understand.

Then came the summons to Lady Vanderkist's room. It seemed chiefly addressed to her mother-in-law, who, however, extended it to Cherry, and proffered a soft, comfortable, substantial arm to help her up the stairs.

There sat Alda, beautiful to behold in white and bright blue ribbons, thinner than formerly, but exquisitely and delicately pretty, and so eager in her conference with her milliner, that she could only give Geraldine a hasty kiss, and sign her to a seat, before appealing to Lady Mary on some point of clashing taste respecting her court dress, which was the present subject of engrossing interest to the younger lady, while the elder evidently did not feel greatly at home or interested in a subject which she said had not come before her since the maiden days of Queen Victoria. Indeed, when Alda became excited in maintaining her own opinion, she put an end to it with gentle but irresistible authority, dismissed the milliner, and insisted upon the repose that Alda was inclined to laugh to scorn.

After an exhibition of the little four weeks daughter, a pretty creature, in whom mother as well as grandmother showed plenty of pride, the two sisters were left to a *tête à tête*, Cherry feeling almost hypocritical when Lady Mary supposed them to be so eager for it.

Rather languidly Alda inquired after everyone at home, chiefly after Wilmet and Captain Harewood, where he was, and what chance there was of his return. Then Cherry talked of the great home subject of interest, namely that the organ was actually ordered; but Lady Vanderkist attended little, and it was safer as well as more entertaining to let her talk of herself; and she seemed to have had a very gay winter, to have been recognized as the great lady of her neighbourhood as well as bride and beauty, and to have had much sporting society at home and abroad, while now she looked forward to a season among the circles which had always been the object of her ambition. No wonder that the cares and joys of Bexley occupied her but little, and that it was not much to her whether Felix was to be a town-councillor. However, she was now among people who considered it an honour to have a sister exhibiting at the Academy, and she professed much eagerness to see the Constellation. 'But what could have induced Edgar to send such a picture?' she added; 'Adrian says it is the maddest thing he ever saw in his life.'

'It takes some study,' said Cherry, subduing her indignation.

'I should think it had taken very little study.'

'You have not seen it?'

'No of course not yet. I shall go as soon as I can, it is so stupid not to be able to talk of the Exhibition; but I don't look forward to Edgar's picture at all, I hear the drawing and painting are so disgraceful.'

'There is an apparent carelessness that enhances effect.'

'Standing up for Edgar as usual, Cherry! But if you still have any influence with him, this is the time to use it. Adrian hears that he has taken up with a lot of tremendous scamps. Indeed, he saw him on the Derby day betting away with all his might. Now he cannot stand that long, and Adrian says I must let him know that when he gets into difficulties, he need not expect to fall back upon us.'

'The last thing he is likely to do,' said Cherry, burning with suppressed wrath.

'Well, give him a warning, and tell him to be careful how he comes in Adrian's way. It upsets me so when he comes in and asks where I think he has met my precious brother.'

'I don't see,' cried Geraldine, breaking out, 'why a place should be worse for one than for the other.'

Alda drew up her head with a little contempt, but instead of flying out as when they were on an equality, she merely said, 'Don't you?'

Then Geraldine recollected herself, and tried to say meekly something about the difference made by being able to afford it; but though Alda was kinder than usual, and changed the subject, there was no more real comfort throughout the visit, and she went home to be unhappy. Here it was as hard as ever to behave properly to Alda. Her presence seemed always to rouse the spitfire propensities, of which Cherry would otherwise have been unconscious; and what was far worse was the misgiving that she had only spoken too truly. Cherry's heart sank, scold it as she would for sinking. Her *will* might adore Brynhild, but her sense assured her of grievous carelessness in the execution; and when she recalled Edgar himself, she knew there was something indefinable about him that confirmed Alda's suspicions.

Her own success had been real and brilliant, but through it all her heart ached with apprehension as she became more conscious of the difference with which her doings and his were regarded, and could not always succeed in attributing everything to personal politeness to herself. She was staying on to take a few more studies, and to collect materials for the illustrations of a serial tale, an order for which Mr. Renville had procured her; and she found herself quite at home at those pleasant little parties at his house, treated as one of the confraternity who had won her standing, and with new comers begging to be introduced. Mr. Grinstead was always there, and a real friend and protector among strangers; and all was delightful except the reserve about Brynhild, and the frequent absence of Edgar, who used once to be always welcome, and like a son of the house.

Even at Lady Vanderkist's, Geraldine found herself a mild sort of lion, when Alda came out into the world and found that her sister was viewed as having done something remarkable.

Not that there was much intercourse. There *was* an invitation to the christening, extended even to Edgar and the school girls; but Lady Mary was more the mover in this than Alda herself. Edgar excused himself, and it was not a very brilliant festivity. Indeed, one anxiety on Geraldine's part was lest Lady Mary's engaging kindness should embolden Angela to break out aloud in the wrath and indignation that stiffened her neck and shone in her eyes at the bare dull christening on a week-day—standing all alone—in an ugly 'pewy' church. A luncheon, at which the health of Mary Alda Vanderkist was drunk, was the only honour to the occasion; and Sir Adrian, though not actually uncivil, looked as usual bored, and left the amiable and gracious to his wife and mother.

Mrs. Underwood was indignant, and abused him all the way home. All Lady Mary's kindness had not hidden from her the fact that Alda was ready to spurn aside the scaffolding by which she had mounted to her present elevation, and was only withheld from so doing in consideration of Marilda's wealth; while Marilda, with her unfailing good nature and instinct of defence towards Alda, declared that all arose out of anxiety lest Sir Adrian should be wearied with them, and bluntly declared, 'You know, Mamma, we are very tiresome people; not like Cherry here, who always has something to say.'

'Oh! Cherry is a genius, but without that people needn't be tiresome, as you call it, to those that brought them up, and made them what they are.'

'We didn't bring up Sir Adrian, Mamma.'

'I'm not talking of Sir Adrian. One expects nothing from a fine young man about town; but, Alda, that was like my own child to me, never so much as asking us to see her in her court dress!'

'She ought to have done that,' said Cherry, who had been reckoning the quantity of pleasure that could have been so cheaply given.

'Now depend on it, Sir Adrian doesn't like his wife to make a show of herself,' cried Marilda, hitting on a subtly delicate motive rather than have no weapon of defence for this favourite cousin. Certainly there never had been a fuller adoption as sister and brother than hers had been of Alda and Edgar from the moment they had been given to her. She respected and trusted Felix, and was free and kind with Cherry and all the rest; but her affection for these two was quite a different thing, and resolutely blind; and this—just as last year with Wilmet—made her comfortable to Cherry, since she too ignored all that could be against Edgar, and fought his battles fiercely when mother or grandmother picked up reports of his idleness, of the ill success of the National Minstrelsy, in which he was somehow concerned, and of the unsatisfactory habits into which he was falling.

Very dull were the evenings when he did not come, and only worn through by reading aloud. No doubt the house in its quiet widowed condition was far less attractive than of old, and that the lively young man should neglect it, even with his favourite sister there, was more to be regretted than wondered at; but whenever he did come, he was greeted with delight, petted and made much of, as if with the desire to secure that presence, though it was not always as much of a sunbeam as of old.

One afternoon, however, he hurried in in a state of ecstasy. A wealthy manufacturer, noted as a purchaser of modern pictures, was in treaty for Brynhild; and Edgar looked on his fame and fortune as made. Three days ago the taste of the cotton-spinner had been denounced as dependant on fashion and notoriety. Now his discernment had gone up to the skies, and Edgar was wandering about the room in his exultation, talking to Cherry of a winter trip to Rome, and ready to promise everything to everybody. Only the next day, however, came out the principal art journal, containing the long expected mention of Brynhild.

Alas! No. 260 was disposed of in two lines as 'the flaming production of a tyro in suspense between the Pre-Raphaelite and the Turneresque, who in the meantime had better study the primary rules of drawing.'

Poor Geraldine! She shed a great many bitter tears over the cruel verdict, while Marilda characterised it as wicked, ill-natured, and spiteful; and when Edgar came to them they received him with tenderness and sympathy that would have befitted his sentence in his own proper person.

He was crushed as he had never been before. He did not abuse his critic. Indeed, he had candour enough to tell Cherry that her editorial experience might have taught her the need of shedding a little life-blood now and then for the public to slake their thirst upon, but this very charitableness almost proved it to be his life-blood.

The intended purchaser had not gone so far but that he could draw back, and this breath of hostility had effectually blown him away. He had broken off his treaty and declined Brynhild.

'I don't blame him,' dejectedly said Edgar; 'all the other critics will yelp in suit, and he would be the laughing-stock of his fellow cotton-lords; but he has done for me. The very sight of "Sold" upon my picture would have saved me.'

'Shall you be worse off than before?' asked Marilda.

'Of course one is, for having been led to make engagements under a deception. But there—never mind. Don't vex yourselves about me. I'm the most miserable dog in the world, and that's all about it.'

'Dear Edgar,' said Cherry, smoothing his hand, 'maybe the opposition paper will take up another line.'

'Not a hope, Cherry. That demolished me long ago, only they were all too merciful to show it to you. This was my last chance.'

He lay back in a sort of collapse of complete depression.

Marilda, meanwhile, sat writing at her davenport, and presently rising, came towards him with a closed envelope. 'There, Edgar,' she said. 'Now put "Sold" on your picture.'

'Polly, Polly, you're a girl of gold!' cried Edgar, starting to his feet. 'You've made a man of me. I must give you a kiss.'

To Cherry's amazement, a little to her horror, the kiss was given; Marilda only bluntly and gruffly saying, 'There then, only take warning, and don't be a fool again.'

'Your warning comes sweetened, my dear,' said Edgar, 'and it ought to save me. I don't mind confessing that I was in a most awful fix. Well, you have Brynhild, and we'll hang her over the drawing-room door for a scare-crow, only don't let in any Sigurds who won't be as good as you are to art out at elbows!—Good-bye, my Cherry ripe. I must betake me to shaking off the toils of the hunter, now that this good mouse has nibbled them through.'

Cherry had not spirit to rally him on his quiet assumption of the lion's part. And her acceptance of his embrace was not warm. To the delicate sense nurtured under Felix, the whole proceeding was as painful as it was strange; and she was longing to have sold her pictures so as to relieve him herself. True, she had many visions, but she would much have preferred freeing her brother herself to seeing Marilda make a purchase to which she was indifferent, palpably for the sake of assisting him.

Maybe he saw the questioning look in her face, and therefore hurried away so fast that Marilda broke out in regret at having failed to secure him for an intended visit to Sydenham the next day, when part of the day would be spent with friends and the rest in the Crystal Palace. It was the sort of expedition Edgar hated, and Cherry's pride rose enough against the notion of his being purchased to be dragged at Marilda's chariot wheels to prevent her from seconding the proposal to write and ask for his company.

She would have been glad enough of his arm through the long galleries. The heartless glare and plaster showiness tired her to death; nor were Mrs. Underwood's friends particularly restful.

When she came home late in the evening, she had hardly energy to open a note that lay on the table; but when she had wearily unfolded it, she screamed with amazement and delight. Mr. Renville wrote to tell her of an offer for the Acolyte, and to propose to her to meet the intending purchaser at his studio on the second day ensuing, at twelve o'clock, to consult about an order for a companion water-colour, the subject likewise taken from the Silver Store, the price of the two together to be £150. Here opened the fulfilment of the longing of her heart, the lightening of Felix's burthen! Her dreams were a strange maze of beautiful forms to be drawn, and of benefits to be heaped on all the world; and her first measure in the morning was to write a dispatch to Edgar, begging him to come and support her at the interview, and almost laying her gains at his feet.

All day she expected him to show himself, full of advice, joy, and congratulation; but he came not. Her note must have missed him, she supposed; and she had to experience the lack of sympathy, for Spooner had come almost before breakfast was over, and Marilda had immediately gone back with him into the City; and Mrs. Underwood was not sure whether it were *comifo* to be elated about selling a picture, and had no council to give between Cherry's sketches of the robin with the wheat-ear, the monk and his olive tree, the blessing of the swallows, or the widow Euphrasia and her straw.

When Marilda did come home, she was more glum than Cherry had ever seen her. She would not even guess why Edgar made no answer, but advised that no one should think about it. Man could not be always dancing after woman. She was in no better humour in the morning, when Cherry expressed her security that though he might have come home too late to answer her note, he would not fail her at the appointment.

No such thing, he did not come for her; nor did she find him at the studio, where Mr. Renville was however a perfectly kind and sufficient protector, in the arrangements with the courteous and gracious old nobleman who viewed it as a duty to encourage art, and intended the pictures to adorn his daughter's drawing-room. The choice fell on Cherry's favourite, the red-breast, and altogether the interview would have filled her with transport if only Edgar had been there to share it. She could not believe him to be so changed as to neglect her out of mortification at the contrast between her success and his own; but the bare idea poisoned the laudatory critique in the Times of her two productions.

It was Mrs Kedge's birthday, when her family always dined with her at her old-fashioned hour of five. When they set off, Cherry faltered an entreaty that they might call and inquire for her brother at his lodgings, but this was so curtly, almost harshly, negatived, that she feared that she had unwittingly proposed something improper. Still there remained the chance of his coming to the festival, where he was certain of a welcome. It would be so like his good nature, that Cherry never relinquished the hope through the hot stuffy dinner, when, after the two elder ladies had sighed, shed a few natural tears, but wiped them soon, over the absence of poor Mr. Underwood, they took to City gossip, occasionally rallying the two young ladies on their silence and abstraction; Mrs. Kedge contriving to joke at her grand-daughter's supposed loss of her 'eart, and at Cherry for having made such a conquest with her hart.

Just as dessert came in, and Geraldine was reflecting with a sort of dreamy despair that it was the hour for driving in the park, there came a thundering knock, and Cherry bounded on her chair, exclaiming, 'There's Edgar!' while Mrs. Kedge cried out, laughing, 'Just like him! I knew he'd be in time for my preserved ginger. Ah! Mr. Hedgar, trust to—What! isn't it him? Who is it, Mary?' handing the card to her.

'Mr. Travis!' Marilda and the maid exclaimed at the same time; and the next moment he stood before the quartette, receiving a cordial welcome from all; for though Mrs. Underwood might bridle a little, she remembered that Alda was safely disposed of, and that he was now an undoubted millionaire depending on no one's good-will. Geraldine was flushed, and quivering between pleasure, shame, and the moment's disappointment; and Marilda's broad face flashed for a moment with a look of indescribable illumination and relief, then subsided into its usual almost stolid calm.

For himself, he looked more like what he had been as Peter Brown's clerk than the Life-guardsman, for he had outgrown the boyish display of ornament, though he had never lost the fine military bearing that so well became his figure; but he now had a grand black beard, which made him more romantic-looking than ever. His countenance was as usual grave, but not so depressed or languid as formerly, and indeed it lighted into glad animation at the unexpected sight of Geraldine, as he wrung her hand with the fervour of a brother. He sat down; but except to drink Mrs. Kedge's health he accepted none of the eager offers of hospitality, but said he was to dine with Mr. Brown at eight o'clock. He had come home on business, and not being able to wind up his uncle's affairs quickly, thought he should have to spend his time between England and America for a good while to come; but he hoped to run down and see Felix, 'and to hear about the organ.' Cherry had so much to tell him about the building of it, and of Lance's delight in the prospect, that she forgot her anxieties for the moment, till he asked after the success of the concert, and she had to tell him of Edgar and his stars. He looked at his watch, and said he should have time to see after Edgar before dinner. 'Ah, do!' said Cherry; 'and find out whether he got my note, I haven't seen him these four days!'

There was a break-up from the dining-room; and Ferdinand, smiling a sort of apology to Mrs. Kedge, offered his arm to Cherry to take her up to the drawing-room, where except on these great occasions no one ever sat; Marilda managed to linger on the stairs, so as to intercept him on his way down.

'Mr. Travis,' she said, 'you will do me a great favour, if you will call on me at our office between ten and twelve to-morrow. Can you?'

'Certainly,' he replied, much surprised; but she flew up the stairs before any more could be said.

She was at her counting-house in full time, sitting at the library-table in the private room, just like her father, opening letters and jotting on them the replies to be made by her clerks, without often needing to take counsel with Spooner.

At ten o'clock a clerk brought up Mr. Travis, and he was soon seated opposite to her, not quite so unprepared as on the previous day.

'Thank you for coming,' she said; 'I knew you were the only person whom I could trust in for help.'

'I shall be very happy,' he began. 'Is it about Edgar Underwood?'

'Do you know anything?'

'Only that no one at his rooms seems to know where he is.'

'Ah!' (as if expecting this). 'Now, I know you would do anything for Felix Underwood and the rest, and can keep silence. To speak would be worse than anything.' He bent his head: and she went on, 'Read that. No, you won't understand it;' then collecting herself, 'Poor Edgar! you know what he is, and how he can't help running into debt. We gave him his tastes, and it is our fault. This year he managed to do a picture, an odd red and yellow looking thing, but very fine, with a lady fast asleep in the middle of a fire. Well, he thought he had sold it, and made sure of the price, when some spiteful newspaper abused it, and the shabby man was off his bargain, and left the picture on his hands. He was so frightfully downcast, and I had reason to think him so hard up, that I thought I'd take the picture off his hands; and so I popped a cheque for a hundred, done up in an envelope, into his hand, not telling him what it was—more's the pity. We were out all the next day, and he called and wanted to find out where we were gone, but the footman is stupidity itself, and could not tell him. He came three times; but we were racketting at that miserable Sydenham, and did not get home till eleven. If he had only come in and waited! The next day came Spooner to me in a terrible rage. Now, promise, Mr. Travis, that this is never mentioned. On your honour!'

'On my honour. Never!'

'My cheque had been presented with the one hundred changed into four. The clerk at the bank doubted it, and had come here, and Spooner came to Kensington about it. I believe I went nearer to a lie than ever I did before; I said it was all right, and stood to it so that they both had to be pacified. You see,' as she saw how shocked Ferdinand was, 'he was in great difficulties, and he only meant it for a trick which would have been explained directly, if only I had not been so unfortunately out of reach.'

'You don't mean that you would overlook it?'

'Well, it seems that I was altogether wrong about the value, as pictures go. Of course I thought it rather too bad, and meant to give him a piece of my mind and frighten him thoroughly; but ever since poor Cherry has been pining, and wondering at his not coming; and yesterday I got this—addressed here, no doubt that Cherry might not see it, but marked private to keep Spooner's hands off.'

She thrust a sheet of paper into his hand.

DEAR MARILDA,

Had I seen you yesterday, I should not be in my present plight. I rehearse continually in my own ears the assault I had in readiness for you for your ignorance of the market price of art. Brynhild may be worthless, but if she be worth a penny, she is worth £250, which was what that gay deceiver was to have given. I had liabilities which I had staved off; indeed, my villain of a landlord only refrained from seizing my goods and chattels on the promise of the cash instanter. Other debts I durst not face. All that was left of your father's bequest is gone in the smash of the National Minstrelsy. County courts yawned on me, and only promptitude could save me. But verily I would not have taken a sheep when a lamb would have sufficed the first wolf, if *one* would have lent itself to transformation into anything but a cool *four*. Your round hand has been the ruin of me, Polly. It must have been the loop of your *e* that undid me. Nevertheless, I had the odd £150 in my pocket to hand over as your rightful change, (and maybe have begged of you,) when thrice I failed in finding you; and as I was coming this very morning—or was it yesterday? I'm all in a maze—I saw Spooner dash by in a cab, and knew it was all up with me!

Don't believe so badly of me as he has told you, dear old Poll. I have put myself out of his reach that he may have the less chance to break Felix's heart. For myself, I don't care a rap what becomes of me; but if it be not too late, I implore you to screen him and poor little Geraldine from the knowledge. Let them think it a simple flight from creditors—true enough in all conscience, as I fear they will soon find.

If it have got wind, I need not beg you to spare them and let Lance know that I am thankful to the 'early piety' or whatever it was that kept him out of the scrape. Some day all shall be repaid; but until then you have seen and heard the last of—your not ungrateful in heart, however ungrateful in deed—the most miserable and unlucky of dogs,

T.E.U.

'Where was this posted?' asked Ferdinand.

'At Ostend. Here's the post-mark.'

'Has he sent back the £150?'

'Oh no; of course he must have that to go on with.'

'It would have been more like repentance if he had sent it.'

'No, no; he couldn't. He would have had nothing to live on. Besides, it makes no real difference. Don't you turn against him, Mr. Travis, for I have no one else to trust to. I can't tell Felix; for it might do him serious harm in his business, and he might not consent to hush it up. Then Clement is a formal prig; and Lance is a boy, and couldn't get away. Nobody but you can do any good.'

'And what is it that you wish me to do?'

'I wanted your advice, first of all; I had no one I could venture to talk to, lest he might think some dreadful thing his duty, and go and tell!'

'There can be no palliating the criminality of the act,' said Ferdinand gravely; 'but for the sake of the—the innocent—' (his lip quivered at the word,) 'it may well be concealed, since you are so generous. Vanderkist might make a cruel use of it.'

'And I think it would kill Cherry. What I wished was—since one can't write with no address—if any one could go after him, and tell him that not a soul knows. I do believe now, after this shock, he might be sobered and make a new start; not here perhaps—'

'I'll go!' cried Ferdinand. 'I'll do my business with Brown, and start by to-night's steamer. Do you know where he is likely to be?'

'His wish has always been for Italy, but it is hardly the season; and my dread is of his going to Hesse Homburg, or Baden, or some of those places, hoping to retrieve this money.'

'I'll look, I'll make every inquiry. I'll never rest till I have found him!' said Ferdinand, with the earnestness of one delighted to have found the means of rendering an important service to his dearest friends.

'I felt sure that you could and would, from the moment I saw you,' said Marilda, 'When your card came in, there seemed to open a way out of this dreadful black misery.'

'Remember,' said Ferdinand, 'it would not be right to bring him home at once on the former terms. You forgive him, and for the sake of his family you do not expose him; but he ought not to be reinstated.'

'Not only for his family's sake—for his own!' cried Marilda. 'He is just like my brother—it was only between brother and sister. But you are right,' she added, as the man's grave look of severity recalled her from her sisterly championship; 'it would only be running him into danger again. He had much better go and study in Italy; and he can be helped there, if he will only keep out of mischief.'

She then mentioned all the haunts of his she knew of in Belgium and Germany; Geraldine might know more, but how was she to be told? Marilda had a perfect terror of renewing the condition into which she had last year been thrown, and besides feared her quickness of eye might discover the secret. She hoped to keep her in ignorance till Ferdinand could send home tidings, and make Edgar write what would be some comfort after the suspense; but when the time that, at the lowest computation, must elapse before anything could be heard was reckoned, they both felt that it was cruelty to keep Cherry in her present state. A week more would be enough to destroy her.

But Marilda, though a strong-minded woman enough ordinarily, shrunk with dismay from telling her. Should Felix be written to? There was no doubt that so soon as he heard the tidings from Cherry, or otherwise, he would hurry up to investigate and to take her home; so that to ask him to come and break it to her was hardly giving him unreasonable trouble. Besides the secret might be safer, so managed. Thus, the two generous spirits who sat in council first destroyed poor Edgar's letter, lest it should ever serve as evidence against him; and then Marilda wrote—

MY DEAR FELIX,

Geraldine will have told you that we have not seen Edgar for some time. From a note received from him, I have reason to believe that debts are the cause of his flight. Mr. Travis is kind enough to follow and see what can be done; but I do not know how to tell poor Cherry, and if you will come up I will meet you at the station at 11.30.

Your affectionate cousin,
M.A. UNDERWOOD.

CHAPTER XXX.

THE SCULPTOR.

'Her heart, her life, her future,
Her genius, only meant
Another thing to give him,
And be therewith content.'
A.A. Proctor.

By the time Felix could obey Marilda's missive, and entered Cherry's sitting-room, she had come to such a state of mind, that not even his pale, fixed, mournful face was needed to make her lie back in her chair, gazing piteously up at him, murmuring, 'O Felix, what can it be? What has become of him?'

'Marilda has heard from him,' said Felix, kneeling down by her, and holding her hands.

'Heard! Oh, why did she not tell me?'

'She feared to pain you. My poor Cherry, nothing has happened to him; but his debts have come to a crisis, and he is gone off to the Continent. That good fellow, Fernan, is gone after him, to see what can be done for him.'

'And he wrote to *Marilda?*' asked Cherry, greatly bewildered.

'Yes; from Ostend.'

'He wrote to her! Did you see the letter?'

'No, she had made away with it. She was so shy and short about it, that, Cherry, I suspect that distress had brought poor Edgar, as a last resource, to try whether she would accept him.'

'Oh!' cried Cherry, starting forward with conviction, 'that would account for it all!' And she told of all that had passed about Brynhild, now ten days ago—Edgar's despair, Marilda's ready assistance, and the manner of acknowledging it; and both agreed that there was strong presumption that he had taken her kindness as encouragement to venture on a proposal. This would fully account for her silence and ill humour; and the delusion, perfectly unsuspected by her, was the best possible auxiliary in guarding her secret, by preventing the brother and sister from pushing her hard with inquiries, and sufficiently explaining whatever was mysterious. Indeed, if Edgar had had the face to make the proposal, there was some grace in the shame that had caused his disappearance; and luckily for Marilda, Cherry was far too modest and shame-faced to allude to her own suspicions. She only longed exceedingly for home, and yet could not bear to leave the readiest place for receiving intelligence.

Felix could not of course rest without doing his part towards inquiring, and went off to Edgar's lodgings, and also in quest of the National Minstrelsy people, whom Lance had assured him to be the most likely to give him information. He came back depressed and jaded, and went straight to his sister's room. She could see in a moment that he had found out nothing.

'Nothing! The National Minstrelsy shut up a month ago. Allen and his family had left their lodgings, and given no address. I tried the post-office, but they grinned at me, and said many gentlemen came inquiring. I went to two or three music-shops, and asked after him and after the Hungarians, but with no better success; no one knew anything about them. Then I found my way to his lodgings.'

'Ah! I wanted so much to have called there, but Marilda would not let me.'

'As well you did not. Did you know that he had his rooms in partnership?'

'No—never!'

'Nor heard him speak of a man—an artist, named Malone?'

'Yes. I have heard of him. He has got two pictures in the British Institution. Poor Edgar wanted me to admire them, but I couldn't; they are Scripture subjects—Ruth and Rachel—made coarse and vulgar by being treated with vile reality—looking like Jewish women out of fruit-shops. He always said Tony Malone was the best fellow in the world, but he never told me he lived with him.'

'I was quite taken by surprise. The poor little miserable looking maid said Mr. Underwood had not been there for ten days; and when I said I was his brother and wanted to ask some questions, she fetched her mistress, who said he had paid up just before he went away, but that he had given no notice, so there was this ten days. Of course this was reasonable; besides, I wanted to bring home his things; so she took me up to his rooms while she went to make out his bill, and I thought entirely that I had come wrong, for I found myself in such a den as you can hardly conceive—light enough of course, but with the most wonderful medley of things imaginable, and in the midst a table with breakfast, and a brandy bottle; a great brawny sailor, half stripped, lying on the floor, a model for Samson, or Hercules, or somebody; and this man with a palette on his thumb, a tremendous red beard, and black elf locks sticking out all manner of ways. And that was the place he wanted to take Lance to!'

'He wouldn't have let it get bad if Lance had been with him. Besides, you old bachelor, don't you know that an artist must live in a mess and have models?'

'Of course, I know that, Cherry. I did not expect things to be what your friend Renville makes them for his young ladies; but the odour of spirits, the whole air and aspect of the place, had something that gave me a sense of hopelessness and dissipation, when I found that those really were Edgar's quarters, and that he had concealed his sharing them with this Malone ever since he left Renville. The man behaved very well to me, I will say that for him, as soon as we had made each other out, and seemed very fond and rather proud of Tom, as he chose to call Edgar; but he is a prodigious talker, and a rough coarse kind of fellow, exactly what I couldn't have fancied Edgar putting up with.'

'I dare say it was out of good nature.'

'Half of it, no doubt; indeed, he gave me to understand as much. Edgar can't but be kind wherever he goes; even that wretched little slavey cried when I gave her a shilling for helping his things into a cab, and she found he was never coming back! I should think he had spoken the only kind words she had ever heard in her life.'

'But this man must have told you something! Had he no notion where he is gone?'

'None at all! He knew thus much, that Edgar came into his room about ten o'clock in the morning—he couldn't tell what day, but we made it out it must have been on Thursday the 3rd—'

'The day after we went to Sydenham. Well!'

'—Looking pale and scared, and saying, "I'm done for, old fellow—I'm off!" That is all he is clear of, for he was just waked and fast asleep again directly.'

'At ten o'clock in the morning!'

'Well, Cherry, I'm afraid there had been a carouse the night before. Edgar had sold his picture, you see, and had cleared off old scores—a few of them, at least. He was restless—Malone said in and out—all the day before; he could not make him out. I fancy he had sent his letter to Marilda, and was awaiting a reply, which she must have sent, or he have called for, early the next morning; and after holding off all day from the jollification in honour of the sale of his picture, and deputing Malone and his other friends to hold it without him, he joined them at the theatre towards ten o'clock, and went to a cider cellar with them afterwards, where I should gather that he was in a state of reckless merriment, but quite sober—yes, Malone eagerly assured me of that, as if that were a merit to be proud of in my father's son! Well, poor fellow!' added Felix, his bitter tone changing to sorrow, 'he seems only to have thrown himself down on his bed without undressing; but Malone, who made no secret of having been "screwed" himself, only knew of his looking in in the morning. He had driven up, it seems, in a cab, which he kept waiting—not ten minutes, the landlady says—and he carried off his violin case and about as many clothes, I should imagine, as he could stuff into his portmanteau in the time—not by any means all; but one thing at least you will be glad to hear of, Cherry, the photograph of my father! Yes, I am quite certain of it; for when Malone was helping me to collect the other little matters out of his little hole of a bed-room, he said, when we came to the mantel-piece, "Yes, that's the only thing he has taken—the photo that stood there; a parson far gone in decline, the very moral of himself—your father, wasn't it?"'

'At least that is a comfort! Poor Edgar, I am sure he will soon write, even if Ferdinand misses him. You have brought his things?'

'Only his clothes, his sketches, and a book or two. His jewellery—he used to have a good deal, I think.'

'Never so much as Fernan, but in better taste.'

'That was gone. I thought it right to take an inventory of what I took away, and get it attested by the landlady and Malone; and I left it with them, in case the creditors should think I had taken anything of value.'

'The creditors, ah!'

'Yes. I have brought a carpet-bag stuffed choke full of bills, as heavy as I could carry, though of course many are the same over again. Time enough to look them over at home.'

'And paying?'

'No. I am not liable for them.'

'But, Felix, you cannot let his name be dishonoured!'

'My dear Cherry, that is talk out of books. I have no right to give away what barely suffices for maintaining and educating the younger ones, for the luxury of satisfying these claims and clearing Edgar's name. It would be robbing the innocent for the sake of the guilty.'

'O Felix, how can you?'

'Guilty at least of extravagance and recklessness, Cherry, though in a generous way. He had paid up, as I told you, for the lodging—all for Malone as well as himself; and when the landlady brought up an exorbitant bill, charging my country innocence three months in advance, Malone fought her with such vehemence, that I never came in for such a battle royal, and was ready to cut and run, only to be quit of the pair of them; and after all she subsided, and was content and civil with only a fortnight in advance!'

'I think a great deal must have been the fault of those musical people. I know Edgar risked some of Mr. Underwood's money with them.'

'All, I believe, that he did not owe, or was not forced to pay immediately, and that was a regular smash; but I do not think he was liable for any of their debts. These looked to me more like personal luxuries.'

'Well, Felix, if you will not pay them, I will, as I can, and when I can.'

'Do not say I *will* not, Cherry, but ask yourself whether I ought either to incur a debt myself, to trench on the capital of the business, or take home the children from school. You know, for we have tried, that stinting more than we do already becomes privation; such as, though we elder ones might willingly endure it for our feelings' sake, exacerbates the younger ones, and really would be unjust towards them.'

Cherry hung her head, with tears in her eyes. 'And is that just to the creditors?' she said.

'Well, Cherry, I cannot say I have much pity for the tradesmen who trust such a young gentleman as Edgar. If it be their system, depend upon it, they have means of compensation. Chérie, sweet, indeed I am not hard-hearted, I would cut off my right hand to bring that dear boy back a free man. When we hear from him—and I have looked over those miserable bills—I may find some means of compounding with the creditors; but I cannot despoil Angel and Bernard and Stella of education or comfort for what he has done.'

'But I can—I will—I may,' cried Cherry, with excitement; 'I shall be able to do it all; Mr. Renville said I might make £300 a year, and that would soon do it! You will not hinder me, Felix?'

'No,' he said, kissing her; 'it's not the way in which your earnings ought to go, my Cherry; but you are quite free, and it will make you happier, I know.'

'And you will not let Marilda help?'

'No, not if it can be helped without wounding her too much. You see she is taking her own measures through Travis.'

'I could not endure her doing it,' said Cherry, glowing with a sort of pride. 'And I am the one who ought. My drawing would have been worth just nothing at all but for him; and all this success is through him, and it is so cruel he can't have it, when it signifies so much more.'

'So Sir Bors always thinks,' said Felix, fondling her; but true to his own faith, he continued, 'But Edgar is not past the age for success yet. Only three-and-twenty, remember, and this grievous lesson may be just the making of him. We know he has a warm heart and plenty of power; and though we must make up our minds not to see him for a good while, he will come home from Italy some day a made man.'

'Oh yes, his sketch of Brynhild showed that he could do anything. Do you know, I think that having such a companion as that Mr. Malone almost accounts for his having gone wrong. If he can only fall in with some real nice companions! If he would board at Munich with some family like the dear Frau Renville's. What a letter we will write to cheer the poor dear fellow up!'

Felix and Geraldine never failed one another in that cardinal article of theirs, trust in Edgar's genius, and in the love that hoped all things, believed all things, and endured all things from him—all things personal, namely, for Felix never entirely overlooked the having tried to tempt away Lance into the life of which one passing glimpse was enough for his fastidious home-bred spirit, unable to appreciate the fascination of freedom and unconventionality. Altogether they had talked themselves into hope and consolation that surprised Marilda, when, after waiting till her patience could endure no longer, she knocked at the door, to ask whether Felix had discovered any clue by which Edgar could be traced.

It was one of those requitals of generosity that are felt inadequate because the generosity is really unsuspected. Felix and Cherry *could* not be as unreserved with her as if they had felt her a sister and one of themselves, and not as one whose bounty Edgar had abused. They did not—nor was it in the nature of things that they could—understand that Marilda's feelings towards him were as fraternal as their own, nay, had the force of exclusiveness, and the tenderness of protection; and so, though Felix replied to her inquiries, it was not with the detail and confidence he had shown towards his sister; and the more she questioned and remarked, the more they both felt inclined to shrink into themselves. In fact, they knew so little worse of him than before, that after the ten days' agony there was a sort of reaction, without much visible weight on their spirits. Felix had business which made it needful to stay another day; and as he was going out Cherry begged him to take charge of a small box containing a cast which Mr. Grinstead had lent her to copy, and she did not like to entrust to any chance hand.

'If you would send in your name,' she said, 'I think he would let you see his studio, and I do so want you to see his figure of Mercy knocking at the wicket-gate.'

'I thought he never did admit strangers.'

'Oh! Geraldine is favoured,' said Mrs. Underwood, with a laugh. 'Depend upon it, anyone belonging to her will have the *entray*. But go, go by all means. They say his house is a perfect little bijou.—Isn't it, Geraldine? She went to a party there, you know, chaperoned by Mrs. Renville, and met Lord de Vigny.'

Felix knew all about it, much better than did Mrs. Underwood—that little select dinner of the *élite* of the world of art and genius, to which Mr. Grinstead had asked Cherry about a fortnight ago, and which she had described with such delight. He had not much heart for strangers and works of art at that moment, but he could not refuse Cherry's commission, nor vex her by omitting to ask to see the studio; so there, in the course of the morning, he found himself, alone at first among the statues and casts—grave and graceful creations—more from the world of Christian than of classic poetry, and if less æsthetically beautiful, more solemn and more real.

He had gone in meaning only to fulfil his duty to Cherry, but he found himself attracted and enchained, and was standing before Cherry's favourite figure of Mercy, drinking in, as it were, the beseeching wistful spirit of faint hope that breathed from the whole figure, when a crimson curtain was lifted, and a gentleman of about five-and-forty or fifty, but grey-haired and looking older, came with a soft tread towards him.

'Mr. Underwood, I believe.'

Felix bowed.

'I am very glad to have the pleasure of making your acquaintance.'

'I am very much obliged for my admission. I should not have ventured, but that my sister was so anxious that I should see what she enjoys so much.'

Mr. Grinstead smiled, and quietly did the honours, while Felix—though, of course, untrained—modestly showed himself full enough of taste and intelligence to be worthy of an artist sister; Mr. Grinstead treating him all along like an honoured guest, and taking him farther into his private rooms, to see some favourite old German paintings, and to offer luncheon.

The house did indeed deserve Mrs. Underwood's term, fitted up with all that carved wood and well-chosen simple colour could do; and with wondrous gems of art—all the refinement and beauty that a bachelor, when he *does* choose, can bring together even better than a lady can.

'How long shall you be in town?' had been an early question, answered by, 'I take my sister home to-morrow;' and then, when it had struck Felix that his host was becoming increasingly thoughtful and absent, and he was trying to take leave, but was always prevented, Mr. Grinstead asked, 'Should I be likely to find your sister at home if I called this afternoon?'

'Not early,' said Felix; 'I think she has some commissions to finish. I am to meet her at five. I am afraid I must wish you good morning.'

'A few minutes longer. Mr. Underwood, I must begin by making you a confession, and asking you a question. Do you think there is any chance for me with that sweet little sister of yours?'

'With Geraldine!' Felix laid hold of the back of a chair, feeling as if his senses almost reeled, though whether consternation or exultation came uppermost, he could not have told.

'Yes,' was the reply. 'I am speaking abruptly, but I am taken by surprise at finding that you intend so soon to take her away. Indeed, I believe these are matters on which long consideration often ends in a sudden plunge,' he added, smiling a little, as if he wondered a little to find himself in a situation that seemed to reverse their ages; indeed, Felix was by far the most embarrassed.

'I do not think she is at all prepared,' was all that occurred to him to throw into the gulf of silence.

'Perhaps not,' said Mr. Grinstead, rather wistfully. 'I see you think the notion a preposterous one,' he continued, with something unconsciously of the elder's tone towards inexperienced youth, though there was pleading in it too; and he put a chair in his visitor's way, and speaking quietly though eagerly, as Felix tried to utter some polite disclaimer: 'I see the disparity myself, though perhaps less strongly than you do. Forty-six does not feel itself so vast an age as five-and-twenty may think it. The truth is this. I was made a fool of, as befalls most of us' (Felix looked more assenting than he knew, poor fellow!), 'and was hit harder than some, I believe. At any rate, the distaste it gave me was invincible, till I met with that wonderful compound of brightness and tenderness—spirit and sensitiveness—I cannot help it. She has haunted me ever since I first met her last year; and if there be nothing in the way on her side, I believe I could make her happy.'

'There is nothing in the way,' repeated Felix, as an honest man, but with a sense of a jewel being dragged from him, and relieved to have something to say that was not all consent. 'It is a very great honour for our little Geraldine to be so thought of, but I think you should be aware that she has nothing of her own, and—poor child—is sadly frail and feeble in health.'

'For that,' said Mr. Grinstead, 'I think you may trust her to my care;' and he spoke eagerly, as if longing to be taking care of her. 'And though I am a self-made man, I have had prosperity enough to be able to secure a comfortable provision for her.'

'Thank you—yes,' hastily said Felix. 'It was not that I was thinking of.'

'I see you are against me,' said the sculptor, perhaps anticipating the answer that actually came—'Selfishly, sir; only selfishly. Geraldine is so much our life and light at home, that your—your proposal was a shock to me; but I see the very great advantage it would be to her, and I could not desire anything better for her.' There were tears in his eyes, and the last words came with a choking utterance.

'I see,' said Mr. Grinstead, 'that I am doing a hard thing by you, and that to hold out the idea of her becoming even more to you sounds like mockery. Besides, I am too far from secure to begin to spare any pity for you. Now tell me, can I see her this evening? Where are you to meet her?'

'I am afraid I cannot propose your joining us then,' said Felix, more cordially, 'for it is to be at the Baker Street Bazaar, about some very domestic shopping; but I believe we shall come home between six and seven o'clock.'

'Very well; you will find me there. You will use your own judgment as to preparing her.'

Very domestic shopping indeed it was. The ancient coal-scuttle, a Froggatt legacy, had three decided holes in it, and Wilmet had a vision of one glimpsed in Baker Street. She would not trust either Felix or Cherry to choose it separately, but conjointly she thought they might counterbalance one another, and combine taste, discretion, and economy; and they were both afraid of failing her.

The very contrast of that commission, and the importance ascribed to it, with the ease and luxuriousness in Mr. Grinstead's house, served to bring before Felix the sense of the promotion for Geraldine that he was so ungratefully accepting. Little tender being, the first to wither under the blight of penury, how could he grudge her the sunshine of ease and wealth, cherishing care, prosperity, beauty, society—all that was congenial to her? No, indeed—he rejoiced. Yet how rejoice—when every time he came in from his work, he felt it a fresh blank when he did not meet her responsive look of welcome, or hear the half-quaint, half-pathetic tones that made much of the tiniest adventure of the day. His heart was sore enough at Edgar's evasion, and to lose Cherry from his hearth would quench its most cherished spark. He had been so secure of her, too. She had seemed so set apart from marriage, so peculiarly dependent on him, that it had been to her that he had turned with a sort of certainty as his companion in the life of self-sacrifice that he knew to lie before him. It was no small part of that sacrifice, that as he went to and fro on foot and by omnibus in the busy streets, he was schooling his spirit to look on the change not as desertion of himself, but as a brilliant and happy prospect for the little sister, who had powers and tastes such as ought not to be buried in the room over the shop at Bexley. He must keep the regret well out of mind, or he could never persuade her naturally, or avoid poisoning her happiness.

Should he prepare her? That must be left to chance. And chance was not favourable, for when he had found his way into the pit at the Baker Street Bazaar, appropriated to ornamental ironmongery, he saw her accompanied by Robina and Angela, whom Mrs. Underwood had good-naturedly sent for to spend her last afternoon with her. There was a sort of pang when Cherry's face greeted him, and her hand nestled into its accustomed hold on his arm just where it had leant by preference these sixteen years; and as she said in her low playful tones, 'Is it not a curious study to see invention expended on making an intrinsically hideous thing beautiful by force of japan, gilding, and painting? You see the only original design nature provided for a coal-scuttle is the nautilus shell, and unluckily that is grotesquely inappropriate! Just look at the row of ungainly things craning out their chins like overdressed dwarfs. I am decidedly for the simplest and least disguised, though Robin is for the snail, and Angel, I believe, for that highly suitable Watteau scene. Which do you vote for?'

'The most likely to satisfy Wilmet,' said Felix absently, knowing he should hate whichever it might be, and wondering who would ever again put so much interest into common things.

'The scuttle of Mettie's dreams appears to be no more,' said Cherry; 'but as Robin always seems to me guided by her spirit, I am inclined to think it safest to go by her judgment.'

'Robin represent Wilmet?' repeated Felix, scanning the plump, honest, sensible face, as that of his destined housewife; and not a bad prospect either practically, though without the charms that specially endeared Cherry.

She thought him absent, feared he had heard some fresh ill tidings of Edgar, and though reassured on that head, lost the zest she had caught up, and the selection was pretty well left to Robina.

There was no opportunity of confidential talk; the children were with them all the rest of the drive, and were to return with them to dinner; and that Angela was much shocked and subdued by the tidings of Edgar's flight did not conduce to privacy, since it silenced the tongue that generally sheltered any conversation! Nor could Felix succeed in hurrying his three ladies: they had a great deal still to do, and awe of Wilmet made them very particular in the doing of it, so that it was not till perilously near dinner-time that he brought them home, and there, on a hurried excursion to the drawing-room to notify the arrival, was Mr. Grinstead discovered. He had called, avowedly to wish Miss Underwood good-bye; and the mistress of the house, with perhaps an inkling of the state of affairs, had asked him to stay and dine. She could not help it, as she said, in excuse to her daughter, who always hated clever men, especially associated the sculptor with all the misery of the day of Alda's rupture with Ferdinand, and also wanted to have had Felix to herself this evening.

So she favoured the party with as little of her civility or conversation as possible; not that it was much missed, for Cherry was perfectly unsuspecting, and expanded into wit and animation as usual; and Mr. Grinstead, to Felix's surprise, was not rendered either silent or *distrait* by his suspense; and Felix himself had learnt conversation as a mechanical art in his trade, and could do his part, with cares and anxieties packed away.

After the ladies were gone, there only passed the words—

'Can I speak to her?'

'I will fetch her.'

'You have not prepared her?'

'I had not a moment.'

'Better so, perhaps.'

Felix led the way to her painting-room, having luckily delayed just long enough not to encounter the two children fetching the purchases for a great display. From this discussion, so dear to the female heart, he snatched the unsuspicious Cherry, with the few brief words that Mr. Grinstead wished to speak to her in her sitting room.

'An order! oh, it must be an order!' echoed among the sisters; and as Angela skipped up after them to fetch some further article to be shown off, there was no opportunity of even a hint except from Felix's agitated face, and the unconsciously convulsive squeeze of the little fingers between his arm and his side. He put her in a chair, and hurried off, disregarding the 'O Felix, are you going?' but shutting the door, and returning to the dining-room to keep a restless watch.

It lasted—what must have been a shorter time than he expected, terribly long as it seemed. Mr. Grinstead came downstairs, and Felix's heart bounded at the first footfall.

The kind, far-seeing, thoughtful face did not betray much. He held out his hand. 'Thank you, Mr. Underwood,' he said; 'I hope I did not distress her much. I have only one entreaty to make to you. If you should find that there is any allowance to be made for the surprise and shock, and newness of the idea, you will be a true friend, and not let pride or delicacy prevent you from letting me know.'

'I will not,' said Felix, ready to promise anything to comfort a man who had lost the Cherry he retained.

'It is nonsense, though,' added the sculptor; 'she is much too sincere and transparent a creature to trifle with feelings. Those innocent things are not to be won so late in life. Go up to her. She will want you. What a rival you are! I will make my excuses to the ladies.'

Felix held out his hand, too sorry for him now to know what to say; and after a strong grasp, they went their different ways.

Felix found Geraldine cowering down in her chair, with her hands clasped together over her forehead. She looked up at him, as if startled by his entrance. 'O Felix, how could you?' broke from her.

'My dear, I could not help it. Has it been so very distressing?'

'Oh!' with a great gasp, 'I'm sure to refuse a man is the most horrible thing in the world—except to accept him! And such a man too—so great and good and kind. You shouldn't have let him do it, Felix.'

'Don't scold me, Cherry; how was I to know you would not like it?'

'Felix! an old man like that!'

'Well, that's decisive,' said Felix, laughing at the tone; 'but, indeed, I did think you admired him very much.'

'So I do—but not in that way—not so as to bear to see him lower himself—and—and have to grieve him—' and the tears started from her eyes. 'But you know, he only could have done it because he saw a poor little lame thing and wanted to take care of her.'

'I think it goes a good deal deeper than that, Cherry.'

'I'm very sorry,' said Cherry. 'How very disagreeable it is that such things will happen; I thought, at any rate, that I was safe from them; and he was such an old man, and such a kind friend, that I was so proud of; and now I have vexed him so—and it is all over.'

'Do you really regret it? are you sure you did not speak only in the first surprise?'

'Felix! you! you to be against me!'

'Not against you, Chérie.'

She interrupted with a cry of pain. 'Oh! don't let anybody call me that till Edgar comes home again!'

'My poor Cherry!'

Then there was a silence; her head was on his shoulder, and she was crying silently, but so profusely that he could not tell whether her tears were all for Edgar or for new feelings stirred in her heart.

'Cherry dear, don't you think we ought to look at it reasonably? If you do not feel as if you cared for him—like a novel—yet still—'

'Hush, Felix! he is much too good to be accepted any other way.'

'I am not sure that he thinks so.'

'I do, then!' said Cherry, raising her head up indignantly. 'I should be ashamed to marry any man without! A lame, sickly, fretful thing like me ought to bring real love at least, to make up to a man for being bothered with her. Come, Felix, have done talking sensible nonsense! I know you don't wish it, so don't pretend.'

'I am making no pretence. It would be a dreadful business for me; but all the more I think I ought to make you consider.'

'Consider! Oh! I'll consider fast enough; that beautiful drawing-room, with the statues, and the conservatory—and a carriage—and going to Italy! Do you think I am going to be bribed by things like that?'

'No; but to have one so fatherly, kind, and tender—'

'As if one wanted one's husband to be fatherly!'

'—And the safe position—'

'I declare you are talking just like Alda!'

'But if you don't like him, there's an end of it.'

'I like him, I tell you; but not so much as the tip of your little finger!'

'Perhaps not, now; but—'

'Felix! You don't want to get rid of me? I know you were right to argue with Wilmet, and persuade her, because she had let her heart go, and only was afraid to acknowledge it; but mine isn't gone, and couldn't go. If I had not learnt to work, and had not a work to do, I might try to think of freeing you from a burthen; but now that I have, why should I upset it all, and wrench myself away from you? When I lean against you, I have got my home, and my rest, and all I want here. I never go away from you but I feel that I *do* want you so; and when one feels that, what's the use of looking out for somebody else?'

'Dear little Sweetheart! Yes!' as she lay contentedly against him, with his arm round her; 'it only makes me tremble, that you should give up a home like that, and risk so much upon my one life. The other boys love you dearly, but they are more likely to make ties for themselves! and if—'

'I should love you better dead than any other man alive!' cried Cherry impetuously. 'I won't do it, Felix! so spare your dutiful remonstrances! I do hate them so, and I know you don't mean them.'

'Mean is not the word, Cherry. The more I hated making them, the more I felt bound to do so.'

'There, then! You've done.'

'Yes, I've done. My Cherry, my Cherry! you don't know how much lighter the world seems to me than it did half an hour ago!'

'O you foolish old Giant! And there come those irrepressible children! Oh! I hope and trust they have not found it out!' cried Cherry, bounding up from her sentimental attitude, as Angela was heard galloping up the stairs.

But there was this benefit in dealing with a veteran, that he knew how to keep his own counsel and other people's. Angela came dashing in. 'Oh! here you both are! Mr. Grinstead said he had forgotten, after all, to give you this letter. He said you had better write to the lady herself. It is a capital order, he said—you've been settling about it, haven't you? What *are* you going to do?'

'I don't quite know, Angel,' said Cherry, seeing the letter was addressed in a strange hand to the sculptor; and thereupon venturing to open it, and finding it contained a request to obtain from Miss Underwood an engagement for a set of studies similar to those in the exhibition, if it were true that these were not for sale. It was from a lady of wealth and taste, whose name was well known as a patroness in the artist world; and Cherry could quite understand that Mr. Grinstead had kept it back, with the feeling that were she his, no toil should be hers for the future.

That was little recommendation. Her first rise out of uselessness gave her more exultation in its novelty than did even the exercise of her art or the evidence of its success. There was something exquisite in the sense of power. She had made up her mind to give Wilmet quarterly the same amount as was charged for Lance, to set aside just enough besides to clothe herself, and that the remainder of her earnings should liquidate Edgar's debts; so that some day she should write to him to come home a free and unburthened man. Viewed in this aspect, that huge carpet-bag, stuffed to bursting with bills, had not so frightful an aspect, but rather seemed to her a dragon to be conquered for Edgar's sake; and Felix laughed at her for tendering him the cheque for her Acolyte, and asking him just to pay off a few of them before leaving town. He had to explain to her that equity and custom required that no one should have the preference, and that she must wait till she could either pay off the whole, or else make payments of so much in the pound.

'Like a bankruptcy! That can't be worth while. Those are your business ways!'

'I fear you little know what you have undertaken. Remember, there is no call to pay any of it.'

'Indeed! Oh! why does not that tiresome Ferdinand write?'

'There has not been time.'

'He could have telegraphed!'

Marilda was likewise much disappointed at hearing nothing; but discussion was trying to her, and she dreaded her cousins' sharp eyes so much, that it was a relief to her to escape them. Nor could they linger, for Wilmet was anxious about Lance, who was exceedingly miserable; and in his anxiety hardly knew what he was about, scarcely what he said.

If Wilmet wished him to feel what a narrow escape his had been, he broke into despair that he had not been with Edgar. The room and the room-mate that had seemed so disgusting to home-bred Felix, had fascinated him by their charming disregard of wearisome propriety, and their congenial eccentric liberty; and the picture of Edgar coming home in his distress to his sleepy, half-conscious comrade made him wretched. He treated regret like censure, and alarmed as much as scandalised Wilmet by longings to have been there to share the wanderings, which, even if they amounted to starvation, could not, he averred, be 'half so hateful as standing behind a counter.'

Perhaps he had never before been so near showing temper as in his arguments with Wilmet, and his determination to defend Edgar through thick and thin; and she was almost relieved when after the disappointment of finding that there was no news from Ferdinand, he collapsed into one of his attacks of headache. Nay, for weeks, though about again and at work, the lad was not well nor thoroughly himself; he seemed, like Cherry, to be always watching for tidings that never came, and unlike her, he made light of whatever could be construed into censure of any taste of Edgar's.

Felix, though unwilling to pain him, thought it might be wholesome to let him see for himself the facts of Edgar's life, and accepted his assistance in sorting the bagful of revelations of self-indulgence and dissipation, which he knew Lance's lips might defend, but never his conscience.

Judging as well as they could by the dates and charges, there had not been much amiss except carelessness of expenditure before Alice Knevett's defection, eighteen months back; but this had been succeeded by a launch into every sort of excitement, so increasingly painful and disgraceful, that Felix declared at times that it was profanation to let the proceeds of Geraldine's pure and high-minded art be spent in discharging such obligations. There were traces of an endeavour to pull up after Tom Underwood's legacy, which would have far more than cleared Edgar, if he had been satisfied to do more than merely pay 'on account,' and stave off difficulties, until the main body of the bequest had vanished between gambling and the crash of the National Minstrelsy.

Meantime the weeks of Edgar's silence and absence were running on to months, and nothing was known. Ferdinand Travis's quest had been an utter failure. Baden, Homburg, Spa, Munich, Paris, Florence, Rome, Monaco, had been searched in vain; ingenious advertisements in the second column of the 'Times' were unnoticed; and though there was no outward difference in the manner of the two who loved him best, each bore about a heavy yearning heartache and foreboding—the one, that there must be something, worse than was known, to lead so affectionate a person thus utterly to efface himself; the other, that some terrible unknown accident, lake-storm or glacier-crevasse, could alone account for such pitiless disregard of home suspense. His relics had been hidden away like those of the dead, with sad reverence; and his name was never mentioned except now and then in low sad tones in a *tête-à-tête*.

CHAPTER XXXI.

THE BARBE BLONDE.

> '"And neither toil nor time could mar
> Those features, so I saw the last
> Of Waring." "You! O never star
> Was lost here, but it rose afar.
> Look east, where old new thousands are."'
> *Browning.*

The first thing that really cheered Lance was an enforced holiday of the organist, when he was asked to undertake the church music in the interregnum. He threw himself into the work, consulted Dr. Miles, who lent him books, and gave him lessons; and the whole current of his thoughts became so soothed and changed, that Felix attended to no remonstrance on the danger of unsettling him, but truly declared that the few hours he weekly gave to scientific music was more than compensated by his increased power of attention, and steadiness of concentration on his business, as if he there found the balance needed by his sensitive nature.

His head too, instead of aching more, as Wilmet had feared, suffered less; but there was a change in him. He had experienced the bitterness of sin, as nearly and as bitterly as was possible to one yet intact. He had looked down an abyss, and been forced to recognise that had he followed Edgar into what he had tried to believe merely exciting, artistic, or free, he could hardly have been spared a flaw in his life. It was when wrapt in the grandeurs of sacred harmony that this sense dawned on him. It was most true of him that 'the joy of the Lord was his strength.' Respectability had no power over him, he had a liking for the disreputable; but his reverence and delight for the glory and beauty of praise seemed, as it were, to force him into guarding his purity of life and innocence of mind, which might otherwise have been perilled by his geniality and love of enterprise. At any rate, after the first shock to health and spirits had passed off, he retained a more staid manner, entirely abstained from his former plentiful admixture of slang, caught more of Felix's demeanour, and ceased from those kinds of sayings and doings which used only not to give his sisters an impression of recklessness because they knew he always did rectify his balance in time.

Meantime another interest arose; for John Harewood had got his promotion, and had obtained leave to come home and try for an appointment. Wilmet had reason to believe him actually on his journey, when one morning, early in October, Lance, who was waiting in the office, was startled by Will's entrance, asking, 'Have you had a telegram?' in a scarcely audible voice.

'No! What is it, Bill?' said Lance, dismayed at his countenance.

'That dear Jack!' and thrusting two telegraph papers into his hand, Will threw himself down on the high desk, hiding his face, with long-drawn gasps of anguished grief, to which he could only now venture to give way; nor did Lance marvel, as he read—

Rameses, Egypt, October 3rd, 2.30 p.m.

Major Harewood to Rev. Christopher Harewood, the Bailey, Minsterham, England.

Boiler explosion. Severe scald. No pain; probably will be none. Dearest love to W.W. and all. Poor Frank Stone killed.

The other, which had arrived at the same time, was dated,

6 p.m.

Charles Chenu, Surgeon, to Christopher Harewood.

Injuries not necessarily mortal, unless from extent. Wanted, good nurse, water-bed, linen, and all comforts.

'There's more hope in that!' said Lance.

'I have none! Don't you remember poor Tom the stoker?

'Twas just what they said of him,' said Will, raising his face for a moment. 'And here they've sent me to tell Wilmet! I—O Lance, I just cannot do it. 'Tis bad enough at home!' and he lay over the desk again, almost convulsed with grief.

'I will go and tell Wilmet,' said Felix, who had come in unperceived by him, and received the telegrams from Lance. 'She is at Miss Pearson's. Is any one going to him, Will?'

'My poor father!' gasped William. 'I don't believe it is any good! But I shall go with him, unless—He sent me on to see whether she—Wilmet would go. You won't let her, Felix? I must go on to see whether I can get a nurse at St. Faith's.'

'I believe Wilmet will wish to go,' said Felix.

'And be the best nurse,' added Lance.

'If there were any nursing to do,' said William, looking at them in amaze. 'I haven't the least hope he can last till we can come out! But my father *will* hope—that's the worst—and wants to have her rather than me. Don't tell her so, though; I don't know what I am saying. Only she should not be persuaded to go! Oh, that it should come to this!'

'I will leave him to you, poor fellow!' said Felix, beckoning Lance to the door, as William again flung himself across the desk. 'I think she will go, and that it will be better for her.'

He was interrupted by the arrival of a telegraph boy with a message to him in his editorial capacity, which threw more light on the accident.

Telegram from Alexandria, October 4th, 7 a.m.

Serious explosion of locomotive engine at Rameses, on the Suez and Alexandria line. Engineer and stoker killed. English officer injured, without hope of recovery.

Felix gave it to his brother, and went on his melancholy way—seeing Miss Pearson first in her parlour, and then sending for his sister.

Wilmet was just what those who knew her best expected. While there was scope for action, she would never break down. She inferred at once that the surgeon expected the comforts he sent for to be of use, and dwelt upon Mr. Harewood's kindness in allowing her to accompany him. As soon as she arrived at home, she scolded William, and made him find sense and hope, which in truth he had only lost when, instead of having to support and comfort his impulsive mother and sisters, he could afford to give way himself. He could now give a coherent account of his father's plans. Mr. Harewood was hastily arranging matters at home, and would be on his way to Southampton by the last train. If Wilmet would go with him, she was to meet him at the station—either with or without a nurse, as she might judge needful. Her decision was against the nurse. She reminded Will that his brother had with him a Christian Hindoo servant, who had already proved an efficient attendant in an attack of fever; and she herself had some experience of scalds, through Felix's accident, and one that had befallen a servant of Miss Pearson's. Expense, the prostrate despair of the family at home, and his own college duties, had alike decided that if she went out, William must remain in England; but he was despatched to St Faith's, where the needful appliances were always kept, and could be made over in such an emergency.

Meantime Wilmet, grave but steadily calm, made her preparations. She devised means of providing a substitute at Miss Pearson's, bethought herself of everything requisite; and when Geraldine pursued her, trying to help, but panting and sobbing nervously, it was only to be put down on a chair, and warned not to knock herself up. The keys were made over to her, but without directions or injunctions; only one soft whisper—'Dear Cherry! after all, you have made me able to do this.'

Felix would not be denied going to Southampton with her. Mr. Harewood was looking out for her at the station, with the resolute mask of indifference that both must assume for the journey. He took both her hands, and said, 'Thank you, my dear; I knew I should see you.' And she said, 'Thank you, for letting me come.' Then she took charge of his plaid and umbrella, and it was plain that thenceforth she would be his guardian daughter.

When Felix and William left the two on board the Havre boat, they knew that the Wilmet of old was gone for ever. She must come back with a great change upon her; but who could guess whether that change would be for weal or woe?

On went Mr. Harewood and Wilmet by steamer and by rail, unable to obtain intelligence, and maintaining absolute silence on the one thought that filled their minds, each solicitously tender of the other's comfort and fatigue, though both tacitly agreed that nothing was so trying as a halt.

When they reached Marseilles, they found the P. and O. agency certain that if Major Harewood were not living it would be known; and they likewise learnt that Rameses was a sort of little French colony around a station that the works for the Suez Canal were raising to an importance it could hardly have enjoyed since it was a treasure city of Pharaoh; and, while obliged to await their steamer, they obtained counsel on the articles likely to be most needful for their patient, and hence they telegraphed an announcement of their coming, and were replied to by the Hindoo servant, Zadok Krishnu—'Not worse.'

At Alexandria they found themselves expected and welcomed. Interested countenances and sympathising greetings were ready for the father and supposed sister at both consulate and hotel; and from the name of the engine-driver, Frank Stone, who had been killed, Mr. Harewood perceived that John must have recognised in him a clever Minsterham boy, and this accounted for his having joined him on his engine, where indeed it was suspected that he had been trying to help him obviate the dangers caused by Oriental indifference and fatalism. The injuries were regarded as hopeless, from the great extent of surface; and there was a kind preparatory intimation that all that could be hoped for was to find life not extinct, for that opiates were required to such a degree that there was no consciousness. M. Charles Chenu was a clever young French doctor; and a deaconess from the Alexandrian branch from Kaiserswerth was in attendance, as well as an Englishman who had been in the train, and all the alleviation possible had been given.

That was all the comfort to be had while waiting for one of the few and tardy trains, which at length set the travellers down at the strange little town of European houses and Arab hovels in the midst of the sand, distinguished by a boulevard and line of palm trees. At the station stood a short brown-faced figure, in white turban and trousers, and scarlet tassel, sash, and jacket, who with a salute half military, half Oriental, inquired in good English for their luggage, and in reply to their anxious questions, told them that the Sahib was lying in the same state of unconsciousness produced by opiates.

The goods, so needful to the sufferer, were all identified, and extracted at a great cost of patience, and the travellers were escorted, amid incomprehensible Arab clamours, across a *place* ankle-deep in sand, to a one-storied building of such unburnt bricks as the Israelites might have made, covering a good deal of ground, and combining the caravanserai and the French hotel. A Greek landlord and his French wife came forth, and the one talking all languages, the other only her mother tongue, but both warmly welcoming the arrivals, and assuring them that *le pauvre Monsieur* had had every care lavished on him—Dr. Chenu was there night and day.

A slender, moustached, brisk young man appeared, asking in French, in a kindly tone, whether they—especially Mademoiselle—could be prepared for so sad a sight as awaited them, but assuring them that the mere fact of life having so long continued had begun to inspire him with a sort of hope.

Mr. Harewood's French was not very available, but Wilmet made reply; and they were admitted into a low empty room, with windows shaded by screens of reed, through which came a dim light, showing a still figure, covered with light linen rags steeped in oil and spirit, which a little square figure in dark blue, with a neat net cap, was changing and renewing as fast as they dried.

All the preparation could not prevent the father from being overwhelmed, and having to turn away to grapple with the shock; but Wilmet, who had all along sustained herself with the recollection of John's reference to her awakening Lance from his deadly lethargy, without pause or shyness bent down, kissed his forehead, and called him by his name; and perhaps the full sense of his entire prostration only broke upon her when there was not the slightest token that she was heard, but the torpor continued unbroken by the faintest movement of the half-closed eyes or lips. Even then she only looked up with a piteous appealing glance to the doctor, who told her that the only chances of consciousness were in the intervals between the passing off of one anodyne and the administration of another, but that hitherto these had been spent in a sort of delirium of anguish, that made the renewal of the opiate immediately necessary.

Hope that at least the familiar voices might penetrate through the cloud still buoyed the new-comers up; but when the moans, restlessness, and half-utterances of dire suffering set in, the eyes opened to dim glassiness, the ears seemed neither to hear nor understand, and there was as much relief as disappointment when the slumberous potion had again brought back the senselessness. Nothing could be done but to moisten the lips and change the rags, and these seemed to dry up on one part as fast as another was renewed. The face had indeed escaped, and so had the back, and for the most part the right side, but the neck, chest, both shoulders, and the whole length of the left side were fearfully scalded, with white sodden-looking spaces, the most fatal appearance of all, worse than even a deep laceration by a splinter above the hip. Day and night Wilmet, the deaconess, and the Hindoo were changing the rags, and fanning, or keeping off the flies; and soon there was a great affection between Sister Hedwige and the young Englishwoman, who shared the same desolate room close adjoining—or rather, lay down there by turns. Wilmet spoke German enough to explain that she was not the patient's sister, but his *Verlobte*, and that in a matter-of-fact, dreamy kind of way, submitting passively to be kissed and cried over by the puffy little elderly German.

Poor Mr. Harewood could give no active assistance, and was in a sad state of isolation, unable to exchange a sentence with anybody except Wilmet and Krishnu. He tried Latin and French with the doctor; but the diversities of accent foiled him in both, and Wilmet had to be interpreter. He was a great charge to her, but a far greater comfort. There were his constant prayers, and the sight and example of his deep resignation; there was the sense of protection and sympathy, the relief and distraction of attending to him, and of gratitude for his care; and besides, he wrote all the letters, for which Wilmet had neither time nor heart. She could keep up while acting, instead of realizing, as the expression of words must have forced her to do; while the struggle in the father's mind, was only not to long unsubmissively for a conscious interval at the last.

An English army surgeon, who came from Malta a day or two after their arrival, thoroughly approved of M. Chenu's treatment, but agreed in his verdict that any other expectation would be futile; recovery, though not impossible where no vital part was injured, was most improbable where nature had so large a surface to repair.

Yet the actual symptoms that would have been immediate doom did not appear, but as one dim sad day rolled by after another, the parts least hurt began to show a tendency to heal; and therewith sprang up a conviction in Wilmet's mind that there was not always a total insensibility to her presence or Mr. Harewood's, but that the face changed at their voices, and that there was a preference for her hand; and then Dr. Chenu began declaring that these English had 'complexions' like rocks, and that if it were not 'the impossible,' there would be hope; and instead of giving his anodynes with the reckless desire to stifle pain, he become cautious, modified them, and only gave them when decisively expedient.

There resulted a gradual clearing of the senses. There were lulls when pain was comparatively in abeyance, and the faculties less and less clouded, the eyes regained meaning, and smiles of greeting hovered on the lips; a sense of repose in the presence of Wilmet and his father was evident; an uneasy perception if either were absent; and at last an exchange of words—conscious words. When his awakening was marked, not by a groan of pain, but by the feeble inquiry, 'Where's Wilmet?' she felt as if she had had her reward.

Once he asked 'Where's your brother?' and when she explained that none of her brothers were with her, he seemed confused and dissatisfied; but his voice died into an indistinct murmuring; and when twice again the same inquiry recurred, she set it down to the semi-delirious delusions that the narcotics sometimes occasioned. She knew that an English gentleman had done much for him at first, and had only left him the day before her arrival; and she had regretted being unable to discover who he was from lips unused to British nomenclature, but had been too much engrossed to think much about the matter. But there were now intervals in which she fully had her John again, entirely sensible, anxious to preserve his consciousness, so as to be desirous of putting off the sedative as long as he could endure the attacks of suffering without it. He could listen, and sometimes talk; and the next time he returned to the puzzling question, 'When did your brother go?' there could be no doubt that he was in full possession of his understanding; and Wilmet answered, 'Dear John, I do not know what you are thinking of; Felix has never been here at all.'

'I do not mean Felix; it was Edgar.'

'Edgar! You never have seen him, you know, dear,' said Wilmet, speaking softly, as one persuaded that he was recalling a delusion.

'I know that I never saw him at home; but he was in the train. He was the first to come to me; he said he would telegraph. Surely he did so?'

'That accounts for the correctness of the telegram!' said Mr. Harewood. 'I remember now that the wording was so well put, that it gave me hope that you must be quite yourself.'

'What was it?'

They could well tell him, for it had seemed branded in fire on their minds for days.

'Yes, that was his doing. I think I only called you *her*,' he said, smiling. 'I could trust to his knowing my *her of hers*.'

'But how did you know one another? Was it in the train?'

'No. Poor Frank Stone recognised me at Suez, and begged me to come with him on the engine. I remember his consulting me about representing the impracticability of some of his subordinates; and next after that I was somewhere on the stones, unable to stir hand or foot—not in pain, but a numbness and faintness all over me, with every sense preternaturally clear, as if I were all spirit. I made no doubt I was dying fast; and when some one came to see after me, I begged him to take down my telegram to my father while I could give it. I remember his start and cry when I gave my name. "Good Heavens!" he said. "You are not Jack? Wilmet's Jack?" and really, I hardly knew; my voice seemed to come from somewhere else; but I saw the face over me that belongs to you all.'

'And did you speak to him? But no, you were in no state for that.'

'I gave what messages I could think or speak; but the numb faintness grew on me, and seemed to gather up all my senses. I did not seem able to care about anything when I felt myself in his hands.'

'Edgar!' repeated Wilmet, still slow to believe. 'Did you call him by his name?'

'I cannot tell; I think I did. I know I no more doubted of its being he than I do that you are Wilmet. Ah! I remember struggling between a sense that I ought, and the growing disinclination to speak, and wanting to tell him to go home, for you were all very unhappy about him. Did I get it out? Did he answer? I cannot tell! No, dearest, I know no more, nor why he is not here. Zadok must know; where is he?'

The Hindoo was summoned, and it was elicited that the English gentleman had watched over the Sahib day and night, sent the telegrams, called in the doctor from Malta, and had acted as if the patient had been his brother, only going away by the last train before the arrival of Mr. Harewood, and then leaving with him a packet only to be given up in case the Major should die without recovering the power of speech. It was claimed, and proved to contain a record of all that poor John had endeavoured to say, but written in a disguised hand, though merely in the spelling of the names betraying that the scribe had been no stranger. It was plain that he had so entirely thought Major Harewood a dying man, as to have made no attempt at concealing his own identity from him, but he had kept it carefully guarded from every one else; and Wilmet's heart smote her as she questioned, 'Would he have fled if it had been Felix or Cherry who had been coming?'

Questions were asked, and both M. Chenu and Madame Spiridione testified that the gentleman who had attended on Major Harewood had been *un jeune homme extrêmement beau—grand et blond*, but they had no guess as to his name, and merely knew that he had gone away towards Alexandria. Both there and at Cairo did Mr. Harewood write to make inquiries, but always in vain; and the trains were so few and so slow, that he could not go himself without a longer absence than seemed fitting to propose in his son's precarious state, when the very efforts that nature was making towards restoration might so easily result in fever, or in fatal changes in the wounds.

The sight of him seemed to be only less precious to John than that of Wilmet. When in comparative ease, it was almost a basking in their presence. After his long years of foreign service, no one could guess, he said, the delight it was to look at them; and when he meditated on the journey they had taken for his sake, he would break out in wondering gratitude, not to be checked by Wilmet's simplicity of protest, 'Of course she had come; she could not help it.'

The pleasure and comfort she gave him were really serving to bear him through. Not only was her touch unusually light, firm, dextrous, and soft, but pain from her hand was not like that given by any one else, when each dressing was tortured; and when his nerves were strung to an acute misery of sensitiveness, her look and touch, her voice and gesture alone were endurable. His first powers of being entertained were shown when she talked, or sang, not indeed as her brothers could sing, but in a low, sweet, and correct voice, that had an infinite charm of soothing that weary sickness. He might strive not to be exacting; but his face showed in spite of himself that when she quitted the room the light of his life went with her, and there was nothing left him but tedium, helplessness, and sore suffering.

She only did leave him for sleep, which she could usually time while he was lulled by the anodyne, and for hurried meals at the table d'hôte, which collected almost every European in the place. Mr. Harewood likewise made a great point of taking her out every evening for a sandy walk on the boulevard under the palm trees, as a preservative of her health, much to the perplexity of the observers. She saw no necessity for leaving John, to plough her way in the hot sand; but it relieved the Librarian's mind, and was besides their opportunity for discussing questions not intended for their patient's ear.

Here it was that Mr. Harewood communicated his difficulty. He had exchanged one course at the cathedral, but could not arrange for the next, and it was imperative that he should be at home by the end of the second week in the New Year. John, though they dared now to call him better, was still immovable, and what could be done? 'Shall I,' said the Librarian, 'telegraph to William to bring out Lucy or Grace?'

'Would that be of any use?' said Wilmet, thinking only of their scatter-brained recklessness in Lance's case.

'They have not your faculties of nursing, my dear; but you see, I don't perceive how otherwise to contrive for your remaining.'

'Mine! I must stay!' exclaimed Wilmet, her little proprieties most entirely vanished into oblivion.

'I knew you would say so. Indeed, I still think nothing else gives a hope of pulling my poor boy through; but in that case, you see, my dear, one of the girls—or their mother—'

'She would be very uncomfortable, and all for nothing,' said Wilmet; 'and William would lose his term. You know,' and only then the colour flew into her cheeks, 'I could do very well alone if you were only to marry us.'

With such simplicity and straightforwardness was it said, that the Librarian had replied, 'The very best plan,' before the strangeness struck him, and he began to falter, 'You have—John has settled it?'

'No,' said Wilmet, crimson, but grave, steady, and earnest, 'it was only this that made me think of it; but if it can be managed without hurting him, it seems to me the most feasible way.'

This form of speech of course only proceeded from unfathomable depths of affection and reserve, and it was understood.

'Dear child,' said Mr. Harewood, 'this is the truest kindness of all. I will not thank you. You and I are too much one with him for that; but I wish his mother could have known what he has won.'

Soft silent tears were dropping fast under Wilmet's broad hat. Maidenliness would have that revenge; and she could not speak. The question of broaching the subject to John overwhelmed her with embarrassment and shamefastness, at the thought of her own extraordinary proceeding. Perhaps an impulse might have led her into proposing it to him, as she had done to his father, but the bare idea of so doing filled her with shame and dismay; and Mr. Harewood, a ceremonious and punctilious gentleman of the old school, thought it incumbent on him to lead his son to make the proposition, so that it might come at least in appearance from the right quarter.

He had to watch his opportunity, for John was by no means always fit for conversation, and when he was, was not willing to dispense with Wilmet's presence; and it was necessary at last to come to, 'I want to speak to you before she comes back;' and then, having calmed the restless eye that watched for her, the Librarian explained the necessities that called him home: and these were fully appreciated by the Major, who owned that it had been much to have had him for these six weeks, but therewith came a look of alarm, and the exclamation, 'Oh, but how about her?'

'She does not think of leaving you. We must consider how to arrange for her.'

'Has not Clement finished his terms? Could not he be franked out?'

'Is there not a simpler way? John, nothing would make me so happy as to leave that dear girl your wife.'

'But you go before the New Year. Father, it is not to be thought of,' he said, with a nervous movement of his right hand, which he could now partially use.

'There is no reason that I should not marry you as you lie there. She would consent.'

'Dearest! she would consent to anything she thought good for me, but the more reason that it cannot be thought of. Look at the wreck I am, and the glorious creature she is.'

'She would not accept that objection.'

'The more need that I should. Even if this place in my side do not, as I expect from day to day, gangrene and make an end of it at once, it can hardly be expected that there will not be some contraction or distortion to make an object of me.'

'Does Chenu tell you this?' asked his father, who had never had the chances so plainly set before him.

'No. Chenu does as well as any one can; but he has not the gift of foresight, and there is no use in taxing his French complaisance by asking questions that no one can answer,' he answered, with quiet calm and patience that almost overcame his father.

'I did not think you were so despondent,' he said.

'I do not think I am despondent,' was the reply; 'I feel as if I had only to lie here and wait my orders from above. I suppose weakness and sedatives blunt the feelings, for I do not regret all that might have been, as I should have thought I should—nay, as I did, in one night of fever in India. I can only feel thankfulness for intervals like this, and the blessing of having you both with me again. Father, I would not have spoken out, but that I thought you knew it better than I.'

'So I do—so I ought, my dear boy; but I cannot cease to hope that your having been so far given back to us is an earnest that God will entirely restore you.'

'That may be yet, but in the uncertainty, it hardly seems right to take advantage of my darling's devotion to bring on her so terrible a blight in her youth and loveliness. Sending her home a widow, Father!'

'Poor child! There would be little difference in her grief; and you should take into consideration that even so, you would leave her freed from the necessity of working at that school.'

'I could do that, without injustice to Will and the girls; and there would be a pension besides,' said John thoughtfully; and his father ventured to add—

'Indeed, I think if your recovery were as partial as you would have me apprehend, it would still only be a matter of time.'

'She would have her eyes open,' said John; but he thought long before he spoke again. 'I cannot trust myself to think of it! It is so great a temptation! My Wilmet! my darling! to waste her strong young life on me!'

Mr. Harewood said no more. He had experience enough to believe such things worked themselves out without interposition; and he would have regarded it as compromising Wilmet's dignity and confidence alike to mention her words. He left the room when she returned, but nothing resulted. John was restless and uncomfortable; and Wilmet, thinking he had heard all, and deemed her forward, was unhappy, and would have become shy, if his perturbation had not brought on feverishness; and that as usual inflamed the hurts into such acute pain, that the doctor gave a stronger opiate than had been needed of late, but which at first only produced distress, moaning, and wandering. They were more anxious about him that night and all the next day, than they had been for more than a week; and only towards the second morning did he become tranquil enough to fall into slumber, which lasted so late into the following day, that Wilmet, after being up all night, was persuaded to lie down during the noonday heat, when she had seen his sleep become more natural, and the distressful expression relax on his countenance.

She lay on her bed in a kind of waking doze, sad, anxious, and vexed at what she thought the consequence of the proposal into which she had been betrayed, feeling desolate, and dreading as much as she desired a summons to return.

Sister Hedwige did not call her till she had had more refreshing sleep than perhaps she was aware of; and then, when she came softly into the room, his eyes shone wistfully into hers, and she knelt down by him to stroke back that stiff sandy hair of his, and cool his brow with her freshly-washed hand. He lifted his as far as he could, inviting her to clasp it; his eyes again looked into hers, and a smile came out upon his face. 'My father has put a very wonderful thing into my head,' he said; then, as the lovely colour deepened on her cheek, 'can it be so, Wilmet?'

In her own calm way she answered, 'Do you not think it will be the best way?'

'For me? No doubt of that, my dearest, sweetest, best darling!' and the feeble force of his fingers somehow caused her brow to bend down to his fervent kiss. 'You look as lovely as—no, ten times lovelier than you did on the stile when you scolded me for telling you so. Why don't you now?'

'Because I am glad my face is a pleasure to you,' she said, glowing, so as to deserve his words, in spite of the effects of her long vigil.

'Ah! sick people are privileged to be foolish to their heart's content. But, Wilmet, let us be wise for once. This must not be till you have counted the cost.' And he repeated what he had said to his father of the likelihood of permanent effects being left.

'You would want me all the more,' she said.

'And you?'

'I should want all the more to be with you.'

Again he smiled fondly on her. 'And more, my love. How easily I may be a little worse than yesterday, and then you would have to go home alone.'

'These things are for always,' said Wilmet; and the tears she had resolved against came in crystal veils over her eyes, and it was vain to squeeze them out.

'I am conquered,' said John, half quaintly, because he was afraid of emotion. 'Here is a hand, at least! My father must manage the rest. I can only be the most glad and thankful of men. Love, this is worth it all!' as she tenderly smoothed his hair with her soft hand in the way he liked so well.

'And oh! how nice it will be as you get better!'

'I can believe I shall, much more than I have hitherto done,' returned he. Then after a happy pause, while she still stroked his head, and they looked into one another's faces with hearts swelling with unspoken prayers, he added, 'But of one thing I must and will be sure—of your brother's free consent.'

She was so sure of it herself, that she only smiled at him; but his was a sort of soldierly punctilio that forbade the profiting by her devotion without the sanction of her family, and his father supported him in it, and wrote from his dictation, detailing the provision which he was making for Wilmet in case of his death and begging for a reply by telegraph, since there was not time for Mr. Harewood to wait for an answer by post, then signing it, with great effort, with three crooked initials.

There could be no doubt as to the answer; and Wilmet went about her preparations with her own peculiar modest dignity. The 'belle Mees' had been a marvel to the French part of the community ever since M. le docteur had shrugged his amazement at *une grande Anglaise magnifique, mais blonde et fade,* coming out instead of a professional *garde malade,* and then found by experience that her hand and head, her nerve and gentleness, equalled those of the most skilful *soeur* with whom he had ever been thrown. And when it slowly dawned on him what were her relations with the Major, his wonder at English institutions knew no bounds. He would have adored her beauty, which grew on him as something marvellous, if he had not been a little afraid of anything so lofty and so still, and so incapable of airy chatter, as he found her at the *table d'hôte.* She produced on him something of the effect of the Pallas of the Parthenon, come across from Athens to undertake his patient, or the goddess Neith as John sometimes called her, when he lay watching her swift needle.

The Deaconess understood her better. Wilmet was much more nearly the stately Teutonic maiden than the Grecian divinity; and Sister Hedwige had had her days of romance, and beheld a Velleda in the noble, self-possessed, helpful woman, who was equal to any of the Fliedner disciples in resource and firmness. The German mind, too, appreciated the betrothal tie; and when Wilmet, who had grown very fond of the kindly, homely *Schwesterchen* consulted her about sending to Alexandria for the bridal white that must not be denied to John's eyes, she wept with joy, promised the willing aid of the Deaconess' establishment in procuring all she needed, and, moreover, a wreath from the myrtle they nourished in memory of home.

69

Wilmet's commission was not needed. She found one of the big boxes that had been in use as tables and seats opened; and Zadok diving into it under the Major's directions, and turning out parcels innumerable, among which appeared a snowy mass of India muslin, exquisitely fine and covered with delicate embroidery.

'There, Wilmet, you know what that is for.'

And with all the good-will in the world, Madame Spiridione volunteered French counsel in the cutting out, and Sister Hedwige German needling in the making; and Zadok, sitting cross-legged at the door, proved himself equal to any sewing-machine, and worked faster and better than either of the European nationalities, as indeed he was the son of a *dirjee*, or embroiderer-man, and had learnt some of his trade, though educated at a Mission school.

Dr. Chenu half despised, half envied the convenience of being married without the production of the registers of baptism, or the consent of either of the mayors or the commanding-officer, and a mere telegram, 'With all my heart,' from the elder brother; but still, Mr. Harewood was obliged to make an expedition to Cairo to arrange the formalities for the registry of the marriage, for which the Consul promised to send an official. The question was whether this gentleman should act as father to the bride, whose choice otherwise lay between M. Spiridione, Dr. Chenu, and Zadok Krishnu, and who much inclined to the last mentioned; but on the last day, by the very same train as brought the secretary, an unexpected arrival took place.

The one interest of Rameses was the arrival of the trains—few and far between. Mr. Harewood used to go out to count and report on the pale faces going westward, and the rosy young ones going eastward, and to capture the mail-bags and parcels that connected this Egyptian desert with the outward world. So seldom did any one halt, that he was amazed, not only to see the secretary, but a slender, black-bearded personage, portmanteau in hand, Panama hat on head, looking not indeed Oriental, but so un-English that it was startling to be accosted with, 'Good morning, Mr. Harewood; I hope your son is still going on well.'

Then it flashed on the Librarian that this was the Life Guardsman who had once ridden over to Minsterham as Alda Underwood's betrothed.

'Mr. Travis! This is unexpected! You don't bring any bad news for Miss Underwood, I trust,' he added, taking alarm.

'Oh no, far from it. I came to try to follow up this trail of poor Edgar. None of the family can,' he proceeded in a tone of apology; 'and as I have time, I can let no possibility go by.—But is it true, what they told me at Alexandria—that I am come just in time for a wedding?'

'Indeed it is, but for a very strange one. I am forced to go home when that train returns; and that sweet girl will not—nay, cannot leave my poor son. I hope it is not wrong in me to rejoice, turn out as it may. They will be delighted to see you.'

Ferdinand was made very welcome. He was a breath from home that made them feel how long they had been exiled. It appeared that he had been at Paris, vainly seeking as usual, when he had received a telegram from Miss Underwood, *i.e.* Marilda, and hurrying to England, had heard all that could be gathered from Wilmet's letter; and here he was, intending to pursue his inquiries in Egypt, and if needful extend his researches to Palestine or India, according to whatever clue he might gain.

Such exertions on the part of a stranger in blood were rather surprising; but Ferdinand seemed to think no explanation needful, and perhaps his American contempt for space rendered the wonder less. At any rate, his coming was a great pleasure. He was almost a brother-in-law to Wilmet, and had belonged to old days in her life, and he was intermingled with John's time of courtship at Bexley, so that to both he was like a relation; and Mr. Harewood was much relieved by his promise to remain comparatively within reach so long as it was possible that he could be of use to Wilmet or her convalescent, as they durst not yet term the bridegroom.

So, as John declared, the wedding was graced by representatives of all quarters of the world. It was on African soil, between two Europeans, and one spectator came from Asia, another from America, to say nothing of the lesser distinctions of France, Germany, Greece, Egypt, and Arabia, nor of the mingling of Aztec, Spanish, American, and English blood in the veins of Ferdinand Travis.

Bizarre as were the conditions, the marriage scene was very solemn and touching. It had proved impossible to wait for Christmas Day, as had been wished; so the 21st of December had been chosen, and the time, the cool early morning, before the heat of the day, and when light could be let in without glare or scorching, such as the noontide even of mid-winter brought.

The room was arrayed as on Sundays, not without thought of the first Paschal Feast—kept at this very place and round about it—and Mr. Harewood had robed himself, and brought out the preparations he had made in case he should arrive in time for his son's last Communion Feast, but which now served for that of his marriage.

John had so far decorated himself that he had caused M. Spiridione to trim his hair, and shave all but his habitual red moustache. There was not much possibility of alteration in his spare, freckled, sunburnt face; and his condition was chiefly evident in the prone motionlessness of his figure on the water bed, covered by a bright striped silk quilt, outside which lay one wasted hand, still scarred and stiff. He was striving to be calm and passive; but every now and then his fingers twitched, and the muscles of his face quivered with strong emotion, so that the doctor, standing behind in military uniform, with moustaches waxed into standing out like a cat's, was anxiously watching him. Krishnu, resplendent in white, red, and gold, was on the other side, with an English Prayer-book, and over a chair his master's uniform coat and medals, of which he would not be denied the display. There too was the Greek, in his unbecoming Frank courier dress, and a few spectators who had crept in at the unclosed door for the strange sight of the English wedding.

Wilmet's matter-of-fact nature and freedom from self-consciousness were great auxiliaries to her composure. Living always in the work at hand, severance from home did not come prominently before her, and still less the strangeness of giving herself, on her own responsibility, in a foreign land, to one who could scarcely raise a finger to accept her, and whose life hung on a thread. Of the lookers-on she never thought; she could only recollect that she was qualifying herself for the entire charge of John, and the only eyes she thought of were that one pair of pale greenish-hazel ones, but for those she took as much pains as Alda had done to face a world of gazers.

The snowy soft flow and straight folds of the muslin, beneath the green wreath on her classical braids of light brown hair, far better became the straight outline than the glossy satin, lace flutter, and formal wreath, of the London bride. The eyelids cast down, the heightened carnation, and trembling lip, rendered her grand beauty as modestly tender as it was majestic, when Ferdinand Travis led her forward, followed by the sober-suited Deaconess, by Madame Spiridione in a Parisian cap, and her little boy in full Greek costume.

Poor Fernan! he had eagerly undertaken the service he was to render to Wilmet, but it must have been a sad reminder of his own vanished hopes; and as he led her forward, his slight but fine form, noble cast of features, and clear dark colouring, so fully equalled her in good looks, that he seemed a more fitting match for her than the feeble helpless bridegroom, never at his best *extrêmement beau*.

However, no such thought crossed the minds of the parties most closely concerned as Wilmet knelt by the bedside—knelt at times when she ought to have stood, or her hand would not have been within the reach of the poor weak one over which her long soft fingers seemed to exercise cherishing guidance, with that sense of power and protection she had been used to wield through life. But though her hand was the firmer, and less nervous, it was a much stronger, clearer, steadier voice than could have been looked for, as if manly tenderness overcame all physical prostration, in which John Oglandby took Wilmet Ursula to be his wedded wife, rising into power and energy, as though even then the impulse of guarding, protecting, supporting, love were strengthening him; and Wilmet, on the other hand, quiet and steadfast though she was, had her eyes swimming in tears, which now and then stole down and dropped unawares on his coverlid, and the tone, though not broken or faltering, was low and choked with intensity of purpose and of prayer. 'Till death us do part,' which he had said so gravely and steadily, came from her with nearly failing breath, as though the words almost took away her resolution.

But the Psalm and the Blessing brought back her calmness, and there had never been any trembling in the hand that held her husband's; there was only thankful affection in the eyes that gazed at him while she still knelt on, and all left the chamber except the faithful friend and faithful servant, who were to share with the newly-married pair the holiest of feasts. And strangely enough, if Wilmet and her home were closely interwoven with Ferdinand Travis's first admission to Christian privileges, it had been Major Harewood's example and occasional words that had first brought the teaching imbibed in a Mission school to bear the fruit of true faith and confession thereof in Krishnu.

So it was a really happy and peaceful wedding-day in that strange far-away land; and John seemed rather the better than the worse for the exhilaration of spirits, and the sense of secure possession he had gained. He was so much delighted with Wilmet's bridal white, that he grumbled if she tried to put on her former dresses, and her first personal expense was the keeping up her stock—he loved so well to see her moving about or hovering over him in her clear pure white folds.

They were quite sufficient for one another; and Mr. Harewood left them by the next westward train. Ferdinand went to see him on board the Alexandrian steamer, and then continued to circulate in the haunts of travellers, for the chance of Edgar having joined a Nile boat, or being sketching among the tombs of the Thebaid. Every now and then he reappeared at Rameses to report how some *barbe blonde* he had been hunting down turned out fiery red; and to communicate his hopes in some other direction. Suez was inquired through in vain; and he could not learn that any one of the name or description had gone to India. Indeed, that country seemed less likely to attract a man of Edgar's tastes than the picturesque and historical Levant; and his artist powers and charm of manner made it not unlikely that he might have been engaged to make sketches.

One hope they had, which died away. The gentleman from the Consulate mentioned that a party of vocalists had been giving concerts of national melodies to the European population at Cairo and Alexandria; and the description reminded Wilmet of last year's meteors. Indeed, it proved on inquiry that Stanislas and Zoraya Prebel were really among them, and that they had gone forward to the East, making a tour of the British dependencies; but when Ferdinand had with difficulty obtained a sight of an old programme, and a description of the performers, it was only to convince himself that Edgar could not have been among them. There was no name like his, and the songs that might have been his were sung at the very time when his *alibi* could be proved at Rameses.

CHAPTER XXXII.

THE NID D'AVIS.

'It is called—I forget—*à la* something which sounded
Like alicampane, but in truth I'm confounded,
What with fillets of roses and fillets of veal,
Things *garni* with lace and things *garni* with eel,
One's hair and one's cutlets both *en papillote*,
And a thousand more things I shall ne'er have by rote.
I can scarce tell the diff'rence, at least as to phrase,
Between beef *à la Psyche* and curls *à la braise*;
But in short, dear, I'm tricked out quite *à la Française*.'
Moore.

One forenoon, soon after the end of the Christmas vacation, Robina Underwood was seated at her desk, working deeply at the solution of a quadratic equation; when from the far-off end of the schoolroom arose that peculiar hushed choked giggle, that no one ever ascribed to any cause but some prank of Angela's, more especially on the mornings devoted to her natural enemy, 'the professor of the exact sciences,' as he called himself; who was in fact a stop-gap in the absence of the University man usually employed.

Robina knew that the more concerned she showed herself the more madcap tricks were played, and she disturbed herself little about the commotion, aware that she should only too soon learn the cause, if it were anything out of the common way. So she did. In the quarter of an hour of clearance and recreation before dinner, plenty of information reached her, couched in boarding-school *lingua franca*.

'Ah! Rouge Gorge, vous ne savez pas ce qu'elle a fait.' 'Une fille delicieuse.' 'Une Alouette superbe, tout a fait Angélique!' 'Et M. le professeur! Comme il etait dans un cire!' (These phrases being chiefly the original coinage of Angela herself.)

71

'*Mais qu'est ce que c'est qu'elle a fait?*' demanded the elder sister, with small sympathy with these ecstasies.

''*Le plus exquis!*' and with volubility far outrunning composition, and resulting in a wonderful compromise of languages, that a new book had been produced out of which the class had been required to work what was described as '*un somme dans le règle detrois tout à tort et à travers; detestable, horrible, vilain,*' to which a chorus chimed in, '*vilain, vilain vilainissimo.*' The question was, If twelve reapers cut a field in thirty hours, how long would it take sixteen? As a matter of course, all but a few mathematical geniuses at the head of the class had multiplied by 16 and divided by 12, and made the result 40; but Angela, having wit enough to see that this '*n'avait pas le sens commun,*' instead of trying to make out the difficulty, had written at the bottom of her slate, what was hastily transcribed for Robina's edification—

> Forty, by the best time-keepers.
> Reapers? I should call them sleepers,
> Lazy heapers, idle creepers,
> And their peepers should be weepers!

All who obtained a sight of this stanza became forthwith weepers with suppressed giggle, and there was a stern, 'Your slate, if you please, Miss Angela Underwood.'

The effects were expressed with all the force the language could convey. '*Il etait comme un lion enragé—il écumait à la bouche—il disait qu'il appellerait Mlle. Fennimore*'—a far greater climax, but after all he only sentenced her to read the rule aloud to the class. No sooner had she touched the book than she dashed it from her, '*Comme la poison*'—'*comme un couleuvre,*' declaring it to be a shocking one, unfit to touch, so that of course the sums came wrong. Most of her audience, all girls under thirteen, for she was the arithmetical lag of the school, had no notion why the title 'Colenso's Arithmetic' so excited her—the master had none at all; and while Angela, who was not for nothing sister to a church candle or to a gentleman of the press, declaimed about heresy and false doctrine, he thought it all idleness and wilfulness, and fulfilled the threat of a summons to the authorities. By them the matter was a little better understood; but the disobedience was unpardonable, even if the testification against the author were not merely a veil for dislike to the problem, and the sentence had been solitary confinement until submission. From this Angela was so far distant, that as the young ladies marched in to dinner her voice might be heard singing the Ten Little Niggers.

It was an unlucky time, for the next day was Marilda's twenty-fifth birthday, and she was going to keep it in a way of her own, namely, by taking the whole family of children of a struggling young doctor, over the Zoological Gardens. It was not a very good time of year, and Marilda's first proposition had been the pantomime, but the mamma had religious scruples about theatres, and it turned out that the Zoo was the subject of their aspirations; so Marilda, securing her two young cousins to help her in the care and entertainment of her party, hoped for fine weather.

From this party of pleasure Angela must of course be debarred, unless she yielded; and her sister was sent to reason with her, but this had no better effect than usual. Robina was a thoroughly good industrious girl, who neither read the papers nor listened to controversy; she cared most for heresies as possible subjects for her examinations in Church history, and had worked problems innumerable out of Colenso. So all she gained was a scolding for consenting to the latitudinarianism that caused correctly-done sums to make sixteen reapers tardier than twelve; and the assurance that no allurement, no imprisonment, should make the young martyr consent to truckle to a heretic. Angela looked exactly like Clement as she spoke, except for an odd twinkle in her eye, as if she were quizzing herself.

Robina knew herself to be too much wanted to give up the expedition, and was sent for by Marilda in time to assist in giving the five children the good dinner that was an essential part of the programme, and which reminded Robin of Mr. Audley's picnic. One little boy, however, seemed bewildered and frightened by the good things, and more inclined to cry than to eat; but he would not hear of being left behind, though, when arrived at the Gardens, he could give but feeble interest even to the bears, and soon fretted and flagged so much that Marilda thankfully accepted Robin's offer of taking him home in a cab, and waiting for her till her rounds with the other children should be finished.

It turned out that he had had a headache and a 'bone in his throat' all the morning, but had kept them a secret of misplaced fortitude; and when Robina had taken him home, wrapped up in her cloak, trembling, shivering, and moaning, she found the mother with the yearling child much in the same condition on her lap; and she was rendering kindly help in putting them to bed (for of course the nurse had a holiday), when the father came home, driven in by a sore throat and headache of his own, and forced to pronounce, as best he could, that they were in for an attack of scarlatina.

Here was a predicament! Robina had never had the fever, nor had any of her home brothers and sisters in any unimpeachable manner. She could not stay where she was, and what would either the school or Mrs. Underwood do with her? After such consideration as the little boy allowed her to give, she wrote a note of warning to Marilda, to be handed to her at the door, and another to be sent on to Miss Fennimore. The note was handed to the frightened hurried maid, and duly given. There was a moment's pause, and then the children were left in the carriage, and Marilda walked into the house. Then there took place what could only be described as a scrimmage. Marilda was determined on carrying all the four home with her, out of the way of the infection, but the mother was persuaded that they must have it already, and would not part with them. If they were ill in another house she would not be able to go to them, and the thought distracted her. The father was appealed to, and between the same dread of separation and scruples about carrying infection farther, he gave sentence the same way, and Marilda was most unwillingly defeated.

She could only take away Robina; and Robina submitted pretty quietly to her decision that her quarantine must be spent at Kensington Palace Gardens. In the first place, Marilda protested that she had had 'it;' and though 'it' turned out only to have been a rash, and it was nearly certain that Mrs. Underwood would be in despair, yet Robin really knew not where else to go, and Marilda was quite as old as the constituted authorities at home. All Robin could insist on was on remaining in the carriage till Mrs. Underwood had heard the state of the case; but considering the rule that Marilda exercised, this precaution was of little use. In five minutes she was called upstairs, a note was sent to Brompton, and she had to make up her mind to a full fortnight of quarantine—and what was worse, of lack of appliances for preparing for the Cambridge examination, her great subject of ambition.

Neither Mrs. Underwood nor Marilda could suppose that it was not a treat and consolation to a schoolgirl to get a holiday; they were as kind as possible, but oh! the dullness of the place! It was much more dull than in Cherry's visits, for she had her own study and her own purpose, and Alda and Edgar enlivened the house; but now Marilda had no pursuits save business and charity, and was out many hours of the day, there was hardly a book to be found, and Mrs. Underwood expected her to sit in the drawing-room and do fancy-work. Meantime she was losing precious time, her chances of marks and prizes at Brompton were vanishing, to say nothing of her preparation for the Cambridge examination, on which her whole start in life might depend.

The doctor's family were all very ill; but she could not think nearly so much about them as of the music she tried to practise, and the equations she set herself, while she reckoned the extra work by which she could make up for lost time. Alas! on the very last day of this weary fortnight, conscience constrained her to mention an ominous harshness of throat; and by the evening she was wishing for nothing but that Wilmet were not in Egypt.

However, Marilda proved herself far superior as a nurse to what she was as a companion. She would not be kept out of her cousin's room, and with Cherry's old friend, Mrs. Stokes, took such good and enlightened care, that the infection did not spread, and Robina, though ill enough to be tolerably franked for life, was in due time recovering so favourably as to be very miserable and wretched about everything, from the Cambridge examination to her own ingratitude. She never had felt so like Cherry in her life.

It was hard to say which was worst, her banishment from school or from home, or the doleful idea presented to her by that kind promise of carrying her to be aired at Brighton for six weeks! It was the loss of the whole term, and all the prizes she had set her heart upon, nor was there any one to sympathise with her, as she turned her head away and hoped no one would find out the tears in her eyes.

It was just as it had been with Lance, she thought; prevented from sharing in the competition that might have won him success in life. And how sweetly and brightly Lance had borne it; but then he had never reckoned on the success she had hoped for, and besides, her nature had not the surface *insouciance* that had helped him. She had more industry, more ambition, more fixity of purpose, and the disappointment was proportionably severer.

Poor child! she lay on the sofa, as Mrs. Underwood supposed, fast asleep, but really trying to work out in her brain puzzling questions, why it was good to be disappointed when one does one's best, why the race is not to the swift, nor the battle to the strong, trying to accept her failure as wholesome mortification to ambition, recalling 'Under Wode under Rode;' but rebelliously feeling that this did not comfort her greatly in the very unnecessary picture her fancy proceeded to draw of herself, with attainments fit for nothing but a nursery governess or school drudge, or a companion to some one duller still than Mrs. Underwood, magnanimously releasing William Harewood from all ties to so inferior a being, and proceeding to die of a broken heart, and to shed a few tears over her own grave; or maybe the still more melancholy conviction, that there were no ties at all that he would or ought to remember.

A postman's knock made her start, and Mrs. Underwood lament that she had been awakened. Presently she was sitting up, receiving a long, narrow, green, thin letter, at which she looked with exultation and delight all over the visage lately so doleful. 'O Mrs. Underwood, it is from John himself——dear John!' was the cry, as her eyes lighted on the address; and her pleasure amounted to rapture as she read the closely-written sheets, in that clear strong neat handwriting that had hitherto always been Wilmet's monopoly.

Alexandria, March 20th.

MY DEAR ROBINA,

I hope this may find you as it leaves me at present, a thankful convalescent, and able to think of undertaking a journey with more motive force in your own person than I can yet boast. My good little French doctor has unlimited faith in the healing virtues of the Pyrenean baths, he being Gascon born, and has even volunteered to help us on our way thither when going home for his holiday—a chance too good to be lost. Malta must be our first stage; and if, as I am told to hope, I can get my sick leave extended, after being sat upon by the doctors there, we shall go on to Bagnères, where we hope to arrive about the last week in April. We think you had better meet us there. Miss Underwood will see about arranging an escort for you; Wilmet is writing to her about it. She also desires that you will rig yourself out afresh, bringing nothing you have used while laid up; and you had better likewise provide the stock of books the Cambridge dons advise, as we shall be very quiet and stationary for some time, and I will gladly do my best to help you, unless modern lights have gone quite beyond the capacities of the R.E.

You see by my date that we have made our first move. Chenu was anxious to get us away from Rameses before the Egyptian plagues should have become rampant, and after Wilmet had found a scorpion curled amiably up on my pillow, she was ready for an immediate start. So, amid the shrieks of the Arabs and tears of the entire establishment, I was carried by Travis and Krishnu to the station, and deposited in a horse-box, that I fancy occasionally transports a harem, our host weeping and kissing Wilmet's hands to the last moment. Poor people! they treated us with uniform kindness. If you can make inquiries about the price of a dinner-service, write me the result; it is a sort of testimonial that might be convenient as well as appropriate.

Here, in this great hotel, we are no longer No. 1, but simple units, and find it so much less enlivening, and more common-place, that we even regret the nightly laughter of the hyenas. I want Wilmet to join a party who are going to pay their respects to the Sphinx; but she will not hear of it, even under the care of Fernan Travis, who has grown quite familiar with that venerable animal. He is an admirable squire for her (Mrs. H——, I mean, not Mrs. S——,) at the *table d'hôte* and is altogether as excellent a fellow as ever lived. I am much struck with the ripening he has undergone since we were together at Bexley, and his deeply conscientious views of his very trying and difficult position. He means to see us off for Malta, and then to make his way to Jerusalem for Easter, for the chance that the throng may attract poor Edgar. Never was search more indefatigable. Wilmet sends her love, but does not write, as she has letters in hand to Felix and to Miss Underwood.

Hoping to see your face as round as ever before a month is over,

Your affectionate brother,
J.O. HAREWOOD.

Write to us at Malta whether you can come, and we will either write or telegraph to you when to start.

On a separate page were directions for the journey; and a cheque was enclosed, the first Robina had ever received, providing amply for journey, outfit, and books.

An hour before, the journey to Brighton had seemed a terrific fatigue. Now a journey to the Pyrenees was only delicious! Her happiness and gratitude were unspeakable. This was not banishment—this was not loss of time—this was perfection!

Wilmet's letter to Marilda, which came at the same time, was a far more anxious one. She described her husband as certainly better, but still with three unconquerable wounds, on shoulder, hip, and knee, that kept him helpless and prevented him from regaining strength. He was always a bad sailor, and she extremely dreaded the voyage; yet it was impossible to remain in the Egyptian climate, for already the heat was fearfully exhausting, and this long, cheerful, well-written letter must not deceive those at home, for it had been written in the cool of the evening, when he always revived, but for the greater part of the day he could scarcely speak or look; and she cautioned Robina against reckoning too much on the Pyrenean journey, since if the military authorities would not give John his leave without his presenting himself in England, they must try some sea-side place there. John's hopeful plans always ran on so fast whenever he was feeling a little better. However, Wilmet herself was very eager to have Robina, who she thought would be a great amusement and occupation to him, and was only puzzled about the escort, since Felix could hardly spare the time, and Clement was in the final agony of preparing for his degree.

This however was settled by Marilda's offering her own maid, who was a practised traveller; and not long after arrived the final intimation. All had been made right at Malta; and Robina, who had by this time had leisure to change her skin, and gather her strength, was to start at once for Bagnères.

She was not allowed any parting with Angela, or any of those at home. It was safer otherwise, and not worth the risk, she was told, and there was nothing to do but submit; and very much alone in the world did she feel when she stood on the deck of the Folkestone boat, with the black-silk maid as her only protector. It was a great plunge into the vast unknown for one solitary little schoolgirl!

Behold! A hand was held out to her, a merry pair of yellowish green eyes twinkled, a wide mouth smiled, a greeting was in her ears: 'That's right, Bobbie! I thought you'd be for this boat.'

'Willie! O Willie! You are crossing? How nice! But you shouldn't touch me.'

'Bosh! I had it long ago! Are you well and jolly?'

'Quite well, thank you. You are really coming?'

'Ay, I thought I'd run over to see Jack, and how Wilmet figures as a bride; and it is a good speculation to get you to do all the French.'

'If I can; but here's Marilda's maid, a perfect traveller's book of dialogues. Mrs. Purle—here is Major Harewood's brother, who is going the same way.'

A gentleman was not an unwelcome sight to Mrs. Purle, who was used to depend on couriers, and who entreated him at once to enforce attention to certain luggage about which she was distressed.

And to Robina, he was simply the most delightful sight in the world. After six weeks of the flatness and tedium of those good ladies in Kensington Palace Gardens, a little youthful brightness, fresh too from home, would have been like the pure sea wind after dull London air, even if it had not been, of all people, Willie, Willie Harewood himself, timing his journey on purpose to escort her!

True, there were always two sets of feelings going on within her; one when she was actually concerned with or about him, when the common-place aspect overcame the remembrance of that evening by the river-side, and left only a pleasant companionship of long standing, with the freedom of family connection and acknowledged preference; the other, when he was out of sight and hearing, and was the standing romance of her life.

It was not a wholly untroubled romance, for she was not certain of her duty. Their promise had been exchanged when they were such children, that it would be ridiculous to mention it, and it might be equally absurd to dwell on it; yet her mind could not help attaching weight to it, and questioning whether her secrecy might not be a fault. Yet it would be unfair, as well as absurd, to avow seriously nonsense three years old, and without any further advance on his part. Without any? That was the question that recurred over and over again to the poor little heart, whenever romance got the upper hand, the heart that *would* one moment yearn, at another fail, at another bound! It was avowed that Willie was very fond of her, and his sisters made that fondness one of their standing jokes; but when Robin remembered the enforced reticence with regard to Wilmet, that was no good sign, and she could never discover whether he remembered the sixpence they had not broken. It was no desirable state of suspense, this consequence of having innocently listened to premature playing at lovers' vows; and though good sense and modesty might mitigate the evil, that very conscientiousness gave her the more to endure.

However, the pain was all in private, and private moments were few, and encroached on by sleepiness and struggles to write letters. They went on too fast for more than fleeting views from the train, only at Paris, after the *table d'hôte* Willie was urgent for a stroll in the gas-lit streets, and on Robina's demur, appealed to Mrs. Purle's good-nature, and brought her out, tired as she was, but enjoying the delight of the two happy young things.

It was too late for sight-seeing, but little recked they; the wonder of the city, then so great and gay, was quite enough for them; the long illuminated arcades of the streets, the masses of trees in their young foliage in the Tuileries gardens, the unaccustomed sounds—thundering omnibus, rushing cabriolet, neighing, shrieking horses, and high-pitched clamour of tongues, filled them with exhilarating amusement. Then the people! Maid-servants in quaint white caps, stately *sergents-de-ville*, soldiers marching to change guard, with clanging bands, knots of talkers gesticulating, parties sitting out on the pavement at the cafés—all was so new and queer, and it was so wonderful to be there with only Will, that Robina could hardly believe she was herself!

Above all, the shop windows! How they lingered and admired, like the frank-hearted children they were! Everything looked so enchanting on those slopes—photograph, confectionery, porcelain, millinery, or jewellery. Oh! the raree-show those trinket-shops in the

Rue Rivoli were to them, as they gazed at the wonderful devices—those earrings and brooches, as flies, as beetles, as fishes, shrimps, and acrobats. At last they came on a set where the earrings represented a little silver bird hovering, and the brooch a gold wicker nest with three pearl eggs, and the same birds standing over it, and Robina's cry of admiration was instantly replied to with—

'You must have those, I vow!'

'Nonsense! they must be frightfully dear.'

'I don't care; you are the bird that must have that nest.'

'But it is earrings!'

'Well!'

'I don't wear earrings.'

'That's no reason you never should.'

'No, no; Wilmet would not like it, and Mamma never did. It is making holes in oneself to wear useless ornaments in,' said Robin, hurrying out her remonstrance without choice of words.

'And the other thing, with the two birds—is that for your nose?'

'No, a brooch.'

'You wear brooches. You have on a thing like a calf's eye.'

'My poor onyx—for shame!' said Robina, not confessing that it was her sole possession in that line.

'Then you shall have those two cockyolly birds.'

'No, indeed. It is a set, and they won't break it.'

'Then Grace shall have one bird, and Lucy the other.'

'Each one earring—you ridiculous boy!'

'And wear them by turns! Come in, and ask the price prettily.'

'No, I sha'n't.'

'I thought you were to speak French for me?'

'Only when I approve.'

'Then here goes!'

And Robin, who was afraid to stand in the street without him, heard him asking, '*Quoi est le prix de ce nid d'avis?*'

Fortunately, or unfortunately, it was a bi-lingual shop, and the purchase was conducted in English; the brooch was separated from the earrings, the change made right, and the little box containing the treasure thrust upon Robina, who could only twit the donor with his *nid d'avis*.

'*Avis* not the French for a bird? If it is not, it ought to be. I thought one only had to speak Latin through one's nose and bite off the end.'

'General rules are dangerous of application in particular instances. There's the first hatch for you out of your nest of advice.'

'If you hatch advice for me, I'll take it.'

'That's a pretty considerable engagement!' said Robina, lightly.

'Your eggs of advice ain't rotten like some folk's.'

'They won't be pearls like these!'

'How do you know? My eyes, Bob, there goes a regular old Dominican, looking just as if he was got up for a charade. What a place this is, to be sure! and how hard to fancy that it is but a few hours from home after all!'

The gift and the few words after it had brought Robina's outer and inner worlds unusually near together; and when she opened her little box in her room, she caught herself kissing the silver birds in a strange thrill of pleasure and yet of doubt whether Wilmet would think she ought to have accepted it.

The long, long journey ended in mazy sleep through the diligence part of the transit, all in the dark, but with a dim consciousness of wheels, voices, and bumps. It seemed quite the middle of the night, and far too troublesome to move, when at length she was extracted by William rather than by her own volition, and something in a white turban appeared before her dazzled eyes in the lamp-light, as stumbling with weariness, she was supported and guided by her companion's arm, and reviving in the cool night air, heard that 'it was but a few steps, and the Mem Sahib was waiting.'

Then a great door opened, and showed a flood of light intercepted by a tall figure, and then Robina found a pair of soft arms round her, and nestling close to a well-known bosom, felt the infinite relief of being off her own mind and with her who had ever been the very core of home!

'My Robin, my Robin! Is she quite well? Oh, this is nice! And Willie—' giving her sisterly kiss. 'Yes, we had your letter, we were so glad. Mrs. Purle, how are you? thank you for bringing her! There's some tea ready—Krishnu will show you.'

And then they were in the sitting-room, with its bright lamp and blazing wood fire, and thorough English tea, and Wilmet in muslin and blue ribbons, as they had never seen her but on rare gala days.

'How's John?' began William, rather blank at missing him.

'Much better—so much better, but I told him not to think of seeing you to-night. He has been in bed more than two hours. And oh, my Bobbie, you ought to be there too!'

'Yes, she's tired to death,' said Will; 'we have been going since eight last night.'

She really was too much tired to speak or eat, and passively submitted, scarcely conscious where she was—nay, at some moments thinking herself in the old nursery in St Oswald's Buildings, in the comfort of being undressed, cossetted, and put to bed by the hands most natural to her since infancy. After a time of weariness too great for right sleep, and of a strange confusion about confessions to Wilmet, she at length lost the feverish element of over-fatigue, and slept soundly till she opened her eyes to realise a little festooned bed in an alcove, white curtains over the windows, strange new street-cries outside, and within, her own box, a sofa, a table, a chair, and a fine clock, which could not be going, for it pointed to half-past ten!

As she was sitting up and looking in vain for some means of washing, the door gently opened, and that dear motherly face looked in. 'Awake at last, my poor little tired bird?'

'O Wilmet, is it really so late?'

'Of course! never mind. Willie is just as bad; there are his boots outside his door still. There, drink this coffee before you dress. Yes, you want it; you could take nothing last night. Let me look at you; are you quite rested, and fit to get up?'

'Oh yes!' energetically; 'if only I saw how to wash!'

Wilmet laughed, and opened a cupboard-door, displaying the requisites, even including a tub, which she had found and purchased individually. After the ablutions she could judge of her little sister better, and thought the cheeks not greatly wanting in their roundness, or healthful freshness; but all the brown hair had been cropped, and the short wavy curls added to the childish contour. It was a prim little schoolgirl figure that stood there in a grey carmelite dress, and black silk apron.

'My dear, have not you a bow or bit of ribbon? John likes colour.'

'Only a blue ribbon for Sunday.'

In a moment Wilmet had hurried to her own room, a rose-coloured snood was round the brown hair, and a little Maltese cross hung by another pair of rosy streamers round her neck.

'And a brooch, my dear. Haven't you one—what's in this box?'

'O Wilmet, I wanted to ask you about it. Willie would buy it for me at Paris!'

'How pretty! There, that will do nicely. Are you ready? John is quite eager for you, now he is at his best.'

So Robin, who meant to have put her question in a very different form, was hurried away, *nid d'avis* and all, and the next moment found herself in the sitting-room, where on a couch near the fire, but commanding a view from the window, lay, half sitting, her new brother, holding out both hands to draw her to receive his kiss of welcome. 'Well, Robin, quite recruited after the scarlet enemy? So you were dead beat yesterday!'

'O John, I did not mean to be so late!'

'You are beforehand with that lazy brother of mine, who tacked himself to your skirts. Just in time for *déjeûner*, a thing always going on here. Is the young Sahib awake, Zadok?' as the white figure with a brown face entered to lay the cloth, but it was at once followed by the young gentleman, exclaiming, 'Good morning, Wilmet; I beg your pardon—I'd no notion of the time.' Then coming to a sudden stand-still, 'Holloa, Jack!'

'Holloa, Bill,' replied John, imitating the tone, with a smile. 'How's my father?'

'As—as usual! But, Jack, old fellow, how—how small you look?' said Will, shocked and overcome into small choice of words, as he stood with a frown of dismay on his face.

'Boiled to rags, like the policeman in the Area Belle,' said John, trying to laugh him into reassurance. 'Did you expect the process to have the same effect as on a pudding?'

'But my father said he was not altered!' said William, turning to his sister-in-law.

'He has gone through a good deal since then,' said Wilmet, wistfully. 'And the sun-burning has had time to fade. If you had seen him before we came into this mountain air, you would only wonder at him now.'

'Besides,' added John, 'you are grateful to a man for looking anyhow at all when he lies like a mummy. And now he is dressed like his fellow-creatures, you compare him with them.'

'And that is only since we have been here,' said Wilmet, proudly.

'And how are they all at home, Bill? How's the mother?'

'Oh, all right; and she kindly insisted on my taking out some Liebnitz to you in case you couldn't get anything in these French places. She fairly took me in this time, and I suggested it was rather tough for you under present circumstances, but she said that couldn't be, for she got it warranted in tins at the competitive.'

'Dear mother!' said John, as they all shrieked with amusement; 'I don't think Wilmet will be at all ungrateful to her. I am afraid the commissariat is a weight on her mind. Now, what do you think of her looks?' demanded John, rather anxiously.

'Well, she is always—just Wilmet—but she is thinner, and not so pink as she used to be,' said the uncomplimentary Will.

'Of course,' said Wilmet, as John's eyes turned on her the more solicitously, 'after the heat of those last weeks in Egypt; and Malta was almost worse, except that there was not the constant warfare with the flies that just kept one alive.'

'It is very warm here,' said Robina, who had left London in an east wind.

'We find it cold up here in the mountains,' said Wilmet, who wore a velvet jacket and thick glossy striped blue and brown silk. 'Dr. Chenu warned us to prepare.'

'Yes,' said John, 'so I sent her out at Marseilles to fit herself out, and what does she come home with but one lugubrious black silk, which she tried to persuade me was the correct thing!'

'And then,' said Wilmet, 'the next thing I found was his bed spread all over with patterns, and it was all I could do not to have enough to clothe all Bexley. I was obliged to get a new box as it is, and luggage is frightfully expensive on these French lines.'

Willie and Robin, though both in some awe of Wilmet, could not help smiling at a speech so exactly like herself, as to remind them of Lance's mischievous averment that she must have married John because it was so much cheaper than sending any one out.

Those four happy tongues, how much they had to tell and to ask, about the two journeys and the two homes, all mixed up together, Bill's tidings being the most recent, and all that was known by letter becoming much more real and interesting by word of mouth.

Cherry? Yes, Cherry was very well, and had no end of a picture for the exhibition, of the maiden spinning for her lover's ransom—she had studied the maiden from one of Ernest Lamb's sisters, but she had put in exactly her own eyes, poor Cherry! There was a picture of Stella and Theodore upstairs for Wilmet Lance had played his violin to keep Theodore happy while sitting. Oh, and had they heard that Lance had really been asked to take the organist's place? The former one had sent in his resignation, and after the half-year that Lance and the choir had worked together, there was a general desire that he should take the post. Mr. Bevan had even written to request it, at £50 a year instead of £70.

'What a shame!' broke out Wilmet 'I hope Felix did not consent! I had much rather he was not paid at all.'

'That was what Lance wanted, of course,' said Robina; 'he wished to give his music freely, as he does not give up the business.'

'But Felix said he had no desire to give either £20 or £70 a year to my Lady, and that he did not accept her as the Church,' said Will; 'and Miles—old Miles was more rabid than ever he was at the Zoraya; and Lance was in a state bordering on distraction for fear it should go off altogether, and he should undergo torture from a fifty-pounder every Sunday of his life, but my Lady gave in; and Lance reconciles his conscience to the lucre of gain by getting a lesson from Miles once a week, and raising the pay on the biggest of those interminable little Lightfoots.'

'George, the intelligent one, that Cherry used to have up to teach,' interposed Robin, 'so that there's another in the shop to make up for any time Lance spends away from it. And when Fernan's new organ comes, whenever it is finished, it will be such a delight.'

'I hate to see him all the same,' muttered Will, with a frown; but the observation was unheeded, as Robina eagerly told how Theodore had one day gone in with his brothers to the choir practice, where he had been in such a state of bliss, and kept his *lieder ohne wörter* so true that they had taken him regularly first thither and then to church, where he accompanied like a little musical instrument, and at last Mr. Flowerdew could not resist enrolling him in the choir, where, seated in front of Felix, and with 'one of the interminable Lightfoots' as guardian by his side, he was safe from molestation from any teasing freak of the other boys, and however much he might comprehend, there was no doubt that his felicity was perfect.

'It has really altered him,' said Will. 'I did not know him when I saw him in his surplice; and indeed he seems to have got a stimulus altogether, between that and Scamp.'

'Scamp!'

'What, they've not ventured to tell you that they've set up a dog!' and Bill and Bobbie both fell into convulsions, in which the Major joined more moderately, at his lady's demure face of astonishment.

'I suppose it was forgotten, when all the wedding letters were being written,' said Robina, rather guiltily.

'And when the mice no longer expected the cat,' said John.

'No, indeed it wasn't that!' pleaded Robina. 'Lance couldn't help it.'

'It was a votive offering,' said Will 'Lance has never ceased to be little Dick Graeme's demi-god ever since he licked him within an inch of his life for bolting Shapcote's plums. You know those dogs of Mr. Graeme's, Jack—beautiful black retrievers with tan legs and muzzles. One belonged to Dick, and no sooner has she a litter of puppies than he must bring up one for Lance, without a hint to him or any one else, till one day he coolly marched in with his dog at his heels.'

'His father was driving in,' said Robin, 'and had no notion the boy had not settled it all. We were just sitting down to dinner when the bell rang, and there was a wonderful floundering on the stairs, and in tumbled Master Dick with this great black beast padding and sprawling after him. Then, while Cherry stood clutching Lord Gerald in one hand and the back of her chair in the other, much as if it had been a wolf, we heard the pleasing intelligence; "He is for you, Underwood; he is Sal's finest pup, and I brought him up on purpose for you."'

'But Lance was not forced to keep him.'

'We could not turn him out neck and crop; and you can imagine the rapture of Angel and Bear, and Lance wished it so much! Even Cherry did not like to vex the boy, and when she began to talk of Felix and the yard, I thought how it would end. But when she said it would frighten Theodore into fits, the next thing we saw was the two rolling on the floor together, Tedo's arms round the dog, and Scamp licking his face all over, and all that satiny puppy hair on the long ears mixed up with Baby's flax. Cherry made a sketch on the spot, and there was no notion of sending him away after that. I don't know whether Tedo cannot do without Stella better than without Scamp, for they seem to understand one another better, and he is not afraid to go into the garden alone with Scamp, though he never would with Stella. It is quite new life to him.'

'As good a thing as could have been devised for him,' said John.

'Poor dear Tedo! yes, I am glad for his sake,' said Wilmet; 'only I hope they don't have him in the house.'

'Don't they,' said Willie, mischievously; 'didn't I nearly break my neck over the black back of him last Monday!'

'But Lance always combs him,' eagerly interposed Robina.

'Yes, Lance is as dainty about brushing and curry-combing him as he is over his own lark's crest when the ladies are coming for their magazines. Oh, Scamp is a great institution; he walks Cherry out every day, and even Felix can't resist if he makes a set at him.'

'Capital! What, not reconciled yet, Wilmet?'

'Not to having him in the house. I am thinking of Mrs. Froggatt's carpet.'

'Ours, you mean,' said Robin; 'besides, it is drugget.'

'And past praying for,' wickedly added Bill, 'since Bernard and I made a general average of the inkstand and Cherry's painting things at one swoop.'

'Abdicated sovereigns should close their ears,' said John. 'No doubt Constantius' doings much disturbed Diocletian over his cabbages.'

'I hope I was not such a tyrant,' said Wilmet; who, though used to raillery from her brothers, had yet to learn to take it from her husband.

'At least I hope you have retired on a cabbage, *mon chou*,' he said.

She smiled, but turned the subject by explaining that their excellent doctor had not only secured these comfortable rooms on the ground floor till the season should be advanced enough to remove to Barèges, but had recommended them to a *confrère*, and had found, what John added was more difficult to get than the savant, a pony and a wheeled chair, in which he was going out at two o'clock. 'And it is past twelve now,' said Wilmet; 'and you ought to be resting.'

'I'll go and look about, and come back in time to put you in your chair, Jack,' said William. 'Come along, Robin.'

'If you are not tired, Robin,' said Wilmet, 'you had better go out. We can only keep along the road; and John ought to get some sleep before he goes out.'

'The cabbage is well drilled, you see,' said John; but he really did look weary, and Robina was glad enough of the positive command.

Her sister had clearly no notion but of turning the children out to play whenever they were in the way; and for the present that was quite enough to send her down, forgetting everything but the charm of the walk and the companionship.

The fresh sunny spring-tide and mountain air would have been exhilaration and ecstasy in themselves, such as she had never known, even if there had been nothing to see, and no one she cared for at her side. And now the ravine, the pine-clad slopes, the scattered cottages, the rocks, the foliage, the blossoming trees, the picturesque figures, above all, the veritable mountain summits, still glorified by their winter snows, cutting the clear blue sky, filled her with a sense of beauty and wonder, enlarging her whole spirit with a new incomprehensible sensation; and William was altogether lifted out of the hair-brained rattle-pate. His frank-hearted nature had no corner for the affectation of sneering at his own loftiest emotions. It was his first mountain, and he was perfectly overcome by it; he raised his hat with an instinct of reverence, and the tears stood in his eyes as he kept silence at first, and then murmured, 'One seems nearer the Great White Throne!'

'I never guessed it was—oh—that there was such a soul in it!' responded Robina, in low awe-struck accents, as if in a church.

'No words ever gave one a moment's sense of it,' he answered; and then they began revelling in individual admiration, climbing and wandering in oblivion of all but the light and shade, the shimmering torrent and sheer rock, the cloud-like hills and deep clefts, till far on the road below they spied a queer high-wheeled pony-chair, a lady in a broad-leafed flat-crowned hat walking beside it, and the Hindoo's unmistakable scarlet and white in attendance.

'Bless me!' cried Will, leaping up, 'didn't I mean to have carried poor Jack to his chair! Time is nothing in these places!'

'Can we get down to them?'

'Of course! Charge, Chester, charge! Give me your hand, and I'll get you down. I say, Robina,' in a lower, graver tone, 'I'm glad we've had this sight together! We'll never forget it!'

Whatever sentiment might be conveyed in these words ended in as English a view-halloo as ever startled the Pyrenees, causing the party below to look up and wave gestures deprecatory of the headlong descent, which, nevertheless, was effected without the fracture of limbs, though Robin arrived breathless, and panting enough by no means to disdain a seat by John's side. He was looking as happy as a king, in the enjoyment of the mountain air and scenery after his long confinement on the parching Egyptian sands; but it was silent delight, and when Robina had recovered the physical agitation of her descent, she had time to feel the heart-swelling at those words, and the afterthought whether it was a stolen pleasure unless Wilmet fully knew how sweet it was to be sent out with Will.

But speaking to Wilmet was no easy matter. She was engrossed with her husband, and never willingly quitted him for a moment, thinking of nothing but as it regarded him, and viewing his brother and her sister more as means for his entertainment than in their substantial aspect. She did indeed follow Robin to her room that evening, to satisfy herself about the child's health; but just as the desperate struggle to begin on this most awkward of subjects was being made, she fancied she heard John's call, and was gone.

Next morning, not only were the two sent out together while the doctor made his call, but William communicated to her the verses that he had sat up late and risen early to relieve his mind of, beginning with—

'Can we ever forget this day?'

To be sure it was all mountain, and would have suited Lance equally well with herself. It was shown to John as a 'March Hare' contribution, and was destined to the Pursuivant; but did it not begin with *we*, and had she not had the first-fruits? The consciousness grew more precious, the conscientiousness more distressed, till it drove her, in her truth and honesty, to the desperate measure of so decidedly begging for a private interview, that Wilmet came at once, supposing her unwell.

'Oh no, no, but—but I wanted to make sure of its being right. All this about Willie.'

'About Willie? He is in no scrape, I hope?'

'Oh no; only I could not be comfortable without your knowing. Those verses, and—'

'You little goose! How red you have turned! I didn't think you could be so silly.'

'It is not silliness,' exclaimed Robina, hotly; 'he said it.'

'My dear! he must know better. What and when?'

'Long ago. That evening at Bexley, just before Lance went to Vale Leston.'

Wilmet fairly burst out laughing. 'My dear child, how can you bring me here to listen to such nonsense? That sort of children's foolishness is silly enough at the time, but to dwell on it nearly four years after is too absurd.'

'I thought it might be play then,' said Robin, 'and everybody would have laughed if I had told; but it never will quite go out of my head, and now and then he says or does something that makes me think he has not forgotten either, and I thought I ought to tell you.' She spoke low and fast, with averted crimson face.

'You are a good little girl, Bobbie,' said her sister kindly, from an immense matronly elevation; 'but it is a pity anything so foolish and mischievous was ever said to you, and you ought never to have thought of it again. You should have left the boy if he would talk such nonsense.'

'I couldn't. Lance said we must not leave you alone,' murmured Robin.

Wilmet gave her little clear laugh. 'I'm very much obliged to Lance,' she said; 'but I am sorry Willie was inspired with a spirit of imitation.' Then, as the mirror betrayed an unconvinced look, 'Has he said anything to you since?'

'I—I can't tell—you might not call it anything. Only that brooch! O Wilmet, you aren't going to be angry with him—he never said anything direct.'

'I shall say nothing to him without far more reason; I never saw any. At home he talks to Cherry.'

'Yes, but—' she was ashamed to say 'he likes me best,' and it turned into 'Everybody does.'

Which Wilmet could not gainsay; and she went on: 'As to the verses, you have sense to see they mean nothing. Willie likes you, of course, and we are all brothers and sisters now; but as for any more, it is the merest absurdity to think of it, and though you mean to be good, my dear little sister, this is just working up a mountain out of nothing. There can't be a more unlucky propensity than fancying everybody is paying you attention, especially if you are not particularly pretty, and have to be a governess, and take care of yourself!'

'I know I'm not pretty,' said Robin, rather proudly; 'and I never shall expect any one to pay attention to me;' and as Wilmet's smile denoted incredulity after this specimen, '*this* is quite different from anyone else.'

'I should hope so,' said the elder sister. 'There now, Robin, you have done quite right to tell me; and now we'll think no more about it, but go on as usual.'

With this Robina had to be content; and if the incredulity was mortifying, at any rate liberty was sweet, and there was a precious underlying conviction that there was something that, if Wilmet would not see, it was not her fault. Conscience was free to enjoy the most brilliant spring her life had known. Throughout the fortnight of William's stay they were out together nearly all day, sometimes climbing near home, sometimes joining expeditions of English visitors, always sympathising in seriousness or sportiveness, and ever ready to fulfil the sisterly part of beast of burden towards his belongings when he wanted to climb any specially inaccessible place, or smoke with the friends he picked up. She always viewed that fortnight as the most exquisite of her whole life!

There was no sentiment in their last walk; for a brother and sister, who were always in the habit of fastening themselves on every one who was seen going out, stuck to them to their own door; but when Will took possession of two water-colour sketches he had begged from Robina, and announced his intention of framing and hanging them in his rooms, to call up before him what without them would never be forgotten, they won for their artist a thrill of delight such as none of Geraldine's far superior performances had ever obtained for her.

Robin had no one talent in any remarkable degree; her drawing was exact and tasteful, but without genius; none of the Underwood sisters, except Angela, had much voice, and her musical powers were only cultivated at the expense of much diligence; but her general ability, clear-headedness, and intelligence were excellent; and John surprised his wife by observing that he thought she resembled Felix the most of them all, both in countenance and character. Robin's—the round ruddy face of the family—like Felix's defined delicately moulded features and fair colouring! John smiled; he never took the trouble to defend an opinion that Wilmet thought unreasonable, but he contented himself with saying, 'There was a good deal of stuff in the Robin.'

She did not flag when her holiday was over; indeed, there was a quiet purpose in her soul that made her dutiful industry doubly hopeful and pleasant. She had a good master. John's nature was hard-working, and the invigoration of cooler air made want of employment irksome enough to give him great satisfaction in the acquisition of a well-grounded intelligent girl pupil to whom his aid was of real value. Their lessons and their subjects multiplied as his strength increased, and though they had plenty of fun and nonsense over them, Robina soon felt herself making such progress as far more than compensated for the two months she had so much regretted. Wilmet, telling them that some day Robin would know how pleasant it was to have nothing to do with teaching, sat by, stitching at a set of shirts for Clement. It was her ambition, as a parting gift, to provide each brother with a stock; she had made those for Felix and Theodore by John's bedside at Rameses, and to be busy with the 'white seam,' and watch John eager and interested, and daily looking less languid and pinched, was entire happiness to her. The walks and drives became longer, and the neighbour brother and sister complained that Miss Underwood could never be had, and was always absorbed by her hard task-master, whom on her side she thought a far more entertaining companion than they would ever be.

The move to the mountain nest at Barèges was made, but the scheme made in the warmth of their hearts in the spring, of William's spending the long vacation there, was not fulfilled. Two objections stood in the way; first his reading for honours, secondly the cost. He could not afford another trip out of the proceeds of his scholarship, and the Major's means were not so large as not to be seriously affected by such an illness; while as Her Majesty's service had not required his proximity to the engine, he could not obtain compensation for his accident. When Wilmet had come to the understanding of the finances she was to administer, she was startled at the free and open hand which might suit a well-endowed bachelor officer on Indian pay, but would soon drain the resources of a man—very possibly invalided for life, and with a penniless wife. Robin would hardly have had that wonderful cheque, if in Malta her sister had been altogether informed of the balance at John's bankers; and when she was consulted on the possibility of giving Bill a run, her reply was the more conclusive, because, little importance as she attached to Robina's confession, she preferred keeping the youth at a safe distance. Neither examination would fare the better for mutual distractions on Pyrenean crags, and both together they would be far less companionable to John than either separately.

Beginning wedded life in prostrate helplessness, John had been as entirely thought for, managed for, and 'done for,' as Theodore himself, during these earlier months; and when he had a will of his own, it was treated with indulgence as a sick man's fancy, and yielded to or not according to his wife's judgment; but as time went on, there was sometimes a twinkle of amusement on his eye-lashes when he submitted, or withdrew an opinion rather than exert himself for controversy.

CHAPTER XXXIII.

A BOOTLESS BENE.

> "'What is good for a bootless bene?'"
> She answered, "Endless sorrow.'"
> *Wordsworth.*

Geraldine was yet to discover how peaceful and happy was her life. For a year and a half, the words at the head of our chapter—whatever they may mean—had been running in her head. That 'bootless bene' was a thing of sudden stabs and longing heartaches; but Edgar had not been a sufficiently permanent inhabitant to be daily missed, as Wilmet was. He had been a crowning ornament of the fabric of the house, not a stone whose loss made a gap, but rather an ever bright, enlivening, exciting possibility in her life, whose criticism and approval had led her on to art, and trained her talent and taste. She never worked at a drawing without an inward moan, and would almost have lost heart, save that he and the clearance of his name were still her object; but for reliance, support, and fellow-feeling, she had more in the remaining brothers than he could ever have given her. Felix and Lance were precious companions, and Wilmet's departure had left her no time for drooping. Housekeeping began by being a grievous responsibility. Cherry could not bargain like Wilmet, nor go down into the kitchen and toss up something dainty out of mere scraps for her brothers' supper; and when she heard that Zadok Krishnu excelled in curry and coffee, she could only lift up her hands and sigh on the waste of good gifts of cookery upon one Major! Martha was a good faithful servant, but odds and ends did not go so far as they used to do; and Cherry never could, and never did, reduce her bills to the original standard, though she brought them on Saturday nights with such misery and humiliation that Felix was forced to laugh at her, and represent that their pinch of poverty was over, and excessive frugality no longer necessary. His position was now what Mr. Froggatt's had been, and his means, with Lance's payment for board, were quite sufficient to bear the difference, even without Cherry's own, which fully covered the diminution through her want of time and of notability. Waste there was not, profusion there was not; but a certain ease there was, so soon as Cherry had learnt, as Lance said, not to believe they should be in the County Court because they had spent a shilling instead of elevenpence-three-farthings. She felt too that home was comfortable to the others. The anxious stinting, though at times needful, had, as Felix hinted to her, been good for no one. Though praiseworthy and self-denying *when* it was needful, the habit had become cramping to Wilmet herself, and to all the brothers it had been an irritation, endured by some with forbearance, but certainly prejudicial to others.

Nobody was afraid of Cherry; but since all had outgrown the bear-garden age, a sympathetic government was best. *Berserkarwuth* might require King Stork's 'Now, boys;' but when the ruler was a lady, and a lame lady, chivalry might be trusted even in unruly Bernard, who had come to an age when freedom was better for him than strictness.

So had the world gone till the autumn, when Major and Mrs. Harewood had to retreat from their mountain abode, but did not venture on wintering in England. They had made up their minds to winter at Biarritz. John would have preferred Pau, but Wilmet set her face against it, dwelling upon the benefits of sea air; and he yielded, but he would not be baulked of a day's halt there. It was a place he had always wished to see; and he would not defraud Robin of the castle of the Foix, and of the tortoise-shell cradle of *le Grand Monarque.*

He could walk now, but only with a stick, and stooping and halting a good deal. His obstinate hip was still troublesome, and his recovery had been retarded by painful methods of preventing contraction. Nor was it yet certain whether he would ever be fit to return to his corps; and though he moved about the house, and discarded invalid habits, he was still so anxious a charge, that Wilmet was quite justified in her vexation at the charms of the old castle at Pau, where he *would* walk and stand about, admiring and discussing history and architecture with Robina and a clever French priest, lionising like themselves. She did catch her sister, and severely forbid her to make a remark that could protract the survey; but the wicked priest was infinitely worse, and beguiled them into places where the ordinary guide would never have thought of taking them; nor was she certain that her provoking John did not perceive and rather enjoy her agony.

At last she got him safe to the hotel, and into the tiny bedroom opening out of their sitting-room.

'It is much quieter there,' she said, returning. 'I have given him the *Times,* and I hope he will have a couple of hours' rest before the *table d'hôte.*'

'Then, Wilmet, would you come with me? I made out the street, and it is very near,' said Robin.

'What street?'

'Alice Knevett's—Madame Tanneguy. O Wilmet,' as she saw her countenance, 'you know Cherry promised the aunts that we would see about her if we went to Pau.'

'Cherry had no right to make such a promise, and I do not mean to be bound by it. Madame Tanneguy does not deserve notice, especially from us! I should have thought you had had enough of her.'

'But should not I be unforgiving to remember that?'

'It is not a matter of forgiveness, my dear. Her marriage was the best thing that could have happened to us. I am absolutely obliged to her for it; but that does not make her behaviour any better.'

'No; but suppose she was in distress?'

'No reason to suppose any such thing! The man was well to do; and of course she is leading that gay life the *bourgeoisie* do here—at the theatre or out on the *place* all the evening—nothing fit for us to associate with.'

'I don't want to associate, and I only think it right to find out.'

'What does Robin want to find out?' said John, helping himself forward with the table; 'some defender for Jeanne d'Albrêt, whom we have heard so run down to-day?'

'O John! why aren't you lying down?'

'Because I have no taste for being condemned to solitary confinement as a punishment for being beguiled by that Jesuit—not even in disguise. I'm going to write to my father. Aren't you going out again?'

'No,' said Wilmet.

'I thought I heard Robin wanting to find out some one for Cherry. These doors aren't adapted for secrets. What was it, Bobbie?'

'I did not mean to trouble you about it, John,' said Wilmet. 'Do you remember about that unfortunate affair of Alice Knevett?'

'Was it to her that your brother Edgar was attached?'

'Yes. Remember, it was a clandestine affair; and these children were made to serve as tools—that is, Angela was; and though Robina refused, she was involved in the scrape, and suffered so much for it that I should not have thought she would have wished to run after her again.'

'Then she married a Frenchman, did she not?' interposed John.

'Yes. After refusing to give Edgar up, and giving us all an infinity of trouble and annoyance, she suddenly threw him over without a word, and ran away with this Frenchman from Jersey. Yet here are the Miss Pearsons expecting us to call on her, Cherry undertaking that we shall, and this child expecting me to go and do so!'

'Do you know anything about the Frenchman?'

'A sort of commercial traveller, I believe.'

'Agent for a wine merchant,' said Robina. 'Major Knevett said there was nothing against his character. Miss Pearson sent the address; it is in the street at right angles with this, about eight doors off.'

'Well,' said John, 'I do not see how you can refuse to satisfy the Miss Pearsons about her.'

'If she were in a right frame of mind she would write to them. While she treats them with such neglect, I do not see why I should encourage her.'

'Cherry said they thought she was ashamed to begin,' said Robina. 'Miss Pearson wrote severely at first, and now wants very much to make a beginning, and to be sure that Alice is not in distress.'

'I think it ought to be done,' said John; 'it is so near, that you can walk there at once with Robina, and at least inquire at the door. I do not see how you can refuse Miss Pearson.'

Nobody had spoken to Wilmet with authority since her fifteenth year, and she did not recognise the sound.

'I do not choose to notice a person who has behaved like that,' she said; 'Miss Pearson has no right to ask it. Take off your things, Robina; I am going to pack for to-morrow.'

There was no temper in her tone, only the calm reasonable determination that had governed her household and ruled her scholars; and she walked into the other room and shut the door, as on a concluded affair.

John looked round. Robina was standing by the table, wiping away a few tears.

'I do not know what to do, John,' she said 'I wrote to Cherry that we were coming here, and would do this. May I have Zadok to walk with me?'

'Your sister is quite right,' said John. 'I am the fit person to go. How far did you say it was?'

'Eight doors, I counted.'

'Then we need not get a cabriolet,' said John, reaching for his hat and stick.

'But you are so tired!'

'Not at all. If we go early to-morrow, this is the only time for doing it.'

Whether she experienced a spark of triumph, or whether she was merely frightened and uneasy, as her brother-in-law came limping downstairs after her, Robina knew not. She had never seen any one but Fulbert fly in Wilmet's face. Felix might sometimes differ and get his way, but that was by persuasion; and the pillars of the house had always preserved the dignity of concord towards the younglings. It was astounding, even considering that he was her husband. So quietly and easily he did it, too, as if he had no notion what an awful and unprecedented action he was committing. Force of habit made Robin feel as naughty as when Fulbert had led her and Lance to see-saw on the timbers in the carpenter's yard; and she could not divest herself of fears of some such reception as had awaited them on that occasion.

Wilmet packed without misgiving. She had foreseen this perplexity when she endeavoured to avoid Pau, and her mind was too fully made up to be overruled by Miss Pearson's ill-judged yearnings, Geraldine's imprudent promise, Robina's foolish impulse, or John's good-nature. It was not resentment, but disapproval. If Alice had jilted young Bruce she should have held the same course. She would not argue before her little sister; but in private John should be brought to a proper understanding of Alice's enormities, and learn thankfulness to his domestic check on Harewood easiness and masculine tolerance.

Then it struck her that those two were unusually quiet in the next room. Some sounds she had lost in opening drawers and moving boxes; but now all was still, John no doubt writing, and Robin—could she have gone to her own room to cry? The elder sister began to relent, and think the moment come for drawing from her a confession of her wilfulness. She opened the door to seek her. Behold, John was not there. No, nor his hat and gloves! Robina was not in her bedroom! Had they absolutely sallied forth in opposition?

Wilmet had never been so defied by anything too big to kick and scream! She stood aghast. Naughty obstinate Robina had wrought upon John! He ought to have known better! He would knock himself up—inflammation would come on—the wounds would break out again, all because of this complication of foolish pity for that horrid little flirt!

Wilmet's tears gushed, her chest heaved with sobs. Why could he not have attended to her? Withal his words came back to her.

He had distinctly bidden her to go; and had she done so, he would have been safe on that sofa. Bidden? yes, it had been a clear desire, courteously and calmly uttered, but decisive; and only at this moment did it strike her that his orders were more binding on her than those of Felix. He had commanded. She had disobeyed, and he had done the thing himself, to his own inconvenience, not to say peril.

Then came vexation. It was not fair! She would have gone anywhere had she known the alternative. Was it kind or grateful, after her long nursing, to risk himself without warning! Nay, could a man use plainer words than 'You ought'—'You cannot refuse?' Yet was she, as a wife, to obey blindly at the first word, against her judgment? Perhaps Wilmet had never known so hard a moment as this first galling of the yoke of subjection—the sense of being under the will of another. How could he run after that heartless Alice, who had been Edgar's bane and Felix's grief? Who could tell what company she kept, or if she were fit company for Robina? And the creature was so disgustingly pretty that she could deceive any man, even Felix. True; but a little moderation on her own part, and she herself—the prudent matron—might have gone forth with her husband, protecting and protected, instead of exposing Robina's inexperienced girlhood and his manly good-nature to any possible contaminations or deceptions. Oh! would they but come!

There was time for many such cycles of vexation, relenting, self-reproach, and anxiety—ever growing severer towards herself, bitterer towards Alice and Robina, tenderer towards John. It was nearly seven o'clock before the slow thud of the stick, and the steps with one foot foremost, proclaimed the return. Zadok was in the ante-room and let them in. She saw John heated and panting; and reproachful solicitude predominated in her voice as she exclaimed, 'You must stay here. You are not fit for the *table d'hôte*.'

'None of us are,' he answered, in a low, grave tone that startled her; and she then saw that Robina was looking dreadfully white and overcome, and trembling violently.

As the girl met her eye, all was forgotten but the old motherly relation; and there was a rush to hide her face on her, and a convulsive sobbing of, 'O Wilmet! Wilmet!'

'Lay her down! I will fetch something,' said John, moving towards the other room. 'She has held up with all her might.'

'But oh, what is it? That wretched Alice! Bobbie, my dear child, lie down! Don't try to keep it in; cry—no, you can't speak. O John! What is it?—Yes, that's right,' as he brought what was needed from the medical resources always at hand for himself; 'only tell me the worst.'

With his eyes on the measure-glass, and his steady hand dropping the stimulant, he said, in an under-tone, 'A duel! The husband was killed; but it was hardly Edgar's fault.'

Wilmet, with Robina almost fainting on the sofa, was wholly occupied in administering the drops, and bathing the flushed face; and the success of her efforts was shown by another cry of 'O Wilmet!' and then a passion of weeping that shook her whole frame violently.

'That is best,' said John. 'She kept it in bravely.' And as the great *table d'hôte* bell clanged, he went to the door and spoke to Zadok.

As he returned, Robina bounded up, nervously exclaiming, 'O John, lie down, do; you are done up!'

But when strength was needed, he found it. 'Not now, thank you, my dear. I have told Zadok to bring us some dinner. That will make less disturbance. We will get ready, and after that we shall be better able to talk.'

Overwhelmed and crushed, the sisters did just as they were told; but Wilmet turned once, and said as if out of a dream, 'Is there anything to be done? Is he here?'

'Oh no! It was months ago—before I saw him. It was forced on him. You shall hear all presently, dearest.'

The gentle kindness restored her, or rather drove everything out of her thoughts but his flushed, weary, affectionate face, and heavy painful tread; and when he grasped her arm to be helped into the sitting-room, and sank with a sigh into his chair, half the world might have killed the other half, so long as he was neither ill nor angry with her.

'Will you see for that poor child?' he said, as Zadok came up with the three couverts; 'she needs restoration as much as any one.'

Robina had washed her tear-stained face, but was only brought to the table as an act of obedience; and all through the meal John was coercing her into swallowing soup and wine, and Wilmet was watching that he did not neglect his own injunctions. Then disposing of Zadok with some orders about coffee, he lay down on the sofa, but by a sort of tacit motion invited Wilmet to give him one hand to play with, and stroke his hair with the other—his old solace at Rameses—and oh! how much it made up for to her! Robina was now quite restored, and longing to relieve her soul, and the narration chiefly fell to her.

'We soon found the house—one of those immense tall old ones—and we rang, and asked whether Madame Tanneguy lived there. "*O oui,*" said they, "*au quatrième.*" We thought that rather odd; and John asked again if she were English, and the *concierge* said, "Yes, assuredly;" and as someone else came just then, we asked no more questions, only climbed up, up those dreadful stairs, so dirty and so steep. I wanted John to sit down and wait for me, but he would not hear of it.'

Wilmet looked at him with moist eyes, and pressed his hand. 'I was accountable for the child,' he said, smiling. 'Besides, there was nothing to sit upon.'

'At last,' continued Robin, 'we did get to the *quatrième*, and rang; and we heard a little trot-trotting, and the door was opened by a queer little French child, that turned and ran away, calling out, "*Maman, Maman!*" and as we went in—O Wilmet! there rose up, with a little baby in her arms, poor Alice, all in black, with a great flowing white veil, like the widow at Bagnères. She knew me directly, and I believe we both gave a little scream.'

'That you did,' murmured Major Harewood.

'And she said, "You—you! what do you come here for?" I did not know what to say, but I got out something about the aunts; and she answered, "Then you do not know, or you could never have broken in on me and my poor orphans!" Really I thought she was mad with grief, and said the aunts would have sent all the more; but she burst out, "No! no! not his sister—his—the murderer of my husband!" and she began to cry. I only thought still she was mad, but—O John, what was it? Didn't you think so?'

'No, I saw that was not the case; but I thought she took you for someone else, and began to explain; and I think the curiosity of making out who I was, and how we came there, did more to bring her round than anything else.'

'But how could this dreadful thing have been?' asked Wilmet. 'You said it once: but it cannot really be true!'

'Too true, my dear,' said John, 'but with much extenuation. It was last September. He really was with those National Minstrels.'

'Ah!'

'But not by name in the programme,' said Robina. 'She went to the theatre with her husband, and there were Hungarian and German songs; but then when the English ballad began—the Red Cross Knight—the first notes overcame her; she had a *saisissement*, screamed, and almost fainted.'

'Just like her!' exclaimed Wilmet 'Then it was all owing to that?'

'I fear so. Edgar looked up, and when he saw her, he broke down. He began again, and got through the rest of his part; but in the meantime M. Tanneguy had been discovering that he was not Alice's first love.'

'Not by ever so many,' muttered Wilmet. 'And of course she shuffled and shifted off the blame to Edgar.'

'If so, she has suffered for it,' said John, with gentle repressiveness.

'And,' continued Robina, 'whatever she could say only enraged him more; he took her home, then waited for Edgar at the door of the theatre, demanded an explanation, and challenged him. They fought outside the town, and M. Tanneguy was wounded; but they did not think it so bad; and, like a brave Frenchman, he kept up to his own door, so that Edgar might get safe away. On the third day he grew worse, and died! O Wilmet! who could have thought it? How will Felix bear it?'

'Remember,' said John, 'that this was fastened on your brother. I don't, of course, look on it as anything but a crime, but it should not be exaggerated. To be insulted and called to account by a fiery Gascon, when you believe yourself the injured party, cannot be easily bearable; besides, Edgar had had a foreign training, not so alien to duelling as ours, and his associates would expect it of him. For the rest, I think he must have won his enemy's heart, for the poor lady said much of her husband's acknowledgment of his generosity, and desire for his escape. I am sure he might well, if he did half as much for him as he did for me.'

'And he had done this when he touched you,' said Wilmet, shuddering.

'Or I should not be here,' said John. 'My dear,' and he held both her hands, 'I wish I could make you look on it in a different light It was not an assassination. To have refused the challenge would have required a sort of resolution that few men are capable of; above all, when all his surroundings would have expected it of him.'

'What surroundings?' replied Wilmet 'No wonder he could not bear to face your father and me! Poor Edgar! wandering about like Cain! And he was such a dear little boy! Papa used to call him his little King Oberon! Oh! I am glad Papa and Mamma don't know it.' She slipped down on her knees by John's side, hid her face in his pillow, and cried, but softly and gently now.

'I don't think it can be less bad to Felix and Cherry,' said Robina, sadly. 'How can we write to them?'

'We had better not do so till I have learnt more,' said John; 'I shall go to the *bureau de police* to-morrow, and make inquiries, and try to see poor Tanneguy's employer, M. Aimery, who seems to have been the only friend that poor young thing has had.'

'Why did she not write?' asked Wilmet.

'M. Aimery did write to her father,' said Robina, 'but he has left Jersey, and the letter was returned; and as to the aunts, you know Miss Pearson did write sharply once, and Alice always took her strictness for unkindness, and never knew how fond of her the aunts were. Indeed, I fancy she has been too ill and inert to do more than go on from day to day.'

'Has she anything to live on, poor child?'

'Her husband had a small interest in the business, and M. Aimery pays her the proceeds every month—a hundred francs.'

'A hundred francs! four pounds three and fourpence for herself and two children!'

'She had to move up from the nice apartments below to this dismal *quatrième*, only one room, and very little in it; and then she was ill for a long time, and the baby was born; and that took up all the ready money there was left. She has been thinking whether she could get any daily-governess work to do among the English; but then, how can she leave the children?'

'Poor thing!' said Wilmet, 'I must go and see her to-morrow.'

'Do,' said her husband affectionately. 'Considering all things, we had better remain here a few days, had we not?'

'Certainly. I will speak about the rooms. Of course we must do our best for her and those poor children. I hope they are girls.'

'No,' said Robin,' boys—Gustave and Achille. Gustave looks preternaturally wise and solemn, with his black eyes and bullet head; but when his mother cried, he went into such an agony, that John had to show him his watch, and give him his stick to ride on, before we could hear ourselves speak. O John, what work you have done to-day!'

'And you too, Bobbie,' said Wilmet kindly, 'you had better go to bed as soon as you have had your coffee.'

Her head was aching enough to make her glad to take the advice; and when she was gone, John lay still, too weary, and yet too comfortable, for the exertion of going to bed; and he was not far from sleep when Wilmet came back from giving her sister the tender care that the shock demanded.

Bitterness and resistance had long been swept away by those terrible tidings; but Wilmet could not forget that she had offended, and gathering herself into a great effort, she stood by the sofa, dignified, but rather constrained, and said, 'I am very sorry about this afternoon, John.'

'You were quite right,' said John, sleepily; 'it was not a business for women alone.'

'That was not what I meant,' she answered. 'I ought not to have made that flat refusal. I did not recollect.'

John roused himself a little, to say, 'I suppose when two people come together who have grown up separately, their judgments must sometimes differ, and there is not always time to adjust them.' These last words were very sleepy again.

'No, I see I ought to have submitted; but I had no notion you would go; I behaved very ill to you, and you did it to punish me.'

'Not exactly,' he said, stirred up at those words. 'It would have been kinder to have told, but you had spoken plainly, and there seemed no time—nor occasion—for—further—Jeanne d'Albrêt—'

Which last words were sufficient testimony of the power of Morpheus. After all, he was inflicting, though he did not know it, a severe punishment. Wilmet was not a self-tormentor like Cherry; but she did not like to have her little mutiny passed over without a reconciliation, and to see him so perfectly unruffled by what had made all the depths of her heart turbid. And when he had 'fallen asleep in her very face,' she had the strongest possible temptation, if not to pursue the argument, at least to demand if he meant to sleep there all night, and rout him into going at once to undress; and when her real goodness and affection would not permit this, to beguile the time with the piece of intricate Pyrenean knitting, which had been the solace of his active nature, when he was good for nothing else. Though she had taught him to knit, those essential differences in the strength and manipulation of male and female fingers, made him particularly dislike to have rows interpolated by either of the ladies, and this she always so far resented, that it would have been uncommonly agreeable in her present mood to have gone on with the work. To abstain was all the harder to a person of her instincts, because no other occupation could be attained without opening a door, and breaking his slumbers; and though Wilmet had plenty to think of, the deprivation of mechanical employment for her fingers was trying enough to take away serenity or connection from her thoughts. Instead of any sort of meditation on the terrible tidings of the day, her mind *would* vibrate between desire to take up the knitting and resolution to let him sleep till eleven.

Perhaps in truth, nothing in her whole life was so difficult to Wilmet Harewood, or of so much service to her, than using such abstinence.

The shock and horror of the tidings when they reached Bexley may well be believed. John, after full enquiry, had written both to Felix and to the Miss Pearsons. Geraldine had perhaps never before believed that Edgar was lost to her, and the blow of regarding him as a murderer had such an effect upon her, that an illness was the consequence, in which Felix had to call in Sister Constance's aid to supplement little Stella's, and conquer the almost exaggerated feeling that for a time threatened nervous fever.

Sometimes, however, a lesser worry becomes a remedy for the effects of a greater, and Cherry's recovery was certainly not retarded by a certain dismay at learning that the forgiving aunts had offered a home to their errant niece and her little ones. No one could grudge them the asylum, but it roused Cherry from bewailing the crime of the one brother to a far more common-place anxiety about the other—a counter-irritant that so restored her health and spirits, that Sister Constance left her to such peace as it allowed her to enjoy. Felix had settled down so quietly—he seemed so entirely to have got over it, that it was hard to have all stirred up and the lady brought back again, freed in so dreadful a manner. No woman can ever estimate beforehand the effect that one of her own sex will produce on a man, however sensible. Her opinion is no gauge for his; and she labours under the further disadvantage that her better judgment is sure to be pitied, if not as feminine spite, at least as feminine incapability of candour; and Sister Constance advised Cherry to abstain from expressing the faintest regret. The good old aunts religiously preserved the secret of the mode of Tanneguy's death; but no one who knew the niece could doubt that the whole story would be at the mercy of whoever chose to cultivate her confidence.

Her arrival was notified by the sending in of a parcel from the travellers, containing Wilmet's sets of shirts for Lance and Bernard and two beautiful shawls in Pyrenean knitting, one for Cherry and one for Mr. Harewood. Felix said very little, but his complexion was still as tell-tale as a girl's. He was restless till Geraldine had called, though he feared to ask her to do so. She was not indeed uneasy about his actions; but only lest his affections should be so far out of his power as to render him unhappy and open the old wound.

Her visit went off better than she expected. She was greatly touched by Alice's delicate appearance and altered looks, and was favourably impressed by her subdued affectionate manner, and her fervent gratitude to the Harewoods, little guessing that it was to Robina that she owed it all. There was so much to hear about the Major's degree of recovery, his kindness, Wilmet's splendid beauty, and the sensation it excited, and all their arrangements for the winter, that Cherry went home in a far more ordinary mood than she could have thought possible.

For some time there was no meeting with Felix. Cherry even began to wish it was over, and off his mind as well as her own.

It came about at last suddenly. Felix opened the house door exactly as Alice was passing; they greeted one another, and shook hands. She had her eldest boy with her; he was leading Theodore, and Scamp, who was at their heels, instantly thrust his tan nose into little Gustave's face, so terrifying the child, that Felix was lifting him in his arms out of the dog's way, when he was startled by a yell from Theodore. The boy had an animal's instinctive jealousy. He had never seen any child but himself and Stella caressed by his brother; and the sight brought on one of the accesses of passion which had begun to seize him since his will and his strength had become somewhat more developed. Felix had no choice but peremptorily to snatch him indoors, leaving Madame Tanneguy and her child, who were both very much frightened, to Lance.

No more effective separation could have been devised, for Alice could not but retain a great horror of that 'dreadful boy,' who, though much smaller than Stella, and with little force in his soft aimless fingers, was still nearly eleven years old, and twice as big as her tiny brown elf. If they had been shut up together, Gustave would have mastered him in a minute; but she of course viewed him as a formidable being; and on the other hand, his face changed at the word 'little boy,' and his blue eyes grew fixed and round, and his soft murmuring to an angry inarticulate jabber, if he did but catch a sight of the little French boy from the window. Geraldine was just beginning to feel that the preventive had come in a curious form, between the two unconscious creatures, when Madame Tanneguy received a remittance from M. Aimery, and could not understand how to get it cashed. So just at the old twilight hour of her former visits she was shown into the drawing-room, and a message was presently sent to beg Mr. Underwood to come up when he was at leisure.

When he came, Geraldine was struck with the peculiar gentleness of his manner. It was gentle to all women and children, but to Madame Tanneguy it had a sort of tender reverence that gave its exceeding kindness a marked character, and was so unlike the good-natured elder-brotherly raillery that used to veil his youthful adoration, that Alice scandalised Cherry by exclaiming, 'How altered Mr. Underwood is! Grown so grave, I should not have known him!' As if anyone would not be grave when approaching the widow made by his brother.

He had minutely fulfilled the little service for her, and no doubt the reverential tone gratified her, for thenceforth she was always coming for the help and counsel that she never failed to find. 'Nobody could advise like Mr. Underwood,' she said; and it was amazing how much she found to consult him about—not only her French investments, but her arrangements with her aunts, her correspondence, and at last whether she ought to bring up Gustave and Achille as Roman Catholics. It so much annoyed him to detect any pleasantry on his submission to her behests, that Cherry and Lance scarce durst glance their half-amused annoyance to one another; and Angel and Bear never fell into a worse scrape in their lives than when they concocted a forgery with the tidings that Madame Tanneguy presented her compliments to Mr. Underwood, and was grieved to inform him that Gustave had scratched Achille's nose. Would he give her his much esteemed advice whether to apply court-plaster or gold-beater's skin?

Felix severely told Angela that to make a jest of Madame Tanneguy's forlorn condition betokened heartlessness, and added to Bernard that all the assistance that he or any of the brothers could afford was no more than her due, and could never atone for the past. Bernard was really awed, and after sulking for the rest of the day, suddenly veered into a certain private adoration of the lady, who by this time, with returning health, was resuming her vivacity. She had discarded her floating crape, and her pretty little head shone in its native glossy jet, while she smiled, chattered, and except that she was a devoted mother, and did her duty conscientiously as an assistant in the school, was the old Alice to all intents and purposes. Nor was it her fault if the original Felix did not likewise revive; she tried many a little art to beguile him into the playful terms of their former intercourse, but he never relaxed that reserved, compassionate gentleness, nor allowed himself to forget that his brother had first loved and then made her a widow. Cherry could have jumped for joy that first time she detected, and saw that Lance did, a shadow of a shade of impatience at those exactions; and finally she settled into the trust that propinquity was the best disenchantment, and that though there was still some romance, it was about the Alice of old visions, not the live Madame Tanneguy, whose obedient slave he would indeed always be, but merely as Edgar's brother, and who was fast, by force of boring and of levity, dispersing all the remaining glamour.

Cherry had her own anxiety, for an inspection by Wilmet was approaching, and very suddenly. At the end of the winter, at Biarritz, the travellers' plans had been deranged by an offer of an appointment at Woolwich, which hurried them home in the end of February instead of the beginning of May, as they had intended, and allowed them only to give one clear day to each of their families. To that day Cherry looked forward with some dread. Certainly the household was not precisely the Babel that Wilmet had found on her former return, but a formidable consciousness of shortcomings that would not bear inquisition beset her, and she had such a frantic bout of tidying, that Lance found her hopping about half dead with fatigue, and Stella nearly smothered with dust; and begging an afternoon's remission from business, he became the merriest and most helpful of housemaids till the operation was accomplished.

After all, the anxiety proved to have been a little superfluous. Winds howled all night, and Major Harewood's well-known discomfort at sea made the arrival dubious till about three o'clock, when, in pouring rain, a fly deposited the voyagers, shaken, battered, jaded, with a prolonged and wretched passage, and each too anxious that the other should rest, to be good for anything but wan smiles and affectionate greetings. They had eaten or tried to eat at Southampton, and nothing could be done with them but to shut them into Mr. Froggatt's state bed-chamber and leave them, promising to be better company in the evening.

Then there was time for Robina, who meanwhile had done little but run about in their service, select and open the boxes and bags containing what was wanted, and introduce the Hindoo, who was put under charge of a young Lightfoot.

Then Lance and Robin had time to stand up in the drawing-room gazing at one another after this thirteen months' interval. Lance held up his hands and pretended to fall back in dismay: 'Robin-a-Bobbin grown into a young lady! Ah!'

'And what's this?' as she flew at him to pinch the thick brown down upon his lip. 'What kind of crop is this?' And they took one of their old tumbling waltzes round the room together, as if to shake themselves into one, while, with the hand that each kept loose, Robin continued to snatch at the new decoration, and Lance to defend and smoothe it down.

'Ay,' said Felix (who tolerated it by a certain effort of philosophy, and the humbling consciousness of being an old Philistine), 'he is cherishing it for the Handel festival. He wants to be taken for a German.'

'O Lance, are you to go to the Handel festival?'

'Yes, Miles has got me a place in the chorus—jolly, isn't it, of the old fellow? I say, Robin, we must get you up there.'

'I—oh! I shall be at Woolwich then, I suppose. Do you know, Cherry, I must only stay till Monday? Those two aren't in the least fit to get into their house at Woolwich without help, and John has begged me—'

'I suppose you must,' said Cherry. 'After all these good accounts, this is disappointing; but how could you all cross on such a night?'

'Why, Wilmet never minded the sea before, and John had made up his mind soldier-fashion, and thought nothing was to be gained by waiting. And when Wilmet had to succumb she would not believe it, and was so disgusted at herself, and so miserable about him, that it did her all the more harm.'

'And you!'

'Oh, I was quite well; but it was horrid enough any way—and poor John had gone from the first to lie quite flat in the gentlemen's cabin, where I could not get at him.'

'Before I go, what do you think of him?' asked Felix. 'One can't judge of his looks to-day.'

'Oh! he calls himself sound—the wounds are all healed at last, but he gets a great deal of bad pain still, either rheumatic or neuralgic; he says it comes from the strain on his constitution, and will take no advice about it till he can see Dr. Manby. Then he's so cripply that he could not have gone on in the service if he were not a field-officer. He says he is quite up to it, but we think it a great experiment. Oh! Felix—Lance—don't go—there can't be anybody this wet afternoon!'

'Yes,' said Felix, 'this is just the time that all the old gentlemen who get tired of their own fire-sides, and all the professionals that can't take their walk, feel inclined to come and prose at "Froggatt's."—But they won't want you, Lance; I'll send if there's anything for you to do.—Good-bye, Robin Redbreast, you do look uncommonly nice!' and he took her round cheeks between his hands, and held up her face to kiss each of them, with mouth and brow, individually and gravely.

'She's the Robin still,' said Cherry, 'only just a little polished up.'

'Developing,' said Lance, stalking round her, and speaking his words deliberately; 'developing—into—the—bloom—of—sweet—seventeen—and of—'

'Not beauty!' broke in Robina. 'I would not be as pretty as Wilmet for two-pence.'

'Not for a major?' suggested Lance.

'He didn't marry her for her beauty,' vehemently responded Robina, 'but for her—her niceness. Her beauty has been always in her way, and a nuisance to her, and—'

'Sour grapes!' quoth Lance.

'Not a bit. It would be a worse hindrance in my branch of the profession.'

Lance did not answer in jest this time; he looked at the bright pleasant-faced girl in her maidenly bloom and fresh stylish dress, and said, 'What a horrid pity it is! she looks ten times more of a lady than ninety-nine out of a hundred of 'em—and there she's to go and grind and be ground just for a governess.'

'Not a bit more of a pity than that—I'll not say that you should be a printer, Lance, but than that anybody should be anything. I learnt my Catechism, you see, to learn and labour to get my *own* living.'

'So you sent Madame Tanneguy home to prevent you from getting into Wilmet's shoes at Miss Pearson's?'

'I should hope I was fit for something more than that!'

'Well done, Bob!'

'I didn't mean—' said Robina, rather distressed, 'but you see I have had a much better education than ever Wilmet could get, and have gone on longer with it; and I can go in for things that girls here would not care to learn; so, as I am not wanted to keep house with Wilmet, it would be just waste for me to come and do like her—poked up in this corner.'

'Ah! you've had a taste of the world,' said Lance, speaking in jest; but Robina, recollecting how he had crushed any ambition of his own, and who *did* veritably feel that though home was home, Bexley was dull and narrow, turned round with moist eyes.

'O Lance, I hope it is not that! You know I have been brought up to go out, and it seems my work and duty; but I think it is a great deal more honourable to stay here because one is wanted.'

'Because one can't help it,' said Lance, pulling her hair and smiling. 'Have you learnt to make speeches in France, Bob?'

'No. But indeed, Lance, I do want to know if you do never get tired of things now?'

'Oh! I've no right; I'm not one of the highly educated ones!' said Lance, in a spirit of teasing.

'Now, Lance, don't punish me, when I really want to know.'

'Taking into consideration the awful slowness and stodginess of the place, and the contempt of one's highly educated brothers and sisters,' said Lance, slowly, but with a twinkle in his eye that somehow made up for the words, 'one *does* drag on life pretty well, by the help of Pur and the organ. The new one is coming by next summer, if there's any faith or conscience in the builder, which I believe there is not.'

'And,' she added, coming near and speaking low, 'did I not hear that there had been a letter from Ferdinand?'

Cherry looked for it. 'Felix took it down to answer,' she said, 'but it was from Sydney. He had seen Mr. Allen.'

'Oh!'

'Yes. He tracked those National Minstrels all over India, Bombay, Calcutta, all manners of places—good faithful fellow—and at last he found they had gone to Sydney, and there, actually, was Mr. Allen, settled down as a music-master, making—I don't know what in a week.'

'But—'

'But there had been a great quarrel, and the concern had broken up; and he did not in the least know where poor Edgar was gone,' sighed Cherry. 'Robin, did you hear what name he sung under at Alexandria?'

'No, Ferdinand only told Wilmet that his name was not in the programme.'

'That good Cacique!' broke out Lance; 'he is about the slowest-witted fellow that walks the earth. I believe he would never believe it was he if he saw anything less than Thomas Edgar Underwood in extra type. If he only would have sent me, I'll be bound I'd have run Edgar down in no time, instead of being always three months behind him, and now off the scent.'

'No, but is he?'

'No, he has not given it up,' said Cherry. 'Mr. Allen did not know whether they were gone to Melbourne or Adelaide, and he meant to try both; and to go and see Fulbert and Mr. Audley.'

'One of them will stumble on him while Fernan is staring about with his nose in the air,' said Lance.

'I am afraid he will only avoid them,' said Cherry sadly.

'And another certainty is that he will have taken some fresh alias,' said Lance, 'while the Cacique is still hunting for Tom Wood. I bet on Fulbert's finding him!'

'Has he parted from those Hungarians too?'

'Ay, there's the question! Should you like a prima-donna sister-in-law, Robbie?'

'No, no, no—don't, Lance,' cried Cherry; 'Mr. Allen said Mademoiselle Zoraya had—the horrid woman—thought much more of Edgar since—' she could only pause, 'but he was far too sharp to be drawn in.'

'That I believe,' said Lance. 'Never fear, Cherry, we shall have him some of these days, with a long beard, a longer fortune, and the longest story—ah!' with a long sigh, 'if I wasn't an organist, wouldn't I like to be a scamp!' The offensiveness of which word was concealed by a sudden embrace of the Scamp dog, who was made to stand on his hind legs, with his feet in Robina's hands, to display his beautiful topaz eyes; and in the midst of the exhibition the door opened, and John came slowly in, leaning on his stout stick.

'O John, I am glad! are you rested? Haven't you been asleep?'

'No; I think Wilmet will sleep if she is alone, so I am going to waste no more time. Thank you,' as Robina put the cushion as he liked it, and looked into his face with inquiry as she detected the well-known lines that showed it was pain that made sleep hopeless. He smiled and gave a little nod, by which she understood that she was to keep her discovery to herself, and that it was not so severe but that he hoped to amuse it away; and he began at once laughing with Geraldine.

'Well, Cherry, you see I've a rival to Lord Gerald.'

'I began to think I ought to offer him to you, though it would go to my heart.'

'As if I would be put off with a slender little wand like that,' said John. 'That's what I call a stick.'

'That's what I call a club,' retorted Cherry. 'I should want somebody else to carry me if I took such a monster;' and they proceeded to a sort of tilt between their two supporters.

'I won't have disrespect to my steadfast friend! She's made of olive tree; her name is Olivia; and I believe Wilmet is jealous of her.'

'Indeed she is,' said Robin. 'When you go out all by yourself, and come in hardly able to speak. That's what he went and did at Paris.'

'When one has got a wife and a sister, one breaks loose sometimes. Here, you little Star, come and speak to me! Why, you were a blackberry-gathering baby when I saw you last! Let me look at you now. How old are you?'

'Eleven and a quarter,' breathed a little voice, as he gathered two tiny hands into his, and a pair of porcelain blue eyes glanced up for a moment out of the most dainty little oval chiselled face and pink-and-white complexion, set in soft brown hair.

'And can eleven and a quarter hatch an egg from the Palais Royal? Not from Bill's *nid d'avis*, but of a bird of larger growth,' as Stella, with a half-breathed 'thank you' rosiness spreading over her face, and lips raised for a kiss, beheld a beautiful blue egg, containing implements of needlework.

John tried to talk to her over it, but could get nothing but monosyllables, and blushes, and smiles, till he released her, and she flew off, 'To show her egg to Theodore,' said Cherry. 'There's some baking going on; and he never stirs from the kitchen while he can handle the dough.'

'What a lovely little fairy it is!' said John; 'but is it wound up to say nothing but yes or no?'

'She is awfully shy,' said Lance. 'Bill can't get as much out of her as you have done.'

'She has not spoken a word since I have been in the room,' added Robin.

'She is a strangely silent child,' said Cherry. 'Sometimes I think living so much with Theodore helps to make her so. She is quick at her lessons, and is a perfect little book of reference; and will talk to me gravely when we are alone; but it never seems to come into her head to chatter. I'm sure Lance and Robin have talked more nonsense in this hour than she has in six months.'

'I've a longing to hear Stella perpetrate a little nonsense,' said Lance. 'When Angel and Bear are at home, and there is a good gabble, there sits the child, her bright eyes smiling and gleaming, without a word.'

A knock at the door. 'Mr. Lancelot, there's the Centry carriage in the High Street.'

'There, you see what it is to be the lady's man!' said Lance, laughing and running down.

'The Centry carriage means your cousin no more,' said John.

'No; she has let Centry to an old general with a large family. She said she knew nothing about country poor, and hated county people; and her mother likes nothing really but Brighton. I think she is quite right,' said Cherry.

'What sort of people are they?'

'Oh! they do very well for the parish; but of course are nothing to us. The General proses over the papers to Felix sometimes, and the daughters have the loveliest eyes in the world.'

'That's Lance,' said Robina, laughing. 'Is he as tender-hearted as ever?'

'Oh yes; or more so; but as long as the ladies *all* have the most beautiful faces that ever were seen, and his attentions are confined to putting attractive advertisements into their parcels, I don't mind.'

'Lance is the most altered of you all,' said John.

'Dear Lance,' said Cherry, 'he has got back a great deal of his sunshine—quite enough to be very delightful to us, though I doubt whether he is always as bright to himself. There is a certain *sehnsucht* in the pieces of music he goes on improvising, that sometimes makes me anxious.'

'You mean whether he has got into the right line,' said John.

'It's no use thinking about that; Felix could not do without him; and he is fit for nothing else now,' said Cherry. 'I fancy when the new organ comes, he will have a love in that and be happy.'

John was thoroughly one of themselves, more eager about Bexley affairs than his wife, though she was thoroughly her affectionate self when she joined them in the evening. She was too much tired, and too glad to see their faces, to do more than repose in the sight; and it was kinder to sing than to talk to either traveller. Even the next day, when the ravages of the storm had been repaired, she had too much on her own hands to have leisure to set Cherry to-rights; and if she perceived any disuse of her pet economies, she acquiesced as if it were to be quite expected, and no more worth a protest than matters at the Bailey, whither she was going the next day. To be sure, there was a kind of implied expectation that she would some day arrive for a general rectification of what could just be tolerated under present circumstances; but this was not a very pressing alarm.

87

The visit was over, the new home at Woolwich begun; and before many weeks were over, it welcomed what father and aunt united in calling a magnificent boy. Felix went with Mr. Harewood to the christening, and found his sister a different creature, lovelier than he ever remembered her. It seemed as if her happiness would have been almost too great for this earth if John had only been as strong and well as he tried to appear. But, after all, Felix really believed Wilmet would have been lost without some one to nurse besides Christopher Underwood, dutifully named after his two grandfathers.

Alda had actually come down for the day. It was the first time the sisters had met since the funeral at Centry Park, and it had cost her an effort, for her third daughter was but ten days older than Wilmet's baby; and she could not withhold a slight plaint at the inequalities of fate, in bestowing only girls where they were less welcome, while the sex of Wilmet's magnificent boy could be of no possible consequence—a remark which so exasperated not only the mother, but the father, as greatly to amuse Felix.

Lady Vanderkist looked very thin and worn, as if much less recovered than Wilmet, who had a beautiful fresh bloom, and was vigorous while Alda was languid; but the brother and sister gathered that her difficulties in coming down were far less caused by health than by disregard to her private wishes and plans. Wilmet regretted that she had not brought her little Mary; and she said she had hoped to do so, but had found she could not have the horses, and did not like to take her in a cab. She warmly invited Wilmet to town, but to Marilda's house, not her own, except for mornings; and she apologized with real vexation for not being able to offer Felix a bed, Adrian expected someone that evening.

She was, of course, beautifully dressed; but Wilmet, in a delicate pale-grey silk and Parisian rose-bud bonnet, was not the foil she used to be; and the two sisters were still a very striking pair, though no one would have guessed them to be twins, so worn did Alda look. She was much kinder to Robina, too, and absolutely eager to hear of every one at home.

But what struck Felix most was this. He had business in London, and went back with her late in the afternoon. At the last moment, Wilmet, wanting to cloak her sister, transferred her baby to his father, who, as he held him, smiled to him with one of those little gestures of tenderness, that express so very much because they are involuntary and unconscious; and after the brother and sister were seated in the fly, when they looked back with a last wave of the hand, Robina alone answered; the papa and mamma were wholly occupied in handing back their treasure with a kiss on either side. Alda went on looking out, and presently Felix saw her handkerchief stealing up to her eyes. Perhaps she thought herself composed, for she turned round and said, with an effort at a smile, 'That's what it is to have a boy! If Adrian had ever looked like that!'

Felix charitably refrained from expressing his accordance with her former sentiment, that it would have been all the same with a girl; and indeed Alda had miscalculated her fortitude, for speaking brought a flood of tears. Felix durst not look at her, and doubted whether to let himself be conscious, but said at last, 'Caresses are no test. Many men do not care for very young children.'

She shook her head; but as they arrived at the station she forced back her tears, bit her lip, and drew forward her spangled veil; Felix brought her a glass of water, and she walked along the platform with him, holding his arm with a clasp that reminded him of the day he had taken her home from Thomas Underwood's, but not a word did she say in the train.

There was no carriage to meet her, and Felix could not resolve not to see her home.

'Oh! thank you,' she said, more warmly than perhaps she had ever thanked him before. 'I've always said one must come to you for chivalry. But it is terribly out of the way; you will be late for the dinner in Palace Gardens.'

'They must forgive me,' he said; 'and I should like to see the last of you.' And as he sat by her in the hansom, he tried to give her a smile, all affection and no pity.

'I wish there was time for you to go in. I want you to see little Mary;' then presently, after an effort, 'You'll not speak of this, Felix. I'm not strong yet; and I suppose daughters always are a disappointment where there is a title.'

Felix supposed it too, and very kindly.

'Is there any chance of your coming to town again, soon?' she asked, 'I am always at home and alone before three.'

'I do not think I shall—no—Lance is going up to the Handel festival, and we cannot be away together.'

'Little Lance! I've not seen him since he used to have his head-aches. But it is no use to think of it, we shall not be in town by that time, the house is so dreadfully expensive. We shall not have one another year. One gets sick of so much going out, and with all these little girls it is time to begin to be prudent.'

Felix had seen enough of Sir Adrian Vanderkist's name on the turf to think the sentence ominous; not that he was afraid of any great crash, but expensive tastes did not accord with estates entailed and the annual birth of a daughter; and he was greatly touched by Alda's collapse of self-importance.

He was late, and Marilda forgave him easily, but Mrs. Underwood was cross. No doubt she had fumed about poor relations having no right to keep her waiting; and though there was something indefinable about Felix that hindered her from manifesting this cause of displeasure, his having been engaged in Alda's service did not pacify her. She considered Lady Vanderkist as extremely ungrateful for not having transported Marilda into those upper circles to which marriage had introduced her, without taking into account that the obstacle lay, not with Sir Adrian, who was ready enough to pay court to riches, but with Marilda herself. That young lady was forming her own way in the world. She had had enough of the Golden Venus line while, for her father's sake, she submitted to it; and she did not choose to force herself into fashionable circles. Country poor and the Lady Bountiful life, that her mother would have accepted as 'comifo,' were distasteful to her; but she had thrown her business abilities into the service of London charities, and was there becoming every year a more considerable power. Her business premises were in St. Matthew's district; and this made her regard herself as a parishioner, and undertake no small amount of service, of descriptions better known to the clergy-house than to her mother, who set down to the accounts of the office many an hour spent in Whittingtonian schools and alleys. At any rate, Marilda had become a much more agreeable person, with more aplomb, more ease, and decidedly less touch of vulgarity, since she had made her standfast, ceased to be dragged at the wheels of the car of fashion, and become the managing spirit of Kedge and Underwood, besides all that St Matthew's knew of.

CHAPTER XXXIV.

THE VICAR OF VALE LESTON.

'Cushions and cloth an' books, takin' the old church right roun',
Surplice, shovel, and broom, they would na ha' fetch'd half-a-crown,
Commandments to boot. They was the only good lookin' things
Wi' yellow cherubs between 'em, and nout but heads and wings.
Parson Myles was a hunter, and could gallop through a prayer,
Right straight ahead over anything, an' stop him who dare.'
Rev. W. Heygate.

There was to be a meeting about the paving of the town: Mr. Underwood, though only twenty-eight, was a town-councillor, and decidedly an influence in himself, as well as through the Pursuivant. He had so worked his way up, that his fellow-citizens accepted him as one of themselves; and his birth and breeding gave him a power which they felt without in the least acknowledging. Besides, his conscientious journalising made him always thoroughly get up his subjects; and he threw himself into the merits and history of asphalt and flag-stones with that 'all his might' with which he did whatsoever his hand found to do.

He was busy on an article to prepare the way for the meeting, when Lance, who had been making selections from London papers, laid the last sheet of the 'Times' on his desk, and silently pointed to the obituary:—

'On the 4th, at Torquay, aged 37, the Reverend Fulbert Bowles Underwood, Vicar of Vale Leston Abbas, only son of Fulbert Underwood, Esquire, of Vale Leston Priory.'

'I see,' quoth Felix.

Five minutes' waiting while he wrote.

'I say, does it go into Pur?'

'Certainly not. What matters it to any one here?'

That was all Lance could get out of Felix; and after a time came the second delivery of the post. All the letters lay in a heap on the office table, just when, as Lance mentally termed him, the longest-windedest, button-holderest of all the municipality walked in to bestow his opinion on the paving question upon Mr. Underwood; and Lance not only had to retreat from the important conclave, but was occupied himself by a succession of customers for a quarter of an hour after its conclusion. When he made another rush into the office, he found Felix still writing away at the paving stones, but with a good deal of red in his cheeks, and a letter lying by his side.

'Read that, Lance,' he said, 'but don't speak till this is done.'

Lance read:—

Vale Leston Priory, May 7th.
MY DEAR MR. FELIX UNDERWOOD,

I write by desire of my poor friend Mr. Underwood, to acquaint you with the death of his son, your cousin, the Vicar, at Torquay, on the 4th of this month. The melancholy event had long been anticipated, as there had been a complete break-up of constitution; and I for one never expected to see him return home alive when he went to Torquay with his wife last winter. Mr. Underwood has felt the loss deeply, though not with the same acuteness as if he had not had such long preparation, and it had not taken place at a distance. He has become much more feeble since you saw him five years ago, when certainly you left a lasting impression. He wishes you to be present at the funeral, with any of your brothers to whom it may be convenient. The time is fixed for next Friday, the 10th, at eleven o'clock. Your rooms will be ready for you on Monday; and if you will mention your train, you shall be met at Church Ewe or Ewmouth. It seems premature to mention it, but Mr. Underwood is so anxious that no time should be lost, that he desires me to intimate to you, that if you can procure immediate Ordination, he will present you to the Vicarage. I do not take this to be as simple a matter as he does, but under the circumstances, and with your studious turn, I should think it quite possible for you to be ready before the Vicarage lapses, and the poor old Squire has evidently set his heart on it, and planned it ever since he gave up hope of his son's life. Congratulations would be out of place at this moment, but I trust that the succession is now secure.

Remember me to my friend Mr. Lancelot—I trust that headaches are with him a thing of the past—and believe me,

Yours very truly,
H. STAPLES.

Lance made all manner of contortions with his visage, read and re-read, indulged in a suppressed war-dance, and finally merged all other sensations in an agony of impatience, as still Felix's eyes and pen continued to travel over his sheet; and not a muscle of his face moved until the last was handed to little Lightfoot, and sent off to the press.

'That's done,' then he said.

'You may well be on the board of paving-stones!' cried Lance. 'Nothing but one of them could have gone on so.'

'It had to be done.'

'I could as soon have done it as flown.'

'Not if you never let your mind loose from it. Now for the letter. Stay, we'll take it up to Cherry. I'll just say a word to Lamb.'

Felix's courtesy to his subordinates always went a great way. The noontide lull of business was beginning to set in, but Cherry and Stella looked up from their lessons in amaze as both brothers came in; and Cherry mutely clasped her hands, and with the word Edgar fluttering on her lips, but as both faces plainly indicated no, she rallied instantly, saying, 'What wonder of wonders is it?'

'Nothing very surprising,' said Felix gravely. 'It is that poor old Fulbert, at Vale Leston, has lost his son, and wants me to go to the funeral.'

'That's not all,' added Lance. 'What do you think of his wanting this here Giant to get himself ordained, and take the Vicarage on the spot?'

'Felix, you could not—not in time.'

'Nor at all. That is not to be thought of; but I shall go through London, take Clement down with me, and see if I cannot get the living for him; but let me read you the letter—I could barely glance at it.'

He read; and Cherry broke out, 'The succession secure! Does that mean to you?'

'I am heir-at-law,' said Felix quietly; 'and it was entailed on me in case his son had no children.'

'He takes it coolly, doesn't he?' said the far more elated Lance, 'but then he's had plenty of preparation.'

'You don't mean that you've known about this?'

'I knew the estate had been entailed on me to prevent this poor man from alienating it.'

'You knew, and you never told anyone, and went on as usual!'

'How would you have had me go on?' he asked, with a certain provoking meekness, that sent her into a laugh, while Lance, catching Stella's wondering eyes, practically answered the question by locking her fingers in his, and whirling her round in a sort of impromptu choric dance, chanting:—

> 'Wrong shall be right,
> And right shall be might,
> When—'

('bless me, what a plague three syllables are!')

> 'When Felix' right and Felix' might
> Shall meet upon Vale Leston height!'

'It is not a height,' interposed Felix.

'The King shall have his own again then,' amended Lance. 'No, I have it. The enchantment is over, and the Frog-prince is about to resume his proper shape!'

'Lance, considering—'

'Blunderbore, considering the extraordinary relief and disburthening of my mind, after labouring under this secret five years come August, if it were not profane, I should compare myself to Christian when the pack dropped off his back!'

'But why was it a secret?'

'For two reasons, Whiteheart,' said Felix. 'First because there was nothing to tell; and secondly, because that "nothing" might have turned several heads. Still, I believe you would have known it long ago, if I had not been ashamed after binding over Lance.'

'Please, may I understand?' entreated Stella, in rather a melancholy voice, as she found her usual mode of observation quite inadequate.

'Understand, my Star! Yes,' said Lance; 'understand that we were all of us kicked out—all of us that were there to kick, that is to say—from the jolliest place in all the world; and now things are coming right, and Felix is going to be a fine old English gentleman who had a great estate! I declare it makes me so poetical I can't get on!'

'You'd better come to me, Stella,' interposed Felix. 'Nothing is going to happen now, my dear. It is only this. The old house where we elder ones were born was meant to belong to my mother, but there was a flaw in the will that left it her, and so it went to the more direct heir; and my father would not go to law because he did not think it right when he could not afford it, and especially as he was a clergyman.'

'O Felix!' cried Cherry eagerly.

'Yes; I have a copy of the letter. And now, the poor old gentleman who had it has lost his son, and has sent me a kind message, as if he wished me to go back there; but that will not be in his life-time, so we need not talk about it. There is nothing to make any change now.'

'No?' asked Cherry, disappointed.

'Of course not. Expectations are not good sustenance. The reversion is possibly very distant, and there may be some mistake about it, after all.'

'Well! one ought to be prepared,' said Cherry; 'but oh! to see you at home—home—yes, Vale Leston is home! O Felix, what it will be!'

'Don't set yourself on wishing it,' said Felix anxiously. 'Remember Pur and the business are our dependence or independence, and most likely are far better and safer for us.'

'Pshoo!' shouted Lance; 'I won't have you talk book!'

'May I tell Wilmet?' entreated Cherry.

'No harm in that; meantime I must get things in train, and then walk over to explain matters to Mr. Froggatt; and as soon as I can get away to-morrow I shall go up to town, and make Clement come on with me.'

'O Fee, one moment! Are we to go into mourning?' Then, as he held up his hand, 'It means more than you think. It shows how much we hold by the connection; and if I understand you, you wish nothing so little as to have it trumpeted about that Mr. Underwood has great expectations.'

'As prudently stated as W.W. could have done it! It must turn on the degree of connection.'

'Is he as near as Tom Underwood was?'

'The same on my mother's side. Yes, put on black ribbons; but, as you say, don't trumpet the thing. Don't begin about it, but if any one asks, explain how it stands.'

The heir-expectant was gone; and Lance, after waiting to indulge in another pantomime of exultation, ran after him, humming:—

'Oh, to see him back again!'

By the middle of the next day Felix was able to leave home, after having seen the Froggatts, whom he treated with as much deference and attention as if he were still accountable to them. The reception of his communication made him glad that he had been silent when the chances were more remote, for though Mrs. Froggatt was ready to cry for gladness at the notion of his taking his own proper place as a gentleman, and had a farmer's daughter's respect for the squirearchy, her husband feared that empty anticipation would spoil Felix for a tradesman, and be injurious to the business, which he viewed with tender pride and solicitude. So he lectured on the uncertainty of prospective fortunes, and the folly of reckoning on them, till it was evident that his confidence would have been sorely shattered had the bare notion been whispered five years earlier. Indeed, his comfort seemed compromised by finding that Felix would not be the permanent property of the business, and he was almost displeased, as if he thought he had allowed it to pass into his hands on false pretences. It was vexatious and disappointing; but he had to be left to recover the first shock, which, after all, proved his love and value for the young man.

Felix did not reach Whittingtonia till late; and on inquiry at the clergy-house, heard that Mr. Underwood was not at home, but the Vicar was. To him therefore Felix went in his study, not sorry to ask his advice. Clement, who would not receive priest's orders for some weeks, was over young for the charge of an utterly neglected parish; but it was dangerous to let the presentation pass by, since only a brother could satisfactorily co-operate in dealing with the old ancestral sacrileges, in case he should ever come in for the property himself.

Mr. Fulmort never spoke while Felix told his story; and the bell for Evensong had begun by the time it closed. Then he said, 'I am very glad, heartily glad. I have been watching Clement, and I see he is not tough enough yet for our work. When a young fellow, of such a length too, can't eat after any hard day's work, instead of being ravenous, he is sure to break down the first time he takes cold or catches an illness, and then he is done for. I should have had to drive him away elsewhere, at least for some years, poor fellow, though none has ever been more like a son to me. Yes, of course he is too young, but he is not the sort of stuff that falls into slackness, and that is more fatal than any amount of blunders and foolishness.'

The last words startled Felix. He had been so anxious to place Clement at Vale Leston, that he had thought of no drawbacks till he was roused to a foreboding of that dour uncompromising rigidity, left to itself, sowing dissensions, becoming a hard master to them all—nay, not improbably alienating the old Squire, and overthrowing all their prospects! Such a future passed before Felix in his transit across the quadrangle, and was met, but not disposed of, by the sense that it was right and just that Clement should be put forward, '*Fais ce que dois, advienne que pourra.*' He had put Clement into his own place to console his father for his own secession to secular work; and if devotion, blamelessness, and earnestness were recommendations, they were not lacking. 'And if he do give offence, and all be left to Marilda,' thought Felix, 'let it go. It would only be for conscience sake. Poverty is better than riches! and I may have to show that I believe so. I only hope that the boy will not do the thing in some pig-headed way, in which it would be hard to back him up.'

Misgivings vanished for the time when his brother was in sight. It was not easy to make him out in the deep perspective of the choir. Felix only knew that a fair-haired head above the average line must be his; but when he came forward to the Eagle, whence he was to read the Second Lesson, and afterwards give his lecture, he was in full view. In his lankiest hobbedy-hoy days, Clement had always looked his best surpliced; and now, with the cassock beneath, the stole over one shoulder, and his black-and-white hood, his figure had a certain dignity, and his voice gave Felix a thrill. The mixture of hereditary tone and unconscious imitation were such that when he shut his eyes he could believe himself a boy at St Oswald's, listening to his father; and even when he looked up the illusion was hardly dispelled, for the half-light brought out the similar moulding of the features, and a hectic tinting. He gave a careful little discourse, evidently one of a series, and the allegory of the Wilderness life with much more depth and poetry than the elder brother had expected.

He had taken care to place himself out of direct view of the young preacher, and his appearance in the quadrangle was an immense surprise to Clement. 'Felix! you here! nothing the matter? What's that? Not poor Edgar?' as his eye fell on Felix's new hat and hat-band.

'No, no—this is for the younger Fulbert of Vale Leston. I have more to say to you.'

'Come in to supper, then. Have you seen the Vicar? Do you stay the night? That's jolly! Here, Fred, you've not seen my brother!'

Fred Somers was known to be Clement's friend. With one of the natures that prefers external to home friendship, Clement had at first bestowed his affection on poor Harry Lamb, and since upon this companion, who had been his predecessor by half a year in everything, and in whom Felix was diverted to see his complete contrast. Mr. Somers was at least five inches below Clement's six feet one and a half, and was a dark, plump, merry little man, who looked as if the Vicar never need scruple about getting any amount of work out of him; and Clement, with a hand on his shoulder, looked perfectly happy, and as if working at St Matthew's side by side with him were all he desired. And very overgrown and boyish Clement looked too at that supper, a very merry one. There were the six clergy, fourteen choir boys, and sundry chance-helpers, mostly talking eagerly, with a good deal of laughter at old and new jokes. Felix, seated by the Vicar, thought Clement far more at his ease, more playful and familiar, than ever he had seen him at home, and infinitely less on his dignity than he ever allowed himself to be with Lance and Bernard.

After supper, the two brothers repaired to Clement's tiny private room, uncarpeted, with a table, two Windsor chairs, and a book-case; and then, when the elder had explained, the younger flatly refused to have anything to do with Vale Leston Abbas.

'I!' he said, 'go to a fat easy-going country living when the need is so urgent here? I to stand alone when I want years of training? It would be enough to ruin me!'

'But the place, Clement. This parish will never be ill-supplied while Mr. Fulmort lives; but people have souls down in the country.'

Clement had not much feeling for souls whose bodies he had never realised; but he answered, 'Very bad for the souls to have an inexperienced priest.'

'Quite true; but observe, it is not the choice between you and such a clergyman as you would select, but between you and no one knows who—certainly a person who could not help in the complication of family and Church property, as only a brother could do.'

'That is all in the clouds,' said Clement. 'I have made up my mind to ten years' service here, and I intend to keep to it.'

'The Vicar says you have not strength for it.'

'Then I shall go on without it.'

'Till you kill yourself.'

'The best end one could come to.'

'No, not if there be a leading of Providence elsewhere.'

'I observe that Providence is generally said to lead in the direction of ease and £ s.d. No, Felix, I am much obliged, but even if this old man would appoint a vicar of decided opinions like mine, I cannot allow myself to be led aside into a path of wealth and luxury contrary to all I had marked out for myself.'

'Are people always meant to do all they have marked out for themselves?' said Felix, as he heard the frequent first person singular.

'When it is the line of self-abnegation.'

Felix could not help smiling, and muttering between his teeth, 'Is it?' Then he added, 'At any rate you will come down to the funeral and see the old place?'

'No! I will not raise false expectations to be disappointed.'

The idea of baffled expectations excited by that long white-faced lad! Even Felix was beginning to console himself, and think Clement might be doing the best for them all, when they were summoned to the Oratory by the evening prayer-bell. As good-nights were spoken at the foot of the stairs, the Vicar asked Felix, 'Have you prevailed?'

'No, sir. Perhaps you will talk to him?'

Mr. Fulmort nodded, and Felix went to his own room. In the morning the Vicar told him that he had not made much impression, but that he had actually made it matter of obedience that Clement should go to Vale Leston with his brother, and not consider his decision as made till he had thoroughly seen the place.

And thus it was that Felix, in different company and different mood from when he had last seen his birthplace, found himself stopping at a little station called Church Ewe, about three miles short of Ewmouth; and there a smart servant came up with his finger to his cockaded hat, and took possession of the two little black bags.

'The beginning of greatness!' observed Clement, who was very benignant towards Felix's prospects, though he would accept none for himself, as they ensconced themselves in the great barouche with the pair of horses.

Felix shook his head. He wanted to hold himself as loose as possible from gazing on the place as an inheritance, at the same time as he greatly desired to see Clement smitten with it, almost as much from jealousy for the old home as with a view to the future.

Their way brought them in on the opposite side from the Ewmouth road; so that the first view was from high ground, whence the lovely encircling valley, the slopes of wood inclosing it, the purple moorland above them, the grey sheen of the river, the high-arched bridge, the noble church, and grand old ancestral-looking priory, partly veiled by fine trees, in the delicate glory of early summer, lay outstretched before them, the shimmer of the sea, and a few white sails far in the distance.

That sense of the eye satisfying the heart, and being as it were at rest and at home, which he had felt at the sight five years before, and never at any other, came over Felix; and exulting in the loveliness, he looked eagerly to see the effect on Clement, but the smooth young face was carefully guarded against relaxing, the light blue eye was steadily set as unmarking anything. Felix was provoked, and then wondered whether the Deacon were like the Moslem who refused to dwell at Damascus, lest he should have his Paradise only on earth. A little local information elicited nothing but civil indifferent answers, that inspired a desire to shake that inanimate figure.

Driving up through the park, beauteous with chestnut blossom, they were shown into the library; and there Mr. Staples came to them, cordially shaking hands, but, as Felix fancied, somewhat critically scanning that long straight coat with the little cross at the button-hole.

'The Squire is tolerable,' he answered to Felix's inquiry. 'I think it is coming out in gout. He will dine with you. It does him good to see people.'

'And Mrs. Underwood?'

'Came yesterday. Mother and brother here too. Ladies dine together upstairs.'

'Are you staying here?'

'No; but I am over as much as I can. The old Squire wants someone, and I don't fancy leaving him too much to Smiles—he's the curate, and has been trying to worm himself in. Will you come to your rooms? Dinner at seven.'

To Felix it was like meeting an old friend to tread the black stair, and the long panelled corridors, all windows on one side, the other hung with portraits, the Underwood red cheeks and blue eyes staring round, and coarse like Marilda. Mr. Staples popped Clement into one wainscotted room, and left him there, but shut himself in with Felix.

'So that's your clerical brother?'

'An excellent hard-working devoted fellow.'

'But very—?'

'Well, rather!'

'And it is quite out of the question for yourself?'

'Entirely so. Even if I thought it right, it could not be done.'

'I thought so, and told the Squire. Unlucky, for things are a good deal involved; and you would find the vicarage income handy, while as for this—why he is a mere boy!'

'So he feels himself. He is conscious of his want of experience, and it would be an infinite relief to him to see it in good hands.'

'Mrs. Fulbert and her mother declare that the Squire promised poor Fulbert to give it to her brother, Harry Shaw, whom you'll see here to-night; but he swears he did no such thing; and on the whole, I think Smiles would have a better chance—he's an obsequious chap, who has been very attentive to the old man all the winter, half their spy, half his toady. However, the Squire would never let either of them have it while there's a parson left with Underwood blood in his veins!'

All the quaint old bedrooms in this passage opened one into the other, and Felix unlocked the door between himself and Clement to communicate the information received, but it apparently took no effect.

The dinner-party was dismal and incongruous enough. Obsequious was a word that exactly depicted little, sleek, low-voiced Mr. Smiles, who though presiding at one end of the table, seemed ready to emulate Baillie M'Wheeble's posture; and the rival candidate, Mr. Henry Shaw, was a red-faced, punchy man, hardly distinguishable in appearance or manner from his farmer kindred, and, as soon became apparent, with such principles as he had, diametrically opposed to those of Clement, who, with his refined countenance and form, looked as if he belonged to some other world.

Mr. Underwood was wheeled in in his chair. He was not a man to give way, but rather to try to talk sorrow down; and the curate and Mr. Staples, knowing his humour, set county politics going, and all joined with a fervour, not to say violence, that struck the brothers as unsuitable. It was more than the Squire, between deafness and the burthen of grief, could follow; he grew abstracted, and presently rousing himself, turned to Clement to ask what had just passed at the other end of the table.

'That the bribery petition will fail, sir,' repeated Clement, bending with the naturally kind and courteous manner due to age, infirmity, and sorrow, and speaking in a clear sweet modulated tone, that evidently struck the old man more than the words.

'You have the family voice,' he said, looking up at him. 'Why, you are a mere lad! You don't tell me you are in Orders?'

'I was ordained Deacon last summer, sir,' said Clement colouring deeply at having to say it loud enough to attract everyone's attention.

'Ah! eh! And your age?'

'Four-and-twenty last March.'

'You don't look eighteen,' said the Squire, with that still infantine face close to him, reddening most youthfully. 'Where's your curacy?'

'At St Matthew's, Whittingtonia,' said Clement impressively, and casting his eyes round, as if, thought Felix, he were making a confession of faith and looking for persecution; but, half to the elder brother's relief, half to his diversion, they had got into a world where there was no thermometer of London churches, and no one knew what the avowal implied. Mr. Smiles asked if it were a Bethnal Green district; and Mr. Shaw observed, loud enough for the Squire to hear, that London parishes were not the places for plain straightforward men, no one was looked at who wasn't got up like a swell to please the ladies; and then they both united in rallying the youthful curate about tea-parties and pretty young ladies; but Clement was as impervious to ridicule on that score as if his head had been cowled and tonsured, and he bore it well, simply and gravely replying that he was too much occupied to go into society. He volunteered no dangerous topic, but showed much more good sense and forbearance than Felix had ventured to give him credit for in the curt answers he was compelled to make; but the old gentleman did not hear these, and began again.

'You've a sister married—eh?'

'Two,' said Clement, for Felix was too far off to be audible and as further information was looked for, 'one to Major Harewood, and the other to Sir Adrian Vanderkist.'

If Felix did for a moment feel that it sounded better than if they had married the butcher and the baker, Mr. Shaw took care to qualify the announcement with, 'Sporting baronet, ain't he? Got three horses at Epsom, I think!'

'What's that?' demanded Mr. Underwood. 'Your sister's husband on the turf?'

'I am sorry to say he is,' said Clement gravely.

'Not getting into scrapes? Any danger of his going on too fast?'

'I think not, Sir.' Felix felt he must shout, knowing well that Clement's regret was directed rather to racing in the abstract, than to any pecuniary peril, and for the first time feeling bound to defend Sir Adrian as a brother-in-law. 'He is a prudent man, and not likely to go beyond his means.'

Which was true. He was not exceeding present means. The evil was the future of the little girls, now four in number; but Clement looked reproachful at the answer he had to repeat to his neighbour, who relapsed into silence for a little while, then asked again, 'Who said one of them had married into a marching regiment?'

Mr. Staples laughed, and came to the rescue this time. 'Regiments never march but when young ladies marry into them; but it is not true in this case, Sir. Major Harewood is in the Royal Engineers, and has an appointment at Woolwich.—Didn't you tell me so?' turning to Felix. 'Have you heard anything from him of this new gun?'—which gun was safely wielded through the remainder of the meal.

After dinner, the Squire went back to his room, desiring Felix to come with him.

He looked much older than before, and made no more effort at cheeriness; as he sighed, settled himself, and signed Felix to a chair near him and his great fire.

'So!' he said. 'So things come round! Why did you not bring the nice little lad that was here before?'

'He and I cannot both leave home together, Sir. He is my right hand in the business.'

'You've not brought him up to your business?'

'I could not help it. That sun-stroke put him back in his studies, and he could not bear to be idle.'

'You must find some gentlemanly line for him; not too old, eh? You give it up, of course, you've thought better of my proposal—eh?'

'Quite impossible, Sir, thank you,' said Felix. 'You are very kind, but I am totally unfit. My education was stopped at sixteen.'

'Don't tell me you can't get through what Harry Shaw there did! Besides, what do we want of a scholar? I'd rather have a man of sense!'

'No Bishop would or could ordain me within the time.'

'Staples did say the Bishops had got more crotchetty now-a-days. How long would they insist on for preparation? I'd get little Smiles to hold it for the time.'

'It is impossible, Sir, thank you, in every way—even if I could think it right.'

'Right? It is not right the things should be separated. I've been crippled by it all my life, and cursed my folly in setting my face against the Church; and you'll hardly get the property in so good a condition as I did. Why, you're bookish already, and look like one of the cloth. Fit! you're fitter by a long chalk than Harry there! Come! think better of it. I'd not mind the cost if they insist on a turn at the University.'

'Thank you, Sir,' said Felix; 'but I cannot do it. It is against my conscience.' And as he saw that this was incomprehensible, he thought he had better bring forward a palpable testimony to the impracticability. 'Besides, I must go on with my work. There are too many of us for me to give over.'

'Many! The lad hasn't been fool enough to marry?'

'No, no, Sir; but there are two, a little brother and sister, at home, and two more at school, besides Geraldine and Lancelot.'

'All depending on you?'

'The four youngest entirely so; Geraldine earns a good deal with her painting, and Lance quite makes his own maintenance; but I could not leave them, nor break up the home.'

Six brothers and sisters were more than any one could adopt on the spot, and Mr. Underwood felt the cogency of the argument. 'Then you absolutely must keep up this confounded trade of yours till the breath is out of my body!'

'I hope to keep it up a long time yet, Sir,' said Felix; 'I have been very happy in it.'

'And—and—there's no other way?'

'Certainly not, Sir, thank you. All I have is embarked in it; and while things stand as they do, I should not be justified in making any change.'

Whatever Felix's kindred might think of his occupation, they were always forced to feel the dignity of his industry and independence. Here was this young man, under thirty, and looking younger than he was, talking of half-a-dozen of young brothers and sisters as a reason, not for accepting help, but for being let alone to maintain them; and actually showing a brother, a clergyman, scholar, and gentleman, visibly superior to what his kinsman had brought there to meet him. This was not a young heir to adopt, foster, and command, but a man to address upon equal terms, and Mr. Underwood put his next suggestion with less of authority. 'If it were not just absolute trade—retail, ain't it? It will be against you when you come here, you see. Could not you get out of it into Kedge and Underwood's firm? That would sound better.'

'Yes, Sir, but I could not throw over my business without a great loss; and it would be undertaking what I don't understand, instead of what I do.'

'Besides,' added the Squire, going on with his talk, 'with your expectations, family, place, and all, that girl of Tom's would jump at you!'

Felix shook his head decidedly, though unable to help a little inward laugh at this revival of Alda's old manoeuvre.

'By-the-by,' continued the old gentleman, 'what's become of your brother that Tom bred up?'

'We knew of him last in Australia, Sir.'

'Next to you, is he or this tall lad you have here?'

'He is older than Clement'

'Poor Tom made too much of him—eh? Well, young men will be young men,' said Mr. Underwood, too full of his own sorrows to think about Edgar; 'but they come round at last:' and therewith he fell into a talk about his own son, whose illness and death he proceeded to dwell upon, as he found he had a kind and attentive auditor; and this lasted till the butler came to wheel him off to his bed.

Felix and Clement paid an early visit to the church next morning, and found it in a course of being muffled in black. 'Seventy-five yards there allys was for every Underwood on 'em,' said Abednego Tripp, who had become much more shaky and feeble, had resigned his market-boat to Kerenhappuch's husband, and was hobbling about the church in a mixed, but on the whole a pleasant and exulting, frame of mind, by no means partaking of the intense disgust with which Clement beheld the sanctuary invaded by the paraphernalia of human woe.

Dr. May, unasked, brought Bernard over to the funeral, which was at twelve o'clock. Neither the father nor the widow attended it; but the incongruity of Edward Underwood's sons acting as chief mourners was prevented by the nearer claims of the Shaw brothers-in-law. The farmer tenants came; but the lack of neighbouring clergy and even gentry struck the brothers in contrast with the overflowing numbers who had flocked to their father's grave, so far from his ancestral home, showing how much more the man can be than the position.

Bernard was staring about him with little endeavour for appearances; and at the first moment that speech was possible, even while the hat-bands were coming off, he looked up in the face of Clement with open eyes, and said, 'My eyes! this is no end of a place! Is it what is to come to us?' Clement hushed him seriously and vigorously, but without much effect. 'Did you know 'twas like this?' he persisted, gazing round.

'I never thought about it. Hush!'

'Why, 'tis twice as jolly a house as Abbotstoke! And the woods! And the river! One might shoot every day, and fish the rest, and be always boating besides!' exclaimed Bernard, enthusiastically, but happily under his breath. 'And ain't there a hunter worth £120 here? Where is he, Clem?'

'How should I know?'

'You've been here all night and this morning, haven't you?' said Bernard, as if he had not thought even Tina capable of such indifference. 'I'll get down to the stables, and find out.'

While Clement was trying to stop him, the summons to a lugubrious luncheon did so more effectually. There Bernard had the opportunity of fraternizing with a Shaw nephew of his own age, and none of the malice of his seniors, who imparted the melancholy fact that the hunter-colt was sold, but undertook to show off the stables; but fate was too strong for Bear, he was captured by his eldest brother, and told that while Dr. May's horse was coming round, Mr. Underwood would like to see him.

The wish was far from mutual, and Bernard was as sulky as his namesake; but sulkiness might pass on such an occasion for decorous solemnity; and Bernard was always one of the show specimens—a big, well-grown, straight-limbed boy, with a handsome Underwood face, not of the girlishly rosy tinting of his brother's, but glowing with a hardy healthy sunburnt hue, and he could not but answer with a sort of glum awe-struck civility the few questions asked him, as to his age, and where he was at school, and then whether he had ever been rabbitting.

'Only once;' and Bernard's face lost its sulkiness. 'Marilda's gone and let her shooting!'

'And you like it?'

Bernard's lips only said 'yes,' but his blue eyes danced.

'Well, some of these days, you must come over and have a day with the keeper, when your brother is settled here.'

The eager face of anticipation fell, and out came at unawares, 'But that won't be till you are dead;' and then the boy began colouring to the ears.

'No, no, I don't mean this brother; but what's his name—the young parson? When he is here, you must come over. And here—' As the Doctor came in to take leave, Bernard found in his hand 'tip' that exceeded even the great days of Ferdinand's munificence!

He sprang out to Clement, who was standing in the porch. 'Oh! I say, Clem, what a splendiferous go this is!'

Again, all he got was a scandalized hush.

'I don't mean *that*. He told me himself! I'm to come over to shoot rabbits, and all that is delicious, when you are a clergyman here! Hurrah!'

'Hold your tongue, Bernard,' said Clement, with a voice of subdued impatience, 'and don't talk nonsense.'

'But you *are* going to be a clergyman here,' persisted Bernard. 'He said so.'

'That does not make it the fact.'

'O Clem, you'd never be so viciously spiteful as not to come! Think of the rabbits and the salmon, and a licence by-and-by!'

'Come, Bernard,' said Dr. May's cheery voice behind; then, as he shook hands with Clement, 'You must find your way over to Stoneborough when you are settled here. Our church is a sort of rival to yours.'

'Not mine,' protested Clement; but the Doctor was in a hurry, and was off. Business was to be done with the family lawyer, and Felix got a hint that he might be wanted after a time, so he betook himself to a nook in the cloister, redolent with old memories, and began a letter to Mr. Audley. Clement, as he really believed with malice prepense, put himself entirely out of reach by starting off for a walk with Mr. Smiles, who, detecting that the London clergyman's mind was far from made up to bury himself in a dull, secluded, straggling country parish, had kindly volunteered to show him the beauties of the scenery.

Nearly two hours had passed, when a tall shadow came across the arch, and Clement's low eager voice asked, 'Have you any money about you?'

'Just about enough to get home with. Why?'

'How near is Ewmouth?'

'Nearly four miles. What *are* you after?'

'I can do it before dinner;' and the long legs seemed about to move off.

'Stay, Clement! What?'

'I must raise enough to get a bottle of port. There's a child sinking in typhus. Don't detain me, Felix. I find there's no help for it. I must have this place,' he added, as if throwing a tub to the whale to effect his escape.

'Stop, ask for some here.'

'No use. Squire forbids all giving in that quarter.'

'What do you mean to do?'

'I must dispose of—of—of—Well, it must be this,' touching his little cross, Ferdinand's gift, and nearly his favourite possession.

'Come! It won't do to make your début at Ewmouth by disposing of your jewelry. I left myself a margin of half-a-crown, and if we walk from the station, that will save two shillings more.'

'That will do,' said Clement. 'Thank you, Fee, you shall have it again. I had given all I had about me in the other hovel. The woman is waiting in the churchyard. I'll send her off, and then tell you.'

Felix accompanied him through the beautiful summer garden to the rough rugged churchyard, where a lean woman in tattered drab-coloured garments by no means accorded with the paradisaical notion of Vale Leston. Her distress was so genuine that she scarcely thanked Clement; but assuring him she could now get what she wanted, she walked off.

Clement sighed, and looked up at the great massive church, not with Felix's pitying love, but like a mighty burthen.

'Well, Clem!'

'Well! I see it must be done.'

'I am very glad.'

'I am sure I am very sorry,' said Clement, with a simplicity new in him.

Before any more could pass, a servant came in search of them to summon them to Mr. Underwood's room. He looked worn and sorrowful, but there was a certain look of pleasure at the entrance of the two young men; and he made a sort of introduction of them to the lawyer, Mr. Wilder, a London solicitor, then turning to Felix, he once more asked if he still declined all idea of eventually taking the living.

'Certainly I do, thank you, Sir.'

'So,' said Mr. Underwood, 'as is only just, the offer is passed on to your brother.'

Clement bowed his head, colouring crimson, and the tears coming into his eyes, as with a trembling lip he answered, 'Thank you, Sir; I will do my best, God helping me.'

It was curious how this weight of responsibility was extinguishing self-consciousness, and making a man of him. The tone of his reply seemed to surprise both Squire and lawyer; and the former said, in an old man's tone of encouragement, 'That is well. No one can say more. Now give us your full name, that we may get on with the formalities.'

'Edward Clement Underwood, B.A., St. Cadoc's.'

'Edward?'

'It is my first name, but I have never been so called.'

'Edward! Strange it should so come about! Well, you may do pretty well here. Small tithes commuted for £420—(Rather a contrast, thought Felix, to the recent difficulty of raising a few shillings!)—a fair provision for a young man; if you are content not to launch out, nor be in a hurry to marry.'

'Certainly not,' said Clement, with an emphasis that made everybody look up to see whether he showed any tokens of having met with a disappointment in love; but if his cheeks were redder than usual, lip and eye were steady and resolute enough.

'I hope not,' proceeded his patron: 'it is the worst thing a young man can do to get his neck into the noose before he has had time to look about him. And there's the Vicarage—been used to enlarge our stable room—will have to be rebuilt altogether; so you had best let your horse keep your residence for the present, and come and look after the old man. I would not be much of a burden to you; but this is a big house, and it is getting lonesome.'

'I will do whatever I can to be a comfort to you, Sir,' said Clement earnestly. 'It is very kind in you, and I will certainly come first to you. Only, Sir, I ought to warn you that I have been bred up in a very stringent school of principles, and that if I come here, I shall feel it my duty to do my best to carry them out.'

Mr. Underwood smiled at the lawyer. 'How exactly boys get the trick of their father. I could think this twenty years back! Well, changes for the worse there *can't* be! Ungrateful set of drunken poaching rascals as ever lived! And as to the church, what notions you may bring there won't do me much harm, so long as you don't bring it about your ears. Only, look you, Edward, a word in your ear. Don't let Jane—Mrs. Fulbert, I mean—cajole you into doing up the Vicarage for her.'

'Very well, Sir,' said Clement dreamily.

'You had better stay on a few days and look about you; I'd send you over to see the Bishop.'

'No, Sir, thank you, I must get back to-morrow. I have little enough time to prepare for my Ordination, but I will come down as soon after as Mr. Fulmort can make it convenient to spare me.'

'Ay, and little Smiles will see to the duty meantime; but I say, Edward, you are inexperienced, and he is a dirty little dog. Don't let him expect anything from you till you've read in. He's got his quarter, and 'tis the churchwarden's business to provide.'

Felix hoped other people did not find Clement's face so intelligible as he did when this turned out to be the warning to inexperience. There was little more to be done, and the conference broke up to give the Squire time to rest before dinner.

'And now, my dear Vicar,' said Felix, linking his arm into his brother's, and leading him to a walk beneath a wisteria-covered wall, 'let me hear what brought you to this laudable resolution.'

'I wish it may be laudable,' said poor Clement, brushing away a couple of great tear-drops; 'I only know I have taken leave of all comfort or ease of mind for life, and I suppose that may be right!'

'I thought,' said Felix, a little hurt, 'that my father's objection to this place was its perfect ease.'

'A good deal has gone to the bad since his time,' said Clement, 'and well it may! I could think of nothing but the traffic in Babylon the Great of "the souls of men," and wonder whether I was sharing in it! Not a word as to my fitness or unfitness, not an attempt at inquiry! I might be the veriest disgrace to my Orders for what they cared, so long as my name is Underwood!'

'And, Edward!' said Felix, 'I can't but be touched to see how the poor old man feels it an act of restitution. It is the best he knows, Clem, his first step, and I am glad you have not baulked him of it.'

'It is a vicious and rotten system altogether,' said Clement, 'and I am not sure how far one is justified in submitting to it.'

'And now, without going into the question of lay-patronage, what brought you to submit to it?'

'I'll tell you, Felix. I set out to walk with Smiles, to see the place, and set Shaw so far on his way home. We went on beyond the village street, where all looks smooth and fair—all roses and gable-ends—like the model place you fancy it, and maybe it was in Father's time. On by the little river—'

'The Leston. Isn't it beautiful?'

'It is like places I saw in Wales. Well, there is another little ravine running down to meet that—very wild—a show place.'

'Blackstone Gulley. Isn't there a quarry?'

'Indeed there is; and *such* a set of hovels round it, run up in a hollow without a notion of health or comfort! It seems the demand for the stone is uncertain; so these wretched quarrymen are half their time poaching and pilfering, a villainous ferocious lot, that do all the harm in the neighbourhood—in fact, the Squire flew into a rage at the very name. He had forbidden anything from his house to be given to them; and even the Miss Hepburns were afraid to go among them. What are you laughing at, Felix?'

'Because I see why Mr. Smiles took you that way. Go on.'

'He took us to the best point of view, but told us we had better not go down, as typhus was raging there. I offered to wait if he had any one to visit; and behold! it was against the principles of both to go unless they were sent for. Mr. Shaw said it was making oneself too common, and Mr. Smiles had to consider Mrs. Smiles and the children. By that time we had been seen, and a woman sallied out to speak to him; and would you believe it, he tried to warn her off with "You see I have gentlemen with me! I always tell you to go to Mr. Tripp!" Then it struck me that I need not stand on the etiquette our Vicar is always so particular about, since it is nobody's parish just now, and I had the offer; so I offered to go and see what she wanted. Smiles said a good deal about the deceitfulness of the women, and the danger of venturing when the men were at home, as if one had never been down a court in Whittingtonia.'

'And was it very bad?'

'Bad, yes. Except that there's clear air and water outside, it is as miserable as anything I ever saw in town, and more squalid and savage. Four huts with cases of typhus! Though after all, it is not worse than our district is in the winter; and it is by tens, while that is by hundreds. Moreover, Ewmouth is getting into this parish, building fast on this side. When I saw and heard those two men, and knew the place would be turned over to one or other of them, I could not leave it to such a fate!'

'Quite right; and not at all what the curate expected.'

'I had thought,' continued Clement, 'that such clergy had become extinct; but I suppose nothing of a better stamp would have put up with the poor man we buried to-day. I had imagined the choice only lay between me and some one who, if without my advantages, would be superior in experience and weight; but now I see the alternative: it is plain that it is a call, though why—why it should have come to me, I cannot think.'

'Perhaps,' said Felix, 'because we are especially bound to fight against the evil our family has allowed to accumulate.'

'At my age, and all alone! I say, Felix,' after a pause, 'can one get the key of the church?'

'The door into the cloister used not to be kept locked,' said Felix, turning in that direction; and then, struck by the loveliness of the lights and shadows, and the banksias trailing over the cloister tracery, he could not help exclaiming, 'There's no place like it! You will grow very fond of it, Clem!'

'I dare say I shall,' said Clement, to whose eyes the beauty seemed to go for nothing, and who was quite past his usual heed to keeping up his dignity with his brothers; 'I dare say I shall when I have worked here a little while; but I had rather have had the dingiest cell in the clergy-house and Fred Somers. Just as I had got back, when we thought we should have such a time of it—working together there, for life perhaps!'

'You might have him for a curate.'

'Fred! He'd never come to "easy duty in a romantic country and eligible neighbourhood,"' indignantly quoted Clement; 'and for my part, with only a population of eight hundred, if I were to set up a curate, I should just give myself over to be a fat, double-chinned, easy-going incumbent!'

'You're a good way from that,' said Felix, looking at the tall slight being by his side; 'but I think you are right. I am as sorry for you as can be, Clem, when I think of your pleasant evenings at the clergy-house, and what it will be with that poor old man; but you see he ought to be cared for as well as the parish, and there is no one but you who can do it.'

'I must try!' said Clement, with something of a gasp.

'Well,' said Felix, who had by this time reached the door, 'I do feel obliged to you, Clement. This helps me immensely.'

It was a great consolation to Clement that one person at least did not congratulate him on the preferment that weighed on him so sorely; but after he had spent some time alone in the church, he had mastered himself, and was quite satisfactory all the evening. Their dinner companions were the widow and her mother. The former did not look very much crushed, though she carried a large pocket-handkerchief; and her mother declared that nothing could have brought her down but her desire to be acquainted with her cousins. Felix could not help thinking of the pic-nic; and before long he perceived the drama that was being enacted. Her great object was evidently to stay on, and continue the ruler of the Priory; and Mr. Underwood was equally desirous to get her, not only out of the house, but out of the village; but he could not quite tell her so on the day of the funeral, and hints neither of them would take. Then she fastened upon Clement, and discoursed to him about *her* charities, and her regrets that during her dear Fulbert's long decline she could do so little; only she knew things were in such excellent hands with the Miss Hepburns, good old ladies, perfectly devoted, treasures for any parish; but for herself—she was only too much at liberty now, she should be delighted to go the round of the parish with him, and introduce him to her own peculiar pets!

Clement could not snub direct; but he only bowed, he did not commit himself; only in all simplicity he did ask about these charities, and only succeeded in raising a mist of words, in which the desirableness of not destroying self-dependence, and the pauperizing tendency of liberality, were the prominent ideas.

Clement ventured a question about Blackstone Gulley; but Mrs. Underwood hurriedly cautioned him under her breath not to say a word about it before the Squire, it excited him so fearfully—the people were such desperate poachers and thieves, and did such wanton mischief! They were evidently viewed as quite out of the pale of humanity.

Little did the lady imagine that they were the chief attraction to the Vicar-elect!

The brothers had to be off so early the next morning, that they made their farewells that night. Mrs. Underwood hospitably told Clement they would be better acquainted; but when he took leave with the old Squire, his hand was held fast, while the broken eager voice entreated, 'You'll soon be back—you'll come soon? You shall have the study, and any rooms in the house you like.—Been down to the stables? Just say which saddle-horse you like best; I'll have him kept for you.'

'Thank you, Sir, but I am a very good walker.' (Felix was glad he did not say he could not ride—a degeneracy in an Underwood that plainly had not occurred to the Squire.)

'Nonsense! Can't get about in this country without a horse. Mind, I didn't mean that you should keep it for yourself. Take a look, if you have not yet, and say which of the two.'

'The quietest!' exclaimed Clement, in a tone nearly of entreaty, diverting to his elder brother, who had had enough pony-back before his eighth year, with a little subsequent refreshment on Mr. Audley's horse, to give him a pitying disdain for anxieties on that score.

'Eh? You are a steady-going parson—don't want a showy beast? That's as young parsons are now-a-days. Well, you shall have the chestnut, very good to ride or drive. Write, I say, as soon as you can fix your day. You might see the Bishop in town. Only don't,' lowering his voice, 'leave me long alone with Jane.'

Just after the hot water had been brought to the brothers' rooms the next morning, there was a simultaneous knocking at the door of communication, and then an equally simultaneous turning of the handles, which was of course ineffectual, till Felix let go, and Clement got it open; and they stood laughing at each other, each holding an envelope, one addressed to F. Underwood, Esquire, the other to the Reverend Edward Underwood, each containing a cheque for £10, and scrawled on the flap of each—'To cover expenses of journey. F.U.'

'Expenses of journey—poor old man!' said Felix. 'It would go some way to a special train!'

'I suppose this is myself,' said Clement.

'Ah, you'll have to resign yourself to be Edward for the rest of your days.'

'Do you mean to take it?'

'Impossible not to let him have the pleasure of it. Poor man, depend upon it he is wishing it had been my father all the time. And it might have been—' Felix's face quivered and contracted. 'No, it won't do to think of that. But, Clem, look here—we won't exactly walk from Paddington; but deducting the one pound five that this really has cost me, you shall take the rest of mine for Blackstone Gulley.'

'It must have cost you more.'

'No, for I was coming to town any way. Did I not tell you that I am to meet poor Edgar's creditors on Cherry's behalf, and settle with them?'

'Poor Cherry! It has been a noble thing for her to have carried out, but one cannot but feel it wasted.'

'No,' said Felix, 'she will never feel it so. Whatever she may do for the future, she will be able to feel that she has been just before she was generous. Remember, she will have sent our name home again cleared of debt. I am proud to owe that to her! Now, whichever of us is ready first must write the old man a grateful note, and we will both sign it.'

'Stay, Felix! I can't have you giving this to my people. I shall have plenty.'

'In time, but I don't expect you will have much in hand for some time; and if the Squire is so furious against these people, you won't like to ask him. Besides, they are my people, in a way, as well as yours; and if this is really the earnest of my inheritance, I should like it to go to them.'

CHAPTER XXXV.

THE OLD SQUIRE AND THE NEW.

'I remember, I remember,
The house where I was born,
The little window where the sun
Came peeping in at morn.'
T. Hood.

So it was that the Reverend Edward Clement Underwood became Vicar of Vale Leston Abbas; and as Geraldine observed, when she saw his whole worldly possessions waiting for the omnibus, he probably carried with him less personal property than any entering incumbent on the rolls of fame. All was contained in one box, one portmanteau, and one black bag, and chiefly consisted in the more clerical of his father's books, his pocket-communion plate in the well-worn case, and a few gifts from St Matthew's, not unaccompanied with cautions on their use.

He spent a few days at home; and Mr. Bevan, who after his five years' holiday had just come home, not only called on him, but asked him to preach and to dine, including Felix in the latter invitation; but both were impossible, as Clement was due at Vale Leston on the Saturday. Thenceforth his family heard little of him. He had never been much of a letter-writer, except when he sent a sort of essay on Church affairs to direct the Pursuivant, and even these nearly ceased, so that, as Lance said, there was no guessing whether he viewed the squire as the wicked world or as a sick old sinner. And with Lance, Clement had had a sort of passage-at-arms. He wanted much to have sent him to the University, and was much vexed when Lance for many reasons declined; but the offer and refusal were unknown—by the wish of both parties—to the rest of the family. Clement said it was all indolence, and passion for that organ of Ferdinand Travis's, which, now it had come at last, had proved transcendently well worth waiting for. Clement viewed it with some jealousy, and predicted that Lance would rue his decision; and Lance could not help resenting what was unjust in the accusation and prognostic, the more for what was just in it. To be sure, his displeasure went no further than the resumption of the impudent old name of Tina, but from Lance that implied much.

Clement as a beneficed clergyman was something tangible; otherwise people were rather disappointed to find Mr. Underwood in his natural place, looking just as usual, and though to one or two close inquirers he allowed that some property might come to him some day, he declared that it made no difference. And when people found no blunders in their accounts, no failures in their serials, and no neglect of their parcels, they left off thinking he must necessarily be demoralised; and though the Tribune sneered more than ever at the organ of a bloated aristocracy, the world in general soon forgot, and then disbelieved, that their attentive bookseller had any 'expectations.'

Indeed, Felix himself had made up his mind, as he told his home sister and brother, that the Squire had still many years to live, and that the inheritance was only to be viewed as a dispensation from laying by for old age, a point on the duty of which he had never decided, having in truth nothing to lay by. The interests he now had in the place, and the security of a welcome, satisfied his affection for it; and he was too much at home in his present occupation to feel impatient to have it ended.

Geraldine found the waiting a greater trial. Longings for the green grass, the purple moorland, the sparkling river, and broad sea would come over her; and she would wonder whether the best years of their lives were to be spent in the Bexley streets, where she could not help fancying the smoke of the potteries more apparent than ever; and whether Felix were condemned to stand behind a counter till he had grown too old to begin a new life. Then she blamed herself, and tried to struggle the thought away; but there was to her an absolute oppression in Bexley summer air, and an uncongeniality in the dull ugly surroundings, that made content an almost impossible achievement; and the anticipation assuredly did not make her happier for the present.

She declared however that Angela was wholesome to her, as a tipsy Helot was to the Spartans. The girl was intoxicated with the prospect when she suddenly plunged into it on coming home for the summer holidays. It seemed nearly as good as her intended Duke, and she talked continually of the horses she would ride, the tours she would take, the balls she would frequent, while Felix would drily build up her castles to some such manifestly outrageous height as to make them topple down headlong with her.

She was not the only Helot. Madame Tanneguy's sympathetic excitement knew no bounds, and she clasped her hands with a gesture learnt in France, as she rejoiced in Mr. Underwood being reinstated, and never would hear or understand that there was no *re* in the case. She would be enthusiastic; she would drop in on Sundays, and question Felix point by point about that magnificent place; and it must be owned that he liked sympathy well enough not to answer her as ungraciously as Cherry would have approved. She even tried to bring little Gustave, that he and Theodore might grow accustomed to one another; but in this she never succeeded, for Theodore having learnt that he must neither scream at nor attack the little Frenchman, never saw him approach without retreating to Sibby in the kitchen, or his brothers in the office.

But Lady Price's demonstrations were much more amusing. She had come home a good deal subdued and more on her guard, and she could take advantage of the former Miss Underwood having been so fully occupied to excuse her past neglect. She asked Felix to dinner, and his sisters to croquet parties indefatigably, and tried to get up musical entertainments which must lead to his singing with Miss Caroline. What to do was a perplexity. Felix did not like to refuse altogether overtures from the Rectory, for he had a warm feeling for poor Mr. Bevan himself; but the horrible penance of singing with Miss Price he backed out of pitilessly on the score of want of time; and as to the garden parties, Geraldine hated them, and would have declined them altogether if Angela had not been wild to go; and Felix and Wilmet both decreed that it would be better for the child to accustom her to a little society than to leave her pining and raving for amusement within her reach. So as long as Angela was at home, Cherry consented to go to the Rectory croquet, and horribly dull she found it. Lady Price used demonstratively to inquire after her sister Lady Vanderkist, and how Mr. Clement was getting on, and would introduce her to two or three of the lookers on; but they were not apt to be of the mould who brought out Cherry's powers of conversation; and she never got on well with any one but the old Miss Crabbe who had once brought Stella home, and who knew the Vale Leston neighbourhood, and could tell her a good deal about it.

Wilmet had never come home to institute her reformation. John's occupation did not give him much leisure, and his mother's kindred sent him so urgent an invitation, that he felt the more obliged to carry his wife among them, because it was an act of forgiveness for his marrying her. One of his mother's sisters had died, leaving him her portion, and the survivor yearned after poor Lucy's son and his little boy. So Wilmet was taken amongst the Oglandby clan, and took all the gentlemen by storm by her beauty, and all the ladies by her domesticity and good sense; and John found himself so taken up with business connected with the bequest, that no time could be made for either of the homes. Besides, it was greatly suspected that as a mother Wilmet was afraid of Theodore and his jealousy, for she never offered to run down without her husband. Indeed, he was carrying on a hard struggle to keep up to his work through the inveterate remains of neuralgic suffering left by his accident, and only those who stayed any time in the house knew how brave an effort were his industry and cheerfulness.

Robina had a capital situation as second governess in a large household, where she seemed very happy; while William Harewood continued to win prosperity and honour at Oxford, ending by obtaining a first class, and becoming a student of Christchurch. Who would have augured the like of Bill?

The most visible effects of the heirship were big hampers of game, which appeared at intervals all through the autumn and winter; and Felix did thoroughly enjoy the carrying over the choicest spoils therefrom to Marshlands, where they gave a great deal of pleasure and a certain kind of pride. Now that Mr. Froggatt had seen no symptoms of the turning of Felix's head, he began to believe in his prospects, and to be a good deal divided between regard for him and for the business.

Bernard was the one who profited most by the present state of things. Not only did he go over twice, for a day, from Stoneborough to Vale Leston, but he spent a week there at the beginning of the Christmas holidays, chiefly in the society of the gamekeeper. So supremely happy was he, and so brilliant were his descriptions to Madame Tanneguy, that by the time they had gone through a Russian scandal process among her confidantes Vale Leston had swelled to the dimensions of Windsor Castle; and Lance and Angel were incited to prepare for her especial benefit a parody of 'Bolton Abbey in the Olden Time,' with Clement in the character and costume of the Abbot, presiding over the like profusion of game.

Not much more could be got out of the boy. He would talk indeed plentifully, but it was all of rabbits and ferrets, pheasants and ducks, horses and dogs. He evidently viewed himself as the Underwood who alone could do his duty by the *feræ naturæ* of the estate; and though his magniloquence was not perfectly trustworthy, the elders gathered from it that the old Squire had really been pleased to find in one of the brothers the sportsman tastes he could appreciate, and had encouraged the boy by telling him all manner of hunting anecdotes, and letting him have the run of the woods. Bernard was small enough to have no dignity to lose, and had galloped on the ponies turned out to grass; but Felix had a curiosity to learn how Clement got on with the chestnut, a question which set the school-boy into fits of laughing. 'Oh! I believe he sticks on somehow now, but just like a pair of compasses, you know. Joe says if he has been spilt once he has been spilt forty times. He knows by the mud on his clothes, you see; but Mr. Eddard, as every one calls him, never says one word about it, but stalks in just as upright as ever, and only once or twice they thought he was a little stiff.'

'But does he go on all the same?' asked Cherry, rather alarmed.

'Oh yes, 'tis dogged as does it; and one can't get about there without riding; such roads, and mud, and water-courses up to your knees. Yes, and Joe doesn't think he's been off for more than a month now.'

'Hurrah!' said Lance, 'I always knew Clem had lots of pluck in his own way! And does he drive?'

'He drives out the Squire whenever it is fine enough.'

Much more could not be made out. The boy had, as Cherry said, a fine singleness of eye. The game was in full focus, all the rest very dim and obscure. Yes, Clem had a jolly room enough. What he did, or whether he went out much, this deponent knew not, only that he believed the church bell rang at eight—he thought Clem rang it himself. Dinner was at seven, uncommon jolly—a capital cellar—and he was with difficulty called back from an imposing enumeration of wines, to say that Mrs. Fulbert was certainly not in the house. Mr. Underwood seldom left his room till the middle of the day, and then, if he were well and the weather fine, Clement attended his airing, then left him to sleep, and after dinner played piquet or cribbage with him. When once Mr. Staples dined there, Bernard had taken a hand at whist, of which he was inordinately proud.

That was all that could be gathered with any certainty, though Bernard did nothing but groan for Vale Leston whenever he was not skating. They had learnt that the Vicar of Vale Leston could ride and play at cards, and they might make the most of that.

Nor did they hear more till the next April, when Felix received the following note:—

Vale Leston Priory, April 29th.
MY DEAR FELIX,

If you can get away I wish you would come down without loss of time. Just after Bernard left us, Mr. Underwood got a chill, and has had a good deal of suppressed gout. The doctor thinks ill of him. I find he never has been a Communicant. Latterly, the sense of wrong done to my father has held him back. It is not satisfactory now, and I long for a priest of experience, but I must do my best, and time and faculty seem failing. Your presence and participation would be a comfort. Can you run down? I will have the 4.40 train met on Monday.

Your affectionate Brother,
E.C.U.

At 4.40 accordingly, Felix beheld a sporting-looking dog-cart of varnished wood, containing a long black figure holding a very big chestnut horse, and stretching out an eager hand to grasp his brother's. 'That's right, Felix! I'm glad you are come!'

'Is he worse?'

'He has been changing rapidly since I wrote to you. Page does not know what to think of him. I've been writing to ask Dr. May to come over to-morrow.'

'You look fagged, Clem. Does the nursing fall on you?'

'We have a nurse now; and he seemed disposed to sleep, so I thought I might come and meet you,' said Clement, who not only had the heavy eyes of broken rest, but altogether had lost the childish contour of face, and acquired the stamp of thought and reality.

'The daughter-in-law is no help, I suppose?'

Clement laughed, but rather sadly. 'They had had a great row over poor Fulbert's properties before I came on the scene at all. She never was anything but a grievance to him. He meant his son to have had Marilda; and when that failed, consented to pay his debts and let him marry this person, on his yielding to take Holy Orders—a miserable business, and he feels it so now. I have tried to bring about a better state of feeling, but I can't feel my way. I think there is more good in her than he gives her credit for; and he fancies she blinds me, and has as good as ordered me never to speak of her again.'

'Then he has quite adopted you?'

'Oh, yes, he is very kind to me,' said Clement warmly, and from what he went on to say, it was clear that he had grown fond of his charge, and found it far less of a burthen than he had expected, though he must have been often crossed, and could have met with little congeniality.

He had been left quite unfettered in action as a clergyman; indeed, the Squire had supported him under the growls of a few malcontents, and though this was chiefly on the ground that State must stand by Church, Underwood by Underwood, and that tenants had no business to think, still it was effective. The only quarrels had been caused by the young Vicar's peacemaking endeavours towards the widow, his proclivities towards the pariahs of Blackstone Gulley, and his backwardness to enter into county gaieties.

'Young men were hardly to be trusted if they were not like young men,' argued the Squire; and he was vexed if he found Clement avoiding a party or refusing a dinner on the score of parish engagements. Indeed, an invitation from a sporting nobleman of a questionable repute was declined at the cost of such offence, that Clement had thought he should have to reconstruct the Vicarage, if not repair at once to sleep in the hay-loft thereof; but after one evening's storm, the subject had never been renewed. To have had more of the animal and less of the spiritual in his young inmate would have been pleasanter and more comprehensible to the old gentleman; and he had begun by a certain distrust of what the military comrades of his youth and the hunting associates of his later years would have declared sanctimonious hypocrisy in so young a man. The first offer—as a mere matter of course—to read prayers to him had been received with a snarl, and a dry 'Thank you, I'll let you know when I require your services.'

Clement had desisted, and strengthened by the Vicar's counsel, had waited to feel his way and win his ground, by many a reading of the newspaper, many a game at piquet, many a prose on the Shaw misdeeds and on county politics, and by what the poor old man had never known before—the genuine filial kindness of reverence for age and infirmity, without interested adulation.

After all, it was the attacks on the young parson's new-fangledness that first led to discussions that died away only to be renewed again, revealing queer prejudices and conclusions based on nearly total ignorance—the ignorance of a careless son of a careless household sixty years back, and since alienated from all religious teaching by the consciousness of one act of injustice in requital of unusual forbearance and generosity.

Clement felt as though he had done nothing, and that the opportunity was fast fleeting. Where he had but stirred the waters, he thought that a man like Mr. Fulmort might have produced real effect; and he was downcast and humble at his own inefficiency, though he allowed that no stranger would probably have been permitted to go so far as he, a youth, an Underwood, and a son of the injured cousin's.

This, Felix's third arrival, was unlike the former ones. He had no need to watch his brother's countenance for tokens of interest; Clement was the one at home, and with his heart in the place, though still he looked as if he thought there was irrelevance in the cry of loving joy that broke from Felix at first sight of the valley in its beauty. The moor, the wood, the river, and the sea, did not go for much with the Vicar—it was the people he thought of, and the damages and deficiencies of the Church struck him infinitely more than the grandeur of the tower and picturesque beauty of the building.

He had no power to make changes in the fabric; and indeed, it had been Mr. Fulmort's advice that in all the alterations which he should introduce, he should carefully distinguish between essentials and non-essentials, including in the former that spiritual support for himself, which was needful to prevent the salt from losing savour, and himself from becoming lowered to his people's level while waiting to raise them, but omitting what would be viewed as mere outward ornament till minds were trained to enter into it.

So, though Abednego Tripp's voice still reigned supreme in the responses, there was a full complement of daily prayer and weekly feast, though the Vicar's very heart ached over the blankness, dreariness, and scant attendance. The main body of the parishioners never indeed openly censured an Underwood, but they viewed these aberrations on the part of 'Mr. Eddard,' as an outcome of gentlefolks' lack of employment 'The last Passon Fulbert, *he* were all for hosses, this here Passon Eddard, *he* be all for churchings,' was the parish judgment; and only now and then were deep-set grafts implanted by his father discovered to cheer his heart.

Indeed, the influences of school, visiting, lectures, and classes, were the more impeded by the influence of the four Miss Hepburns.

'Ah!' said Clement, as he touched his hat to a tall grey and russet form, 'there goes one of the trials of my life! All the religion in the parish was kept up by those good ladies, and now they think mine worse than none. They call me "Poor young man!" Yes, you may laugh, Felix; but it is they who prevent me from making way. If they were only Dissenters, I should know what to be at; but they have deserved all the love and reverence of the parish all these years, and now they turn it against me!'

'Knowingly?'

'So far as that they sigh at me, and warn people against trusting to ordinances, as if I ever taught any such thing, or as if people needed to be told *not* to go to church.'

'They don't do that?'

'Not exactly; but it amounts to an excuse for not going. And if I object to one tract, they ingeniously substitute another just as bad. I can't turn them out of the school. They were so much disgusted when I got the Sunday school out of the Lady Chapel into the Vicarage, the stable you know, that I was in hopes they would cut the concern; but no, they go on like martyrs. Their object is to counteract me. They have as good as told me they think it their mission.'

'Do you argue?'

'Oh yes, I did so plentifully the first six months, but they always assumed I said something I never even dreamt of. They even went to Mr. Underwood, but I don't think they got much out of him,' said Clement, laughing a little. 'Of late I have had no time to go near them; and my one comfort is they don't think Blackstone Gulley a place for ladies, and fancy we have nothing to do with the East Ewmouth suburb. I don't know why I should rejoice, though! The place there grows every day, and into heathenism.'

No wonder poor Clement was fagged, melancholy, and discouraged. His life was lonely. There were no gentry in the village but these ladies; and he—with his strong opinions and assertion of his office—was exactly the person to be as heavy a trial to middle-aged ladies of opposite traditions, and accustomed to a semi-pastorate in the neglected parish, as ever they could be to him. The neighbouring clergy, except one overtasked incumbent, on the farther side of Ewmouth, were of their way of thinking, pitied them, and stood courteously aloof from the new-comer. Stoneborough was too far off for much intercourse, and even there his peculiarities stood in his light, and his position as the guest of his invalid kinsman prevented him from bringing a friend to stay with him, or arranging an exchange to give himself relaxation. He had not even been able to go up to Cambridge for his M.A. degree, and had not once slept out of the Priory. Of this he did not complain, but no doubt this isolation had assisted in his depression and belief that he was failing utterly, and doing nothing but mischief.

It seemed to be an inexpressible relief to talk to some one who could understand him; and perhaps he had never so enjoyed his brother's society before.

The butler met them at the door, saying that Mr. Underwood was awake, and asking for both him and 'Mr. Felix;' and Clement led the way at once to the sitting-room, where the old man still was daily wheeled, for the restlessness of rapid failure was on him; and the sight of his wan puffy-looking face and the sinking in of his whole figure startled Felix, even after what he had heard. He lighted up a little at the sight of 'Edward,' and held out a cold damp hand to Felix, complaining of chill; nor could he bear to lose sight of the younger cousin again. Every moment he wanted his help to change his posture or alter his pillows; and when the brothers were called away to dinner, Clement would hardly have gone save to obtain an opportunity of telling his brother that he saw much change in this short time, and to despatch a message for the medical man from Ewmouth.

He, however, said nothing definite, but administered an anodyne, and promised to come early, advising Clement to leave the night-watch to the nurse, as causing less excitement, and perhaps with a view likewise to the visible effects of a long course of anxious and disturbed nights.

But in the early light of May morning, Clement was standing by his brother's bed-side, saying in a low agitated voice, 'Felix, I think the end is coming. His mind is clear, and he wants to see you. I think we ought to have the Celebration. I hoped to have brought him to send for Jane—in fact, I have sent. You must judge if we ought to wait.'

Felix had less experience of the approach of death than the young clergyman, but the ashy sunken face and hollow breath assured him that there was no time to lose. The old man was sensible, and perfectly knew Felix, but was too much oppressed to speak much; only after a time he said, with an odd kind of smile, 'That boy Edward does more for me than ever my own, poor fellow—like his father—glad he has his place—he's not next to you?'

'Not if poor Edgar be living, sir.'

'Don't let a scamp come between him and the property,' gasped the old man; but Felix felt no need of answering.

'Wish my uncle had signed his will,' was the next murmur. 'Edward and Mary would have done better—maybe, my poor boy, too. Is Edward there? I say—you lads—never drive a son into the Church, whatever you do.'

It was a remote temptation, but there was an echo of repentance in the warning. No more was said till all had been made ready. Old Tripp had been sent for to make up the number; the household contained no Communicant. The dying man made each brother give him his hand, and said, 'Peace with all, isn't that it? You, both of you, Felix and Edward, I did use your father and mother as I ought not, though somehow I thought at the time I had the right, but I believe I have suffered for it all my life; and I ask your pardon as I would ask theirs.'

'Indeed you have it, as I know you had theirs,' Felix said. 'My brother knows as well as I, how no word like bitterness was ever allowed amongst us.'

'Did Edward forgive me at last?'

'Not at last,' said Felix; 'he had done it so much at first, that he never thought of it.'

'And,' added Clement, 'will you not send a message to your daughter-in-law—to Jane, sir?'

'To Jane? Much she cares! Well, if you say I must, and if Edward forgave me, I suppose—Tell her I'll do my best to forgive—but if she had never got hold of poor Fulbert—God forgive me—what am I getting to? Only mind she doesn't do the same by you. Ay, I'm at peace with her and all of 'em! Only don't let her come. God have mercy on me?' The cry was, at least, half bodily.

And so the holy rite began in dark doubt and dim trust and hope. How unlike the bright cheeriness and the joy that no man could take away from Edward Underwood's last Communion! This was the last interval of clear consciousness. All that day he was dying, with just perception enough to cling to Clement's presence and voice, as almost unceasingly the young man held him up, and prayed with and for him with the earnestness of one who held intensely full faith in the might of intercessory prayer to aid the spirit in the doubtful strife, often supported by the thought of the prayers that were rising in so many churches far away for the struggling and the dying.

Felix was with him at times, but no one could do much to aid his physical exertion; and it was needful to keep guard over Mrs. Fulbert Underwood, as long as there was mind enough left for her presence to cause emotion. It had been right of Clement to send for her, but she was a trying element in the day, though not loud or coarse, but tearful and affectionate about the dear old Squire's former kindness and the wretched misunderstanding that had come between. There was every reason to believe her a harpy, but at this moment she could not show her talons; and Felix was divided between sense of humbug and fear of injustice during the long uncongenial *tête-à-tête*. The only breaks in it were from the doctors. Mr. Page was backwards and forwards the whole day, and Dr. May came in the course of the morning; but they could do nothing but apply these resources of science that seem but to lengthen out the death agony. However, the greatest refreshment of that day was a turn under the wall with Dr. May, hearing how highly he thought of Clement's whole conduct towards the old man.

'I don't say the lad is altogether after my cut,' said the Doctor. 'We old folks used to think ourselves up in the steeple, and now we find these young ones think us down in the crypts. I'm afraid he may be bringing a hornet's nest about his ears, but that's all outside; and for the rest, nobody could have had such an effect on poor old Ful Underwood without something very genuine in him.'

'That is quite true,' said Felix; 'Clement has startled us sometimes, but we have never done otherwise than respect his thorough sincerity; and he always shows to the very best in any trouble or trial.'

'Ay,' said Dr. May; 'and I'll tell you another thing I've been slow to find out. It's not one youth in a hundred that if he is moderate enough to stop with what satisfied our—my—generation, has anything in him. Why, as I saw it well put the other day—Ethel was delighted with the notion—King Arthur tried to work up the Round Table, and because Christian chivalry had raised that generation, comes the Quest of the Sancgreal to lead them higher. 'Tis one of the tests of life whether we will take to our Quest and let others take to it. Tying them down to our Round Table does no good at all. But what am I talking of? You are one of these boys yourself.'

'I suppose I am,' said Felix; 'but I own I should be happier to see things as my father would have had them.'

'Somehow I saw it in you. Veneration has fixed your standard, I take it; and you've had all the cares in the world to sober you. But depend upon it—I've seen it many a time, in my own boys as well as others—enthusiasm carries on the work, and where that is, you may be only too thankful to give a loose rein. A young man must have it out one way or another; and we may well be thankful if he gives it to the Church, even though he may run into what seems queer to us.'

Felix laid up the conversation for himself and Geraldine, and thought it over many times that long day.

Not till late in the evening was the unconsciousness such that Mrs. Underwood could be admitted, and it was not till two in the morning that the struggle was over. Clement had scarcely tasted anything since the hurried, interrupted dinner the previous day, except what his brother had almost forced on him at the bed-side; and he was so stiff, spent, and worn out, that Felix could think of nothing till he had seen him safe in bed.

Nor was it till the clash of the knell had sounded several times, that at eight next morning, Felix gradually awoke; and only slowly did the strokes, as he mechanically counted them, recall to him that the event had happened—that he was in his own house—his mother's rightful inheritance—and that his years of toil and effort were over! To say that his first thought was not exultation would not be true. The recovery of his natural position, and the possession of such a home for his sisters, could not but rejoice him, though with it came the sense of responsibility, and of a perplexing knot to be untied, a knot of wrong to be undone at *any*—yes, at *any* cost. 'Even if it leave us as poor as heretofore,' he spoke to himself, 'God grant me to prove my faith in His word as to poverty.'

Ere the tolls had ceased all the multiplied honours they could pay to sixty-five years and Squire-rector, Felix saw Clement, instead of sleeping, on his way to the church. Felix followed thither ere long, and the brothers met at the churchyard gate.

'Well, Clement,' said Felix, as their hands met, 'you have led this to end better than one durst hope.'

'It had all been working long before,' said Clement in a trembling voice.

'It has been a terrible time for you. Are you rested?'

'A little stiff and achy—but that will work off, thank you.'

'And now, Clem, you must stand by me, and help me in what is to be done.'

The two brothers stood looking at the fine old house, the cloister connecting it with the church, the spring beauty blossoming round; Clement put his hand on his brother's shoulder, and said, in a half apologetic tone, 'After all, I can't help being glad it has come to you at last.'

It may be doubted whether any congratulation pleased Felix so much. 'I am glad to have known it so long beforehand,' he answered. 'I hope we shall be enabled to see the right and do it.'

Clement looked at the church and at the village; and again, with warm impulse and tears in his eyes, exclaimed, 'I cannot help being glad. Now I have some hope for my poor people.'

'We will do our best,' said Felix; 'and you will bear with me if I disappoint you.'

'Nay,' said Clement, the tears nearly choking him, 'the really best thing for the place would be, if you would let me give up, and appoint old Flowerdew.'

'What! be driven away by the clan Hepburn?'

'Not that, exactly, except that an older man, who had not made such a wretchedly bad beginning, might make all the difference. Till you are settled in here, you will not conceive the mess I have made of it all.'

'I see you have had a great strain on you; you will look on it differently when you have rested.'

'I don't know,' said Clement. 'It is not that I don't care for the place, Felix,' he added, pleadingly; 'I do now, with all my heart and soul—it *is* my charge, and must be—only if I could learn a little more, and get rid of a little of my youth and priggishness before I come back, it would be so much better for the people.'

'Of that last article I think you have got rid considerably.'

'I'm sure there's been enough to take the conceit out of me;' and perhaps he proved it by adding, 'But I leave it to you, Felix; I know you think it may be essential to your plans that a brother should hold the vicarage, and if so, of course I would go on, knowing too what an immense difference the influence of this house will make, and the having you to turn to for advice.'

'If we can live here at all,' said Felix. 'I do not in the least know the rights of the property.'

Nor could he tell till after a good deal of talk with the lawyers and looking over of papers. The funeral was to be on the Saturday, and conducted exactly like that of last year. Felix thought the present no time for a protest against the seventy-five yards of black cloth. 'Though this is the last of it,' he said to Clement, 'I'll have no church put in mourning for me.'

He saw very little of his brother, for the house was a good deal beset with Shaws; and besides, Clement, who was to go up to London on the Monday, had a good deal of parish visiting and business in arrear to make up, and so far from resting, scarcely sat down or ate. He would accept no assistance at the funeral, but every one remarked how ill he looked. Afterwards there was a public reading of the will, which named Felix as sole executor as well as heir; and added to the provision for the daughter-in-law by the settlements a charge of three hundred a year on the estate so long as she should remain a widow. A few very unkind things were said by the Shaws, which Clement was young enough to mind a good deal, after all his peacemaking efforts, and which made Bernard's eyes flash.

Bernard was to stay with his brothers over the Sunday; but he must have found it a dull evening, for Clement had a sermon to write, and Felix was deep in calculations till long after the boy had yawned himself off to bed.

At last Felix knocked at Clement's study-door. 'Up still! Clem, you want rest.'

'Not I. But I have just finished. How do things turn out?'

'Fairly,' said Felix, showing him a paper where he had drawn up a statement. 'The property altogether, you see, has been counted at four thousand five hundred a year. Well, out of that Mrs. Underwood has eight hundred a year, and the involvements of Fulbert's debts reduce it a good deal more, so that Mr. Wilder says I must not reckon on more than two thousand three hundred at present, and of that nine hundred and fifty is the great tithe, and the rent of the Glebe farm is three hundred and seventy. Blackstone Gulley belongs to the estate, and could not be sold; but the speculator gave a round sum for a twenty-one years' lease, which will not be run out these four years, so we can do nothing about that at present. Now, Clem, this nine hundred and fifty a year—I'm not going to make it over to you bodily. I think that, with the Glebe Farm, your income as Vicar will be quite as much as is good for a parson.'

'I suppose so,' said Clement, laughing; 'I never felt poor in my life till I had four hundred a year, and I should be poorer still if I had fourteen hundred.'

'No wonder, if you subscribe to everything, and pay for whatever is wanted in the parish instead of asking those who ought! I believe four thousand would not make much difference to you, or four hundred thousand either,' said Felix, who had come to some appalling discoveries as to Clement's ways of dealing with money.

'Perhaps not,' he answered, good humouredly; 'but what do you mean to do? To be your own ecclesiastical commissioner?'

'Something like it; at any rate, not to put it out of my own hands till I see the best way, and that there will be time to do while it is putting the church and the Glebe cottages into a proper state, and setting the Vicarage to rights. Perhaps first of all should come a school-chapel for Blackstone Gully; and as I reckon that all this will take six or seven years, by that time we shall be able to judge what is most wanted—a church and endowment for Blackstone, or for that Ewmouth suburb, or both; and when that is done, I would make over the rectorial rights to the living.'

'O Felix! I never durst think of anything—so like a dream!' said Clement, looking up at him.

'And you will stay here, Clem? I think you must; for you see I can hand over the rent of the glebe, and settle these things with you, taking my time about them in a way I could not do if the incumbent were not my brother and my next heir.'

'But I am not your next heir.'

'I have made you so. I thought it right to draw up a very short will, leaving everything to you, with John Harewood as executor, to save the dead lock there would be in case of my coming to some sudden end. I can perfectly trust to you to do right by the sisters and Theodore; and if Edgar, poor fellow! should come home, I know you would hand over to him what is really secular, and you would feel to be his right. But, Clement, you need have the less scruple at my doing this, that I have come to think there is little likelihood of the dear fellow being alive.'

'Indeed!'

'More than a year ago, Fulbert sent me a scrap of newspaper with an account of a man being found murdered by the bush-rangers. He had been robbed, and there was nothing about him to lead to his identification; but the diggers he had last been with called him Ned Wood. Fulbert went to the place and made all possible inquiries, but could find out nothing, but that he had been noted for singing, and was light-complexioned. Fulbert himself believes it; and I think nothing else would have led Fernan to give up his search. I thought it so entirely vague and improbable, that I let no one but Lance see the letter; indeed, I so utterly disbelieved it, that it did not dwell on me at the time; but the longer we are without hearing, the more I am driven to believe it.'

'You have not told Cherry?'

'If it were a certainty, I could not tell her half what Fulbert heard. I have never spoken to her about it. I will not take away her hope on such grounds.'

'I think you are right. I do not think anything of this story myself.'

'Nor I, at times when I think of "the child of so many prayers,"' said Felix. 'But with such a dreadful possibility, never to be cleared up, you see it would never do to leave things unsettled; so I just did this for the present.'

'Yes, it can be altered at need,' said Clement, with a long breath.

'This house,' said Felix, returning to business, 'is clearly our own; and you will go on with us of course for the present, if we can live here. It has certainly been a priory, but I do not therefore feel bound to restore that; I have read and thought much about those religious houses, and I think that there is no call to give them up as things now stand.'

'If?'

'I must talk it over with some of the financial heads. Of course I wish it for the girls, and my own duty seems to lie here; but if it will not do, I must let the place till the entanglements clear themselves.'

'Let the place? What! and go on with the business?' cried Clement, in consternation.

'I must keep on the business any way.'

'Felix! Impossible! In your position—'

'I cannot have the position if I cannot have the business. Look at it: here is Bernard to be educated, and Lance to go to the University, and four girls without any provision worth naming, besides Theodore; and how is all to be done out of less than a thousand pounds a year, with this house and grounds to be kept up, and where people are used to see five thousand spent?'

'Could you not sell the business?'

'Of course I could; but judging by what I have gathered during this year, the capital I should receive would not bring me in anything in proportion to what I make now; and I cannot afford to lose so much.'

'I don't see that you are a bit better off than you were before!'

'Rather worse, as far as money goes.—But this place! You don't feel the charm of it half enough. What will it not be to Cherry, and little Stella? I do think Cherry will get along here; though Wilmet will say we ought not to try. But I shall pay off all the servants on Monday, and we'll start on a new tack.'

'Yes; I believe they have preyed awfully on the old Squire. There's not one I should wish to keep, in-door or out-door.'

'Then we would begin on a smaller scale, and harden ourselves against traditions. I would get a real good assistant for Lamb, go backwards and forwards, and keep on the Pursuivant myself as before.'

'The Pursuivant is all very well. It is a valuable influence: but can't you keep that, and drop the retail affair?'

'I can't give up three hundred a year for the honour of the thing.'

'But if I live with you, could you not keep the rent of the Glebe farm as my board?'

'You certainly have been sumptuously maintained here, but hardly at the cost of three hundred and seventy pounds! No; I think it would be only fair that you should give a hundred towards the housekeeping, as Mr. Audley used to do, and something more for your horse; but to take any more would only be robbing the Church under another form.'

'I don't like it! It will do you harm in the neighbourhood. You will never take your proper place;' then, as Felix half smiled, 'you wonder at these arguments from me? Yes, but I know the neighbourhood better than you do, and I do not like to see your influence and usefulness crippled.'

'That may be; but the choice lies between being looked down on for being in trade and continuing in this wrong to the Church.'

'Surely we could live at small expense here! We have all been used to frugality.'

'Yes, and I have seen that stinting has not a happy effect. In such a house as this, we cannot live as we have done at home. We can do without display, but plain hospitality we must have, and debt would be worse than trade. Ah, Clem! the old home has made you the exclusive aristocrat again! Recollect, such a restitution must involve sacrifice of some sort. We must have the Underwood "rood" some way or other. You are ready enough to let it be in money and luxury, but can't you let it be in—what shall I call it—consideration? That is, if it does make any difference, or if we find it out.'

'You'll find it out fast enough from the Miss Hepburns,' muttered Clement.

Felix laughed 'Poor Clem! Hepburns first and last! I'm sorry to disgrace you!'

But during that laugh Clement had bethought himself. 'I beg your pardon, Felix; you are a lesson to me. I did not know that it was the world that was arguing in me. To go on working in trade in order to make restitution to the Church is heroism I did not grasp at first.'

'Perhaps,' said Felix more lightly, 'it is all reluctance to give up being somebody at Bexley for the sake of being nobody in Ewshire. Don't look so unhappy, old fellow; University men and beneficed clergy, like you, think much of what I was inured to long ago. Come, put out your lamp, and come up to bed; I am sure you can't finish that sermon to-night.'

'If I did,' said Clement, shutting it up, 'it would be to say I was not worth ever to preach again!'

Perhaps Felix, who had entirely disbelieved the report of Edgar's fate till his mind had in a manner become accustomed to the idea, had underrated the amount of shock that it would give Clement, who had never been half so much attached to poor Edgar as himself; nor perhaps might it have done so, but for the unnerved overstrained condition to which the year's solitude and responsibility, the months of nursing, and the days of severe fatigue, had brought him.

Felix was wakened from his first sleep by the strangled scream of nightmare in the next room, and hastening in, broke the spell, and found that poor Clement had been dreaming out what he had told him, and had deemed himself bound, gagged, struggling to come to Edgar's aid, and ask his pardon for having done him some horrible injury, the load of which did not at first pass with awakening.

'No,' he said, when he had entirely resumed his waking powers, 'it is too true! Things never were as they ought to have been between us! Who knows what difference it might have made!'

'Of course,' said Felix, thinking that to talk it all out would conduce to Clement's quieter rest. 'We can all look back to much that we would have had otherwise; but I trace the original mischief to those days when Mr. Ryder, young and eager, talked out all his crudities to the cleverest boy in his school, just as he had done to his Oxford friends. He feels it himself, I think. He gave unintentionally a sort of resource against whatever was distasteful, and made all the scepticism that the poor dear fellow was exposed to abroad not seem a mere foreign aberration. Somehow he was afraid of what religion might do to him, and so took refuge not so much in doubt, as in knowing it was doubted. The only thing that I ever knew touch him, was something Lance said to him about refusing to go and live with him in London.'

'Yes; his brightness did good, where my assumptions only added to the general contempt.'

'Still, the more I think, the more I do believe that whether we ever know it or not, so sweet and loving a nature must come right at last.'

And there in the dark those two brothers knelt down together and in deep undertones uttered a few clauses of intense prayer. Then Clement said in a broken voice, 'Felix, *do* keep your present room, and let us say this together every night.'

And the elder brother's only answer was such a fatherly kiss as he gave the younger ones. They remembered that night long after!

On the Sunday Clement was not only exhausted and unwell, but could not help allowing it, for he fainted after his first service, and was forced to allow himself to lie by whenever he was not actually needed, letting Felix spare him whatever was possible. Thus it was that the new Squire astonished the natives by taking the Vicar's Sunday class in the stable that served for the school. By-the-by, instead of receiving such a lecture as used to be the penalty of intrusting his own Bexley boys to Clement, he was now dejectedly forewarned that the Vale Lestonites did not know half as much, and had the more reason to think it true because such an extraordinary proceeding on a Squire's part filled them with blank speechless amazement.

The congregation were equally full of wonder, approaching to incredulity, when their new Mr. Underwood stood forth surpliced, and read the Lessons. He had done the like often for Mr. Flowerdew; but he would not have thus amazed the villagers on this first Sunday if he had not been really uneasy as to their Vicar's powers of getting through the services. And it really was a memorable thing, to Clement at least, to hear his full clear beautiful voice setting forth the delights of the Land of Promise, the goodly houses and fields, and the warnings that he was verily taking to himself against the heart being lifted up, and forgetting, or turning to serve the gods the former nations had served—the gods may be of family pride, and pleasure, and ease, and comfort. To Clement it seemed as though he read the whole magnificent chapter of Deuteronomy like a manifesto of his own future course, declaring all against which he meant to beware. It was just as, when he had to seal up a bundle of papers that evening, he took up a big old white cornelian seal with the family shield, and said, squeezing it down into a deep well-prepared bed of red sealing-wax, 'There, I never did that before; I couldn't be liable for armorial bearings!' And as Bernard exclaimed, 'Yes, now you are a gentleman out and out!' he answered gravely, 'Not forgetting the motto, Bear. Remember what we take up.'

'There's no sense in those old sing-song saws,' boldly averred Bernard.

'Perhaps you'll know better some day.'

Felix went himself to St Matthew's with Clement, and had a private conference with Mr. Fulmort, the result of which was, that the senior curate, very glad of a breath of May loveliness, went down for three weeks to Vale Leston, while the Vicar thereof refreshed his spirit at St Matthew's, and that when he went back again he was to take with him the Reverend Frederick Somers, to stay till the family move should bring him other companions.

The only sister within reasonable distance was Robina; and Felix could not deny himself a call on her, especially as there were no further considerations about incommoding the family with her relations. He was shown into a big drawing-room, not at the moment inhabited, but with the air of being used by easy-going happy people; and almost immediately in flew the neat trim black-silken personage with the sunny round face he had come in search of.

'Felix! dear Felix! how nice and good to come in all your glory! Lady de la Poer was in the school-room, and she told me to ask you to stay to luncheon. Do, pray! I want you to see her and Grace, and my children.'

'Very well. If I do, can you come out with me afterwards? I want your help.'

'Oh yes! I am sure I shall be able. I'll ask at luncheon, if Lady de la Poer does not offer.'

'Have you spoken to her?'

'Told her? Of course. We had quite a festival in the schoolroom, and all drank your health in cowslip wine. We had had a whole lot of cowslips sent up from the Towers; and their papa came in, and wanted to know if Mr. Underwood were not worthy of a more generous beverage. Oh, I wish he were at home; I want you to see him!' ('And him to see you,' she had on the tip of her tongue, but she thought he would not like it.)

'And when are you coming home?'

'When you all go to take possession. I would not lose that for anything. I am to have my holiday then.'

'Holiday! You are coming for good.'

'Don't you think,' she said, looking up in his face, 'that after all this education on purpose for a teacher, it would be a shame to throw it all up and come to live on you?'

'That was just one of the things I value this inheritance for, Robin. There's no fear but that you would find plenty to do.'

'You have three to do it,' she said; 'and the more Angela has on her hands the better she will get on. I have been thinking it over ever since you wrote, Felix, and I cannot see that your having an estate makes it right in me to live dependent when I can maintain myself. It would not if I were your brother.'

'You are not going in for women's rights, Bob?' he said, smiling.

'Not out-and-out. But listen. What you have for us is just the run of the house, isn't it?'

'Well, yes,' he hesitated. 'It will take some time and prudence to make a provision for you, you horribly wise bird!'

'Then would it not be foolish to come and eat up your provision at home when I can do something towards making one myself; and I am really very happy?' and there was colour enough in her cheek slightly to startle her brother.

'Oh, if you are too happy here to come away—'

'Don't say that! she cried. 'I like it, for they are all kind and bright; and I never had such a friend as Lady Grace—and I feel as if I were doing a duty; but—oh no!—'

'Don't be so horribly discomfited, my dear. Only when young ladies are so happy away from home, and want to make a provision—My dear little sister, I beg your pardon—'

'Stay, Felix; I must tell you now, that you may not fancy anything so dreadful as that it is any one here.'

'Then there's an "it is," after all!'

'No! oh, I don't know! I tried to speak to Wilmet, and she would not let me; but when we were both ridiculous children, a little foolish nonsense passed between him and me.'

'Whom?'

'Willie!'

'Will Harewood? I thought that was all the Bailey nonsense.'

'I can't tell,' said Robina, leaning against him and looking down. 'Do all I can, I can't forget the sort of—of promise; and I've never been sure whether he meant it, but—but I think he did. O Fee! is it bad of me?'

'My sweet Bob,' he said, and kissed her, 'I am glad you have told me. I never thought of such an affair being on your little mind. I must say I wish it had not happened.'

'No, don't say that,' said Robina. 'It does not worry me;' and she laughed at the very sound of the words. 'Why, can't you see how happy I am? and I *mean* to be. I know how good and nice he is; and if he doesn't remember, or can't do it, there's no harm done. (This was in a tone brave because it was incredulous.) But if ever it did come to anything, I should like to have something to help on with.'

'Very practical and business-like, my bird! And I am afraid it is a sign it goes deep!' he said musingly.

'Deep!' she said, looking up to him, 'of course it does! It would be very odd if it did not! But that will only make me glad of whatever is good for Will; and I think the waiting is all right. I do want to have done something for him! The only question is whether it will be bad for you at Vale Leston to have a governess sister.'

'There's worse than that, Robin,' said Felix, gravely, 'for the Squire himself remains a bookseller!'

'You don't mean that!'

He briefly explained.

'That quite settles it,' she said. 'I could not go home and live in idleness while you were working on.'

'I believe you are right, Robin; but I am disappointed. I did reckon on my sisters living like ladies!'

'Isn't three enough for you,' laughed Robin, 'to set up in a row and wait upon, as Stella does on her dolls?'

'Precisely so. I don't think I could have let you turn Effective Female on my hands, if you hadn't a pretty little feminine aim of your own.'

'For shame, Felix! Don't ever think about that again! Only tell me when to ask for my holiday.'

'There are a few repairs that must be done at once; besides I've made a clean sweep of the servants, and turned in old Tripp's daughter to do for Clement. I don't think we can possibly be ready for a month or six weeks.'

By this time the gong was sounding; and Lady de la Poer came in with a kind and friendly greeting. Felix soon found himself in the midst of a large family party of all ages, full of bright mirth, among whom Robina spoke and moved with home-like ease, and he himself took his place as naturally as it was given to him. Lady de la Poer knew a little of Ewshire, and talked to him about it in the pleasantest manner, giving the sense of congratulation without obtruding it; and she, without waiting to be requested—proposed Miss Underwood's going out with him, proclaiming that she would herself take the children into Kensington Gardens.

Then, while Robina was gone to prepare, she said, 'Your sister told me she does not wish to leave us. I said I could not consider the answer as final till she had seen you. Perhaps I ought not till she has seen your new home.'

'Thank you,' said Felix. 'I confess it seemed to me startlingly prudent and independent; but when I came to think it over, I could hardly say that the child is wrong.'

'We were very glad, as you may believe, to find that she was happy enough to be willing to stay on. Indeed, we both feel the benefit not only to the little ones, but of the companionship to the elder girls. Grace is especially fond of her, and I hope it will be a lasting friendship.'

Felix coloured as one very much pleased, and made some acknowledgment.

'There's a sturdy fearless good sense, and yet liveliness, about her,' continued the lady, 'which has already been of great use to Grace, who is naturally all ups and downs. However, if she changes her mind among the attractions of home, we promise not to feel ill-used.'

'What is Mamma saying?' exclaimed Lady Grace in person, entering the room with Robina as her mother was speaking. 'Is she pretending that we shall not feel ill-used if Miss Underwood deserts us? No such thing! I shall never forgive her—never! If you try to persuade her, mind, it is at peril of being haunted by the ghost of a forlorn maiden, pined to death for a faithless friend!'

'You don't half like to trust her with Mr. Underwood,' said her mother, laughing.

'I told you how good he was, Gracie,' interposed Robina.

'He is pretending to consent, and he means to undermine me! It will be just like Beauty and the Beast. Your sisters will do their eyes with onions, to work on your feelings; and then you'll stay on, and find the poor Beast—that's me—at the last gasp!'

'That will be when she goes home,' said Felix, laughing. 'I promise to bring her safe back now, Lady Grace; but surely you have enough sisters of your own to spare me mine!'

'Now listen, Mr. Underwood. It is true, as a matter of history and genealogy, that I've got five sisters; but Number Two—that's Mary—is married, and no good to anybody; and Number One—that's Fanny—is always looking after her when she is not looking after Mamma. Then Adelaide, whom nature designed for my own proper sister, is altogether devoted to Kate Caergwent, and cares for nobody else; and as to the little ones—why, they are only nine and ten, and good for nothing but an excuse for having Miss Underwood in the house! Now is not it true that you have three sisters already at your beck and call?'

'Two, I allow; but the third is hardly at any one's beck.'

'What, that most entertaining person, Angela? I don't think we have had such fun in the school-room since Kate's maddest days.'

'My dear, I think you have a remnant of them,' said Lady de la Poer. 'Let Miss Underwood go; I am sure her brother has no time to spare.'

'I hope,' said Felix, when they were in the street, 'that Angel has not been exposing herself there.'

'No, no, not much,' said Robina, hesitating. 'The first time or two she was asked to tea in the school-room she kept me sitting on thorns, and liked it—the wicked child; but after all, there is something about their manners that keeps her in check; they are so merry, and yet so refined. I think nothing improves her so much as an evening with them—except, indeed, when there's any external element.'

'External element?'

'Anything that—that excites her,' hastily said Robina. 'But is not Lady Grace delightful?'

'She seems passionately fond of you—or was it a young lady's strong language?'

'Oh, she means it, dear Gracie! She is lonely, you see. Lady Adelaide is rather a wise one, and she and Lady Caergwent read and study deep, and have plans together, and leave poor Grace out; and they all tease her for being so excitable.'

'Well, I thought she was almost crying while she talked her nonsense.'

'Just so I think her the sweetest of them all, because she feels so easily; but her sisters do snub her a little. And my Lady herself—is not she exactly one's imagination of a real great lady?'

'*Crême de la Crême?*'

'Yes, perfect dignity and simplicity, and as tender and careful a mother all the time as a cottage woman. I never felt any one so mother-like, even to me.'

'I can quite believe that. Yes, if you *are* to work, you could hardly do so more comfortably.'

It was a concession, and Robina had to put up with it; for as they turned into Piccadilly he changed the subject by demanding, 'Now, Robin, what shall it be? Seal-skins?'

'Seal-skins in the height of summer?'

'I thought all ladies pined for seal-skins. We have half a column of advertisements of them at a time.'

'You don't want to extend the business to them?'

'No, but to give one to each of my sisters.'

'They are a monstrous price, you know. You should have heard Lord de la Poer grumble when Addie and Grace had theirs!'

'Fifty pound will do the five, I suppose?'

'I thought there were heavy expenses, and not much ready money.'

'There's enough for that, and I mean it. I shall not know that I have come into my fortune till I have taken home something to show for it.'

'I wonder what Wilmet would say.'

'Wilmet is not my master, and a chit like you had best not try her line. It won't do, with your face and figure.'

Robina could only laugh, and feel that she was still Felix's child, and if he chose to be extravagant she could not stop him.

'Which shall it be?' he continued; 'seal-skins, or silk gowns, or anything of jewellery?'

'Jewellery would last longest, and none of us have got any,' said Robin; 'but I believe you like the seals best.'

'I want to stroke Cherry in one. And wouldn't Wilmet look grand? She hasn't got one, has she?'

'No. I was out with her and John last winter, when she dragged him past the shop.'

'I thought you were aping her! Well, I've broken loose, and she will have no choice now.'

'You don't mean to include Alda?'

'Poor Alda! Seal-skins have ceased to be an object to her; but I have had a very warm letter from her.'

So Robina was only allowed the privilege of assisting in the selection of the smooth brown coats and muffs. Felix insisted on despatching Mrs. John Harewood's to her at once; and he wanted to send Angela's, but yielded, on Robin's representation of the impossibility of her putting it away in any security from the moth. His exultation in his purchases was very amusing, as he stroked them like so many cats, as if he were taking seisin of his inheritance. And when, some hours later, he sprang out of the train, and was met by the station-master with, 'Mr. Underwood! allow me to offer my most sincere congratulations,' and everybody ran for his luggage as never before, he still clung close to his precious parcel, like a child with a new toy, even to his own door, which was suddenly opened at his bell, Sibby crying aloud, 'No, no, Martha, not a sowl shall open the door, barring meself, to me own boy that's come to his own again, an' got the better of all the nagurs that kep' him out. Blessings on you, Masther Felix, me jewel, an' long life to you to reign over it!' And she really had her arms round his neck, kissing him.

'Well done, Sibby, and thank you! Your heart warms to the old place, does it?' and he held out a hand to the less demonstrative Martha, who stood curtseying, and observing, 'I wish you joy, Sir.'

By that time Stella had flown upon him, Theodore was clinging to his leg, Lance half way downstairs, and Cherry hanging over the balusters.

'You villain!' were Lance's first words; 'why didn't you come home by daylight? All the establishment waited till the six o'clock train was in to give you three times three!'

'And now you are come,' added Cherry, 'stand there, right in the middle! I want to see how a Squire looks!'

He obeyed by planting his feet like a colossus, tucking his umbrella under his arm like a whip, putting on his hat over his brow, and altogether assuming the conventional jolly Squire attitude, which was greeted by shrieks of laughter and applause.

'Now let me see how a Squire's sister looks,' he continued, opening his parcel, and thrusting Stella into the first coat that came to hand, which being Angela's, came down to her heels.

Cherry shouted, 'Like the brown bear!' and Scamp began to bark, and was forcibly withheld by Lance from demolishing the little brown muff that rolled out; while Felix turned on Cherry with the jacket meant for Stella; and she, in convulsions of merriment, could do nothing but shriek, 'Cyrus! Cyrus! Cyrus!'

'Well, then, take the great coat, puss,' said Felix. 'Here, Stella, let me pull you out of that! That's more like it!'

'My dear Felix,' continued Cherry, in great affected gravity, 'are these the official garments wherein we are to be installed? Nearly as severe as royal ermine.'

'Don't scold, Whiteheart. I had enough of that from the wise Robin before she would help me choose them. I had set my heart on them.'

'Dear old Giant!' cried Cherry, craning up to kiss him; 'he couldn't believe he had a landed estate till he had seen it on our backs! But,' she added, fearing to be disappointing, 'I never knew before what it was to be sleek and substantial. If ever I did covet a thing, it was the coat of a seal.'

'But how is Mr. Froggatt, Lance?'

'As well as can be expected,' was Lance's reply. 'He congratulates with tears in his eyes, says you deserve it, but bemoans poor Pur, till I am minded to tell him that I'll stick by him and the concern; for really I don't know what else I'm good for, and honest Lamb couldn't write a leader to save his life.'

'I'll walk over to-morrow, and set him at rest,' said Felix. 'I could not drop Pur if I would.'

'I'm so glad,' said Cherry. 'I felt quite sad over the proofs, like casting off an old friend.'

'Or kicking adrift the plank that has brought one to land. I knew Cherry would have broken her heart to part with Pur.'

'Besides, it is a real power and influence,' added Cherry; 'and it is so improved. We had up a whole file of it for years back. Willie Harewood had lost some of his earlier March Hare poems, and thought they were there; so he and I hunted over reams of ancient Pur, and couldn't find them after all. I believe you had declined them; and they would have been lost to the world if Lance hadn't written to Robina, and she had copies of them all, laid up in lavender.'

'And they are the most splendid of all!' said Lance.

'Only too good for the Pursuivant,' laughed Felix.

'Well,' said Cherry, 'Will and I held up our hands to find how stupid Pur used to be four or five years ago, when you were in bondage to Mr. Froggatt's fine words and his fears.'

'Yes, and had no opposition to put us on our mettle,' added Lance. 'The Tribune was the making of the Pursuivant; I'm inclined to offer it a testimonial. By-the-by, Felix, are you prepared for a testimonial yourself—or at the very least, a dinner in the Town Hall, from your fellow citizens? They're all agog about it.'

'On the principle that "as long as thou doest well unto thyself men will speak good of thee?"' asked Felix. 'No,' correcting himself, 'that's hardly fair; there's kind feeling in it, too; but perhaps they will let me off when they find it is not a farewell.'

'Not!'

'Now, Cherry and Lance, I want you to look at this statement. Clement has seen it, of course; but I don't want it to go any further, except to Jack. It is enough to say that I find the property a good deal burthened, which is only too true.'

'You don't seem to have much of a bargain!' said Lance, coming round to read over Cherry's shoulder.

'The question is whether Cherry can trample on Underwood traditions, and keep house for a thousand a year where people expect three or four times the sum to be laid out.'

'I thought you reckoned things here at five hundred.'

'Hardly so much. We shall have to get our old bugbear, the superior assistant. Besides, Lance, now's your time. You must begin to get ready for Oxford at once.'

'I?' said Lance. 'No, thank you, Felix. Clement offered me the same last year, but my head wouldn't stand grinding nohow. No, if you stick to the old plank, so will I. I was more than half wishing it before, and ready to break my heart at leaving the organ to some stick of my Lady's choosing, only I didn't know what you might think due to the manes of the Underwoods.'

'The manes of the Underwoods must make up their minds to a good deal,' said Felix; 'but is it really true that you do not think yourself fit for study?'

'No, but music I can combine with the work here,' said Lance; 'and that would save the superior assistant, and you will be free to make a gentleman of Bear.'

'Yes, that must be done,' said Felix. 'Even Stoneborough will not do now. He is such a cocky little chap, that the only chance for him is to get him to a great public school, where this promotion will seem nothing to anybody.'

'My poor little Bear! I am very glad,' said Cherry. 'And he is still young enough; yet it hardly seems fair, when all his elders had to earn their own education.'

'Such as it was!' interjected Lance.

'Yes,' said Felix; 'and when I remember the sighs my father now and then let out about Eton or Harrow, I feel bound to give the benefit to the one who can take it; but I don't like the spending two hundred a year on that boy, and then leaving you, Lance, to all the drudgery, and a solitary house.'

'That matters the less,' said Lance, 'because I am busy with the choir and with practice two evenings in the week, and should be more, if it wasn't for doing the agreeable to Cherry.'

'He'll turn into a misogynist, like Mr. Miles,' laughed Cherry.

'No, he'll be consumed by an unrequited affection for all the young ladies that come in with the loveliest eyes in the world,' said Felix.

'He'll set the March Hare poetry to music, and serenade them with it,' added Cherry.

'No, I shall cultivate the Frogs,' said Lance. 'It would be too bad to have left the poor old boy in the lurch.'

'Yes, that has weighed a good deal with me,' said Felix. 'I'm determined that they shall come and stay with us at the Priory as soon as we can get it in order, and before the winter. I'll bring them up myself. You see, Lance, whenever I take a turn here you can be at home.'

'Home! he has begun already!'

'It was home to me first, and I always feel that it is whenever I come in sight of it. Lancey, boy, when I think of leaving you here, it seems letting you sacrifice yourself too much!'

'Nonsense, Blunderbore. You can't give this back to the Church if we don't keep off your hands; and next, that *coup d'état* addled my brains so far that I'm good for no work but this that I have drifted into.'

'Then, Cherry, you must help me make an estimate of the expenses, and see whether we can venture to live at the Priory, or whether we must let it, and go on here for seven years.'

'Oh!' They both looked very blank.

'I'd rather live on bread and cheese in the country,' said Cherry.

'So had I,' said Felix, 'if the manes of the Underwoods are appeasable. One step is a riddance of all the servants; I wonder how many you can do with. Five maids and five men I paid off, only keeping on one man, to look after Clem's horse and see to the garden.'

'By-the-bye,' said Lance, 'George Lightfoot begged me to state that his sister is at home, and always had a great wish to live with Miss Underwood.'

'Let her come and speak to me, then,' said Cherry; 'though I am afraid she must moderate her expectations. It seems to me that except for the honour of the thing, this is another version of our old friend—"poortith cauld."'

'Our best friend, maybe, Cherry,' said Felix, 'if we can only heartily believe it?'

'His bride, as truly as St. Francis's,' thought she; 'and without the credit of it.'

CHAPTER XXXVI.

POSSESSION.

> 'And while the wings of fancy still are free,
> And I can view this mimic show of thee,
> Time has but half succeeded in his theft—
> Thyself removed, thy power to soothe me left.'
> *Cowper.*

Though Felix had gone to town both in going to Vale Leston and coming from it, a much shorter way was feasible, only necessitating a couple of hours' delay at a junction.

This was not so entirely inconvenient, on Felix's twenty-ninth birthday, which had been fixed for the general migration to the new home, since Robina was to meet the others there from a country house of Lord de la Poer's, seven or eight miles off, and Major and Mrs. Harewood, and their two sons, would be in the down-train that was to pick the party up. Not only were they to assist in the taking possession, but they had secured lodgings for three months at the Glebe Farm. 'It will be such a good thing,' had Wilmet said, 'to settle them all in, and put Cherry and her housekeeping on the right tack.'

'My dear Wilmet, I am perfectly sensible of the admirable monarchical constitution Kit and I live under; but my principles are against annexation, and if you extend it to Cherry's house, I shall carry you off at once to Buckinghamshire, or to the Hebrides!'

'I only meant to help,' said Wilmet, with a little dignity; then changing her tone as she saw a smile twitch his moustache, 'and you shall be judge what is help!'

Clement was already at Vale Leston; and Bernard, declaring that no one should catch him again at that filthy hole, Bexley, had repaired thither as soon as his holidays began. Martha, Amelia Lightfoot, and a superior housemaid of Wilmet's selection, were gone on to make ready; also a young gardener, whose face had pleased Felix when he came to advertise: and half the Underwood family were at the station, together with Willie Harewood, Sibby, and Scamp—the latter chiefly in the service of Theodore. Sibby was useful in other ways; but she was, as ever, to have the chief charge of the boy by day, be his refuge from strangers, and attend to his meals, it being one of his peculiarities that he never could or would eat at the family table. And Scamp, though Lance's property, was so much Theodore's delight, that separation would have been cruelty; and Lance had resigned him with free good nature, and not without hopes of Scamp's brother as an inmate, for Dick Graeme himself had been articled to a surveyor, and was to live and board with Lance, his mother declaring her conviction that this was the best security both for his moral, and his rather fragile physical, health. One of the 'everlasting Lightfoots,' as Angela called them, had married a nice young wife, and was to occupy the lower rooms, and *do* for them.

So there were nine individuals seeking what pastime the junction afforded. The Squire—Felix's present nickname—was, to every one's amusement, seated at the table in the waiting-room, writing a leader with the rapidity and abstraction peculiar to himself. A leather couch was occupied by everybody's hand-bags, umbrellas, and parasols; a cage of doves, a basket of the more precious flower-roots, and another with a kitten, under Geraldine's protection; while she endeavoured to keep Theodore happy and not troublesome by a judicious dole of biscuits to be shared with Scamp, whom he held in a string—until, at Lance's step on the platform, the dog rushed out after him, dragging Theodore after him—Cherry limped after Theodore, Felix hurried after them all, and Lance took Theodore by the hand, and led boy and dog wherever it pleased them to go, and they could go safely, while Stella rushed to satisfy herself of the welfare of her kitten and birds.

Except for such interruptions, the public was mostly concerned to find a place whence to behold Robina's arrival. 'What will she come in!' said Stella. 'A carriage like the Centry one?'

'Rattling up in an old fly,' said Will, gruffly.

'Will is jealous of the swells that have proved so attractive!' said Angela. 'Aren't you burning with curiosity to see them?'

'Not in the least! I know quite enough of them.'

'Know them?'

'A couple of tufts at Christ Church. Not a bad oar—but a regular stuck-up fellow!'

'Which? or is the description collective?'

'Look, Angel!' cried Stella, as an open waggonette, drawn by two handsome black horses and full of a merry party of young people, came dashing up; a cockaded servant opened the door, and a youth in summer costume sprang out.

'That's him!' quoth Will.

'Lord Ernest!' responded Angela.

Then the well-known figure of their own Robin was handed out by him, and lastly one of the other damsels, whom Angel identified as Lady Grace.

'They are not coming in here!' exclaimed Bill, grimly.

Nevertheless they were; the waggonette drove off amid nods and smiles, and Robin and her two companions were the next moment in presence, and Will was forced to shake hands with Lord Ernest, while Lady Grace went through the same ceremony with Felix and Angela, indeed with every one. 'I know you all, already,' she said; 'I'm so glad to have seen you, if only to warn you not to keep *her*.'

'Are you going our way?' asked Cherry, feeling the bright charm of manner.

'No; we only came to see her safe into your hands. Come, Ernest!' But he was enthusiastically admiring Scamp, and inquiring how to procure the like; and it was some minutes before he shook hands with Robina, saying, 'Then you'll let Gracie know whether one is to be had for love or money?'

'I thought you were to have one of the brown setters?'

'Well, why not?'

'One can't have more than one dog of one's heart,' said Angela.

'They must compete for that honour, then. Dogs, as well as other beings, must earn their place by their qualities. Eh, Gracie?'

'You foolish boy!' was his sister's reply. 'Come along. Good-bye, my dear little Copsey. If I don't get a letter every day I shall be convinced that your sisters are putting onions in their eyes.'

'What bright creatures!' exclaimed Cherry.

'What did she call you?' said Will

'Copsey. Oh, Copse, Underwood—the children all call me so. It is my pet name.'

'Insufferable impudence!' muttered Will. 'And what were you thinking of, Lance, to talk of getting him a dog of that breed, when you know Graeme would as soon sell his children?'

'Was not he very proud of the Richborough keeper coming over after them?'

'Those weren't sold.'

'I beg your pardon. Dick told me what he got for them.'

'One may do a thing for a neighbour, that one wouldn't for a chance stranger at a station.'

'You Red Republican!' said Angela.

'It is enough to make one a republican in earnest.'

'In *earnest*, indeed!' mischievously echoed Angela.

'To see a shallow young tuft expecting to get whatever he chooses to ask for, and every one else encouraging him in it—even those who should have more sense!'

'Meaning me!' said Lance, putting an arm in his and walking him off to the end of the ticket-taker's little platform; but they had no sooner turned back than he exclaimed, 'There's that fellow again!'

There indeed he was, with 'Here's your parasol, Miss Underwood. Of course you know the guilty person?'

'Mine was almost exactly like Lady Caergwent's, thank you!' said Robina, comparing the plain blue sun-shade with the one she held.

'Except that hers is minus the tassel,' said Lord Ernest. 'You plainly don't understand the principle of barter and exchange.'

'What? Always to take the least scratchy slate, and longest slate pencil!' said Angel.

'That's an essentially school illustration that *I* should not have dared to make,' said Lord Ernest.

'Nor I,' said Angela, 'but for the blissful fact that I'm no longer a schoolgirl.'

'I envy you,' he said, with something like a sigh. 'Your wings are grown!'

But there Robina uneasily said, 'You are keeping Lady Caergwent all this time without her parasol.'

'There, you see!' he returned, in a half pathetic tone of appeal, which made Angela laugh excessively. 'But, indeed, there's no fear; she and my sisters are in Long's shop, and will spend the next two hours in debating whether print in spots or stripes best conduces to the morality of their old women. That's the next stage after leaving school is it not?' turning to Angela; 'the first use to be made of your liberty!'

'To wear stars and stripes?' she asked, with a little wilful gloss.

And so with desultory nonsense they went on; Robina more than once interfering, and trying to send Lord Ernest off, but always hovering about them, in a certain ill-at-ease condition. Felix, having posted his leader, and taken his tickets, came out on the platform, and watched the group with a shade of perplexity.

There stood Angela, the bloom of seventeen brightening her pale colouring, and her play of feature and beautiful mischievous dark grey eyes making her face full of attraction. A knowing little black Tyrolese hat, with a single peacock's feather, was tipped over her forehead; her mass of flaxen hair was in huge loops, tied with crisp streamers; and her tall figure, in the same silver-grey as all the sisters had agreed on, looked dashing, where Robina's—with the adjuncts of a shady hat and a good deal of falling black lace—was quietness itself. Robina's face, still round, honest, and rosy, had grown more womanly, and had a distressed uneasy aspect, as she stood a little aloof, not quite mingling in the conversation, but yet not separating herself from it. The youth who was talking to Angela was dark haired, with rather aquiline features, but with that peculiar whiteness of complexion which is one of the characteristics of old nobility, and though not exactly handsome, with a very pleasing countenance, and an air of birth and breeding, a decided contrast to the figure who regarded them from a little distance. William Harewood had developed into a much bigger man than his brother, but he had not the advantage of John's neatness of figure and soldierly bearing. He had his mother's odd looseness of make, as if his limbs had got together by accident, and his clothes ditto. John's hair was of the pale sandy hue; but his, including long whiskers, was of the darker, more fiery tint, which Lance, at his politest, termed cinnamon. To be sure, he had a huge massive forehead, under which his yellow green-flecked eyes could twinkle and sparkle; and his wide mouth, when grinning from ear to ear, was an engine of fascinating drollery, while a few deep thoughts or words instantly gave majesty to the whole face, and extinguished all sense of its grotesqueness; but at present, as he leant against one of the posts of the platform, a heavy ill-humour had settled upon his countenance, which made his whole look and air more befitting a surly navvy than a first-class prizeman, tutor of a distinguished college, and able to get more aristocratic pupils than he wanted for his intended reading-party on the hills of the upper Ewe.

Felix had stood for some moments, looking on, wondering what it all meant, when the bell rang, the train swept up, the doors flew open, and John Harewood sprang out among them.

'A crowded train!' he said. 'There's only room for three in there, with Wilmet; Krishnu and the nurse have been keeping the places. Here, Cherry!—Here, Robin!—What, Stella! all this live-stock?'

'Oh, yes, please, *please*, Robina, take the doves; I can't trust them or my pussy with any one else.'

And past various self-concentrated people, intensely aggravated at exchanging the companionship of one baby for that of two doves and a kitten, the sisters were bundled, to find Wilmet watching for them, with her elder boy asleep on her knee, a great serene good-tempered fellow, with her features and clear skin, and though with true Harewood hair, a Kit to be proud of.

'But where's Angela?'

'There—running after Lance.'

'In that hat! Angel? I saw her as the train came up, and never thought of her belonging to us. How could you let her make such a figure of herself?'

'Nature is partly accountable,' said Cherry, in an odd sort of voice. 'And—Well, she brought home the hat, and it does become her. She can be very picturesque!'

'I'm no artist,' said Wilmet, remembering her husband's caution, and abstaining; then, as the train began to move, 'Ah! Willie will be left behind! No; he made a rush! How foolish! What's the matter with him? He seemed in a brown study.'

'He is out of sorts,' said Cherry. 'I believe he is very much put out with Lance for not going to Oxford.'

Robina looked up eagerly. 'He must have wished it very much!' she said, catching gladly at this explanation of his ill-humour.

'Yes,' said Cherry; 'nothing would have so relieved him from the sense that Lance blighted his prospects in his service. He came down persuaded, I believe, that he and his big head could shove Lance through all the passes, just as he could put him over a gap.'

'Everything comes so easy to him, that he has no notion how hard it is to Lance,' said Robina. 'John says Lance is right, but I am sorry—'

'So Felix wrote,' said Wilmet, 'and one can only acquiesce. Oh, and before this good little traveller wakes, tell me all about the dinner.'

'There's more that you have not heard about,' said Cherry, triumphantly.

'The inkstand!' said Stella. 'O sister! they have given him the most splendid inkstand!'

'Who? The Bexley people?'

'Yes,' said Cherry, 'a regular testimonial. They kept it a great secret; only Mr. Lamb came blushing in one day and borrowed one of the old books with the coat-of-arms in it, so that I thought something was brewing. Half the town subscribed—all Felix's young men's class, and quantities of his old scholars; and there's a little silver knight on the top, with a frosty silver pennon with the Rood upon it.'

'The Pursuivant himself?' said Robin.

'Yes, standing on a pedestal—a match-box, I believe, with such an inscription on it that Felix is ashamed of it; and we have had such a fight about its standing in the drawing-room or being suppressed in his study, that Felix said at last that we were like Joseph's brothers in prosperity, and wanted the warning, "See that ye fall not out by the way."'

But the quarrel had not been a serious one, to judge by her happy face.

'It is very nice, very nice,' said Wilmet, 'and I am not at all surprised. I thought they must do something of the kind. Was it given at the dinner?'

'Yes; it was brought in when Mr. Postlethwayte began his speech. He is Mayor this year, and he was so kind—he came and asked us whether we should *object* to go with Mrs. Froggatt, to sit in the gallery. *Object*, indeed! I wouldn't have missed it for anything in the world; and we were just above our dear old fellow's head, where he could not see us, which was all the better for him.'

'Was he nervous?'

'No; he said there was a reality of kindness about it all that made him feel it as friend to friend. So the Minsterham reporter said too. Felix brought him in to tea, because we are to have his report for Pur. He said he had never seen such genuine feeling on all sides. He wanted to call it an ovation. And Felix puzzled him so by declaring that inapplicable, unless it had all been mutton.'

'And Mr. Bolton did send ever so much venison,' put in Stella; 'and a letter besides, because he could not come himself. Mr. Postlethwayte began by reading it.'

'Yes; that was all the right and proper thing,' said Cherry; 'all civility about his valuable supporter. As well might he say, for hasn't Pur fought for him through thick and thin—and suffered too! But it was Mr. Postlethwayte who had his heart in it. There, Stella, you can say it all off by heart like a little live page of Pur. Tell Wilmet what he said about example.'

'He said,' rehearsed Stella, 'that Felix had set a noble example of considering no means of independence derogatory, and only manifesting his birth in the high sense of honour which, in the name of his fellow-citizens, he confessed to have been no slight stimulus.'

'Well done! That was much for Mr. Postlethwayte to say.'

'Oh! everybody said everything!' answered Cherry. 'Mr. Bruce went on about the paper. Poor dear old Pur, he never had so much good said of him before, and every word true; but the real beauty of the thing was the Frogs.'

'I am so glad Mr. Froggatt could go.'

'He said he would not have missed if he had had one foot in the grave. I really was afraid, once or twice, Mrs. Froggatt would have embraced us then and there in the gallery, before all the people. How she did cry, dear old lady!'

'She was thinking of her own sons, poor dear!'

'Partly; but I do think half was pride and pleasure, and that sort of feeling that grows up of unanimity. I can't describe, but it is like a spirit mastering all. You will read in the report; but it does not give a notion of the kind of glow, and the ecstasy of the cheer, when Mr. Underwood of Vale Leston was given out—the looks of all the faces! Oh! I can't describe it—one seemed obliged to sob for gratitude! And then, in the lull at last came his voice, so clear and sweet and strong, and taking them all by surprise. Now, Stella, go on!'

'Felix stood up,' said Stella, with a pretty little tone of enthusiastic imitation in her low sweet voice, 'and said perhaps it was not regular to criticise the manner of such an honour as they had done him, but he must say that he had rather they had proposed him as Underwood of 14 High Street. For if his good friends thought they were disposing of him with a long farewell, he must tell them they would not be rid of him so soon. For he said that for the means of fulfilling his new duties he must look in great measure to his old sphere, and their unvarying friendliness. What a noise they did make then! and when he went on to thank them for their kindness in treating him as one of themselves, though without any claim of long standing. And then wasn't it nice when he went on about Mr. Froggatt!'

'Can't you see, Wilmet,' continued Geraldine, 'how being altogether moved and excited, all sorts of things came out that he never could have said in cold blood? About the gentleman he said it was all owing to—his accepting him when he was a raw friendless lad, giving him an opening for exertion—patience—kindness. You'll read it, but if you could only have seen and heard when he said he should always esteem the connecting of their names among the dearest honours of his life, as it had certainly been the proudest. He told us afterwards that he saw a face looking as if it sounded like humbug; so he added louder, "Yes, as much the proudest and dearest, as what one may hope is personal is better than what comes by the accident of birth." And he could not believe that any honour could bestow on him the pleasure he had felt when he first saw the names of Froggatt and Underwood together. Whatever he had done or hoped to do, he felt to be due not only to the first start, but to the long thorough training in diligent habits of business. As Mr. Bevan said afterwards, it was the most beautiful outpouring of gratitude without false shame. And Mr. Froggatt, who had not the least expected it, was quite past speaking. "Gentlemen, my feelings—" he said, and broke down, and every one cheered, and he tried again, but only got as far as "Gentlemen, my feelings—" and put his hand on Mr. Ryder's arm, and begged him to say it for him, something about "a thousandfold repaid." Mr. Ryder made a set speech of it, all very true and good, really the best of all, looking so in the Pursuivant, but nothing to "Gentlemen, my feelings—" and the great sob.'

'Dear old gentleman! is he more reconciled to the losing you all?'

'Yes, he is so much pleased to keep Lance, and that Felix does not throw it all up. Indeed, if we could have given up Bexley it would have been a great difficulty, for Felix feels that he took the duties of a son upon him.'

'It does to a certain degree qualify one's regret,' said Wilmet. 'As John says, one would not take the responsibility of saying a word of remonstrance; he is no fanciful lad, but a man well used to practical questions; but I still am sorry he should so cripple himself by acting on scruples Papa never entertained.'

'We can hardly be sure of that,' said Cherry. 'That old letter to Mr. Staples looked as if he were doubtful. When I told Sister Constance—I could not help it, though Felix had not given me leave—she seemed quite overcome, and then she pointed out how right it had all come, for in the ordinary course of things most likely this restitution would not have been possible. If he had been brought up as an eldest son, and we had all had an expensive education like other people, not only should we all have grown into acquiescence in an unavoidable sort of abuse, but there would have been none of the power of independence that enables him to do this; and there would have been settlements and all manner of things to tie it up. Remember, too, that dear Papa was always thankful that he did not have the trial of unmixed prosperity.'

Those were the last words before there was a slackening of speed; Wilmet resumed the one Kit, Stella the other, Robina wielded the doves, and gathered the parcels, a tall fair head under a big black hat nodded and smiled welcome, and the little station seemed to flash with greeting, as in another moment the halt was made, Clement wrenched open the door, swung out Stella, holding fast by the basket, and set her down with a kiss, next putting forth a long tender pair of arms to lift Cherry down, and then receiving his nephew and holding him while Wilmet and Robina extracted the other impedimenta, and the other two-thirds of the party hurried up, amid touching of hats and services of porters, Bernard and Angela flying upon one another, and luggage pouring out of the van.

'I hope there's room,' said Clement, surveying the numbers. 'I brought everything on wheels that I could get beasts for.'

And making Kit over to his father's hand, he conveyed Cherry to a corner of the big barouche with post-horses, and then hurried back to pack in Wilmet and her boy. He would have put in Robina and Major Harewood, but they both cried out that this was the place for Squire himself. Clement and John dragged him from some selection of boxes in a recusant but passive state, and deposited him opposite to Geraldine, as she merrily called him 'to enjoy the novel sensation of riding in one's own coach.'

'Theodore!' he remonstrated; but Wilmet's eyes grew uneasy, and Clement said, 'Better let Lance and me take him. You'll have a noisy welcome, and he had better not have the first brunt. Here, Tedo, jump up by Lance; see my big horse! Ha! I see Angel and Bear have climbed to the box. Now then, Robin, in with you! Can you make room for Stella?'

So having packed the barouche, Clement sent it off with a dash, taking John and Will Harewood as well as his two brothers in that dog-cart that fitted him so oddly, while Sibby, Krishnu, the nurse and baby, and the luggage, were disposed of in a sort of break which would hold everything, and came soberly behind with a farm-horse.

It had been well done of the brothers to relieve Felix from the charge of keeping the peace between Theodore and Kit, and leave him free to enjoy the arrival with his sisters, and to be happy in having Wilmet with him, the sharer in all his earlier exertions, and the best able to enter into his recollections, though at first she failed to recognise the old landmarks he pointed out, and Cherry sat dreamily smiling, owning that she recollected nothing in particular, but all was lovely and delicious, and not like a strange place, but as if she belonged to it.

Then came the summit of the hill, the church tower, and the river, and the rich valley stretched before them; and as there was a halt to put on the drag, up came on the breeze a clash and peal. 'The bells! the bells!' cried Stella; and Wilmet held up the finger to her boy, 'The bells, Kit, the bells for Uncle Felix! Listen!'

'Don't you ever forget,' cried Cherry, bending to kiss the wondering child; and grasping Felix's hand in irrepressible agitation, 'Oh! how often I have wondered whether we should live to see this day!'

113

'Thank Heaven that you share it, Sweetheart,' fervently whispered Felix; while Bernard and Angela turned round, and screamed to them to look.

And there was a big arch all across the road, all greenery, big white and orange lilies, and 'Welcome' and 'F.C.U.'s, and a flag on the church tower, and a tremendous onset of drums and trumpets, obstreperously hailing the conquering hero, who had to take off his hat and bow to the mounted array of some dozen tenants and their sons, all the cavalry of the estate turned out to meet him. 'Master Kistopher' was hardened enough to military bands not to mind this at all; but it was well that Theodore was a little behind, for the lungs of all Vale Leston Abbas, and more too, united in the cheer as the arch was reached. 'Oh! I hope they won't take out the horses!' cried Cherry, more than half frightened, while Bernard and Angel danced up and down with ecstatic cries of 'Jolly! jolly! Here's the whole place turned out! They'll draw us up to the house! Hurrah! hurrah!' bowing so graciously, that Cherry, in a counter paroxysm of diversion, called to them that they would be taken for the man and maid if they appropriated all the enthusiasm.

Happily no one was venturesome enough to meddle with the horses, but the whole population attended the carriage up to the house, making so much discordant uproar, that the reception was a very questionable pleasure to the nervous; Cherry was between laughter and sobs, and Wilmet had to spend much pains in persuading her boy that it was all excellent fun.

At last, upon the stone steps stood Felix, with Cherry on his arm, Theodore in his hand, nine altogether out of his twelve brothers and sisters round him, on this the threshold of the home of his forefathers. There he stood, bare-headed, moist-eyed, thanks to Heaven swelling his heart, thanks to man fluttering on his lip, as he heard the fresh shout of welcome, and the old men's 'There he is! God bless him!'

'Well may they say so!' whispered John Harewood to his wife. 'Here, at twenty-nine, he stands a stainless knight, with a stainless shield, as though he had not had to fight his way, and bear up all these around him!'

Felix meantime, withstanding Theodore's terrified tugs at his hand, put him into Sibby's care, to be taken as far as possible from the human greeting, and to enjoy that of the bells; Clement, with a prevision of the welcome, had provided a supply of cider, wherewith he and the other gentlemen proceeded to administer draughts to the health of the new master, who was allowed to do nothing but stand on the step to make a tableau, as Bill said, with his sisters, and return by look and gesture the tokens of welcome and the cheer, which Clement, gathering his choir, contrived to render considerably less inharmonious.

Then Felix, feeling that some words were due, and trained a little by town-council exigencies, spoke forth. 'Thanks, thanks with all our hearts, my good friends and neighbours. We did not expect so hearty a welcome, and I am sure we shall never forget it. As far as an earnest wish and purpose to do my best will carry me, I will try to deserve it; but you must bear with me if I often unavoidably disappoint you, and do not come up to the old golden age of this house. Any way, let us do our best, one and all, to live here to the glory of God, and in friendliness to one another. Then it will go hard if we are not very happy together.'

The bright smile and joyous hope in his face awoke a shout of 'Yes, yes!' and another cheer, followed by a farmer's voice proposing the health of the ladies, with the homely addition from another quarter, 'Bless their sweet faces!' and an observation which the Major delighted to overhear—'That there tall one, with the child by her side, was a right-down comely one, just such as our ladies up here did used to was.'

Health to 'Mr. Eddard' followed, surprising the new comers who had not learnt to accept the Vicar's parish name. It drained his provision of liquor, and gave him the opportunity of saying, 'Thank you sincerely, dear friends. We are old friends, you know, and I need say no more, only that now we have seen the good time coming, you had better wish the travellers good-night, and let my sisters rest. You will all be better acquainted soon.'

'Well managed, Mr. Edward,' said Felix, smiling, as Clement, for the first time able to speak to him after dismissing his flock, ran up the steps looking heated and radiant.

'There's another thing I've done, Felix,' he said, rather breathlessly. 'I've got a supper for the ringers in the long room. Martha is much displeased about it, but it is the only chance of breaking the neck of the drinking at the Rood without making you unpopular.'

'All right, Clem, thank you. Well! you look better than when I saw you last!'

'I'm quite jolly, thank you;' and indeed, the fagged air of depression had changed to hope and sunshine; he had grown quite sunburnt, and as Cherry followed up the compliment, had turned into a vigorous country parson instead of a white town-bred one. He was acting as a sort of host. 'This way, Wilmet. You must settle about the rooms, Cherry. It was all guess-work between Martha and me. There's some tea in the drawing-room by this time.'

He led them quickly through a large hall, paved with black and white lozenges, into a sort of conservatory passage, glazed on one side, and containing old orange-trees in tubs, and more recent fuchsias and geraniums, a great curtain of lilac Bougainvillia drooping at one end—making the girls shriek with ecstasy, and reproach Felix with never having told them of it.

'I am afraid I had forgotten it,' said he. 'I never went into this part of the house on my last two visits.'

'It was Jane's territory (Mrs. Fulbert),' said Clement, 'and I am afraid she has dismantled the room a good deal. The one hundred pounds you allowed her to choose as her own furniture came chiefly out of that, and the valuable things poor Fulbert had in his smoking-room. It was an odd choice, but I thought you would not mind that, and the valuation man looked sharp after her. I kept out of the way of the squabble.'

'I know where I am now,' said Wilmet. 'There's the garden-door at the end. And here is the drawing-room door. Ah! it does look empty.'

'Oh, never mind tables and chairs. The window!' cried Angela, flying forward to the eastern one, a deep bay, cushioned round, and looking out on the sloping lawn, gay with flower-beds, in pleasant evening shadow, the river sparkling beyond, and with a sidelong view of the bridge on the one hand and the church on the other. Two other windows looked to the south, also into the garden.

'At least she has left the piano,' said Lance.

'It was valued at eighty pounds, which would have made too large a hole,' said Clement. 'Also she has left a chair for you to sit on, Cherry. Are you tired?'

'I haven't time! I can't grasp it! Home! So exquisite, and all ours. Oh! the pictures! That lady, with the bent head over the rose, and the arch pensive eyes! She can't choose but be a Sir Joshua.'

'Right, Cherry,' said Lance, mounting a chair and turning to the back; "'Lady Geraldine Underwood, 1770. J. Reynolds.'"

'The Irishwoman that gave you eyes and mischief. Your best possessions,' said Will.

He looked at Angela. Did he forget that neither Irish eyes nor mischief were Robina's portion?

At that moment Stella, who had gone up to the hearth, exclaimed, 'Edgar!' then checked herself, at the sound of the seldom uttered name; but Felix and Wilmet had both sprung to look.

'I remember,' said the latter.

'Is it my father?' whispered Stella.

It was one of a pair of the largest size of miniatures in Ross's most exquisite style of finish, thirty years back, just before the marriage of Edward and Mary Underwood. He, still a layman, was in a shooting-coat, with a dog by his side, and with the look of life and light, youth and sunshine, that had never left him—indeed, none but the little ones who had never really seen him could have hesitated for a moment; but it was different with the fellow-portrait. If Felix and Wilmet had not remembered 'Mamma's picture,' they would hardly have connected the bright soft smiling rose-tinted girl with the toil-worn faded image on their memories. Wilmet's tears gathered; and Felix murmured to Cherry, 'One feels that the life was killed out of her! She looks as if one would have died to save her a breath of care! Oh! to have brought her back!'

And with a wistful sigh he looked at Stella, the most like the portrait, though none of the sisters really reproduced it; indeed, the peculiar caressing and relying expression could hardly have been brought out, except by a petted shielded life, free from all care or hardness. Wilmet was on a more majestic and commanding scale; something of the darling child expression was in Geraldine, but intellect and illness had changed both the mould and colouring of the features. Robina was of the round-faced, round-eyed type, only refined; Angela like no one but Clement; and even Stella was not only too small, but too thoughtful, to recall that flower-like careless loveliness of Mary Underwood's maiden bloom.

'It was hard on you not to have had these,' said John.

'I suppose,' said Felix, 'that they were done for my uncle, and that my father thought them too valuable to take away.'

'Better so,' said Cherry, quietly.

'Yes,' said Lance; 'to have had these before one's eyes would have made one ready to fly at that man's throat,' glancing at the old squire in uniform.

'And now,' said Cherry, 'they are smiling their greeting to us.'

'You'll turn out the Squire, won't you, Felix?' added Lance. 'You won't keep him here, gloating on his victims?'

'Certainly not, if he suggests such ideas,' said Felix. 'It is Cherry's domain, though, and she must decide whether to banish him.'

'Oh! oh!' screamed Angela, who had meanwhile followed Bernard out of the room. 'Come here, all of you! Felix, we must have a ball! Nature and fate decree it.'

Felix laughed, gave Cherry his arm, and the procession moved on. 'Tripp says this conservatory was glazed for a surprise to my mother while she was on her wedding tour,' said Clement. 'You know this wing is the recent part of the house, built by my old great-uncle, when people had come to have large notions as to drawing and dining rooms. Here's the dining-room, but we shall go in there for severe tea presently. This is the middle period, the Stewart style part,' as they came back into the wainscotted hall, rising to the top of the house, with a staircase opposite to the front-door, and a handsome balustraded gallery running round the first floor.

But Angela's discovery was a great arched doorway, mantled only by a curtain, and leading into the only really ancient part of the building (except one turret). It was a very long room, with dark oak floor, six arched and cusped windows looking into as many arches of the cloister that ran along it, and black wainscot panelled walls, and oak beams, painted with coats-of-arms. So long was it, that the billiard table at one end, and at the other Clement's table laid out for the ringers' supper, made little show in it; and Angela, pouncing on Will Harewood, waltzed wildly with him up and down the shining floor, while Bernard learnedly expounded to Stella the games at billiards he had enjoyed with Mr. Somers there, and Lance went straight to the organ at the farther end.

'Ah! if you can do any good with that!' said Clement. 'I have been trying, but have only driven it and myself distracted!'

'How well I know the place!' cried Wilmet. 'Oh, if Alda could see it! I remember your driving us all in a team here, Fee!—Yes, Kit, trot, trot, all along. It is as if I saw you, Cherry, taking your first run alone there.'

'Better than now, I fear,' said Felix. 'Why, Cherry, woman, we must lay down bridges of matting for you,' as he felt her clutch his arm.

'Are all the floors so dreadful?' she sighed, as Clement next opened from the hall door into the library, with only a bit of carpet as an island in the middle. The library ranged with the drawing and dining rooms, though older. It had a window and a door into the cloister, and two windows to the east, and was surrounded with caged book-shelves. Here stood an harmonium, and the table and deep window-seats were piled with the miscellaneous parish appurtenances of the nineteenth-century pastor.

'You had better have this room, Felix,' said Clement; 'there was so much to do that I could not get my traps moved after Somers went.'

To which Felix replied by insisting that Clement should retain it. The door into the cloister, communicating with the church and churchyard, made it particularly eligible for the Vicar; and the study, on the opposite side of the hall, the Squire's favourite sitting-room, with the two south windows, would suit him and Pur,—the better that the adjoining room, where old Fulbert had slept in his infirm days, would serve as a housekeeper's room for Sibby and a retreat and home for Theodore. It opened into a passage leading to the offices.

'Never mind them now,' said Clement. 'Let Martha recover before we face her. I don't know which she resents most, the supper, or my sending in Kerenhappuch to help her. You all will be glad to find your nests, ladies,' he added, as poor Cherry surmounted each slippery shallow step, clinging hard to Felix's arm, while Angela and Stella had flown all round the upper story, and were helping Bill to laugh at the round-eyed range of ancestors in the corridor.

'Here I put you, our grand company, Mettie,' said Clement, opening the door of the handsome bedroom of the drawing-room wing; 'the nursery is up over, as I daresay you remember.'

'As if I did not!'

And up to it with one accord they all went, Cherry and all—for the stairs were close by, and of deal. At the moment of entrance, Felix, Wilmet, and Cherry, broke into a simultaneous shout of delight, as they beheld, staring at them in open-nostrilled pride, the rocking-horse of their youth. In one moment Cherry's arms were round its neck, Wilmet had her boy on the saddle, Felix was gently moving it, and patting its dappled sides with the tenderness of ancient love.

'This at least is unprofaned! I suppose no child has mounted it since we five hung rocking on it altogether that last morning!'

'I should like a ride now, dear old Gee-gee,' said Cherry, half sentimentally, as Kit insisted on being taken down to go to his Emma and his tea; and to her surprise and fright, her brothers snatched her up, and deposited her on its back, between screaming and laughing; and hardly was she lifted down, before Wilmet was on her knees, as Lance said, worshipping the doll's house over which she and Alda had broken their hearts, and setting all the the chairs and tables on their legs again.

The very cribs in the inner nursery were all in their old places; and to the great amusement of the rest, the four who had the honour of being natives, each sat down upon his or her own; and Felix and Wilmet had quite a little quarrel which owned the favoured cane-sided one, where one could poke one's fingers through.

'One's fingers—or rather two's fingers—are rather too big to decide that question now,' said Felix. 'However, you can take possession by deputy, Mettie, and some day Alda shall fill them all.'

'Ah! to meet her here!'

But there was one more sadly missed—the King Oberon of the nursery, whose star of cracked glass still marked one of the panes. Kit was the first to see it, trot up to point, and say 'Naughty!' but no one answered him, and Felix struggled back to a cheerful tone to say, 'After all, cane crib and all, I was not here to the last; I slept in Papa's dressing-room after Clem came to the fore.'

'Mamma's room was the one over the library,' said Cherry, as they descended.

'Here it is!' with transomed windows, trailed over with vine and Virginia creeper, one towards the river, and two towards the church, and Cherry's own particular boxes were in it. 'Oh! my dear Lord Chamberlain,' she cried, 'this is the place the master ought to have!'

'I had rather be on the other side, Cherry,' said Felix. 'It is better for Theodore that Clem and I should have rooms opening into one another, as he will look to him when I sleep out.'

'And I thought the dressing-room would serve for Stella,' added Clement. 'Why, she is quite pink!'

'Have I really a room to myself?'

'There are enough in the house for that, my little Star,' said Felix. 'I suppose you will hardly make a further progress now, Whiteheart?'

'Only let me show her the Prior's room,' said Clement, taking her to the floor above the billiard-room. It had been a smoking-room in the last reign; the windows were hung with heavy curtains; there was both a stove and a cheerful grate in it, a thick carpet and cushions in the windows, and a high screen, to cut off the draught from the little window into the south transept, where the Prior of old used to hear Mass, if indisposed.

'I have been purifying this room, literally and metaphorically,' said Clement, thinking of the pictures he had removed, and the air he had let in. 'It will make Cherry a capital painting-room.'

'Oh! but it is too much! You must not give me all the best rooms in the house.'

'Who should have them but our lady of the house?' cried both brothers.

'And after all, there are conveniences in not painting in the drawing-room,' said Cherry. 'May I tell, Lance?' as they both fell into a transport of laughter. 'You must know, Willie there insisted that I should do Cleomenes after the battle, when he would not go into his deserted house. He used so much moral compulsion, that though I knew that a Greek warrior was as much beyond me as an archangel, I only feebly objected the want of a model; and Lance, in a spirit of classic friendship, said he would sit. So one afternoon—there he stood, with his trousers turned up to his knees, and his shirt-sleeves up to his shoulders, no shoes or stockings—the table-cover gracefully disposed with a big shawl-brooch on one shoulder for a chlamys—leaning on Sibby's long broom-stick by way of a spear, endeavouring to compose his face as if his wife were dead, and his children in captivity, and he just beaten horse and foot, and going after them.'

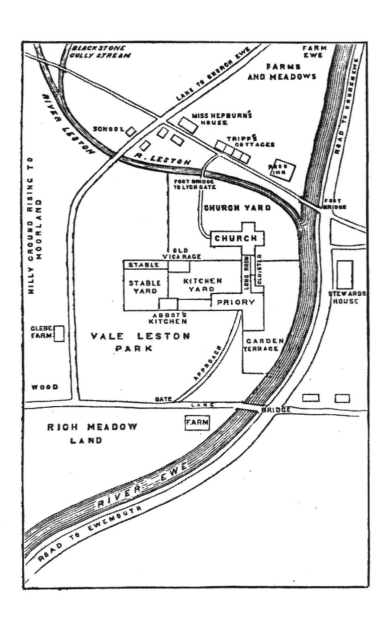

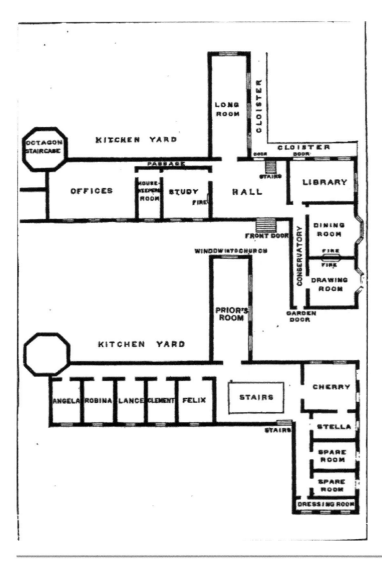

'Cleomenes is no laughing matter,' sternly interposed Bill.

'Cleomenes was not, but Lance was. Well, I was just making a study of his foot, never dreaming of anybody getting in but by the street-door, when of all things in the world, up comes Miss Pearson herself—Miss Pearson, senior! and three girls! They had met a mad ox in the street, or some trifle of that sort, had bolted into the shop nearly in fits, and this unthinking Felix had popped them through the office to be still more scandalized upstairs.'

'Poor Miss Pearson!' said Lance; 'I shall never forget her gentle "Do I intrude?" going off into the wildest scream. And I couldn't escape by the other door, for Cherry had her easel up against it. She could only shriek "He's sitting!" technically, you see, like an old hen, or a schoolmaster, for I wasn't sitting at all.'

'Well, you need have no such catastrophes here,' said Felix, when the laughter began to subside; 'but your progress has been long enough; now we have landed you. You younger fry, you must shake into your rooms as you choose.'

'I secure the octagon turret-room at the end of the corridor,' cried Angela.

'And I shall hold to my room with the rum ceiling,' said Bernard. 'It is as good as the barrack at home! Come and see, Lance.'

'I ordered tea at seven,' said Clement, 'that Felix might be ready to speak to the ringers after it. You must take us in hand, now, Cherry; that is my last domestic order.'

So Cherry was left with her little sister. There was a little bustle of unpacking at first; but by the time Cherry was ready, she missed all sounds of Stella, and looking into her room, saw the child standing by the window, gazing intently out in a kind of dream, which ended in her running up to Cherry with a gasp of ecstasy, and hiding her face against her. 'O Cherry!' she said, 'I did not know it could be so—so—so exquisite!' and her bosom heaved with the struggle of new emotion—she who had seen nothing but Bexley suburbs in her little life.

'It does seem almost impossible to believe we are really always to live with these lovely sights,' said Cherry. 'It is like getting into the Promised Land! Why, my Star, it quite overcomes you!'

'Oh! if Tedo could—could—' It was a sort of moan that burst from Stella, followed by a shower of tears.

'Ah! Stella, sweet! We all of us miss somebody. It is not the Promised Land yet, for there you know there will be Ephphatha indeed!' and Cherry strangled her own sob, as her supplication went up that all might be as well there with her heart's grief as with Stella's. 'Besides,' she added, cheerfully, 'Theodore will be happier here; he will have more liberty and more pets.'

'And he likes the bells,' said Stella; but there was a wistful yearning look on the sweet face, as if the excess of pleasure increased the longing for companionship in her twin.

Cherry took her hand to encounter the dread waste of slipperiness before her; but in further proof who was the lady and the darling of the house, no sooner did her door open, than Felix hastened across from his room, Clement strode up from the library, John Harewood's head emerged from his dressing-room door; but Lance was beforehand with all, for he was close by, helping Golightly the gardener to carry the boxes as near as possible to their destinations.

He bore her off in triumph, with so much laughter, that the consequence was a slip, and a shout of warning displeasure from the elder brothers.

'No fault of his,' cried back Cherry, holding tight to him. 'Only if four brothers at once will make me so proud, I can but have a fall.'

'Aren't you prouder now?' said Lance, as they trooped into the dining-room. 'There's a table to sit down at the head of!'

What a glittering array it was of glass and silver and brightly-coloured china; and the profusion of country fare—roast fowl, green pease, yellow butter in ice, virgin combs of transparent liquid golden honey, mountains of strawberries, great jugs of milk and cream. There was no formality indeed in the Amen that responded to their chaplain's grace.

'Good creatures verily,' ejaculated Felix, as he took up carving-knife and fork.

'Is it a feast for his birthday?' whispered Stella, 'or is it to be always like this?'

'You see,' said Cherry to her neighbour, the Major, 'we remember when we used to have a quart of blue milk, and save for the babies.'

'I say, Felix,' cried Angela, 'have we got a farm, with cows, and turkey-cocks, and turnips, and all sorts of jolly things?'

'Stunning!' said Bernard; 'and an old bull with a ring in his nose, that would toss you as soon as look at you!'

'That home farm is a difficulty,' said Felix. 'I believe I ought to get rid of it, for I know nothing of farming, and have no time to learn.'

'Oh, let me manage it, if that's all!' said Angel. 'I'll get a smock-frock and big shoes, and a long whip, and get up at four in the morning.'

'Seriously, I hope you can keep it in your own hands,' said Clement. 'There's no getting milk otherwise. You might as well ask the farmers' wives for their hearts' blood. There's a child that I baptized soon after I came; the mother is sickly, and had lost two before. I found her feeding it with some mess of pounded acorns, and recommended milk, but found I might as well have talked of melted gold. Even when I offered to pay, it could not be done—would break up the cheese-making. I thought of buying a cow and some hay, and putting her in the Vicarage; but when I saw a great jug of hot milk come in with my coffee every morning, I ended by getting a mug and carrying it down every day; and really the child has lived.'

'But, Clem,' said Angel, with a sort of affectation of solemnity, 'wasn't that a difficult case of conscience? Weren't you stealing Mr. Underwood's milk?'

'No; for our old *régime*—not to say St. Matthew's—had taught him to go without,' said Felix, smiling, for he had seen the mug in force.

'Till the new Squire came, and I could unblushingly prey on him,' rejoined Clement.

'Whereby I propose,' said Major Harewood, 'that we drink the health of the said new Squire—with all birthday wishes—and long may he reign!'

'All birthday wishes, Felix,' responded Wilmet, who, like some of the others, had begun tea with a glass of claret. 'Do you remember this day thirteen years, when Robin did not know what a cold chicken was?'

'I remember it well,' said Felix, gravely. 'It seems to me to have been the last day that I was a boy. Thank you,' as each bright face nodded at him. 'Haven't I made speeches enough? Well, then, Ladies and Gentlemen, many thanks to you for coming here to-day. It's little good this place would be to me without you. And—' from the playfulness a sudden emotion came over and thrilled his voice—'may God grant we may still be all as happy together as we have been these thirteen years!'

'I would not have missed this for anything!' was John's very warm aside; but a little afraid of emotion, he added, 'Yes, you are worth looking at. You certainly are a right goodly family.'

'Seen in the light of prosperity,' said Cherry.

'He need not be accused of that,' said Wilmet. 'He never saw so many of us together before.'

'Except the first time,' said John, 'when I thought you would never have done coming into the room.'

'Poor John!' said Felix, 'I pity your blushes. I wonder you were not frightened away at once!'

'And it was not Robin's fault,' said Cherry. 'Do you remember, Bobbie, the agony you were in, till you grew desperate, and stopped Clem and me by speaking out?'

'Robin could have had nothing to speak about,' said Wilmet, with a resumption of her old manner that tickled the others exceedingly.

'*In*deed!' quoth Lance. 'Bill remembers his confidences by the river.'

'Moonshine!' growled Bill, but scarce heeded, for John had turned to his wife with a droll injured air of condolence, saying, 'Ah! my dear, these little secrets will come out; but we must make the best of it!'

'And talking of rivers and moonshine,' cried Angela, 'we'll have a turn in the boat. Hurrah for the boat! Come, Bear—come, Bill—I want my first lesson in rowing.'

'Stay,' said Felix; 'that eddy where the Leston comes down makes the river not safe when you do not know it. Now, girls, all of you, remember once for all that I desire you will never go in the boat without some one who can swim, nor take Theodore without me.'

119

He seldom gave a direct command, but there was enforcement in his tone; and John added, 'Quite right. I see it is a stream not to be trusted.'

'It is just a device to hinder our going at all,' pouted Angela.

'And swimming is a mere hindrance to drowning aisy, if you are to be drownded,' added Bill.

'Do you know,' added Clement, 'that

>"To Leston and Ewe
>   Underwood pays due,"

in every generation?'

'Where did you pick up that adage?' asked Felix.

'A prophecy, a prophecy!' cried Angela. 'What fun! I shall hold up my head more than ever, now we have a saw of our own! What fun!'

'Where did you hear it?' repeated Cherry, who as well as Stella looked discomfited.

'I did not hear it,' said Clement, 'the people were far too polite to tell me; but it was administered to Somers by way of warning, after some eccentric proceedings in the boat with Bear. They say an Underwood is drowned in every generation—I suppose since the sacrilege.'

'Prove the fact,' said Felix.

'Somers and I did try to make out,' said Clement, 'between registers and monuments. We found one Lancelot in 1750, with a note "Drowned" attached to his name, and a conglomeration of urns and water-nymphs—Leston and Ewe, I presume—scrambling about his monument in the south transept; and the old Squire had told me that the crayon young lady in a cap in the library was our old great-uncle's intended, but was drowned in crossing the ferry at Ewmouth, before the bridge was built. She is not very pretty; and I was going to have put a photograph in her place, but it seemed to me profane, when she had hung there so many years for the poor old faithful lover to look at.'

'The Ewe seems to have been in overhaste to claim its due, before she was an Underwood,' said Angela.

'Quite enough for an adage,' said John; 'one real Underwood, and one intended.'

'However, as I do not mean the rivers to get their due through any fool-hardiness,' said Felix, 'you must attend to my rule.'

'And I think it renders boating reasonably safe,' added Clement. 'There are no holes, and the only danger is when there has been a good deal of rain to make the currents strong; otherwise it is quite safe for a tolerable swimmer. I learnt at Cambridge, and Bear is a perfect cork; but I did not know you could swim, Fee.'

'I improved my opportunities at Ewmouth five years ago, when unluckily Lance could not.'

'I should try again if I were to be much here,' said Lance; but the general voice dissuaded him; and at the same time Tripp knocked at the door—the summons to the Vicar and Squire to visit the ringers at their banquet.

'You had better go to bed, Cherry,' said Felix, as he rose; 'you look like a white rag.'

'Triumphs are tiring processes, to say nothing of making tea,' said Cherry; 'but I don't want to disturb Sibby just yet.'

'I'll put you to bed, if you like,' said Wilmet 'I want to send Emma down, and keep within hearing of the children.'

'Oh, that will be most delicious of all! So like old times!' And the two sisters went off, to be happy together, and coo a little delight in their Squire and his beautiful home, mingled with a domestic consultation how the bared drawing-room could be inexpensively rendered a pleasant family gathering place.

'A little chintz will do a great deal,' said Wilmet; 'we will see about it.'

Which assurance set Cherry's mind at rest on that score, for her belief in Wilmet's notable abilities was boundless. 'But what is the matter with Robina?' she added after a few minutes, recalling the events of the day. 'She is so silent, and has a distressed anxious look I never saw about her before. I wonder whether she regrets the not coming home for good.'

'I am not sure,' said Wilmet; 'I am inclined to think she is sorry to be away from Repworth Towers.'

'O Wilmet! impossible, unnatural!'

'I never do quite understand Robin,' said Wilmet. 'She seems the simplest, soberest girl in the world; and yet I suppose that folly of Alice's put things into her head, for she has a strange propensity to think people are paying her attention. Even at Barèges I saw symptoms of it, which I put a stop to at once.'

'I can't think it of any one so honest and sensible as the Robin.'

'I know it, unfortunately; and it is the more curious that she has only moderate good looks, and no other tokens of vanity. It is particularly unlucky in her position.'

'You don't imagine there's anything going on!'

'I hope not.'

'I have a great deal too much confidence in the Robin to suspect her.'

'Not of consciously doing wrong, but of having been flattered, and now perhaps in a difficulty. However, I shall say nothing till we have seen more. She may be only tired.'

Felix—with all that was on his hands—had likewise noted the absence of the Robin's chirp, and looked for her when he came back from the ringers' supper, to which Clement and Lance had followed him. They then went off to Clement's library for a consultation about some music; and Felix, repairing to the drawing-room, found nothing there but a lonely cockchafer, knocking his head against a lonely lamp on the lonely round table in the centre—not an enlivening spectacle; but hearing steps on the gravel, he went out, and found John pacing under the wall with a cigar, and Bernard emulously following in his wake.

'Where are all the others?' he asked; 'it is not far from ten.'

'Wilmet went up to the babies,' said John; 'the others are about somewhere.'

'Larking about,' added Bernard, with superior wisdom. 'Well, John, you were saying—'

Felix was too thankful to have Bernard doing anything so sensible as to talk to John to interrupt them further, and turned away. He stood for a few minutes to enjoy the strange repose of the exquisite loveliness of the scene—the summer sunset, not yet entirely died away, but tingeing the northern sky with pure light, while the great moon, still low, silvered the river, and defined the grand outline of the church.

And this, not only a scene to be gazed at, but the home he had reached at last—the home so long withheld!

'Entering into rest,' he said to himself, for the repose of mind was great. 'And yet—

"Your rest must be no rest below."

No, home duties—higher duties, still more—forbid me to make this more than a resting-place—not rest. "There remaineth yet a rest for the people of God"—yet a home, but its shadow here is very sweet. Let it not beguile me!'

Just then Angela's laugh, a very musical and yet a very giddy one, like a rapid peal of silver bells, caught his ear; and in the moonlight in the churchyard he saw her tall light figure, and what could be none other than Will beside her. He was vexed. She was bare-headed, and the churchyard was open to the village on the other side, and had a public pathway through it. He walked quickly towards them, and called as soon as he could do so in a low voice, 'Come in directly, Angela. You know this is not private ground.'

'O Felix, we have found such a delicious ghost! Don't you see its white wings?'

'Angel thinks it is her own kin, a fossil cherub,' said Will. 'Why aren't you all out? 'tis not a scene to be wasted, especially with Angels and Ministers of Grace to defend us.'

'Minister of *Grace*—that's Robin,' laughed Angela.

'Hush, Angela! come in,' said Felix, severely; 'this is no place for nonsense—especially unkind nonsense,' he added in a lower voice.

She did not answer, but the church clock began its chimes—sweet, mysterious, tender—given by some musical Underwood long ago, and sounding in the dark quite unearthly, while the long deep tones of the ten o'clock that followed came with awe upon the ear. Will was heard to give a long sigh, but no one spoke as they all came back to the drawing-room, which was full enough by this time—four gentlemen, hotly discussing a cricket-match by the chimney-piece; Wilmet knitting on a stiff chair in the corner; and Robina, under the lamp, hard at work on some point-lace on a green roll.

'Putting out your eyes, Bob,' said Felix, feeling the need of saying something kind to her. 'What are you doing that for?'

'Lady de la Poer has some point de Venise that she can't use because one ruffle is wanting,' said Robina, 'and I have made out the pattern. I want to take it back with me and surprise her.'

'It is all willing sacrifice when one puts out one's eyes in a marchioness's service,' said Will's voice from the window.

Robina looked up resolutely. 'Very willing when one is grateful for a great deal of motherly kindness,' she said, steadily, and yet with a certain sadness in her voice.

'Oh yes! a handle to one's name makes a little civility go a great way.'

'You know nothing about it.' The voice was steady but indignant, and there was a flush of deep colour on the cheeks.

'It is quite true, Robina,' said John. 'It is one of the trials of life, that when we live in two different worlds, the inhabitants of the one are apt to resent and misunderstand our feelings for the other.'

They were all grateful for this generalization; and Felix now spoke of the household prayers. 'I had not begun them,' said Clement; 'I thought the real master of the house should take the initiative.'

'Set up the domestic halter, as Mrs. Shapcote says,' added Lance.

'We might make that organ available,' said Felix, 'and screen off the end part of the long room where it stands, for a permanency.'

'Yes, there's rather a nice window down there with our Rood in it—nothing incongruous,' said Clement, 'if Lance can only cure the organ.'

'Meantime, I suppose we had better have the servants in here, and use the piano.'

'They will be all dispersed, and not like to come in,' said Wilmet.

'Possibly,' said Felix, 'but I shall go and see. I have a feeling against beginning our first night in our new home without some collective commendation of ourselves.'

'If we had but an authorized form for dedicating a new home, like the Russian Church,' said Clement.

'You have not thought of anything in especial. Well, see.' And he pointed to some marks in the prayer-book he left in Clement's hand, while he left the room for a word or two, which he thought would better prepare the household than a peremptory bell.

Clement was struck, as indeed they all were, with his selection. There was the Psalm, 'Except the Lord build the house;' a short lesson (the reading of which Felix reserved to himself), namely, the words from Deuteronomy, against the presumption of prosperity; and the Collects, 'Prevent us O Lord in all our doings,' 'Charity,' 'the sundry and manifold changes of the world,' and 'things temporal and things eternal;' and then came the hymn—it was, 'Lead Thou me on.' Felix believed he had heard its echoes in his little bed that last Sunday night, and therefore wished for it, though it seemed a strange choice for the new house. How Edward and Mary must have felt that 'one step enough for me,' when they went forth with their little ones into the moor and fen! But in this hour of restoration, was it still to be a looking forth into mist and fog, led only by the kindly Light,

'Till through the dawn the Angel faces smile.'

Some who looked at those pictures felt as if they had had a foretaste of those angel faces.

121

'And,' said Kerenhappuch to her father, 'to see Miss Mary's sons, those dear young gentlemen, all a standing singing together like so many lambs—it was just a picture like the three chorister boys. I says to myself, "Keren, this 'ill be a blessed place. If this isn't the angels come down after all!"'

CHAPTER XXXVII.

INVASIONS.

> 'He muttered, "Eggs and bacon,
> Lobster, and duck, and toasted cheese."'
> *Phantasmagoria.*

'When did Bernard Underwood say his people were coming?'

'On Wednesday.'

'To-day! That's right. I can take you over to-morrow to call on them.'

'So soon!'

'Welcomes can't be too soon.'

'If one is not settled in?'

'The furniture was left to them.'

'That's all men know about it!'

'I know this, that if I don't go to-morrow, I have not another free day for a fortnight.'

'It is all very well for you. I daresay the man-kind have a room in some trim, or don't know it if they have not; but to fall promiscuously on the female sect, with their little amenities in an experimental state of development, is the way to be obnoxious. Can't you go solus, and make pretty speeches?'

'No, Ethel; it must be attention here from woman to woman. It may help them to start in the neighbourhood.'

'I submit. How are we to go? What is the distance?'

'Twelve miles. Suppose we went by railway, and took a boat up from Ewmouth. What do you say to that, Daisy?'

'That I have had quite enough specimens of the family in Master Bernard and his clerical brother.'

'You liked the former specimens well enough. Eh! Do you remember Daisiana?'

An angry flush rose to Gertrude May's cheeks, but she tried to answer composedly, 'The man-kind, as Ethel calls them, are no matter; but what can woman-kind be, after a life-struggle to preserve gentility over a stationer's shop?'

'The more reason they should be susceptible to mortification from their father's old friends,' said Dr. May, as he left the room.

'No, you can't get off, Daisy,' said Ethel. 'It must be done, and I only wish it could be a little later, for fear we should inflict more vexation than pleasure.'

'No; it can't be helped. He is going to run a-muck and take us in his train,' said the spoilt child, shrugging her shoulders.

On the Thursday morning, at the Vale Leston breakfast-table it was, 'The first thing is to make the drawing-room habitable before any one calls.'

'No one will presume on such barbarity till after Sunday!' exclaimed Cherry.

'Unless the Miss Hepburns should—' said Wilmet.

'No,' decidedly stated Clement; 'they told me they should wait till Monday.'

'And your library is as respectable as it is in the nature of the male animal to keep its lair,' said Cherry; 'so I don't mind if a gentleman comes, such as Captain Audley.'

'You need not trouble yourself about Captain Audley,' interposed Bernard. 'Never calls on ladies by any chance; hates 'em worse than poison.'

'Bosh, Bear! We met him at a picnic,' quoth Lance.

'That was long ago, and it grows on him; and it's monstrous hard lines on Charlie, now he's big enough to be spooney, that he never will go anywhere among humans. He's gone off in his yacht now to shoot seals, and cut the Arckey—Archey—Archidiaconal meeting.'

'Archidiaconal? He's not a churchwarden, is he?'

'What is it, Clem? You know. A whole lot of fine ladies and swells and dons and big-wigs coming to Ewmouth to go on about Gothic arches, and Roman camps, and Britons' bones, and all that sort of rubbish.'

'Does Stoneborough derive archæology from arches?' said Felix.

'Perhaps he thinks Archidiaconal functions consist in looking after them,' added Will.

'I remember now,' said Clement; 'there is really to be a meeting of the Archæological Society at Ewmouth, and it is to be apprehended that they may make a descent upon this place.'

'Happy hunting grounds,' said Felix. 'I only hope they will give us due notice.'

The bare idea quickened the breakfast. By ten o'clock a survey had been taken, and Cherry had thankfully accepted Wilmet's assurance that there were sufficient resources scattered through the house to repair the ravages of Mrs. Fulbert without more serious expense than that of a piece of chintz; and having resigned the command into her hands, beheld her consulting Clement on the possibility of being driven into Ewmouth, which he undertook to do in person in his dog-cart without loss of time. An exchange of all the other existing vehicles had been arranged for one roomy waggonette, and a basket pony-carriage, fit for Cherry to drive if ever she took courage—they had only been kept to meet the exigencies of the arrival *en masse.*

By a quarter to one Dr. May had landed his daughters at the garden steps, and was walking them up to the cloister door, when they were greeted with a hideous whistling bray, followed by the apparition of a figure with a pink and white shirt and grey legs, a great deal of dust and brown moustaches, upon inflated cheeks puffing vigorously through a big golden tube, which he next proceeded to spy down with one eye, and through that telescope became aware of one of the new comers, and uttered an ejaculation, 'Dr. May, by all that's lucky!' at the same time, using both eyes more naturally, he perceived the two ladies, blushed up to the eyes, and came forward with an apologetic greeting and hands far too dusty for any grasp less eager than the doctor's. 'Grown out of knowledge, but you're an old friend, I see.'

'I'm sorry to be in this awful mess, but I want to get the organ to rights before Saturday, when I must get back,' he said, as he led them through a world of organ-pipes, scattered here, there, and everywhere, and conducted them straight to the drawing-room. There the scene disclosed a giddy fabric, consisting of the round table, pushed up to a window and surmounted by a chair, and that again by a footstool, on the top of all a lady, dropping a measuring-tape to the floor, where a little girl was holding it by the ring at the end. The floor was bespread with slippery glossy lengths of chintz, patterned with pink and purple heather, on which a third sister was performing with a big pair of scissors in a crawling position on the floor, and a fourth was supplying the yawning shelves of a chiffonier with books. Ethel's prognostic was justified to the full.

'Wilmet!' exclaimed Lance, 'take care! How could you? Why didn't you send me up?'

'I should not have trusted you; but now you may help me, down.' And there she became conscious of the guests, but with a curious simplicity and dignity, she took no notice of them; while they thought it best to engross themselves in shaking hands with the lame sister, with her who scrambled up from the floor with a red and fagged visage, and with the little one, who, amid all the dust and confusion, looked as dainty and shining-haired as if she had been newly adorned for a feast.

'Here she is on the ordinary level of society!' said Geraldine. 'This is Mrs. Harewood, Dr. May—Wilmet, whom I think you remember.'

Wilmet had brought her composure down with her, and astonished the visitors therewith, as well as by the rare quality of her beauty, reminding Ethel of the fair matronly dames of early Italian art, both for her silence and her substantial stateliness. Nor was there the least flutter or affectation about Cherry; she thought the adventure fun, and had seen in a moment what sort of treatment was suitable to the present company, so she merrily observed, 'Now that Lance has given you a pleasing peep behind the scenes, won't you come to a less dismantled region?'

'It is only the consequence of resigning oneself to one's gentlemen,' returned Ethel. 'If I had had my way, you should have had time to "big your bower."'

'Ah! but we could not afford to miss a kind welcome,' said Geraldine, with the little pathos of sweetness that was such an attraction. 'My brother is surveying his new domains, but he will come in almost directly to early dinner. You are come for it? You'll come and take off your hats. Lance!'

Lance had fled, so soon as he had extricated Wilmet from her perilous attitude. No wonder; particular as he was about young ladies, his déshabillé, nearly as bad as that of Cleomenes, must have been dreadful to him; and it was Wilmet who gave Cherry an arm over the oak floor. They put Dr. May into the library, where Clement came to light; while they took the daughters upstairs, where they were almost as much pleased to see, as the sisters to show, the beauties of the quaint old house, and were perfectly sensible of the well-bred simplicity, playfulness, and absence of all false shame, so entirely different from what they had expected.

Ethel had been prepared to spend her day in a state of good-humoured forbearance and repression of Gertrude's intolerance. Instead of which she found herself in that state of ease which comes of accordance of tone, and she saw—what she had never beheld before—in her keen unvenerative sister, who had never formed any kind of attachment out of her own family and not many in it, the process of falling into an enthusiasm. That lame Miss Underwood, like an old fairy with her ivory-headed crutch stick; her marked eye-brows, thin expressive face, with its flashes of fun and plaintive sweetness, youthful complexion and pronounced features, was—what Daisy called—'so uncommon' as to strike her fancy, to a wonderful degree, and she had hardly eyes or ears to spare for anybody else; when at the sound of the dinner-bell, which had a charming little extinguisher of its own at the top of the octagon tower, the whole of the party were exhibited in the dining-room—Felix and John Harewood from a round of inspection with the bailiff; Angela from the kitchen-garden. She had been set to work unpacking books with Robina, but becoming discursive, had flown off to a tour on the leads with Bernard. 'So much less considerate than Stella!' sighed Robin, left to the tasks that could only fall to the quietest and strongest female of the family. For one happy half hour she was cheered by Will, who volunteered help, gave her all the volumes wrong, or put them upside-down, then lighting on Chaucer, read aloud Palæmon and Arcite, with comments, until Angela burst in, and whirled him away to shake an apple-tree for half a dozen urchins, with whom she had made acquaintance in the churchyard; and Robina had toiled on alone till, on Wilmet's return, she was swept into the furniture vortex.

Dr. May's heart, like Ethel's, warmed to the long table so like their own best days; and the perfect absence of pretension in the plain leg of mutton and vegetables delighted them eagerly. Moreover, he was dazzled by Wilmet's grand beauty, and the general comeliness of his old friend's family, while he talked with immense satisfaction to Felix and Major Harewood; but some strange change had fallen on Daisy.

She had been only fourteen at the time of her escapade on the Kitten's Tail, and now at nineteen the presence of the gentleman concerned in it seemed actually to keep her silent, so that she did not respond to the advances of her nearest contemporaries, Robina and Angela, one of whom had a good deal more manner and the other a good deal more assurance than she could boast; and though Lance had reappeared in irreproachable costume, she daunted his attempts at conversation by her evident determination to listen to the elders' discussion of architects.

'Aren't you going to the Church?' asked Robina, finding him leaning against the cloister door when there had been a move to show the Church to the visitors.

'No use in crowding them up with all the ruck. I shall strip, and go back to my organ-pipes. I shall not come here much. 'Tis no use being in a false position.'

'Nonsense. A false position is pretending to be what one is not.'

'Here I pretend to be on equality, and am shown my place,' said Lance, disconsolately; for he was very soft-hearted, and had an immense turn for young ladies.

'You're annihilated by a breath,' said Robin; 'besides, it was only shyness.'

'Shy? You should have seen her last time!'

'That's the very reason. If you only knew how horrid things done at one end of one's teens feel at the other!'

However, with Robina things were mending. Will had recovered his temper. There had been nothing to remind him of the obnoxious family at Repworth, when the pointlace had yielded perforce to the heather-patterned chintz, which was crackling about in all directions under the needles of all the ladies, and even of Krishnu. Everybody, except Angela, who said it hurt her fingers, was at work at petticoats for ottomans and robes for armchairs, or coats for curious settees routed out from upstairs, while Wilmet used the sewing-machine on the curtains, to supply the place of the brocade borne off by Mrs. Fulbert, and brought to light exquisite tamboured work of Lady Geraldine's that happily had been entirely unappreciated in the last reign.

Robina was stitching away the next day, when she had a treat. Bill came after her with the blottiest of all rolls of MS., being an essay to prove that the sun, the dawn, and the clouds, were *not* the origin of everything and everybody everywhere in legend and mythology, and he wanted a pair of ears to which to read it, so that he might hear it himself before submitting it to John. Lance was perpetrating worse screeches than ever with his organ-pipes, and could not Robin bring her needling out of the sound of them and listen to a fellow?

Ample space was no small privilege to a family accustomed to be cramped and crowded, and there was a pleasant sense of expansion in sitting down under the cedar-tree, with Bill luxuriously spread on the grass.

Such a sense Felix had in sorting his papers into the numerous drawers and pigeon-holes in his ample study-table, trusting himself not to make them so many traps for losing things, since he did not hold with Bill, that it is best to have no partitions, and have only one place to search through. Clement was making over to him the memoranda of the transactions conducted in his absence, when horses' feet were heard at the front-door, and Clement reconnoitring at the window, said, 'Mr. Milwright—the Rector of Ewford—no doubt it is about the Archæology.'

'A friend of yours?'

'Not particularly. I sat next him at the Visitation, and as the Charge ended, he touched me and said, "I'll show you the only bit of fourteenth-century glass in the choir;" and when we came out, and he heard my name, he said, "I congratulate you on the possession of the finest specimen of Cistercian architecture in the rural deanery." I'm afraid he minds his ecclesiology more than his ecclesia.'

By this time the entrance was effected of a lively well-bred man of middle age, not at all the conventional antiquarian, though still with one master idea. He apologized for his early call, but explained his purpose, namely to ask permission to conduct a party of the archæologists over the Church and Priory, and to make a preliminary inspection at once, to compare his old notes and prepare fresh ones. They were both willingly granted; and Felix went to summon his sisters, who would gladly profit by the primary survey without a crowd, and be delighted to learn the traditions of the place, which were necessarily a good deal lost to them. When the pair under the cedar looked round on hearing voices, Robina exclaimed with surprise and recognition of the guest.

'How do you know him?' asked her companion.

'He was staying at the Towers last winter. He was once a curate at Repworth.'

'Will he know you?'

'Not so likely as if he had seen me as a brass; but I must go and speak to him.'

'Such an enchanting encounter in your exile!'

'Nonsense! I only don't choose to seem ashamed of my vocation,' she answered rather proudly, as she came forward to join the party, for whose benefit Mr. Milwright was drawing the plan of the original Priory with his stick in the gravel. Felix was about to introduce her, but she held out her hand, saying, 'I have had the pleasure of meeting Mr. Milwright before at Repworth. I am one of the governesses.'

He made civil acknowledgment, but would hardly have cared if she had avowed herself kitchen-maid there. He knew only that two intelligent auditors had come up; and all were soon absorbed in the interest of his discourse, an entirely new pleasure to most.

To read in the peculiarity of the dog-tooth round the pointed arch, as clearly as in Arabic figures, the date when the church was founded, and to bring out stone by stone each fresh stage of improvement; to see when a building prior came from France, and put in a flamboyant window in the south transept; when a sturdy baron atoned for ravages in Brittany, by giving that perpendicular tower and cloister; and when, in a spirit of renovation, the last effort broke forth in those marvellous fan pendants in the Lady Chapel—these were feats delightful to enter into, and it was amusing as well as instructive to see the ecclesiologist poke into rubbishy corners, and disinter fragments of capitals and mouldings, sedilia and piscinæ, altars, and prior's coffin-lids with floriated crosses, giving an account of their origin as confidently as if he had had a pre-existence as a brother in the Priory. Moreover, his intentions furnished an excellent pretext for doing away with the seventy-five yards of black without outraging the squire's memory; indeed, Clement undid a good deal of it to facilitate the researches, and no one could pass it without a sly tweak to detach another nail.

'I'll keep the hatchment over the door as long as man can wish,' said Felix; 'but the Church in mourning I cannot stand.'

'And I think the three-decker might come down too,' added Clement. 'It is clearly within the chancel, and is your undisputed property.'

In which opinion Mr. Milwright, as a Rector, confirmed him, and likewise bestowed some good advice as to the manner of the intended restoration. 'The worst of it is,' he said, 'it can't be done under some thousands; and there's so much work of that sort about, the public is nearly wrung dry. However, it would be the very time to set a subscription going.'

'Paying toll,' said Felix, drily. 'No. I think the Rectory ought to do it gradually.'

'Oh, I beg your pardon.' And Mr. Milwright recollected that he had heard something of young Underwood being in trade, and concluded that he had made a good thing of it; and when on the way to the house some question was asked as to what was usual on such domiciliary visits, he did not scruple to say that a luncheon was usually bestowed by the inhabitants.

The visit to the house was still more entertaining. The long room was explained to be the remnant of the old hospitium below, with the Prior's chamber above; but the cellar was the oldest part of the house. Felix had been thither to take stock of the wine, and had only carried away a sense of the elaborate arrangement of the bins, and the ages it would take to consume their contents; but Mr. Milwright passed all these, and finally made a set like a pointer at a big beer-barrel, pointing to a low door behind it. Golightly was sent for to assist in moving it, which he did with great reluctance, asserting on the authority of Mrs. Macnamara (Sibby) that it led to nothing but ruins and foul air.

'Ah!' said Mr. Milwright, 'I am glad my friend Dobby is not quite forgotten.'

'Indeed, Sir, if you mean to imply that I ever was actuated by such a superstition!' cried Golightly, giving all his strength to assist his young masters; while Angela capered about in delight at having acquired a ghost as well as a prophecy, and Felix recollected having been threatened with Dobby by a young nursery-maid. The door proved to lead to a vaulted passage cut out in the solid rock, and ending in a beautiful semicircular chamber with melon-like divisions, uniting in one large boss at the summit, carved with the five stars which had been the shield of the Priory. The bad conscience of some despoiling Underwood had probably led to the idea of a walled-up monk, whose phantom was accustomed to take his walks abroad, rattling a chain, under the pleasing name of Dobby.

But the vault was a grand possession, and the access to it was to be made as favourable as circumstances would permit. Mr. Milwright next showed that the big knobs at the posts of the balustrade of the staircase unscrewed for the insertion of flambeaux, since the builders of the mansion, following instincts bequeathed from times of peril, had put their banqueting-room at the top of the house. All that was now divided by floor and wainscot into the long corridor and a rabbit-warren of rooms, had once been a banqueting-hall, the ceiling of which, in the upper story, still showed handsome chequer-work of plaster mouldings, the intersections alternately adorned with roods and crowns, L.U., and J.R. The octagon tower at the end was of earlier date, and had formed a part of the principal entrance, flanking one of the two great gateway towers, of which only one stump remained, built into a wood shed.

And, as to the Prior's kitchen, a splendid octagon, with eight arches for as many fires, and a chimney in the middle, it had been so hemmed in with sheds and leans-to, that though it existed as a coalhole, no one had yet explored it. Geraldine was ashamed, both as housewife and antiquary; but she had been so much engrossed during these two first days that she had by no means learnt all the ins and outs of her new old home, of which all felt much prouder than before, and on the renovation of which Mr. Milwright preached as earnestly as that of the Church.

He took leave, having greatly excited the whole family as to the coming feast of antiquities, and their own especial share of it.

'What shall you do about this luncheon?' asked Wilmet, when the party next assembled round the long table.

'Give it,' briefly answered Felix.

'It will be tremendously expensive.'

'An elegant cold collation from the pastrycook at Ewmouth would be; but I don't see why we should not have a few cold joints. Eh, Cherry?'

'Like our celebrated supper to the Minsterham choir,' responded she.

'You neither of you know what it will lead to,' was the old phrase into which Wilmet relapsed.

'Never mind her,' interposed her husband. 'She is demoralized by regimental déjeûners.'

'It serves you right for dragging me to them,' retorted Wilmet.

'I don't do so to please you, my dear, but because I can't have Major Harewood said to mew up his handsome wife out of sight.'

'I own,' she said, not quite pleased, 'I am afraid of this affair being more expensive than Felix imagines. If it is done at all, it must be done properly.'

'Of course it must,' pronounced Bernard. 'If it is to be a snobbish concern, I wash my hands of it. I shall go off to Jem Shaw out of the way!'

'I'll tell you how to make it snobbish, Bear,' said Cherry. 'To have the very same waiters in the very same cotton gloves, handing about the very same lobster-salad, in the very same moulds, and and tongues in the very same ruffles, with the very same carrot and turnip flowers on them, that have haunted the archæologists at every meal.'

'Bravo, Cherry!' broke in Will. 'Commend me to the unconventional woman!'

'Whereas,' proceeded Cherry, still directing herself on Bernard, 'no snob ever had such a place as the hospitium, nor such a salt-cellar as Amelia showed me this morning, and which I'm sadly afraid was filched from my Lord Prior, nor such wonderful old China plates and dishes, with all the acts of the romance of the willow pattern.'

'It's all plates and dishes so far, with nothing on them, like a Spanish don,' said Lance.

'Stay a bit,' said Cherry. 'We'll get a big piece of hung beef, and break into Mrs. Froggatt's parting gift of hams. Then Will and Bear shall kill us some rabbits, and they and the pigeons in that delicious old dovecote will make no end of pies; and what with the chick-a-biddies in the yard, and the unlimited lobsters Tripp talks of, and a big dish of curds and cream, and Wilmet's famous lemon cheesecakes, and all the melons and the cucumbers, and the apricocks and mulberries, the purple grapes, green figs, and dewberries, I think Bear's snob will be rather surprised! Then we'll have clean plates on the side-table, and let the gentlemen fetch them for the ladies; and if John will lend us Zadok, and Miss Lightfoot and Mr. Golightly act according to their names, I think we shall manage it all without any outgoing except for the solid eatables.'

'And drinkables there are enough and to spare in the cellar,' said Felix; 'and John must sit in judgment on them. It seems to me a clear matter of hospitality to feed hungry and tired people who turn up at one's house, and they must be content without mere display. In fact I see how to pay for such a feast as Cherry's genius sketches, and our tickets into the bargain. I'll write up to the "Old World," and offer an account of the whole concern.'

'Learning is better than house and land,' muttered Will.

'But it makes extra work of your holiday,' objected Wilmet.

'Reporting comes as natural to me as listening,' said Felix; 'besides, I mean this to be only a sketch at the end of each day. I won't go as a reporter this time, it is thrusting it too much down people's throats; and besides, this is rather out of Pur's line.'

'I shall do it for that,' said Cherry. 'I won't have poor Pur neglected.'

'We must have my father up here,' added John. 'What a banquet it will be to him!'

'He might deliver his mind of his lecture on mediæval seals, which got so much too learned for Minsterham,' added Will.

There ensued a dispute for the possession of the Librarian. Major and Mrs. Harewood meant to move off to their lodgings at the Glebe Farm on the Monday, for even these two days showed that Theodore and Kit were incompatible elements in the household. The poor little uncle's uncertain conscience had been so far reached, that he knew he must keep his hands off; but to see the child noticed by any one he loved was misery to him, and 'Master Kistofer' was by no means safe from being the aggressor. He viewed all toys as his exclusive right, and did not scruple to snatch from the astonished fingers; and as he was active and enterprising, and could climb stairs and open doors, it was never certain where he might next appear, nor would he obey anybody except his own natural lawful authorities. Poor Stella was continually on the alert; indeed she was the greatest sufferer, for her only weapon against her nephew was coaxing, the sight of which excited Theodore to a passion of jealousy; and though she never uttered a murmur, she was undergoing a perpetual agony between them. The only safety was when Kit was in the charge of Zadok, whose dark face was Theodore's horror, and another reason for relieving the Priory of the establishment. John apologized for the luxury of such an attendant as Krishnu. He had brought him home with the idea of letting him study at St. Augustine's, but his care had become a necessity during that tardy convalescence; and when it proved that his attainments were not up to the St Augustine's mark, and that he had no strong inclination to make them so, but shrank from leaving his master, the decision was welcome. He was northern mountaineer enough to bear the climate; and Wilmet declared that he did the work of half there besides his own proper business. He certainly was invaluable in those days of bustle and arrival, and would have been more so but for the unlucky feud between Kit and Theodore. However, the farm was so near, that the safe members of the family could be together almost as much as ever.

Visitors thickened. The reported excursion of the Archæological Society made every one feel that it was expedient that the first call should have been previously made. Sunday was the limit Even the Miss Hepburns came not till that day; Clement merely presented them when he brought down his imposing staff of new assistants to the horse-boxes that so conveniently partitioned the classes, and gladly made over the big boys to the well-practised Squire—a set of little stolid urchins to Angela, and all the infants to Stella. If he hoped his display would induce the former teachers to withdraw, he was mistaken; their close white-trimmed bonnets still kept guard over the girls.

On the Monday they called, and kept on safe commonplace ground, like the ladies they were, and grew so cordial that Wilmet proposed walking back to see the invalid and introduce Robina, her namesake godchild.

The girl's staid looks and manners gave great satisfaction, in contrast with Geraldine and Angela, who were thought flighty, and demonstrations were made which led to the explanation that she was only on a visit at home. 'A governess!' The four ladies were horror-struck. 'So selfish of Mr. Underwood!'

Robin swelled up like her kind preparing for duels on the October lawn. 'My BROTHER!' she said, in the emphatic tone that never meant any one but Felix.

'It is entirely her own choice,' added Wilmet.

'Nothing should have induced him to consent,' said Miss Isabella, decidedly.

'We did not see it in that light,' said Wilmet. 'He has worked so hard for us all, that we are glad to do anything to relieve him.'

'It can't be necessary!' exclaimed Miss Bridget, who always spoke breathlessly, and looking appealingly to Isabella.

'Not absolutely necessary,' said Wilmet; 'but you know that so many would be a burthen on a much larger property.'

There was a gasp all round at this, and Miss Isabella warmly said, 'My dear Mrs. Harewood, do not let yourself be blinded. We know perfectly what the property is, and allowing for Mrs. Fulbert's settlement and any follies of the poor young man, I can assure you there is no reason your sisters should not remain at home, which is the only proper place for young women. I speak to you, as the married sister, who, as your brother Edward tells me, have acted the part of a mother. It is your bounden duty to protect your sisters.' (Wilmet had to frown at Robin, who sprang up in her chair.) 'Of course your brother is meaning to marry;' (The negative went for nothing.) 'You cannot expect anything else; but still it is his first obligation not to cast them off, but to provide a home for them near at hand—the only becoming thing.'

'Home is quite ready for us all, always,' cried Robina. 'My brother would never let us want that; but while I can, I had rather maintain myself than be a burthen upon him.'

'Ah! my dear, that is a dangerous because plausible spirit of pride and independence. As those who have tried can tell you, very little suffices single women, who have long ago broken with the world.'

This beautiful sentiment was received with an assenting breath by the other three, while Miss Isabella triumphantly added, 'And that your brother is bound to provide.'

'I saw it stated,' continued Miss Martha, 'that no one worthy the name of man will permit the ladies of his family to go out into the world for maintenance.'

'A man that provideth not for his own household,' whispered sadly even gentle Miss Hepburn.

'And, Isabella—tell them,' pursued Miss Bridget, 'from facts we know—'

'Yes,' said Miss Isabella, striking the nail. 'If it is alleged to you that the estate is not sufficient, I warn you that there must be something wrong about the matter.'

'You know,' said Wilmet, feeling it almost wrong to extend the misdeeds of the dead so much, 'the estate does not come clear.'

'I allow for that, but I know from Mrs. Fulbert herself what that is; and, pardon me, that is no sufficient plea, and you ought not to be allowed to think it is. Why, the Rectory alone is twelve hundred a year!'

Was Felix's secret to be kept at the expense of his character? However, Miss Martha brought some relief, by saying, 'And of course it can't be true that those persons who were staying with Mr. Edward were monks, come down to take possession of the Priory and restore it?'

The sisters laughed, and Wilmet explained. 'They were former fellow-curates of his. They came down to help, because he was so much knocked up.'

'Then,' said Miss Isabella, hushing some further observations that evidently quivered on her sisters' tongues, 'we may assure our friends that there is no truth in the preposterous rumour of a so-called restitution.'

'Certainly not of the Priory,' said Wilmet.

'Nor the Rectory?' chimed in Miss Bridget.

'I am hardly at liberty to answer,' said Wilmet. 'I do not know what my brother means to do, nor will he act hastily; but I know he has strong feelings about tithes, and that all the rest wish to be no hindrance in the way of what he thinks right.'

'To sacrifice his family to a scruple!'

'Quite fanatical!'

'And we heard he was so sensible!' mourned the sisterhood; while their spokeswoman returned to the charge.

'You remember, my dear lady, that the wealth which corrupted the clergy was curtailed by the wisdom of our forefathers?'

'Tithes!' breathed Robin, for here she thought they had an indisputable stronghold.

'We are not under the Jewish dispensation,' said Miss Isabella, with a half severe, half triumphant expression; 'but I see how it is. I have traced it all along—the system of works.'

'Yes, Isabella; you saw from the time that Mr. Edward, dear misguided young man, took from the poor dear children that precious hymn,

> "Till to Redemption's[1] work you cling
> By a simple faith,
> 'Doing' is a deadly thing,
> 'Doing' ends in death."'

So sighed Bridget; while Martha added, 'If Mr. Underwood would only come to discuss it with Isabella, I am sure she would convince him.'

'And then you need not be sacrificed, my dear!' said the eldest lady.

'Nor his position in society!' added another.

'For you know, Mrs. Harewood, it is hardly fair towards the neighbourhood to connect it with trade. Our county people are not accustomed to it.'

'I daresay not,' said Wilmet, who had risen during the last sayings. 'Good-bye! I will tell my brother what you say.'

'Do so, my dear; I cannot bear to see a family I have known so long, suffer for, I must say, a mere Judaizing scruple!'

Robina uttered two gasps on her way home. 'Doing ends in death!' The other—'Single women who have broken with the world!'

Confession to Felix of the betrayal of his purpose was needful. He took it coolly enough. 'Never mind! We can't charge poor Fulbert's memory with such a *deficit;* but there are not many who will probe so hard.'

As Cherry saw, he could stand its being talked of much better as a very chimerical and unjustifiable action than even as simple honesty. 'Do you mean to encounter them?' she asked. 'I see now the meaning of Perseus going among the Graiæ,-for they seem to have but one eye; and I think poor Clement would be glad if they had but one tooth.'

'No,' said that misguided young man; 'don't be unfair on them. They are not in the least spiteful. Miss Martha is the only one who has the gossip in her, and her sisters always repress her. They are very good women, and I believe I have learnt much from them.'

He said it with melancholy candour; and Robina indignantly recurred to their unconscious worldliness about what was due to the county; to which Clement replied, that he feared that they would find that Felix's resolution *did* cost them something besides mere luxury.

Cherry understood this when the Staples family called. The father was all that was warm and cordial; and his wife meant to be the same, but she patronized. She expatiated on the rapacity of Mrs. Fulbert in carrying off so many handsome articles, and gave a sort of 'all very well' commendation of the substitutes. And she proffered recommendations to shops and servants, and the use of her name, and even chaperonage, in a manner that made Cherry shrink into herself with dry thanks. It was credible that Mrs. Staples pitied the present Underwoods, and thought they had been so much damaged by their present circumstances as not to know how to do justice to their promotion.

The daughter Felix and Lance had liked best was married to Mr. Welsh, the member for Ewmouth, a self-made man, and great shipowner, who, though disappointed that working among the people had not imbued Mr. Underwood with popular politics, was friendly and pleasant; and his wife, a merry prosperous young matron, much more lady-like than her mother, and drolly vehement in her new opinions, was only vexed that the new comers declined her dinner-parties, and could only be engaged to lunch on the first great archæological day. She knew nothing about archæologists, but she should keep open house, and it would be great fun.

Very different were the next visitors—namely, Sir Vesey Hammond, the patriarch of the county, the undisturbed forty years' member, the very picture of a country gentleman, white-haired, clear-eyed, ruddy-cheeked, tall and robust, all vigorous health, and bringing an almost equally beautiful old wife. Theirs was a real welcome. They had come fifteen miles to give it; for had not Sir Vesey been a friend of great-uncle Fulbert, and had not Mary been the admiration of both? Did not Lady Hammond recollect the twins, and was not she equally ready to do homage to 'Master Kistofer'? Nay! did she not even appease any lurking furniture regrets, by exclaiming, 'I am so fond of this room, and now it looks like old times. I never could like it as Mrs. Fulbert Underwood made it, but now it is so bright and fresh and liveable! Ah! there's the dear old treble-seated settee again. I must go and sit in it for old acquaintance' sake!'

There was a wonderful matronly charm about her, with her dark eyes that had last none of their softness, her snowy hair, and her sweet old face; and all the sisters drew round, unspeakably attracted by the motherliness that gave them a sense of what had been so long wanting to them.

Her husband seemed to be satisfying himself that the new squire's politics neither disgraced him, nor he his politics. Cherry caught an echo of—'tells me you have been editing a Conservative paper.'

'Yes, Sir; I do so still.'

'I am glad of it. You are a benefactor to the country!'

Wherewith Cherry had to respond to the old lady; and when next her ears were open county matters had set in, and the baronet was hailing a useful auxiliary, and pressing Felix to come to dinner, next Thursday, to be introduced to the lord-lieutenant of the county; and she found herself included by both in the invitation.

There was a pause for an answer, and the colour came into Felix's face. 'You are very kind, Sir Vesey; but my sister is rather an invalid, and I am still in business—only backwards and forwards here. In short, as I told Mr. Staples just now, we cannot afford dinner visiting.'

'I understand,' said Sir Vesey, quickly and kindly, and no doubt crediting poor Fulbert with a good deal. 'We are quite out of distance for mere dinners. Fifteen miles is far too much for driving home at night; but could not you and your sister come and spend a couple of nights? We would meet you at the station.'

Lady Hammond not only backed the invitation with all her might, but guessing perhaps that the lame invalid wanted help, extended it to a second sister. It was impossible to decline, it was not a case of reciprocity; and when Felix mentioned his acceptance to Mr. Staples, he found the worthy man as gratified at his adoption by Sir Vesey as if it had been a personal compliment.

Robina was the other sister who was to go; for, said Cherry, 'She has customs and costumes adapted to high society, which can't be said for all of us!' Robina thought Angela should benefit by the introduction, but Felix declared that he could not trust Cherry to her—a cruel stroke which she did not quite deserve, for she had a good deal of the nursing instinct.

The expedition was chiefly memorable to Cherry in that she first saw Felix there as a country gentleman, and could judge of his appearance among others. The party was, however, mostly of the higher order of 'county people,' above the mark of even the original Underwoods, more of the London-going type of which members are made. They and their woman-kind were not as full of talent and brilliancy as Cherry's artist friends, but had none of the stiff dullness of her cousin Tom's circle. They were well bred, and had no lack of sensible and fairly intellectual talk about the subjects of the day, and all were intimately at home with one another. All the gentlemen, and most of the ladies, were addressed by their host like one who had known them from boys and girls. Yet though every one was so intimate, there was no exclusiveness, and the two girls were at once let into the circle, as it were, and made one with the rest of the ladies; in truth, Cherry effected one of her usual conquests, and quite subdued Sir Vesey's heart as he drove her from the station. The dinner and appointments would not have been pronounced by Mrs. Tom Underwood *comifo;* they lagged a good deal behind the complications of delicacies, and vessels, and implements, which modern luxury delights in multiplying, and the dresses were of a quieter style than Cherry expected, so that it by no means fulfilled her awful notions of a state dinner in the country.

And how did her own Squire hold his place compared with others? Looking at him critically, as she tried to do, she saw that his complexion was devoid of the embrowning of sun and wind, his hands were over-white and delicate, and too many cares had pressed on his young shoulders not to have rounded them; so that he did not look like the active athletic men who had led an out-of-door life; but in look, movement, and tone, he was as thorough a gentleman as any one. Evening dress was perhaps most favourable to him, for he had rejected, with a sort of dislike, all semi-sporting morning costumes; and there was a little precision in his neatness, not like the ideal squire, but thoroughly individual in him, and the effect of his doing whatever he was about in the best way he could. When Bernard once declared that Felix's dress looked as if it were always Sunday, Stella gravely made answer, 'I think it is always the Fourth Commandment with him!' In which, perhaps, the little woman found the key of his nature.

There was no lack of ease about him; he did perhaps say 'Sir' more than is the ordinary custom, but this had rather a graceful effect to an elderly man; and he had no backwardness in conversation, but was as well-informed and intelligent as any newly-arrived squire could be expected to be, or more so. If he did not shoot, or hunt, that was his own affair: these were not men of the calibre to appreciate nothing else; they felt they had got a sensible, honourable, practical man among them, and accepted him as a fellow-worker for the welfare of their county. If he did sell books elsewhere, that was nothing to them; they felt he was a gentleman, and that was all they wanted.

Perhaps it was altogether more gratification than enjoyment, where all was so new and strange; but the second evening was pleasanter than the first, and the last breakfast made them like old friends. The introductions during those two evenings had been very opportune, in giving a little foothold among the denizens of the county before the great gathering of the antiquaries.

Ewmouth had been selected as head-quarters, on account of its castle, its church, and a bit of Roman wall, besides a Roman villa, and several curious churches within distance for excursions. The names of readers of papers were very promising, and included 'Mediæval Seals, by the Reverend Christopher Harewood.' These lectures were to be given in the mornings; in the afternoons the excursions were to take place, and one evening there was to be a soirée at Mr. Welsh's.

Tickets for the week cost a guinea. Felix took one apiece for himself and Geraldine; and Wilmet, not caring for such things, made her ticket over to Robina. This week would nearly finish William Harewood's holiday. A few days later he was to meet a reading-party at a vast old farm-house called Penbeacon, in the moors at the source of the Leston—five miles off, but still in the vast straggling parish, whose acreage little corresponded to its population.

Clement and the Harewoods, meantime, spent their leisure moments in routing in Abednego Tripp's rubbish holes, and bringing out quantities of fragments of lace-work canopies, heads of saints and demons, and shattered Priors' coffin-lids. The black cloth came down; two divisions of the three-decker were stored away in the hay-loft over the vicarage-stable. The third and lowest was to serve Clement for his sermon, and Abednego must make the best of a place in the choir. As to the trumpeting angel at the top of the sounding-board, Felix was so constant to it, that he carefully dusted it, proved it to be really rather graceful, and set it up against the wall in his own bedroom. Will Harewood declared it was the idol representing the Pursuivant, and he rejoined that he only hoped that the Pursuivant might sound in accordance with that trumpet.

[1] The real word is too sacred for quotation. (*Author*)— (*transcriber's note*: "real word": 'Jesus', in the original hymn (J. Proctor and I.D. Sankey, 'Nothing, either great or small').

CHAPTER XXXVIII.

K. T.

> 'So black of hue,
> With orange tawny Bill.'
> *Midsummer Night's Dream.*

The town-hall at Ewmouth was a good fifteenth-century building. The common herd sat on chairs and gazed at the speakers behind the table on the dais. There were the Lord Lieutenant and the local peer (he with whom Clement would not dine), Sir Vesey Hammond, and Mr. Welsh, together with Geraldine's old acquaintance, Lord de Vigny, who was sure to turn up at every sort of *dilettante* gathering in the kingdom, made words on the benefits of local research, and compliments on local hospitality; and then some wise man gave an excellent compendious sketch of the history of the city and neighbourhood, notifying the connection of the spots it was intended to visit, beginning with the Castle that very afternoon. Meantime there was not much opportunity for greetings; people were all in rows on the same level, looking into the fabrics on the crania of their neighbours in front.

'That's the way with ladies,' said William Harewood; 'they'll go anywhere to see one another's bonnets. That's the real point, whatever the excuse may be.'

The remark was made in all good humour. Everything had been smooth all these ten days. Had not Robina copied out his whole essay in her beautiful clear script, and tied it up with purple ribbons? Had she not toiled early and late at effective shaded diagrams of his father's seals? had she not listened intelligently to his own supplemental lecture on the unconscious poetry those queer devices expressed? and had she not rescued an important letter of his from the slit in Clement's S.P.G. box, which he was always taking for the post?

The lecture over, there was a dispersion to lunch at various houses or hotels. The Underwoods were of Mrs. Welsh's party, where Geraldine was made much of under Lady Hammond's kind protection, and Robina remained in enviable obscurity at a side-table. Lady Hammond's age obliged her to ascend to the Castle afterwards in her carriage, and she insisted on taking her lame young friend with her. Every one else walked—Robina with her brother and Will, for both the Major and his father had fallen in with old acquaintance and gone their own way.

Other parties debouched from other streets; and as Robina climbed the Castle hill, she was aware of Lord Ernest de la Poer in the act of greeting her.

'You here!' she exclaimed.

'I am at Eweford with Milwright.'

'But your reading!'

'Here I am, improving my mind.'

'Hardly in the needful manner.'

'Nay, but why is this holiday month to be all play and no work to every one but dis here unlucky nigger?'

'You've not earned the right to play.'

'Nor ever shall at home. You know what a farce it is to "call it either work or play."'

Felix did not wholly like the tone of this dialogue, but just then a brother of the press entreated a few moments' conversation. It was to ask for a recommendation, which he was now in a condition to give; and he was obliged to leave his sister to Will's care, intending speedily to overtake her.

Meanwhile, Lord Ernest went on, with somewhat less of reserve, 'Now I put it to you, which is which under the K.T. influence—Greek or croquet?'

'The last is not her influence.'

'No, nor her nature, but her uncle's drill into complaisance. She is a victim to filial piety, and drags me to the same shrine.'

129

'Just what she does not want to do.'

'No, but now you are gone, the games would never end if one didn't get her through a hoop occasionally.'

Robina averted her head, for there was a general halt and a silence, and a voice made itself heard, explaining that here was the Roman masonry.

The Castle was a large place, containing the county hall, and having likewise a small garrison of artillery to take care of the sea defences, on which modern science had of late been busy. The lecturer led his flock literally from pillar to post, stopping to expound all points of interest, and handing round drawings and photographs. There was nothing to do but to follow, and hope to fall in with some of the others. Of Geraldine there was no hope; old Sir Vesey had tucked her under his vigorous arm as soon as she stepped out of the carriage; Lord de Vigny had claimed her as an acquaintance, and her lameness gave her *brevet* rank for the nonce, for she was thrust into the forefront among the dames of high estate, and had a near view of everything. Felix had vanished; and Will, whose arm would have been very convenient to Robina in the throng, hung a little aloof, wearing an almost quaintly desperate air of surliness, while Lord Ernest hovered close, speaking to her at every pause in the lecture.

This uncomfortable trio were far in the rear, and a good deal jostled about, without very clear ideas where they were going or what they were seeing. Now it was along a moat; now out on a rampart with a green slope open to the sea, a very living looking cannon in the embrasures; now gazing up to a machicolated turret, then dragged up its spiral stair to be handed out on a leaden roof, and get a grand view, and a general impression that one of the King Henrys had done something there; then diving down to a doleful dungeon, where somebody had been starved to death, but as it was not true, it did not signify who it was. Such were all the ideas that Robina or either of her cavaliers could have given of their perambulation of Ewmouth Castle. It was lucky for the Pursuivant that they were not its caterers.

By the time she had ascended a dusky stair into the great hall of columns, which had never been a chapel, Robina found that the tour was ended, and moreover that Will—as well as all the rest—had been lost in the throng, and that no one was near whom she knew but Ernest de la Poer.

'I wonder where they all are!'

'We had better stand near the door,' he answered; 'they must pass this way.'

They waited while the stream of people flowed past; and when an acquaintance came, who was going to shake hands with Robina's companion as one of the many brothers, she piteously asked for tidings of her party.

'I saw Miss Underwood in Lady Hammond's carriage at the other door.'

'That accounts for it,' said Lord Ernest; 'I saw there was an eddy in the flood. Shall we go across?'

The move was a relief, and Robina hoped to find Felix waiting for her at the other door, for the hall was emptying fast, and they were the last to make their exit by the opposite porch. Not only were the carriages gone, but the foot-passengers; and the policemen were shutting the doors behind them, so that there was no returning across the hall.

'I will go round to the High Street again,' said Robina. 'Some of them will be sure to come back to look for me.'

'Where did you have luncheon? Will not they be there?'

'At Mr. Welsh's; but I don't think we were to go back there. We were to get in at the inn where the carriage was to be put up, only I don't know the name of it. My brother drove there after setting us down.'

Lord Ernest applied to a policeman for the name and locality of the principal stables. 'The Antelope,' he said; but it proved to be in the opposite direction to Mr. Welsh's, and so distant that Robina doubted whether Felix could have gone thither. She begged not to delay her companion; and he answered, as she knew he would, that he was quite at her service; indeed, she was quite at her ease so far as he was personally concerned, and if it had been any other town in the kingdom except perhaps Bexley, Oxford, or Minsterham, she would sooner have trusted to him in a difficulty than to any one whose name did not end with wood. He was too considerate to worry her with talking during the quick walk, and with some difficulty he caught a busy ostler, who averred that Mr. Underwood's carriage had not been there at all—no, not the horse, which he knew perfectly well. He evidently thought the new Squire's family rightly served for deserting their ancient haunt, and he ran away instead of answering whether there were other yards nearer Mr. Welsh's.

Nothing remained but to retrace their steps up the steep High Street that climbed the Castle cliff, meeting many a load of happy people who had found their carriages. Presently they came full on Mrs. Fulbert Underwood, who had been one of the callers in the last week, but who would have passed without recognition, but for Robina's despairing entreaty, 'Could you tell me where our carriage can be put up?'

'What! Rosina Underwood! I am surprised!'

'I have missed the others in the crowd at the Castle. I thought I should have met them at the Antelope, but our carriage has not been there.'

'*We* always put up at the Antelope,' said Mrs. Underwood; 'there may be inferior stables, but I do not know them. I have not been to all this lecturing—I don't like such things for ladies; but I can go round by Vale Leston, and set you down.'

'No, thank you. I could walk if that were all, only I must find the others, for they will not go without me.'

'Oh! if you are better off—I did not see that you had a beau. Mr. Harewood?'

'No,' said Robin, in her fiercest straightforwardness, 'Lord Ernest de la Poer. You know I am his sisters' governess. He is kindly helping me to find my brother and sister.'

'Oh! I leave you in good hands. Good-bye. If I meet any of your party, I will mention that I have seen you.'

Robina had been reddening all the afternoon. She was crimson now, but she was resolved not to make things worse by visible discomposure.

'Who was that obliging lady?' asked Lord Ernest.

'The last Mr. Underwood's daughter-in-law,' said Robin, so angry as to disclaim connection as much as possible; 'perhaps one is well off to have only one odd sort of relation.'

'I see a man who dined with Milwright yesterday,' exclaimed Lord Ernest. 'He may not be above all inns but the Antelope.'

He charged across the street, and brought back intelligence of a Fox's Brush in Castle Street, and of a short cut through a narrow alley and the churchyard; but there seemed risk of another miss, and besides, something like a waggonette was discerned near the top of the hill. It proved to be a break full of strangers; and by that time Robina, though bravely breasting the hill, was so tired and breathless that Lord Ernest offered his arm, but was refused with a certain weary sharpness.

At last the corner of Castle Street afforded a view of another hopeful looking vehicle a good way down; and at the same moment, Felix, very pink, hurried up from one quarter, and Will Harewood, fiery red, dashed down from another.

Felix had been to the Antelope by the by-street, and had met Mrs. Fulbert, then had posted after to overtake them; Willie had been all round the Castle, trying every gate in vain; Mr. Harewood was on the quest in another direction.

Robina thanked her escort, Felix did so more coldly, Willie gave a savage little bow, and they parted. Cherry was waiting in the waggonette, with the Major, who might not be overwalked, sitting on the box, holding the horse; and as Will was about to plunge after his father, Cherry called, 'Pray put on your hat! you look like a mad hatter instead of the March hare.'

'Enough to drive one mad,' muttered Will, sharply, pulling his hat nearly down to his eye-brows, and disappearing just as his father came soberly back from inquiry at Mr. Welsh's.

This time it was decided to drive down the High Street—always a slow operation, since it required a drag; and Felix left the reins in John's more practised hands, through the difficult navigation. They drew up at sight of Will in confabulation with Mrs. Fulbert, not much to the improvement of the serenity of his manner as he bestowed himself within the vehicle. Geraldine begun taking all the blame on her own bad chaperonage, and pitying Robina for being heated and tired.

'Well she may!' said Will, 'after galloping all over the place with that donkey.'

'A four-legged donkey might have been convenient,' said Cherry, laughing; 'but how came you to be left to him? I thought you safe with the Squire.'

'The Squire was called off to speak to some one,' said Robina.

'And I am afraid you were remiss, William,' said the Librarian.

'She seemed well satisfied,' he growled.

'I think you forget yourself,' said his father, gravely, as if his first-class son were still a little boy. The most courteous of men himself, he was always trying to teach manners to his family, but had egregiously failed excepting with the Major.

That Robina's adventure was relished by no one, might be gathered from the fact that none of the five alluded to it, and no objection was made when she came down the next morning in a stay-at-home garb, and announced her intention of remaining to assist in preparing for 'the spread' of Wednesday.

Cherry could not help remembering Wilmet's allegation that Robina was apt to attach much importance to ordinary attention; but at least if there were an error, it was on the side of precaution; and Cherry had so many qualms of conscience at taking her pleasure and devolving the trouble on Wilmet, that she was glad to leave so effective an assistant.

The day's entertainment was Mr. Harewood's lecture and another in the morning, and then a sort of picnic at the Roman villa. Lord Ernest found the Vale Leston party out, and Cherry thought he looked a little blank; but he took to cultivating her, and in the absence of her more distinguished cavaliers, made himself very pleasant, though she discerned that he cared not a rush for its baths and mosaic pavements; but she liked him so much, and thought him so genuinely kind and attentive, as to acquit him of all but humane courtesy to his sisters' governess, only hoping Robina so understood it.

That night Felix was dutifully writing his summary of the proceedings of the day, when a knock came to his study door, and as his boding soul anticipated, it was the prelude to Robina's entrance. With a solemn directness, not unlike that when she had dealt the death-blow to his early dream, she thus addressed him: 'Brother, are you very busy, or can you speak to me?'

He felt a cold dismay, and only said, 'Well!'

'It hardly seems right even to tell you, but I have this letter, and I want you to help me.'

'A letter!'

'Troublesome ass!' was at the tip of his tongue, but he was thankful it had gone no further, when Robina answered, 'Yes, from Lady de la Poer, and from Grace. You brought them from the second post.'

'You are in no scrape, I trust?' he said, somewhat relieved, but not enough for warmth or encouragement.

'Not that I know of,' said Robina, 'though I don't know whether I shall be able to go back after this.' And the tears came into her eyes.

'And what is *this?*' said Felix. 'Don't be afraid to tell me, my dear; I know you mean honestly.'

She seemed to have some difficulty in beginning, and finally put a note with a coroneted cipher into his hand. He read—

MY DEAR MISS UNDERWOOD,

I hope you are in full enjoyment at home. I believe Grace keeps you fully informed of the doings here, so I will not waste time over the wherefore of the inquiry I feel constrained to make—among other reasons, to satisfy myself of the children's truth. Cecil has told Lady Caergwent, on Susan's authority, that his brother Ernest told you that K (or C) T were the two most troublesome letters of the alphabet, an unmitigated bore except in cricket. As you know, Susan always holds fast to Cecil; and for their sakes we trust to you to tell us what was said or misunderstood. We should, of course, apply to Ernest himself, but he went on Thursday to the Ballford cricket-match, and we do not know how soon he will return: otherwise I should not disturb your holiday. Susie and Annie seem lost without you; and I rather suspect that idleness was in this case the mother of mischief, though some foundation there must have been, and I am sure you will let me clearly understand what it was.

131

Yours very sincerely,
FRANCES DE LA POER.

Felix drew a long breath; then smiled, and asked, 'What does it all mean?'

'Don't you see? K T. Katie—Lady Caergwent.'

'And did you really receive this extraordinary confidence?'

'Not quite like that.'

'Is this your Countess in her own right, who was said to be engaged to one of the De la Poers?'

'To Lord Ernest, yes;' and to Felix's satisfaction, there was no shrinking from his eye—she looked clear and innocent. 'The slip you sent me from that paper was altogether impertinent and premature. There is no engagement yet, but there is to be.'

'In spite of this opinion about the letters of the alphabet?'

'That is no more than one of Bear's growls. You must know, Lady Caergwent is an odd girl. She is only twenty, very clever at any headwork, but curiously childish about anything real. Her uncle and aunt, with whom she lives, were obliged to go abroad with Mrs. Umfraville's sick brother; and she is a ward in Chancery, and could not go, so she has been at Repworth all the summer. I believe the elders have settled it. Colonel Umfraville says if she does not marry young she will never marry at all.'

'Are you in his confidence too?'

'No, but Lord de la Poer talks to Lord Repworth, and he tells Grace. They are all open-hearted; and, except Lady Fanny, none of them can help talking.'

'Well, I didn't know *mariages de convenance* went on still.'

'No, indeed; they really like each other. No one could doubt it some time ago, when they were not thinking about it; and there is a sort of understanding that it will be, though it is not to come on formally till he has done with Oxford. Well, that understanding has spoilt every one's comfort.'

'I should think so!'

'Will you not see, Felix, that they really care for one another, only he is a little ashamed of the good match, and its all being made up for them. Then this summer has been unlucky: he was to read with Mr. Crichton, the Curate, a very clever man, a friend of Lord Repworth, who teaches Cecil and some of the girls Latin.'

'Is he married?'

'Oh dear yes!'

'Then he is a K T?'

'Twice over, by name and nature. It would have done very well for Lord Ernest to read with him, as he did last year, if they had been let alone. Not that Lady Caergwent wants to interrupt. Her uncle has taught her a good deal of those kind of things; indeed, she spurred Adelaide up to it, and only wanted to work with her and her brother.'

'Spurring leads to recalcitration—eh?'

'If you would only understand. She is not at all what you are fancying. She is a sort of intense child. She is slight and feminine, a great coward, as nervously excitable as Cherry, and showing it more, so that her eagerness quite overdoes people. Then, she is very shy, and so much hates to take the initiative, that people think her proud and ungracious. I soon found the only way to set her at her ease was to behave as if we were two girls on equal terms. It is so provoking, when she has just been the life of the whole schoolroom, to see her shrivel up as if a stranger was a blight—especially a shy one. And the more she makes a conscience of being agreeable, the worse it is, for the nervous fright paralyzes her. There never was any one with so little presence of mind. She can't get on without being under somebody's wing. And another unlucky thing is that she has no dexterity of hand, and hates all games that turn on it, like croquet. There's no keeping out of them, for there is a garden-party at Repworth to all the neighbours every Tuesday in the summer; and there would be quite a fuss among the natives if Lady Caergwent did not show herself. I believe her uncle put her under a solemn promise not to sit in the pollard in the park with Addy all the afternoon. So she plays like a martyr, infinitely worse than among ourselves, and some one always has to get her through to end the affair. The last day before I came home I had stayed in with little Susan, who was upset with the heat, and had been naughty enough to be kept in as a sort of sedative penance. I thought she was asleep on her board when Lord Ernest came in. Now, Lady Caergwent had been all the morning poking out some dates and marking some books she knew he would want; and she had left them with me for him to take when he came in for the two hours' reading he always was to take before dinner, and which *she* never let him off. If I had seen at first how hot and fuming he was with the bother first of her croquet and then of her hints, I should have put off executing my commission; but unluckily I gave my message, and he broke out, "Crichton, croquet, (pronouncing the t,) K T for ever—the most intolerable conjunction in the alphabet—nothing tolerable spelt with them." I laughed, and said, "Is cricket in that *cate*gory?" and he answered, "The only one that is not an unmitigated bore."'

'But, Robin, what would Wilmet say to your having him gossiping in your schoolroom?'

'It is not my schoolroom, it is Miss Oswald's, and the brothers are all tame about her like their sisters. Indeed, this was a mere accident; and when I found he meant to stay and grumble, I made an excuse about looking for Annie, and left him. Now hear what Grace says:—

"We have an awkward mess just now, and I hope you can help us out of it. You know how Papa dislikes that cricket mania which makes playing at a match a sort of public duty, to which everything is to be sacrificed; and how the boys say he would not mind if Colonel Umfraville had not worked him up. At any rate, as it was understood that Ernest was reading, and could not play in matches, the Breretons need not have summoned him fiery-cross fashion to their Oxford eleven. Kate broke out in the middle of breakfast, that it was a great shame, and she hated bondage; and he was provoked to answer, 'So did he.' Mamma hushed it down; but Kate's blood was up, and she never knows when to let a thing alone, so she hunted him into a corner after breakfast, and argued with him; and you know no man could stand that."

'No, indeed,' said Felix. 'It is quite enough to have to marry a Countess!'

'Don't, Felix! If you could only see the slight clinging thing! It all comes of her eager faith in her uncle. It is imploring, not domineering.'

'Well, go on; was that what drove him here?'

'Gracie goes on—

"They must have been very near a quarrel, for she rushed off, and unluckily came full pelt upon Papa. She did not speak, but he had seen tears in her eyes, and that brought it to a crisis. He accused Ernest of trifling with her, and amusing himself with everybody else; and Ernest made some answer that I am afraid was very foolish, and went off to Ballford. I met him in the hall, and he said things were past endurance, he should like to enlist as a private soldier, and he did not know when he was coming home, but I thought he only meant whether it would be Saturday or Monday. Kate was vexed, but would not show it; and when she found Cecil dawdling in a fit of the nothing-to-does, she suggested some sensible employment, and that exasperated him into telling her Ernest had gone away because he said that all K Ts were horrible. I don't think Kate would have mentioned it; but she turned white, and Addy was there, and was furious with Cecil, and it came to such a row that Mamma came in. Cecil stood out that Susie heard him say it to you, and Susan added that it was because Kate is so tiresome at croquet, and set him such a long lesson. Mamma thought she should have it out with him if she went to fetch him home from Ballford and had him all to herself; but when she came there, he was gone, and none of the Breretons could tell where. I fancy it may be to Eweford, for Mr. Milwright wanted both him and Repworth for his ecclesiological meeting. If you see him, pray talk to him and send him home, for Kate has been in great trouble about it, laying the blame on herself, (as well she may,) and she has actually written to her other uncle, Mr. Wardour, to propose going to him. It is very horrid. Papa feels keenly that she has been—what he calls insulted in his house by his sons; and yet we can't do much, because—oh why is she not only Kate Umfraville? The light is gone out of her brown eyes, and she looks as she did before the Colonel came home. She wants to be too proud to show it to us, but there is no pride in her, and she can't act it. If you could only get at that boy and send him home, it would all come right. There's the whole story: I hope it will not spoil your pleasure; but if you have a scrap of time, write, and comfort your poor loving

G. DE LA P.'"

There was an odd look in Felix's face as he said, 'Poor young man!'

'It is too bad of him!' said Robina, hotly.

'And are you armed with a long whip to send him back to his Countess and his book?'

'Please, Felix, be in earnest! It is a serious matter.'

'Because it concerns such exalted personages.'

'No,' said Robina, the tears burning in her eyes, 'because Grace is my friend, and Kate Caergwent a dear bright girl, who must not have her life spoilt—nor he either. Felix, you never were unfeeling before!'

'Have you let them know where to find their truant?'

'I had begun a letter this morning, but had no time to finish.'

'But you can give your evidence on the K T case by to-morrow's post.'

'Yes, if you can get my letter to Ewmouth before nine o'clock.'

'I will take care of that; and then you will have done all that ought to be expected of you.'

'Oh! I must speak to Lord Ernest.'

'Really, Robina, I am so thankful to see you so well out of the scrape that I don't see why you should thrust yourself into it. Surely, when the boy's parents know where to find him, they are competent to act.'

'Don't you see, they will not get my letter till the day after to-morrow, and by that time Lady Caergwent will have gone. Now, if he would only go back to-morrow of his own accord, it would have a much better grace. Why do you laugh, Felix?'

'I profess not to understand lords and ladies,' said Felix, recovering his gravity; 'but I doubt the effectiveness of the remonstrance, and I greatly fear your burning your own fingers.'

'There's no fear of that,' she said, with dignity. 'It is a duty to friends who are dearer and kinder to me than any one here believes!' And the tears started on her cheeks.

'Of your duty you are the best judge. I see you must have been discreet, to have earned so much affection and confidence. I own I should have thought the fewer who meddled in such a concern the better! and that—though I daresay it is very shocking—there was something rather wholesome in the poor boy's exertion of free will.' He was near laughing, the whole affair struck him as so ludicrous, especially Robina's look of dismay.

'Oh! His sisters! Lady Caergwent! His mother, and all! Oh no! If I don't try my utmost to get him home, I should feel treacherous—as if I were encouraging him here.'

'Honestly, do you think your being here has anything to do with his coming?'

'N—no! At least, I think the sight of you all so bright and pleasant at the station put it into his head. He is very much amused with Angela; but—oh no! I am certain he does not come after any one—least of all me!'

'There is one person who seems to think otherwise, if I may judge from his manner,' said Felix, tentatively.

'It is very unjust and unfair!' cried Robina, flaming up. 'He ought to know and trust me better. I will not heed such unworthy fancies. A son of the house, indeed! He ought to know that if there were no other reason, I should think it dishonourable.'

'Yet was it not on that account that you stayed at home to-day?'

'Yes,' she said more softly; 'but that ought to content him. I cannot give up a duty for unworthy suspicions.' And her neck bridled, and her eyes shone with hurt dignity through her tears.

'Well, Robina, you know best. You understand your own affairs, I suppose, and I see you are really trying to act rightly and honourably. I will give you any opportunity I can of speaking to this youth, though, for your own sake, I should strongly advise your only giving him his mother's letter, and letting it speak for itself.'

Robina shook her head. It was useless to argue it further. Like a woman, and a young woman, she was resolved to run all risks in her friend's cause, deeming it ignoble to make any concession to William's unfounded jealousy, and not appreciating Felix's doubts of any young man, especially one in a chafing refractory mood, going back to the yoke at the behest of his sisters' governess.

Felix did not like it at all, but he was always slow to act where he did not understand his ground; and the tone of the two letters showed such confidence in Robina, that he felt that her prudence might be trusted; while as to William Harewood, an unrecognised engagement did not deserve consideration from the family.

So he kept her counsel, and let things take their course, on the busy confused morning that preluded the first attempt of the family at an entertainment.

Breakfast was enlivened by a discussion whether precedence was to be respected, and next what that precedence was. 'Ought the Baron, or the Marquis's younger son, to come first and take Miss Underwood?'

'The Baron, I hope,' said Cherry. 'Old men are twice as nice as young ones, though your friend is very pleasant, Bobbie. Which is it to be? You are the experienced one.'

'Not I,' said Robina. 'Of course I don't dine late, and they go into luncheon nohow, as I should say was the best way here. Let Felix take Lady Hammond, and leave the rest to settle it. Depend upon it, they know their places better than we do.'

'"Ladies and Gentlemen, sort yourselves," as the parson said, when he had married five couple all at one go,' said Bernard.

'Don't they sometimes stick in the door-way curtseying? They do in books,' said Cherry.

'Not out of them,' said Robin. 'If there is a choice, I think age gets it more than actual rank.'

'There's nothing Lord Ernest hates like dowagers,' cried Angela, 'when all the jolly girls are out of reach.'

'What do you know about it, Angela?' said Felix, rather sharply.

'I've heard him say so twenty times. We are prodigious allies, and it was very sly of Robin never to tell me he was coming. Bear and I would have got up Dobby for his special edification.'

'You will do no such thing, for him or any one else!' broke forth in displeasure from Felix.

Angela shrugged her shoulders. 'Our Squire has grown very peremptory since he came to his kingdom,' she said; and perhaps he thought so, for he said to her at a quiet moment, 'Angela, perhaps I should have given you credit for not meaning what you said. You must know the impropriety of playing tricks on our guests, more especially when concerned with the world of spirits.'

The words appealed to the more accessible side of her nature, and she was silent. He considered whether to warn her about Lord Ernest, but was deciding that it would only excite her to further mischief, when he was summoned to admire the preparations that had absorbed the home party all the previous day.

The screen, a high wooden carved one, entirely cut off the end of the long room appropriated to the household prayers. The long table was laid with the fine old damask, the wealth of plate, glass, and old china, to which the substantial cold viands, and the jellies and creams, compounded by Wilmet and her ingenious Krishnu, were now to be added. The only failure had been in the unlimited lobsters, which had been all absorbed by Ewmouth itself; but then, Marilda, hearing all about it from Lance on his way through London, had actually sent them last night two venison pasties and a grouse pie, ready made, besides a great deal of her best fruit.

All stood admiring except Geraldine, who cried, 'Oh, that big epergne! Oh, those dahlias! They are just like a pincushion, or Protheroe's window! Stella—Bear—Bobbie—for pity's sake get me some fuchsias—traveller's joy, Bougainvillia—anything trailing—and I'll get a little of the stiffness out before Wilmet comes, and then she'll never find it out! And where's my salt-cellar? Oh for Lance!'

When Wilmet came upon the scene, she found Cherry seated as the centre-piece on the table, contending with the difficulties of adorning without concealing the curious old salt, the table-cloth bestrewn with green leaves and fallen fuchsia bells, and the epergne, the triumph of her art, the subject of her distant admiration at the last dinner party of the olden time, (Clement's christening feast,) relegated to a much inferior station, its formal glories of purple and crimson quilled dahlias obscured by loose streamers of passion-flower and hoary clematis.

Other people besides Robina had something to bear that day, but there was nothing in which John's influence was more shown than in the mutual forbearance of Wilmet and Geraldine. The latter took the initiative with a torrent of thanks and apologies; and Wilmet, remembering whose house it was, submitted with a good grace, and concealed her vexation by hurrying to the kitchen to take the jellies out of their moulds. There at least she was supreme. Martha was only too glad to have her to sympathize with her new glories, and for her sake could even bear with 'that there blackamore chap.'

Robina, in a nearly sleepless night, had decided on giving William a word or two of explanation as to her having a message from home for Lord Ernest; but in the rush after flowers, Angela had carried Bill off to rob a wisteria of its second bloom, and by the time they came back, Felix was hurrying his party into the waggonette.

Only the gentlemen went; the ladies had enough to do at home, since it was only too true that Cherry's improvements had doubled their work, and she felt herself the more graceless that she could not run about to supply the labour she had created. Indeed, all were watching lest she should overtire herself; but she was one of those who never feel weariness while excitement lasts.

The last jelly was scarcely in its place, the last wine-glass adjusted, when Angela announced a carriage turning over the bridge; and the long approach up the lane, and down the drive enabled Cherry, by the united efforts of her sisters, to cast her housewifely slough, don her white dress and mauve ribbons, and seat herself in the drawing-room, with Clement as her supporter.

Luckily Cherry had never been afraid of people, and she faced the inroad with great composure. This proved to be only the advanced guard, namely, Mr. Milwright, bringing Lord Ernest and a fellow ecclesiologist with whom he wanted to hold a private discussion over the fragments of a shrine in the south transept; and Clement went to show his discoveries.

So cruelly were opportunities wasted, that Robina was in the far end of the west wing, dressing herself and Angela, while Lord Ernest was having a twenty minutes *tête-à-tête* with Cherry, whom he consulted as to joining Will Harewood's reading party, and told her that the Vale Leston choir was renowned as the best in the neighbourhood; and that old Milwright, being unable to go in out-and-out for the mediæval, let things alone, and was content with two fiddles and a flute. Wherefore he should walk from Eweford on the ensuing Sunday, to this—simply the most charming place he had ever seen. Whereupon Miss Underwood innocently invited him to luncheon between the services.

Robina could only come down just as Felix returned, immediately followed by the whole multitude, exceeding the expectations of the family so much, that Marilda's pasties were a comfortable reflection, and Wilmet's imagination fell to reckoning knives and forks. Places at the table must be hopeless for many; and when Felix, in desperation, offered an arm to Lady Hammond, he left a chaos behind which he hoped would, as Bernard said, 'sort itself.'

People must have been quite as curious about the Underwoods as about their Priory, for the most improbable guests had come, even the undesirable peer, whose earldom complicated matters. He assumed, however, that the eldest and handsomest bonnetless lady must be her of the house, and accordingly gave his arm to Mrs. Harewood; Lord de Vigny, who knew better, took his old acquaintance, Miss Underwood, and dipped her once more in the dear old world of art; the others paired somehow, and, as Robina had foreseen, Lord Ernest left himself behind with the common herd, who, after the seats at the long table were occupied, betook themselves to the cushioned embrasures of the windows, and to catering for themselves at the side-board, where, happily, there was no lack of supplies. It was great fun, and Angela agreed with Lord Ernest in pronouncing it so much jollier than a wedding-breakfast, as there were no wretched victims to be turned off. If there were any victims, one was Robina, who was penned up in a corner by Mr. Henry Shaw, doing his best to be polite; and the other was Will, who had on his hands two ladies, a gushing mother and daughter, who had just discovered him to be the author of those delicious songs, signed March Hare!

The discourse, the occasion of all, began in the long room, Mr. Milwright taking up station after station, while people herded round to look at what he pointed out. This tour must be Robina's opportunity. There were a good many stragglers from the troop of listeners; and among them was Angela, keeping close to Lord Ernest, and delighted to take him on a counter round, displaying all the charms of her new home.

This Robina had expected. She knew that it might be said that the two young Miss Underwoods were running after that young man, and she wanted to speak as soon as possible, to put an end to the pursuit. So when Angela had led him to a shed where resided an owl captured in the church tower, she took the bull by the horns. 'Angel, I have a message from Repworth to deliver. I must ask you to leave us a little while.' And she opened the door leading into the walled kitchen garden. Angela shrugged her shoulders, but fell back.

'And so you have betrayed me? Could not you let a poor fellow breathe a little free air for once in his life?'

'Read that!' was all her answer.

The effect of his mother's letter resembled that on Felix; he burst out laughing, much more unreservedly exclaiming, 'Well done, Cecy!'

'But it is not what you said!'

'Wasn't it? Then my words fell short of my thoughts. What was it the King of France said when he had got away from captivity or Catherine de Medici (his K Ts, you see)—"I am yet a man and a brother."'

'Please don't make light of it. Grace is in such distress.'

'There generally is a commotion when a prisoner breaks loose. I thought better of you, Miss Underwood, than to suppose you a detective in disguise.'

'I only want you to realize how wrong it is that you should be here.'

'I assure you it is all for the family honour. *Tout est perdu fors l'honneur.*—That was the fellow's sentiment—wasn't it?'

'I don't see the application.'

'Don't you? Sha'n't I be ploughed to a dead certainty if I go on trying to carry this on at home!' said Lord Ernest, much more seriously. 'How about *l'honneur* then?'

Robina could not deny the danger, and knew not how to answer. He saw his advantage, and pursued it. 'Was not reading, under the circumstances, a delusion? You won't speak treason? Never mind, I see it in your eyes. You know that between all the K Ts within and without doors, it was providential that I retained sufficient combination of ideas to effect my escape before I was quite distracted.'

'I don't think you guess the distress you have caused,' said Robina, gravely.

'What, Gracie has written you a deplorable letter? Gone to the bad entirely, am I? My mother weeping, my father wailing, my sister sobbing, our K T wringing her hands—' Then, as she moved decidedly away, with a gesture expressive of deep displeasure, 'Nay—I declare they are re-assured. Even if you haven't—I have written to my father; and they know by this time that the vortex I have rushed into is nothing worse than a conglomeration of antiquarian old fogies.'

'Oh! if you have written—' she began, feeling that Felix had been right, and she herself more or less of a goose.

'Yes. I have written to explain that my brain won't stand being beset within doors and without, and to propose joining Harewood's reading-party.'

Robina fairly started. 'Do you know if he will have you?'

'I hope he can. He is a crack coach, you know, little as he looks it. Wonderfully able man when he makes the most of himself.'

'I think he has as many pupils as he has room for,' said Robina, highly gratified, but hoping to avert what might drive Will beyond all bounds.

'I hope not. Your sister seemed to think it might be managed.'

'What, Angela?'

'No; Miss Underwood—is she not? The one who was in the room first. What a delightful countenance she has, by-the-by, it strikes me more than Mrs. Harewood's. It is a rare thing to meet so much beauty afloat in one family.'

However complimentary, he must not be allowed to run on in this way; and his monitor returned abruptly to the charge. 'I allow that it is hard to read at the Towers; but before you make any other arrangements, I think you ought to go home this very evening and explain things. There is a train at 4.11, at Church Ewe.'

'Have you got a policeman outside to give me in charge to?'

'No,' she answered, with some anger; 'but Lady Caergwent is going away to-morrow!'

His first impulse was a little whistle of dismay; but he caught it up, and coolly said, 'Joy go with her, a K T clasm! You have not let Grace cram you with all *that*?'

By this time Robina was thoroughly sensible of the false position she had got herself into, and had only to get herself out of it as fast as she could, so she took the path between the espaliers and scarlet-runners which would soonest lead back to public haunts, saying decidedly, 'I do not want to hear anything about it.'

'It seems to me,' said her companion, with more of the man than he had yet assumed, 'that having entered on this, you should allow me to remind you that this *is* a free country, and these are not the days of family compacts. I will not go home, to be badgered whatever I say or do. I will strike out my own line, and work for myself.'

'But your father—!'

'If I know my father, he will like me the better for it. The Colonel has a way of making him see things in his point of view, and it was a tidy little plan; but there are not so many men in this world born for prince-consorts, and they have not got hold of one of the sort. There, now, you have discharged your duty! You may tell Grace what I say—the whole houseful, if you like.'

'Very well,' said Robina coldly, glad to have nearly reached a door opening upon a laurel path. 'It is of no use to say any more. You have written, and I have no more to do with it.'

'I didn't think you were on the enemy's side!' he proceeded, as if pleading with her displeasure. 'I know you are one to like a fellow the more for having a spark of independence. Come, you may as well say so; it is in your nature, I've seen it, and you owe me compensation for all that you have rehearsed to me in the spirit of the K Ts.'

This was in a tone between warmth and raillery, that made it very difficult to know how to reply; and all she could think of was, 'You can be the only judge of what is right and manly.'

'There then!' as if he had done with the subject. 'Oh! don't open the door. Let us have another turn. I want to tell you about my plans. This is almost as good as losing ourselves.'

'I can't,' said Robina, with much repressive displeasure, 'I am wanted. I only came to show you your mother's letter;' and she plunged into the laurel-walk.

'Then I am much obliged to my mother's letter,' was the reply, in a tone that conveyed more than the words.

Therewith, at the other end of the path, were seen Mrs. Fulbert Underwood, Miss Martha Hepburn, and Mr. Harry Shaw. They met; Robina shook hands; Lord Ernest moved his hat; but though 'Jane' made a low curtsey, her observation was marked—'Oh! so you have lost yourself again, Rosina!'

'My name is Robina, if you please,' she exclaimed, glad to have something to contradict.

'Ah! I never can remember! It is so peculiar!'

'Peculiarly pretty,' said Lord Ernest. 'It puts one in mind of all sorts of pleasant associations.'

'It is Scottish, after Miss Hepburn,' said Robina, severely turning from him.

'Yes,' said Miss Martha. 'It is a very old name with us, but we never called my sister by it; we call her by her name of Elizabeth, it is less romantic but more sensible.' And Miss Martha, frightened at speaking so like Isabella, laughed a little to diminish the stern effects.

Robina hoped to shake off Lord Ernest by joining them, and said politely, 'I did not know you were here.'

'Harry and I thought we would just come over to see what the learned men think of the poor old place; but after all, it is only Mr. Milwright, and one can hear him any day, so we came round just to have a look at the old conservatories, which I used to dote on.'

'You have had some luncheon?'

'Yes, thank you, we got some cold pigeon pie. My dear, what a pity your sister did not apply to me! I could have recommended her to Patakake, who always did things for us. Whom could you have had?'

'Kerenhappuch,' said Robina solemnly, for, in spite of all her trouble, she was awake to the fun of the thing, and she greatly tickled Lord Ernest by the tone and the name.

'Well, so Miss Martha said, but I could not believe it. Done entirely at home?'

'Yes.'

'Excuse me, my dear Ros—Robina, but it was a mistake in a position like yours.'

'I am sorry if anything was not good.'

'Oh! that's not it. It is style that is the *thing*, especially in your position. It will not do to fall short of it!—You agree with me, my Lord, air is everything.'

'I much prefer good food,' he answered; at which Harry Shaw broke into a hearty laugh, and Robina could not help joining. Perceiving, perhaps, that his dictum would go for something, Lord Ernest gravely added, 'If good food and good taste combined are the right thing, I am sure we had it to-day. I never saw a more thoroughly pretty or graceful set out—so well appointed too.'

And though the two ladies agreed that the poor young man was very far gone, and that there was something artful about that girl, yet it silenced the lamentations for Patakake. Mrs. Fulbert declared it wonderful how those girls had managed it—but, of course, they had been brought up to such things; and Miss Martha—more good-naturedly—made it known that 'that young nobleman had never seen anything equal to it for style and good taste!'

'Of course, simplicity was a relief after the jaded life of a man of fashion,' added Miss Isabella.

'What, the Earl was there! What a pity those young people should get into such a set!'

By the time the lawn was reached, the discourse was ended, and people were scattered about on the garden-chairs, partaking of further refreshments handed by Krishnu, who had assumed his white and scarlet, and had an imposing effect, leading forth sundry footmen in diverse liveries as his assistants. Lord de Vigny had detected Geraldine's studio, and insisted on seeing her portfolio. She had somewhat flagged since her object had been attained, and among the excitements of the last year; and the old gentleman gave her a real scolding for wasting such powers in little desultory half-finished memorial kind of sketches. It was impossible not to laugh at the exaggerated feeling of the kind old courteous amateur; but after all, the stimulus was good for her. She did not exactly accept the assurance that it was the first duty of her life to produce something every season for the Exhibition; but the fresh eye, and the criticism, which had reality in it, though it was complimentary, stirred her up; and she felt that it was not doing justice to the gift of which she was a steward, to shrink, as she had done of late, from the train of attention and detail which the maturing an original subject cost her, besides that contributions to the housekeeping were really felt by all that could work for themselves to be almost due to him who toiled so freely for them and for his conscience. As to the neighbours, they only then and there discovered that the little lame Miss Underwood was an exhibitor at the Royal Academy, and that the queer old nobleman, with the loose grey hair, raved about her drawings. They regarded her the more or the less according as they most esteemed genius or gentility; and as Miss Martha Hepburn said, 'No one would ever have found it out.' 'As if they expected me to go about in a white turban and a palette on my thumb, like the pictures of Angelica Kaufman!' said Cherry, laughing, as Angela reported this speech while the home party stood under the porch, after seeing off their last guests.

There was plenty of indulgence in self-gratulations, and a universal contribution of the observations each had received, almost all resulting in declaring their house-warming a great success. In the midst, some correspondence of eye between Robina and her eldest brother, brought the colour into her cheek as she drew nearer to him. He held out his hand to her, and when the others dispersed to their rooms, they began to walk together under the wall.

'You spoke to him?'

'Yes. Oh! I wish I hadn't. You were right. He had written to his father, after all!'

'Then it is off your mind?'

'Yes. No—it would be—' She fell into a terrible tangle of hesitation and broken words, out of which he thus interpreted,

'You found the situation awkward?'

'Oh! I ought not to complain, for it was my own doing when you warned me, and I don't believe he meant it; but—but—it just amounts to this, that I can never freely say again that he never said, or tried to say, a word like flirting—to me. And I suppose it is my duty to tell, and—give them all up—'

'I suppose you had rather not tell me what he really said?'

'It was not words so much as manner—assuming that I was on his side at heart, and half laughing at me all the time. Then, when he had told me quite seriously that the family compact was all nonsense, he grew a little more like that—wanted me to hear his plans, and stay away from the rest—said it was as good as our being lost.'

'Is that all?'

'Yes; except that, when I said why I began, he answered, "Then I am much obliged to my mother's letter."'

'Then, if there is no more, you had much better let things alone. If he has written to his father, a post or two will decide his recall; and in the meantime, such a confession, though quite conscientious, would only make you ridiculous.'

'Yes, I see that. I had much rather not. Wilmet thinks I am always fancying such things—but you don't, Felix! I only wish it were—'

'I don't think you so silly, my dear,' said Felix. 'No one can judge of manner without seeing it; but so little as you have to tell seems to me nothing to cry out about, and your confession might be misunderstood.'

'Of course I don't want to do it; but to keep it back when I write seems treacherous.'

'Don't write!'

'Not to Grace?'

'She knows you are much occupied; and even if she do think you a little remiss, really even such a dreadful idea seems to me preferable to any fresh reports coming between this young man and his family, at what may be the turning-point of his life.'

'I should not send a false report!'

'You could not help sending an excited one; and if it were the actual short-hand notes of what passed, word for word, what could it do but give all the ladies something more to talk about? If Lord de la Poer be the same man in private life as in public, he and his son will understand one another much better without the interposition of any women's tongues, or pens, however kindly-intentioned.'

'So he said—that his father would understand, and like him the better for being independent.'

'For my part, I could not understand what you told me!'

'He is so fond of Colonel Umfraville, and would be glad to see one of his children like a son to him. I can't help hoping it will come right, for poor dear Lady Caergwent's sake.'

'Then, once more, let it alone!'

She obeyed, with a sigh. It was a quiet evening, Felix and the Harewoods went to the soirée; and the next day was that of the excursion to Stoneborough, for which Robina had not much heart, but that dreadful imputation of being apt to make a fuss about nothing prevented her from backing out. She did not understand William, who had dropped his surly petulant manner, and was only exceedingly grave and quiet, keeping out of the way, and looking dejected and subdued. She longed to speak to him, but he specially avoided her, and this time Felix made her his special charge, transferring Cherry to John Harewood's guidance. Both understood, almost without even a glance, that he wished to be free; and Cherry could not have had a more devoted cavalier than her brother-in-law, who never left her, except when the ascent of the Tower made Gertrude May hang back, declare she had had enough of that, and beg to take Miss Underwood under her protection, to rest in her sister's drawing-room.

And there Gertrude, in one of those curious accesses of confidence that congeniality sometimes produces, poured out a great deal of what was most individual to herself. Daisy had never set up a friend before, and had always been rather contemptuous of intimacies; but this was a case of love at first sight. Geraldine was about six years her elder, and not in the category of 'tiresome girls,' and while her sister's beauty was talked of, no one said much about her; so Daisy fancied this a discovery of her own, and became devoted to her, especially when she began to touch on Felix, and found that for hero-worship nothing could rival the sister. Geraldine had her reserves, but to find such a listener to the achievements of Felix was enough to open all her heart. And when the interruption came at last, all Gertrude thought of was when and how to meet again.

Nothing worth note befell Robina; and on the Saturday the only event was Mr. Harewood's departure, and his son's disappearance immediately after. It turned out that he was walking to Penbeacon to make his final arrangements; and when regrets were expressed that he had not borrowed a horse, John warned the proprietors against trusting a beast in Will's hands; and Wilmet declared that, in mercy to his pupils, she should drive over next week and see whether the rooms were fit for anybody. Clement spoke well of them, but she had little faith in him.

On Sunday, just as the church bells were calling, and the Priory ladies were proceeding to the bench they had placed in the south transept, when leaving the chancel to the choir, there appeared the not very welcome outline of an aquiline young profile, with loose shining brown hair, peering about over the big oaken boxes that fenced up the central aisle; and it was Angela who popped up her head to guide him to a local habitation.

If it were true that Vale Leston rejoiced in the best choir in the neighbourhood, Ewshire could not be well off, thought those who were used to the Bexley organ and choir under Lance's presidency. Clement had done a good deal in the past year with his boys, and had a good schoolmaster as organist; but the best voices did not appertain to the best men, and those best men, being the most imbued with Hepburnism, viewed the gallery as a much more honourable place than the chancel, and would infinitely rather have sung in a dissenting chapel than in a surplice; but though they were little cultivated, and were still in what their vicar called motley, his voice, with the Squire's practised one, and Will's with its old chorister training, told enough to make the general effect far above the country average, and to merit the admiration with which Lord Ernest replied to Angela's exaggerated despair at the dissonances.

On the way through the Cloister he contrived to say to Robina, 'I've heard from Papa—it is all right.' She could only reply, 'That is well!' with a real look of congratulation, though she felt that the use of the strictly domestic appellation was another dangerous implication of familiarity. After dinner she crept up to her own room, resolved to give neither encouragement to him nor offence to William, thinking it hard that the latter's last Sunday should be spoilt. The school would, she knew, keep Angela out of mischief, and Cherry would look after the guest if he deserved to be entertained. What had become of poor Lady Caergwent?

Perhaps the sun was too hot in her southern room, for Robina grew restless over her books, and wandered into Cherry's painting room, gazing listlessly from the windows. Then she saw a sight that surprised her—Will and Lord Ernest under the cedar, in a conference that lasted till the smallest bell began to ring.

Felix was still more surprised by Will's address to him some hours later.

'I just want to know one thing. Do you want that young fellow licked into shape—that young De la Poer?' he added, meeting Felix's look of blank amazement. 'He wants me to take him in hand at Penbeacon. I told him I did not know if there was room—I really don't; but the real question is—' and there he came to a dead stop.

'The real question is—' repeated Felix.

'Whether you think it a good thing?' continued Will, his head bent over a cat's-cradle of string in which he had tied up his fingers.

'A very good thing for him, and pecuniarily not a bad one for you.'

'Botheration! that has nothing to do with it. Can't you see what I mean? Is it good for—her?' and the poor little monosyllable came out with a sort of groan.

Felix pitied him enough to help him forward with, 'For Robina, do you mean? You are under a misapprehension, if you think it makes any difference to her!'

'Then you don't approve of it? You don't want to put a stop to it?'

'There is nothing to put a stop to, that I know of!'

'Ah! then you don't know!' said Will, lapsing into deep dejection.

'I know she would consider what you imply as dishonourable and treacherous!'

'No, no!' cried Will, vehemently; 'no such thing! Your sister in your house—as well-born a lady as any in England—a match for any man in the realm!'

'There are other reasons, besides her position in the family, which would make her think it treason to encourage what, I believe, has no existence.'

'Ah, then—you don't know what—' and again he stopped short between dismay and oppression.

'What do you mean?'

'No, no; you shall not have it from me. I'm only sorry I said a word.' And the poor fellow was going away.

'Hold, Bill! Tell me what you mean? I believe I can explain it!'

'There's only one expla—No; what am I saying? She has every right. You'll hear it soon enough!'

He was turning the handle of the door, when Felix said, 'If you mean that Robina spoke to him in the kitchen-garden on Thursday, I know all about that!'

'Indeed!' His face altered instantly.

'She had a letter from his mother that she thought he ought to see. She told me what she intended.'

'Queer people, to find such a channel of communication,' said Bill, gruffly. 'And that was all?'

'The whole.'

'Well! I never meant to act the spy; but I'll tell you how it was, Felix. I had heard all Milwright's prose, and was sick of all the humbug; so I went into your study for a little peace, and there I heard Theodore fretting awfully in the next room—'

'I know. You were so kind as to take him out.'

'He wanted you, and he wanted to be out; and he was plagued and bothered at so many strangers about, and Sibby was nearly demented with having to keep him quiet and wash up the thingumbobs. So this watch—it belongs to John, came from his aunt's; but I've got it while mine is refitting—and it plays all manner of tunes. Theodore will come anywhere after it; so I got him into the kitchen-garden, thinking there would be peace there, and into the old root-house, and there what does he do but go to sleep on my knee!'

'Yes; he had had a bad night. I was writing later than was good for him, and he was excited by the preparations.'

'So while I was pinned down, I saw—from the little window—those two walking up and down at the further end of the garden,' and he made a gesture of utter despair. 'It was no good showing myself—I was out of hearing; but—And so,' he added, 'I thought if I could anyway conduce to making him fit for her, it was all I could do for her.'

'Very kind! but you might have trusted her!'

'Trust! If I had any right!'

'She thinks you have!'

'She!' and the face lighted up. 'You don't mean that she holds to *that?* Of course you know nothing about it, though? Some childish nonsense passed years ago, but I never durst believe she remembered it.'

'She knows it ought not to bind you, but—'

'Bind! What should bind but the love of my whole heart, ever since I knew I had one? I durst not speak again of it. When I came to perceive what I had done, I thought it not fair towards her to renew it, till I had the means to keep her as she ought to be kept; for you know I've not got a preserve of old aunts, like Jack!'

'Quite right, Will!'

'And when she had been among all those swells, how did I know what she might not be wanting to take up with—never being much of a fellow to look at, any time?' he added wistfully.

'I think you might have known her better!'

'You see,' he broke out, 'I don't want her to be held to me only by what took place long ago, when she was a child of thirteen. That would be a downright shame, and I never meant to remind her till I had a home to offer her. There have been times when I made sure we understood one another; but to this hour I don't know whether she likes me a bit better than John, and if she—likes—this young man better—she has a perfect right!' concluded poor Will, with a great sob from his big honest chest.

'That you had better ascertain!'

'Do you tell me so?' he exclaimed.

'I am not exactly the person to tell you to do so; but though I honour your conduct with all my heart, I think the mutual uncertainty is causing you both much unnecessary unhappiness and anxiety.'

'I can answer for one! But she? People always preach that long engagements wear out a girl's life.'

'If you were sixteen and thirteen over again, I should say, "Don't!" very decidedly; but having gone so far, I think you had best go on. I really believe that not only would an understanding be a great present relief, but that an avowed engagement would be a great comfort and protection to her.'

'I'll never let her go back to that drudgery!' cried Will.

'That you must settle with her,'

'Then I have your sanction?'

'Yes; but I'm not your father!'

'Oh! he'll be jolly and glad! He never interferes with anything in reason! I wonder how Wilmet will look!'

'That must be ascertained by experiment. We must shut up now, Will, or poor Tedo will have another restless night. Good-night!'

'Pah! I should like to go out and halloo!'

'Write a poem instead, and work off the steam!' said Felix, turning down the lamp to get rid of that most unpoetical-looking poet.

Will had announced an intention of walking to Penbeacon in early morning, and when rallied by Angela on having overslept himself, the great audacious slap-dash fellow proved to have turned as shy as a girl. He kept on blushing up to the ears, looking sheepish, and losing opportunities from sheer awkwardness. If the space had been as small, or Felix as punctilious as at John's courtship, the crisis could hardly have come on; but Felix had put off going to Bexley, to see the affair through, and was resolved that the mutual infliction of misery should last no longer. So finding matters in *statu quo* at dinner-time, he ordered the waggonet, and declaring suddenly that he would protect Cherry through the visits she had to return, he packed in three sisters, declaring, with a twinkle in his eye, that he knew Bobbie wanted to finish her sketch of the church. Clement was gone to the far end of the village, and Bernard was fishing, so that the coast was clear.

But the drawing went on in solitude under the cedar for a quarter of an hour; and when at last a sort of irresolute saunter resulted in a big loosely-built personage reclining on the grass at the sketcher's feet, a good many more minutes were spent in pulling up tufts, while she was too glad to have him there to suggest that he was doing the work of a dozen chaffer-grubs. Indeed, she soon saw that he was ill at ease, and her painting felt the influence of his restlessness, which began to alarm her, though she durst not disturb it. He might mean to have it out with her—he might be composing a poem—to which last opinion she inclined when he at length lay prone on his back, his straw hat entirely over his face; and she expected either a heroic utterance, or a hasty demand for a pencil and a page of her sketch-book. Instead of which, after a deep sigh, came the portentous words—'Double-distilled donkey!'

'Indeed, I don't think he's quite that!' justice compelled her to say.

'There! I knew how it would be! Nothing but an unmitigated idiot could have thought otherwise for a moment!'

'Thought what?' said Robina—not exactly liking to consider the 'unmitigated idiot' meant to apply to herself, the most obvious antecedent.

'Why, I was ten thousand asses for coming out here!'

'Indeed!'

Something in the tone of that 'indeed' raised him to a sitting posture, with his arms embracing his knees, a resolute and deplorable attitude. 'I say, Robina, tell me at once, and put an end to it, whether you care for that sprig of nobility!'

'I!' she cried, her eyes flashing. 'How can you suspect me!' and indignation made it sound like—'insult me!'

'Don't be in such a fury with a poor fellow that has been driven nearly to desperation!' said William, putting an elbow on the chair where her apparatus stood.

'It was your own fault!' said Robina; she meant it to be sternly, but it was softly. 'I wanted to explain to you, but you never would let me!'

'I did not know that you—I mean, that I felt that I had no right to ask!'

'O Willie!'

'Robina! Robin—dearest! Are you thinking of that evening?—Bah! what's this?' as his start forward upset the chair against him.

'The water I was painting with! Let me wipe it. It is making a green stream over your face!' at which they both laughed hysterically; and what Will tried to do to the hands that were drying his face may be inferred from—'Now, don't! Let me do it properly! Be quiet, let me look!' And as he half sat, half knelt, she turned up his great freckled face with her hand under his chin. 'There's a green drop still in the corner of your left eye! Let me take it out.'

'The last drop of the green-eyed monster, I promise you, Robina. Now, don't you know what they always do to good little boys, who have had their faces washed nice and clean?'

'But you haven't been a good little boy! You were very naughty, making me ever so unhappy!' and, smiling as she was, there was a tear not green in her eye.

'Ah! You could never have been so wretched as I was; not knowing whether what was my deepest earnest was child's play to you, and not daring to ask.'

'Just like me!' she whispered.

'And now, is it not like waking out of a horrible dream, or getting out of a mist of darkness, to find that we have had one another's heart ever—ever since? my Robin—mine own—mine own!'

'Oh! indeed it is! I don't think we quite knew what we were doing then, but it has only grown as we have grown older.'

'And will grow for ever, Robina!'

'I trust so!'

'Isn't this rest?' he said presently.

'After all those worries! Oh! I must tell you about Lord Ernest!'

'I don't want to hear a word about Lord Ernest, or Lord Anybody! Bless me, I forgot! I was to let the fellow knew if I could have him up at the farm; and in fact I was waiting to know whether you wanted him made a man of for you!' and Will laughed merrily. 'I'd have done my best, Robin!'

'I do want him made a man of, but not for me,' said Robina, stroking his face, by way of reward for a generosity she could not speak of. 'You'll do it, Willie?'

'He'll be off with it, now!'

'Nonsense! that had nothing at all to do with it. He had been trying to read at home, and it did not answer.'

'Never does!'

'He got bothered, and came to Eweford in a fit of temper. The family did not know where he was, and I thought I ought to show him their letters, and let him see how vexed they were. Felix said I had better let it alone, and I found after all that Lord Ernest had written to his father.'

'Felix knows about us. How is that?'

'I was uncomfortable at his not knowing. I once tried to tell Wilmet, when I was afraid I ought not to keep the *nid d'avis;* but she said I was a silly child, and would not listen.'

'How lucky! What a delicious time we had at Barèges! It is like a stream of sunshine in my mind. Won't we go there again some day! That would have settled my business, even if there had been no summer evening at home. I've got your sketches up in my rooms, and this one will follow them.'

'If you haven't gone and spoilt it! Look! There's a great dab of blue, that you made me make, half way up the church tower.'

'Make it Clement, in a sky-blue scarlet vestment, pronouncing a benediction!'

'For shame, Willie! that's as bad as Angela. Besides, he isn't gone up as high as *that* yet!'

'Make it a forget-me-not, then!'

'Up there! and as big as the window?'

'Make it something! I won't have it washed out. It marks the prime moment of my life—when I came from darkness into sunshine. You must come some day and do our Cathedral from the meads, and I'll show you where I cut out our initials and 1861.'

'No! did you?'

'Of course; and all the more because you would not break a sixpence. You will now?'

'With all my heart!'

'I declare I haven't got one now! Only a three-penny bit, again.'

'Here's one!' said Robina. 'Give me the three-penny, and then it will be half from each.'

'That's not the right arrangement,' said Will, as he frowned horribly over the difficulty of dividing the coin. 'I say, I'll get you a ring to-morrow, though it won't be such a one as Jack's.'

'No, it will be much better!' said Robina, taking the scissors at her chatelaine, (from a Repworth Christmas-tree,) and snipping a lock from his head, while he was still struggling with the sixpence. 'There, I shall make that into a ring! Yes it is the only one I will have—the only gold I care for.'

'If you call that gold, it is decisive,' said Will, laughing, as she twined the ruddy thing in her fingers. 'You must have something to set it in?'

'Yes; I must wait till the chestnut horse comes home, for a few hairs of his mane for a foundation—black would show through.'

Bill protested in favour of 'a real one,' but without much effect. Was not the sixpence yielding at last? and had she not that precious bird's-nest, which she had not dared to wear during his displeasure, unwitting that this grieved him the more? They were very earnest over the old-fashioned ceremony of the sixpence; they scratched a W and an R on each moiety, and made a hole, and Robina undertook the finding a cord for each. It was playfully done, but with great depth beneath.

'It has been the homely token of a great deal of simple trust!' said Will.

'And I am sure we are poor enough!' added Robina.

'But you will never go back to that abominable harness?'

'Indeed I must! No, Will! Cannot you see how wrong and foolish it would be to be living on Felix, with nothing to do, and no one wanting me?'

'No one?'

'Cherry is all the world to Felix, and teaches Stella. Angela takes the parish work; and it would be a sin and shame to waste my education in dawdling here. Even dear old Lancey is too much taken up with his music to want me to keep house for him. I should only be in his way; and I do not want to enter on all the questions about society there!'

'No; Bexley would not do for you!'

'And when I am getting one hundred pounds now, and am to have one hundred and fifty after Christmas, when Miss Oswald goes, would it not be sheer waste and laziness to come and prey on Felix, when I might be earning a nice little nest-egg to furnish our house with?'

'That's to coax me; but I can't stand your working for me!'

'I might as well say I can't stand your working for me, you silly fellow! You don't see me crying at your keeping pupils at Penbeacon.'

'Yes, but I'm the right one!'

'I declare you've been learning of my godmothers, who say it is unworthy of a man to let his womankind work. A regular Mahometan notion, isn't it? And I shall get my holidays whenever you are available. Don't you see?'

'I see it exactly in Miss Hepburn's light. Men must work!'

'And women weep! Eh? I've no intention of weeping! I much prefer working, and I do no more than is wholesome for any person's well-being. I believe it is Green-eyes again?'

'No; I'm not afraid of you, my own, own steady-hearted Bird! I never would have been, had I known whether you viewed that evening walk as play or earnest. I've done with that sort of trouble; but I should like to lift you out of all the drudgery of work-a-day life, and give you all that heart could wish!'

'The heart of a bird of paradise!' said she, looking into his face; 'the heart of a robin red-breast gets much nearer what it wishes when it is working—working for you, you know! Ay! that's so sweet, that you want to get it all for yourself!'

'My sweetest Bird! before you have talked me quite out of my senses, with your poetical way of putting it, let me say that you and I don't work on equal terms. There's the rub!'

'Oh! You're ashamed of the governess?'

'No indeed, dearest; but that you—you—equal to any in birth—should be in an inferior position!'

'Lord Earnestlypoor!' announced Amelia, in one single word, as she advanced on them from the house, with the gentleman following. 'He asked for Mr. Harewood.'

Up they sprung, holding out their hands.

'I thought I might walk over for my answer,' he said, with a sense of interrupting something.

William gave a conscious laugh. 'I'm afraid I've not been up to Penbeacon yet.'

'I think,' said Robina, rallying her powers, 'we had better make our avowal at once. Lord Ernest, we want your congratulations. We have been engaged this long time, and my eldest brother has just given us leave to make it known.'

Good breeding and self-command might perhaps be what prevented all sign of aught but frank friendliness. 'Indeed! I wish you joy with all my heart. Does Grace know?'

'I am going to write to Grace.'

'She will be very unselfish if she rejoices.'

'I don't think it will make any difference for some time to come,' said Robina.

'You see,' said Will, 'we neither of us have anything; and she will have it that she is so happy among your sisters, that it is no hardship to go on as she is.'

'My mother will say that it is as great a compliment as ever she received.—Well, Harewood! when you can think of such sublunary matters as pupils, will you let me know? I wouldn't have interrupted you, but I had no notion anything so interesting was going on!'

He was so genuinely simple and hearty, that Will was impelled to try whether he still wished to be his pupil, by asking whether he would object to sleeping at a cottage. 'Not in the least!' he said, 'it would be rather jolly! All I want is for you to work me up. I feel more bound than ever not to come to grief, now they have let me take my way,' he added, with frankness satisfactory to both.

Will entered into particulars of the accommodations, and Robina interposed warnings against his statements till verified by her sister's inspection. These two were really lovers of too long standing to be overwhelmingly engrossed, but were rather like beings lightened of a heavy load of suspense; and when the question between the two gentlemen began as to the books he should write for from home, he diversified it by saying to Robina—'I brought my father's letter. Would you like to see it?'

Probably he had meant to read selections, and gave it to her only because this was impossible, and he really wanted to justify his recent words.

Lord de la Poer fulfilled the assertion that he would not be displeased with his son's independence, provided he should persevere in exertion. There was a kindly expressed but not the less real warning, that the examination at Oxford would be the test whether this were a manly spirit or mere restive impatience. Full permission to read with Mr. Harewood, or any one he preferred, was given. Mr. Crichton had perceived that the system of study at home did not answer. 'When the class-list comes out,' wrote the Marquess, 'it will be time to consider of the future; but I promise that you shall not find yourself withheld from any suitable course, by any wishes that may have been prematurely expressed. That whole subject may be considered as closed. If your present plans are inspired by any other views, I trust to your treating me with confidence.'

That was the only sentence in which any suspicion could be detected. How Robina rejoiced that Felix had prevented the confession that would have been so ridiculous now! Of Lady Caergwent there was not a word. If Lord de la Poer knew of any grief at the defection, he regarded himself as in honour bound not to betray her.

Robina was waiting to restore the letter for a pause in the discussion of Greek plays and moral philosophy, which was the prelude to the licking into shape, though in externals the tutor looked by far the most in need of the process, when Amelia made another incursion, and this time announced, 'Miss Hepburn'—who proved to be two of the sisters—Bridget and Isabella; but introductions not being the prevailing custom at Repworth Towers, Robina did not feel called on to make any, and indeed William had been at Vale Leston as long as she had. But they had never met face to face before, and the ladies resented the omission, returned the bows stiffly, and when she said, 'My sisters are gone out to make morning visits,' the answer was, 'Yes, my sister Martha saw them, and we thought you would be alone.'

'Thank you. Will you come into the drawing-room, or do you like sitting out-of-doors?—Willie, please ring, and ask for some tea.'

'No, thank you! We will not disturb you. We did not know you were engaged!'

Will took the word technically, and started; Lord Ernest kept his countenance with difficulty; but Robina had sense enough to understand, and say, 'I only stayed at home to finish a sketch. These afternoon lights and shades are particularly becoming to the church.' And Lord Ernest, bringing some chairs to the rescue, applied himself with ready courtesy to make talk, though praise of the choir was hardly a happy subject to start. He did his best with Miss Isabella, while Robina faltered through ten minutes of cold commonplace with Miss Bridget.

About a quarter of an hour later, Major Harewood, who was working out the problem whether prudence would allow him to exchange military engineering for high farming as the Squire's agent, looked up at the sight of his wife in hat and parasol.

'Are you going out, my dear? Is it not too hot?'

'Only to the Priory.'

'There's nobody at home. Kit saw "Uncle Fee" and all the aunties going out in the carriage.'

'Not Robina. Miss Isabella Hepburn has just been here, to warn me that she found her sitting on the lawn, alone with two young men!'

'Bernard and Theodore?'

'No, no; of course she knows them by sight. I shall go down. I expect it is that young De la Poer; and either Robin does not know how to get rid of him, and will be glad to see me, or else she ought to be!'

'Those are the ladies that are said to have but one tooth,' said John, taking up hat and stick.

'There's no need to disturb you. Only I feel it the more expedient to be near. I am much vexed at this beginning. I never expected it from Robina. She is worse than Angel!'

'Poor Robin! There's been something amiss with her all the week, as well as with Bill. I wonder if there is anything in the Bailey joke about them?'

'Most certainly not,' said Wilmet; 'I am much more afraid of the other thing. I always thought her choosing to stay at Repworth suspicious!'

'I don't believe it! I saw them come up after she had been lost at Ewmouth, as innocent as lambs! Her manner was perfectly simple and natural.'

'I don't understand Robina's manner,' said Wilmet.

Walking down the hilly slope of the path, they presently were aware of a pair with arms and hands doubly interlaced, in the fashion peculiar to the circumstances.

'John!'

'Wilmet! Was there never a blackberry lane in our lives?'

'Not without—Robina!'

They turned, but without confusion, without loosing of arms, or if Robina had attempted it, it was checked.

'Oh! there you are, John!' exclaimed Will 'So you see we have settled it at last!'

'I do not know what you mean,' said Wilmet, gravely.

'O Wilmet!' said Robina. 'I told you all about it, long ago, at Barèges.'

'If you consider that as any intimation—' she began; but her husband interrupted her. 'I suppose Felix has yet to hear this?'

'Oh no!' both cried; Will adding, 'Felix created this vast solitude on our behalf!'

'Your father?' added Wilmet.

'He went away a day too soon; but there's no fear of him, is there, Jack?'

'You all seem to me demented!' said Wilmet aghast.

'Nay, Mettie, if you knew it at Barèges, you can't say a word!' said John, much amused.

'Always sending us up the mountains together!' added Will. 'No one ever gave me such a happy time of it!'

'Giving me leave to keep the brooch!' continued Robina, chiming in with their humour.

'Why, 'tis your doing,' summed up the Major; 'and I trust it is a good work for both!' he gravely proceeded. 'I wish you joy, with all my heart, though I fear I must wish you patience too!'

'And prudence!' put in Wilmet, but softening into sweetness. 'Dear Robin—dear Willie—don't think I don't care!' as she gave a sisterly kiss to each. 'It is because I do care so very much for both that I am anxious!'

'Anxiety was your meat and drink so early in life that you can't shake it off now!' said John, affectionately; 'and Harewood as I am, I should share it with you, if I didn't know that Bill's choice much resembles her elder sister!'

'You may say that!' observed Will. 'Why, she wants to go on in harness at Repworth!'

'That is wise!' responded Wilmet.

'But, halloo!' cried John, 'did your friend see double, Mettie?—or what have you done with your other young man, Robina?'

'Walked him to the little gate! He came to settle about reading with Willie.'

'I say!' cried William, laughing, 'did the Graiæ go and send Wilmet to put on her Gorgon's head, and charge down on us? I thought they were looking as sour as verjuice!'

'You see,' proceeded Wilmet, 'we must all be careful! It won't do to fancy one can do anything in the country. These old ladies don't do it out of ill-nature, like Lady Price, but they are almost worse!'

'However, Mettie, as these poor things have been subjected already to one Oxonian and two hags, I think you and I had better relieve them of our presence, and let them finish their walk in peace.'

Putting things together, Robina thought she had not wholly escaped doubt at Repworth, for she received no letter between the inquiry into the K T case, and the answers to her own communication, and these so overflowed with affection and cordiality, as to suggest that they were a reaction. Lady de la Poer wrote warm congratulations, and spoke of her eldest son's high opinion of Mr. Harewood; she was rejoiced at Miss Underwood's decision to return to her post, and she gave a few words of thanks for the explanation about the children's chatter: 'Susie has been well lectured on Russian scandal!' was her conclusion.

Lady Grace was rapturous enough to think she had seen the future dawning at the station. Poor Grace! she certainly was rather gushing, and probably it was the contrast that made her so devoted to the staid Robina. She let out that she was 'so glad to write again. Mamma had advised her not, for fear of more misunderstandings, till it was settled about Ernest; and now he must bring Mr. Harewood to Repworth for her to see. As to Kate, she was still at the Towers; the Wardours had the small-pox in their parish, and could not have her.' Grace had evidently been put under some reserve as to the Countess; but there was a note from herself—quaint and hearty, like all she did, and with a little sadness in it. There was no such intimacy as to render it necessary, and Robina interpreted the writing of it to mean that there had once been bitter feelings towards her, and that this was their recall.

MY DEAR MISS UNDERWOOD,

Gracie tells me you have been well employed. I heartily wish you joy. A university tutor seems to me as mighty a power of influence as any in existence, but I suppose it is your mission to spoil him for that. Lucky girl that you are, to have work and brothers and all! You don't know how much it saves you from. One brother is all I would have asked, if only to prevent me from signing myself,

Yours affectionately,
CAERGWENT.

The secret history must evidently wait for Robina's return, and before that there was a great deal of conscientious hard work at Penbeacon, the tutor resolutely refraining from walks to Vale Leston, except when, on Sunday, he and his whole party marched down to what he called 'prayers and provender,' at Vale Leston. Also there was one, only one, picnic given by the Penbeaconites to the Vale Lestonites, during the week when the Squire inexorably went to Bexley, and sent Lance to be the merriest of the merry on the last of August, and to make acquaintance with the hares and partridges on the 1st of September.

At the end of that week, in the early charms of September, with the sheaves glorifying the fields, the fruit glowing on the trees, the pears drooping in russet drops, the apples piled in red and golden heaps, the geraniums and verbenas flaming on the lawn, Felix brought Mr. and Mrs. Froggatt, for what was probably as happy and exultant a visit as ever they paid in their joint lives. To see Felix in his glory was almost as much to them as if he had been their own child, and they were intimate enough to make it possible to provide for their entertainment perfectly to their satisfaction. The home-farm, which was to be let to Major Harewood, with a tariff for the articles needed for family consumption, afforded Mrs. Froggatt great amusement in studying chickens and ducks; and the agent's house, a pretty cottage on the opposite bank, was being improved at John's expense, so as to be ready for occupation as soon as he could effect his retirement and break up from Woolwich; and every one knows the resource house-building is to the leisurely holiday-maker. Indeed, Mr. Froggatt wanted nothing but his book and newspaper, and a little talk and garden fancying; and the petting Cherry and Stella gave him. The tender reverent affection all the young people showed to both, as to their true friends and benefactors, warmed their hearts.

One state-dinner—in spite of his disavowal of dinner visiting—Felix had always resolved to give, chiefly for the sake of the satisfaction he knew Mrs. Froggatt would for ever feel in it. He had to pick the other guests, but he secured a sufficiency. Dr. May had promised himself and his two daughters. Of Mrs. Staples Cherry was afraid, but Mr. Staples came, and Mr. and Mrs. Welsh, which was the more amiable in him because there had been a time in his life when Mr. and Mrs. Froggatt would have been far above him. Lord Ernest came down from Penbeacon, and thus, with the Harewoods and the large home-party, the numbers were quite imposing; especially with the display of all the plate, champagne, ices, Krishnu, and even Cherry's abomination, a hired waiter in white gloves!

It was not thrown away. Mrs. Froggatt was indeed a little awed in the Bismarck brocade and blonde cap she would have been so sorry not to have aired; but Dr. May found the way to her heart, even before dinner, by admiring the testimonial inkstand which adorned the drawing-room writing-table, and its story and all it led to lasted more than half through dinner, and Gertrude caught echoes even while fraternizing with Major Harewood over her brother in the engineers. After dinner, good-natured little Mrs. Welsh, to the manner trained, took to entertaining the old lady, and though the style was too electioneering for Cherry's taste, it suited the purpose exactly, and made Mrs. Froggatt pronounce her a very pretty and affable young lady.

Even if there had been less enjoyment at the time, that dinner-party would have been one of the chief events of Mrs. Froggatt's life. She never wearied of dilating on it to all the friends who called on her, on her return. 'She should have thought it a privilege only to see that dear young gentleman in his proper sphere; but for him to treat the old people as he might any lord in the land, and show himself as attentive, as filial, she might say, as if he still had his bread to earn!' and there she always began to cry.

'One effect your dinner-party has had,' wrote Lance to Cherry, 'it has wholly destroyed the small remains of Madame Tanneguy's peace of mind. What she does not believe of the glories of the Priory it would be hard to say. She angled full two half-hours for an invitation last time the Squire was here, between her affection for you—and then poor little Achille's health. And the effect upon that stony-hearted old Giant was, that he sent two ten-pound notes to Miss Pearson, with a request to take lodgings for her and the children at Dearport for a month. Wherewith Miss Pearson trotted confidentially to me, to assure me that she could not use them, since nothing on earth ailed Achille. I advised her to keep and apply them; for not only do I know he would not take them back, but it is no bad form of intimating that she may change to any air save Vale Leston. And the absurd part of it is, that the more she aspires, the more poor Lamb casts his hopeless sheep's-eyes at her!'

CHAPTER XXXIX.

FOUR YEARS.

> 'Yet there are some resting-places,
> Life's untroubled interludes;
> Times when neither past nor future
> On the soul's deep calm intrudes.'
> *Jean Ingelow.*

That Penbeacon pic-nic became an institution, and was one of the pleasantest annual events in what were on the whole very happy years.

Care, exertion, and self-denial, were indeed still needful; but the two latter were perhaps ingredients of happiness, and care would not have been avoided if the Underwood view of duty had been the world's views of what became Vale Leston Priory. A strenuous endeavour to keep up appearances, and compete with grand neighbours on an uncertain three thousand a year, would probably have been more wearing than living on twelve hundred—partly earned by honest labour—and improving the cottages, planting a school-chapel at Blackstone Gulley, hiring a house for the purpose at East Ewmouth, and restoring the church by degrees.

As for exertion, to be an Underwood of the late type would have been harder work to Felix than his hours of Pursuivant or days at the office, though in truth the labour was sometimes considerable. It was not immediately that the two young men at Bexley could get on without constant aid and superintendence in the business: he was always the working editor; besides which, he was already important at Bexley, and soon was found too good a man of business not to have a good deal of county administration devolved upon him. Trade and public affairs did so far clash as to be a strain, but not more than was compensated by sense of usefulness and consideration, and giving zest to the delightful snatches of leisure in his lovely and cheerful home.

Self-denial? Felix and Geraldine would have disputed that. They had grown up to a style that made simple plenty and moderate ease luxurious, and superfluities never even suggested themselves as needs. Perhaps the lack they were most concerned about was inability to 'keep up the place' in the trim and dainty order it seemed to call for. The smoothness of the grass in the park was dependent on the convenience of John Harewood's dairy farm; and though the garden between the house and river was always in beautiful order, in the shrubberies there was a fine struggle of natural selection; the kitchen-gardens were made to pay their way, and the ranges of conservatories were cold and empty, except one necessary refuge for tenderer plants, and one maintained at Clement's expense for Church-decorating flowers. Golightly was greatly distressed at having no underlings but one old woman, one small boy, and half the man who looked after the horse and pony, or sometimes—what was worse than none—some subject to whom the Vicar was applying the labour-test. The worthy gardener truly represented that three men was the minimum for such grounds, and gave warning when he found that justice could not be done them; but after Felix had found him a much superior place, he declined; he could not find it in his heart to leave the place to an untrained labourer, who would not even know how to help devastating it. This sense of what was the garden's due caused him to bestow an immense amount of personal toil on it; for indeed it was observable that whoever worked for Felix always did so with a will, stimulated no doubt by the master's example, as well as by his hearty appreciation and acknowledgment of good service. In this there was much real economy.

The farm did well in the hands of Major Harewood, who had adapted the agent's house to his own needs. It was just on the other side of the river and road; and a boat, commonly called 'Lord Ullin's Daughter,' brought it within five minutes' reach, going round by the bridge taking about three times that interval. The land was chiefly rich pasture; and John was growing learned in short-horns, and Wilmet upon butter and cheese, while Clement's wish was realized by a parish cow.

The calculations as to the scale of living were justified by the result. Lighter household tasks were natural to the young ladies. They kept their own rooms in order, dusted the books and ornaments, took care of the household linen, and performed delicate cookeries, so as to keep down the number of needful servants; and the occasions were few and far between when their hospitality extended beyond the addition of a few guests at their ordinary meals, or a garden-party, with its pretty and inexpensive refections.

People who restored their church and built schools, without begging for subscriptions either directly or through a bazaar, but continued in trade, and cut off superfluous luxuries—servants, horses, and dinner-parties—were a fertile subject for wonder and gossip in the neighbourhood. Society growled, contemned, and remonstrated, by the mouth of Mrs. Fulbert Underwood, and the defence of her misguided family was a heavy charge to Wilmet for the first year; but no one worth caring about really took umbrage, and after a time people accepted them on their own terms. A beautiful lawn, full of sprightly youth, of looks, spirits, and talents, above the average, could not fail to be popular, and an old county name went for something.

Cherry was proof against dinner-parties. Health was no longer an objection, for either Vale Leston had the virtues of native air, or the Bexley potteries had merited Alda's vituperation, for Cherry's ailments were more rare, and she had much advanced in strength and vigour. Felix declared she was growing quite handsome; and he, though not exactly the ideal squire, had acquired much more of the robustness of manhood, and had lost the appearance of fragility he had shown in earlier years, though he retained the fair youthful complexion which sometimes made people hardly credit that his tens were three. He sometimes dined out alone; but Cherry considered dress and reciprocity to settle the question of abstinence for her. Angela was, however, so wild about Ewmouth balls, that John victimized himself and his wife rather than create a grievance, but even his tolerance was sorely taxed.

Was the blame to be laid on prosperity for the difficulty of dealing with the two standing anxieties—Angela and Bernard? They had not been the most docile subjects in the days of comparative poverty, and their heads were certainly turned now. Bernard could not be convinced that expensiveness was not the proof of being a gentleman, and in three years at Harrow cost his brother more than Clement, Fulbert, and Lancelot, all put together, in their whole nonage, had ever done, besides the scrapes that Lance helped him out of. He had no sympathy with Felix's purpose in economy; not that he had reflection enough for a sceptical habit of mind like Edgar's, but he considered it a hardship that the whole family should be stinted and impoverished for what he was pleased to term Tina's maggots; nor could anything persuade him that he himself was no richer than before, and equally dependent on his brother's bounty. There was no positive harm in him, but as genius and taste alike lay in the line of cricket, he cared not for distinction of other kinds, but was content to scrape through the school without disgrace. His farther destiny was a moot point, while he scorned cheap colleges and halls, and Felix insisted that a distinguished one was only to be attained through a scholarship.

Angela was a greater puzzle. She was still much what she had been in childhood, alternating between the fast and the devotional. She was Clement's right hand in the parish, in the schools, Sunday, day, or night, and with even more than Wilmet's nursing instinct, the prime doctress of the village, and enjoying the cure of a broken chilblain as much as a waltz. To take a medical degree had become her ambition in turns with the dukedom, the opera, and the Sisterhood. Therewith she was the most saucy and idle of creatures. With less regular good looks than most of the family, she was more sought after. Figure did much, the hop-pole had become lithe and graceful, and her dress was always becoming, as well it might be, for her bills were never within bounds. She said she could not help it, and certainly her adventurous nature and rapid movements occasioned numerous catastrophes to her wardrobe, though not enough to account for the discrepancy between her accounts and her sisters'. Her charm lay in droll dash and audacity, and the irresistible glance of her eyes. Even Christopher and his little brother Edward preferred her to all their other aunts—the night-school was gathered by her as to a magnet, and better than all the Vicar's arguments and the Squire's influence had her coaxing prevailed to get the choir into surplices. She was by far the most formidable as well as the most unscrupulous adversary of the poor Miss Hepburns, who viewed her with pious pity and horror as the natural outcome of the system they deprecated. Indeed, whether she were Clement's greatest help or hindrance was doubtful. He could not have a friend to stay with him, or obtain the assistance of a curate, without furnishing prey for Angela. Fred Somers, after a six weeks' visit, went back to St Matthew's with his peace upset, and an understanding that the two friends must never meet again in the haunts of that dangerous siren. A few more such experiments convinced the Vicar that unless he wished the village girls to remark that 'Miss Angel was carrying on with another young man,' he must do all the work himself; and his present amount of services, Sunday and weekly, at the parish church, and Blackstone Gulley, were quite up to the mark of any one man's powers, besides his attempts at East Ewmouth. Here Felix had no property, and therefore could not check the eruption of small tenements, which broke forth on some fresh field every spring, containing independent, often surly inhabitants, always changing, and rapidly outrunning the powers of the undaunted young Vicar. The two parishes were so entangled that the difficulties as to territory were endless, and the endeavour at a week-day service was not encouraged or assisted by the incumbent of the nearest district, who feared Clement's 'views,' and had been staggered by Angela's ostentation of them.

Angela was the greater heartache to Clement, because she had been trained in the same system with himself, and was inclined to carry it to lengths that even he thought extravagant. There might have been some disadvantage in his inexperience when she came into his hands for direction only at the end of his first year of priesthood, and he would fain have kept her in Mr. Fulmort's keeping; but difficulties had prevented his insistence, and this he increasingly regretted. For in spite of all his efforts, his relations with her were lapsing into what he had always scouted as the popular notion of confession. It was technical, as far as he could see devoid of repentance. Angela contrived to separate the brother and the priest; she would go through any formula, accept any discipline, but mechanically; but she would not endure exhortation, and if he ever attempted to check her boisterous spirits, she scouted him as Tina. Sometimes he wondered whether she sought him only because the practice belonged to what she called an 'out-and-outer,' and Felix retained doubts of its universal expediency.

Did Angela suppress Stella? Never were sisters less alike. Princess Fair Star, as the brothers called her, was still very small, with a lovely little face, tinted like fine porcelain, and hair and eyes more deeply coloured than those of most of the family; hair still snooded and in shining curls, and pensive eyes shining with a lustre of their own. She was the help and handmaid of the whole house, especially of Geraldine, with whom she still did regular lessons; and she was very diligent in all her doings, turning out her handiwork with delicate finish; but she was not enterprising, the very pains she took rendering her slow to undertake, though she spent much time in finishing Angela's odds and ends. She still continued the family lexicon, for even if she could not answer a query off-hand, she could always hunt it down, and the reply was generally ready in the soft low musical voice. Her laugh was noiseless and not frequent, for though never fretful nor depressed, she was only gently merry, pensively gay; and though now and then a quaint remark would drop into the whirl of family fun—and she was no inconsiderable element in games—she was always as happy, if not happier, in the garden or the woods with Theodore, their pets and flowers. She was devoted to the garden, its trimness was in great part owing to her; and as Golightly said, 'The bookets for the 'ouse was Miss Stella's province, and them for the church Miss Hangela's;' and of live-stock the twins tended a curious variety—rabbits, doves, cats, dogs, canaries, dormice, and owls, besides wounded creatures, rescued, cured, and released. Stella's quietness was a great ingredient in taming them; John Harewood called her the only feminine creature devoid of propensity for making a noise, and Felix, their silent Star

'Up above the world so high,
Like a diamond in the sky.'

Sometimes she would talk freely to Geraldine on any unusual excitement, but if she conversed with any one else, it was with Theodore. No one who watched the pair could doubt that they had more mutual understanding than the boy had with any other person—even Felix, for whom his love was like a dog's devotion to his master. The out-of-door life and country air had been beneficial both to mind and body, and Theodore was much healthier and stronger, made progress in the little that he could be taught; could utter a few words, comprehended more than he could pronounce, and improved in self-control. His conscience was developing in some degree, and his delight in the Church services and music less unintelligent.

Perhaps Stella was content to be the longer a child because each advance into life was further away from Theodore; and she had never yet shed such sorrowful tears as when Clement decided against presenting him for Confirmation, in the inability to trace whether the comprehension that Stella maintained, and Felix believed, were not an illusion of their loving imagination.

Yet strangely enough, Theodore was confirmed after all. He was as usual among the choir-boys, walking in procession with them, and materially aiding them by his perfectly true though wordless chant. His nearest companions were candidates, and he moved instinctively with them to the step; nor had either brother the heart to interfere as they saw him kneeling—for though he could not renew the vow, why might he not receive the Seal? The tickets had been previously taken, so there was no obstacle; and when explanation and apology were afterwards made, they were met with encouragement not to debar the innocent from his Christian privileges because of his lack of power of expression.

Indeed, the Bishop, who had been dismayed at the institution to the family living of another Underwood, and he such a young one, was not a little gratified and surprised at the changes he found going on in Vale Leston—no longer one of the dark hopeless spots of his diocese, though of course the work, both moral and material, was gradual. Felix had done nothing in advance of the means that the great tithes brought into his hands, and had begun with the needful repairs of the cottages on the Rectory property, and the crying needs of Blackstone Gulley; but the Church restoration was gradually going on—the Vicar, Marilda, and John Harewood, all claimed a right to assist, and another year or two of the great tithes would accomplish the full detail of the plan of restoration he had set out with.

Meantime he had made many real friends. The one whom he had reckoned had, however, been disappointing. Captain Audley had exerted himself to leave his cards, but when he had reason to believe no one at home. He was friendly when he encountered Felix, and sometimes on the spur of the moment asked him to dinner; but the ladies he ignored, except that once when Cherry and Angel were driving past his house in a shower, he rushed out and offered an umbrella.

His son, however, soon haunted the Priory, as affording all that home lacked. He was a nice lively lad, dark and brisk, and not the less welcome because there was much to recall the Charles Audley who was striving to bring light to the 'black fellows' of Carrigaboola. He was avowedly Bernard's friend, but he was regularly tame about the house, walking in at all times during his vacations, in a way that could not be grudged to one whose home was so dull. Certainly it was a pleasant house to young men; Wilmet sometimes murmured a little when all Will Harewood's pupils appeared there at luncheon every Sunday of the stay at Penbeacon; and the old ones invariably turned up again, especially Lord Ernest, who had taken a second class and got into a government office, and yet always managed to appear at each Penbeacon pic-nic.

The first shadow which came upon Vale Leston was good Mr. Froggatt's death, a grief really deep to those who owed so much to his kindness. It was a touching thing to see the four fine young men, who looked on him like a kinsman, gathered round his grave. Felix and Lance were far more to the widow than her own nephews; and when married nieces wanted to take her home, and single ones to live with her, she—not without misgivings as to the nature of the attraction—declined all, preferring to face her solitude at Marshlands, in the security that dear Mr. Lancelot would walk out to see her once or twice a week, and that still dearer Mr. Underwood would come out whenever he could.

It ended in Lance doing more than this. He had been a partner ever since he had come to years of discretion, and now found himself the legatee of all Mr. Froggatt's remaining interest in Pursuivant or business. Ernest Lamb had lately lost his father, and having come into possession of a slender capital, was in condition to become one of the house, as indeed he was excellent in whatever regarded the trade, though incapable of more than the most mechanical newspaper work.

The new arrangement of Underwood and Co. had hardly been made than the world was electrified by the announcement of Mr. Lamb's engagement. That Madame Tanneguy had been adored by him ever since her arrival was known to all; but hitherto she had only vouchsafed a distracting smile at long intervals, and had laughed at him with her intimates. Her opportunities were not extensive, but she was as pretty as ever; and she turned the heads of one or two brothers of her pupils, had at one time a promising little flirtation with a sentimental young partner of Mr. Rugg's, and never ceased to dream of an invitation to Vale Leston, which she was quite sure Geraldine alone withheld poor Mr. Underwood from giving. But Gustavus and Achilles were growing rather big for inmates of a young ladies' school, Madame Tanneguy was weary of the drudgery, and no such positive release as Ernest Lamb offered had come in her way. His mother's opposition could be set aside, between coaxing and unwillingness to quarrel; and though he was some years the younger, he did not look it, nor could there be any doubt that he would be the best of husbands, and a kind and conscientious father to the boys; and the aunts, though drawing up their necks a little when they spoke of it in private, could not deny that it was a subject of thankfulness—making their future retirement come within the bounds of possibility.

'Guess the proposal I have had,' quoth Felix, when next he returned from Bexley, and Cherry drove to meet him at the station with the pony she had named Master Ratton, in that sort of tender defiance of painful association found in those who own an exile.

'Eh! You don't look humbly cock-a-hoop, so I gather it was *not* to stand for the borough.'

'Why don't you say the county at once? No, it was of a less public nature.'

'Oh, then, I know! To give up the house to the happy pair. What? You don't mean that it really was? That beats everything!'

'Well—it is undeniable that those are large quarters for Lance, his cat, and his fiddle.'

'I do believe you have been and gone and consented! Well?' with a sigh, as if she did not know what might come next.

'As it was purely out of consideration for Lance, I referred it to him.'

'Oh! it was all for Lance's sake—was it?'

'Entirely!'

There was a dryness in the last two replies, that pacified Cherry a little.

'How Serious Mutton must be translated, to have the face—'

'He hadn't!'

'What? Alice did?'

'Yes. I believe that he had refused; but, you see, when Lance's comfort was at stake, she was not to be withholden by a scruple or two.'

'Come—tell me how she managed it. Did she write?'

'No; she chose her time. Lance was gone to that Minsterham affair, reporting—Lamb out of the way—when I heard a playful sort of little tap at the office door, and there she stood, smiling and blushing.'

'Blushing!!!'

'I'll not insist, but so it appeared to me. I assure you she did the thing to perfection—smiled and hesitated, and said she thought it was a pity to let *mauvaise honte* stand in the way of what would be so much better for Lance and all of us.'

'What, she wanted to have the house and *do* for him?'

'As one of the family!' then, taking no notice of Cherry's 'Faugh!' he went on, 'It was curious to look at her as she sat there, and think of the difference she was able to make; yet in many ways she is superior to what she was then, and certainly prettier; but I own that my feelings for her *then* seem an unaccountable infatuation.'

'Accountable only because you never spoke to anyone else, and did not rave about the customers, like Lance. I am glad you were in triple brass, though—and I can't help enjoying her having come to sue for the shop that she used to despise.'

'Fie, Cherry!'

'I declare! I believe you have gone and consented, after all that bravado!'

'I left it to Lance. Don't be furious, Cherry; the boy has had more loneliness than is good for him since Dick Graeme has been in London, and as he has his own notions about companionship, I was not sure that he might not catch it.'

'I have a better opinion of Lance.'

'And justly. But what he wants to do is to leave the old house to Madame, and betake himself to Mrs. Froggatt. He says—truly enough—that every evening he has free of his choir-practice, penny readings, and all the rest of it, he should go out to look her up, and that this would simplify the matter, and nothing would do the poor old lady so much good as seeing him.'

'That's true; but to be going out there at all times, and in all weathers!'

'That is nuts to him! Don't you know he has got a velocipede fever? He has set up a thing that he calls Plato.'

'Un play toe, I should have thought.'

'It is Plato, because Mrs. Harewood announced that he and Bill had come all the way to Minsterham, each upon his own philosopher.'

'I declare they make up things for that poor woman.'

'Or she makes them on purpose for their diversion; but at any rate, Plato is lord of the ascendant just now, and demands exercise as if he were flesh and blood. I own I was glad to see the boy in a craze again.'

'And letting Pur alone. It was very droll that the passion for making that diurnal instead of weekly, set in with him just at the same age that it did with you.'

'Yes. I am much obliged to Alda for nipping my plans in the bud.'

'The dignified weekly purr is not to change into a little petulant daily mew!'

'No. It was a manifestation of restlessness, like his wanting new stops for his organ, or being annoyed when there is a murmur against over-elaborate music. I am afraid the fact is that he has outgrown the whole concern, Cherry!'

'You never did!'

'That's nothing to the purpose. He has done all he can do with his present means, and no doubt he is thrown away down there.'

'He never says so. And it is quite hard to get him here.'

'I wish I had not consented to leaving him there. That boyish coolness and audacity that used to rush into all kinds of society are quite gone, and there is no persuading him that he is not in a false position among our neighbours.'

'He gets more into society at Bexley than ever you did.'

'Oh yes, he has quite made his place there; but there's no denying that he has been left behind; and though he says not a word, there's no doubt that since he went up to Oxford he has felt it a good deal more. Well, in a couple of years at latest, the Rectory affair will be settled; and if I can get Blackstone Gulley into my own hands, I may be able to set him free.'

Lance had been to take a musical degree, and had spent a week with William Harewood at Christ Church; and it might be true that the vague spirit of enterprise for which Bexley afforded so little scope had become remarkable since that time. However, no more was heard of it during the preparations for installing the bride in the new home. Robina came for the first fortnight of her holidays to take her leave of the old rooms, and help in the removal of his belongings to Marshlands, where the arrangement was as great a pleasure as poor Mrs. Froggatt was capable of receiving. Moreover, Robina assisted in another great change. Miss Pearson had—by Felix's management in conjunction with some others interested in middle-class education—been enabled to retire; the house and good-will of the establishment being made over to the governing body of Miss Fulmort's school. Two ladies were provided from thence, who undertook to make a home both for young teachers and daily governesses, and were likely to raise the standard in Bexley. They were old friends of Robina, and she did much to settle them in, and pave their way. After this Robina went to Minsterham for one of the brief visits that were never satisfactory, for Grace Harewood had made a foolish marriage in the town, and Lucy did not improve, but became louder and more daring, her native cleverness only making her more unrefined and less simple than her mother. The Librarian never wondered that his son soon escaped to his pupils at Penbeacon, and the Vale Leston neighbourhood.

Before Robina had been many days at home, one Saturday forenoon when she was undergoing Cherry's third attempt to satisfy unreasonable Will with her portrait, while assisting Stella's German, Angela rushed in—'One to make ready, two to prepare—one, two, three, if not four swells—not away, but here—Hammonds, et cetera.'

'Here? Not imminent? Lady Hammond always sends notice.'

'Imminent? They are prancing up the drive! Only I cut across in "Miss Ullin" to give warning. Shall I administer any orders to the dinner, Cherry, before I make myself scarce?'

'No, thank you, there is quite enough. Just take my painting-apron, that's all,' said Cherry, as coolly as Lady de la Poer would have heard tidings of such an inroad; but when Amelia announced, 'Sir Vesey and Lady Hammond in the drawing-room—and two more ladies, Ma'am—shall I lay the table for them?' she quietly answered, 'Yes, I suppose so.—Stella my dear, will you see if there is fruit enough in?' And Stella stayed behind, while Cherry descended, aided by Robina's arm.

Felix was already in presence, and the moment the two sisters appeared, a slight, brown, hazel-eyed girl in mourning exclaimed, 'O Miss Underwood, this is just what I hoped!' and eagerly kissed her, while Lady Hammond introduced 'Lady Caergwent' and 'Mrs. Umfraville,' the latter a peculiarly sweet-looking elderly lady in widow's dress. There were apologies for this sudden descent, telling that, on hearing how near Vale Leston was, Lady Caergwent had been so eager to see the Priory, that she had wrought with Sir Vesey, and prevailed.

Yet she did not seem to be profiting by the opportunity, for she merely sat by Robina, looking, thought Cherry, neither like a Countess nor a woman of twenty-three, but much more like a girl of eighteen—petrified, all save her great eyes, by shyness; and Felix regarded her precedence as not only unnatural but unlucky, with so unconversible a subject, when he had to give her his arm, and seat her at his right hand for the mid-day meal. Be it observed, that the veal stewed with asparagus, and the pie that was to be cold for the morrow, as fully justified Cherry's calmness, as did the pile of strawberries and glasses of preserves her trust in Stella's handiwork.

Clement came in late and astonished, and with a very hazy idea who the strangers were, just as Sir Vesey was saying, 'Now, Lady Caergwent, Mr. Underwood will be able to answer your question.'

She coloured a little, and rather hastily asked whether there were any tradition of French architects having been employed in the church, for she had been struck with the foreign air of the tracery of the south window. Not a little surprised, Felix soon found himself in the midst of an architectural discussion, which taxed all his knowledge on the matter, and stirred Clement on the other side into the ecclesiastical aspect of the question; and all three fell into an eager talk, when suddenly there was a general lull, and the young lady's voice was heard saying, 'There is no heart or beauty in what is not symboli—' and there she came to a full stop, and looked at Mrs. Umfraville with a start of embarrassment, requited.

Appreciation of their church was no slight merit with any of the Underwoods; and in the lionizing that ensued, the guest had eyes and tongue full of architecture, romance, and history, even spying and identifying a heraldic badge that supplied a missing link in the history of the building. Angela thought it flagrant pedantry; but Clement was so struck with her keen interest in all his arrangements, and her real reverence, that he unlocked the grille of the chancel, offered her to try the tone of his organ, and in spite of her total ignorance on that head, he asked if 'Miss Umfraville' would not like to see the choice needlework from St. Faith's in the chest in his vestry. There she had no lack of ideas; she examined and asked questions evidently with practical views, and could be hardly got away to continue the tour, when she again satisfied him (and more) by indignation on behalf of the monks—not sentimental, but evidently straight out of Dean Hook's version of the dissolution of the abbeys; and yet there was a quaintness and originality in the way she put it, that amused Felix greatly.

In the painting-room an entreaty was preferred to see Miss Underwood's drawings, which were indeed more worth looking at than when Lord de Vigny had stirred her up. She always had at least one real work in hand, and a good many studies. She was finishing a water-colour of the scene in The Lord of the Isles, when Ronald's betrothal ring falls at the feet of Isabel Bruce in the convent.

Lady Caergwent stood before this as if it touched some responsive chord; but her aunt was busy with the portraits. Geraldine's emulation had been fired by the cluster of miniatures in the drawing-room, and she had undertaken to commemorate the present family in the same style. She had produced very fair likenesses of Felix and of Wilmet, besides her half-finished crayon of Robina, and a still better one of Mr. Froggatt, which she was copying for his widow. Mrs. Umfraville was delighted with these, and wished she could get anything as good of her Kate, whom photography always represented as a fury, and portraiture as a doll; but by this time Lady Caergwent had got Robina in the recess of a window, asking, 'Are you still at Repworth?'

'Oh yes.'

'And how are they all?'

'Quite well, except that Lady Susan does not get over the remains of measles.'

'Poor little Susie! What a monkey she was! but oh, I want to hear about Gracie, and if she is more eager than ever.'

'She is very much sobered and subdued by reality.'

'And what's he? I always thought Grace would marry a great block, and ripple and splash round him.'

'No, he is a little brisk satirical man, who laughs at her when she gushes.'

'What chance is there for them?'

'Not till he gets preferment.'

'How tiresome! Ah! I forgot! Is not Mr. Harewood here?'

'At Penbeacon, but he comes here every Sunday. He knows Mr. Pemberton very well.'

'Poor Gracie! Lady de la Poer wrote to Aunt Emily that she thought it well that her steadiness should be tested; but it must have been hard to see Addie go off with flying colours. How does Addie get on as a chieftainess?'

'I had a letter from Gracie this morning. Do you like to see it?'

'Is she there? Do tell me how to say the name. I see there must be a hideous roll in the bottom of one's throat.'

Robina gurgled. 'That was allowed to pass for it when we had a lesson in pronunciation on pain of not being allowed to be bridesmaids.'

'Not a creature have I seen to tell me about the wedding.'

'Kate, my dear,' said Lady Hammond. 'No, you need not look so blank; that is, if Robina will kindly let us take her home with us. Her brother and sister are so good as to come to dine and sleep on Monday.'

For so it had been settled during the colloquy in the window, Sir Vesey and his lady being no doubt very glad to find a play-fellow for his younger visitor.

Colonel Umfraville had died after a long illness, rather more than a year previously, and this was the first time his widow and niece had come from home. The Hammonds were very old friends, but Mrs. Umfraville still shrank from general society; so that when Felix and Cherry arrived they found themselves the only other guests besides the Harewoods, who had come earlier in the day.

No sooner had Cherry been conducted to the room, which, as usual, she shared with her sister, than Robina said, 'You are going to be asked to take Lady Caergwent's likeness.'

'My dear, I am not the sun, to do it in a minute!'

'And make a Brigand's Bride of her. No, you are to have her at the Priory.'

'Are you gone crazy, Bobbie?'

'Be conformable, and you shall hear.'

'I'll hear, but I don't promise conformity.'

'Now listen. Nobody can do her fit to be seen; and Mrs. Umfraville wants a nice water-colour like Mrs. Welsh's, which was exhibited. I said I did not see how it could be managed; and then she asked if she might not come to us for it; and Mrs. Umfraville let me know that she would be very glad, for she has to go on into Wales to some old maids, who would be horribly fussed if she brought Kate.'

'Well, we are old maids and old bachelors to boot. Why should not we be horribly fussed by a live Countess running about the house?'

'Because she would be tame; and because you have common sense.'

'Oh, I thought you would say, because you were used to act keeper to the species! In herself she may be inoffensive; but what sort of a tail does she bring after her?'

'Six running footmen, eh?'

'Don't be saucy, Cock-robin. One grand maid would be bad enough, scaring Theodore, and upsetting Sibby. No, no, Rob! leave countesses to those who can live as sich.'

'You need alter nothing. You may do as Bear says you do—eat boiled pork and greens every day at one o'clock—and she'll like it! She and her aunt always do dine early; and as to her maid, she is a little Repworth thing, just promoted from waiting on us in the school-room. I'll answer for her. The very attraction is, that you'll leave her in peace, and not beset her with dinner-parties.'

'She doesn't keep a duenna, then?'

'Duenna!'

'Well, heiresses in books always do. And in this case it seems to me that the article would be desirable.'

'Oh, we settled all that! Wilmet is equal to as many duennas as you like. She will come and do all the chaperoning.'

'Do you mean that she has undertaken it? Then I can only submit, provided the Squire does.'

The Squire made a few wry faces, but consented, with all a man's superior philosophy towards domestic disorganizations of which he does not feel the brunt. Besides, both he and Wilmet were proud of Cherry's talent, and the esteem in which Robina was held; and Mrs. Umfraville had been confidential with Wilmet, saying how glad she was to see her child willing to go among youth and brightness. The girl had, she said, never made young friends except the De la Poers, and her Wardour cousins, who had married, and gone out of reach. She had no suitable neighbours, and 'circumstances' had hindered her being much in London; and loss of her father-like uncle had not so much taken away her spirits—for she was always bright—as given her a distaste to society. She hated entertaining people or seeing strangers; cared for nothing but her aunt, her books, her walks, and her poor; was oppressed with the business of her property, and was altogether so studious and indefatigable at three-and-twenty, and so averse to gaieties, that her aunt feared she would never act up to her position, unless her habits of seclusion were broken, and had therefore forced herself to come on this journey with her. But there had been no real thaw till she heard of Vale Leston and met Robina. Wilmet was not a little gratified by hearing, at second-hand, Lady de la Poer's praise of the young governess as a valued friend; and it was plainly to her charge that the precious niece was committed.

When the visit took place, the Countess was soon forgotten in the companion. At first, Felix was a little ceremonious, and she a little shy, watching the family party as if they were acting a play; but as the strangeness wore off, she began by being diverted, though silent from long disuse of family chatter, and soon plunged in, with as droll and eager a tongue as ever wagged.

Then Cherry found her face quite unlike her first reading of it, and had to begin all over again. It was altogether, as Bernard said, a jolly time. That young gentleman was, for the first time, smitten. His devotion to himself and cricket had never before been disturbed; and he had reached his eighteenth year without regarding woman as intended for any purpose but to wait upon him. But bright eyes, merry smiles, genuine fun, and mayhap the rank that gratified his vanity, began to avenge the wrongs of the sex; and Bernard was enslaved enough to amuse and edify his brothers and sisters—all the more, that the simple-hearted Countess was perfectly unconscious, thought herself immeasurably older than the great, handsome, idle fellow—half an inch taller than the Vicar, by-the-by—stood on no conventionalities with him, and when released by her task-mistress, would run down-stairs to call him, nothing loth, to give her a row on the river, to blow away the fumes of the painting-room. Quite unawares, she effected a victory for Felix; for when she assumed that since he was going to Oxford it must be to Keble College, and he found that she regarded it as very stupid to do anything else, he entirely forgot all his former objections, and was only too happy to gratify her.

Even Clement expanded more than usual, for he had never met a more congenial spirit. Lady Caergwent's enthusiasm went much deeper than externals, for she was well read in Church history, and a practical worker in the present, being at Caergwent, that teacher, register office, manager, letter-writer, &c., which the lady-of-all-work to a parish must become, whether clerical or otherwise. 'There's Tina boring her with shop!' would Bernard mutter, in a paroxysm of jealousy.

'Quite the reverse,' said Angela. 'She is the most thorough Goody I ever came across, not excepting Clan Hepburn!'

It was not with any design of captivating sympathy, but because Lady Caergwent had an unusual number of interests, and was intensely eager about each in turn. Landlord cares were discussed with Felix, as Church matters were with his brother. She was too headlong and unguarded not often to say ridiculous things, but nobody more enjoyed having them caught up and laughed at; and when Felix had made gentle fun of some of her impetuous political economy, she looked up to him like an elder brother. With the sisters she was soon as much at ease as in the De la Poer schoolroom, making Robina her friend *par excellence*, but apparently observing Angela, who, having no one to flirt with, was at her best, and was drawn out by the 'Goody' sympathies.

'Robina,' said Lady Caergwent, entering her friend's room at that confidential moment, near 11.0 p.m., 'you know all about everything!'

To which monstrous assertion Robina assented.

The next question was equally abrupt. 'Do you know that Angela wants to go into a Sisterhood?'

'Oh! I thought that had gone off.'

'No, indeed! It is to be a very strict nursing one;' and as Robina smiled a little, 'I cannot but believe I know the cause.'

'It always used to come on when she was going to be particularly naughty.'

'Robina, I can't understand it in you; you do not seem like an elder sister to pooh-pooh all higher aspirations in a younger one, or to have no sympathy with deeper feelings.'

'You will only think the worse of me for not believing in the deeper feelings,' said Robina; 'but indeed, I think I know Angela.'

'How odd it is! Then it is true that elder sisters never can do younger ones justice!' said Lady Caergwent, looking at Robin in a meditative kind of philosophical way, which made her laugh, and say, 'There, it is no use to say anything!'

'I would not, but that I am going away; and I want you to promise that if—if you see that any scruples hinder her happiness, you would tell her how entire all *that* is at an end.'

'If I do,' said Robina, much pitying, but much diverted at the romance that could ascribe either forbearance or self-sacrifice to Angela.

'*He* comes here, doesn't he?'

'He came down last summer, but I saw no symptoms of anything—to signify,' added her conscience; 'in fact, I think he prefers Cherry.'

'I hope,' said poor Lady Caergwent musingly, 'that some day or other, when we are all old women; Gracie, Addie, and I, may meet and smile at all that is gone and past. I can laugh now, even while I am sorry, to recollect my absurd presumption. I had the influence, delusion on my brain, and believed mine the only right way, and dragooned every one about wasting time. I am glad he asserted himself! What he has done since showed how nonsensical I was. Does he like his work? no one tells me.'

'You know what his chief said.'

'Oh! what?'

'To Mr. Welsh, the member for Ewmouth, so it is quite impartial—that he never had a better fellow to stick to his work, or more clear-headed. Yes! and we all think—here, I mean, as well as at Repworth—that he is so much more of a man. Felix really talks in earnest to him now, and so does his father. His nonsense is gone.'

'Oh, that's a pity.'

'I don't mean sensible nonsense, but you know his old absurd way.'

'Yes, of course that unlucky state of things was as bad as possible for him. He would have been the poorest stick in creation not to have broken loose. I have had a life-long lesson, and I hope it will save me from getting hard and narrowly resolute, as authority makes single women.'

'You could hardly do that with Mrs. Umfraville before you.'

'Hardly! dear Aunt Emily!' cheered and cheering all the while; 'as long as I have her, nothing can go *very* wrong with me. I never thought I could have enjoyed myself again away from her, as I have done here.'

'I am so glad, dear Kate!'

'If I could get any of you to Caergwent! But people are always going to be married.'

On the Sunday, William Harewood, now a deacon, descended from Penbeacon to church and dinner, with a train of five pupils, bringing intelligence that the senior, who had been at the original pic-nic, and was at Penbeacon for the last time, must leave it at the end of the week, and entreated that he might not miss the entertainment.

There was a general acclamation. Lady Caergwent was wound up to enterprise pitch, and, as an ardent botanist, was delighted with the flora she was told to expect there; and Cherry only bargained for time to make the pies and send for Lance. It was the only home-gaiety he would willingly partake, because they always kept it to themselves instead of making it serve as civility to the neighbourhood.

Lady Caergwent, after having much appreciated the Sunday-school in the loose boxes, looked on, rather bewildered, at Angela's 'carrying on' with four pupils at once, chattering, laughing, defying, and being defied, in a manner, which, if it dissembled grief, was wonderfully successful. To these was added young Charles Audley, coming up the river in his skiff, for Evensong.

'Ha, Charlie, you're in luck! Hurrah for Penbeacon!'

'Are you going? Then the Kittiwake sha'n't sail! I've missed your spread every time through that everlasting tub, and the Skipper shall hear reason!'

'Oh, I thought nobody asked you!'

'As if your sighs had not been wafted on the breeze!'

'Puffs to swell the sails and transport bad rubbish!'

'What day is it to be?'

'Wednesday; but you've got no ticket. We are desperately select.'

'By-the-by, you've got a regular tip-topper, haven't you? Old Patakake invited me under his breath to gaze at the Countess of Caergwent in Mr. Underwood's carriage.'

'Ay! but we are bound by awful pledges not to regale the country bumpkins with the sight of a real countess at feeding-time.'

'Then I shall repair to Harewood for an invite. Isn't this the girl that was booked for young De la Poer?'

'Most ineffable bosh! It went the round of the papers, and my brother sent it to Robin, who contradicted it flat. She'll never marry anybody, and he'll never marry her!'

'Indeed! Why so?'

'He was wanted to. Isn't that enough?'

'He *was* wanted to?'

'Yes, poor wretch! till he cut and ran for dear life, and never thought himself safe till he had got to the top of Penbeacon. That's the way you swells *doos* it.'

'I'm no swell, thank goodness!' said Charlie, chucking a stone into the river.

'No swell! A swell*ing* at least! I always regarded you as a sacred personage, condemned to *noblesse oblige*, and all that!'

'Catch it obliging me to what I don't choose!'

Such was the conversation, whose sounds would have amazed Lady Caergwent, even more than did the sight: not that there was intentional hypocrisy in Angela—she never acted a part, but showed herself exactly as she felt at the moment, 'only more so,' and the moments were so little in harmony.

Another person who was scandalized was Wilmet, who, in her capacity of chaperon, was spending the evening at the Priory; and when she found that this addition to the party was viewed as a matter of course, sought Felix out, and declared that she would have nothing to do with the affair unless it were made quite clear that Captain Audley was aware of the extent of the intimacy.

Felix himself had once or twice doubted whether some steps ought not to be taken, for the eldest brother having died and left only daughters, Charlie was heir to the baronetcy, and old Sir Robert and his wife had a reputation for haughtiness and exclusiveness. Their grandson never went near them if he could help it, only enduring a duty-visit by the help of shooting; and their son was even more slack, having, in fact, never entirely forgiven their coldness to his young and passionately-loved wife. If there should be anything more than fun and froth in all the quips and cranks, jokes and pranks, among the young people, there would assuredly be an explosion, and silence on his part might justly be deemed unfair encouragement. Maybe, his was an over-scrupulous mind, for he was already uneasy enough to make the strength of Wilmet's remonstrance unnecessary. The fact of another eye than his own having remarked it, was enough for him; and although he gave Mrs. Harewood little satisfaction at the moment, the next forenoon he jumped off his horse at her door, interrupting her unprosperous attempts at making her eldest son remember six times four—

'Five minutes, Mettie!—Yes, Kester, you shall ride round to the stables if you be off now.—I've asked Captain Audley to Penbeacon.'

'You don't mean that he will come?'

'Far from it; but it was the easiest way of suggesting that I wished him to see for himself.'

'With what effect?'

'That of being civilly shown that I was a fool for my pains.'

'Do you mean that he does not care?'

'Not a straw. I can't make out whether he thinks the Somerville-Audley blood beyond precaution, or whether it is all indolence, and dislike to hinder the boy's amusement.'

'Did you speak plain enough for him to understand?'

'Oh yes, he understood—very nearly laughed at me, and changed the subject. So now I must leave it; I can't forbid the young fellow the house, and a warning to Angel would only precipitate it.'

'It is hard that one's sisters should be sacrificed.'

'My dear, everybody is not as much *au grand sérieux* at that age as we used to be. The Skipper, as Charlie respectfully calls him, may be right, and there may be nothing in it; or if there should be, that Angel of ours has quite strength and spirit enough for a struggle, and maybe a disappointment. The truth is,' coming nearer, and looking mysterious, 'we know nothing at all about it, and had best let it alone.'

Wilmet's face of expectation melted into pardon for being teased; but Kester, shouting, 'Uncle Felix, come!' put an end to the conference, rather an odd one to be taking place at the moment when the Countess was beguiling the constraint of sitting, by dreaming over Isabel Bruce, and the magnanimity of rescuing the intended recluse by—Alas! she had never had a ring to throw at her feet—only that whisper which Robina seemed unwilling to convey.

CHAPTER XL.

A K T STROPHE.

> 'When shall we three meet again,
> In thunder, lightning, or in rain?'
> *Shakespeare.*

Lance did not appear on the evening before the picnic, and announced by letter, the next morning, that he could not get away. Felix regretted not having as usual changed places with him, but could hardly have absented himself from such a guest as the present without discourtesy; and Cherry, looking at the blunt brevity of the postal-card, feared that the high-sounding title of their new friend was adding to Lance's almost morbid sense of being in a different sphere from their surroundings. However, she had little time to think; for their only other guest, Gertrude May, had come by long promise to sleep at the Priory the night before; and the party were collecting in the hall, while the waggonet, a farm companion being allotted to the chestnut for the nonce, the Harewood phaeton, and Master Ratton with his basket, were marshalled at the door.

'The Vicar says there is going to be a thunder-storm,' said Lady Caergwent, in rather a solemn voice.

'The Vicar always has a thunder-storm coming whenever it isn't a fall of snow,' returned Bernard.

'Hush, Bear! Kate won't have the Vicar's name taken in vain,' laughed Angela.

'Angela! Is not that expression a rebuke to itself?' whispered Cherry.

'There's not a symptom of a cloud,' added Gertrude, 'but the heat is overpowering.'

'Yes!' said Cherry. 'Lance could hardly have gone in such scorching as this.'

'We shall find mountain-air at the top,' said Robina, 'when once we can get there.'

'And the storms there are magnificent,' added the deep voice of Clement, as he strode out in broad hat and alpaca coat, pausing to put his despatches into the letter-box, and inspect the barometer.

'Let that poor thing alone, Clem,' called out his eldest brother. 'We mean to enjoy ourselves.'

'Are you affected by thunder?' the Vicar asked, seeing that Lady Caergwent did not look very happy.

'Not affected really, but I don't like it at night, or out of doors,' she answered; 'but I don't think there can be a storm to-day.'

'Never saw weather less like it,' added Bernard decisively, gazing up at the sky, as if to dare it to thunder. 'Hollo, Charlie! what have you annexed!'

For Charles Audley appeared walking up from the river, very hot, and holding upon its back, like a baby, a huge blue lobster, which impotently flapped its fringed tail, brandished its claws, and waved its whiskers.

'What do you propose to do with that marine monster?' asked Cherry.

'Eat him, to be sure! He's my contribution. I bought him of old Jenny as I came up. Take care, Kester! he'll grab you as tight as the Mayor of Plymouth. Have you a basket, or anything to put him in?'

'He's alive,' said Cherry, recoiling.

'Of course. In civilian costume, you see. Of course the natives up there have some sort of kettle. I've done dozens of lobsters in the yacht.'

'What fun!' cried Angela. 'He shall go on the driving-box, to be made lobster-salad of. Get a basket; Kester, let his whiskers alone—ridiculous creature!'

'Oh!'

It was a soft little breath, but Charles turned round. 'You're not afraid of him, Stella! See! his claw is tied. Don't you like it?'

'I'm not afraid; but I don't like it.'

'Like Kate's thunder-storm,' laughed Angela; 'not afraid, but she doesn't like it.'

Stella stood her ground: 'I don't like keeping the poor thing in misery.'

'Nay!' said Angela. 'Why don't you send that cruel boy to restore it to its native element?'

'That would be nonsense,' steadily said Stella; 'but I think it would be kinder to have it killed at once, than to jolt it all the way up there.'

'Now, Charlie, it is absurd to yield to that child's tender-heartedness. She is a perfect Brahmin, and can't believe that those cold-blooded fishy things don't feel.'

'I believe the sentiment is general,' said Lady Caergwent, eagerly but nervously: 'though I had not the resolution of Princess Fair-Star,' she added, aside to Cherry; who rejoined, 'Not being sure whether it might not be the native custom to consume raw lobsters. Oh! here come Wilmet and Eddy; so let us pack. Lady Caergwent, do you prefer dignity or landscape? for that perch by my brother is the best for the latter.'

'Landskip, to be sure. You delightful person!' cried her Ladyship, springing to the driving-seat.

'May I invite you, not to our skip, but our springs, Cherry?' asked the Major.

'No, thank you,' said Cherry, who had seen a pair of wistful eyes lose one spark at the Countess's ascent, and another at this invitation. 'My springs rival yours; and Gertrude and I mean to be snug behind Master Ratton.'

Gertrude's face beamed delight as she took the other place; and the Vicar ingeniously coiled his length into the out-rigger at the back ready to spring out on any emergency of gate or hill, in spite of his apparent absorption in the newest and most strongly-flavoured of Church journals.

In consideration of Ratton's small capacities, he had the start, Cherry leaving the rest to pack as they chose; and when, on the first long ascent, she was overtaken, it was first by the Harewoods, the Major leading his horse, and Wilmet and her youngest son in front, Stella and Kester behind; and the foremost of the waggonet-load was walking beside, with his hand upon the back-seat.

The larger vehicle was empty, all but the driving-seat, where Lady Caergwent and Felix were talking so eagerly, that Cherry laughed, and said, 'I wonder what nut they are cracking?'

'Is she not dreadfully clever?'

'Most curiously simple. Whatever is in her head, out it all comes.'

'Your brother likes it!'

'There's a great deal of it, to be sure, but it is so original, and genuine, and funny; and besides, she is easily daunted. Robin says her uncle kept her in great order, but she was devotedly fond of him; and whenever she catches herself going too fast, she starts and stops, as if he were looking at her.'

'In order? Not a spoilt child and heiress—a Lady Clara Vere de Vere?'

'No, indeed! Lady Clara took Tennyson's advice, and began teaching the orphan boy to read, and the orphan girl to sew—operations she much prefers to entangling simple yeomen. Eh, Daisy! did you think she had a simple yeoman there?' said Geraldine, in an amused but rather indignant voice, as she perceived symptoms of confusion.

'Oh no, never really! but when one's brother has a sister-in-law who assimilates all the gossip of the place, one can't help hearing. If mouths could but be stopped!'

'Which they can't; but they can be confuted.'

'How, by her marrying?'

'Certainly not,' said Clement, from behind, much disconcerting Gertrude.

'I thought him lost in his ecclesiastical organ,' said Cherry, laughing. 'I believe nothing would have roused him but such an enormity with regard to his live Countess Marilda.'

'I merely think,' he protested, 'that Lady Caergwent perceives how much more she can do for the Church as a single woman.'

'I agree,' said Cherry, 'to the unlikelihood of her marrying—most especially, I know whom it won't be, let them have their heads together as much as they will. See them now—not a bit of the view will they see! That's right! prod them with your parasols! Make them look round, or they will miss the great view of the castle and the estuary.'

'Felix will never do that,' said Clement, 'He seems to me to value people according as they appreciate the scenery of the Ewe.'

'He never got over Marilda's knitting all the way up the river.'

'Or Mr. Bruce's saying, "You've a snug little box here, Mr. Underwood, if it wasn't so close to the river." Felix's face was a sight—just as he had got to the turn down the hill, which he says comes as a fresh delight to him whenever he comes home.'

'No wonder, there's nothing like it!' said Gertrude. 'Ah! they have stopped to look.'

'Click, click! gee-up, Ratton! we'll pass them again.'

So they did, Lady Caergwent calling out, 'Ah! I pity you. You are too low to see this glorious sight.'

'All very well talking,' called back Cherry; 'but who had to be poked to make them look at all?'

'Ay! What do you think they were doing!' shouted Angela. 'Sounds reached us about Casuistry and Jeremy Taylor.'

'You could hear nothing in the din that came up to us,' retorted Felix, looking round.

Indeed, Lady Caergwent was in her element. She liked nothing so well as a kind of discussion on character, a sort of fitful Friends in Council, plentifully interlarded with historical or fictitious allusions; but she did not often get the opportunity, for her historical tastes were so much more vivid than most of her contemporaries, that she always had to guard against seeming pedantic; but, thanks to Felix's habit of keeping a solid book in hand, and always thoroughly getting up whatever he had to write about, he was a man of great range of information, and could reply to her bright crude fancies with depth or sportiveness as occasion served, enjoying the tête-à-tête as much as she did.

Meantime, the horses climbed higher still and higher, rougher still and rougher, till the final gate was opened; the wheels emitted only an occasional creak on the soft bent-grass, and the breeze refreshed the travellers, who were soon hailed by all the pupils and all the dogs, and conducted to the Penbeacon saloon. This was a deserted slate-quarry, where the mounds of rubbish were old enough to be covered with hawthorn, mountain-ash, travellers-joy, and exquisite wreaths of bramble, so as to afford shade at any period of the day; and around was a delicious carpet of soft grass, thyme, eye-bright, ladies'-fingers, and rock-rose. Beneath lay the whole panorama of the Ewe valley and the estuary, the bridge spanning it, and the Castle jutting out into the sparkling sea, where here and there a sail, white or umber, or puff of steam, glided along the blue. The intense clearness of the air rendered the scene a fresh joy to those who knew it best, and entranced the new-comers, though they were told they would see it still better when they had climbed to the top of Penbeacon, which, with tracking the source of the Leston, was a regular part of the programme.

Operations could, however, only begin with preparations for the meal; and while Felix, Clement, and Major Harewood drove on to deposit horses and carriages at the farm, there was a general unpacking of hampers, Cherry securing that which was to be untouched till dinner-time, by sitting upon it.

'I say,' observed Will to Robina, as he opened one of the letters that they had brought up to this unpostal region, 'here's a go! He may be coming to-day!' and he signed towards Lady Caergwent, who, with Bernard, was compounding a salad.

'Impossible! To-day?'

'That depends.'

'Knowingly?'

'Not unless it be through you.'

'I have not written since she came.'

'So the daily fire has slackened.'

'Mr. Pemberton enjoys that.'

'And once a week is deemed enough for me!'

'Old stagers such as we are! But, seriously, Willie, what can bring him?'

'The scent of Penbeacon!'

'I thought he was in Scotland.'

'Yes, but his two months' holiday was up on Monday; and when he came to London, his office was painting, or white-washing, or something, so he got a week's grace; and London being a desert, he said he should look in at Lady Mary's, and then run on here; but when he left, doubtful.'

'Then it depends on how he likes it at Lady Mary's? Have you mentioned it?'

'No, I knew I should catch it from you if I did.'

'Discreet boy! I have hopes of you. In the uncertainty we had better keep it to ourselves. It would only put her into a tremor, and spoil her day.'

'Poor girl! I hoped it had gone off, for I see small prospect for her. He is getting on well, likes his work, and will hardly run into thraldom again, since he broke loose in time to make a man of himself.'

'Don't you envy him?'

'Yes, when you fiddle for an hour over every knot in that string! Let me cut it and have done with it.'

'Remember holy poverty, Sire, as the Lady Abbess said to Louis XV. over the jam-pot; or rather, remember that this has to be packed up again in six hours' time.'

'Don't make me remember six hours hence. This is my prime day of all the year, and I can't recollect any end to it.'

'There then, can you carry that pile of plates without a catastrophe?'

'A K T strophe is what is apprehended.'

'Come, you two,' called Angela, 'affection is misplaced over the crockery. Here are plates wanted to weigh down the table-cloth; there's a ruffling gusty wind that gets under it.'

'Illustrating the earthquake theory,' said pupil No. 1, who was keeping it down with his knee.

'Or thunder-storm practice,' responded Pupil No. 2.

'Not a word more about thunder!' cried Angela. 'Lady Caergwent hates it; and as she views our Vicar as a mild embodiment of all the General Councils, the regular Clementine prediction has upset her already. I say! what are you doing? Apricot-tart at first course!'

'Apricot-tart, you don't say so! Three cheers for Miss Underwood!'

'Don't let blind enthusiasm put its foot into it.'

'Or you'll have to eat it all.'

'What a temptation!'

'Wasn't he already a greedy beggar, who stuck at no trifles! Don't you remember his tucking in the apples at the fair that the elephant wouldn't have?'

'And swallowing nineteen fresh eggs to clear his voice for the concert!'

'I say, Miss Underwood, what songs have you brought?'

'And what's to become of the Der Freischütz song without your brother Lance?'

'Can't the Squire take his part? His voice is a capital one.'

'Oh yes—he is thrush to Lance's nightingale—not so high—fuller in the lower notes—and he can't play such tricks with it,' said Angela; 'but whether you'll get him is another thing. That Countess of ours has no more music in her than an owl!'

'Can't she be suppressed? Whoever heard of a Penbeacon picnic without a song?'

The feast took place with all the merriment produced by the combined forces of seventeen people, not one of whom had reached the middle point of life; but when it was over, the sun was still so powerful, and the air so sultry, as to bring to mind that this festival had taken place earlier in the year than usual. No one was willing to quit the luxurious nests in the bracken, and the ceremony of mountain-scaling was deferred till after the songs for which the pupils clamoured, and Lady Caergwent heartily said how unlike fine old songs in the open air would be from the tiresome drawing-room performances, that seemed to her an invention for interrupting interesting conversation. In the pause of preparation, she made, however, some inquiries whether the arrow-head she had been told about grew on the intended path, and if not, how it could be reached.

'I'll show you the way,' cried Bernard eagerly. 'It is only down there,' when he heard the place.

'*Only!*—my dear Kate! I don't let him inveigle you—it is nearer two miles than a mile and a half,' said Robina; 'and all through stony thickets and bogs—and in this heat! We will try to drive you there, or send for it.'

'I'll go; I'll be back long before they've done singing,' said Bernard. 'What is it like?'

Lady Caergwent hesitated; but he would take no refusal, and having been told it was white, had three roundish sort of petals, and arrow leaves, and grew in the water, the lazy youth, who would seldom move an inch in a sister's service, went striding down the hill side, with his coat over his shoulder, and his pugaree streaming behind him. Cherry was afraid he would incur Lance's fate; but Felix laughed, and said he was glad to see he could do anything for anybody; and besides, the sun was becoming less fierce.

So Cherry hastily sketched his retreating figure as a feature in the drawing she annually made of the group at the quarry during the music. Gertrude May had a fair ear, and good though not much trained voice, and she was exceedingly happy, for even without Lance the Underwoods' singing was a remarkable and beautiful thing. To make William into Polyphemus, and hear him thunder out 'Ruddier than the cherry,' while Felix and Angela served as his Acis and Galatea, was always a part of the programme, and it was all Wilmet enjoyed, for were not her boys—even though they were hers—boys of the period? Had not her son Edward come, against her better judgment, because his papa wished it? and had not his combined fatigue and restlessness come to a pitch where there was nothing for it but to take him away to the farm-house, and let him have the sleep he had missed in the forenoon?

Then, even in her first outline, Cherry missed three figures; and when, after completing her general sketch, she returned to touch up the individuals, Kester, who had been portrayed running up and down a mound with the dogs, was asleep against his father; nothing was to be seen of Will but a pair of black knees peeping out of the bracken, and the head of Scamp's brother Chaff, who was sitting on his breast; and Lady Caergwent had vanished altogether. She was further becoming sensible that the shadows were less sharp, the light less clear, the heat heavier, and presently that a great black cloud had mounted far into the sky behind the quarry and the hill; and beginning to think that Clement's prognostications might be justified she was waiting for the end of Lance's setting of 'Mont Blanc is the King of Mountains,' to call attention to the fact that Penbeacon was borrowing his vest of cloud, when the announcement was made by a vivid flash of lightning, followed with appalling rapidity by a peal of thunder. No one stirred till the thunder had rolled itself away. Then everybody said, 'There!' and started up, just as a few big rain-drops splashed down. Kester woke with a scream of fright; and his father, throwing a plaid round him, ran off with him towards the farm. Felix and Clement had both sprung to Geraldine, and were helping her up. There was a mile of open hill and stony road to the farm—a long walk for her under any circumstances; and no one had any protection bigger than a sun-shade. There was another terrific flash and burst of thunder, and the hail-stones came rattling down, so large as to give sharp blows.

'She can never walk it,' said both brothers at once. 'Cherry, you must ride!'

'Oh!' gasping, 'you can't.'

'Can't we? Haven't we often? There!' and in a moment the hands were clasped, queen's-cushion fashion, beneath her, the necks were bent for the arms to be thrown round them, even as had been done many a time in childhood before, only then Edgar had generally been one supporter. She hardly felt the beating of the pitiless storm; and when the wind, hail and roar of the tempest came with a terrific deafening whirl, she felt a strange sense of security; and even when the most fearful of all the flashes seemed to burst into the ground close before them simultaneously with the discharge like a thousand cannon overhead, and she heard Clement's whispered ejaculation, her first feeling was, 'All together—together!'

The others all darted past them in the general *sauve qui peut.* Wilmet, watching in anxiety at the farm-house porch, received first, half laughing, half panting 'Oh! isn't it jolly?' Angela and the longest-legged pupil; secondly, her husband, with their little son in his arms. 'This is like an Indian storm,' he said, and sat down, a good deal spent, and breathing hard.

Then came, dashing in together, the main body—Gertrude May, four pupils, Stella with Charles Audley; and they had no sooner recovered breath, than in came William and Robina, who had been delayed by Robina's attempt to secure the table-cloth, which had been blown so entirely over her, that Will had had some difficulty in releasing her from the flappings. They satisfied Wilmet that Cherry and her bearers were quite safe, and at the entrance of the lane; and John thereupon started up, and declared he should go and relieve them, but at that moment they were seen at the gate, Cherry on her own legs, and Felix and Clement, all in a glow, on each side of her. 'It was so nice,' she said, as her sister anxiously met her. 'Only think of having two such brothers! Oh no, I'm not frightened—no, nor in the least wet!'

Nobody was wet, for the hail-stones had rebounded, and one or two that had been captured were wonders worth preserving, had that been possible, looking like nitre-balls. Felix was drawing a pencil line round one on a piece of paper, when Robina exclaimed, 'Where's Lady Caergwent?'

'Didn't she come first?'

'I thought she was up-stairs.'

'No—no one came in before Angela,' testified Wilmet. 'Is every one else here?—Bernard?'

'He must be sheltering down by Lang's pool. Never mind him! But she! So afraid of thunder too!'

'Unpardonable!' burst out Felix, in dismayed self-condemnation, as he again pushed his head as deep as it would go into his hat, and hurried out again, Clement and William after him; John was going too, but his wife caught him—'No, no, there are quite enough! Remember the neuralgia. See, it has turned to pouring rain!'

And John submitted, for three strong men could do all that could avail one young girl, even under possibilities terrible to think, not only from the lightning, but among those dangerous places, steep slopes, and sharp precipices, where a stranger, blinded by hail and lightning, might so easily stumble. The farmer was at market, and his wife could only offer her 'odd man' when he should have done milking; but Mr. Harewood knew the place thoroughly by this time.

It rained in torrents as they set out, the thunder-cloud blotting out all but the path under their feet, though the lightning was more distant. They searched the quarry, and shouted, 'Any one here? Lady Caergwent!' But the mocking echoes only answered, 'Here!' and 'Gwent!' while they searched in vain—till 'Holloa.' Was it a response? Felix shouted. Another 'Holloa!' but hardly from feminine lungs—certainly not from any one suffering any damage. No—there was something tall struggling up the hill through the rain. 'Bear! you've not seen her?'

'Who? Why in the name of wonder are you getting a shower-bath gratis out here?' said he, panting up to them, his arms full of something shiny, and battered, and green; and, as a word or two explained—'Looking for Lady Caergwent! Every one missed her'—the boy's eyes flashed so that Felix really thought he was going to knock him down. 'Left her out here? Why, savages wouldn't have done it! If I had but been there! Dear, sweet girl!'

Just then, something dark was seen lying under a rock, and slightly moving; Clement silently pointed in horror, Bernard gave a sort of howl, waved them all back as unworthy to touch her, and leapt forward. He soon came to a stand-still. It was one of the rugs on which they had been sitting, which had drifted there, rolled up by the wind.

'I begin to hope she may be in the cart-shed,' said Will. 'Let us go on there.'

Bernard strode with a certain tragic authority in advance, as they proceeded, scrambling over a low stone wall into a steep sloping field, scattered with stones and sheep, not easily discernible from one another in the downpour, save for some getting up and running away, while the others remained motionless. At length appeared a fabric of rough stones, rougher piles, and roughest slates, a kind of shelter thrown over the angle of the wall. Through all the rush and roar came a murmur of voices, and through the drifting streams of rain, two figures were discernible, one heather-coloured, the other grey. So much the others had seen, when Bernard, with a sort of tiger-bound forward, shouted, 'You rascal!—Never mind, Lady Caergwent, I am here!'

'Holloa, Bernard!' said a cool voice.

'De la Poer!' and Bernard stood transfixed, not even joining at first in the general clamour of, 'So shocked!' 'You here!' 'How could we miss you?' 'I never was so sorry!' 'It was all my own fault!' 'Oh, never mind,' &c.; but when his voice was heard again, 'Lady Caergwent, if I had been there, this should never have been! These brothers of mine!'

'Not a word more till she is safely housed,' interposed Felix. 'Don't you see how drenched she is?—Will you trust yourself to me after this inexcusable neglect, Lady Caergwent?'

'I told you it was I who lost myself,' she said, with a most forgiving radiance in her eyes, glancing through the dark hair that flew about her hatless head.

They wrapped her in the cloak they had brought, and tied the hood down over her hair with a handkerchief; but when Bernard would have proffered his arm on the side unengrossed by Felix, he found himself forestalled, and could only fume in the rear—such of his denunciations of the general barbarous carelessness as were not blown down his throat again by the wind being received by Will Harewood, with comical little sounds that nettled him exceedingly.

156

The contention with wind, rain, stones, and torrents, was far too severe for any one else to attempt speaking, while the blast swept round the hill side as if trying to whirl them off their feet; and even when the lee side of the barn was reached, Lady Caergwent was too breathless to do anything but gasp out that Mr. Underwood must not blame himself—it was her own fault, and all right.

A whole cluster of anxious faces crowded the deep porch, to receive the dripping figures that came in, looking, as the delighted Kester said, like the cats that became pools in Strewelpeter. Some used their first breath for laughter, others for the long pent-up apologies, which were cut short by Wilmet and Robina bearing the young lady up-stairs to be dried.

The room was homely, for their hostess was not of the advanced order, and had no fine daughters. She appealed to Mrs. Harewood on the expediency of bed, warm water, and something hot; but the Countess, her eyes dancing through her plastered elf-locks, laughed all to scorn, only begging for the loan of some clothes. However—will she, nill she—while struggling with the soaked adhesive sleeves of her jacket, a foot-bath and big ewer, and a tray of various beverages, made their appearance, putting her into fresh fits of mirth, as Robina tugged at the refractory garment, and Mrs. Hodnet endeavoured to add lumps of sugar at every polite refusal of the negus.

'Lady Caergwent, the bed or the negus?' said Wilmet, at last, with full authority.

'The dagger or the bowl? The bowl then, if you please, when my hand comes out. I'm like Agamemnon now. Oh!—there!—thanks, Copsey. I hope the rest of the coats of the onion will come off easier. Thank you! oh, so much, Mrs. Hodnet! That will be beautiful!'

Herself of the squarest proportions, Mrs. Hodnet was bustling about to find something wearable by the tall slim girl. At last, after her best violet silk had been found impracticable, a linsey skirt and a soft silk shawl seemed possible materials; and she withdrew to superintend the preparations for tea; and Wilmet departed likewise, from the mixed motives of believing that the two girls wanted to be left to a *tête-à-tête*, of uneasiness as to the whereabouts of her sons, and desire to secure the swallowing of the like portion by Felix and Clement.

The moment the door was shut, Lady Caergwent threw both arms round Robin, and hugged her tight, with a long sob-like sound of 'O Copsey, Copsey!'

'Then it was—'

'Yes—yes—yes! Did you know?'

'Willie told me he might possibly come; but it was too uncertain to mention. We thought Lady Mary would be sure to keep him.'

'Mary was from home.'

Robina longed to ask more, but did not quite know how, and applied herself to make the best of Mrs. Hodnet's toilette apparatus, in dealing with the hair, which the tempest had deprived of every fragment of head-gear. 'Shall I twist it, or do it up in long plaits?'

'Any way for me to get down again! Oh, how little I thought it!'

'Felix was in despair when he found you were missing; but you see the first thought of all my brothers has always been Cherry.'

'Quite right—and you see I wasn't there at all. You know my ears are stupid, and though there's more sense in your music than in most people's, it did not put out of my head some marsh-cinquefoil I thought I had spied as we went by; and I fancied, while you were singing, I could creep off after it, without all the fuss of the gentlemen wanting to get it for me. No one saw me, and I did find some delicious things, only I'm afraid I lost them. On I went, from one to another, like the bad folks in an allegory, away from the rocks and the singing, lured by the flowers in the bog—till, sure enough, I lost my way, and the sharp wall of rock above me, which I thought part of the quarry, turned out to be no such a thing. There, to bring in the demoniacal element, a horrid little black cow came up and stared at me. You know what a goose I am about horned monsters; and I thought the whole herd would be coming home to be milked, so I didn't stare the beast out of countenance, as I am aware is the correct thing; but as there was a high ledge, a sort of shelf in the precipice, I scrambled up out of the way. I suppose the animal had never seen a young woman in such a position, for not only did it stand in contemplation, but two or three of its congeners came up and stood gazing at me, out of their spiteful, curly, shaggy faces, with white pointed horns, like the imps of the piece. Then it struck me that these were not quiet christianable kine going home to be milked, but horrid Scottish cattle at pasture, keeping no hours at all, but free to stand staring till I dropped on their horns. So I put whatever dignity I had in my pocket, and squalled, fancying you were all round the corner, but the only effect was to make the brutes toss their heads and stare the harder.'

'Did you see the storm gathering? Behind the hill, as we were, we neither saw nor thought of it till that first grand peal; I was so sorry for you.'

'Somehow, I minded it less than I should have thought. The grandeur and the solitude took some of the nonsense out of me; but the hail was very bad; it knocked me about so; and the wind tore at me like a human fury. After my hat was carried off, those hail-stones would have been quite dangerous, but that there was a good thick bower of traveller's joy (well-named) up above; and one comfort was, the demons didn't like it, stuck up their tails, and galloped off. I thought none of them could have the face to run at me in a thunder-storm, and I tried to come down, but I found it was a Martinswand on a small scale; and I could get neither up nor down. So I remained, the butt of the elements, waiting to make another effort till the wind would let me alone. At last, I saw a human being in the distance, battling with the wind. I thought it was Bernard coming back, or if not, I was past caring; so I called, and it came. I only thought of Bernard, and it must have thought itself in for an adventure with an escaped lunatic, or wild woman of the woods. "Trust yourself to me," he said; and then I knew the voice. But it was like a dream, for I didn't seem surprised at first. At least, I don't know; I think I must have made a fool of myself somehow, for he was coaxing and comforting me, till somehow he got me to the shed, and I came to my senses a little, and thought he was only pacifying me; so I asked whether I had really been in such a dreadful state, and said I was all right, and that he need not go on. "Why should I not go on?" he said. Oh, I dare say it was very nonsensical—but don't you and Mr. Harewood talk nonsense sometimes?'

'Egregious!' said Robin, laughing, and kissing her. 'Oh, I am so very very glad, dearest!'

'He said, the longer he went on, the more he found he really did care for me in spite of it all, horrid and disgusting as I had been.'

'Was that the nonsense?'

'No, you thorny Copse, but his pretending I was all right!'

'Ah, he has thought so this long time! I have been sure it wanted very little to come right.'

'Oh, tell me! for while they were dragging me through the storm, it came over me that maybe he was just surprised into it, and that I ought—I ought not—'

'Who is talking nonsense now, Kate? No—if you had been at Repworth you would have seen how altered he has been—ill at ease, as if something had gone out of his life—only able to bear his restlessness by hard work.'

'Ah! is it not a pity to spoil him for his work?'

'You will find him work enough.'

'Make him a land-agent!'

'A good deal more. You will give him power that he is much fitter to use now.'

'Well, there's plenty to come before that. Dear Aunt Emily! I say, Robina, nobody ought to be told before them all, you know. There, thank you! what a deliciously queer figure,' as she looked in the glass, 'and what a pair of cheeks! The farm-house port has flown into them! Am I to put on these stockings? That dear woman's legs must be as big as her bed-posts! I wish people wore peasant costumes here! A pair of horse-hair butterfly's-wings now on my head, a striped petticoat, and orange stockings! At least it is better than when I jumped into a pond out of the way of the thunder, and Lady de la Poer put me to bed! Dear people! I could jump, but for these elephant-slippers, to think of getting back to them.'

'Oh, please—let me get that skirt straight.'

'Very well! Do I fidget horribly? I beg your pardon, Robin; but how can one stand still when one is all fizzing with gladness! When I think of the old ache, when he came here—and when I found it was not you, I thought it must be Angel—I really came, hoping to find out, and—'

'Throw the ring at her feet!'

'You witch! only I never had the ring to throw! Oh, this is much better than being magnanimous! Is that your ring? His hair? How charming! Ernest shall give me nothing else!'

'Ah, there will not be time for yours to wear out! Mine has had two renewals, though I always keep part of the old foundation.'

'Dear Robina! I wish—no, it's not right to wish that; besides, it's a horrid place. I suppose Mr. Pemberton must have the first living that is going at Repworth.'

'Yes. We think of a grammar-school, or a mastership, somewhere, when Willie's five years at Christchurch are up, and we have made up enough for a nest-egg.'

'That's what I should like! Ah! am I talking of what I know nothing about?' and she gave an earnest kiss. 'There, I'm presentable now! May Ernest only be in the farmer's leathern gaiters!'

'No chance of that, with so many gentlemen to equip him. But for your feet, you would do very well.'

For the fault of Kate Caergwent's face was want of glow, and this was fully supplied. The two plaits were picturesque, and Mrs. Hodnet's shawl of crimson silk, and the dark skirt, made a becoming garb; but walking was not easy, and the descent of the stair was a series of flaps, as she came into a sort of vestibule, containing staircase and big clock.

'Hermione descends to the sound of soft music!' exclaimed Lord Ernest, springing up to meet her; and they both stood still to laugh.

'Hail, hail, all hail! was the music,' she said.

'Yes, Miss Underwood,' grasping her hand mightily. 'I give you infinite credit for the *mise en scene*.'

'Undeserved!'

'Nay, stage-effect could not have been exceeded, though perhaps things went rather to the verge of sensation.—Katie, you are flushed still! Ought she not to be put between blankets, and dosed with water-gruel?'

'Then we ought "all to have a little water-gruel!"'

'There's a sumptuous tea-fight preparing in there. They've fetched the hamper, and Mrs. Hodnet is producing all the delicacies of the season!'

'Is Lady Caergwent there?' and Bernard came forward to meet her; while Lord Ernest paused to answer Robina's congratulating eyes. 'Yes, when I found that it was her own self, there was no helping it. I forgot all about earning her better opinion. I could only ask her forgiveness. I shall tell my father I owe it all to you.'

'Nonsense!'

'I do, though. If you hadn't all been what you are, I should have made an irrevocable ass of myself.'

'As—oh dear!—some one else is doing,' said Robina to herself, as she caught the words Bernard was addressing to the Countess, standing in the door-way of the great farm kitchen. 'I am only sorry for what you were exposed to in my absence.—My brothers are dreadfully cut up about it, but I know you'll overlook it. They are excellent fellows, but you see they have never had any advantages.'

An ineffably funny glance passed between Lord Ernest and Robina, who had a strong desire to take Mr. Bear by the shoulders and shake him, only unluckily her head was only on a level with those same broad shoulders.

'I never could have overlooked it, if they had left Geraldine to look after any one else,' said Lady Caergwent, with some of the hauteur she could assume, and very decidedly moving forward, but with the flowers in her hand that Bernard had brought her.

The party far exceeded the capacities of Mrs. Hodnet's parlour, where the lodgers usually sat, and were much more happily disposed of in the great kitchen, one of those still flourishing in old farm-houses, spacious though low, with a stone floor, a long oak table, and benches and a dresser glittering with metal and fine old earthenware, a great hearth with a lively fire, and a deep latticed window making quite a little chamber, where stood the small round table and two chairs, the leisure resort of Mr. and Mrs. Hodnet, the one with pipe and paper, the other with work-basket of socks. A door opening into the serviceable kitchen revealed a vista of garments hung up, a red glow behind them, a girl of the farm-servant type scuttling about, and the more active spirits of the party darting to and fro. In the room the long table was laid for tea; Cherry and Will were chatting on either side of the fire, Major and Mrs. Harewood were enjoying the delight of their offspring in an oft-renewed fiction of being shut into the hamper, lost, and discovered; and Felix was amusing Gertrude May with the mysteries of Moore's Almanac on the wall, and the account of his own fruitless endeavours to promote a taste for something less oracular.

He came up as the Countess scurried in, and said, with a frankness not quite answering to Bernard's description of his despair, 'I am very sorry for our neglect, Lady Caergwent, I am afraid it caused you to be in a very unpleasant predicament; but my sister is so far from strong, that she is apt to be our first care.'

'It would be a horrid shame if she were not,' said Lady Caergwent brightly. 'I should not have been and gone and lost myself!—You've not caught cold, Geraldine!'

'Oh no, I was best off of all, riding home in state. It comes, you see, of taking such poor shiftless beings up to the top of mountains.'

'It was a grand adventure,' said Lady Caergwent, rather hastily; 'I'd not have missed it for the world!' And then suddenly conscious of what that might convey, her colour deepened still more, and she made her way to the Darby and Joan nook by the window, sat down, looking out, and murmuring something undeveloped about the weather. Lord Ernest came to help her study it; Felix thought it expedient to continue his elucidations of Francis Moore; Robina came up to the fire, and slid her hand into Will's, and a look and smile passed between them that Cherry comprehended as well as they did. Only Bernard came forward with a footstool he had routed out from under the dresser. 'Won't you have this, Lady Caergwent? the floor is cold.'

'Thank you very much.—Yes; and Addie finds her hands full?'

'She's the jolliest little lady of the house!' and Lord Ernest found himself a perch on the round table, with one foot on the other chair.

Bernard returned to the charge. 'Here's one other flower not beaten to pieces,' he said, after applying to the green things he had left in the porch.

'Thank you,' but hardly turning her head from Lord Ernest, who was describing some one as 'Yards high, of course; three inches beyond what any one need be in reason,' meaning of course the Scottish chief; but Bernard was not quite sure whether this was not personal, for conceit in a state of irritation can make strange appropriations.

While he was standing just so far away as his sense of good breeding required, grim and discomforted, Angela darted in, crying, 'Mrs. Hodnet is teaching us to make furmenty. Come and see.'

'Too many cooks may spoil furmenty as well as broth, Angel,' said John, as no one seemed disposed to move.

'How stupid you all are!' she exclaimed. 'Come, Kate, don't you want to study furmenty?'

'I can't study anything but sitting still till I get my boots,' said the Countess, with languid decision.

'Bootless toil,' murmured her cavalier.

'You'd better come, Lord Ernest,' persisted Angela, 'Enlarge your mind! 'Tis a classical dish, always made on wake days.'

'Thank you, I never presume to enter those penetralia,' he answered, likewise with unconscious distance in his tone—excited, perhaps, by the familiar abbreviation of the young lady's name.

'If you are so curious about it, Angela,' said Felix gravely, 'I wonder you do not attend to it!'

'Oh, it is stirring! I left Charlie at it, to console him for the loss of his lobster. I only came out of pure and unrequited philanthropy.'

And she sprang back to the outer kitchen, philosophizing, 'What a queer thing it is that when two swells get together they must be on their dignity, and act as if they came out of some other planet.'

'Better be a swell than a cinder,' said Charlie. 'Mrs. Hodnet, is this stuff stirred enough? I've been at it like a galley-slave till my arms are ready to drop.'

'I'll stir the infirmary!' loudly declared Kester, intercepted on his way by his uncle Will, who hoisted him up, in an ecstasy of amusement, as a 'true grandson of his grandmother, which he wasn't.' The two rooms resounded with merriment, and Felix regaled Gertrude with a few of Mrs. Harewood's proverbial malapropisms; but the pair in the window remained utterly unconscious of all that was passing.

'The odd thing is,' said Angela confidentially to Charles Audley, 'that I know those two regularly hate each other.'

'It looks very like it!'

'Oh, that is to keep up appearances before the outer barbarians. I know what each thinks of the other. You clumsy boy! those plates will all be down, then what will you say to Cherry?'

'That I am overcome by appearances. What hollowness do you not reveal to me! I say, Bear must be overcome too! What makes him stand there like a grisly monument?'

Kester and Edward were, at that moment, permitted to summon the company by a performance with the bright warming-pan, as if they were hiving bees; and as Lord Ernest jumped off the table, with a look of fury and dismay Bernard pounced on Stella, who happened to be near him, and almost dragged her out into the porch. 'I can't stand it any longer, Stel. Say I'm gone home.'

'Are you ill, Bear?'

'Ill? no; but that confounded puppy—'

'He isn't lost, Bear, he is fast asleep under Cherry's chair. You need not go after him!'

'Hang it! Didn't you see? That brute of a fellow has been and squashed all the flowers! I'm sure he did it out of spite, and be hanged to him!'

'Hush, Bernard, don't!'

'A man can't mince his words when he's driven distracted! When I went through fire and water to get them for her, and it was all his jealousy, because he saw her pleased.'

159

'But I don't think those were your flowers.'

'Weren't they, though!'

'I thought you went to get arrow-head?'

'Well—'

'And that is great water-plantain on the table. There are quantities of it by the churchyard.'

'She never said it was not right.'

'Perhaps she would not vex you.'

'Bosh! You don't know anything about it, Stella; I'll soon find out.'

So Bernard stalked back, followed by his little sister, just as seats were being taken, with no further exclusiveness, but with the Countess on one side of Felix, and Gertrude on the other, and Lord Ernest by Geraldine's side. They had tried to get Mrs. Hodnet's company, but she would not consent to do anything but fry rashers for them.

'Lady Caergwent,' said Bernard's voice, 'were those the wrong flowers?'

A silence. 'You were very kind to get them for me.'

'Then they weren't arrowhead?'

A still more awful silence. 'Oh! let me see, where are they? Perhaps—'

'Lord Ernest de la Poer sat down upon them,' returned Bernard, in such a tragic voice, that convulsions of suppressed laughter began to prevail; 'but here are the remains, such as they are.'

'I am very sorry,' said the Countess, more than half choked as the faded, squeezed, limp water-plant was extended to her; 'but I can't flatter you that it is—no—it is not arrowhead.'

'Arrowing, isn't it?' of course muttered the witty pupil.

'But it was just as kind in you,' proceeded Lady Caergwent, conquering her paroxysm, and looking up with great sweetness in her hazel eyes. 'You went all the way for it, and were caught in the storm, and I am just as grateful to you.'

'You shall have some before I sleep!' and he was off like a shot.

'Oh! he isn't really gone!—Stop him, Mr. Underwood!—Stop him, Ernest!—How can you all sit there laughing!'

'It will do him a great deal of good.'

'Felix!' cried Cherry reproachfully from the other end of the table; 'when the poor boy has had nothing to eat!'

'And he's got my new boots on,' ejaculated Pupil Number 2. 'They'll punish him.'

'It's a great deal too bad,' said Lady Caergwent, flushing up. 'Cherry, what can I do? Indeed, it wasn't on purpose.'

'Don't you think he could be stopped, Felix!' entreated Cherry, tender over her boy. 'Is not there some short way to the garden?—Willie!'

'Impossible, Cherry,' said Will. 'No doubt he will go home instead of coming back here.' And to his neighbour—'Don't distress yourself. It is the first time I ever saw Bernard stirred out of the grand simplicity of his *self*-devotion.'

'Where's the Vicar?' broke in Lord Ernest, while Lady Caergwent looked far from consoled. 'You've not sent him after any water-weeds, have you?'

'No, a vicar never gets a clear holiday in his own precincts.' said Will. 'I've rigged him out to go to some cottagers up here—and if they know him for their shepherd, it's a pity.'

For besides being a shorter and more loosely-built man, the Oxford tutor, though not unclerical, had not the peculiar ecclesiastical look of the Vicar of Vale Leston.

'What have you done to Bernard?' said the voice of Clement himself, as he came in, certainly a good deal transformed. 'I met him galloping down the lane, and saying he should walk home, and you were not to wait for him.'

'You didn't turn him back? O Clement!'

'He hasn't quarrelled with any one?' said Clement, anxiously surveying the ranks; 'he wouldn't tell me.'

'Only with humanity in general,' said Felix. 'He brought Lady Caergwent the wrong plant, and has rushed headlong to repair the mistake, without knowing a bit better what the right one was. It is his first essay in chivalry, and he is having it strong,' he added, smiling, as he turned to the lady.

'Never mind, Kate,' added Angela, with her usual questionable taste, 'it's only a bog and not a whirlpool that you've made him plunge into; besides, it isn't the Ewe, so he isn't due to it!'

'Will you take his place in the waggonette, Lord Ernest?' asked Cherry. 'Where's your bag?'

'My bag—I declare it must be at the bottom of the Lady's Rock! We'll charter a boy to go and look for it.'

'We will stop as we go by. There are plenty of relics to pick up.'

'For hospitality's sake,' said Will, 'I might mention that the room next the Apple-chamber is at your service.'

'Thank you, since you are so kind, Miss Underwood, I'll come. I want to see your picture. What are you doing now?'

'A little portrait work,' said Cherry, smiling and blushing, and looking towards her subject.

'There,' quoth Lord Ernest, to Robina. 'Did not I tell you it was a Kit-Cat-astrophe!'

'Oh!' said Gertrude, little aware of the by-play, 'I forgot to ask if you had been going on with Edith of Lorn?'

'The maiden all for-lorn,' was another aspiration of the witty pupil.

'That's just the usual aspect of the Maid of Lorn,' said John, 'only Geraldine hasn't done her at all, only the last flutter of her cloak.'

'Quite right,' said Lord Ernest; 'that young person always struck me as taking the oddest way of reclaiming her young man, by charging down the hill at the head of all the stable-boys, grooms, and helpers.'

'I confess,' said Felix, 'I should have been harder to seek after that exploit than when all the bridesmaids were singing.'

'No doubt,' said Will, 'he knew best. How often had she scratched his face in Artornish Hall?!'

In the midst of the laughter a low silvery voice was heard saying to her neighbour, 'Please read it. You really ought.'

'Only one does get it so thrust down one's throat in the Hebrides,' returned Charles; 'but I'll try.'

'I agree with you, Stella, it is almost profane of them,' said Lady Caergwent; 'only one plays with what one loves best.'

'The maiden all forlorn got the best of it at last,' said Angela.

Which made some of them blush, and others make a move to recover the remnants of the feast. Wilmet wanted to take her boys home to bed, since the rain had ceased, and the carriages were brought out.

'Shall I offer Master Ratton to those two?' asked Felix of Robina, 'or is it too barefaced?'

'As yet, till the elders know.'

'Then you must come with me in the basket, Bob. I shall make Clem drive the waggonette home; he knows the ground better than I do.'

There was a good deal of summer lightning all the way home: but Lady Caergwent, tightly packed into the waggonette, never started at the shimmering sheets of pale light. Nay, she loved them all the rest of her life.

And the arrowhead, which she found in a jug outside her door in the morning, received full justice, and was in fact the last botanical specimen ever added to her collection.

The proverbial 'dull elf' alone could fail to figure the ensuing days, with the semi-concealment of what everybody knew, but no one was supposed to know before the authorities. How Lady Caergwent sat up at untimely hours, pouring her heart out to Robina; how Bernard became melancholy and misanthropical, when cruelly snubbed by Lord Ernest—'I could have had some pity on him,' was the reply to a remonstrance, 'but for that speech about his brothers.' Angela, on the other hand, made such endeavours to rescue poor Lord Ernest from being bored, that Cherry, in constant fear of her exposing herself, told her how matters stood, when she became furious and scornful at his supposed weariness of toil, and the succumbing of his resolution. Clement endured it much better, being quite willing that any one but the clergy should marry, and knowing Lord Ernest well enough to believe that he would only make the lady a stronger pillar of the Church.

After a few fresh touches had given a new and different reading to the portrait, and after a Sunday of bliss that cost Will and Robina some gulps of envious philosophy, there was a return to the Hammonds, and a tremendous croquet party to kill off all the neighbourhood before Mrs. Umfraville's return.

That lady's thankful comfort was only alloyed by sorrow that her Colonel could not see the fulfilment of his chief wish, while she felt that the four years' estrangement had improved both in manliness and womanliness, in forbearance and humility, and the matrimonial balance would be far easier of adjustment.

Of course invitations and promises to attend the wedding were made in the heat of the moment, and these were kept in October by Felix and Geraldine as well as Robina, who a second time dazzled Lady Vanderkist by her appearance in the list of bridesmaids. It was the last thing before she, with the whole De la Poer party, went abroad for the winter for the sake of her little delicate pupil, Susan, who had been ordered to spend the winter in the Riviera; and ever considerate, when Lord De la Poer asked his daughter Grace's Mr. Pemberton to join the travellers at Christmas, he also asked William Harewood; and Robina was the best off, for the curate could not come when the tutor could.

Mrs. Umfraville made a great deal of Mr. and Miss Underwood at Caergwent, and they much enjoyed their visit; but it was always a subject of regret that these outer interests seemed to make Lance feel at a greater distance from them. Something was amiss, though it was not easy to make out what it was, and he never allowed that he was uncomfortable, nor weary of his bicycle or of Mrs. Froggatt.

CHAPTER XLI.

CHESTS AND HEARTS.

'Waketh a vision, and a voice within her
Sweeter than dreams and dearer than complaint—
Is it a man thou lovest, and a sinner?
No; but a soul, O woman! and a saint.'
Frederick W.H. Myers.

One snowy November night Lancelot caught cold, and aggravated the ailment during his organist's duties on Sunday so much, that though he resigned himself to Mrs. Froggatt's attentions on Monday, she soon found herself obliged to supplement them by Mr. Rugg's; and her letter on the Wednesday caused Felix to bring Angela to nurse him through a sharp attack of pleurisy, complicated with bronchitis.

All went well, and by the week before Christmas he was fit to be taken home, uniting in persuading Mrs. Froggatt that her care was necessary to him *en route*, chiefly because he and his brother could not bear to leave her to her widowed Christmas. She came, but nothing would induce her to stay beyond Christmas Day; nor would she even wait till Felix returned with the New Year to Bexley, to busy himself with the accounts, about which Lance was concerning himself too much for his good, writing such characteristic notes that when, half way through January, Felix came home, he was disappointed to find so little progress made towards recovery. The great musical brow, big blue eyes, straight nose, and brown hairiness, seemed to have lost the cheeks from among them: there was a weary yearning look in the eyes, and the whole demeanour was languid and dejected. Lance just crept into the painting-room at noon, and spent the afternoon by the drawing-room fire, talking a little at times, or amused by Wilmet's baby; but her boys were too much for him; and though he liked Stella's music, he was fretted by Angela's careless notes, and had not energy to play for himself. His voice indeed was scarcely serviceable even for speaking, and its absence always made him unhappy. A reader only in the way of business, books and newspapers were distasteful; and though he could not be ill-humoured, he was evidently a heavy burden to himself; sad and listless; he neither ate nor slept, and yet the actual symptoms were not unfavourable.

'He does not get on,' said Felix, as he and Clement stood consulting in the library.

'He sleeps so badly, and has two hours or so of bad cough in the early morning, and that seems to exhaust him for the day.'

'So you wrote, and I told Rugg, who said that would wear off gradually; but I cannot see that he is mending.'

'Nor does he think so,' said Clement.

'Rugg declares that there is no reason he should not entirely get over this, and he never gives any encouragement he can help. I shall not rest till May has seen him.'

'I should have sent if you had not been coming.'

'So he is low about himself, dear fellow! Have you had it out with him?'

'Nay, he seemed to me quite willing it should be so. If he is not, I don't know who should be! He never seems to have been from under the shadow of his cathedral. I believe he rather puzzled Miss Isabella the other day!'

'You don't mean that she has been at him?

'Yes, she affected an entrance when no one was on guard but poor little Stella, who was dreadfully upset, and told Cherry all about it. It seems the good lady is shocked at our all deceiving him.'

'And took it on herself to warn him?'

'And to inquire if he were a Christian, and into the foundation of his hope—all which he seems to have received as a kindness. Stella says he answered that he was quite aware of his condition, but he did not think there was much need to grieve himself or others over it. Indeed, she—Miss Isabella—told me herself that he is a heavenly-minded young man.'

'Yes, they met in the inmost heart of things, without battling on the outworks. When I look back at that boy's life, I do not feel as if I deserved him; I ought not to have let him sacrifice himself to that life at Bexley.'

'It was his own doing, poor fellow! and he sees his mistake.'

'None of us could realize at the time the force of contrast,' said Felix; 'indeed, I should have thought him the last person to have been affected by it.'

'I did not mean that only. I meant the higher service,' said Clement, making Felix suspect that his consolations had been so applied as to deepen the depression, and resolve the more to write to Dr. May.

So two days later, with a certain passiveness, as though the physician's visits were a matter of course, Lance, who had just finished his tardy toilette, obeyed the summons into the library, and submitted to the examination, which ended in an assurance that there was no tendency to pulmonary disease, and that care and patience would soon subdue the remains of his illness.

'Thank you, Sir,' in a perplexed half-incredulous tone, as he leant back, not troubling himself to ask a question as to the treatment.

Dr. May waited a little, then looked steadily into his face. 'Now, Lance, we doctors ask startling questions. You've not fallen in love?'

'Not particularly,' said Lance, without a particle of blush, even if he had had cheeks to blush with.

'What does that mean? Generally?'

'I never let myself go in for it. It was of no use.'

'Without letting yourself, then?'

'No, indeed!' returned Lance, almost petulantly; 'I never had the chance. How should I? It would have been something to care about.'

'This fellow does not half believe in me,' muttered the Doctor.

'Lance, do you remember consulting me before, when you thought your brains were addled by the sun-stroke?'

'They might as well have been, for any good I have done with them.'

'I thought you were one of the lights of Bexley.'

'A nice sort of light, and place too,' muttered he, with scant courtesy; but the Doctor caught an idea from the dull weary tone.

'It must be a dullish sort of life,' he threw out.

'Can't be helped,' in the same tone, almost conveying that it was merely his own affair. 'It was my own doing; and I've been like this before, and come round.'

'Your chest has been as sound as a bell before!' said the Doctor, with a little wilful misunderstanding.

'My chest,' with a sound of contempt.

'If not your chest, what?'

'My—myself. The Everlasting Everything,' said Lance, with a sort of impatience, covering his face with his hands, as though—had twenty years been subtracted from his age—he would have begun to cry.

'My dear boy,' said the Doctor, 'never mind me. Have it out. You don't like to complain to your brother, and you can't stand the life you are leading?'

'No use to say *can't*,' said Lance, looking up, with his brow contracted; 'I must and I will, if I am to get well. I got over it before, and I shall again, I suppose, when my strength comes back. I made my bed, and must lie on it.'

'You mean that you chose your present business?' said the Doctor, trying another leading question.

'Ay. My brothers, as soon as they could, both offered me to go to the University and take Holy Orders! but, as Clem said, my hurdy-gurdy was a new toy, and I was as proud as Punch of it, and thought life offered nothing better; besides, I was always a dolt at classics, and thought they would split my head.'

'Are you ever reminded of that sun-stroke?'

'Less every year; but summer sunshine still makes me sick and giddy, and now and then extra work brings on a racking headache.'

'Take my word, your instinct was right. You could not have stood college work.'

'So I thought; but if I had scraped through, it would all have been over now.'

'Very likely,' was the dry answer.

'Well, it would have been worth dying for. I did not know what I was giving up.'

'In position?'

'Partly. I was a mere boy, and did not see the difference as I do now I have been with Will Harewood at Oxford, or when I come here. I keep out of it as much as I can, for it's just a mockery to go and mix with their friends here, and talk to a pretty girl, when I know she would not touch me with a pair of tongs at home.'

'More shame for her, then. Have you no society at home?

'Oh yes, plenty of nice fellows—professionals, I mean, and a dinner with the upper-crust now and then,' said Lance, laughing; 'not much in itself, but making me cock of the walk in our own line—trade, I mean. Nice girls there are, too—if one had seen nothing else—but then, they keep out of the way, and the others make themselves such fools. It was good fun once; but one gets sick of it, as one does of everything else.'

The vein of confidence had been found at last, and a mere demonstration of sympathy was enough to draw him on. 'I seem to have got to the end of my tether with everything—Pursuivant and all. Even the organ, I can do no more with it as it is; and it is no good crying out for more stops, for nobody cares. I have worked at the science as far as Miles or my own study can take me with my present means; and as it is, I know more than there is any power to use in my squirrel's cage, yet I can't go on into what there is beyond without giving my whole self to that and nothing else.'

'Is that out of the question?'

'It would bring in no return; and I am not a gentleman at large, nor am I sure of the right and expedience of it after all, nor whether the craving is to praise God or please myself. What I have seen behind the scenes at musical festivals—ay, and before them too—has made me doubt whether the most perfect music gets put to its full use.'

'Or ever can be here.'

'Ay. Practically, the anthem, chant, and hymn, have the direct devotional use; and that they may serve it, they must not too much go beyond the average musical capacity of your congregation.'

'Quite true. You have thought it all out,' said Dr. May. 'I wish more organists saw it so.'

'That's just what the St. Oswald's people say I don't! Well, you see what it is. My poor brother Edgar told me how it would be when I would not be a regular professional.'

'How what would be?'

'Why, that it would all get intolerably slow and flat, and that I should not be able to bear it. It is true enough, but I got over it once.'

'And as you say, you will do so again. The life you embraced upon principle may for a time be distasteful, but the restlessness under it can only be a trail. If I understand you right, Lance, your motto has been

"If I forget thee, O Jerusalem,
Let my right hand forget her cunning."'

'Stay, stay, Dr. May. I don't regret that first decision—not at all—but the other—when they offered me to study for Holy Orders. I find I was like a soldier, who thought playing in the band was fighting in the ranks!' And Lance lay back in his chair, and shaded his face with his thin hand.

'And that has been preying on you all this time?'

'Perhaps. I am for ever coming on facts about crime, misery, ignorance—here, there, everywhere; and I know that with a little perseverance and resolution I might have been a priest, doing the only work worth doing—and behold, all I have done—has been—to gratify my passion—for music—and call it—dedicating—' He had begun to cough distressingly, and could not go on.

'If I had not known it was more spirits than lungs, I would not have let you go on,' said Dr. May, when Lance could hear again. 'Your present life is irksome, and you think you may have done wrong in not making an effort for the higher service?' Lance nodded assent. 'But remember, non-commissioned officers are as much needed as commissioned ones, and your Pursuivant is no mean weapon. It is really easier to find clergy than thorough-going lay-men in a position like yours; and from all I can gather, if you had tried to fight your way to Ordination, you would only have broken down, and done nothing. So be content, my boy. You have honestly put the higher duty foremost, and it will come right somehow.'

'Only—'

'Hush! If the thermometer gets above 50 degrees, take a turn in the cloister. Fresh air will do sleep and spirits the most good; only lay up entirely, and blister on any symptom of return of pain. But go about the house, and get back to family habits as you feel up to them, not

163

troubling yourself as to what is to come after. I'm wrong! You are *never* to ride outside a velocipede in the rain again. That pleasure is for ever forbidden! Somewhere about the end of the east winds you may go into questions of the future, though to me it seems that your post is one of rare value and influence. While—as for the "not impossible she," for whom it is worth while to go in in particular—depend upon it, she is waiting for you, and will fall in your way yet, even if, as Captain M'Intyre felicitously expresses it, your veins were filled with printers' ink! I should be ashamed to think it could be otherwise. Now rest. Don't speak.'

'Only one thing. My voice—will it come again?'

'Your voice? Of course. You spoke very well before I let you wear it out.'

'For speaking—oh yes—but singing?'

'Singing? Your throat was a good deal affected. Your voice—what kind? High tenor, did you say? Ah! those are very soon damaged; but one can't tell; don't go trying experiments on it too soon. Happily, it is not a vital question with you.' And as he saw the lip tremble, and a tear in the eye, 'Don't fancy I meant to prepare you for its loss; I dare say you would rather lose a good deal besides.'

'I believe I had.'

'Let it alone then, and guard your throat.' And with a few more counsels as to the treatment, Dr. May left him, and much consoled Felix and Cherry by assurances that the lungs were fast recovering, and that the spirits would follow them. And he then proceeded to give a message that he was to deliver contingently upon his patient's state—namely, the offer of a visit from Gertrude. His little granddaughter, Margaret Rivers, was at Dawlish, in so sad a state of suffering, that he and Ethel were to go and be with the parents; but Gertrude was not wanted, and would gladly bestow herself upon Geraldine.

'You'll take care of her,' he said, with the solicitude that fathers never lose for their youngest daughter. 'You have no young lords nor precipices to put in her way, I trust.'

'Lords, precipices, and thunder-storms, are equally improbable just now,' said Cherry; 'the tithe-dinner and school-treat are the most brilliant entertainments in prospect.'

'I shall tell her to mind you like an Ethel the second. By-the-by, Ethel says she never saw any one so good for the child. She was our spoilt one—at least, so Ethel says; though I'm an old fool of a father, and never saw it, and you are said to have put the womanliness into her.'

'I'm afraid I don't deserve the compliment. "I speks it growed."'

'To tell the truth, so do I,' laughed the Doctor.

Geraldine in her secret soul thought the development in maidenliness due to something besides age, for she knew what was the great bond between herself and Gertrude May; and bethinking herself of the entire extinction of all remaining sentiment for Alice Knevett, she could not but speculate on the possible results of the coming visit, and recollect that to shrink from them would have no such excuse as in the former case.

The announcement was not received with acclamation. Angela did not like Gertrude May. Both were high-spirited free-spoken unconventional girls, in whom something of womanly grace was as yet slow in coming; but Gertrude was more essentially a lady, though louder voiced and less naturally graceful; nor had she a particle of flirtation, but disliked young men, and was unpopular from irony and exclusiveness; whereas Angela was thoroughly the girl of the period in a highly stimulated state.

'Bother!' she exclaimed. 'She is nearly as bad as Miss May herself.'

'Indeed!' said Felix, in a much offended voice.

'As good then, and that's as bad!'

'Stuck-up, like all the Mays,' put in Bernard.

'They have been very good-natured to you,' said Felix again, in a tone of reproof.

'Soup tickets,' muttered Bernard.

'Take care, Bear,' said Cherry. 'Small minds repudiate gratitude.'

'Then Bernard's bound to entertain her,' said Lance.

'Catch me,' quoth Bernard.

'Perhaps she may alleviate his pangs for the faithless Countess,' suggested Angela.

'She!' The unutterable contempt of that monosyllable set all laughing, and he indignantly reiterated, 'She is stuck-up enough for ten countesses and duchesses to boot.'

'The monotony of Bear's ideas was always striking,' said Felix.

'He's got but one pole to run up, poor Bruin!' said Angela. 'Now, I could have found ever so many objections.'

'Only that it would be a queer way to welcome Cherry's guest,' said Clement, in reprobation.

'As if you liked her yourself, Clem!' exclaimed Angela, 'when Stoneborough is altogether in the rear, and not one of the whole crew belongs to the E.C.U.'

'Is it impossible to be courteous to any one out of the E.C.U.?' said Clement so gravely, that the laughter was renewed; but Cherry had the uncomfortable certainty that if there had been a show of hands it would have been on Bernard's side. Clement and the Mays had never harmonized; and Lance, who was always reluctant to face his sister's young-lady associates, now had no escape, and was ready to feel everything an oppression, so that his silence was an act of forbearance.

It was a good sign, that when Clement came in unobserved from Evensong, he found Lance at the piano, making twilight beautiful with something wonderfully yearning and mournful, but with a deep underkey of resolution ever waxing stronger and stronger. Clement leant on the settee, listening till his eyes grew moist; and when the cough forced the musician to desist, and come back exhausted to the sofa, he asked, 'Where did that come from?'

'It is a Largo of Beethoven's in C Major. I fell in love with it when we had C—— at Minsterham.'

'Dr. May has done you good.'

'I don't know. I see he thinks my voice done for.'

'I would sooner have your fingers than your voice, Lance,' said Clement, appreciating the grief as Dr. May could not, never having heard those notes.

Lance shook his head. The trouble was too deep and real for speech.

'Sooner or later we shall have our voices in perfection,' said Clement. 'Meantime, who knows how good it may be for you to be parted from that beautiful thing!'

'My golden idol!' Lance broke out in a sort of laughing coughing sob.

'At least, you have the comfort of knowing you never prostituted it to any ungodly purpose,' said Clement. 'You always treated it as His goodly gift.'

Lance made no answer. Perhaps he felt at that moment that his voice had been the chief thing that made his dull life pleasant to him, and that to be either dumb or an offence to his own delicate ear was a lot to which he could hardly resign himself. Clement went to the piano, and softly sung 'Angels brightly shine forth.'

Angela came into the room with a light as he ended; Lance started up, and hastened out of the room.

He was rather worse than better for the next day or two, and shuddered with annoyance when Gertrude May's wheels approached. He would not, however, vex Cherry by shirking the early dinner, where Gertrude, a bright mixture of blue merino and swans' down, was making fun of her precise brother Tom's inclination to escort her on this her first solitary journey, when she knew it was only 'because of his friend at Ewmouth, who is equally crazy about microscopes and such unpleasant things.'

'As microscopes?' said Felix.

'That depends on what you look at. Now Tom is making perquisitions into the germs of all kinds of diseases and infections, and is never so happy as when he gets an excuse for driving over to Ewmouth.'

'Is there anything so scientific there?'

'Mr. Elsted, the chemist. He was a fellow-student of Tom's, but he hasn't nerve enough to practise; so he is a kind of stickit doctor, though he has science at his fingers' ends—the right place for a chemist, you'll say—so very sensibly he took to that line.'

'We must make friends with him,' said Felix.

'Do! It would be a great kindness. He is really very much of a gentle—' where she awkwardly stopped, and caught herself up, colouring to the ears.

'Which cannot be said of all medical students,' said Felix, greatly helping her out.

'No! And as Tom could not come himself, he has given me a precious little box to carry, which the post would squash. Don't be afraid; it isn't the plague, or the small-pox, or anything—'

'I thought of going to Ewmouth this afternoon if you like the drive,' said Cherry.

'You don't trust me! You want to be rid of Pandora's box.'

Of course there was more fun about it, resulting in the timid being only half certified that it contained only some slides of glass; but Lance took his part in the teasing, nor did he forget—what Cherry took care to tell him on her return—that Gertrude had shaken hands cordially with the chemist under the very shadow of his purple jars.

Gertrude's spirits were not much affected by her niece's illness; and she had been so seldom from home, that this was a new experience, from which she derived as much freshness as she brought. The Squire was always her hero, and with him she was always on her best behaviour, as if trying to redeem her performance on the Kitten's Tail; while he treated her—like all his sisters' friends—with the gentle playful courtesy that had first begun with Alice Knevett. A musical evening seemed to have thoroughly fitted her in among the inhabitants, and in the forenoon she repaired quite naturally to Cherry's painting-room.

'That's right, I have designs on you.'

'Me, myself me, or in character?'

'In character. I catch every one. One gets so tame and unreal without fact.'

'But you'll let me write to Ethel. It feels so queer without the old thing. I'm not sure that my head is on the right way.'

'Pray write. You ought to be doing something.'

Just then a pair of slippered feet came noiselessly to the door, and with 'Good morning, Miss May,' Lance came in, his sister exclaiming, 'How early! You have not had your sleep after breakfast.'

'No, but I slept a good deal later this morning, which is a better thing,' he said, advancing to a big arm-chair. Gertrude had hoped for a snug morning with Cherry; but he looked so wan, pinched, and shadowy in the morning light, that there was no grudging him the content with which he sank into his place, nor the anxiety with which Stella was sent down to hasten his beef-tea.

'Have you made your capture, Cherry?' he asked.

'I was beginning when you came.'

'Then Miss May has not seen your contribution to the "Rights of Woman."'

'I have only escaped from the subject at home. Mrs. Harvey Anderson has been getting up a meeting for the Ladies' Suffrage, and wanted Ethel to come to it.'

'O for her likeness!'

'What can you want of it?'

In answer, Cherry produced two cartoons. One was a kind of parody of Raphael's School of Athens, all the figures female, not caricatures, but with a vein of satire throughout. The demonstration on the floor was an endeavour to square the circle; some of the elder ladies were squabbling, some of the younger furtively peeping at themselves in pocket-mirrors, or comparing ornaments; some in postures of weariness, one gazing eagerly as if responding to some signal, another mimicking her teacher, a third frowning at her rival's success. There was no air of union or harmony, but something of vanity and vexation of spirit pervaded all.

The companion was arranged on the same lines, but the portico was a cloister, and the aisle of a church was dimly indicated through a door-way. The figures and occupations were the same, but all was in harmony. The maidens, though mostly in secular garb, wore the cross; the central figure, in matronly beauty, was portioning out the household tasks, while in the place of the harsh or sour or tyrannizing disputatious ladies were women, some in hood and veil, but others in ordinary dress, all dignified and sweet, while the damsels were smiling happily over their employments, for the most part the same as before, but in a different spirit. The demonstration on the floor was no longer impossible. It was the circle of eternity spanned by the Cross; the quizzing and teasing had ceased, the loiterers were at their needlework; the rivals were united; the girl, whose glance down the grove had been furtive, was now standing in the door-way, openly watching for the little male figure in the distance. Both were in rough bold outline, almost scrawled, and here and there dashed with pen or Indian ink; but Geraldine's masterly hand showed wonderfully in the grace and expression.

'I don't know whether I shall make anything of it,' she said. 'I sketched it in a kind of frenzy; and Felix is bent on my going on with it.'

'It would do for Punch, if for nothing else,' said Lance.

'For shame!' exclaimed Gertrude.

'No, it is a great compliment,' said Cherry; 'but what the Squire wants is to have them in the Exhibition. Now I mean No. 1 to bring out—'

'The lesson of Tennyson's Princess,' interrupted Gertrude.

'In part, but going further into life. I mean that while woman works merely for the sake of self-cultivation, the clever grow conceited and emulous, the practical harsh and rigid, the light or dull, vain, frivolous, deceitful, by way of escape, and it all gets absurd. But the being handmaids of the Church brings all right; and the School of St. Sophia develops even the intellect.'

'You'll have to write a key,' said Lance.

'I leave that to you gentlemen of the press. I don't expect that many will enter into it, but if only a few do it will answer its purpose, and be worth doing. I want to know whether it conveys its meaning to a fresh eye.'

'Let me see,' said Gertrude. 'Woman working every one for her own hand, is all nohow, either grim or silly, the laughing-stock of gods and men; while working for the Church makes all harmonious, and sets each in her place.'

'It might as well be man as woman,' said Lance.

'More so, I believe,' said Cherry; 'because marriage gives woman a head; so I think the married ones at least do not suffer so much in character from misbelief. Family life affords a sort of religion to those who do not know the truth; and so while man kept them in subjection, they did not need to think it out, as the single ones must do now.'

'The Church provides ties and object for them,' said Gertrude. 'Ethel would like that.'

'Clan Hepburn would more than ever warn one against making an idol of an abstraction,' said Lance. 'I couldn't help asking them what they thought of the Bride in the Revelation, and they warned me against taking the figurative literally; but they are deeply good old girls, though your St. Sophia has not had the training of them.'

'Not consciously,' said Cherry. 'They did her work, though, in the dark times; and if she had thorough hold of them, they would not be meddling with the clergyman's province.'

So saying, she produced two more finished copies, the building elaborately put in, and some of the faces and figures worked up evidently from the life. Wilmet was the lovely matronly presiding spirit; Stella, the damsel in the place of one of the beautiful boys in the foreground of the School of Athens, though it had been hard to make her look naughty enough for the first. Gertrude, to her great amusement, recognised Lady Caergwent: 'So that's the use you make of your countesses?'

'It arose a good deal out of a talk with her about the dedication of our powers; and she sent me a horrible photograph to do her bad self by.'

'I declare you must have got Ethel's nut-cracker photograph for the original of that forbidding astronomical female with the compasses. Why! her improved state is Ethel herself, only not quite sweetly odd enough. Did you mean it?'

'No; I only found it coming like Dr. May.'

'She shall sit! And I'll be one of the wicked ones, whenever you please.'

'Then you must be a good one too.'

'Oh! I don't promise that. It is much flatter. Let me be the one who is taking off Urania Ethel's gestures. I declare you are too clever; the constellation you've turned up on the globe is *vulpecula et anser*.'

'No, you fancied that, Gertrude.'

'No such thing! See the stars really make a little W just like it in the sky, and observe the moral. Instead of a he-fox running off with the goose, the vixen will thus run away with the gander.'

Cherry had not laughed so much for weeks, Lance not for a year. Stella's shoulders shook over her German exercise, and her voice suggested: 'It ought to have been in the Southern Hemisphere, for the world turned topsy-turvy.'

'The Southern Hemisphere is stupid, where it got out of sight of the dear old funny folks that named the stars. What shall we have in the world set right?'

'Andromeda on the rock,' said Stella, 'and Perseus coming to let her out!'

'There's Perseus then coming down the walk,' said Gertrude.

'I hope that's me!' said Lance.

'Then you must be *Anser!*'

'*Anser!*' said Cherry. 'If he appears at all, it must be as Athene's Owl.—What great eyes you have, my dear!'

In a moment she dashed into her first draught an owl, comically resembling Lance; 'the twinkling blink in its eyes looking out of that indefinite bushiness,' as Gertrude said.

'Against the beard movement, Miss May?'

'There's only one moustache in the family!'

'Diplomatic,' laughed Cherry.

'Not wholly,' said Gertrude. 'One does go by one's brothers; and I like to see people's expression.'

'But,' said Lance, 'I trust at least I'm the owl of the church tower, though I can't hoot any longer.'

'Athene's ought to be prying down with superior contempt upon the ladies in the Academy.'

'Inspecting them!' said Cherry. 'Hearing them pronounce *vicissim we-kiss-im* in turns, and making a note.'

'I declare,' cried Gertrude, 'I've got the very man for the bad owl. How lucky I brought my photograph book!' She flew back to her room, and returned in a moment with her album. 'I brought it to show Geraldine our New Zealand children, and Leonard's pupils,' she said; 'but just look here. Transplant him, Cherry!'

The photograph represented a handsome, complacent looking, gentleman-like man, with certainly large eyes and an aquiline nose, and bushy beard, but nothing else owl-like about him.

'Who is he? What has he done?' asked Cherry.

'Done! He's a school inspector! Don't you have inspections here? Not under Government? O thrice happy people! If ever you *do* wish to see my dearly beloved sister Ethel in the position of a toad under a harrow!'

'But why, you have got her harrow in your book?'

'He isn't our proper district harrow,' said Gertrude. 'He's badderer and wusserer nor that! He's my sister Mary's brother-in-law, and Tom's bosom friend!'

'Worse and worse!' said Cherry, laughing.

'Exactly, for he comes down for Sundays! He is the youngest of the Cheviots by a good many years, born after they had got prosperous, and cockered up beyond all measure—went and got everything a man could go in for at Oxford—horrid fellow—and then turned school inspector, and writes smart articles in Harvey Anderson's Magazine.'

'Rupert Cheviot; I know the fellow's style,' said Lance; 'but may I ask why he is in your book?'

'Because Mary gave me the book, and stuck him in so fast there's no eradicating him; but I shall paste him over before long. Luckily, he generally talks to Ethel. They are always fighting, and I believe she likes him; and he doesn't know what to make of such a clever woman being so narrow, you see.—Now, an' you love me, Cherry, put him up there—an owl, inspecting the Academy!'

Just then, Angela burst in to say that Major Harewood wanted Felix to come and see about the new barn, and Felix had sent to ask if Miss May would come out before the warmth of the short day was past.

'That's hard,' said Lance, as she went; 'you'll lose the light.'

'Never mind, there will be plenty of time. The pensive face is what I want. It can be rather fine.'

'Rather!' in an indignant tone.

Lance slept in the third room in the corridor, opening into Clement's, as Clement's did into Felix's—an arrangement convenient in the earlier stage of his convalescence, and enabling Clement still to take care that his fire never was let out.

'I say, Clem,' he said, from his bed, the next morning, 'you haven't such a thing as a spare razor—mine were left at Marshlands.'

'No, I haven't.'

'I wish you would see if Felix has.'

'Are you mad, to want to begin shaving now?'

'Not at all. It had better be done before it gets thicker, and I have to go out.'

The application brought Felix in, demanding, 'Are you gone crazy, Lance?'

'I thought I might as well titivate myself for the tithe dinner this evening.'

'You need not trouble yourself about that. You'll not dine with us; and if you did, the farmers would excuse you. I thought you were only too glad of an apology for cultivating that furze brake.'

'One may as well be fit to be seen.'

'Exactly my sentiments,' said Felix; 'but you must submit for the present. If you say any more, I shall lock up all my razors from the raving lunatic.'

'Yes,' added Clement. 'Would you like an axe at the same time, to cut off your head?'

Lance subsided; and Felix walked back to his room, and smiled to the risk of his own cheeks over his shaving, as he muttered, 'Tithe dinner, quotha?'

The tithe and rent dinner were always combined soon after Christmas, and the Squire and Vicar had agreed that it was best not to make it a wholesale entertainment at the Rood, but to have a civilized party in the Priory, bringing the guests into the drawing-room afterwards. The numbers of superior tenants were not sufficient to make this unmanageable, and the compliment was appreciated. One or two elderly men might have preferred devouring the value of their tithe at the inn, and enjoying subsequent tobacco and spirits, but most liked the being treated as gentlemen; and the evening was always an odd mixture of boredom, amusement, and gratification.

The audit occupied most of the day, and the dinner was at the primitive hour of six, the ladies of the house appearing thereat. Gertrude, who was worked up to think it capital fun, was warned to deck herself in her best; and she rejoiced that Ethel had enforced preparations for possible gaieties, so that she could appear in a pink silk, presented to her for Mrs. Rivers's last public occasion, and a wreath of clematis.

Her splendours were not thrown away, for the Squire met her on the stairs, and exclaimed, 'That's right, I'm grateful to you;' and next moment she saw Mrs. Harewood uncloaking, and revealing the black velvet her husband always urged on her, and a set of pearls that had not seen the light since the last old aunt retired into old-maidenhood. The Vale Leston opinion was that Mrs. Harewood was the finest woman to look at who had existed since her great-grandmother, Lady Geraldine.

Lance was in the drawing-room when the ladies came in after dinner, shaking out their plumes and relating their experiences. Angela had talked hunting with a young farmer whom she wanted to allure into the choir, though Cherry doubted whether Clement would like to have him there. Cherry had given Mr. Hodnet an account of the Caergwent wedding, in which Penbeacon had had so much share, and had received a lament over Mr. Harewood's absence that winter. 'He was a gentleman that was strong in the pulpit.'

'That's his tincture of Irish eloquence, and the *go* that he has in him!' said Angela.

'I believe the poor people do prefer his preaching to Clement's,' said Wilmet.

'On the variety principle, I believe,' said Cherry.

'Of which they never get enough,' said Angela.

'After all,' said Cherry, 'inherent poetry does tell more than one guesses upon an audience.'

'Ah, ha!' said Lance; 'I've got a novelty in that line for you.'

'From Will? You don't mean that you've been revelling in the second post?'

'Ay! Some one fetched it from Ewmouth, just as your knives and forks began to clatter. I was just thinking what notes predominated, when in came this budget from San Remo. It is satisfactory to hear that while my Lord and my Lady think it the dullest place in the world, our two lovers find it simply delicious.'

'Is that the subject of the poem?'

'It might be,' said Gertrude.

'Only it would be hard on my Lord and my Lady,' said Angel.

'The question would be,' said Cherry, 'how long it takes to be so used to one another that localities cease to be indifferent.'

'How long does it take, Wilmet?' saucily asked Angela.

Wilmet did not choose to answer; and Stella's voice quietly mentioned how Lizzie Bruce and her lover broke off their engagement after being shut up together for a whole wet Sunday.

'How very lucky for them!' said Gertrude.

'They agreed it would be impossible to spend life together,' said Cherry. 'But what is the poem, Lance?'

'The Song of the Electric Wires.'

'Nonsense!'

'They do sing,' said Gertrude. 'I have often wished one could make something of those Æolian-harp sounds.'

'Have you?' said Lance. 'I've tried ever so often to get them on the violin. I'll show you.'

It was the first time he had spoken of touching his instrument; but Wilmet intercepted Stella, who was going as a matter of course to fetch it, by saying the sound would make the farmers expect a dance.

'So much the better,' said Angela. 'One waltz with Harry Palting, and my victory would be complete.'

'It seems,' proceeded Lance, 'that poor Bobbie held herself ready to start off with Bill in case I had been worse; and when the telegraph relieved their minds, the reaction showed itself in these verses.'

'Which Bobbie was there to secure,' added Cherry. 'I wonder how many of his get lost for want of her to copy them out, and make him polish them.'

'When a man hasn't a spark of vanity he misses a very good working machine,' said Lance.

'Spurring machine, you mean,' said Gertrude.

'Let me have them, Lance; you can't read them,' interposed Cherry.

Strange as was the subject, there was a wild airy grace about the lines, by turns joyous and pathetic, and really going well to the fitful music of the winds upon the wires. Lance went up to the piano, and struck a note or two; and that wonderful power he possessed over the instrument brought the very expression, if not the sound, and made Gertrude exclaim with delight, 'Oh! do make a song of it with a piano accompaniment; I am sure you can.'

'If *you* tell me I can,' said Lance, flushing and smiling, though perhaps aware of more technical difficulty than she knew; but the opening of the dining-room door, and the warm greeting of his brother's tenants, broke off his promise.

He worked so hard and so merrily the next day in preparing the Christmas-tree for the schools, in spite—foolish fellow!—of warnings, chills, and catches of breath, that at the moment of projection, he was quite overcome by the throng, noise and glare, and forced to beat a hasty retreat to the drawing-room, whither Miss Bridget Hepburn soon pursued him.

Finding him for the first time on the sofa, looking worn out she viewed his assurances that he was really much better as a melancholy delusion, and warned him against being beguiled by false hopes out of that blessed frame of mind. John Harewood, divining what she was about, presently came in to the rescue; not that he could remove her, for she was burning to communicate a semi-confidential piece of information, namely, the intended marriage of Mrs. Fulbert Underwood to Mr. Smiles, whose sickly wife had been dead about a year. The other two sisters were communicating the same intelligence to any one they could catch in anything like privacy all the evening. It was not at all unsatisfactory intelligence, for on the strength of Clement's appointment having caused his resignation, Mr. Smiles had expected him to supply all his most pressing needs, from educating his son to paying for his wife's funeral. The worst of it was that it was hardly credible that Mrs. Fulbert would be so foolish as to bestow her handsome jointure upon him and his seven children; but as he had just taken a curacy in a popular watering-place, there might be attractions; and at any rate, Clement would be exempted from finding funds for his move.

Lance could not help feeling that if to be weary of everything and indifferent to the future were a blessed frame, he had certainly lost it, and it made the subsequent night of pain and distress all the less endurable, as well as the captivity to bed and blisters that ensued; nor was it till Sunday evening that he could return to the painting-room, where all the family collected as they dropped in one by one from Evensong and the subsequent choir-practice, and stood and lounged about in the Sunday gossip, deaf to all to the manner born.

Felix came in last, having been looking at his letters, for he never had time to do more than glance at a few of the more interesting in the morning.

'It is true,' he said quietly.

'What, about Mrs. Fulbert? Has she written?'

'Yes; a great deal about the love she always had for Mr. Smiles's dear little family, and an entreaty to me not to deprive her of the three hundred a year that she was to forfeit by remarriage.'

'Was she? cried Bernard. 'How jolly!'

'So it seems, though I had forgotten it. She keeps all the settlement, of course.'

'I remember about it,' said Clement. 'Her husband begged his father to do something for her; and he detested her so, poor woman, that it went very much against the grain with him, and by way of some solace, he must have made this charge on the estate contingent on her remaining a widow.'

'You'll never go on with it, Felix!' exclaimed Angela.

'I hope it will not break off the match,' added Cherry. 'There are some people whom one would willingly bribe to keep out of one's way.'

'They do it knowingly?' said Gertrude.

'I imagine so; Smiles managed to know most things.'

'Ay!' said Angela. 'But you see he went on precedents. He knew what Alice Lamb had effected, and had some personal experience of this Vicar!'

'Felix! you are not going to be so absurd!' expostulated Bernard. 'Why, it would keep a hunter!'

'Or a curate,' said Angela.

'Still more amusing to you, Angel,' retorted Bernard.

'But, Felix, *do* promise me you'll do nothing foolish. For my personal satisfaction,' pleaded Angela.

'That is a promise no one can be warranted in giving, Angela.'

'He's afraid of himself!' cried Angela. 'She has only to get him into a corner—like Alice.'

'Then it is well I am going away to-morrow.'

'Very unreasonable,' muttered Lance.

'What, to be so soft—I think it is indeed! I don't care for the money, but how those critters will triumph!'

'He never said they would have it,' said Cherry.

'Oh! if he is only teasing.—What are you going to do, Felix?'

'I do not know. I must look at the terms of the will.'

Gertrude looked triumphantly at Angela, as much as to say, 'Could you not trust his common sense and justice?'

But Felix put a stop to the conversation by asking Lance whether the usual Sunday evening hymns would be too much for him.

'Not at all,' he said, 'provided Angela would sing nothing she had not studied;' and then finding Gertrude took this as a hint, he was dreadfully distressed, and nearly implied that dissonance from her was better than harmony from any one else. She, on the other hand, was as ever, greatly impressed with the sweetness of Felix's voice, and refused, as they went down to supper, to believe that Lance's could be better.

'I do not know that it is in what you heard to-night,' said Cherry; 'but Lance had some notes that none of them could come near, except—' and there she paused, thinking of the voice that still at times she longed for with inexpressible longing.

Gertrude was full of pity, though disappointed to find that Mr. Underwood was going away so early that he bade her good-bye as well as good-night, in spite of her protestation that she should be up to see him off, and binding over Stella, who was always the morning star of early travellers, to wake her in time for his 6.30 breakfast.

It was not far from that time when Felix, coming into Lance's room, was struck with his refreshed and brightened look even at this his worst time, a sort of indefinable look of hope and recovery.

'You have had a good night?'

'Yes; I slept till just now. I believe this last bout of mustard has done me a power of good. The tightness is gone as it never went before.'

'That's the best news I've heard yet.'

'Better than Mrs. Fulbert?'

'Oh, I was coming to that. I have looked at the abstract of the will this morning, and I don't feel myself in the least bound to continue the annuity. Then I have been going over things this week; and what with the falling in of the Blackstone lease, and the winding up of the Rectory business, I shall be likely to get into smooth waters sooner than I expected. So if you can hold on to the end of the year, I will then, if all goes right, do whichever you please—give up the concern at Bexley to you, or let you have an allowance to enable you to go on with your music.'

'Have I been grumbling?' said Lance.

'Can't one see a thing without its being grumbled at one? It is a hard life, yours, Lancey. I did not understand how hard till I took this taste of it, and I am heartily grieved at having let you go on under it till you broke down. I must try some other plan for you when you can go back.'

'No, no; don't upset Mrs. Frog. Summer will be coming, and I prefer her to Mrs. Lamb any day. Give her my love, and tell her I'm mending. Not that I see any sense in your going,' he added, but somehow a little less freely than usual.

'You want to see Lamb's report of the speeches at the sessions? Any commands?'

'Yes; I want some music-paper, and my portfolio of violin music. If you are sending any books, it might come at once. And tell Ellis he had better not attempt that anthem from the Creation next Sunday, unless Speers is come home to take the tenor.'

'I might do that.'

'You don't mean to stay over Sunday?'

'It is of no use to be always running backwards and forwards; I like a Sunday at the old place now and then,' said Felix. 'Good-bye, Lancey; let me find you twice yourself when I come back!'

'I could not thank the old Giant,' said Lance, when Cherry looked in on him; 'but will you tell him, I feel as if he had taken out the stopper that bunged me up from everything. Only it is absurd of him to go into banishment just when this place is so uncommonly pleasant?'

Cherry thought she could guess, and that it was not so entirely distrust of Mr. Lamb's capacity as it was convenient for the family to suppose. And after all, Lance was protesting from dutiful habit of unselfishness, but it may be doubted whether he *really* was quite as sorry as usual to part with his brother.

The early rising to see him off had been effected; but his absence did not disturb the good spirits of the party. Lance was gaining ground quickly, and resumed more of the ordinary family habits every day—sustaining his spirits the better when left behind on their all going out, because Gertrude May did not unite with Angela in abusing the weather for not bringing a skateable frost, and far less in running wild after a sight of the hunt. Nay, she decidedly snubbed that great handsome idle fellow Bernard for abusing Felix and the Fates for not mounting him, and sat soberly at home at her music lesson, when he and Angela went off upon the chestnut and Ratton, to see the meet and bemoan themselves. Gertrude had been slow to exhibit her music before the Underwoods, and had good-humouredly justified Angela's exaggerated excruciation, owning that she had never had any teaching worthy of the name. Lance had diffidently offered a few hints, and they were not accepted as Angela was wont to receive his criticisms; so they developed into instruction, delightful to both, even though much of it consisted in unlearning!

And when the little niece had rallied, and Dr. May fetched his daughter home, Lance did not flag, but was once more the bright Lance of former days, and spent his time between Pursuivant work and labour over some musical achievement, dividing himself between a blotted score, his violin, and piano, using by preference Theodore as a critic, with Stella to interpret his gestures.

CHAPTER XLII.

A HALCYON DAY.

'They had been much together; and one for ever bears
A name upon the loyal heart, and in the daily prayers;
The other but remembers, when the pleasant hours are past,
That something has been sending them so sweetly and so fast.'
S M.

On Whit-Monday forenoon 'Mr. Underwood' was announced in the drawing-room at Stoneborough, and Gertrude May's face, which had at first clouded at the pre-prandial intrusion of any visitor, brightened at the name, but lost a little eagerness when the entering visitor proved himself to be only Lancelot, shaven now all but his moustache, and with an air of entirely recovered health, justifying his declaration that he had no desire to see the Doctor professionally, and had been quite well ever since his return to Bexley at Easter. He was now on his way to keep his holiday at home, but had made a deviation 'to show that I have tried to obey you,' he said, proffering to Gertrude a roll of music, the stiff paper cover beautifully and delicately adorned with a daisy border, with pen-and-ink etchings in the corners illustrating the receipt of telegrams for weal or woe, and the first bars were made to resemble the wires and posts, the notes, the birds perched thereon, the whole being of course William Harewood's poem set to music. So beautiful and elaborate was the finish, that Gertrude was startled and confused; the meaning flashed on her, and the sudden recoil roused the contradictoriness of her nature. The earnest look abashed and frightened her, and with a sort of anger she coldly said, 'Very pretty, very nicely got up.'

'I think it may suit your voice,' said Lance wistfully.

'Thank you' (more nervously, and therefore more coldly), 'we will order some copies.'

Lance, after a moment's pleading gaze, dropped his eyes, coloured, and stammered, 'Not that.'

Ethel came to the rescue with praise of the etching, but this availed little; Gertrude spoke not a word, and Lance, though making some kind of reply, clearly did not know what he was saying, and presently took leave, in spite of Ethel's entreaties that he would stay to the early dinner, and to see her father. He made answer in a bewildered voice about not meaning—and getting home; shook hands, and was gone.

'That was not gracious, Daisy,' said Ethel.

'I'm sure I didn't want it,' said the spoilt child.

'You need not have hurt him.'

No answer but scarlet colouring.

About half-past three he was at the Priory, just as the whole party and Charles Audley besides were standing on the lawn, with rugs and cloaks betokening boating intentions. His first impulse was to shrink away like some wounded animal, but he had been spied, and was eagerly hailed—'O Lance! just in time! Here's the four-oar coming out! Clem and Angel want to go up the river to Tranquillity Bridge, and we are taking them.'

Lance would have done anything rather than betray his wound, so he took his place in the boat, and tried to shake himself into the present; but Felix thought he looked tired, and would not let him take an oar against the stream. Then it occurred to Cherry to ask whether he had had anything to eat. No, he believed not; but he was resolute that he wanted nothing, not even a draught of cider, which Angela mischievously recommended as they passed the 'Hook and Line,' a little tea-garden public-house, a favourite Sunday resort of Ewmouth idlers, and a great scandal and grievance to the Vicar, but secured, like other abuses, by a lease. A boat, belonging no doubt to some holiday-makers, was moored at the steps; but as it was the day of a great Maying at East Ewmouth, most observers of 'tide time' were likely to be there absorbed.

Angela amused herself with wild proposals to Charlie Audley to repair thither in disguise together, talking nonsense that greatly annoyed Clement, and was far from pleasing Felix or Cherry; but she was in so reckless and defiant a mood, that they could only hope that she might work it off at the oar. Her arms were strong as well as long, and rowing was a pastime she loved, having been franked as an A B S ever since she had taken lessons at a swimming-bath. The day was delicious, with clouds chasing one another so as to make fleeting lights and shadows on Penbeacon and the hills beyond; the clear brown water sparkling in ripples or lying in deep pools, shadowed by the woods that came down to the bank in the early green of spring, flowering may, mountain ash, and wreaths of blushing eglantine overhanging the margin, or where the space was open, revealing meadows all one golden sheet of buttercups, while the fringe of the stream was the feathery bogbean and the golden broom, mixed with tall sword leaves of the flag and the reed.

Shaded at length by a picturesque high-backed one-arched bridge, the boat waited while Clement and Angela went on their cottage visiting.

Charlie did not, as Cherry expected, invite Lance to promenade the bank with a cigar, but applied himself to helping Stella in collecting a grand nosegay of every sort of flower and grass within reach. The others remained in the boat: Lance leaning over the gunwale dreamily watching the ripples, apparently half asleep, lulled by the monotonously sweet humming of Theodore, and the songs of the birds in the woods; Cherry was sketching, and Felix rested musingly.

'Tranquillity Bridge,' he said. 'I always fancy it must have been named by some pious builder imbued with the spirit of the Pilgrim's Progress.'

'An unconscious poet,' said Cherry.

'Yes. Such a tranquil rest, amid such perfect peace and loveliness, without one discordant element, is one of the choicest boons of life.'

Lance swallowed a sigh; and Cherry answered, 'The very movements and sounds are all peace, though full of life.'

For a gold-billed moorhen was swimming among its little ones at the margin of the reeds at the bend of the river, and a sapphire kingfisher darted across the arch.

'Halcyon days,' said Felix.

'Oh no! Halcyon days precede storms.'

'Maybe they give strength for them. Times like these are surely foretastes of perfect bliss.'

'How does that prepare for storms?'

'Not only by calming nerves and spirits, but by giving some experience of the joy beyond—ay, and sense of love and confidence in Him who has made all so exquisite for our delight.'

It seemed to come from his heart, drawn forth by the grateful enjoyment of that sweet Whitsun hour.

Cherry held up her finger as a ring-dove began to coo from the thicket, making fit answer to one thus resting in the Feast of the Comforter; Theodore cooed in return, and the bird seemed to be replying. Even the tumult of pain and grief in Lance's breast was soothed by the spirit of the words and scene, while he felt the contrast, like an abyss, between himself and the others.

But when the rest of the party came gaily back with talk and laughter, inaction had become intolerable to him. He wanted to take Angela's oar, but she would not hear of giving it up, and Felix resigned his, while Cherry owned that she preferred having him at the helm when going down the river.

Theodore, with a shout, held out his hands for Stella's flowers, and she gave the whole into his hands, Charlie for a moment looking disappointed; but as the twins sat together, and the little fellow drew out the flowers singly and dropped them into his sister's lap, while she whispered their names, it was evidently perfect joy to both. Some, such as the bright spires of broom, he greeted with a snatch of nursery song, though otherwise the pair were scarcely audible as long as the nosegay lasted, and that was for a long time; but when Stella had made it up again, only leaving the broom to him, he returned to his usual hum, and this time with the tune of 'The strain upraise,' which had been practised that morning for Trinity Sunday, and which met the sound of the bells ringing for Evensong.

'That's rather too much!' exclaimed Angela. 'We shall be taken for some of the pious, a singing of hymns.—Come, Tedo.'

'No, no,' said Felix, 'I'll not have him interfered with.' And he hummed the tune.

'That's always the way when Baby goes out with us,' muttered Angela, audaciously singing out at the top of her clear soprano—

'Six o'clock is striking,
Mother, may I go out?
My young man is waiting,
To take me all about.

First he gives me apples,
Then he gives me pears;
Then he gives me sixpence,
To take me round the fairs;'

thus effectually silencing both the others, the one from sense of discord, the other from serious displeasure. At that moment, shooting from behind the bend of the river where stood the Hook and Line, came the other boat. Excited probably by the song, the young men in it shouted 'Come on! Who'll be first! We'll take a couple of your sweethearts aboard, to make fair play! We'll have your nightingale!'

'Next he gives me bacon
And eggs to fry in the pan,
And no one there to eat them
But me and my young man.'

sung they lustily, as on they came, as fast as the current, assisted by twelve vigorous arms, could carry them.

A few strokes would have gained the garden landing-place, but the pursuers' velocity was reckless. One moment as they passed the eddy of the junction of the Leston, and the end of the four-oar swung round into the middle of the river, there was a shock, a shriek of many voices; and just as John and Wilmet Harewood were crossing the lawn to return to their own cottage, they beheld both boats upset, and fifteen persons struggling in the midstream.

Even as the collision took place, Felix had seized Theodore, and after both had been drawn down for a second, rose again, making vigorous strokes with one arm for the bank, reaching that of the churchyard, where it was built up high and steep; but with one of the violent efforts of a supreme moment, he grasped a branch of the overhanging willow tree, swung himself up by one arm till his feet had a hold, and he could launch himself partly over the iron rail, and deposit his burthen on the grass, when climbing over, he reached down and dragged up Geraldine from the arm of Clement, who had closely followed him.

By that time both the other sisters were safe; Charles Audley, thoroughly at home in the water, had directed himself more skilfully, holding Stella by her shoulder, to the garden landing-place, further off, but of easier access. Indeed, she had not lost the power of helping herself, when Wilmet's arms clasped her on the steps; and only a few moments later, Angela, who had kept herself afloat, was likewise landed, with very little aid from Charles.

Lance's rescue was harder. He could not swim at all, sank twice, and rose the second time a little way down the stream, where John Harewood grappled him and brought him to the steps, helpless and at first unconscious. Of the other boat's crew, two reached the bank alone, another had saved his fellow, a fifth clung to his oar, and was guided ashore by Clement, a sixth was drawn out insensible by young Audley; the last was still missing, and John, Charles, one of the other lads, and old Tripp, were all striving to find and rescue him. Four figures lay insensible, three more were struggling back to life—the servants rushing down; Wilmet, supporting Lance in his gasping efforts, took the command. 'Angel, Stella—don't wait, back to the house. Change instantly.—Amelia, go with them, give them something hot, never mind what, and put Miss Underwood to bed.—Yes, Clement, carry her to her room; and you—don't do anything else till you have changed—Felix, we'll take Tedo to the laundry; it is hot, and flannels can be warmed sooner.—Golightly, you and Martha take this one.—You two the other.—Follow Mr. Underwood—Yes, dear Lancey, you are better. They are all safe. Shall I help you up? That's right. Lean on, my dear, more than that; don't be afraid, I'm strong enough; there, you get on very well.'

Before they had made many steps, a shout proclaimed that the last sufferer had been found; and while he was carried between his friend and Tripp, Wilmet hastily insisted that her husband should hurry home and change his clothes before doing anything else, and relinquishing Lance to Charlie to be helped up-stairs, hastened to the scene of action in the laundry, where the four lifeless figures were stretched on the ironing tables. The other three young men were sent to be between blankets till their clothes could be dried; and Felix, after having laid down his unconscious burthen, lingered for a moment, till Wilmet ordered him off to change his dripping clothes, when he obeyed without a word.

Clement, half-dressed, was finding garments for Charlie, and insisting that bed was the place for Lance, when there was a sudden call at his door, and as he opened it Angela stood before him, exclaiming, 'Come this instant!' and as he followed her flying steps, he beheld Felix on the stairs, sitting propped against the balusters, holding a handkerchief to his mouth covered with blood. He had been standing, supporting himself against the post at the bottom, when Angela had first found him, and had so far helped him up; but the effort had evidently been agonizing, and increased the bleeding so much, that she had tried to place him safely, and hurried for aid. He could do nothing for himself, but Charles Audley coming to their assistance, they brought him to his room door, where Angela, crying, 'Ice! ice is the thing!' dashed away to the offices, where she heard voices.

'Miss Angela, you mus'n't come here.'

'Quick, Martha, the key of the ice-house.'

'Hice-ouse! bless you, Miss Hangela, 'tis 'ot as is wanted.'

'It is ice for the bleeding. It's a blood-vessel! It is Felix. I must have the key.'

But Martha, always despising Angela, and now all the more with her hair streaming below her waist, simply did not hear, and hurried away with her flannels. Angela rushed after her, but only heard, 'You can't come here.'

As she was raising her voice for a more peremptory cry, she saw John Harewood returning. He understood in a moment, made entrance, obtained the key, and while she fetched the ice, he hurried to the scene of the most pressing and grievous need.

By the time she brought the ice, the drenched clothes had been removed, and Felix was in bed, and the remedy she had obtained did at last check the flow of blood, but there was not only exhaustion but evidently very severe pain. 'Where?' He put his hand to his right side; and at that moment, to their infinite relief, they found among them Dr. Thomas May, the professor, who—on his way home from a visit to his friend the chemist—had been met in the village and brought to their aid even before Page, who was out on his rounds.

The verdict of the first moment was that the hæmorrhage was not from the lungs, and indeed the patient showed no difficulty in speaking after the first faintness. Had he felt the hurt on throwing himself over the rail? He thought so, but could not recollect; it only became disabling when he tried to go up-stairs, and that brought the bleeding—'but Theodore! Pray go to Theodore!'

There was no withstanding his anxiety, only the Professor directed the unsuccessful endeavour to make the posture easier, and ordered fomentations as the only present alleviation, except perfect stillness. No judgment could be formed as yet, and he therefore gratified the ardent desire faintly breathed forth, while the great drops of pain stood on the brow. 'Please, see Geraldine! And when Theodore comes round, bring him here! Clem, see it is so; he will be pacified in sight of me.'

Clement promised, and made it plain that it would be better for both; and then he took the young doctor first to Geraldine, who, once in bed, could not leave it without assistance, and was chained there in terrible anxiety, with Stella as her messenger; but her agony of suspense was her chief ailment, and after saying all he conscientiously could to soothe her, Dr. Tom was guided to the laundry, where he vanished.

Long, long was news watched for from thence. Even those who went in quest of hot water learnt nothing, till at last Charlie heard that one of the young men was reviving, and presently he was carried up to the spare room.

Another quarter, another half-hour dragged by. Felix renewed his entreaty for Theodore's presence, but messenger after messenger returned not. First John went and came back no more, then Clement was called for and never returned, and Felix became so restless under the impression that Wilmet would choose to put the child to bed unhappy in Sibby's room, that Lance could only carry down his mandate to the contrary. Then when the next access of watching and anxiety was visibly increasing the suffering and danger, Angela left Stella in charge, and went herself to represent that the dire suspense must be relieved before it did further harm.

The ear was in a state of agonized tension, and caught a sound. 'Open the door, Stella. Hark!'

She obeyed. There were voices; Wilmet's—Clement's. 'You go!'—'He will bear it best from you!' they said.

She heard no more, for Felix had started up on his elbow, and the blood had again rushed to his lips. She called for help. All were about him, there was no checking it, for seconds—for minutes. His face was deathly, his hands cold. Clement, holding him on his breast, whispering prayers, felt him more prone and feeble every instant; all believed that a life was ebbing away far more precious than the little feeble spark so easily quenched.

When a respite came, it was with a hand on the pulse, and with an anxious face, that the doctor durst signify to them that this was relief—not the end as yet; but as Clement laid the head back the furrows of pain had cleared, the brow had smoothed, the breath came without the stifled groans, the position was less constrained, and when Angela ventured to say, 'He looks more comfortable,' there was an air of assent and rest, the worst of the pain was evidently relieved for the time.

Stella stole away with the tidings to poor Geraldine, whom she found sitting up in bed, trembling so that the whole framework shook, and totally unable to move from it, without the appliances that assisted her lameness. Before long, Wilmet was able to attend to a representation of her condition, and could bring her wonted remedies, and what was even better, her strong soft arms to enfold the little frail quivering frame, and her sweet, steady, full voice to assure her that Felix was undoubtedly better, and not suffering near so much.

And when Cherry was quieted, and Wilmet would have returned, the little handmaid said, in an imploring voice, 'Where is dear Tedo? mayn't I go to him now?'

'My dear child!' exclaimed Wilmet, in pitying consternation, 'then you don't know?'

Cherry saw what was implied! How else could the helpless darling have been left by all!

'It is so?' she said.

Wilmet bent her head.

Stella gave a kind of moan.

'Yes,' Wilmet said, 'It is nearly three hours since. The Professor said there might be hope for two. One young man is getting better at last, Page is with him. We went on trying—John says for two hours and a quarter, and Sibby is going on still; but there is no hope now; and when I heard about Felix—Stella, dear child, where are you going?'

'Mayn't I help Sibby?' The voice was so plaintively imploring, the eyes looked so mournfully earnest out of the loose damp mass of dark brown hair, that it seemed cruel to answer, 'Stella, dear dear little one, indeed you must not, you can't go there.'

Instinctive obedience recalled her; but still she pleaded, 'He must get better! He was such a little moment under water! I think he is afraid to open his eyes because I am not there, nor Brother. Do let me try! I'm sure he would know me.'

'Stella, sweet, indeed I would let you if I could; but you can't go to the laundry, there are strange men about, and they are making up a bed for young Light; he can't be moved. The hope is quite gone, my dear, it was such a feeble little tender life.'

'And there could have been no pain or fright,' said Cherry.

But she broke off, as poor little Stella collapsed with her face between her hands, sitting on the floor, lost in her hair, not speaking, only a great stifling smothering sob heaving up, as if the oppression of her first grief were crushing, nay strangling her.

Wilmet knelt down to gather her into her motherly arms, and whisper comfort, but this was not what she wanted; she somehow slid away, stood up, and said, 'Please, may I go into my own room? I want to be by myself.'

'To your room and your bed, my dear,' said Wilmet. 'I am going to send you both some tea.'

Cherry only had visits from the maids, with tea that refreshed her, but from which Stella in the inner room turned away. The summer twilight had passed into night before a long black figure looked in. 'Asleep, Cherry?'

'Oh no, Clem! I knew you would come.'

'I am sorry not to have come before, but there has been so much to do.'

'And he?'

'Tom May thinks his pulse stronger, and was struck by the look of rally about his face when we came back after supper.'

'Who is there now?'

'Wilmet and the Professor. May will let no one sit up who has been in the water. I care the less because with my door open it is almost like being in the same room.'

'But he is better?'

'Not in pain,' said Clement; 'and May thinks that there are no ribs broken, though there is a great bruise. Much may be only violent sprain, and it may be only some unimportant vessel that has given way; but he is too weak and tender yet for anything like examination. However, as long as the bleeding does not return, he is gaining every hour.'

'It was that dreadful scramble up the bank!'

'That quite accounts for it; and he must have twisted himself as he threw himself over the rail. No one could have done it in cold blood, even without dear Baby's weight.'

'And after that he pulled me up! Clem, it was you that saved me, and yet I could not thank you if—O Clem!' She laid her head on his shoulder, struggling with horror at the bare notion of life without Felix.

He was very sorry for her. He had always loved her the best of his sisters, yet he felt himself so inadequate to fill to her the place of their eldest, or even of the lost Edgar.

'My poor Cherry!' he said, stroking her damp hair; 'but thus far God has been very gracious to us, and we will take hope, and trust Him. Think how much worse it might have been. So many in danger, and the only one taken so surely gone home!'

'Ah! I can only think how happy we were so short a moment before. He said halcyon weather came to bear us through storms; but oh! it makes it worse.'

'You will not think so when you see our little one's countenance, sealed with his Alleluia! The vacancy is gone, and there is a wonderful depth in his face, as if his Ephphatha had come to the guileless lips. Sibby and I have been dressing him in his surplice, and laying him under the Cross in the Oratory with his broom blossoms in his hand. Sibby says he was still clutching them when Felix gave him to her. Poor Sibby, she says her heart stood still then; but she would not cease from trying to restore him till long after we all knew it was vain; and when I made her desist, for the sake of young Light, who must be kept quiet, I thought she would have broken her heart; but at last she seemed to feel the soothing awe of the dear little face; and she has got her beads, and means to keep her vigil over him all night.'

'Does *he* know?'

'Wilmet fancies not, and is on the watch for his asking; but I am sure he understood, when I thought he was fast going, and told him Theodore was "safe home." I am sure it made it easier;' and as Cherry winced and shuddered, he added, 'This calmness after the suspense was over was really what did him most good. He is better every hour, and no one else of ourselves at all the worse except Lance. When the alarm was over, we found him shivering violently, and hardly able to hold up his head. I believe that his danger was the greatest of all, and that he could not have been saved but for John; the stream was carrying him down against the bridge.'

'O Clem! help me to be thankful! But is not one poor fellow really taken?'

'Yes, a fine young lad about Bernard's age. He had been under water so long, that we never had much hope; but the whole frame seemed so made for vigour, that Page thought there might be a return, and went on with Krishnu's help for four hours—nor did Sibby leave off till after that. They were a party of clerks and shopmen from Spiers and Hart's. The four who are gone home are very subdued and grateful. The father of one came out in a fly and took them all back, though I thought it rather a risk for the lad who had been so long insensible.'

'Then there is one in the red-room.'

'He had had some blow, and was too much done up to move; but Page says he will be all right to-morrow. I am more afraid for the one in the laundry, and have got Kerenhappuch to sit up with him. The poor boy who is lying by our dear child was a clerk of Hart's; Audley was going to see about sending to his people. He went off in his skiff a couple of hours ago.'

'There's eleven o'clock! O Clem, I ought not to keep you from resting.'

'This is rest, Cherry.'

'Only leave me something to rest on.'

'What shall I say to you?'

'What you like. There are matches.'

'I need not read.'

And he murmured over her Psalm, Collect, thanksgiving, and prayer, half quoted, half from his own heart, and then stood to give her his blessing of peace, and his kiss, which left her hushed, softened, comforted, attuned to meet whatever might be coming.

Again he was at her door in early morning, with tidings of reassurance. Felix had spent a quiet night, without recurrence of bleeding, and though too feeble almost for speech, and unable to make the least movement without pain, he had so far surmounted the first danger, that Professor May meant to go away on the return of the carriage he had sent home at night, and, unless telegraphed for, would not come again till Thursday, only enforcing absolute quiescence though not forbidding speech. Clement had seen a great improvement in looks, and Wilmet had consented to lie down on her husband's coming to take charge of the patient.

'And Lance?'

'He is getting up to come to Church, though he has had a bad night, and he looks anything but fit for it. He says he must come even if he has to go back to his bed.'

'Surely it is too great a risk.'

'So I told him, but he declares he has caught no cold, and that it is all headache and feverishness, which fresh air will relieve. I don't know, but I can't withhold him.'

'Whit-Tuesday! I had forgotten. Sunday seems to have been ages ago!'

'And how are you, Cherry? Did you sleep?'

'In a sort of way; I am quite well, if only any one would come and help me to get up! I can't bear lying here any longer. Do try to send me one of the maids. I can't disturb that poor little dear; she is asleep at last. Take my heart with you, Clement! After all, it is a sacrifice of thanksgiving this morning.'

Clement was wont to gather his small daily congregation in the Lady Chapel, where never since the family migration had the early Holy-day Celebration been so scantily attended. It was in unison with the many beyond that he made his Commemoration, his oblation, his intense intercession, in the dewy light of the early summer morning, his apparently low yet really powerful deep-pitched voice sounding far down the aisles and among the pillars in the nave.

The blessing echoed beyond the enclosing screen, and presently Lance rose from his knees and moved slowly westwards. If for a space he had felt some of the joy of holy comfort on the renewal of the sacrifice of self, soul and body, love and hope, before the Lord of life and death, yet he was more conscious of the oppression of the sickly odour of the drooping greenery and faded flowers that hung trailing on column and poppy-head, and which compelled him to leave the Church, though every step down the nave seemed to increase the load of sorrow, anxiety, and wounded affection, beneath which head and heart had burnt and throbbed the long night through. If he had reinforced patience and resolution, he could not yet feel the benefit.

A slight sound made him raise his eyes. Whom did he see catching at a bench for support, with white cheek and dilated eye? Whose voice exclaimed, 'You! you safe then!' Whose hand, so strangely cold, grasped his with convulsive eagerness, as her lips formed but did not utter the inquiry, 'Who?'

'Our poor little Theodore,' he said. 'My brother is better this morning.'

'Theodore! I never thought of him!' she gasped. 'Two lives—one in great danger—the note said—Tom's man could not tell which—I could not bear it—I had behaved so ill to—'

And she was cut short by a violent though hushed fit of weeping, while he exclaimed incoherently, 'No! no! don't think—I was a fool—oh! don't cry—don't—it is all over now—and this is so good and precious! Oh! please don't cry! Come in to Cherry! Take my arm.'

'Oh!' between her sobs, in a panting whisper. 'I never meant that. But I should have died if I had not come with the carriage to find out. I went in here to wait. I meant no one to know.'

'You must come in now. Cherry is well, and up.'

'I can't! I ought not! Don't let any one know.'

'Indeed you must come in! Think of the comfort to Cherry. Besides, you will hear of them all. Come.'

The tone was most persuasive, and Gertrude felt that she must yield; indeed, she trembled so much as to need the support of his arm as he took her along the cloister into the darkened house, up the stairs to the Prior's room, where he was glad to find preparations for breakfast; and placing Gertrude on the sofa, he was knocking at Cherry's door, when he heard the tap of her stick as she came along the gallery from a visit to Felix.

She had only been allowed to give him ocular demonstration that she was well and afoot, and exchange a kiss and five fond words; but the welcoming smile of gladness had so enlightened his face, that she was cheerful enough to be able to meet Lance's eager face and gesture as he threw his arm round her, whispering, 'She's here, Cherry. She's come in May's carriage. That most dearest—!'

And before she had fairly recollected who was most dearest to Lance, she was borne away into the room, to see tearful eyes, and crimson face, find them hidden against her, and be almost stifled in Gertrude May's embrace.

The explanation was made in more detail than in the church. Tom May, on finding that he must stay, had scribbled a pencil-line to his wife—'Terrible boat accident; two lives gone, fears for two more. Send the other horse for me to-morrow morning.'

The groom was only sure that it was the Squire of whom scarcely a hope was given, and another brother drowned, which he could not say, except that it was not the clergyman. Dr. May and Ethel were spending the night at Abbotstoke; and Gertrude, after hours of tossing under remorse for her discourtesy, and misery of suspense, found waiting unendurable, and obeyed the impulse to rise and go with the carriage.

'Indeed,' she said, looking up to Lance, 'it was very wrong. I could not believe anything so exquisite had been done for me.'

'As if anything—'

'But haven't I been punished!' she went on, not pausing. 'Oh! to think I never—never could unsay it, nor ask your pardon!'

'Pardon!' he gasped, turning as red as before he had been pale, and holding a chair for support; and before he could say another word, the impulsive girl cried, 'And oh! it is all my selfishness, bothering him when he looks so dreadfully ill.'

'No, no,' broke out Lance, afraid he was frightening her away, and still almost beside himself. 'This is perfect healing.'

'Don't talk nonsense,' broke in Cherry, half comprehending, but a good deal alarmed, and therefore assuming authority with some peremptoriness; 'the truth is, you are both famished, and must have some breakfast this instant.' She poured out coffee, and then moved to provide eatables. Lance's instinct was of course to help her, but his hand shook so much that he had to relinquish the bread-knife. 'Yes,' said Cherry, as she took it from him; 'no wonder! When did you eat last?'

'I—can't tell. Somebody made me swallow something hot and abominable when I came in, and my head has never stopped going round ever since; but I don't care now.'

'No doubt it saved you from something worse.—You know he was longer in the water than any of us.'

'I don't know anything,' said Gertrude. 'I thought Mr. Underwood—'

Then it had to be explained—that is, as much as Cherry and Lance knew. 'Some tipsy fellows racing us—the shock—the helpless plunge;' then Cherry had felt the instant security of Clement's arm, and was drawn up the bank.

'How beautiful it was!' said Gertrude softly, 'that care for poor little Theodore first, and then you!'—and softer tears came into her eyes. 'It is just like all his life.'

'Just,' they both said, gratefully.

'And how does he look?'

'Perfectly white, dear fellow—lips and all,' said Cherry; 'and he speaks so slowly, and only just above his breath; but his eyes watch one about with all their grave brightness.'

'Grave brightness,' whispered Gertrude to herself, while a sweet satisfied look passed over her face. 'Did he know how it was with the poor little one before he—was ill?'

'No,' said Lance; but he could now add that when Felix had seen Clement about to go to church, he had said, 'Remember me, and give thanks—above all for dear Baby.'

Never perhaps had Gertrude shown such soft shy tenderness; and Lance confirmed the trust that Theodore could scarcely have felt a pang, for he said that in his own case the drowning had been far preferable to the coming back to life, when Wilmet had seemed a cruel tormentor.

'Who was it that brought you out?'

'Who, Cherry? I never asked!'

'Oh!' emphatically exclaimed Gertrude; then in a murmur under her breath, 'or what would it not have been to me?'

'It was John Harewood,' said Cherry.

There was a knock. Professor May, at his principal patient's entreaty, had come to inspect Miss Underwood. His amazement at the spectacle of her companions was unbounded, and did not make him merciful to Lance, whom he meant to have next visited in bed, and whose throbbing pulses, varying complexion, heavy eyes, aching limbs, palpitating breath, and untasted meal, all indicated that he ought to have been there. The reproof was not like the rough uncompromising scolding Rugg was wont to bestow; but with quiet irony Dr. Tom impressed on Lance that getting up had been a recklessly foolish pastime, in which he might have been permitted to indulge so far as his own insignificant welfare was concerned, but that he could not be permitted to inflict another serious illness on his family. The only thing that was proper by them was immediately to repair to his bed, and there await the upshot of his imprudence, so as to mitigate the effect as much as possible.

And then summarily carrying off his sister, Tom began as soon as they were outside the gate, 'This is simply the most extraordinary proceeding I ever heard of.'

Gertrude held her tongue.

'May I ask whether my father is in the habit of permitting these freaks when he is visiting his patients?'

'I beg your pardon,' she answered. 'I forget the unapproachableness of your patients when they are my dearest friends.'

'Oh, indeed!' Then presently, and as if for fear the groom should hear—'*Les demoiselles font beaucoup de choses mal à propos à l'heure qu'il est, mais je vous conseille de ne pas avouer votre préférence à si haute voix.*'

'I don't care,' she said, scorning the veil, 'who knows that I glory in appreciating heroism.'

'The heroism of getting upset in a boat!'

She deigned no reply; and he waited, trusting to her feminine nature to make her begin again, but silence was her only refuge from angry tears or words, and she kept it till the Church Ewe station was in sight.

'Thank you,' she said. 'I'll go home by train.'

He had visits to make, and was glad to be quit of her, but with elaborate cold care came to the station, found that a train was nearly due, and waited with her. He must have done so for the purpose of saying, 'Mind! these are estimable persons, but that is no reason for dropping self-restraint.' Then, as her pout nettled him, 'Nothing is more disgusting or unmaidenly than pursuit of one in a lower walk of life.'

'Walks of life are what men make them.' And they treated each other with dignified silence till the train came.

'Well,' said Dr. May, on hearing his son's story, 'the Press is king now-a-days, and one daughter is his tribute.' The Doctor still liked to tease Tom.

Meantime, Lance, in no condition to resist, had betaken himself to his own chamber, but only to find the housemaid had left the bed in the most approved sanitary state—so long as it was not to be lain on. Not sorry for a dispensation from captivity, he extracted his private horse-hair pillow from the pile of bed-clothes, and came back to the painting-room, where Cherry cleared her large sofa, and covered him up with her Indian silk quilt, he smiling blissfully, and observing, 'Isn't she the dearest girl in the world?' Cherry might have heard a great deal, had it been possible to her to sit and talk when innumerable messages were coming for her. When she had answered the first, he began again with 'So sweet and generous.' Then came the second which involved a note. When she looked at him again, he only smiled. She next had to go down to the kitchen; and on her cautious return she found him asleep, breathing like a child, and a colour—not fever—coming into his cheek.

'Poor fellow!' she sighed to herself. 'I wonder if there is any hope for him; but if the notion only bears him through to-day, it is a blessing!'

Poor Cherry! Such as this was all the nursing she was good for. Her nerves made her not to be trusted alone in a sick-room, not to do equal damage to herself and the patient; and she could only sit with the door ajar, writing notes, and acting as referee to countless questions, all in an undertone out of respect to Lance's slumbers.

And there meanwhile sat Angela, trusted to fan Felix, refresh him with a strawberry or spoonful of iced lemonade, bathe his face with eau-de-cologne, or catch his slightest wish, cares so congenial, that she liked them for a stranger, how much more delightful for 'my brother;' and though she knew more clearly than anyone save John and Clement how precarious his state was, youthful buoyancy viewed the danger as the cause of future triumph. To be a lady-doctor was surely her vocation! What a pity Charlie was heir to a baronetcy! And he had finally saved her—though she had kept herself afloat—*he* might be allowed the honour of her rescue; and if it made him her fate, Lady Audley, M.D., should obtain a magnificent triumph over conventionality, far beyond all her former conceptions.

When Clement came into the room at noon, she would not give up her place. Felix looked up to him, and said, 'You are seeing to things!'

'Yes—' interrogatively.

'Try how near that willow it can be.'

'I will.'

'How about the inquest?'

'At the Rood this afternoon. Never mind about that.'

'Only see there is no injustice to those poor lads! It was our own doing;' and as Clement looked amazed, 'if our boat had not swung round;' but the earnestness with which the words were spoken brought a thrill of pain that cut him short; and they wiped his brow, and sprinkled him with scent, and watched anxiously till the lines about the eyes and mouth began to relax, and he smiled thanks back, then closed his eyes.

Clement left the room unheard, for the heat of the day compelled the opening of window and doors. He had only just became conscious that from the moment of the accident he had never had leisure to consider the cause; and he went across to the painting-room, where he did not find Cherry; but Lance awoke at his entrance, sat up, and in answer to his apology and inquiry pronounced, 'There's wonderful virtue in sleep. I don't think any of the ills Tom May threatened me with are coming to pass.'

'Your head?'

'No worse than I'm well used to, thank you. How is it in there?'

Clement told him what had just passed, adding, 'What do you remember?'

'My notion,' said Lance, 'was simply that we were overtaken by a lot of scamps too excited to perceive what they were about, and egged on by Angel's unlucky song.'

'I doubt the "excitement" being of the technical kind, unless the water had a very sudden sobering effect.'

'Indeed! Well, considering that you were in your shirt-sleeves, their not perceiving that we weren't in their style was not so wonderful. So Felix says we ought to have cleared them. Ay, I do remember the swinging round now.'

'An oar must have missed the stroke, and brought her stern foul of the other.'

'He must have seen who it was,' said Lance.

'Yes, but as the point is to exonerate these fellows, there seems no need to drive it close home among ourselves.'

'No, *she* need never know exactly what she has done,' said Lance.

'I did not say she never should,' returned Clement; 'but the public need not. In fact, we have nothing to say. Felix, in the stern, may have seen, but I did not.'

'And Charlie Audley?'

'If he knows no more positively than we do, you may be sure he will not draw inferences. I wonder he has not been here yet, by-the-by.'

'You don't mean to forewarn him?'

'Certainly not.'

'No, it would not be right. All we determine is that it shall not be known through us, if we can keep truth and justice without,' said Lance; 'and if appearances are to be trusted, he is likely to be as ready—or more so—to shield her as any one of us.'

'I believe that is as great an absurdity as any of the rest,' said Clement, gloomily.

CHAPTER XLIII.

PRINCESS FAIR-STAR.

'But the little Stars we found (out)
Down amongst the Underwood.'
Jean Ingelow.

Even while Lance and Clement were in discussion, Charles Audley had paddled up the river, and mooring his little craft at the landing-place, had taken the path to the garden.

There, beyond the cedar, so as to be hidden from any one upon the river, sat Stella, decking a cross with lilies-of-the-valley and white lilacs. Scamp was lying by her, and her doves parading and cooing on the grass and cedar boughs beside her; but the utter droop and dejection of her young figure were altogether out of keeping with the summer surroundings; the shining head was bowed, and the heavy eyelids with broad red rings around them showed that she had wept and wept on for hours. She did not hear the step on the soft grass, for her low sad voice was murmuring, 'My Tedo, my darling, my baby, is this the last thing I shall ever do for him?'

Then Scamp wagged his tail and crested his ears in greeting, and the doves circled about, and perched higher upon the cedar tree, while Charles, holding one of the flat sweeping boughs back, stood looking down at her, as hardly knowing how to greet her, and with a tear gathering in his eyes. She stood up, and looked up to him meekly and sweetly, with a touching sort of welcome, as she held out her hand, saying simply, 'You saved me, and I never thanked you yesterday.'

Instead of speaking, Charles lifted the little hand in both his to his lips and cheek for a moment, as if nothing else could express how he prized that chance; but if Stella thought at all, it was that it was a kind action of comforting.

'Your brother is better,' he said, having inquired at Page's door.

'Yes, he is better. I saw him, and he just spoke; but he does look so bad!'

'He will soon mend now,' said Charles, with the confidence of one who knew nothing about it. 'And you are all alone?'

'They are all busy or resting or something, and I want to do it all for Theodore myself—my own own darling!' The last words were a moan to herself, as she sat down in her low chair and resumed the little cross.

'May not I help a *little*?' softly entreated Charles, sitting down on the grass and quietly handing her the flowers, ready arranged in bunches, with a leaf. She did not speak, but seemed to like it. There was a loneliness about her that again struck him, so that he could not help half blaming those who had left her to herself; and to account for their absence asked after Lance.

'He is up, but he seems very poorly still,' she said; 'he is lying down in the Prior's room.'

'And they have left you all to yourself?'

'I like to be alone. Nobody did care for him like me. They were all very kind to him. I don't think he knew the sound of a rough word, my dear little gentle Tedo! but nobody understood him like me, nobody could make him understand—' and she rocked herself backwards and forwards under the load of her first real grief. It was very sad to the young man to watch, and he hardly knew what to say, as again he took her hand. 'Well, now he can't have any troubles, you know, Stella, he's a great deal happier than ever you could make him.'

'Oh yes, I know that. Only it is foolish. I can't think how he gets on all alone! I know it is very wrong, but if Felix or I had gone with him it would not seem so strange for him. Yes, it is very silly,' she added, half laughing, but crying again, 'but it *will* seem hard to fancy he does not want me.'

'He is not the only one to want you,' muttered Charles.

'Oh no! There are plenty of them. I want to be thankful, indeed I do, but no one ever can be so dear! Never mind,' she added in her unselfishness, perceiving that her exceeding sorrow was causing grief and perplexity, 'it can't be helped; I do know he is happy, and I'll learn to bear the being left alone.'

'Never! if dearest love can make up to you—dearest, sweetest little one!' cried Charles. 'There!' as he took both her hands, and her wistful wondering eyes were raised, 'don't you see some one who wants you every moment, and that all your brothers put together can't love you a quarter as much as I do? There! there! Only do just promise, Stella, never to talk again of being left all alone while you have Charlie.'

'I don't think I can,' said Stella, in a dreamy wondering voice, 'for you are so kind.'

'And you'll let me try to comfort you?'—a dangerous proposal, for he did not in the least know how he should have set about it if she had not answered, 'I think you do,' as if it rather surprised her, bringing such an approach to caressing as would have startled her at any moment when her heart was not so yearning for tenderness and sympathy. And there was a reaction the next moment, as finding herself guilty of forgetting Theodore and his cross, she gave a moan of pain—'Oh, my Tedo!' and went on with her work; but she let him wait on her with the flowers, and now and then a little squeeze of the hand, and he knew he must be content with that much. Presently she said that she ought to make something for 'that other poor one, or it would look so unkind when his mother came.' In this task she could brook more help, and she spoke more over it, with a sweet soft languor that had an infinite pathos, as if somehow the acute anguish of her loss had been softened, and she were resting in the strange new peace which she did not yet know for joy, but which had filled her heart. She was so very young, so very pure, so very unconscious, that Charlie, almost as young and not much less simple and innocent, was as tender and reverent of her and her grief, and the state of her guardian brother, as though she had been one of her own white flowers—those last sprays she let him take from her hand when all was done, and they went together to carry the wreaths and crosses to the Oratory.

The large heavy curtains that separated the hall from the long room were let down, and the screen, a tall wooden one, as usual cut off the Oratory. Here the chairs had been removed to make room; and close under the Cross, to the eastward, were the two tables that had been covered with white to receive the two who had so lately gone forth full of life.

On one of the chairs sat Cherry, endeavouring to obtain some record of that unearthly loveliness of expression, chiefly for Felix's sake. She had just done all she durst, and produced a drawing that would not look like such an utter failure away from the original, when these two came in, Stella leading the way in gentle awe, very sad indeed, but still not with that utterly drooping downcast look of leaden grief which had in the morning shrunk from all comforters who could only believe, not enter into, the intensity of her mourning for her twin.

Cherry, in the corner, almost hidden by the chairs, could not tell whether her presence were perceived; but in truth the child was so simple, that she would probably have done exactly the same whether her sister was present or not, and Charles had no eyes for aught save her. She knelt down for a moment, with her face in her hands; then she kissed the white brow set in fair hair, and seemed to expect Charles to do the same, as a great favour to him, after which she let him help her to lay her cross with the wreath round it on the breast, and change the now closed Star of Bethlehem that lay under the waxen fingers, as well as that withered spray of broom. Once more she knelt, and whispered the Lord's Prayer: and he did the same, imitating her in everything, a grave kind of light on his young brow. It was very solemn and beautiful to see them, and Cherry watched them almost with awe.

When they rose, Stella placed her decorations on the longer broader form on the other table, but whispered that Clement had bidden her not to look at that face.

They went away hand in hand, and parted upon the lawn, for precious as each other's presence was, they, in their reverence and inexperience, felt as if his coming in to the family meal might be an intrusion, which neither could propose. So he bade her tell her brothers that he should meet them at the Rood.

'I shall hardly see you just yet,' he said, 'though I shall come to the door every day, but never—never think yourself alone, dearest, dearest, dearest one!' And after holding both the little hands for some moments in his, he drew her up to him for one second, then was gone.

No one saw Angela standing at the garden door, with contracted brows and bitten lip. As she crossed the hall, there was an entrance at the front door; but she darted up-stairs, and it was Stella who first greeted Bernard, who had been telegraphed for by Charlie, and came home awed, subdued, and terribly alarmed by the report he had heard at Church Ewe. 'But I see it was all clack, after all, and no harm done,' he said, as he looked at his little sister's face. 'Only why do you frighten a fellow by having all the blinds down?'

And Stella, horrified at her own disloyalty, could hardly find utterance to explain that it was but too true; and when she led Bernard to the Oratory, somehow it was all the happy and glorious side of her twin's removal that dwelt with her, while he, who had been in a rough way very fond of the little helpless one, and had never faced death before, broke entirely down with 'Poor little chap! I wish I'd been better to him! I meant to have got him a new thingumijig last half—but I spent—I wish I hadn't now. It seems so odd not to hear him humming.' And he yielded at last to a fit of crying; and when Stella spoke softly of the present joyful songs, he said, 'Ay! ay! that's all very well for you that were always good to him, and never kicked him about; but if I'd only known—'

And yet it had always been the most hopeful part of Bernard's character that he had never been really unkind to Theodore, and very rarely even impatient, even when teased by a fit of imitation.

The mid-day meal was the first family assembly since the same hour the previous day, and it did not collect all the members at the same time. Angela was only sent down after every one else had done, constrained by Wilmet's command, enforced by a word from Felix. Cherry had lain in wait for her, to ask necessary questions about her mourning, for no circumstances were likely to make Angela brook the having orders for her dress given without consulting her.

'There's a box of hats and bonnets in Sibby's room, if you would look at them. The bonnets are all one worse than another; but if you would see if you would like one like mine or like Stella's—'

Angela jumped as if she had been stung. 'Stella's! certainly not.'

'I have not chosen a very childish one for her. This will make her more of a woman.'

'Don't go chattering on!' broke out Angela. 'Don't you think *I've* not got enough upon me without your worrying me out of my life with that little humbug!'

'I don't think you know what you are saying.'

'*You* don't, Cherry. That's the way people are always taken in by a little sham softness and simplicity. I hate such snakes.'

It struck Cherry that Angela must have drawn the same conclusion as had occurred to her for one moment as she saw the hands clasped. The bitter word applied to their darling Fair-Star offended her not a little, but she made a great effort to ask kindly, 'Has anything vexed you, Angel?'

'Vexed!' as if the word were utterly inadequate. 'No, not one thing more than another! Have done, Cherry! You mean it well, but I can't stand it!—No more! I've had enough to keep me going;' and she threw down her knife and fork, and gulped down a tumbler of beer.

'You need not hurry. Wilmet is with Felix.'

'As if I didn't know that!'

There was a look and tone about her as if she were brimming over with inconceivable misery, to which every word added; and Cherry felt quite powerless to deal with her as she darted up-stairs.

And just then came the feet of many men, treading as gently as they could. John Harewood regretted for a moment that Stella and Clement had not delayed their arrangements till after this inspection, yet it might be well that these rougher spirits should see how little gloomy they had made the sleep of the innocent. The young men too were evidently struck by seeing that their comrade had not been neglected any more than the child of the house, and Stella's cares were thus not thrown away.

Clement, Bernard, and John Harewood had just crossed the churchyard, and were turning up the road to the village inn, when Clement perceived that Angela had joined them, and turning back to her, he said, 'My dear, you are not thinking of coming?'

'I am.'

'There is no need. Here are quite witnesses enough.'

'No. No one knows what I do,' she said, with face as hard set as marble.

'Has Felix spoken to you?' he said, understanding better.

'Only what you heard. That was enough.'

'It is a right purpose, Angela,' he said, kindly: 'but really you need not expose yourself to this. We can quite exonerate the others by showing that our boat swung round at the last moment, and that is all that signifies. We neither saw nor knew why.'

'And I did,' said Angela.

To check her was plainly impossible. There was the sort of seared look of misery about her face which had before struck Cherry, as if she were perfectly indifferent what might happen to her, and hardly heard what was said; and Clement could only make a gesture indicating that he had no choice, when he met the astonished glances of the others.

The Rood was almost as old as the Priory itself, and the inquest was held in a curious old pannelled room. The other boat's crew had brought an attorney to watch the proceedings, evidently anticipating that undue blame would be imputed to them, to the damage of their character even if nothing more came of it.

The first to tell his story was the Reverend Edward Clement Underwood, who merely explained the manner in which they were seated, the sudden challenge from the six-oar, and how just as he had thought the boat clear, he had felt whirled round in the eddy, the boat was struck in the stern, and went down. His brother Theodore was instantly taken out; Francis Yates, the other sufferer, not till the last, he could not say how long.

Charles Audley then spoke of the shouts and violence of the pursuit—admitting, however, that it would have been harmless had not the boat turned so as to expose her stern in the midst of the two streams. An oar must have missed the stroke, but whose it was he could not say; and he finally mentioned having brought out poor Yates, who had been sucked down by the eddy, and carried to the opposite bank. The Coroner asked in a complimentary voice whether he had not been more successful in other cases; and Charlie, colouring, allowed that he had brought two more out of the river.

There Angela started up. Clement had tried to keep her till she was called for, but the Coroner, seeing her agitation, courteously expressed himself willing to take her evidence. Her cheeks were crimson, and she spoke breathlessly. 'I only want to say it was nobody's fault but mine. They would not have raced with us if I had not begun singing. And then they would have cleared us, but I got frightened when we came to the meeting of the currents, and my stroke failed. That made the stern swing round. And I am ready to take the consequences.'

'No consequences need be apprehended, Miss Underwood,' said the Coroner, a kind old man. 'No one can impute blame to a young lady for a very natural alarm; and every one must feel this voluntary explanation extremely honourable to you.'

He was making a cruel cut if he had only known it, but he was full of consideration for her; and the young men themselves gave their evidence in a very different style from the defensive and offensive one intended; nor was the question of their sobriety, on which they had brought up the landlord of the Hook and Line, even alluded to, before the verdict of accidental death was returned.

Clement had the feeling that this was the most generous action of Angela's life, and yet she had carried it out in so defiant a manner that it was not easy to give her full credit; and before he could address her, she had sped away, between skimming and striding, and was across the churchyard before he had reached the door.

Bernard relieved himself by a low whistle.

'Well,' said Charlie, 'I thought her pluck indomitable. I never supposed that she capsized us.'

'Why, whom did you think it could be?'

'Well, if you must know, I thought Lance just the spoon to do it—a musician, and he'd been looking moon-struck all day.'

'Much you know about Lance! Why, I'd have taken my oath beforehand it was nobody's doing but Angel's. It's just the way with that sort of girl that runs into what she's no call to—'

Lance meantime was having a brief transaction with the reporter of the Ewmouth paper, and then was detained by warm expressions from the other boat's crew, who had been quite disarmed, and were eager to tell of their sorrow and their sense of the kindness and 'handsomeness' of the treatment they had received—speaking to him, indeed, a great deal more freely than they could have done to his brother the Vicar, as being far less removed from their own sphere, and giving him valuable data for dealing with their comrade, young Light, who still lay very ill. Clement had visited him in the morning, and had found him gruff and reserved, and showing decided objections to clerical visits as such.

These lads seemed more careless than free-thinking, as they allowed that Light certainly was; and they were now much impressed, and eager to speak of poor Yates's steadiness and goodness. Indeed, he had not even meant to go to the Maying, and they had been in the act of chaffing him for the abstinence which they now longed to have shared. It was the greater comfort, because his poor mother had just been brought over by her son's master, who would take charge of her till the funeral. She was in the strange mixture of fuss and grief that never shows to advantage, and when taken to see her boy was divided between gratitude at the honours paid to him and dread of their novelty, and the ground where it was easiest to meet her was his real dutifulness and affection.

Attention to the poor woman and other calls hindered Clement from any interview with Angela, whom indeed he hardly saw till the night vigil which he was to share with her. The day had not been unfavourable, except from the exhaustion produced by the afternoon heat; and Bernard's brief visit had exceedingly dismayed him. He declared that he had never seen any one look like *that* but a fellow who had been really killed by a disastrous blow at foot-ball, and put all his auditors in the lowest spirits by a series of tragic anecdotes; until Mr. Page, at his evening visit, declared that he saw more real improvement than he had dared to expect.

Felix could not bear to see two watchers losing their whole night's rest; and as Angela was unpersuadable, Clement, to content him, lay down dressed on the bed in the next room, and being thoroughly tired, was fast asleep, when in the middle of the night an access of pain returned, probably from some inadvertent movement in slumber. Felix forbade Angela to summon his brother; but ere long the agony increased so much, that, with a lip stiff and straightened by the struggle to suppress a cry, he said, 'Help me!' and as thinking he wanted to change his posture, she offered her arm and neck, he released another sob of anguish, and answered, 'No! no! Say—prayers—what I can't recollect.'

Her lips quivered, but no sound came. However, Clement, with true nursing instinct, had been roused, and stood over him, uttering at intervals the supplications after which he had been feeling in the distraction of acute pain, and the look of having lost something passed away. The fomentations were renewed; and at last, just as Lance was dressing to go for Mr. Page, a faint but free voice said, 'Don't go, it is getting better;' and in ten minutes more, the paroxysm had passed into a sweet sleep, which lasted till long after morning had risen.

Clement would not leave him again, but Angela refused every sign of dismissal, and sat cold, hard, stiff as a statue, with open fixed eyes, and cheeks so wan as to be almost green in the light of dawn. He watched her with almost as much anxiety as the sleeper; and when at four o'clock their watch was relieved by John and Wilmet, he followed her to her own door, and said, 'Angel, my dear child, I am afraid you are very unhappy.'

'Well, why not? Good-night, or morning.'

'Should we not both be better able to rest if you would let me do what I can for you?'

She laughed—a horrid painful scornful laugh it was. 'Much good that would do. Such a trouble as this!'

'Yet, Angel, would you but try! There is no grief or penitence too vast—'

The laugh again. 'So one says till one tries, and then one finds that one hates it all! all! all! No, I tell you, Clement, I won't be bothered now! I can't stand it.'

And she locked her door.

Even Felix, who in spite of that one attack was evidently stronger, must have remarked her manner, for he asked Wilmet whether there were anything amiss with Angel. 'She is grieving over her share in the accident,' said Wilmet. 'I hope it may be a turning-point with her.'

No doubt he thought over this; for later in the day, when Angela was sponging his face and hands with warm water, and exclaimed at sight of a red mark on his arm, 'Did you hurt yourself there, Felix?' he answered, 'No, it is the old scald. Do you remember our talk then?'

'You can't go on as you did then,' she hurriedly said.

'Then don't look as you did then,' he said. 'Remember, visible results are often merciful aids to correction.'

She perpetrated a hard stiff smile; and from that time shunned being left alone with him, and sometimes when the exterior family thought her in the sick-room was really shut up in her own, for she avoided the presence of the others as much as possible, and when among them showed an irritability and unkindness to Stella that Cherry could hardly bear to see. She could hardly answer an inquiry after Felix from her with common courtesy, and roughly took things out of her hands to prevent her bringing them into the room, when a moment's sight of her sweet face would have been no harm but rather good to her patient.

By Thursday much of the pain, tenderness, and disability to move were gone; and Tom May was well satisfied, not only thinking the first danger over, and ascribing the chief remaining damage to a sprain, but wishing that Felix should be lifted to a couch, where he could be a good deal cooler than in his bed. It was lucky that Wilmet and Cherry had resisted Clement's desire to present all the old Squire's invalid machinery to the hospital, for there was great comfort in the easy-going wheeled couch with angles of every inclination on which he was brought to the window. Bernard longed to draw up the blind, instead of his 'seeing nothing but that black cross and the old trumpeting angel under it,' as he said.

'My trumpeting angel is a dear friend,' said Felix. 'He says a great deal.'

Felix was obedient to the order to be moved, and showed that he was less prostrate in strength than had been anticipated; but his passiveness struck those who knew him best as not so much the langour of weakness as of sorrow. What Clement had rightly deemed no ill news in what seemed his own last struggle, was a sore grief in his recovery. Little Theodore's loving dependence was greatly missed, and saddened the thought of returning to the family.

Nor was he the only mourner. The first practice of the choir-boys without him ended in a positive howl; one of them was reported to have said Master Theodore was a little angel among them; and the intimation of Stella's desire for broom blossom brought in such an accumulation of golden flowers as might have covered the whole family.

Sibby added to Clement's perplexities by announcing her intention of not going to mass any more barring at Church. She would cast in her lot with her own children, the darlin' above all that was the Lord's own lamb; and she hadn't need go further, when here was Master Clem, as good a praste as any of her own clergy that was.

Though this was precisely Master Clem's own view, he could not tell whether he were encouraging an act of schism or an act of Catholicity; and he had not much choice, for praste as she owned him, he knew that the least opposition would make him in his old nurse's eyes no more than the long white boy she had victimized and allowed to be victimized by all his brothers. He wondered whether to write to the Priest at Ewmouth, who had certainly never attended to Sibby like his brother at Bexley, nor exerted himself to encourage her weekly tramp to mass. Altogether, though touched and warmed, he was by no means so elated about his convert as Clan Hepburn would have thought proper.

Those good ladies, in spite of their belief that there was a regular *chapelle ardente* round poor Theodore, and that the Vicar and the Papist woman spent their time there in telling beads and sprinkling holy-water, were too kind-hearted not to come daily to inquire, and some one always went down to them. On Friday, when they were shown into the drawing-room, they found Angela kneeling by the hearth, burning some papers in the fire-place.

'Felix was better,' she said; 'he was being dressed, and was to be taken into the painting-room, it was so much cooler;' but even as she spoke, the hard silent misery of her face went to their hearts.

'You look sadly worn, my dear,' said Miss Bridget kindly. 'I hear you are the best of nurses, but you must not be overtired.'

'Oh! nothing hurts me!' with her horrid little laugh.

'Fatigue of body is a rest to pain of mind,' said Miss Isabella; 'but there is even a better rest, if you only knew your way to it, my poor child.'

'And I fear it is studiously overlaid and concealed,' sighed Miss Bridget.

Angela looked from one to the other; then exclaimed, 'There's not a bit of help or comfort in anything! It is of no use talking. Nothing—nothing will ever touch it.'

The vast grief she meant, and Miss Isabella understood her. 'Yes, truly there are times when all we have trusted in falls—falls away and leaves us alone.'

'And hating the humbug!' cried Angela, though even as she spoke she was startled at her words; but the hard wretchedness of the past days, when all she had been wont to hear of as comfort seemed but child's play to the intensity of her grief, had exacerbated her against the whole system in which she had been bred, so that the very sight of Clement brought an angry sense of mockery.

Miss Bridget was shocked at the language; but her sister understood better. 'Yes, Bridget, the dear child is feeling the desolation that sooner or later comes to all who have been content with unrealities! Most cruel, but better than the delusion.'

Bridget quoted, 'He feedeth on ashes; a deceived heart hath turned him aside, that he cannot deliver his soul, nor say, Is there not a lie in my right hand?'

'Ashes! ashes indeed!' cried Angela passionately, as she looked at the black paper with grey crumbling edges that had once been a song, where she thought she met Charlie's heart. 'The more one cares the more hateful it all grows!' and she crushed the fragments into tinder with the paper as she spoke.

'Dear, dear girl!' cried Isabella Hepburn; 'even as you crush that paper, throw aside all these vain shows that cannot profit, and simply cast yourself where Help is to be found!'

The real tender kindness, the promise of help, attracted the heart weary of its misery, and yet spurning all the love and help that had longed to aid all these days. She could in some strange way open to a fresh person when the heart was closed to her own kindred; besides, it was better to have the circumstances blamed than herself, and the effect of the good lady's appeal was to make her groan, with tightly compressed hands, 'Oh! no one can tell—no one can reach near the depth of this unhappiness. Think what I have done! and what it has cost me! And then it all seems—words—words—words—'

'Words—yes, till you find Him only in whom is Power to comfort. Is he not rousing your heart by this utter destitution and powerlessness to comfort, so as to bring you at once to lay the load on Him?'

The fervour of her voice carried force; and Angela said, 'If I could—Not to find it all words again—'

'Poor child! Did He ever turn from such as come to Him? Take your Bible in your hand, and at the foot of the Cross—not the material cross, of which you have been taught to make a plaything, but the spiritual Cross—cast your sorrows and your sins; believe, and be healed.'

'Believe! believe!' broke forth the girl. 'I suppose I do believe! I very nearly didn't when I found it all sounded so inadequate and empty!'

'He only can be her Teacher,' whispered Miss Bridget; but her sister, with true warmth of love and hope, said, 'He is teaching her;—but, dear Angela, we will do our best by praying for or with you, or pointing the way to the best of our power.'

At that moment Stella came in, and after quietly giving her hand to the visitors, she said, 'Please, Angel, Clement wants to know if you have the key of the walnut-press.'

'No! I don't know,' she crossly said, after feeling in her pocket in vain.

'Most likely it is in the pocket of your blue skirt,' said Stella. 'May I go and look?'

'No! I won't have my things pulled about! I don't believe it's there. What does he want?'

Stella reluctantly answered, 'We are getting the Church ready; he wants the pulpit-banner with the triangles.'

To the visitors this sounded like profane play at such a time. 'Poor child!' they said; 'are these the devices that fritter away the deep lessons of grief?'

'Stella has devices enough,' muttered Angela under her breath; but the little maiden answered, 'We don't want to be sad;' but, spite of the pensive gentle tone, it seemed to the Hepburn sisters mere levity and desire to escape sorrow.

However, they rose to take leave, telling Angela they would always be at her service; and as she accompanied them through the hall, came Clement on the wake of his messenger, in distress for the key. She dashed impetuously up-stairs—found it where Stella had suggested, and flew down again with it.

'There! I've done with it! I'm sick of it all!'

'What?' asked the astonished Clement.

'I loathe it all,' she repeated. 'It is all of a piece—all ashes instead of bread.'

'You are not mimicking the Hepburns,' said her brother. 'I beg your pardon,' he instantly added.

'Mimicking! No, but like them I have learnt to rate all this frippery at its worth! If you had any depth of feeling, you would loathe it as I do. But that's the way you palter with truth and reality—deceiving and deceived.'

The voice and flash in her eyes directed these last words on Stella; but cutting short the reply that Clement was beginning, she again flew up-stairs, leaving the other two aghast.

'This is a new phase!' said Clement.

'I wonder if grief drives people into a sort of distraction,' said Stella, in a tone of excuse.

'Had the Hepburns been talking to her?'

'Yes; I thought she looked, when I came in, as if they had been some comfort to her.'

'Ah!'

She had never heard such a sigh from him. In amaze she said, 'They are so good. I thought great troubles made little differences be forgotten.'

'True! It is their genuine goodness that makes me fear.'

'If that made her quite—in earnest?' asked Stella.

'I wish Mr. Fulmort could have come before Monday!' ejaculated Clement. 'She's past me!'

Then it struck him that he was talking to little Stella as to a woman, and looking to see whether she had become one, he saw new depths in her eyes. 'Well, Stella, if she deserts I must trust to you,' he said. 'Have you seen much of her state of mind?'

'Not much,' said Stella. 'I think,' and her eyes filled with tears, 'that it is so much worse for her than for any of us—that she is like one bruised all over, who can't bear the least touch, and it comes on her all the more to-day, because she has been occupied by Felix hitherto, and now he wants her less.'

'But is not she specially unkind to you, Stella?'

'Oh! don't call it that. I believe she can't bear to see me, because I put her so in mind of dear Baby.' And the bright tears dropped.

The simple-hearted child had no idea of any deeper and more personal cause of irritation; nor was it possible to pursue the subject, for whereas the innocent's entrance to Paradise was not to cost the central feast of the Christian year one wreath, Angela's defection threw much toil upon her. The funeral was to be late on the Saturday afternoon, for the convenience of poor Yates's friends; and all must be finished before, with the help of Bernard, Lance, and Will Harewood, who had come down, like the brother he was, and was a welcome assistant to Clement, just as Angela's secession seemed like the last straw that would break the camel's back!

The best exhilaration was perhaps an occasional visit to the painting-room, where Felix and Geraldine were so peacefully thankful to be together again, that they hardly breathed a word to one another. And there was comfort too in finding how much the tone of young Light was softening from its hard defiance. Lance, who had a good deal of experience, and was to the young tradesmen at Bexley much what he had been to the choristers at Minsterham, had devoted himself to the sick lad, and had certainly produced an effect upon him.

Felix was recovering strength quickly. As there was an awkward step into the painting-room, he begged the next day to perform the journey on his own feet; and though he needed both the balustrade and Clement's arm, and was still sharply pained by any sidelong movement, this was wonderful progress in so few days. Here he meant to be during the funeral, and to hear the service through the window opening into the transept. There were many dissuasions, but he was for the first time resolute on his own will, both to listen and to be alone. 'It is not nearly so likely to overcome me,' he said, 'as if any one were with me. I shall lie quietly back, and listen as to a most soothing strain!'

'Yes,' argued Cherry; 'but why risk it?'

'I cannot do the last thing for my boy, but it is the nearest I can come to it! The son of my right hand, as Father said! So he has been; I only know now what an incentive his dependence was, and how this loosens me from the world.'

'Please don't say that! We have been too much frightened, and you are getting well so fast.'

'I think so!' he acquiesced, but without much elasticity. 'Yet it was a great element of thankfulness that night, and is so still, though the air seems empty without his constant music.'

Many a note of praise was to come to his ears that day, as the choir preceded their little member across the lawn to the Church gate. Their voices predominated in the Psalms; and the Lesson, read by Mr. Colman, the vicar of poor Yates's parish at Ewmouth, was almost inaudible through the window; but the Lord's Prayer at the graves came to his ear like 'the voice of many waters;' and the final hymn, the same which had been last on Theodore's lips, was sung by the tones of a multitude, and thrilled mightily through the summer air.

Felix was not the worse, though afterwards three doctors came up and tormented him, ending by allowing him to do whatever suited his own feelings and discretion, only bidding him not persevere in what pained him, and to rest thoroughly between every exertion. He asked no questions, and seemed quite satisfied; but Clement was more explicit in his inquiries in private, and was told that where there was so little power of examination, it was impossible to certify whether any harm was done beyond the undoubted sprain, and that this might make itself felt for months, even years, without anything but muscles being in fault; nor could either of the May physicians detect any cause for alarm, except a vague impression that the countenance was more changed than was accounted for by the pain or loss of blood. There had been from the first an indescribable stricken look, less evident now as the face varied with animation, but recurring in repose, and taking away that youthfulness that had endured so long.

Nothing of all this was said beyond Clement's study; the others remained happy in the verdict of remarkable improvement. Dr. May had brought a note from his daughter.

DEAREST CHERRY,

I long to come, and dare to think I should be welcome, but Tom will not let Papa bring me. At least I know it is all right. I knew it would be. Lives with so many bound up in them are not so lightly wrenched away. The world cannot grow dark by losing the selfless. All my soul is with you. Your dear little Theodore has not lived in vain. Your ways—all of you—to him have been bitter reproof to me. Write to me all I cannot pick out of Papa. I hope Lancelot is looking better. Tell him I shall try his 'Lightning Messages,' as soon as I can play them without my eyes swimming or my voice getting upon the howl.

With my dear love,
Your affectionate
G.M. MAY.

Cherry gave the note to Lance to read, expecting to hear no more of it; but he brought it out in the late evening as she was settling some Pursuivant business with him, in preparation for his departure by the early train on the Monday. 'Do you want this?' he asked.

'You may keep it if you like.'

He sighed, holding it close. 'I say—does he know—the Squire?'

'Of her coming over? No; I don't think any one saw her.'

'He ought. I had begun to think so before, but this note convinces me on whose account she came.'

'I don't imagine she knew she came on any one's account in particular.'

'All the nicer of her, but so much the worse for me. Look here, Cherry. Did you know I had been at Stoneborough on Monday? Well, she showed plain enough how it was. Every hope seemed gone—crushed—done for. I was so dazed, that if you said it was I who upset the boat, I shouldn't wonder. I had lived upon the thought ever since Christmas. O Cherry, I do love her so!' cried the poor lad, quite beyond his usual reserved self-control.

'Yes; she is very bright and sweet,' said Cherry, by way of sympathy.

'The Daisy! the light of every place she goes to!' he went on. 'How different she made it all last winter! and I was fool enough to think—Well, it is no good to talk of Monday morning, but it was just falling from Paradise to the abyss; and all the night after I was savage with them all for having dragged me back—nearly mad more than once, I believe. Then in the morning, when I had just stumbled out into church, not able to put two thoughts together, but with only sense enough to know that if I laid my love and my life on the Altar as best I could, God would take them and make the right thing of them somehow—I looked up, and saw her in the morning sunshine clinging to me—the dear thing—then I did believe God had given her to me.'

'Dear Lance! still—'

'No; I understand now. The fancy bore me up from I don't know what, till I had got myself in hand again; but when I look at it reasonably, I see she was glad to find me alive, out of common humanity, and because she thought she had vexed me; but as to the real feeling, this note shows plainly enough where that goes.'

'If it were so, there would hardly be such openness of expression.'

'Do you think so?' (eagerly, then catching himself up). 'No; it is only that the consciousness has never been brought out.'

'I don't believe *he* will ever voluntarily bring out anybody's consciousness.'

'Then he ought! Why is he to debar himself from happiness, and disregard other people's feelings? I tell you, it is positively wrong to keep hanging about him and hampering him. You would do much better to leave him to be happy, and come and let us get on together as we can at home. You might make it just tolerable!'

'My poor Lancey,' said Cherry, smiling, 'things are hardly so far advanced; but if they were, you would be my best dependence.'

'But you'll tell him? And let no fancy stand in the way of his—of their happiness.'

'Tell? You mean of her coming over? Very well, if you think it right. Nay, indeed, it is not the wish to keep him to myself, but the assurance of his resolution—and, dear old Lancey, I don't like your going back to the old mill without the bird in your bosom.'

He hid his face in both his arms as he sat over the table, but recovering himself, said, 'Never mind! Hoping for him is *some* hope, and there's too much on hand for being down in the mouth. It will all come right somehow,' he repeated, secure in that faith, even under his sense of disappointment; but after all, is not a generous consent the best balm in disappointment?

After this conversation, Cherry and Lance were struck, amid a somewhat astonished congregation, when the next day, the Vicar in his pulpit gave out in his clear ringing voice, like a trumpet proclamation, his text, 'And His Banner over me is Love.'

The church was quite full. The beauty of its musical services had of late rendered it a resort from Ewmouth, and the present occasion had attracted every one connected with the persons concerned in the accident, as well as many of the curious. Mr. Colman, whose despair was the young clerkhood of Ewmouth, had protested against having to preach; and indeed Clement felt that he had a word to say, for had not the week been one of intensified feeling, and deepened experience? Yet even his brothers and sisters were not only sorry when they found this task unexpectedly lapsing on him, but feared that he was hardly adequate to the occasion. In general he was a careful preacher, very exact, and rather tediously accurate in citing arguments, much given to similitude and mystical interpretation, and instructive and interesting in a certain degree; but without much fire or individuality, and, as the Hepburn clique asserted, deficient in the root of the matter.

But his voice made Cherry look at him, and his countenance not only glowed with unusual colour, but had a dignity and impressiveness that assured her that she should hear something different from usual, after a text so unlikely for a funeral discourse.

After twice proclaiming that Banner under which he served, he slowly and distinctly spoke those other words, '"One shall be taken and another left. They say unto Him, Where, Lord?" Yes! Strange, startling, arbitrary, as seem often the calls to the soldiers in Christ's army, each is at its true time, for the choice is made in Love.' Then came the description of the mighty host, of their Leader and their conflict, steadfast in the Name that the day's Feast glorified, going forth conquering and to conquer, but, strange contradiction! under the Banner of Love. Love, by which their Captain had won, the work to which all were enlisted, the weapon wherewith each was to fight. Love had been their Captain's weapon, but they needed another, namely, Faith—for who could fight for a vision—who, without reliance on his general? Cause and Captain, and His power to save to the uttermost, were dwelt on in a few ardent words; and then came the picture of the serried ranks, standing fast in one army, warring as one band against darkness, foulness, cruelty, and all other evils, each fighting his individual battle in private, yet even thus striking as much for the cause as for himself. So they stood, soldiers in a campaign, aware that any moment might snatch them out of the ranks, yet also aware that not one would be taken save at the right moment when his warfare had come to the crisis. Our forefathers of old believed in glorious maidens who floated over the battle-field as choosers of the slain, and bore hero-spirits away to the Home of Triumph in chariots of light, to dwell among the brave. Like them we believe in the Triumphant Home, where dwell the brave who have stood steadfast in faith, joyful through hope, rooted in charity, bright in purity, dashing down the arrows of temptation that glint against their armour. Like them, we believe in a Chooser of the slain, bearing us, one by one, from our several posts, with longer or shorter warning, exactly when our warfare is accomplished, our individual battle is, or ought to be, won.

'Is or ought to be! That is the point. That is it on which depends the awful question, "Where, Lord?" which He who has seen beyond the grave, left unanswered. Where? Less than a week ago, on one of the days especially given to us for joy and gladness, in the very height of our mirth, came the moment of danger to fifteen of us. For thirteen of us, thanks have been today returned. "Where, Lord?" has not been said of us, but has not its echo been with us? Where? When I look back on duties neglected, on self-complacencies, on purposes fulfilled on the surface but not in the spirit, on cold-hearted devotions, on a thousand treasons against the Banner of Love, I can only cry out, "Where Lord?" and bless Him that it is the Lord my Redeemer, Who looks mercifully on His unprofitable servants, of whom the question is asked, and Who has spared me for a little space. He calls in due season. But whether the summons be welcome or the reverse, does not depend on its finding us in sunshine summer pleasure, or upon a bed of pain. No—it depends on whether we are really in our camp, our face to the foe, our ensign above us, no treason or desertion at heart. Then, spite of short-comings and failures, with the Banner over us that is Love, we shall know that death is victory; and "Where, Lord?" will be answered for ever by "Him Who liveth and was dead, and is alive for evermore."'

Felix, from his window, caught the texts, and noted the breathless hush. The Vicar of Ewmouth said, as he took leave, 'Thank you. You have touched hearts I could not reach.'

And Lance followed Clement to the library, and begged for the sermon for the Pursuivant. 'I know they would read it at Bexley, and if they care for it as I do, it ought to tell. I never heard you go on like that!'

'Here are my notes, but they will do you little good; I could not write last night.'

'You came up late enough, though!'

'I had to make it up in thought and prayer.'

'A better thing, it seems,' said Lance. 'It is a sermon to set one going, however things look!'

He was nearly at Bexley the next morning by the time Felix had fulfilled his intention of coming down-stairs, and had taken his seat in the Squire's chair before the writing-table, but with his back to the door whence the musical hum would never more issue. Cherry wanted to have put it off; and Clement had proposed an exchange of sitting-rooms; but he had said such things were best faced at once, while no association made much difference.

Cherry was with him, looking over the letters of inquiry and condolence, and sorting out those which she would answer at once, or he undertake by degrees—looking too at the first Pursuivant in which for at least twelve years he had had no share, and which, he said, told him more about the accident than he had yet known.

'Lance has fared better than could have been hoped,' he said. 'I feared for both chest and head.'

'I believe he was very ill the first night,' said Cherry.

'Then—was it my fancy, or did not I hear Gertrude May's voice?'

'How could you hear it?'

'Through the open window, at the hall-door, as Tom May was going. Did she come over with the carriage, good girl?'

'Yes; but we never guessed that you knew it.'

'Many things were borne in on me in a passive sort of way,' said Felix, 'and among them the trust that she was as good an elixir to the boy as in the winter.'

'Quite true! I believe the glow she excited saved him from an illness; but he has come to another conclusion since.'

'Well—what?'

'I should not tell you, but for his entreaty. He thinks she cares less for him than for you.'

'Nonsense! He may put that out of his head, poor boy.'

The colour mounted in his bloodless cheek, but the decision of the tone satisfied Geraldine.

At that moment, however, the door was gently opened, and Stella, her cheeks more deeply tinted than their wont, quietly said, 'Brother, Captain Audley is here. He wants to know whether you are well enough to see him.'

Cherry divined what was coming; but Felix exclaimed, 'Captain Audley! How kind! Tell him I am quite ready.—But you had better make yourself scarce, Cherry; the poor man has met one lady already, and I can't answer for the consequences of his falling in with another.'

There he was interrupted by her contention with his instinctive impulse to rise and give her his arm—a token of improvement; for whereas yesterday he had apologised whenever she crossed the room without him, to-day he began getting up, but was checked by the twinge betrayed by lips and brow, and as Lord Gerald had been fortunately left ashore, Cherry professed to have her most constant supporter.

Another moment, and Captain Audley crossed her, and bowed to her, as she repaired to the drawing-room, from the window of which she saw the two young things, not idling—Stella never dawdled—but cutting flowers, and filling the whole stock of vases which she had brought out, to renew the cheerfulness of the house for its convalescent master.

The sight was pretty, but Cherry wondered whether she ought to go out and protect her little sister's peace, deciding however, that whatever harm there was must have been done already, and that accessibility was her best condition for the present; and so she sat down to begin some of the numerous letters, though their subject was most incongruous with that of her anticipations, and she wrote with divided attention, till Felix came into the room.

'Cherry,' said he, deliberately placing himself on the settee, 'Had you any notion of this?'

'Only the last day or two, very dimly. Has it come to anything?'

'That I want to ascertain. Which did you think it was?'

'The poor little star, I'm afraid.'

'Why afraid?'

'Because there must be breakers ahead, and that poor little dear need not have been molested for years to come.'

'Is she molested?'

'Look! Ah, no! you can't turn; but if you could see them on the lawn!'

'She is such a child. She might be with him as simply as with Will.'

'I'm afraid that is over. Is not the Captain dead against it?'

'No; that's the odd thing. She seems to have vanquished him on the spot by one glint of her bonnie blue een, and he has not the heart to say No; but the worst of it is, he has no power.'

'He should not have let his son loose here.'

'So he allows, and that I saw clearer than he—which I did not, for my suspicions were in another direction, and I fear not without cause, on one side at least.'

'That's the horrid part of it!'

'So persuaded was I, that I went on at cross-purposes at first, and had to ask point-blank which of my sisters he meant, but I don't think I betrayed Angela. What is to be done about her?'

'Oh! tiresome love! Why could they not let you alone a little while? I think Angela has some notion, and that it must be what has made her so very queer.'

'Perhaps! I thought it was her share in the disaster, poor girl!'

'That would not have made her almost spiteful to poor little Stella.'

'Where is she now?'

'Gone to the penny-club business as usual.'

'I hope this will be over before she comes back. I must speak to my little one, only first let me hear what you think about it. The Captain has been most straightforward with me. He explained that he never was a favourite at home, and his marriage was a case of extorted consent. His wife was never cordially treated, and he could not forget the slights she received. Neither party wanted the other, and he had got into his lonely yachting existence, when, unluckily for him, his elder brother's death has rendered him and his boy important. The widow lives with the old people, and he thinks they want Charlie to marry the daughter. They want him to spend his vacations with them, and he is always shirking.'

'I have heard him bemoan himself.'

'The worst of it is, that if the old people take offence, they are likely to leave the bulk of the property to the grand-daughter. The Captain says he hates it all, and would freely let it go; but at Charlie's age, it would not be right to let him incur such a forfeit blindly.'

'They are both too young for anything.'

'Precisely so; but the thing must be either suffered or not, and it is a mere subterfuge to call it nothing, and let him be always about here. If the child knows nothing, the boy's mouth could be stopped, at least till he has taken his degree. I came to see whether that be still possible. You think not? Well, I have some hope of her simplicity. If not, what think you of this? We tell them they are a couple of babies, and bind the fellow to keep away somewhere till he has taken his degree, when it will either have blown over, or he can judge whether to take to a profession and endanger his prospects, and there will be some test whether he really cares for the poor little dear.'

'I'm afraid there is trial for her any way!'

'The difficulty I foresee, is in keeping the Captain up to anything. If he were set against it, our part would be much easier; but he seems to have surrendered at first sight of our Fair-Star, and he is weaker, more impulsive, and undecided than I could have conceived.'

'He has been indulging his feelings all his life. I should not wonder if Charlie were the more sensible.'

'Our other baby! So! I must see how far it has gone.'

'No! I'll call her. Don't move.'

'A shocking reversal,' resigning himself, 'but I believe you had rather. I don't mind walking; it is getting up and sitting down that beats me. Don't startle the child. There's still hope that he has not stirred the waters.'

Cherry had no such hope, as she stood at the conservatory door, calling Stella. Both came up to her; and as she sent the girl to her brother, Charlie looked at her with an anxious 'Well?' as the colour deepened in his honest face.

'I think your father is in the study,' she evasively said.

'Come, now, Miss Underwood, I am sure you know all about it. What sort of a chance have I?'

'I don't think you ought to have any chance at your age. Indeed, Charlie, I do wish you had let it alone for the present.'

'I assure you, I didn't know I wasn't going to let it alone; but what could I do when I found the dear little darling crying enough to overset a mill-stone? One couldn't but do one's best to comfort her; and when I found I had really got over the line, and been making sheer love, I could not but have it out and go on with it.'

'Then was it only that moment?'

'No! no! no! I'd known her for my Star, my light, my darling, ever since I can't tell when; but of course I knew what a shindy there would be, and as long as I could come here and look at her, I could have gone on quietly till I was of age, and could fight it out. Only when it came to her being lonely—'

'Do you think she knew it for what you say?'

Charlie shrugged his shoulders, laughed, and coloured.

'And your father?'

'That *is* comical,' he said confidentially. 'He was dead against it! hummed and hawed, called me no end of fools, said I should be cut off with a shilling, and told me how my grandmother bullied my poor mother. I'd hard work to haul him here, and he said it was only to beg the Squire's pardon, cram full of objections. Well, there was the darling girl gathering forget-me-nots in the garden, with Scamp and the doves round her. "That's she, bless her!" says I. "Is it she?" says he; and with that, he whips out of the skiff, leaving me to moor it, you see, looks her full in the face—I believe he hadn't seen a young lady to look at since my mother died—"Are you Charlie's little Stella?" says he; and behold, there he is, giving her a regular paternal kiss, before I could get quit of the boat. And when one's own father is all right, who is to make objections?'

Stella's examination had been short. Felix held out his hands, took hers, and gazing into her blushing face, said, 'Look at me, my child, and tell me if you know what Captain Audley is come for.'

She hung her flower-like head, and answered, 'I think I do.'

'And what do you think of it?'

'O Brother,' the eyes overflowed, 'I didn't know it was *that*, when he came and was so good to me, or I would not have been so unkind in all the trouble. I only thought how nice he was. Indeed it was not forgetting Tedo.'

'No, indeed, my sweet; that was the last thing I meant. Only, since you do know the meaning of it, tell me—whether you like it.'

'Like! O Brother! It did just seem to take away all the unhappiness. I couldn't help it, you know!'

'Ah! No, no, my dear, you didn't hurt me. Now will you be patient, so as not to get Charlie into trouble, and trust me?'

'Trust you, Brother?' in a tone of wonder, as if it would have been impious to do otherwise; and then she faltered, 'I thought Captain Audley didn't mind it *much*—for, Brother, he kissed me.'

'He is ready to like you with all his heart; but he has a father too, and can't do all he pleases. So you may have to be kept waiting to grow older.'

'Oh yes,' said Stella; 'I know I'm too young, and I could not go away from everybody for a long long time.'

So the edict was given in form, with more assumption of authority on Felix's part than had been his wont towards his sisters' lovers; but he saw it was the best way to spare the little maid from what might prove trifling and end in disappointment, and the young lover from unfair usage of his grandparents, and its punishment. Someone must be resolute, and the father would not; so the brother had to depict the impossibility of fostering an attachment between an undergraduate and a child, under the certainty of displeasing the head of the family.

Charlie argued that it was hard his father's consent should not suffice—that he cared not for the property—he would go to his uncle in Australia, become printer's-devil at Bexley—anything to be free to win his Cynosure, while his father seemed far more disposed to applaud him than to say, Nonsense; and it fell to Felix to explain that whatever course Charlie might decide on, it must not be till his Oxford career was ended, and that till then there must be neither engagement nor correspondence, and the vacation must be spent elsewhere, since daily meetings in present circumstances would be a wrong towards all parties concerned.

Captain Audley could not gainsay that this was both reasonable and honourable, and even reminded Charlie of an invitation from Lord Liddesdale, to pay a visit at his foreign embassy in the long vacation. Meantime there was to be nothing to bind either party; but as Charlie had to return to Oxford that night, a parting interview was allowed in the drawing-room, in which he raved a good deal, and she was very quiet and rational.

Then Felix was left to repose, which he so sorely needed as to have to give up both coming in to dinner, and driving to meet Mr. Fulmort.

'Sisters' lovers are tough customers,' he said. 'Thank you, Cherry,' as she elevated the front and lowered the back of his chair, so as to render it a couch; 'it is well for me that you would have nothing to say to the sculptor.'

She kissed him silently; and as she looked at the pallid sunken face, with the eyes closed, she recollected her declaration that he must be more to her dead than any other man alive, and though far from retracting the sentiment, she wished she had uttered nothing so ill-omened.

The effect on Angela was the present anxiety; and it was impossible not to feel it staved off by the announcement, through a school-child, that she was staying to dine and spend the rest of the day at Miss Hepburn's. Whatever this might portend, it was a present relief to Cherry, though Clement looked very gloomy upon it; and the Vicar of St Matthew's had not been many hours in the house before Cherry, rather to her own surprise, found herself invited into Clement's library, to assist at a council over the perplexing girl.

Neither brother nor sister could say more than that, up to the moment of the accident, she had been in her usual state of ultra-observance and ultra-gaiety, alike wilful and exaggerated, and that on finding herself the real delinquent in the fatal catastrophe, she had petrified into hard fierce reserve. On Sunday alone had she been at Church, and then had been absent from the Feast where all the family had met; she had thrown over all the little ecclesiastical offices that had been her pride and pleasure, and repelled all sympathy, except perhaps that of the ladies to whom she had been most opposed, and whom she had derided and contemned for years. Indeed, she might be said to have hoisted their flag, for the cross round her neck had been discarded, and her hair had descended from the stupendous fabric which no asseveration would avail to persuade the Miss Hepburns to be of native growth, and was now coiled about her head—with an effect, certainly, preferable in itself, save for the signification. Things were come to a droll pass, that the absence of Angel's lofty coiffure should be complained of by one vicar to the other; but Mr. Fulmort had been Angela's first guide, who had prepared her for Confirmation and Communion, and Clement had from the first looked to him to deal with her; but Mr. Fulmort was scarcely encouraging. 'Nothing will be gained by forcing me on her,' he said. 'If I cannot draw, driving will be of no avail.'

'If Miss Isabella has got hold of her,' said Cherry, 'she is likely to imitate the people in books whose first act of virtue is shunning their priest; and when Angel's conscience gets on the side of perverseness, there is no saying what she will not do.'

'One is so in the dark!' said Clement.

'I think I can guess the process,' said the elder clergyman. 'Only actual experience teaches that no system is infallible.'

'Of all plans of education, I should have chosen hers!' said Clement.

'So we trusted to the framework!'

'And how admirably it has answered with Robina, and many more.'

'As far as we see; but this is what I imagine this poor child's history. She has more vehemence and energy than depth, and her musical taste found ritual so congenial, that excitability passed for devotion, in spite of the lack of trustworthy fruit of submission or self-discipline.'

'I believe it did.'

'So she is in a manner justified in complaining that she was allowed to trust to the shell alone. She has been content with the outward form all this time; and when real sorrow makes her find its failure, she is naturally distrustful of the whole teaching that was to her mere surface work.'

'Nothing could be more ungrateful, or improper, than to charge it on you, Sir,' cried the younger vicar.

'Less unjust than you think, though there may be some human nature in it too. When my sister collected those girls, we thought, like most who try experiments, that we had a set of puppets, on whom certain wires must produce certain results—and if we saw untoward specimens, charged it on the want of our system.'

'The system is not ours, but Divine.'

'There was a Divine system in the Wilderness, but with how many did it succeed?'

'According to that,' said Clement, 'nothing would be anybody's fault.'

'And,' said Geraldine, 'did it not succeed with all the mighty men who overlived Joshua?'

'True; but even of that generation, who had never seen Egypt, there were many who lacked faith to drive out the Canaanites. It is the same story over and over again. People who have been led out of something like Egypt, are apt to think those secure who have never been from under the shadow of the Cloud, and have known no bread but manna. We forget how much depends on being "mixed with faith in the hearers."'

'Faith cannot be given from without,' said Clement.

'Certainly not; but looking back at our dealing with our earlier pupils, I suspect that we worked away with the peculiarities we had newly discovered, rather than with the great universal foundations. I am sure we did so with you, Underwood: though happily there was stuff enough beneath to prevent us from doing more than make you unnecessarily priggish.'

'Geraldine can testify that that was done to your hand, Sir,' said Clement, laughing. 'I believe I should have made any place I cared for odious in the ears of my family.'

'We did not know how much party spirit we infused, fancying that once in our groove all must go right. Now, I believe Angela ought to have been held back. She would have done better in a commonplace well-principled school.'

'I don't think her teachers were deceived in her,' said Cherry.

'No; but the observances which she genuinely enjoyed deceived herself. Probably at a dull bare service she would have been naughty and uninterested, but then she would have known her religion for what it was worth. I don't say that I see what ought to have been done, if we could begin over again; but I do see that she has found out her unreality in the time of distress, and concludes that the fault is in what we taught her. To use another metaphor, she thinks that because the Cross has been decked with flowers, it has been no Cross at all; but I trust she is learning the way thither.'

'By casting aside the means?' said Clement.

'Because to her they had not been means, but mirages. If I understand rightly, this is her first true awakening.'

'But is it to be a regular case of conversion?'

'I hope so. I pray so.'

'Is she to be left to these women, to learn contempt for the Sacraments and the Church?'

'Are they Churchwomen?'

'After a fashion! I don't believe they hold a single Catholic doctrine.'

'They never say the Creed—eh?'

Clement looked abashed.

'If she were likely to be led into an act of schism, it might be needful to interfere; but if they seem to be bringing her to the sense of repentance and individual spiritual contact, which is the essential need, resistance would do more harm than good.'

'Why should she not come the right way?'

'Do you remember Ezekiel's pure springs, which the evil shepherds had fouled with their feet, so that the flock could not drink thereof? Without classing you among evil shepherds, whatever I may do with myself, is it not natural to turn from what has been without benefit?'

'By her own fault. And is she to follow their ways, without check or warning?'

'They are communicants?'

'Four times a year. Frequent Celebrations seem to them superstitious and formal.'

'And irreverent,' added Cherry.

'Is it not doubtful whether our poor girl have been reverent? Should not we perhaps be keeping her back for a time?'

'Not for their reasons.'

'No; but if she be in the way to what she needs and we have failed to afford her, it seems to me that while it is within the Church, we had better abstain from distracting her attention by trying to make her do things in our own way.'

'*Our* way, Sir?' said Clement, whose mind was never rapid; 'it is the right way. I cannot understand sitting still to see my sister carried off into ultra Low Church.'

'Better that than incur the risk of taking party spirit for zeal and diverting her attention from vital religion to the excitement of persecution.'

'There's nothing that would gratify her more,' said Cherry.

'It is exceedingly mortifying,' added Mr. Fulmort, 'to see one's own child going over to a rival battalion, which disesteems our ensigns and war-cries; but by your own account it is no worse—the army is all one. And for ourselves, nothing can be more wholesome. I wish it all fell on me, since the mismanagement began with me; but unluckily it comes most heavily on you, both as brother and parish-priest.'

Clement was of course disarmed and humbled. 'No doubt you are right, Sir: I will try to accept the personal vexation as my due; I did not know how much it biassed me. Shall you take no notice?'

'I shall express the interest I feel as old friend and guide, but I shall not insist on confidence.'

He could afford to bide this time, for he contrived to give a parson's week, on finding how heavily this sad Whitsuntide had told upon Clement, coming at the end of a clergyman's hardest half-year. Change could not be had, for Felix was not fit for a journey, and was still so much disabled as to be unable to put on his clothes unaided; but nothing could be better for both brothers than the presence of this friend, bringing them fresh interests from the great arena of conflict between good and evil, and giving warm sympathy and satisfaction to their efforts in their own field. One of his scholars, at least, he confessed to have far surpassed his expectations. He had never expected to see his tall, docile, self-complacent chorister all the man that the Vicar of Vale Leston Abbas had become; but on the other hand, Angela, once almost his devotee, eluded him by every means in her power, and never willingly opened her lips in his presence. When at last he succeeded in catching her, and expressing surprise that she was rushing away when the church-bell was ringing, her reply was, 'I've done with those things!'

'With prayers?'

'With heartless forms.'

'So I should hope.'

'Let me go, Mr. Fulmort; I don't want to be ungrateful, but it is all one great mistake.'

'I am afraid you have found it so.'

His tone was sad, and made her exclaim, 'You feel it too, then? Oh, come and learn as I have learnt—see as I have seen!' Some men would have laughed at this sudden reversal of the order of things; but Mr. Fulmort felt the matter far too seriously, and the sound of inquiry he emitted encouraged her to go on. 'Oh; the hollowness of my old life—the utter lack of all aid or light when the hour of darkness came—the misery, the agony, that racked me all day and all night, when all you told me to trust to proved broken reeds. Would that I could proclaim to all what it was to see at last in Whom—in what assurance lies peace!'

'Yes, my child,' he said. 'There truly lies the only hope. May you be able to grasp it firmly, and for ever, and render the fruits of faith and repentance apparent in your life.'

'I shall never put my trust in my own works again. I hate them—I loathe them.'

'You cannot do better than repent, and bring them for forgiveness.'

'To the foot of the Cross?'

'Certainly.'

'Then you really see the hollowness and emptiness of the system of thinking them pardoned by a man's voice?'

'Did I ever tell you they were?'

She was a little conscience-stricken, but rallied enough to say, 'It is the whole principle of auricular confession, to which nothing shall ever bring me back. Not the utmost persecution!' and as he smiled a little, she added, 'It was all form and human intervention.'

'If you can say so from personal experience, Angela,' he replied, 'it proves how lamentably I have failed to express my doctrine and intention, and how vain it is for me to try to converse with you. Indeed, I only attempted it because I knew you had had a great shock, and were unhappy.'

'Unhappy till I turned my back on the world and its vanities, and beheld the true and simple way of salvation! Would you but let me show it to you!'

'My dear child, do you think I have feebly tried to follow my Master all these years, and never seen it? If I have so totally failed in guiding you to it, my words alone were in fault, and it is well that the one Truth has been brought to bear upon you. I thank Him for it, and pray that some day you may be led to *full* truth.'

There he quitted her; and she could report that Mr. Fulmort had tried to get her under his direction again, and that she had almost brought him to own the emptiness of the system that he inculcated. That he did not was, Miss Martha decided, wholly owing to the Old Adam.

CHAPTER XLIV.

THE FIDDLER'S RANCH.

'The *Vater Unser* that I said
Before I went to school,
The prayers come ringing in my head
Like ripples in a pool.'
Veritas.

Angela's conversion, as her friends did not scruple to term it, had this happy effect at least of extinguishing her passion (if so it might be called) for Charles Audley. It was swallowed up in the general excitement; and once or twice Cherry had reason to think she had persuaded herself that she had voluntarily renounced him among other earthly vanities, such as her chignon, her church decorations, and her balls.

If she still felt any jealousy of Stella, it only showed itself in a pitiful contempt of the poor little unawakened creature, so contentedly deluded by ceremonies, and drifting into the jaws of this wicked world; but it was memorable that though she always opposed Stella's opinion, were it only on the weather, she never attacked her direct, nor reproached her, probably out of a certain discomfort which the little maid's simple answers always gave her.

Stella was Clement's mainstay this summer in the thousand and one inconveniences caused him by Angela's conscience in the thousand and one parish affairs in which she used to be his prime helper, but where she now disentangled the material and the spiritual, after the example of her advisers, though with a sauciness and vexatiousness of which they were incapable. Luckily no idea of pining after Charlie seemed to occur to Stella, and she devoted the time once spent on poor little Theodore to the many tasks that Angela had left on her hands and considered just fit for such a foolish little thing.

Any secrecy as to the possible relations with Charlie had proved unachievable, at least within the family. Charlie might be banished, but his father carried on the courtship with unblushing assiduity, viewing Stella as his special property, and being never happy without seeing her two or three times in a week. In truth, after so many years of morbid seclusion, the society of a family home—such as he had never known—was so delightful to him, that he could not stay away, and almost exposed himself to suspicion of being in search more of a wife for himself than his son.

The Kittiwake, where never woman had set foot, and where Charlie, in spite of Angela's bantering solicitations, had never ventured to invite her, was urgently pressed on the whole party for any excursion imaginable; and when it became evident that both the Captain and Stella greatly wished it, the seniors consented to a day's sail along the coast, it being decided in council between Wilmet and Cherry that sea air might bring freshness back to Felix's looks.

The morning was all that could be wished, but the post brought an appointment from a man of business to see the Squire respecting some land which was to be secured in East Ewmouth, for the foundation of buildings that might serve to Christianize the straggling population there, making a fresh district from both parishes. For it was to this purpose they had decided to devote the tithes cut off from Vale Leston, since the new tenements actually stood in that parish, and the work at home was now forward enough to enable the extension to be made.

Great was the lamentation at this inopportune arrival; but Felix owned himself glad of it, and did not look equal to a long day's fatigue. Clement also remained to assist at the consultation, and after the conference, walked to the spot with the agent.

Returning soon after the hour for the second post, Clement went to the study, where, as he entered, Felix, who was seated at his writing-table, lifted up his face from his supporting hand, very pale, and with eyes swimming in tears, but with a look of rest and relief that reminded the Vicar of that which had responded to the tidings that their little Theodore was beyond the reach of harm. He held up something, saying, 'Look!'

'The photograph of my father.'

'See there,' pointing to the corner.

'T.E.U. Edgar's copy! Is he found?'

'Thank God! There is hope that the lost is found!' He rested his head against Clement, heaving a mighty irrepressible sob, physically painful, but full of relief. Those two had become inexpressibly much to one another during these four years, and far more during the last six weeks.

'From Travis?' asked Clement presently, observing the handwriting of the letter on the table.

'Yes, good faithful fellow! Would you read it to me, Clem? I cannot get on;' and he cleared his eyes of the blinding tears. 'I could only see that there was hope at the last.'

'Of finding him?'

'Not here. No. He begins by telling us the dear fellow is dead. I think it was something violent, and that he tried in vain to save him. Let me hear, that we may see whether there be anything we can spare Cherry.'

Clement thought Felix even less fit for any shock or agitation than his sister, but he could only make him lie back on his couch, whence he watched with earnest eyes for every word.

The narrative is, however, here given more fully than it could be written, especially as one portion of the history was reserved for Marilda alone.

Ferdinand Travis had inherited a considerable claim to mining property in the south-eastern portion of California. He had gone to America, intending to dispose of it, but had ended by settling down there, naming it Underwood, and doing his best to exert an influence for good on the lawless races he found around him. He had enough in common with them to obtain a partial success where another would have failed; his little township was thriving, and to some degree civilized, and he had even been able to obtain the building of a church and residence of a clergyman with a kind of mission to the Indians. All around him was safe and peaceable; but between him and the nearest cities on the Pacific lay a tract subject to the forays of a tribe in the tiger stage that precedes the abject decline of the unhappy red-skins.

190

The district was gradually becoming settled, but neither village nor traveller was secure from horrible raids and savage massacres, and save by letter-carriers, who trusted to speed, the region was seldom traversed except by parties numerous enough to protect themselves.

Such a surveying party Ferdinand had joined, intending to transact some affairs at San Francisco; and on the third day of his journey, when descending a steep hill-side, the war-shouts of the Indians were heard, and presently about thirty beplumed and painted savages were seen evidently triumphing after a victory.

The travellers scarcely uttered a word, but settled themselves in their saddles, and drew their revolvers, then charged the foe with the full impetus of a down-hill gallop. It was the affair of a moment; the Indians threw themselves on their horses and scoured away like the wind, while the new comers found that they had been exulting over the slaughter of only two men and one little child, whom they had been proceeding to mangle after the custom of their tribe. One victim was quite dead, and already scalped and scored; the other, though senseless, stripped, and gashed in many places, was still breathing, as was the child—a boy of six or seven, though shot through the breast, and the mark of the scalping-knife already begun on his head.

The keen wiry dauntless fellow, who acted as guide, driving two of the party in a much enduring waggon, opined that they came from Fiddler's Ranch, about two miles off, and recognized the living one as the Fiddler himself—the best company, he guessed, between this and the Atlantic. It was a service of danger to lift the bodies into the vehicle, for the Indians might be hovering about in ambush to fall on the rescuers in great numbers; but the transit was safely performed; up to the stockade and ditch protecting the township called Fiddler's Ranch, whence issued a population of the rudest description, vituperating the Indians, and bewailing 'poor Tom the Fiddler and little Jerry, the smartest, cutest little critter that side of the mountains.' 'Pretty nigh gone, stranger; bring him in, lay him by the side of his father; those brutes of Injuns fix their work off too handsome—best if neither opens his eyes again.'

A low frame-house, the outer half-store, also post-office, newspaper office, photographic studio—such was the place into which the father was carried, Ferdinand following with the child into an inner room, where were some appliances of comfort, a neatly ordered bed, a few chairs, a table, and some drawings fastened to the wall—among them a photograph that arrested Ferdinand's attention. Had he not gazed at the likeness from his bed in Mr. Audley's room? did he not know it in the family parlour, and in Clement's cell at St Matthew's? It was the likeness of Edward Underwood!

He turned hastily to the bed. Yes, the face, weather-stained yet ghastly, overgrown with neglected beard, stained with blood and dust, still showed the delicate chiselling of eyebrow and nose, the Underwood characteristic!

Such remedies as the Ranch afforded produced tokens of reviving power, and Ferdinand could not believe the wounds necessarily mortal. The rest of the party were about to pursue their journey, and through them he sent the most urgent entreaties and liberal promises that could induce a surgeon to take his life in his hand, and cross that dreadful waste. The signature of F.A. Travis was well known in the West.

While Ferdinand was washing away the soil from the face once so fair and brilliant, bringing out more of the familiar features, consciousness returned in groans; and when at last the lids were raised, and showed the well remembered deep blue eyes, the first word that struggled articulately from the lips was, 'Jerry! Baby!'

'Here!' Ferdinand laid the nerveless hand on the little flaxen head, still motionless.

That was enough at first, but as the tide of life began to flow more freely, Edgar called the child again; and as no answer came, used his hand to feel, writhed his head to look. 'Jerry!—what—asleep? They've not hurt him!' The last words in a tone of full sense and anguish.

'He does not seem to suffer,' said Ferdinand. 'I have sent for a doctor, and I trust to keep you both up till he comes.'

'A doctor! Here?' with a contemptuous groan. 'Help me, I must see him!' with a vain effort for a fuller view of the child, who was on a sort of crib by his side, lying with closed eyes, and a beautiful waxen death-like face. 'Lift me!'

It cost sobs of agony, though that seemed lost in the intense gaze. 'Is his wound there?' he asked, looking at the bandaged head.

'That was the scalp-knife, but it has done little harm. *The* wound is here, but the ball passed out at the back.'

'And is *here*,' said Edgar, laying his hand on his body. 'I had him before me on my horse, as we always went, my brave boy! One week more, and we should have been beyond the miscreants' reach!' and he sank back with a piteous wailing moan, too weak and shattered for demonstrative grief, though utterly crushed. 'Put him by me,' he added presently; 'if there be any life left in him, he will like it.'

'I am afraid of hurting you.'

'Nothing will make much odds now. We are both done for, and I am glad it is both, if it was to be. My poor little chap, we couldn't do without each other!'

Then, as Ferdinand placed the child where his restless hand could stroke the cheek, tender parental pride revived. 'A jolly little face, isn't it? if you saw it like itself. Oh, if I could see those eyes open for once!'

There seemed a revival of strength; but with the knowledge of the bullet-wound and the six frightful gashes of the Indian knives, Ferdinand felt that a few questions must be risked, lest this should be a delusive rally, and speech suddenly fail. 'You know me, Edgar?'

'Fernan Travis! Ay. You're not much altered! But how did you know me? I'm not much like the swell I used to be! Ah! I see!' as Ferdinand signed towards the photograph. 'How are *they* all?'

'All well, when last I heard. Longing only to hear of you.'

'Better not.'

'And this is your boy. His mother?' he added, with more hesitation; and it brought a fierce look.

'Never had one in any real sense. She left him at ten months old—always hated him. But he's all right. You'll find the certificate in that old green case.'

'Of his baptism?'

'No. Such matters don't come handy here, and she wasn't one to concern herself about them. I don't know that she was the better for that! No: it's my marriage lines! I kept them for his sake, though I gnashed my teeth at them often enough.'

'Pray let me baptize him!' entreated Ferdinand, with an imploring accent, contrasting so curiously with his bronzed face and black beard, that Edgar again smiled, saying, 'You've not turned parson?'

'No, but this is a case of necessity.'

'Oh! all's one to me,' interrupted Edgar, with a sort of instinctive sneer to cut short a Clementine discourse; 'since this business must come to their ears at home, they may as well be at peace about one of us.'

'And his name?'

'His eyes—you'll never see them—but they have so much little Cherry's wistful look, that I've called him Gerald; you may tack Felix to it. No mockery! He's been the happiest little soul that ever was born, happiest maybe if he goes on as he is, knowing nothing about it.'

As Fernan repeated the Lord's Prayer, first learnt from Lance, the tears gathered and softened Edgar's eyes, and made a mist as he saw the pale brow sprinkled, and heard the Holy Name.

'You said that once for him. Let me hear the old echo again. I wanted to teach him, but it never came right.'

Ferdinand was so thankful that the doxology came from his heart, though at the moment he saw that the poor child had been almost baptized in blood, for Edgar's caresses had displaced the bandage and some bright red drops had started, and mingled with the water, and he could not help silently tracing the cross with his finger before kissing and wiping it away, and re-adjusting the handkerchief. 'He is warmer,' he said. 'See, his lips are less deathly.'

'The death flush,' said the father.

'It need not be. I will try the brandy again. I thought we got a little down before.'

'I tell you he shall not be tortured! Why should he wake to an hour's conscious misery? I could not bear it! I say I will not have it done!' and he stretched out his hand as in protection.

'Nay, why should not he live? There can hardly be any vital part here, and it has just missed the spine. Let me try!'

'To make him a wretched orphan. Another burthen to Felix.'

'That need not be a scruple now.'

'He has not married Marilda after all!'

'No; but he has come into the property.'

He was surprised at the effect of his words, 'What! what! Felix! Vale Leston?'

'Yes, he has been living there these four years.'

'Not married?'

'No.'

'Then that child is heir to all! Bless me! Felix at Vale Leston! It makes one believe in a Providence at last.'

He anxiously watched Ferdinand's endeavours to restore his little son, as though divided between the wish for his life and the apprehension of his visible suffering; but though the stimulant was certainly swallowed, and produced a slight revival of pulse, the lethargy continued.

Edgar's own wounds, except the rifle-shot in the body, were the lacerations with which the Indians mark their victims, not mortal in themselves; but he never admitted any hope for himself, and though for one day and night his recovery seemed possible, after that the wounds assumed an appearance which the experienced inhabitants, many of them fugitive Secessionists, pronounced to be fatal.

He talked a good deal at times, and was eager to hear all Fernan could tell him about home; and though he gave no connected history, it was possible to piece together the sad story of his life from his rambling talk.

The sight of Spooner, the manager, in a cab, had convinced him that his forgery had been detected, and he could hardly credit the assurance that it was known to no creature save Marilda and Ferdinand himself, whom she had instantly despatched to assure him of pardon and secresy.

'No! did Polly do that? A golden girl I knew she was; but that's sublime! Yet I might have known she had held her tongue, since Felix and Cherry are alive and well! Good old girl. I say, Travis, you must have her after all. She deserves it!'

His relief was intense, when he thought of his son, in finding no brand affixed to the name he had never dared own again, except at the two most unhappy events of his life, his duel and his wedding.

'Ourselves, our souls, and bodies, to be a reasonable, holy, and lively sacrifice,' he said. 'Those were little Lance's words—the chief reason he assigned for burying himself at Bexley. A fanatic craze of course, but I never got the words out of my head, and I'm sure I've been the sacrifice, soul and body, though not what you'd call a holy or a reasonable one! Well, whatever hindered him, it was well for him!'

He explained that Allen had been a feeble speculator, but plausible, of personal good faith, and perniciously sanguine. His schemes had chiefly devoured Thomas Underwood's legacy, while as to the other debts, Edgar treated them lightly, and though he was much moved at Geraldine's exertions to pay them, he called it an infatuation in Felix to have allowed it.

After his flight to Ostend, Edgar had joined Allen's company at Strasburg. Failure had disgusted him with painting, and the free wandering life had long fascinated him, while with the Zoraya he had a standing game at coquetry. Though her name was Hungarian, she was almost stage-born, and her nationality was harder to analyze than Ferdinand's. She had sung ever since she could speak, and been bred to the boards, but as, in spite of her splendid beauty, she lacked dramatic talent, and her voice had been too early strained, she was never more than a third-rate prima-donna, with airs and graces that were Edgar's sport and titillation, while to her he was the handsomest and most gentlemanly man in the company, with wit and breeding of which she was half afraid.

When Edgar found that the unhappy occurrence at Pau was known, he asked eagerly after Alice, blessing the kindness that had brought her home; but he lived where life was held too cheap to make him greatly heed blood-guiltiness; nor had he deemed the wound more than the just penalty of forcing the duel on him, viewing the fatal result chiefly as an accident. But Zoraya had seen Alice shriek and faint, and Edgar falter and blush, and knew that this pretty English doll had been the cause of his killing his man. Thenceforth passion and jealousy awoke in her, and made her whole being centre in the determination to turn his trifling into earnest. Her beauty became more striking, her songs more effective in the absorption of her soul, and her eager pursuit became as often oppressive as amusing. When he had remained in Egypt with the apparently dying Major Harewood, nothing could persuade her that the Englishman was not connected with Alice; and when he joined the troop again, she hailed him like a truant slave returned to his bondage.

Why had he not broken from it? Had the telegram announced Felix, he could not have helped lingering for a sight of his face in spite of everything; but Wilmet, in her cold severity, and her grief too, he could not encounter, especially as Zoraya had threatened to descend upon him and 'imagine the meeting.'

So he drifted back to the 'company,' which had by force of custom become a sort of home, and was his sole resource. 'Rattle-snake and frog,' he said; 'of course the frog succumbs at last.'

But that had not been till the retirement of the Allens had left him to the mercy of the Prebels, and when the absence of Mrs. Allen's unimpeachable respectability left the company at the mercy of scandal; and a little exaggeration of evil report, with a few tears and heroics, brought him passively to surrender his hand to his pursuer, and they were married in New Zealand before proceeding to America to 'star it' in the Southern States.

Even then his affectionate nature would have opened to family love; but with the attainment of her object, Zoraya's passion ceased, and she viewed him as a master to be resisted. His ideal of a wife had been formed on very different women, and incensed her imperious temper; and when her violence was met by cool sarcasm, she was lashed to frenzy. Her repugnance to motherhood completed his disgust. He deliberately told Fernan that first and last he had never seen a spark of even animal yearning towards the infant, only angry impatience of the discomfort and inconvenience, and contempt of the pleasure it gave him. She was enough among the advocates of advanced women's rights to learn to admire her own scorn of maternity, and but for an old negress, whom he had hired on the poor little thing's unwelcome entrance into the world, its chances of life would have been few.

So they had rubbed on, till at Chicago Edgar had fallen ill with inflammation on the chest and throat, and was left voiceless, hovering on the verge of decline. He was still confined to his room when he received a note from Zoraya to inform him that she could not be burthened with the support of an invalid, and had therefore made other arrangements, in pursuance of which she enclosed a deed of divorce. To him it was liberty, and satisfaction that she had not heart enough to rob him of his child, but it was also destitution. However, there was compassion enough for the sick and deserted vocalist to render landlord and doctor merciful, and he was allowed to liquidate his debt by taking portraits as soon as he could reach the drawing-room of the boarding-house and wield his crayons.

'I don't know whether the divorce would hold water at home,' he said; 'but keep it, to guard the boy. If he is heir to anything she will scent it, like a vulture, carrion. Stay, while I can sign it, you draw up a form, giving the custody of him to my brothers, and forbidding her having anything to do with him.'

He was uneasy till this was done. His success at Chicago had given him hopes of gaining a livelihood with his brush, but he soon found photography too strong for him, and could meet with no employment as a violinist. His health was too much shattered for settled exertion, and though he said little of his struggles and sufferings, they must have been frightful, as he dropped from one failure to another, striving as he had never striven before, till he actually became a teamster to a party prospecting far West. 'I can't think how they came to take such a screw!' he said; 'but I believe they forgave me my child for the sake of my fiddle. Such a child as it was too, not eighteen months old, but never fretting for a moment. Most of the way I carried him strapped on my back, and always felt his little hand in my beard, and heard his voice in my ear as blithe as a katydid, and he was always ready to play, till he was a regular pet-kitten among them. Ah, well, Jerry, you and I have had good times together. How will he ever stand the high polite at home? Pah! You must have him out now and then, and let him breathe the prairies, and gallop after the buffaloes.'

It had ended in Edgar's settling down on this spot, having found the Editor of the 'Soaring Eagle of the Far West' closing with a favourable offer at the other end of the Continent. 'Tell Felix I took to his trade,' he said. 'Take home a sheet or two to be preserved alongside of the Pursuivant in the family archives. It is dated Violinia, a free translation of Fiddler's Ranch. Before I came, it used to be Broken-head Ranch; but it got the other name when I took to playing to hinder my boy from hearing more foul tongues than I could help. Take Lance my violin. He may some day make it over to Jerry, if he has a turn that way, though maybe he had best not.'

Perhaps nothing he said was sadder than this, considering what music could have been to him.

It appeared that though the wonderful spring of health in that salubrious air had made his first years there enjoyable, he had begun to feel the lack of all good influences as his child grew older. What he heard with indifference from his comrades, was shocking when echoed from the tender lips that brought back the thought of home; and when Gerald began to ask those deep questions of why and wherefore, life and death, that we only cease to wonder over as we grow used to them, Edgar, who had never reflected before, only undergone a few intellectual impressions and influences, answered as one bewildered; and when the fair head nestled to him, longed to see it bent over the clasped hands, like the heads so like it at home. He tried to teach; but prayers, cast off half a life-time ago, came not at his beck, and the very framework of the religion he had never attended to, and then thrown aside, had almost passed from him. Fragments floated before him, and his perplexity became longing to clear his mind; and when the foul habits and language of the Ranch came prominently before the child's growing perception, he had resolved to remove to where order and decency prevailed. He had answered an advertisement offering employment as an editor in a more advanced settlement, and was in the act of riding to an isolated station to collect his debts before his departure, when the attack had been made.

It was as if he had been just turning back from the husks which the swine did eat, and making his first step from the far country; and perhaps he thought so himself, for when Fernan's kindness as well as his own suffering had demolished his proud irony, he said, 'A fellow like you carries his Bible as a charm. Read me the old story of the younger son. It is not an original idea to ask for it, but the cadences have rung in my head ever since that "Pater noster" of yours.'

It was as if the old irreverence must still tinge whatever he said. Very perplexing it was. Was it repentance, that self-condemnation for wasted kindness? Was it faith, that increasing craving for Gospel messages? Was it prayer, the entreaty for the forms whose words, all broken, haunted the memory of the clergyman's son? He showed neither fear nor regret; he knew he had his death-warrant, he had made a bad business of life, and was weary of it—he, his thirty-second year not yet complete—he, the most gifted of the brothers. He sent no direct message, either to ask pardon for himself, or protection for his child—perhaps he was too secure of both to feel the need, for he spoke more and more of Felix and Cherry—nay, seemed to be talking to them when fever obscured his mind. Over and over recurred Lance's answer, 'a reasonable, holy, and lively sacrifice,' as if it had been the riddle of his life—or again the opening words of the Lord's Prayer, running into 'I will arise and go to my Father.'

The loving hearts must trust to the Father, Who can meet the son even while yet a great way off. And it was well for them that kind Ferdinand dropped the veil over the day when the doctor came too late for alleviation, though in time to save the child, as the lethargic trance gave way, and the moan of 'Daddy, daddy!' began. The last conscious light of the father's eyes met those of the boy; his last word replied to the feeble call. So Edgar Underwood passed away, and Ferdinand buried him beneath a pine-tree, amid many evidences that he had endeared himself to the rude spirits around, who mourned him in their rough sort, with many an anecdote of his ready wit and good-nature, and many another of little Jerry's drollery, simplicity, or courage.

The doctor recommended transporting the child to Sacramento before recovery of his senses should aggravate the danger of the journey. The spine, though not actually touched, had received a shock, and would require most careful treatment, beyond his own skill. So a bark cradle like that of a papoose, had been constructed, and slung to Ferdinand's shoulders so that he could raise it in his arms and break the jolting of the waggon over the roadless waste. When clasped in a pair of kind arms, with a beard to put his hand into, and a soothing voice to hush his moan, he did not waken to miss his father, though more than once he asked how soon they should arrive, and many times begged to go to bed.

The best surgeons of Sacramento and San Francisco had consulted over the little fellow, and pronounced that the spine had escaped by so little that the nerves would long feel the shock, though it might be outgrown in time. They thought he might be removed as soon as the external wounds were healed and the constitution had somewhat rallied. A nurse had been obtained, but at present the boy would endure no attendance but Ferdinand's, and seemed satisfied and lulled into a half-conscious doze by his English voice and accent.

All that Edgar had said about his son being Felix's next heir was omitted in the letter; but Ferdinand said he supposed that Felix would wish the boy to be brought home as soon as he could safely travel, but if not, he should be sure of a loving home at 'Underwood.' If he were not to be received, a telegram should be sent to Sacramento, but there would probably be time for a letter, since weeks might pass before a move would be prudent. Of course, too, all respecting the forgery was suppressed, and only written to Marilda, who was attending her mother on her yearly visit to Spa.

Clement read the letter through without pause or remark, though his voice shook and thickened when he read of Edgar feeling about for the Lord's Prayer, and Fernan helping him. Truly, the last had been first, and the first last. He was disappointed too, not to find more to justify the hope that his brother had evidently gathered.

Felix lay back all the time, his eyes fixed with a kind of unseeing steadiness on his own photograph of his father, hanging against the wall. His hands were clasped over his breast, sometimes trembling slightly, but never unlocking. 'Thank you,' he said; 'there seems nothing to keep from Cherry.'

'She might imagine much worse things if she did not see the letter.'

'If we prepare her, and give it to her to read, it will be almost a comfort. Call her in when they come home. No, I will, or she will take alarm for me.'

Care for Cherry seemed his first thought; and Clement said, 'It is well we never told her what we thought about the Australian report. How much it has spared her!'

'Ay; mark the time, Clem! It was spring, five years ago, just when you and I began those prayers, that he was left with a little child to lead him. How often that is brought about!'

'I am glad he named the child after Cherry,' said Clement, willing to blink the full reply, for never having been able to love Edgar as did his elder brother, he could not as entirely 'believe all things and hope all things.' He felt the terrible deficiency, knowing that Ferdinand would have put foremost whatever truth would allow him to say.

The indirect reply made Felix shrink from that heart's core of the subject, unwilling to hear the faint qualified hope that conscience would suffer his brother to utter, dashing the comfort that he had embraced.

With a heavy sigh he began to lament the great unhappiness that had come upon one so formed for light and sunshine. Edgar and Lance had always been of the same temperament and tastes, and yet they had been the two arrows, shot by the same hand, but of such different course.

'A very sinister blast came on one!' said Clement.

'Yet, change their places,' said Felix. 'Lance would at fifteen have stood the foreign college, and I doubt if the Minsterham choir would have been good for Edgar!'

'The real key lies in those words that haunted poor Edgar. The sacrifice must be to One or to the other—the Rood, or the heavier weight,' said Clement.

'Heavy indeed!' sighed Felix, as if the severity cut him, giving way to a sobbing groan. 'Such a life, and such a death! Our father's pride—the flower of us all! O Edgar, our nursery king, that it should have come to this! What would not I give to have been where Travis was, if only to cry, Alas! my brother!'

And as the beautiful features, gallant bearing, and winning speech, so affectionate when most blameworthy, came over him, his enfeebled state broke down his ordinary reserve, and sorrow had its course.

Then came a long stillness while Clement wrote to Lance; but when the bell rang, Felix rose to accompany his brother; and when Clement, perceiving how painfully he moved, would have dissuaded him, he made his usual answer, that 'After a time, there is no use in favouring a strain.'

His management of himself was right, for after the quiet little service, almost a duet between the brothers, in which both could afford to falter or choke when the *De Profundis* came among the Psalms, Clement found him standing under the willow-tree, quite himself again, as he looked at Theodore's little green bed, with Stella's wreath of white roses. No doubt his thoughts were on the lone unhallowed grave parted from them by half the world; but he would not risk his self-control again, and took Clement's arm without speaking.

The twilight of the July evening was falling when the waggonette came to the door with rippling laughter and merry voices, calling to the two brothers who stood in the porch.

Clement went forward and lifted Cherry out, then left her to Felix. It was too dark to see faces; but silence was already taking effect, and when she found herself beckoned into the study, she knew her brother was strongly moved, and was too sure of the cause by intuition to utter her former cry, 'Is it Edgar?' only she trembled as Felix made her sit down on the sofa, and placing himself beside her, said, 'My Cherry, our long waiting is over;' and then while her fingers closed on the hand that held them, he calmly told her the facts.

She bore it better than he had expected, unknowing how he himself absorbed her chief anxiety. Indeed, the hours which had intervened had brought him to so resigned and thankful a tone, that it almost hid from her the full force of his tidings. She asked for the letter, and then rose in search of light.

'You would like to go to your room,' he said, and gave her his arm, both too much absorbed to remember that he had not helped her upstairs since the accident. When he had kissed her, and shut her into her room, he leant for some seconds on the rail, and his face was contracted by suffering, more physical than mental.

He was at the evening meal, and so was Cherry. She would not have her supper sent up, she wanted to be in his presence, and be supported by it. She was so far stunned, that the horrors that would yet haunt her for many a night had not dawned on her imagination; but when he said, 'It is well,' she felt it so, but she needed to look at his face to be soothed and comforted—yes, though it was terribly pale. The colour, save in chance flushes, had never come back, and to-night the whiteness was like marble, but the quiet strength and peace seemed to hush, bear her up, and quell the wailings of her heart.

And when John Harewood came full of anxious inquiry, he really thought the tidings had overcome them less than his own wife, who had never quite recovered the effect of her exertions at the accident, and coming home over-tired, had been quite crushed by the intelligence— the more because, like those whose judgment was stronger than their yearning over Edgar, she did not trust much to those few tokens of penitence. And Angela was not withheld from loudly blaming Fernan for not having, as she assumed, insisted on proclaiming the sinner's Hope, and when assured, that no doubt he must have done so, though he did not set down his own words, she shook her head, and said, 'How could he, when he did not know it himself?' There she was silenced by Felix, and went to the Hepburns for sympathy.

For the rest, the family spoke little of the new loss. Felix quietly busied himself in the arrangements that the discovery of of his new heir made him think desirable. Mrs. Fulbert's remarriage, and the lapse of her annuity, made him better able to carry out his plans at once; and if his heir were not Clement, it was necessary to make the arrangements more definitively.

Of course the little Gerald was telegraphed and written for. He must be welcomed and loved, but he was on the whole dreaded as much as hoped for. The Mays spoke of the self-reliance of the best-trained colonial children; and what could this poor boy be—the deserted son of the singing-woman—but at best a sort of 'Luck of Roaring Camp.' Wilmet infinitely pitied Geraldine, and rejoiced that the river lay between, to keep Kester and Edward out of the way of corruption.

CHAPTER XLV.

THE MYRTLE SPRAY.

> 'He smiled, "Shall I complain if joy go by
> With summer days and winter follow it?
> If He who gave the gladness I have known,
> Shall take it from me, shall I make my moan?
> Nay, for it all is His, the joy, the pain,
> The weeping and the mirth, the buoyant breath
> Of happy toil; the mist on weary brain;
> The turmoil of our life, the hush of death:
> And neither life nor death—things near nor far,
> Shall sever us from Him whose own we are."'
> *Autumn.*

The Vale Leston waggonette was waiting at the Ewmouth Station to meet the express on an August afternoon, and in it sat Geraldine, her heart in her eager eyes.

Felix was coming out of the station with—oh! what a robust, brown, bronzed Ferdinand, and between them, a little fragile, shrinking figure, dragging his feet with a certain stiffness and effort. That was all she saw till he was lifted in Fernan's arms to her kiss, and passively endured it.

'Will you come by me, Travis?' asked Felix, ascending to the driving seat.

'Will you stay with your aunt, Gerald?'

'Oh, come! don't leave me!' in a plaintive voice, were the first words Cherry heard from her nephew.

'I believe I had better. He feels the jar less,' said Ferdinand, seating himself within, and lifting the child on his knee. 'Geraldine, I say,'—bending forward and indicating Felix—'is he all right?'

'O yes! quite! he only feels the strain a little now and then,' she asseverated.

'I did not know him till he spoke,' said Ferdinand. 'He is grown so much stouter and so pale.'

'We are all getting middle aged, you know,' faintly laughed Cherry.

'Not you, Geraldine, I never saw you looking so well.'

'That's the place. It has done us all good—only strains are endless worries, and he can't take as much exercise as usual. He has thought so much of your coming too—he will be much better now it is over. Little Gerald! little Gerald, our dear little boy!' said she, trying to take the small thin hand that lay on the little black knee, and to look beneath the broad grass hat.

'Take off your hat, my man,' said Ferdinand; 'let your aunt see your face.'

The child obeyed, and sat leaning against his friend, holding his hat in both hands, and gazing full at Geraldine, out of a pair of eyes, which, after what she had heard, rather disappointed her by not being of the family blue, but soft liquid brown; but the skin was delicately fair, and the features of the true Underwood cast, strangely startling her by recalling Theodore, not the mindless Tedo of daily life, but such as he had lain in the Oratory only with those great mournful eyes and a soul intensely looking out of them. The hair too was very light, of the same silkworm fineness as Theodore's, and falling in the selfsame masses of glossy waves. Ferdinand parted these aside caressingly, and showed a curved red scar that made her shudder and ask 'Is it well?'

'Quite. It did not go deep, and even the other is entirely healed now,' said Ferdinand, 'though its effects are more lasting. However, he found his legs on board ship.'

'Are you tired, my dear?' she asked, feeling as if another moment of the gaze of the big sad eyes would make her cry.

'I'm used up,' he said, piteously, but though the phrase was Yankee, the weary tone was English, and gentlemanlike.

'Poor dear little man! We shall be at home presently, and then you shall rest, and have tea.'

A smile broke out on the little face—a smile approving him truly as Edgar's son, as, glancing up through those long black eye-lashes, he asked, 'Are you Chérie?'—(not Cherry, but Edgar's own exclusive title for her).

'Chérie! To be sure I am, my own dear, dear little boy,' and the tears started while she smiled.

'Then will you tell me the rest of the stories?'

'What stories?'

'The story about the poor man that had the burthen and went the long journey, between the lions and up the hill Difficulty. When Daddy couldn't remember, he says you know it all.'

She withstood the impulse to call out to Felix, knowing that a turn to look back always hurt him, and only said, 'Yes, my dear, I'll tell you all my stories. What a traveller you are! how did you like the sea?'

'All but the womanfolk,' said the boy gravely.

'Oh! Gerald!'

'You're not womanfolk,' he answered.

'Eh! what then?' she asked, endeavouring to look into the brown eyes, but their black fringes were down now, and he nestled to his protector, into whose ear he whispered what was repeated to her in a sort of aside:

'She's just Daddy's Chérie, the darling.'

How well she knew them for Edgar's words! She longed to have him in her arms, but she saw by the manner in which Fernan held him that the strong support was needed to break the vibration of the carriage. 'Did you carry him so all across America?' she asked.

'Nearly. Even Pulleman's cars shook him, and he could bear it less then than now. The voyage did him a world of good, and every one was kind to him, but he's as bad a misogynist as ever Lance's Miles. There were but five women at Fiddler's Ranch, and only one white, and they called them all aunts. You'll have to drop that distinction! And may I keep him in my room till he has had time to get used to the strange house?'

'And the strange beings,' said Cherry. 'It will be a great blow to Sibby, who had begun to cheer up at thought of him; but as she never had Theodore at night, she may bear it better.'

'Ah! that loss must have been much felt, though no one could wish it otherwise.'

'No one has felt it so much as he,' said Cherry, glancing up to her brother. 'He had really the mother's love for the weakest. I wonder if he will see the likeness I do! I feel as if Tedo were come back, with what was lacking.'

'And Stella?'

'Oh! Stella—' she suppressed with difficulty, 'has another interest,' and changed to—'Stella has turned into a woman, and is the most helpful person about the house.'

'Whom shall I find at home?'

'The regular domestic establishment, including Bernard, but Lance comes on Saturday, and Robin—she has not been at home since September, but the De la Poers have all settled down at the baths at Töplitz, and his Lordship is coming back on business, and escorts her to London, where Lance meets her. You'll find Will Harewood too—good fellow, I know he thought Clement overtasked, so he has taken no pupils this year, except that he is coaching Bernard for Keble College, and says he is come to learn parish work, and you would never believe what an excellent clergyman old Bill makes.'

Here they reached that spot where ten years previously the charms of Vale Leston had first broken on Felix, and this time he could not help looking back to call out 'Look, Fernan! Hold Gerald up to see the place.'

Ferdinand lifted the boy to look over the empty side of the driving seat, exclaiming himself 'How lovely! There's nothing like an English village!'

'It's a ranch and not a city,' said the boy.

'It is home, Gerald, your home,' said Felix, trying to get a view of his face, which expressed more wonder than admiration.

He looked puzzled as they drove over the bridge, and when they came among the grass and trees of the park where John Harewood's fine short-horns were grazing, he asked 'Where's the store?'

'He has only heard of Bexley!' cried Cherry. 'Not here, my dear; uncle Lance takes care of that.'

'And the paper?' asked Gerald, much to her amusement, but just then they drew up at the door, where all the rest were assembled to meet them, including Wilmet and her boys, who were both dancing about, shouting at the top of their voices for a drive round to the stables. It was too much for the new-comer, he clung to Fernan with a scream, burying his face in his breast, and trembling all over, and Fernan, saying he was always frightened at any sudden outcry, asked leave to lay him at once on his bed, and let him sleep before there were any more introductions.

Felix showed the spare room, and after an interval Ferdinand rejoined them, saying the little fellow was asleep. Cherry asked if she should sit by him.

'No, thank you, he does not mind being alone, and as long as he sees my portmanteau he will know it is all right. It is numbers and noise that frighten him, I sometimes think he has never got the Indian war-whoop out of his ears. They talked of his bravery at the ranch, but that is all gone now.'

'From helplessness, very possibly,' said Felix.

'That is fast improving, but his nerves have had a shock that does not pass off. Besides, I find the poor little fellow somehow fancied he should meet his father here. I had no notion till now that he supposed he was going back to Fiddler's Ranch and the old life when he heard of *home*.'

'It must have been all like a long horrible dream,' said Cherry.

'I don't understand it,' said Ferdinand; 'he was scarcely sensible when I took him away, and he called me Daddy till his mind grew clearer. He seems always watching for some one. I did explain it all, and then I thought he understood, and he knows what death means, but somehow he does not realize it with regard to his father.'

'Very likely,' said Wilmet, 'his impression varies according to whether he is well, or tired and feverish.'

'I never thought of that!' said Fernan, 'I believe it is so—for when he is pretty well, he is the smartest little thing I ever saw, always asking questions, and reading! I believe he read every book on board! And he was very funny there, ready to talk to any one, provided it was not woman.'

'Has he any religious feeling?' asked Clement.

'Yes. He said his little prayers—poor Edgar had taught him that—and, and I thought you would like me to tell him what I could.'

'No one has so much right,' said Felix. 'Fernan, I have been remembering the time when I was angry with Mr. Audley for taking you into our house—as I thought to corrupt Lance.'

'Well, I did my best, or worst, to corrupt Fulbert,' he said smiling; 'and if you and Lance had not been what you were, you would have seen me in much truer colours. I had no training like what Edgar gave his boy. You will find him a wonderfully good little fellow, marvellously shielded from evil.'

'You think he may safely play with our boys?' asked Wilmet.

Fernan smiled sadly. 'Play, poor little fellow, he is a long way from their play as yet! But he is a far safer companion for them than I was for your brothers. He has hardly ever spoken to a child of his own age; I believe there was one black baby and one half-caste papoose in the Ranch, but childhood was not otherwise represented, and he was afraid of the few we had in the steamer.'

'He must have been a most incessant charge,' said Felix.

'But I don't think I ever enjoyed anything so much,' said Fernan. 'I wish you didn't want him!'

'You see how little Cherry could spare him,' said Felix. 'But you will make us a long visit, till he is quite at home.'

'I thank you; I *couldn't* go till he has grown happy with you—happier, I hope, than he has been with me, poor little man; but as soon as I can, I shall run up to London, and there's a matter I must go to Spain about before I return far West.'

'At any rate this is your home in England, Fernan. You know we can't thank you, but you are more than ever one of ourselves.' And Felix held out his hand for a tremulous grasp of Ferdinand's.

Gerald did seem in great need of his friend when he awoke. He recoiled in dismay at the stairs. 'Oh! those dreadful things are here too!'

For he had never seen a staircase till he was carried down that of the hotel at Sacramento, and his limbs had so far been affected by the spinal damage that he could only as yet move with difficulty on a level surface, and needed to be carried down with his eyes shut, that he might not see the giddy height. He consented to sit by Chérie at the evening meal, and was not ungracious to the other members of the family, comporting himself discreetly, gazing out of those enormous eyes at the novel scene, and fraternising with Scamp, who adopted him at once as an Underwood.

He had made up his mind as to his eldest uncle, and when they rose, crept up to him and, putting his frail little lizard's hand into his, said tentatively, 'Blunderbore!' and as Felix started, hardly knowing whether to laugh or cry, he added, 'I want to see the Pursuivant,' uttering all the syllables with great clearness and deliberation.

Much delighted, Felix took him into his study, when he examined the last roll of proof with profound sagacity, and said eagerly, 'I can fix off a sheet for you,' accepting his uncle much more as editor than as squire.

The introduction to Sibby was tolerably successful, he detected that she talked like 'Kerry Micksey,' his chief playmate at the Ranch, and she was the only person he accepted as an aunt. Felix was too glad to be dubbed Blunderbore again to object to the familiarity; they taught him to term Clement the Vicar, and the others went by their unadorned names. It was remarkable that Bernard, though growing up into a fine manly beauty much resembling Edgar's, did not seem to recall any association; but on the Saturday afternoon, when Cherry was sitting with him under the cedar-tree, a low sweet whistle made him start, scramble to his feet, and as Lance came forward, he threw himself upon him with an ecstatic shout of 'Daddy, daddy.' And as Lance stooped down and gathered him into his arms tenderly, saying 'Poor little chap,' no doubt the tone and gesture kept up the delusion, for he clung in a rapture that it seemed cruel to disturb. 'What shall I do, Cherry?' said Lance, much distressed. 'Oh! my poor little fellow, if I could but change myself!'

By that time doubt had wakened, the arms were unwound from his neck, and Gerald, after a moment's contemplation, gave a sad low cry, struggled down, and hid his face on Cherry's lap, then lay passively against her while she fondled him with her hand, taking no notice in word, except by distinctly letting him hear his uncle's name. 'Lance! how came you so early, and where's Robina? Felix is gone to Ewmouth, thinking to meet you by the express.'

'We got off from town earlier than we expected; and walked from Church Ewe, and meeting Bill in the village, of course I stepped out and left them to their bliss.'

Lance looked well, and spoke as if he had attained to steady if not high spirits. In fact, though asking anxiously after Felix, he was plainly gratified by the entire trust and satisfaction shown in himself as a substitute; some of his articles in the Pursuivant had been a success in the circle that cared for them, and one on an important subject had actually been copied into a London paper, a distinction that had not so often befallen even Felix as not to make it exhilarating. What made far more difference to him, Mr. Bevan had finally resigned, and the new rector had a bright young wife, who had been a school friend of Robina's, and both had accepted Lance on terms of equality, so that he had more access to society than had ever been his lot before, and found himself treated as an important ally in all matters for the benefit of the parish. His life was evidently far more cheerful than in the previous year, and he had done what he had declared he should do—'got over' his fit of depression, i.e. resigned himself, and therefore recovered a certain power of enjoyment as well as interest in his work. Cherry reproached him with never having come home since Whitsuntide.

'No possibility of getting away,' he said.

'Not with Mutton as a *pièce de resistance*.'

'Mutton's Madame requires recruiting at Dearport and the frequent solace of her cosset.'

'O Lance! what a boy you are for being put upon.'

'Don't row me, Cherry, I get enough of that from Mrs. Frog. By-the-by, she's going to let Marshlands for a year to the squire while he is enlarging his house, and we are to have Prothero's rooms. The dear old Croak says she'll not have me catching my death on that nasty velocipede another winter.'

'Ah! if you had but brought her back to our old quarters! You should never have allowed the Giant to let Madame in! But tell me, Lance,' she added in a different tone, 'has she shown any feeling?'

'Lamb was in a state of mind about telling her, and wanted me to do it, which I declined, so he fetched Miss Pearson, and came down quite proud to tell me she had had hysterics. What a sheep it is, to be sure! He adores whatever she does! And then her spirits and health required the parade at Dearport.'

'You don't believe in it?'

'I only know that whenever I had to go to Dearport I always saw her best bonnets bobbing about among the ladies, or met her on the parade with Gussy and Killy looking like princes. I called to see Sister Constance one day, I thought she would like to hear about you all. And, Cherry, did you know that Angel had sent back her medal as an associate, and without a word?'

'Just what I should have expected.'

'They did not like to write about it till they knew more. Now I believe the chaplain has.'

'She has said nothing about it. In fact, she is much more with the Hepburns than at home, and they have really done her some good. She was quite meek when we fell in with all the Walshes' guests the other day. I wonder whether she will thaw to Robina! Ah! here they come!'

William and Robina were walking arm-in-arm, deeply content to be together, but grave and subdued.

'How still it all sounds!' was Robina's exclamation, and though the others smiled, it was with a sigh at the thought of the low humming that they all missed.

The hush over the house struck her more than anything. When last she had been at home the whole place seemed vocal with unrestrained life and mirth, all the brothers and some of the sisters went about whistling or singing, every one was always shouting to every one, Stella's doves cooing, the clock chiming, Theodore a continual musical-box, but now, though chimes and doves had not ceased, the soft undercurrent was gone, and so was the gay ring of mirth.

'It is as if there were something quelled,' she said, pausing for the word, when she went out for a turn with Will in the light of the broad harvest moon, rising red over the woods.

'So we are,' said he. 'There is something about the place that reminds me of going into the garden when everything is lying broken and weighed down by a storm, the sunshine making diamonds of the drops, but rain-drops still.'

'Angel is so different,' said Robin, 'and Felix's looks appal me: and yet Cherry seems easy about him.'

'So would you be if you had seen him two months ago,' said Will. 'I don't think any one is really anxious about him but Clement.'

'Oh! if it is only Clement, I don't care.'

'Working under Clement gives a very different notion of him,' said Will; 'you can't think how much I find I have to learn now I come to the real practical thing, among simple folk. It humbles me as much as it refreshes me, after the forcing-house at Oxford. I say, Robin, how long is this to go on?'

'How long?' echoed Robina sadly.

'Nay, listen: Clement is going to set up a curate in the new house, as is to be, and £200 a year. I am sure of pupils.'

'Please don't ask me, Will. It is so very hard, and my better sense won't let me.'

'Then put away that better sense, as you call it, I don't.'

'I can't put away the recollection of my father dying of toil and privation. I should feel it killing you to consent.'

He felt rather than saw she was crying as she leant against him, but he tried to laugh and say, 'I am a tougher subject, Bobbie; we've neither of us been tenderly reared. Besides, here it would be different.'

'Yes, because we should prey on our families. No, Willie, I made a solemn resolution never to drag you down, and I will keep it.'

'You're far too wise for me,' he began, displeased.

'Don't be foolish, and break my heart over it! Oh! Willie, if you get angry, I can't bear it now, it is all so sad.'

The mute caress answered, but each was a little relieved to say 'Hark,' as the silence was broken by the sharp wail of Edgar's violin, which Lance was handling to ascertain in what condition it had arrived.

'Is your voice all right, Lancey?' asked Felix, as he spoke of the choral meetings.

'Just what I want to know. I've not sung to any one I could trust to tell me the sound of it. Miss Grey likes it well enough, but then she never heard it before, and I don't know whether the best high notes have not thickened.'

'What will you try? said Clement 'I'm not sure that "Chloe's disdain" did not show you off as well as any.'

'Then Angel—where is she?'

'Angel anathematises light and profane songs on the eve of the honourable sabbath,' said Bernard; 'I wish she was here to have her ears pulled.'

'No, it is not so much that,' said Cherry, 'as that she cannot bear secular music since that unlucky song. But here's Stella, the universal stop-gap, to be Chloe.'

It was a fine old seventeenth-century dialogue song, a sort of heir-loom in the family—the lady's part full of the pert coy disdain that passed for maidenliness, the swain's of a pathetic steadfast constancy, and there was a variety in the expression that had always given scope for the peculiar beauties of Lance's voice. But as he sang it now, it was not only as a musical exercise or 'crack song,' the manly melancholy stirred the depths of a sad but resolute heart that could hardly have otherwise poured itself out. So two of the hearers understood it, and Cherry, clasping Felix's hand, found the pressure returned.

It was only Clement who, as the last sweet quiver died away, was disengaged enough to say, 'You seem to me to have gained instead of lost.'

He muttered something about a German air left upstairs, and ran away.

'I'm afraid it is Philomel against the thorn,' murmured Felix in his sister's ear.

And Clement, in an undertone, uttered the two words 'whosoever hath,' and Stella, of course mentally supplying the continuation, perceived that he was thinking how the voice treated as a means of praising divine glory had survived in its purity and freshness under the same danger that had been fatal to the gift that had been the temptation and ruin of its owner—a thought better suited to Clement's stern sad nature than to his little sister; and instead of answering, she began to play Mozart's requiem.

It was long before Lance returned. 'It was that poor little Gerald,' he said. 'I wish I had thought of it—when he heard the violin, he thought his Daddy was really come at last. I nearly tumbled over the little white bundle in the gallery. Poor morsel, I suppose he was almost asleep, for when I picked him up, feeling like just nothing at all without his clothes, he firmly believed I was Edgar masquerading; and the more I coaxed him in the dark, the more he implored me, "Oh! Daddy, don't go on, be Daddy, I know you, I do! 'Tisn't play," till he almost broke one's heart—I thought I should have to call Fernan.'

'And how did you manage him, poor darling?'

'It was curious. One of those shouts that they give in the harvest when they clear the last sheaf in a field came in, and made him shudder in horror. "The Indians," he said, and then, after I had told him what it was, I said, "Yes, you heard the Indians once, didn't you?" and he answered, "Oh! yes, Daddy told me, 'Never mind, my brave boy, it can't last long. Shut your eyes, and say your prayers!' and he held me tight, tight."'

'Then that is the last recollection he has of his father! A noble one!' said Felix, with a sound of thankfulness.

'So I told him,' pursued Lance, 'that Daddy was right, and it hadn't lasted long. I just told him the real story, and how his father gave him to Mr. Travis to bring to us. I told him how poor Edgar used to teach me to play on his fiddle, and I think he really was relieved to lose the confusion about identity, and he knew me at last for the Lance who used to sing "Jim Crow." I told him all I could, and looked at the marks on his poor little back and breast. How did he live, Fernan?'

'I can hardly tell; I suppose life is very strong in a healthy child, and that torpor of benumbed nerves saved him much pain.'

'I fancy poor Edgar had told him a good many stories about us, for he asked me all manner of odd questions about home, and I am to take him there when he is well. Meantime I had to sing him to sleep—"like that," he said, poor little fellow; and he started Sibby's old croon that used to be Baby's name for her.'

'The child has adopted you, Lance,' said Felix, when he saw Gerald riding down to breakfast in the new uncle's arms, with an arm round his neck and his head on his shoulder. 'Should you not like him to be your godfather, Gerald?'

'No, Gerald, that can only belong to Mr. Travis, and your uncle Felix.'

'Travis, of course,' said Felix; 'but for me, it would be too like a parent, and—' he paused, but went on: 'You ought to have that tie—you who brought out that final saying from his father. Never let him forget it. It is so perfectly the spirit in which to meet the unavoidable.'

He certainly had a power of transmuting into comfort all he heard of this beloved brother. It had been decided that the boy should be admitted into the church on this, his first Sunday. Ferdinand was anxious that it should be, like his own baptism, his first sight of the interior of a church, and had been preparing him for it all the way home, so that he knew a good deal more than had yet been made to adhere to his cousin Kester, and his replies had a flavour of St. Matthew's that delighted Clement. It did not seem right that the thing should be done in a corner, and in the first strangeness numbers would make less difference than after he had learnt to know the faces round him; so they resolved to face the full congregation at once, large as it was apt to be in the afternoon; for there had of late arisen among the young men of Ewmouth a fashion of walking out to church at Vale Leston, attracted partly by the choir and partly by the preaching.

It was too long for Gerald's feeble limbs to be kept standing, and though he was tall for his age, Ferdinand Travis took him in his arms where the questions and replies startled the unprepared. 'Who baptized this child?' when the answer, 'I did,' came from the jet-black beard of the great American merchant, more like a Spanish grandee than ever; and 'With what matter was this child baptized?' was responded to 'With water'—there was a thought of the blood that had oozed forth and mingled with the 'lucid flood,' and Clement's voice trembled with emotion as he certified that all was *well* done, and as he signed the cross, it was where, in anticipation, Ferdinand had marked the rood, and as Geraldine's eye traced the little coronal that the cruel knife had scored, her whole heart went into the thought.

'Thus outwardly and visibly
We seal thee for His own;
And may the brow that bears the cross
Hereafter bear the crown.'

Strange was the entry in the parish register regarding the child whom his uncle treated as heir of his house and name, but at whom every one looked with compassionate misgiving, so weird were his great pensive dark eyes, so thin his cheeks, so feeble his movements, so complete the contrast to his sturdy cousin Christopher, the one all mind and the other all body.

Felix wished for London advice for him, and, as there was to be a clerical meeting on Tuesday at Richard May's, proposed to drive with Clement as far as Stoneborough to ask the two physicians what they would recommend. Lancelot only discovered this intention just as he was stepping into the boat in which Bernard was going to take him to Ewmouth to meet the train—probably he fancied his face quite impassive, but it was far too transparent for him, and there was a curious gust of expression passing over it when Felix asked whether he had any commands for Stoneborough. 'N-not—at least, my—my—remember me to them. That's all! good-bye.'

Then he expended his energies on the oars, and snubbed Bernard into silent smoking, meanwhile he was calculating the increase of means that had accrued to Felix, and would surely render marriage possible.

Felix found his call happily timed, for Dr. May received him with, 'That's right. Just as the last patient has made his exit. Nay—not the last. I fear your side does not seem to have mended.'

'Not much, thank you.'

'So I see, but wait a bit. You are Tom's concern, and I shall get into disgrace if I go into it without him. You can stay?'

'Yes, I ventured to think you would house me while Clement is sitting in council.'

'That is well. I need not go out till after dinner. Gertrude is at home, but Ethel is gone to Cocksmoor to see after feeding the divines. Don't you find that an uncommon excitement to the clergywomen? Well, have you got the poor little boy?'

'Yes, a sweet little fellow, but in an anxious state. The spine seems affected still, and I want to know to whom you would advise me to show him—I must get some one while Travis is with us to tell what the American surgeons said.'

'That's another matter for Tom. He knows the present leading men better than I do. I'll send up word to him to look in when he gets back from the hospital.'

'There is a third matter,' said Felix, with a blushing smile, when the message had been despatched, 'not so professional.'

'Eh?' said the doctor with arrested attention.

'It is this,' said Felix in the deliberate manner of one who had long conned his part. 'Should you regard it as intolerable presumption in my brother Lancelot to raise his eyes to your daughter Gertrude?'

'Your brother!!!'

'Yes, sir. Lancelot. I could release him from the retail business and make over the Pursuivant to him. He would have rather more than £500 a year, and if—'

'Lance!' again exclaimed the doctor. 'So it is Lance! I beg your pardon, I had been hoping it was yourself.'

'You will hardly hope that long, sir.'

'What do you mean? That hurt? What has been——'

'That will wait. Do not let me lose this opportunity,' said Felix, rather breathlessly. 'It is not only my health. For all essentials, whatever you are kind enough to think of me, Lance is *that* and a great deal more, and he is deeply smitten, poor fellow, and needs affection and happiness so much,' he continued, a little hurt at the smile that played on the doctor's features, and broadened into a laugh.

'Well, I've no right to complain after setting the lad on.'

'You, sir?'

'Ay. When he was brooding and moping in the winter, fancying no girl would look at him, I told him, by way of shaking him up, that I should be ashamed of one who stuck at his occupation. It is like giving a boy a gun, and wondering when he brings down your tame jackdaw. One ought to have experience by the time it comes to one's youngest, but I suppose I should never get it if I were the father of the fifty Danaides.'

'May I gather that you would not think the disadvantages insurmountable? I know it does not sound well, but Lance is in a better position than mine was. He is a good deal thought of in the town; is intimate at the Rectory; and if he lived in the country, and dropped the retail, I can answer for it that there would be plenty of society such as your daughter would care to have. If I foresaw mortification, it would not be right to expose her to it.'

'Somehow my girls care rather too little than too much about society,' said the doctor. 'I shall be the sufferer. How I shall catch it from Tom and the rest!'

'Thank you, sir.'

'Not so fast. Stay a bit. How far has it gone? The boy has not spoken to her?'

'Not in so many words. He does not dare, and I could not venture to encourage him till I knew what you thought. Indeed he has been chained to Bexley ever since I have been laid up.'

'He is a thoroughly nice fellow,' allowed the doctor; 'he let out a good deal of his inner self to me last winter. If worth were to have it——'

'He would stand first,' said Felix eagerly. 'To tell you what he has been to all of us these——'

'Hush, here comes our professor. He was fuming like quicklime at Daisy's escapade the morning after your accident. A wholesome preparation.'

About an hour later the dinner bell brought down Gertrude and her nephew Dickie. She started, and a thrill of colour passed over her face as she met Mr. Underwood at the table, and, laughing rather nervously, begged him to excuse deficiencies, as Ethel, the cook, the parlour-maid, and all the best knives and forks were gone to Cocksmoor.

It struck her that her father was grave and silent, but her heart was, as usual, full of Vale Leston and Cherry, and she catechised him next on all the ins and outs with which her visit had made her familiar, he replying in detail with his natural quiet humour, though whenever Lance's name came up, he could not help colouring a little. He delighted and excited Dickie with Bernard's cricketing feats, and the doctor waked into interest from his abstraction. He had to go out directly after, taking with him Dickie, who now held the holiday privilege of being his charioteer.

'You had better take a rest after your drive,' said the doctor to Felix. 'Nobody will disturb you in the drawing-room.'

Felix willingly reclined in the great easy chair, only begging Gertrude not to think it necessary to leave him, and as she wished nothing better than to stay, she took her work and sat down. At first all was still; he had put his head back, with closed eyes, in the relaxation of complete lassitude, but his countenance did not give the impression of sleep. It was weary and exhausted, though placid, and gradually an expression of reflection came over it, deepening into anxiety and perplexity, until after about twenty minutes he opened his eyes, and looked at her with a pleasant smile.

'I hope you are rested,' she said.

'A good deal, thank you;' then, after a pause, 'Did I tell you that Lance has quite recovered his voice?'

'I am glad; I have never heard him.'

'You must, then. Cherry shall manage it next time he comes home. He has been kept much too close this summer, but we must make a different arrangement.'

'Not your changing places!' cried Gertrude, 'you don't look fit!'

'I am afraid not,' he answered with weary acquiescence. 'Your father and brother have been overhauling me, and I believe my effective days are over for some time.'

'Oh!' she started, and said in an imploring tone, 'Cherry said the sprain was almost gone.'

'The sprain is,' said Felix, 'but there's something beyond. It may go on for some time, but the result is very doubtful.'

She rested her chin on her hand, her eyes dilated by the shock.

'So, you see,' he proceeded, 'I am anxious to lose no time in getting matters into order, both as regards Vale Leston and Bexley.'

'Oh!' she burst out with a cry; 'don't, don't, don't go on like that—just as if it were somebody else.'

The sound of misery convinced him that he was acting for the best in killing at once any embryo aspiration directed towards himself; more especially as he felt her more capable than any one he had met since Alice Knevett of stirring what he was resolved never to allow to be stirred. Never would he have risked this *tête-à-tête* but for his recent interview with the two physicians; and her sorrow touched and warmed the inmost recesses of his heart. He leant forward, saying, 'There is so little actual suffering that perhaps I feel as if it were somebody else. I have been expecting this, and there have been a weight and weariness about me which make the thought of rest not unwelcome.'

'Oh, no, no! You are quite young. Papa and Tom couldn't have said it was so bad. There can't be no hope.'

'No, there is just a chance of things taking a different turn.'

'Oh! they will! I know they will! Please don't give yourself up. That's the worst thing for any one.'

'I don't do that;' and as she came and stood by him he looked up in her face, saying, 'there is so much kindness in the world that one would gladly not leave it, if only not to grieve one's friends.'

'I wish,' with a half-angry sob, 'you wouldn't talk in that horrid resigned way.'

'This will not do, indeed, my dear.' Her weeping made the word slip out as in reasoning with one of his sisters, but it brought her colour, and the tint was reflected in his own as he said, 'I beg your pardon.'

'Oh! please, I do like it so.'

He found himself on perilous ground, for he was exceedingly drawn towards the girl, whose warmth gave him a greater sense of sweetness than ever had Alice's most gracious moments; and it was with strong effort that he preserved a sort of fatherly tone.

'Sit down again; there is a great deal I should like to tell you, if you have patience to listen.'

Patience! She would fain have listened for ever. He told her the more slowly, in order to give time to rally, the history of the family struggles, dwelling at each turn on Lance's manful part in them, and resolute sacrifice of taste and ambition, and coming down to his own inheritance at Vale Leston, with all that it had involved. The fact was that it was needful to let her perceive that he had never had it in his power to marry, and never intended it; that the only mode in which he could both do his duty by his brothers and sisters, and make restitution of the church property, was by continuing his business, being economical, and raising up no fresh claims on the estate.

Probably she did not at the moment take in the idea of this affecting any relations with her, for she exclaimed, with that hot petulance which in her was never unbecoming, 'I see, it's too late; you've spent everything on everybody else, and lived for everyone but yourself.'

'I wish I had.'

'I don't think it fair!' she passionately exclaimed. 'Why should everything come on you?'

'Perhaps, when one's forefathers have done a great wrong—ignorantly, may be—it must come on some one. I have been struck by seeing how seldom the lay rectory has gone in the direct line, and I am glad to prevent it from being bound about that poor child's unconscious neck.'

'I was wrong,' she whispered under her breath, in a sudden change of mood, as the simple-heartedness of his manner impressed her. 'You are as devoted as any of those old people.'

'Not I,' he answered. 'I have had a particularly prosaic, prosperous, comfortable life of it;' and then, thinking the scene had lasted long enough, he said, 'I should like to call on Mrs. Thomas May. Is it permissible to go through the garden?'

'How can you?' she exclaimed.

'Thank you, I am quite rested' (he might have said, as much as he ever was).

'I meant, how can you go and make trumpery trivial calls.'

'It did not answer in the year one thousand to sow no corn, in expectation of the end of the world,' he answered. 'Spiritually, as little as materially.'

He tried for his dry gentle manner, but was too much moved by her grief to make it natural.

'I'll come with you,' said Gertrude, leaping up.

He took his hat, and she a parasol, and they crossed the garden in silence till, almost at Tom's door, she exclaimed, with a choking gasp:

'Oh dear! oh dear! if there were anything I could do for you!'

'Thank you,' he answered affectionately, with a smiling trembling lip. 'One wish is very strong with me. Things may not be prepared for its fulfilment while I am here—but when it comes before you—you will remember what you say, and I think it will be granted.'

She turned, half petulantly, and plucked off the myrtle leaves.

'Are you going to give me a piece of that?' he said, smiling.

She broke off a spray in full flower.

'Thank you,' as he put it in his buttonhole. 'Perhaps some day you will see this again. Then remember.'

CHAPTER XLVI.

SOUR GRAPES.

> 'Hast thou forgot the day
> When my father found thee first in places far away?
> Many flocks were on the hills, but thou wast owned by none.'
> *Wordsworth's 'Pet Lamb.'*

The London surgeon met Tom May and Page, and gave every hope of little Gerald's ultimate recovery, though for the present there was not much to be done except watching him, and encouraging such exertion as did not excite or fatigue. Cherry was so anxious about the examination, its result and the directions she received, that she never perceived that the doctor spent a much longer time in the study with her brothers than was needed on the little boy's account.

This, her preoccupation and bliss of ignorance, was a relief to both Felix and Clement. They believed there would be ample preparation, and not only were willing to defer paining her, but would have missed her cheerfulness, and wished to spare her the protracted suspense that might undermine her health and power of meeting a crisis that might be deferred for weeks, months, nay years, or possibly might never come at all; for there was a chance that treatment might disperse the evil. The suffering did not increase, and was not constant, but only brought on by sudden movements or in certain attitudes, and any token of it was always laid to the credit of the strain. No one could fail to perceive that Felix was more inert, more grave, and, if possible, more gentle, but the acknowledged injury, as well as the loss of his two brothers, might account both for this and his disinclination to the ordinary summer gaieties. No one indeed, wished for them, now that

Angela professed to have broken with the world, and Geraldine's whole mind was absorbed in the anxious tendance of the little nephew, who preferred her to all others, and was continually needing to be soothed or amused, with a precocious intellect stimulated by all he had undergone, and at the same time with spirits and nerves too much shattered to bear the least strain on mind or body. Edgar's child she must have loved, but this little tender, fitful, dependent creature, used to be the half-comprehending recipient of his sad memories and confidences, was inexpressibly dear to her.

There was hardly any visiting that summer, except the calls of a few friends, and in September Felix decided on asking the two Lambs to the Priory. He had business affairs to arrange with his partner, and thought it would be unforgiving to mortify the wife by excluding her from the invitation, so he braved Cherry's absolute indignation. Poor Cherry! had she known all, she would not have exploded as she had hardly done since her girlish contentions with Alda. 'It is really weak to give that woman her wish, and at such a time.'

'I am sorry for the infliction on you, Cherry.'

'You know very well that is not what I care for. It is the insult to dear Edgar's memory to have her here pranking herself off.'

'I cannot quite see it in that light.'

'No, you always had some infatuation about her: you sacrificed Lance to her when you let her into the house at Bexley, and now you are letting her fulfil her aim of coming gossiping here.'

'One can only try to do what one feels to be right, Cherry. I am very sorry, but I cannot be guilty of a marked slight.'

'The more marked the better, I should say.'

'Hush, Geraldine,' sternly interposed Clement; 'you forget yourself.'

She was greatly startled, for she had thought him entirely on her side.

'I understand her,' said Felix, as usual unable to bear reproof to his sister. 'No one can be more fully aware than myself of poor Mrs. Lamb's underserts, but Cherry will one day perceive that this is the very reason I do not choose to treat her with mortifying neglect. If it be a foolish fancy of mine, my dear, please bear with it.'

She was entirely disarmed, burst into tears, undertook to do whatever he wished, and apologised for her crossness, but in private with Clement, she could not help expressing her wonder and annoyance.

'You had better say no more about it,' he answered, 'or you will be sorry.'

'I shall say no more, but it is impossible that you should not think this a great pity and mistake.'

'No, I don't.'

'I know I was wrong in flying out in my old way,' said Cherry, humbly. 'Perhaps there was more female spite in it than I know, and I am thankful to you for catching me up. Of course this is Felix's house; he invites whom he pleases, and I shall make them welcome; but still I think this is a very unnecessary attention, and if you had seen as much of her as we have, I think you would have enforced my opinion.'

He smiled a little sadly, and let it pass, and Cherry inferred that even a cassock could not guard the male sex from weak toleration of a pretty woman. Yet her loyalty was so strong that, when Wilmet's surprise and aversion were expressed with equal plainness, she maintained her brother's right to practise romantic generosity in his own house, especially since his prudence had abstained as long as any speculations could be thereby encouraged.

The visit was to last from Saturday to Monday, and in due time Mrs. Lamb made her appearance, pretty, youthful, and charmingly dressed, with her husband looking so proud of her as almost to overpower his bashfulness.

They were a great contrast, he so honestly simple and affectionate, adoring every word she uttered, however alien to his nature, and she with the claws full grown that poor Edgar had detected in the kitten. Indeed she was not unlike a handsome sleek cat or managing wife, an excellent and tender mother, dainty and demure, but not by any means indisposed to give a sharp scratch with her velvet paw.

When she exclaimed with playful surprise, 'Oh! what a queer old place. So different from what I expected!' or, 'Looking into the churchyard! It would give me the horrors in a week! Such a melancholy noise from the river!' Cherry might conclude that the grapes were sour, but the admirable Lamb was solaced by his wife's sweet preference for her humble home. Such scratches as would have been patent to that good man were reserved for his absence, as when she bewailed the low tastes of such a promising young man as Lance—Cherry made some effort to discover what she could possibly mean, and found that the low tastes signified his preference for Mrs. Froggatt's company, and his assiduity at the Shakespeare Club and Penny Readings.

Of course she commiserated Wilmet for her children's red hair—predicted that Gerald would be a cripple for life, and lamented Angela's being 'sadly gone off.' Angela did in fact avoid the lady as much as possible, and on the Sunday afternoon went off to what she had in her unconverted days was wont to term the Hepburn Methody Meeting, i.e., a Bible class with exposition and prayer held by the good ladies in their own dining-room, an institution dating from the darkest ages of the parish.

Their green-shuttered house looked out upon a space shaped like a triangle, grassy, and formed by the divergence of the Blackstone lane, the nearest approach to a village-green possessed by Vale Leston. Angela was lingering after the dismissal of the class, discussing Will Harewood's sermon, which by-the-by, the clever Miss Isabella much preferred to the Vicar's, probably because Will, a far larger-minded and more intellectual man, was a great deal the most metaphysical, and had more points of contact with her, when the sound of a bawling voice, interspersed with the singing of a hymn, became audible through the open window, and a procession consisting of a pale-faced young man, one old one, three able-bodied women, and four little girls came from the Ewmouth road, and having arrived at the triangle, the young man mounted a log of timber and began to preach. Sounds ensued which made the invalid Miss Hepburn exclaim: 'Oh! there are those people again! There will be an uproar! Oh! my dear, shut the window, and come into the other room!'

'What for?' demanded Angela, who was trying to hear.

'My dear, you can't think how dreadful it was. Such a noise, and that terrible Timins set his big dog at the preacher, and the poor old Squire said it served him right, and would not commit him.'

'Such a thing might be stopped in a moment,' cried Angela. 'Couldn't you, Miss Isabel?'

'My dear, I did not feel free when it was the message of the Gospel.'

'I didn't mean the preacher, but the persecutors. You could stop them directly.'

'Go out there! A lady, my dear Angela!' cried Miss Bridget

'One does not stick at trifles in such cases!' cried Angela.

'Trifles!' was echoed round her.

At that moment a coarse derisive laugh made Miss Hepburn scream and Miss Martha fly to shut the window, while Angela caught up her bonnet saying, 'I'll soon put an end to it.'

'My dearest Angela, you are not going out; your brother would not like it.'

'Lydia never asked what her brother liked by the river-side,' said Angela, hastily fastening her head gear.

'Oh! don't let her go. Isa—Bridget—they'll hurt her. My dear! Stop her,' entreated the sick sister.

'Miss Underwood going out to a Ranter!' cried Miss Bridget.

'Your brothers will never forgive us,' sobbed Miss Martha. And Miss Isabella laid hands on her. 'It is not proper, Angela, I cannot suffer it.'

'I cannot suffer violence to be done to one who is preaching that Name for petty scruples of worldly propriety.'

'They'll throw stones—She'll be hurt,' sobbed Miss Hepburn.

'You know better, dear Miss Hepburn,' said Angela, turning with a smile.

In another moment she was gone, out into the road.

There was a hush at once. The boys all turned round, and the nearest, a lively mischievous fellow, accosted her with a touch of his hat, and evident sense of high desert. 'Us aint a bin listening to that there chap, ma'am. Us be going to send he off faster than he came. Us don't want none of his sort.'

'How do you know that, George?' responded Angela, to his great amazement. 'How do you know he has not the very message you have been wanting so long.'

The boy opened the roundest eyes. If any opinion was strongly established, it was the ill savour of ranters in the nostrils of the gentry.

'Squire'd be against it, ma'am,' said an older man, 'and Mr. Eddard! Us knows our dooty better than to hearken to such like trash.'

'For shame, Brand,' returned the young lady. 'How dare you speak so of a man who comes in that Name. Now! Here I mean you to stand and listen. Who can tell what good he may do us?'

'Miss Angela' was the universal favorite with the village youth, having fascinated them from the first; and if they had of late remarked any change in her, it was set down to 'taking on' about her brothers, and her defence was undisputed quite as much from attachment as from sheer amazement. The preacher had, on the apparition of the tall lady in black with the lightly waving crape streamers and mantle, expected a rescue from insult and violence, but a warning to depart; and his amazement was great when she took a position in advance of the rabble rout, and signed to him to go on.

He was a man above the average of his class, and his discourse was considerably affecting Angela, when down the lane from Blackstone Gulley came Robina, Stella, Bernard, and Will Harewood, showing Mr. and Mrs. Lamb the beauties of the country.

'Holloa, what's the row? A fellow jawing away somewhere!' quoth Bernard.

'I thought you had no dissenters here, Robina,' said Mrs. Lamb.

'No more we have,' stoutly affirmed Robina, in spite of the strange voices on the blast.

'What's that?'

'An obliging mission from our neighbour.'

'Soon to be refuted by our boys,' added Bernard, 'most likely a cricket ball is flying at his bumptious head by this time! Hollo there!'

For he turned the corner and stood in blank amaze.

Alice tittered.

Robina and Stella were prepared for anything from Angela.

Even Will only perpetrated a long whistle, and the observation 'This is coming it strong.'

Bernard's measures were more decisive. After the first shock he marched forward with the peremptory admonition, 'Come, my man, be off with you, we allow none of this here.'

The young man stood his ground. 'By what authority Sir?'

'I'll soon show you—I say—You here, little Pryde, run down and tell the policeman to step up.'

'Stay Bernard,' exclaimed Will, 'this is nothing the police can interfere with.'

'Don't tell me that, canting and ranting here on our ground,' cried Bernard, with a fine development of the insolence of the lord of the soil. 'Pity you're a parson, Bill (and Lamb a sheep),' he added under his breath, 'or we'd have a jolly good shindy. All you're good for is to walk off the ladies. Here, Angel, you mad party, go with him, I say, the joke has lasted long enough.'

'I shall not move, Bernard, I am here to protect this good man from insult.'

'I tell you 'tis the very way to make me insult the impudent scoundrel to see you standing there among the rabble, making a spectacle of yourself.'

'Neither you nor any one else will touch him while I am here,' said Angela, heroically moving nearer the preacher, and further from her brother. 'He is giving us the message that is too much obscured, and I will not have him silenced. I only wish you would listen! Go on, if you please.'

But the unwonted style of this interruption had disconcerted the ardent missionary more than unlimited rotten eggs could have done. The young lady's presence, though embarrassing, had been stimulating; but when three gentlemen, including a clergyman, were added to the audience, all his confidence in his mission could not bring back his eloquence, and, addressing himself to Angela, his only attentive hearer, he said, 'The tenor of our discourse has been interrupted; thank you, Miss, we will resume on a more favourable occasion.'

'When I'll bring down the garden engine,' muttered Bernard, clutching in vain at his sister as she stepped forward to shake hands with the preacher and say, 'We are greatly obliged to you, and I am sorry you should have been so interfered with.'

William, premising that he was not the parish priest, turned to walk with the amateur in his own profession, as much because he was curious about this phase of life as to see him courteously off the ground—while Bernard was scolding and deriding Angela on what he deemed her most monstrous aberration of all, and Angela marching on, impervious alike to displeasure and ridicule. Mrs. Lamb was trying to condole with Robina, and Robina was coolly stating that Angela was quite justified in using her influence to prevent the man from being assaulted.

The fame of Mr. Froggatt's state-dinner party and of another on behalf of Mr. Bruce had reached Mrs. Lamb, and, on the strength of it, she had freshly trimmed her wedding dress, and was greatly aggrieved to find her labour lost; disregarding her husband's representations of the recent bereavements and Mr. Underwood's state of health, and insisting on attributing the slight by turns to Geraldine's spite, and to the meanness that hindered the family from enjoying their fortune when they had got it.

Though Geraldine had withheld this indulgence, aware that a long late dinner would be a great fatigue to Felix, she believed in dilution, and had arranged to gratify her guest so far as to take this opportunity of inviting one or two Ewmouth families who hardly ever had a day in the country except what they spent at Vale Leston, and whom it would have been almost unkind to deprive of their summer treat.

So on Monday afternoon there was a gathering on the lawn large enough to be a formidable spectacle to at least one pair of eyes in the Kittiwake's gig as she came up the river, and to evoke a strong expletive from a mouth whose fringes were grizzled enough for it to have learnt to be less impulsive.

'Can't be helped, skipper. Come on,' laughed the joyous youth at the prow in the ease of summer attire. 'What, hasn't your domestication proceeded further? One would think you were the one newly caught from the bush.'

'I shall set you ashore and come back at dark when the bear fight is over.'

'Not a bit of it! See here she comes, the little darling Star, bless her,' as over the wire netting, that guarded the croquet balls from the river, sprang the little figure attracted by the well-known boat.

'Oh! I'm so sorry,' was her apologetic cry to the captain, then stopping short, the bright colour flew to her cheeks.

'Well you may, to have such a mob to receive what I've brought you, my pretty. Yes, yes, no mistake about him,' as Charlie bounded to her side; 'but what's this? who's this big fellow in the yellow beard? Did you ever see anybody like him? He looks as much astounded as you.'

'You didn't say it was Stella!' ejaculated the tall, powerful personage designated. 'She was just toddling when I went out.'

'You're Fulbert then!' she said, looking up as she was folded in a big brotherly embrace.

'Yes, to be sure, you pretty little thing. I declare you are a beauty after all! And who's this?'

'I can't expect to be remembered,' said the white-whiskered sunburnt clergyman in a broad shady hat and green shade over his eyes.

'But I think I remember your voice,' said Stella, 'Oh how glad my brother will be!'

'And Lance, is he here?' cried Fulbert, eagerly.

'No, but every one else is at home.'

'At home! I believe so,' grumbled Captain Audley. 'I thought myself secure from launchings out this year.'

'It is only the Colmans and Strachans and Parkers, just to amuse Mrs. Lamb. I did not warn you, for I thought you were yachting to-day.'

'I was on board, going to sail this morning, when I got a telegram from Charlie, and just as I expected him to turn up, who should drop in but these two, fresh from Liverpool. Charles, this one, I mean, not *ours*, thought it best not to startle my mother, and came here first, so I brought them over as soon as they had eaten a mouthful, and now I'll take a cruise up the river till it is all quiet.'

'O no, please don't be so unkind,' pleaded Stella. 'I'll take you to my brother in his study without coming across anybody. He went in as soon as we began to play at croquet. Here, through the laburnum path.'

She led him by the hand in a passive condition, highly amusing to his son and brother, and Fulbert followed in a state of bewilderment.

'What an exquisite place!' exclaimed the elder Charles, catching sight of the cloister through the trees. 'What a treat to see old walls! It is like Oxford.'

'Pretty?' said Fulbert, 'I can't think how any one can stand being cramped up by all these walks and enclosures!' and indeed his great robust swinging step seemed to spurn them. 'All well?' he asked.

'Doesn't he know?' said Stella, pausing and touching her crape.

'Yes, yes, my dear,' said Captain Audley, 'they understand all that.'

'But Fulbert is more than half lost,' said the uncle, 'and for my own part I can't realise this as your home.'

'I shall be glad to get to Bexley,' sighed Fulbert. 'However the elder ones can't be so altered! I should know old Fee anywhere!'

They had reached the house, and Stella left them in the hall, saying she would find Felix. Fulbert would have followed her, but was detained by the captain, with the words, 'She knows best. I told you he had never been quite the thing since.'

Fulbert stood still gazing in amaze at the lofty dark oak hall and broad staircase so utterly unlike the narrow entry that had been home to him, but the study door opened and forth came a figure with outstretched hands, bright face, and glad welcome. 'Ful! Dear old boy, come at last!' and the boyish handclasp of departure was an eager kiss of greeting between the men. 'Mr. Audley! My great wish! Do the others know? Have you seen Cherry?'

'I'll send her in,' quoth the captain, and rushing off in his excitement and hatred of scenes, he marched into the thick of the fray, where Cherry, amid mammas and Hepburns under the cedar, was astonished by a voice in her ear, 'Your brother and mine are in the study, go to them. I'll take the teapot.'

'Your brother?'

'Charles. Eyes brought him home—Fulbert with him. Good morning; you'll excuse Miss Underwood: her brother from Australia.'

Cherry could only gasp something about pardon, relinquish her teapot to the valiant skipper, snatch up Lord Gerald and hurry off at her swiftest pace, finding, under the appropriate shade of the orange-tree at the conservatory door, Charlie and Stella. 'Oh! it was not you he meant,' was her inhospitable greeting.

'No, no. The Charles worth having *is* here, and Fulbert. We are gone to look up the rest.'

This did not look much like it, but Cherry stumped on, and came in sight of the three in the hall, still silent in the first wonder, Felix with one hand on the table, gazing at the new comers in silent extasy, while they looked as if scarcely able to speak under the shock of his appearance—those wasted enlarged features, that transparent pallor with the grey shades round mouth, eyes and temples, the figure that lost elastic slenderness without gaining strength, and the hair thinned though still shining. Cherry was used to it, but she saw how it had startled them, and that all three were like men in a dream, which she broke by her cry of—'Fulbert, Fulbert! Mr. Audley! Oh! Felix, is not this joy?'

Fulbert started round, relieved at his first real recognition, and his big arms were round her, his great beard sweeping her cheeks. 'Cherry! you at last! Little Cherry! But you've not got a proper crutch.'

'So much the better,' said Mr. Audley, amused at the complaint, 'she is a stronger little body than when you left her.'

'And where did you drop from?' Felix was the first to ask.

All was quickly explained, Fulbert keeping hold of his sister all the time. Mr. Audley's eyes had suddenly failed him, and the doctor had urged his going home at once if he hoped to save them. Fulbert, who had long been meditating a run home, resolved to see him safe through the voyage, and thus they had set forth suddenly, preceding their own letters. The inflammation of the eyes had subsided, and they were somewhat better. 'Though,' said the owner, 'I hope it is their fault that you look so altered, Felix.'

'He will soon get back his looks,' said Cherry. 'He is ever so much better. You heard.'

'Yes,' said Fulbert, 'Captain Audley told us. Poor little Theodore. The only wonder is that he lived so long—Who comes there?'

'You know me, Fulbert.'

'Wilmet? Yes, only grown grander than ever. But bless me! I thought they told me. No—Lance isn't here, and couldn't have got like that. Who is it, I say?'

'Have you forgotten little Bear?'

'Great Bear, rather,' said Mr. Audley. 'You've made good use of your time, Bernard!'

'Oh! here's *the* long lad,' said Felix. 'You'll not mistake him.'

'Aye! I should know Tina,' said Fulbert. 'He always did look the parson. Who's missing now—Robina?'

'Robin is here! Oh Ful, Ful, you're very big, but your face is just like the old times when you used to clamber up the timbers in the yard!'

'That's right, Bob! Now I begin to believe I'm come home. You're as jolly as ever.'

Just then a shout of 'Mother!' and a vigorous patter of boots ended in the bouncing in of two red curly mops of hair, whose owners were pursuing a squabble of 'I will' and 'I won't,' and pulling at the opposite ends of a string as they charged against Wilmet, in loud appeal and protest. 'Softly, softly, Kester, Eddy, look at your uncle!' was the motherly unperturbed rebuke, a hand on each shoulder, 'There's your uncle Fulbert. Oh Kester, right hands.'

'Never mind,' said Fulbert, not more eager for the greeting than the two nephews, who began again, 'Mother, make Eddy'—'Mother, Kester won't'—and reeled out of the room still twisted up in the string, Wilmet after them. 'Like a pair of puppies in leash,' said Felix.

'How many are there?'

'These two, and a little girl.'

Then came a sound, not without sweetness, though still a whine—'Chérie! I want Chérie, O Chérie, they've got my lasso,' and tottering and shuffling in came the little black figure with the white face and clung to her. Both travellers started. 'I thought they said Theodore—No, he'd be bigger,' exclaimed Fulbert.

'It is Gerald, poor Edgar's boy,' said Felix. 'Here, Gerald, here is another brother of your father—and here's a dear old friend.'

The delicate hand held out by Gerald was as unlike as possible to the brown puggy paws of his cousins, but he entreated still 'Don't let them have my lasso, Chérie. It's grass, and Fernan gave it me!'

'I'll come, Gerald dear, I'll get them some whipcord—I must go back to the people; I hope they'll soon be merciful and go—Oh! the heart's joy of having seen those two!—Yes, dear boy, I'm coming, I'll take care they don't take it away.'

'Cherry and her master!' said Bernard.

'Blissful bondage,' said Felix. 'Have you seen them all yet, Fulbert? No—where's Angel?'

'Little Pryde has chopped his finger with a reap-hook, and she's gone off with Miss Bridget to see about it,' returned Clement. 'Suppose we walk and meet them, Ful—Felix will have his talk with Mr. Audley.'

And Robina and Bernard departed to the game, while Felix led his friend into the study, saying in exultation, 'Our Cherry looks a heartier woman than ever we expected, does she not?'

'Wonderfully improved. I only wish I could say the same of you! Is this the effect of the accident?' as Felix, having placed an arm-chair for Mr. Audley, subsided into his manifestly invalid resting place.

'I believe so. But how about your eyes?'

'That is what I cannot tell. They have mended since I have given up reading or writing, but I durst not accept the Bishopric till I knew whether they would be serviceable.'

'Albertstown?'

'Yes, I've been offered it. Any way, I should have had to come home; and it was very good in Fulbert to come and take care of me.'

'An unspeakable delight and gift to have you both!' said Felix, 'Most thankworthy!' he added almost to himself, 'how good in you to have come to us!'

'More pleasure than goodness. My mother hates surprises and shocks, so I had the day to spare, and I longed to see your domains. What a delicious place! Not even Cherry's sketches made me understand the charm.'

'We have so much to show you! You will think me absurd about it, but I own I never see anything comparable to it.'

'I shan't think you absurd! Imagine what this room, with its air of age and quaintness of carving, is to a man who has seen nothing venerable these thirteen years.'

'And our church. But that you must not see without our Vicar.'

'I hope to give thanks for our return there. Robert said he would give us all the evening here. How much good you have done him. I think his adoration of little Stella is quite equal to Charlie's.'

Felix smiled faintly. 'Ah! you seem to have come to help us anent that affair! I am very glad to be able to put it into your hands.'

'I'm afraid they are not very influential.'

'At least they belong to a head that can be trusted,' said Felix, smiling. 'I'm not sure the poor lad ought to be here to-day.'

'I fancy he gathered hopes from Lady Liddesdale which he thinks justify him,' said the uncle. 'Should you consent if he got a secretaryship at the Embassy?'

'I should feel as if one of my greatest cares was relieved! I have tried to do right in the matter, but it is a hard one. I should be thankful indeed to see my little one cleared from this perplexity, and I begin to trust I shall. Everything seems to be so remarkably smoothing itself, as it were winding itself up.'

'Felix, I don't understand your tone. I can't see you distinctly, but I am sure more is amiss with you than Robert told me.'

'I was on the verge of bleeding to death after the accident,' said Felix, 'and I fancy the treatment I am going through keeps me low.'

'Treatment, what for?'

In a few technical words he repeated what he had told Gertrude.

'You speak with certainty!' exclaimed his friend.

'No, it is too much out of reach. They are trying to disperse it, and if that cannot be done, there would be a fight of strength of constitution. It seems to me hardly to get better or worse since the mere muscular strain passed off, only paining me on provocation, and telling chiefly in weakness and lassitude. It is curious how everything in my life seems drawing to a point, so that somehow I feel as if I were permitted to bind up my sheaves. Here is poor Edgar's fate certain so as to enable me to make arrangements about the property, and his child to be Cherry's object, making me far happier about her. And here you are; I have longed to pray for your being here to help us both when the crisis comes. You will?'

'I will! I will. So far as I dare to promise!'

'Remember. She knows nothing of this, only Clement. I could not get along without him. Poor Clem! Do you remember how we used to laugh at him? You will marvel at the strength and wisdom that have grown up in him. I rejoice to have come to such dependence on the brother I understood and perhaps liked least, and it is the same with Cherry. She has learnt to lean on him.'

'More than on Lance?'

'Lance, our lark and our sunshine! Dear Lance, I think he may have a home of his own, but his affairs are not yet susceptible of discussion,' said Felix, smiling. 'Altogether, I have been strangely blessed in these brothers and sisters of mine. The love and affection I have had from them, the willing loyalty that has been the spirit of them all, strike me as wonderful.'

'Wonderful, because those who do most are generally the worst requited.'

'And now, the dear little fellow is taken whom I could least have borne to leave,' added Felix. 'The missing him was very sore to me at first, but I am glad now. All were good to him, but it was effort to all but Stella and myself, and even with Stella it could not have gone on. There are only two for whom I have real anxieties, and there is good stuff in both.'

'Alda?'

'I was not thinking of her. She never seemed my charge like the rest. No, Angela and Bernard, but so much has righted itself that I have the more faith. I believe Bear may be all the better for losing his dependence on me. He wants to be forced into manhood.'

'Felix, I wonder whether you are right in thus giving yourself up. It makes me doubt if I ought to have left you alone to the charge. It must have gone very hard with you.'

'Not at all. I have had my full share of happiness. A most happy, peaceful family, and latterly in this delightful place! my first, dearest home, the spot I must always have loved best! and Cherry! Truly, too, both here and at Bexley, I have had that blessing of Joseph, whatever

I have done, the Lord hath made it to prosper. You left me Mr. Froggatt's assistant, I think, and each step since has been no small enjoyment in itself.'

'Yet you are content that all this should end! Your father was, but his had been a sadder, more laborious, unsuccessful life, and I own I marvel at you, so fresh in this position, with life before you—You are—?'

'Thirty-four this last July.'

'That is early youth to most men.'

'No doubt something is due to the perpetual weariness and "do nothingness" that belong to the complaint, and make me feel getting done with it all. Soon I shall free myself of being rector here, the endowment of East Ewmouth is settled, the building begins in the spring. A long minority will right the estate, and work off its burthens, and I have had unexpected opportunities of putting things in train; but if I go on, the task of making both ends meet must continue hard. I suppose recovery would bring back zest and vigour, but as I am now, it is like a lame horse at grass, shrinking from a return to the load, the mire and the ruts, and the assurances of rest acquire a sweetness they never had before. If I had only done my part fully, and could say to my father, 'Behold me and the children thou hast given me!' but when I count my hundred thousand errors, and remember what makes up for them, it seems little if the last passage should be a hard one, as I suppose it will. Oh!' breaking off short, 'I should not have run on like this. It must be the worst thing for your eyes.'

'This is an odd way of helping you,' said Mr Audley, struggling for composure. 'I ought to be thankful to see you like this, but I am selfishly disappointed. I had reckoned on seeing you in the prime of your usefulness and honors, and happiness.'

'Here's plenty of happiness,' returned Felix, with his brightest smile; 'and I've not yet given up the uses nor the honors of Squire Underwood. In fact, I hear the carriages coming, and must go and see the people off. Will that serve for honors? it would have seemed like them twelve years ago.'

Uneasy about the eyes that had been swimming in perilous tears, he continued, changing his tone from the thoughtful to the lively: 'It is our only entertainment this year, of course, but I was forced to have Lamb here on business, and we thought it would please his wife.'

'Is she?'

'Yes, Alice Knevett. Prettier than ever,' he answered. 'Will you come out, or shall I leave you for these few minutes?'

The longing to watch him prompted Mr. Audley to follow him, though with little mind to face any one, and in a few moments it hardly seemed credible that the man who had been speaking of carrying the sentence of death within himself was the same who was so cheerfully and easily going through the friendly courtesies of a host—pausing with a face full of quiet humour to point out Captain Audley acting beneficent rover, though it was his first time of touching a mallet since he had been a guardsman, and croquet a novelty of high life.

Here too came the introduction to Major Harewood, never seen before, and the Reverend William, last seen as Lance's shock-headed friend, a terror to Wilmet and Cherry, and frightening the babies with his mesmerism.

It was still light enough for the grand tour, and Felix, though leaning and resting at every pause, would not be denied the going through the whole, showing it off with a kind of affectionate exultation rather increased than diminished since the day of taking possession. The character of the place had altered a good deal since that day when he had first seen it. It must be owned that some of the perfect trimness of turf and shrubbery had gone, and that some stable windows were broken, and their yard grass-grown, and the Vicarage Sunday school had an aspect which thirteen colonial years could not prevent the baronet's son from feeling at first sight a little disreputable. The half-finished Rectory of the future, where the Curate for whom Clement was advertising was to live, was on the glebe land on the other side of the church. Altogether, the house and grounds might be in less dainty order; but there was a look of life about every window, and the lawn was glowing with the bright tints of geraniums and verbenas, while dog, cat, kittens, and doves, to say nothing of the human creatures, imparted an air of gladness and animation, and the Virginian creeper on the cloister hung like a magnificent purple curtain over the scene. The dreary deserted aspect of church and churchyard which had at first so disheartened Clement was entirely gone, and the last September lights and shades showed themselves on tower and pinnacle, and gleamed on stained glass as somehow sunshine *does* seem to fall on what is loved and prized, as if inanimate things responded to affection.

In the part of the cloister wall that lay within the churchyard precincts were two or three memorials of Underwoods who did not lie buried there, and to these Felix had added a brass cross with an inscription bearing the names of Edward Underwood and Mary Wilmet his wife. Mr. Audley looked at these earnestly, marvelling all the more at his friend's resolute content in his exclusion from this lovely spot, and from thence he was led to the little grave, now marked with a white marble cross, bearing on the foot the word 'Ephphatha.' What better could have been wished for that little helpless being? Fulbert was of course more interested in the willow tree. He swung himself over the bank and calculated the height with wonder, demanding of Felix how the feat had been possible to him. 'I can't tell,' answered he, 'I have wondered since. It was very foolish of me not to have done like Charlie. He was the hero.'

'Ah! Charlie is a regular fish, at home in the water or out,' said his father, well pleased.

And they looked at the 'fish,' who was standing a little way off, with Stella beside him, with down-cast eyes. He had made two attempts already to pour out his plans on Felix, who had cruelly answered that he could listen to nothing till the examination was over, and consent gained, and ruthlessly cut him off from all private interviews, not choosing to give anything that could be construed into the most tacit encouragement—but not able to find it in his heart to interfere with the present enjoyment, though it was not in the bond.

As to the church, now brought to all the glory that reverent hands, careful taste, and well-judged expenditure could give it, the contrast was not small from the dreary bepewed building, and all its native beauties were unobscured or renovated. Very happy were Clement and Cherry in pointing them out one by one, and telling the story of the fragments whose forms had guided the restoration, and Felix sat by on a bench, enjoying the evening mystery of soft darkness as it fell on the archings and vaultings, and putting in his word now and then in the pleasant history of the four years' work.

'Yes, Felix, I do congratulate you! Nay, more! I shall give thanks for what I have seen to-day,' said Mr. Audley in a low voice, as they went to robe for even-song.

And Felix added, 'Thank you. But pray for me, too.'

It was well he had an appreciative admirer for his dear Vale Leston in Mr. Audley, for Fulbert, untrained in antiquities, and with colonial 'nil admirari' ways, did not enter into the charms of grey walls, nor understand ecstasies over the proportions of arches, while even in the house, he agreed with Mrs. Lamb that oak wainscot was dismally dark, and that the furniture was worn and old-fashioned. He could not feel at home. 'It was all very fine perhaps,' he said, 'but it didn't seem natural,' and he eagerly accepted the Lambs' invitation to return with them to Bexley. 'I can't help it,' he apologized, 'I'll soon come back, but I shall not know I'm at home till I've seen Lance and the old house. It's all different here, and you are all grown such swells, and the little ones are so big, and Blunderbore looks as if he had been lost for a month in the bush, and I sha'n't get my bearings till I've been down to the old place, and seen Lance and the fellows there.'

So almost as suddenly as they had come, the Australian visitors vanished, leaving behind them only the security that they were within reach. Captain Audley went with his son and brother, and quiet was left to prevail at Vale Leston. The first break was a message brought in the forenoon to the study, where Felix saw to letters and attended to business more slowly and with more pauses and effort, but not less effectively than heretofore. 'Miss Hepburn would be glad to speak to you, sir.'

'Which Miss Hepburn, Amelia?'

'Miss Isabella, sir.'

'She has found *this* out, and is going to exhort me as she tried to do to Lance,' thought Felix, as he desired that she should be admitted, and with some masculine perverseness, not only rose to greet her, but placed himself in a common upright chair to listen to her. He found himself mistaken, she had not come to speak to him on his own account.

'You are aware, Mr. Underwood, that from one cause and another, we have had some influence with dear Angela, more I fear than has been quite palatable.'

'In some ways you have done her a great deal of good,' said Felix, wondering what was coming.

'Nay, not pot-sherds like ourselves, but the way we have been privileged to point to her, dear child, but I am glad you think so. I fancied that you were all in opposition.'

'I think,' said Felix, 'that the poor child had got into a state of unreality and self-deceit, and that after the shock of last spring your kindness helped her to the true foundations which she had somehow missed.'

It must have been a temptation to Miss Isabella to enlarge on the danger of concealing that true Foundation, but she had a point and purpose, and besides, the Squire looked as little in need of being taught where to find that Verity as any one she had ever met in a biography, so she went on, 'It was, I am thankful to believe, true conversion, and the dear child is indeed a sincere Christian, but young people are so enthusiastic.'

'She is excitable, and sure to go to the utmost length in whatever she does,' said Felix, beginning to expect to hear of the ranting.

He was right. Miss Isabella wished him to be aware that she and her sisters had done their utmost to withhold Angela from rushing out. He replied that he was not afraid it would occur again. William Harewood had talked to the man, and thought him disconcerted, and likely to carry his ministrations where there was more neglect. However, Miss Hepburn explained that this was an offshoot of a great revival which the Plymouth brethren were organizing at Ewmouth. One of their great lights, a merchant captain who had given up everything for religion, was about to preach, and Angela had set her heart on hearing him. His tracts had been widely diffused among the Miss Hepburn's friends, and the warfare about disseminating them in the village was still recent. Angela, who had once made holocausts of as many as she could capture, was now their ardent admirer, and had insisted on making part of the audience of their author. Now the Miss Hepburns would as soon, no sooner, have gone to the opera as to a dissenting chapel, and there had been a vehement argument, resulting in their pupil declaring her intention of going with a farmer's widow who liberally hovered between Vale Leston Church one half of the day and Ewmouth chapel the other.

It was shocking to Clan Hepburn to think of forsaking the Establishment, and even more so to imagine an Underwood, a lady, a clergyman's daughter and sister, at a revivalist tea-meeting in a dissenting chapel, and in full council they had decided that it would be unjustifiable not to warn the head of the family, and absolutely conniving at the monstrous proceeding.

'Thank you sincerely,' said Felix: 'it shall be put a stop to.'

'I sincerely hope that may be possible,' said the lady, 'but where the dear child thinks her conscience is at stake, she is far too regardless of remonstrance.'

Felix smiled, having found this the case whether her conscience were at stake or not.

The encounter must be fought out, not on Miss Isabella's grounds but on his own. He knew it must have come some day. He had not spoken a serious word to her since she had rejected his consolation two days after the accident, and knowing that she was under other guidance, he had not interfered, feeling less equal than ever to a war of words with the perverse and perplexing girl.

How near the conflict was he did not know till at dinner, when on Bernard's asking her to pull up the river with him, Angela replied that she was going to drink tea with Mrs. Lake.

This was one of the gracious acts performed from time to time, but it sounded enough like a subterfuge to make Felix feel grieved and indignant, but he held his peace, and so did Clement, while Robina exclaimed, 'Almost my last evening, Angel!' And Cherry laughingly accused her of devotion to Mrs. Lake's elderberry-wine. Colouring deep crimson, Angela burst forth in a combative tone, 'Well, I suppose I may go where I like.'

'O, yes, my dear,' said Bernard, 'to meet that nice young man, who was holding forth on Sunday. Only, when it is a fixed affair let me know, and I'll have a suit of tar and feathers in readiness.'

Angela's neck was burning by this time, and she crumbled her bread savagely.

'Is the party in his house?' whispered Will to Robina.

But no one took up Bernard's remark, all feeling that the matter could not be made game of, and when they rose, Felix said, 'Angela, I want you in the study.' She could not choose but obey, and before she was fairly in the room, or the door closed, made another outburst, 'Brother, I have no intention of deceiving you; I only did not choose to have it out before Bernard and all in the middle of dinner.'

Felix, in his slow careful manner, deposited himself in the Squire's chair, and said, 'Sit down, Angela.'

'No, thank you, I have not time. I only came that you may see I am not deceiving you. I am going with Mrs. Lake to hear Captain Gudgeon,' she replied, with a glow in her cheeks and a gesture as of noble defiance, somewhat disturbed by his extreme gentleness.

'You had better sit down, my dear,' he said.

This actually put an end to her war-dance. She seated herself, but tried to resume her challenge by saying, 'I shall be at home long before ten.'

'Certainly,' said Felix, quietly, 'you will.'

'You understand that I really mean it?'

'No doubt you do at this moment, but I forbid you to do any such thing.'

'I acknowledge no commands superior to conscience,' she said. 'I have made my appointment.'

'That I will arrange for you.'

'You can't.'

'The pony-carriage is coming round at three, and I shall go and explain to Mrs. Lake that you remain at home by my desire.'

Mrs. Lake's farm was at the end of a lane all stones and ruts, and it was well known in the family that nothing hurt Felix so much as a jolt.

'No! no! You can't think of it,' cried Angela.

'I shall walk over the worst places,' he said.

'And that's the whole! Felix, pray don't!'

'I must, unless you will submit otherwise.'

'That's taking an unfair advantage,' she said, with tears of anger in her eyes. 'You know it is leaving me no choice.'

'Thank you. That is very kind. You had better take that pen and paper and write to Mrs. Lake.'

'You know your power,' she said, petulantly. 'If you were well, I would try it to the uttermost!'

With a fraction of a smile he said, 'We will talk it over when your note is written, but it is hard to let poor Mrs. Lake butter her muffins all the afternoon in vain.'

This view of preparations for a tea-party made Angela smile a little also, and that did her good. She sat down at the table, and hastily wrote—

DEAR MRS. LAKE,

I am sorry to say I am prevented from joining you to-night.

Yours, with great regret,

A.M. UNDERWOOD.

She showed the billet to Felix, who made no objection, but rang, and gave orders for its despatch.

'Thank you, Angel,' he said. 'I do not scruple to avail myself of your consideration for my side, because, as long as my authority over you lasts, I am resolved to prevent you by any means in my power from doing wrong.'

'You know I have ceased to think with you on that point,' said Angela, not without hopes of extorting permission after all.

'I know you have, but you are young enough to be prevented from committing an open act of schism before you have grown wiser.'

'You speak as if I wanted to become an out-and-out dissenter, when I only wish to hear a man whose writings have done so much for my soul, which was starving—yes, starving before.'

'Perhaps sleeping would be the fitter word.'

'Sleeping or starving, it comes to the same. Forms, routine, and ordinances assumed to be everything, and did me no good—how could they? And in the awakening! Oh, brother, would that I could make you understand the joy—the ecstasy of looking straight up to my Saviour, and the incomparableness of what brightens and quickens that gaze. Then you could never try to keep me back for mere forms and distinctions!'

'Nay,' said Felix, gravely but fervently, 'it is because I *do*—I hope—love and look up to my most blessed Lord and Master, that I can permit nothing that rends and breaks the Unity of His Body, which He gave us to guard and cherish here.'

'Unity is not external—it is only in the spiritual Church of the faithful, in their hearts. It is I who want to keep it.'

'By going to those who have parted asunder from us?'

'I never said I was going over—only to hold out a hand of fellowship—to hear and learn.'

'I'm afraid your hand of fellowship is hardly strong enough to unite the two bodies, Angela. Don't you think it might end in your being led captive, like certain silly women we have heard of—ever learning and never coming to a knowledge of the truth. That is what I want to save my sister from.'

'Then it is Wilmet's old "what it may lead to!"'

'Exactly, her old wisdom. See, Angela, I cannot tell how long I may have any authority; at any rate you will be of age in a few weeks, and then I do not know what you may do, for there is something very dangerous in your passion for excitement. I have thought a great deal about you, my poor Angel, for yours is the disposition that has always made me the most anxious of all, especially since the shock that has cast you loose from your old bearings; but all I can do, while I am still responsible for you, is to restrain you as far as possible, both because I think going among schismatics wrong in itself, and because I hope the delay may give you time to be steadied, and to perceive that the Divine appointments of the Church are not darkenings, but lamps of faith.'

'I think you are in earnest, Felix,' said Angela. 'Miss Isa says you and Lance *are* true Christians in spite of it all! Tell me honestly now. Your objection is not because it is unladylike, not fit for Squire Underwood's sister.'

He laughed, 'Really that never occurred to me.'

'Then I don't mind. I say, did Miss Isa put you up to this? Yes? I can't understand. It was she who first opened my eyes to the light, and taught me what true Christianity is, showing me the hollowness of all I had lived in, and bringing me from darkness to light. It was she who gave me Captain Gudgeon's books. They are beautiful. Will you look at them?'

'Very well.'

'She does not think, like you, of what you call schism, only of its not being proper for ladies. She says we can read at home, as if that were like living words, and that we ought not to mix with "that kind of people," as she calls them. I can't understand such worldly nonsense in a person like her.'

'Many people let the world get a curious grip of their conscience,' said Felix. 'Perhaps we who have lived so long beneath the line don't estimate the strength of scruple, but in this case it may be well that even inferior motives should prevent the breaking their Communion with the Church.'

'You think that outward Communion preferable to an enlightened spirit. There we differ.'

'No, Angela. The soul must have life and enlightenment, or else it is like one asleep in the midst of a feast, under a lamp, but there is no sure way of keeping up that life and light except by the means and in the union our Blessed Lord appointed.'

'Then comes the question, how do you know that these means, precisely in your own way, are what He meant?'

'By unbroken historical evidence of the Church universal—by the Saints that have been formed through them. Nay, shall I say it, Angela, by personal experience ever since I can remember. I can no more doubt of the grace, comfort, and strength imparted through them than I do of the refreshment of food or of air.'

'Tell me, if you don't mind, a little more precisely what you mean.'

'I mean so far this, that a perplexing question, when taken there, is apt afterwards to clear itself. One sees the way to what seemed impossible, and I am also sure that one's first impulses in unexpected trials become much safer and more trustworthy under the influence one then imbibes. How should they not?'

'That's not the heart, it's all outward,' said Angela, impatiently.

'Nay, is not the outward action connected with the abundance of the heart? As to the rest, my dear Angel, I don't think anything that I can say will express the blessing except "O *taste* and see how gracious the Lord is!" What would life or death be worth without it?' And his face spoke more than his words.

'Well,' said Angela. 'No good came to me till I banished those things away, and knew my load of sin, and Who has taken it. I can't bear anything between Him and me.'

'Nor I,' said Felix. 'Angela, my dear, are you sure your discovery is not exactly what our old way was meant to teach you?'

She hung her head. He had enough experience of her to know that pressing her was useless, so he leant back giving way to his fatigue, and she sat on playing with a paper-knife, till at last she said, 'Brother, do you remember my scalding you?'

'Certainly.'

'When I would not let you pardon me, and you didn't want to.'

'Rather oddly put, but I remember.'

'Well!' coming and kneeling by him, 'I terribly crave for pardon now.'

'My poor Angel,' as he tenderly kissed her brow, and as she rested it on the arm of his chair, stroked her fair hair. Presently there came up a sort of choked whisper, 'for isn't it worse than we thought?'

'May be so, Angel, but you know that came of my own stupid choice of a landing-place, so that is my private affair.'

Her instinct had gathered more than she had been told, and her eager wilful chase of excitement and defiance of Clement had been the vain resource of a sadly foreboding, half-broken heart, dwelling vehemently on the whole mass of past sins, as if putting them in one vague heap dulled the unbearably acute sense of the one act of vain flightiness that had produced such consequences, and now, though she guessed enough to be unwilling to agitate him, the comfort of the avowal and of his caress was infinite.

He partly perceived how it was, and waited a little before saying, 'I look to you as my great help if this comes to anything. You are the family nurse.'

'Oh!' she came still closer, and presently said, 'please tell me just what it is; it can't be worse than guessing.'

He told her.

'I thought so,' she said, and still knelt with her head against his chair for a long, long time, till the door was opened and Clement came in, not seeing her, as she sat on the ground on the further side.

'The pony-carriage is come round; but here's a pretty business. It is all over the parish that Angela is going with Mrs. Lake to Gudgeon's conventicle. Halloa!'

'How can you come and upset Felix?' was Angela's cry as she sprang to her feet.

'Gently, Angel,' said Felix, laughing; 'don't be so like Tabby guarding her kitten from Scamp: Clem is tolerably aware by this time of what does me harm. She has been very good to me, Clem; she has given it up to please me.'

'Because I should have been a brute if I had not,' said Angela. 'Mind, Clement, I'm not convinced! I should like to have fought it out, but——' her dignity quite gave way, 'I don't care. I can't vex him, there—I nev-er, never will!' And she dashed away, struggling with sobs.

'A dangerous undertaking, if it were likely to last longer,' said Felix; 'but even while it does, the restraint may be wholesome.'

'Then you have stopped this?'

'Miss Isabella warned me. One good thing is that the good ladies' opposition was on motives that rather sap her faith in them.'

'Does she know about you?'

'She had nearly found out already. Nature designed her for a nursing sister. I rather hope she may yet turn that way, but the load of a sore heart is very heavy on her, poor child.'

'If she is getting into confidence with you, I have hope,' said Clement, sighing as if his heart were sore enough as he looked at his brother.

'If I can only be allowed to tide her through this searching time of trouble and put her into better hands,' said Felix, 'I should be glad indeed; otherwise I should fear her becoming one of the ladies who drift through every variety of exciting religion.'

From that time he submitted to be watched and waited on by Angela, with an exclusive vehemence that was almost fierce. She attended to his very eye, and for the present so entirely centered her fervent nature upon the 'not vexing him,' that he had to think twice before expressing the most casual and careless wish, lest she should turn everything upside down to gratify him.

To only one other person did Felix speak of his own state, namely, Bernard, who, as Will Harewood foretold, egregiously failed in obtaining admission to Keble College, and took his rejection with the utmost coolness, seeming to think he had made a great concession to family prejudice, and that now something must be found to enable him to pass through the university with the same gentleman-like ease as through Harrow.

Not in the least crestfallen, he stood warming his back at the study fire, and mentioning one or two colleges whose requirements he thought not unreasonable. That Felix should haggle about expense, and have delusions that the university was meant for work, he could endure as the innocuous thunder with which governors must be allowed to solace themselves, while youth listened good humouredly to the growl.

The thunder, however, took an unwonted form in the quiet reply. 'Either you must get a scholarship, or you cannot go to Oxford. You had better study harder than you have ever done, or else turn your mind to some other maintenance. Hitherto, you have depended on me, but Gerald's guardians will not have the same power.'

'Gerald's guardians!' he exclaimed, as the import flashed on him. 'You're all right, except the old sprain!'

'I am afraid not, Bear. There is serious damage, and though I do not wish to distress any one, especially Cherry, it is right you should be prepared to get on without me, as you know I have absolutely nothing to leave you.'

'I say, is this fancy, or have you had the doctor?'

'Four.'

'Four doctors! That's enough to account for anybody thinking anything the matter with him. Cheer up, Squire,' and he assumed a superior air of wisdom and encouragement that made Felix look amused enough to persuade the boy of the effect of his words—'don't be croaked out of spirits. Sprains are nasty things, and go on no one knows how long; but I'll bet anything you like that nothing else is the matter with you but the doctors, and poking over that desk. It's a splendid day, I thought of going up the river. Will you come?'

To which Felix consented, and Bernard, when repairing to Geraldine to propose her joining the party, said, 'It will be good for the Squire. I say, what makes him so down in the mouth?'

'Of course, he is disappointed about you.'

'Pish! I didn't mean that, but about himself and the sprain.'

'I don't wonder, dear Felix!' said Cherry. 'It is very wearing to feel it at every movement, and it is depressing to be so set aside from active life. I only wonder at his patience.'

So Bernard continued to repose in his consoling fiction of low spirits, but he was so far amenable as to think himself 'grinding frightfully hard' with a tutor at Ewmouth, and dislike of the said grist impelled him to propose going out to Carrigaboola; but after a day's shooting with him, Fulbert declined the proposal in no measured terms, when he had seen Master Bernard's daintiness of equipment, disgust at difficulties, dependence on luncheon, and distaste at loading himself with anything that could be carried by another.

And Cherry? How did the quickest witted of all avoid the shadow of the cloud visible to so many?

Partly there was the resistance of a sensitive mind, after hosts of imaginary panics, to a real fear—partly her brother was on his guard against distressing her, and often commanded his countenance, when if alone with Clement, it would have betrayed the pang, and besides, her charm of manner often beguiled his weariness; but above all, her want of perception was due to her absorption in little Gerald.

The child needed careful attention, varying from day to day under a succession of petty ailments, only to be dealt with by assiduous tenderness. To train his vivid intelligence, to amuse and occupy him, to guard him from the aggressions of his cousins, and to soothe him under pain or nervous restlessness was quite one person's work, and engrossed Cherry, whom the little fellow preferred with exclusiveness that increased to petulance whenever he was suffering. She was seldom to be seen without him, and was always occupied with him, and her unselfish brother was content that she should thus be weaned from him, and wind her affections round another object. Yes, even though she could no longer be entirely reckoned for Pursuivant work that *must* be done, and now more than ever no one could do like her; though Gerald's call would break off her writing for him, and either she came not, or he enjoyed only her divided attention in his walks and drives.

'It was better so,' he said, when Clement was vexed and indignant. And truly he was anxious enough about the frail little child to have none of the jealousy of invalid number one towards invalid number two.

Marilda's eager, almost peremptory claim had little chance. Cherry was almost furious at the tone in which the warm-hearted heiress wrote demanding the boy, as if his father had been her brother and not theirs, and nobody could care for him save herself. If Felix had not had more coolness, there might almost have been a breach. As it was, his grateful but decided reply that Edgar had entrusted his son to his brothers and sisters in a manner that would not justify them in resigning the charge, so offended her that a marked silence followed.

CHAPTER XLVII.

THE TASK OVER.

> 'If you might, would you now
> Retrace your way,
> Wander through stormy wilds,
> Faint and astray?
> Night's gloomy watches fled,
> Morning all beaming red,
> Hopes smiles around us shed,
> Heavenward away!'
> *Lady Nairne.*

Felix, Cherry, and Gerald were taking one of their slow drives with Master Ratton, when a tall horse passed them, and with the shout 'As right as a trivet,' Charles Audley the younger waved his hat and rode on, leaving them to meditate on his announcement. 'A three legged article,' as Cherry said, 'hardly suited the felicity he seemed to intend.'

Charlie had not gone in for honors, but had obtained the flattering assurance that he would have had them if he had tried. The announcement, backed perhaps by some mediation of his uncle, had brought an offer of a private secretaryship from Lord Liddesdale, and therewith armed, he had made the awful plunge at the Hall—his father and uncle both waiting to defend his independence.

Behold! Sir Robert and Lady Margaret had comported themselves like lambs. Either the scheme for Charlie's union with his cousin had been a figment, or they were glad to get the sole hope of their house married at all, or they were gratified by Lord Liddesdale's estimate of him, and had learnt wisdom by the ill effects of former opposition. Anyway their consent had been startlingly facile. They heeded birth more than wealth: Stella, with her own legacy and Theodore's, was not unportioned, and an Underwood of Vale Leston had such undeniable county blood that they never connected the younger Charles's ravings with the alarms that had elicited their consent to the elder Charles's expatriation fourteen years ago. Moreover Lady Liddesdale, who had been the young man's confidante, had promised to be a mother to his bride. She had just married off her last daughter, and wanted a young companion, and she offered rooms at the Embassy, and whatever Charlie could wish for his wife in the way of help and kindness.

So here was the young gentleman in tempestuous ecstasy, announcing that there could be no delay, for he was wanted at the Embassy by the middle of February.

The elder brothers and sisters expected to see their nestling distracted by the summons to a distant home in a strange land, but her equanimity amazed them all. She was Charlie's property, and it was only natural to be claimed. 'Every one did,' she said, and she would have been quite as contented to go with him to a City lodging or to the Australian bush as to the splendours of the Embassy.

Wilmet thought her too young to realize what it all meant, and held that she ought to wait a year or two; but Felix would hear of this as little as the captain, having no doubt that the calm, self-contained, thoughtful nature would be equal to whatever it might be called on to meet; and though Charlie was the younger in character, he was a thoroughly good, trustworthy fellow, nor would they begin with an independent home. Besides, was not Lady Liddesdale own sister to 'Sister Constance'?

The announcement of this splendid engagement mollified Marilda, who wrote heartily, and offered services either of hospitality or of choice of wedding clothes. Stella could not bear to leave home, but she was overruled. It was due to the Ambassadress that her outfit should neither be countrified nor left to Marilda's taste; so Wilmet took her to London for a week, and by Felix's desire expended the child's own original inheritance from her father in garments that might not disgrace the suite; the chief difficulty being that Stella had made Charlie consent to her completing her year of mourning for her brothers—a terrible grievance to Mrs. Underwood. Wilmet was meantime the recipient of all Marilda's views as to the folly of Felix's rejection of her offer to Gerald, over whom she absolutely seemed to yearn—and she caught at the invitation to the wedding as at least affording her a chance of seeing him, if not of bringing his uncle to hear reason.

The marriage was to take place on New Year's Day, and as soon as the bustle was over, 'Sister Constance' was actually coming to Vale Leston to arrange for the branch of the St Faith's Sisterhood which was to be established in connection with the future Church of the Comforter at East Ewmouth. She was to choose among houses to let the temporary abode of the sisters, but in the first place was to have a few days for the young friends, who now ranked as old, and on Charles Audley the elder.

The oculist's verdict had not been hopeless, but it had obliged him to give up all prospect of a return to a climate so noxious to the eyes as that of Western Australia. His visit to his home had made it evident that his place was no longer there. His parents were old and self-occupied, and had little in common with him, chiefly depending on their daughter-in-law, a complete woman of the world, thoroughly alien to the clergyman who had spent his strength on wild 'black fellows' and rude convicts. He was more trouble than pleasure to any of the party, and deemed it inadvisable to endure the penance of idleness and uncongeniality in their stately halls, since they gave him no opening for being of use to them; and his brother, who would not leave him, was always miserable there. Once the pet at home, 'poor Charles' was mourned over for his peculiarities, and coughed down if he endeavoured to explain them.

So as Clement was in the usual case of country Vicars, curate-hunting in vain, Mr. Audley proffered himself as a 'demi-semi-assistant,' able to do a good deal without book, and thankful for a refuge from total inefficiency. Clement was rather shocked at finding himself in such relations towards his old Guardian, almost a Bishop elect, but rejoiced in the counsel and support of his experience even more than in the actual aid, which indeed he greatly needed. And to Felix, the intercourse with his first friend was the greatest delight, while there was a rally in his health in the autumn that made even those who knew the worst hope the evil was averted, and every one else viewed him as recovering.

Perhaps he ventured a little too much in the greater sense of strength, for Lady Hammond being unable to go out, and warmly anxious to see the young couple, he took the long drive thither with them, and a few days later went to a public meeting. There was an attack upon Church influence in the Ewmouth hospital, and he went late, expecting only to have to give his vote, but he found a storm raging such as he did not expect, and his side of the question so inefficiently defended by its few lay representatives, that he stood up and spoke for nearly an hour with all his remarkable force and facility.

'I don't agree with you, Underwood,' said Mr. Walsh, as Felix, flushed and panting, waited till the rush to the door was over to get to his carriage, 'but you ought to be in the House; and that's much for a man to say when you've just been the means of beating him. You are one of the few who can make any life or sense out of the old cause.'

Clement was far from knowing whether to be glad or sorry, as Felix made answer with very little more than a languid smile. The speech certainly had, as the saying is, 'taken a great deal out of him,' and was Cherry's *cheval de bataille* whenever any of the wedding guests found fault with his appearance.

There was a grand family gathering, bringing together all the surviving brothers and sisters, for the unexceptionable baronet connection had even induced Sir Adrian Vanderkist to bring his wife and two eldest children, who were to act bridesmaids, together with Robina and Angela, Gertrude May and Miss Audley. Geraldine and Marilda had paired off on the score of age, and little Mary Harewood was to wear a modified edition of the bridesmaid's white cashmere and stars of Bethlehem, whose green leaves gave the only colour the little bride would permit. The calmly decided manner in which she obtained her own way against fashion and conventionality amused everybody. Felix had hoped to have brought Ferdinand Travis and Marilda together on this occasion, but as soon as he found that Alda was coming, he had thought it better to abstain, and was rather relieved when the clerk at Peter Brown's sent information that Mr. Travis had left Barcelona, it was not known for what place, and so that his letter could not yet be forwarded.

The Vanderkists arrived late on the Monday, and the next morning Bernard conducted Sir Adrian to the covers he had been nursing up for this great occasion, Fulbert stalking along with him, thinking how hardly pressed stay-at-home people must be for something to do, if *this* were a sort of duty.

That last day of the old year was that on which Felix attained his object of signing away the lay rectory. The action was so unprecedented, and involved so many complications, that his strenuous efforts had only succeeded in getting the needful documents brought down from London with the marriage-settlements.

'Let me witness that,' said Mr. Audley: 'I am glad to have eyes enough at least for such a sight.'

Felix's face was calmly happy as he wrote the 'Felix Chester Underwood,' laid his finger on the seal, and spoke the 'I deliver this as my act and deed,' by which the Rectory returned to be Church property.

'It is a great load off my mind,' he said, handing the pen to Mr. Audley and William Harewood, who said nothing to him, but merrily shook hands with the new Rector, joking him on the additional substance and consequence the title called for, jests the readier because they all knew them to be empty, since East Ewmouth carried off the surplus tithe, and he only obtained the title and the power over his Chancel. Then Felix required their witness and the lawyer's to the will which the numerous recent changes had necessitated, and they afterwards carried the lawyer off to see the buildings, while Felix might rest till the arrival of the other parties to the marriage-settlements.

However, they had not been gone long before a gentle knock came to the door. 'Alda, my dear, are you come to pay me a visit?' and Felix met her affectionately, and drew a chair for her close to his own.

'I thought I might come when your business was over,' she said. 'I have scarcely seen you.'

'Have you been over the house? You remembered it! You have seen your little girls in our own cribs at last.'

'Yes, I have so often wished to come, ever since you have been here. You quite understand that I should have been so glad, only journeys are so expensive, and we are so many.'

'I see.'

'That is one of the few ways in which I can save,' she said. 'It is such an anxiety to have so many daughters.'

'Seven now?'

'Seven! Adrian says it makes us ridiculous. Poor children! That's what I came to speak to you about, Felix. I want you to talk to Adrian.'

'About what?' asked Felix, not sanguine of either talking the daughters into sons, or their father into preference of the sex.

'About some provision for them,' said the mother; and there ensued an explanation that nothing was secured to the children but her own portion from uncle Tom, while as to the estate, so long as there was no male heir, Sir Adrian could do as he pleased with it, and at the rate of his present expenditure there would be little left for his successors; and Alda, with some vague idea of Felix's helpfulness, had come to beg him to persuade her husband to insure his life, contract his expenses, or do something that might secure her children from dire poverty. She began with a wife's natural reticence and a guarded voice, but gradually, as the home sense of being with the brotherly protector of earlier days wrought upon her, she dropped her caution, and disclosed the harass of her life. Her husband, it seemed, was more and more devoted to the turf, and the display he thought needful to his position, but while he grudged his wife every outlay needful to maintain that ostentation, he was still more unwilling to allow her the requisites for the health, comfort, and education of the children.

'He thinks anything will do for them,' said Alda, with a dismal sharpness in her voice; 'he can't bear spending on anything but himself.'

'No, no, Alda, it is hardly well to put such things into words.'

'I would not except to you, Felix; but indeed it does me good to have it out. I get so disheartened, I would let everything take its chance, but for my poor little girls. There is a wrangle over every cheque! If I try to save in the housekeeping, he is angry about the dinners, and I can't ask for money to pay bills without being blamed for extravagance. Indeed, whether I get it or not, he is always cross with me all the rest of the day. I'm ashamed to see all here in black, but he would not let me do more than just wear a little slight mourning myself, and that for a short time. He would not hear of it for the children. Felix, when I see your peaceful faces and unruffled ways, I feel as if this were a world of peace.'

'You must contribute gentleness yourself, my poor Alda.'

She had never answered him so humbly. 'Indeed I am obliged to try, but you know I never was the good-tempered one at home, and it is very, very hard when one is never very well, and always harassed and anxious. I don't think, in the worst of times, Wilmet had to spend more thought on pinching here and there to make both ends meet than I have, and at least she had the comfort of keeping out of debt, and was thanked and not despised! Will you speak to Adrian, Felix; of course not letting him guess I told you, but beginning as if of yourself about the children?'

'My dear, I can hardly promise, but whatever I can do for you I will. Your little maidens seem to be sweet little, well-trained children, and if they grow up united and affectionate they may be happier on small means than you suppose.'

'The dinner of herbs and stalled ox,' said Alda; 'I have thought of Mettie's rice stews many a time when I have sat quaking because there were no truffles in the soup. Dear children, I am so glad they seem nice to you. I do believe they have the good tempers of our family; there are never any quarrels, and their grandmamma is so fond of them. I do try to keep them good, and'—there were tears in her eyes—'it does make one think more about *things* to have those little ones round one.'

'That is the blessing little Gerald brought to poor Edgar,' said Felix, pressing the hand she had laid upon his knees. 'The greatest of all.'

'When I see you I know it is,' said poor Alda; 'but sometimes I think if I had not been brought up religiously I should be happier, I should not think things so bad; and then Adrian is never so cross as if he thinks me wanting to be serious, or to make the children so. It makes him dislike our being with his mother, though nothing is such a comfort to me.'

'My dear, comfort will grow if you go on striving to submit meekly; do your best with your children, and look beyond.'

He was really more hopeful about Alda than he had ever been. Just then she said: 'One thing more. Mary and Sophy are old enough to need a governess. I have managed so far with a *bonne*, but I have neither time, spirits, nor ability to teach, and Adrian would be furious if I asked him for a proper salary. Do you think Robina would come to us—to live of course as my sister, on an equality? The delight and comfort it would be——'

To poor Alda, thought Felix, but Robina ought not to be sacrificed. 'It would not be right to ask her, remembering her engagement.'

'What engagement?'

'To Will Harewood.'

'My dear Felix, you don't mean that you have consented to anything so foolish! How are they to live?'

'They have been for the last four years endeavouring to save. He makes a good deal by his pupils, and by his writings, besides his fellowship, and she adds something from her salary. They mean to get £5000 together between them—her salary, and his fellowship, pupils and books—and then take either a parish or a mastership at a school.'

'It seems to me sheer imprudence,' said the old Alda, half peevish at the opposition; 'I did think she might have been glad to leave strangers for the sake of her sister, and her natural position.'

'You forget the difference the salary makes to her prospects. She has £150 a year, and it would not be right to ask her to give it up, considering——'

'I can't see why my children should be sacrificed to William Harewood!'

'Perhaps not, but Robina might. No, Alda, it will not do. The De la Poers have made her so happy that she feels Repworth another home, and I should not like to ask her to leave it till she marries.'

'It is hard,' sighed Alda, in a tone not unlike those heard over the shop of Bexley; but then followed another question: 'I want to know what you think about Marilda?'

'About Marilda? You know she is coming this evening.'

'Yes, but about her intentions.'

'I did not know she had any intentions.'

'You see it is plain she will never marry now, and I used to be nearer to her than any one. Don't look so amazed, Felix! I know she is only of my age, and of course it is not so much with any immediate expectations as for the sake of the influence there might be on Adrian. We used to see a good deal of her at one time, but I believe he tried to borrow money of her, and she spoke out in her rough way, so that he grew angry, and made me hold aloof; but now I am sure he wants to make it up with her again, he was so much put out about that little boy.'

'Little Gerald? How or why?'

'For fear she should want to adopt him, or make him her heir. Oh! Felix, you will do nothing to promote that. Remember, my poor little girls are just as near to you.'

'There's no fear of my promoting anything of the kind,' said Felix, coldly; 'Gerald is provided for. No one here will scheme for him.'

'Don't be displeased with me, Felix,' she said, more meekly. 'Only if Marilda should say anything——'

'The child whom dear Edgar expressly left to us we should not give up to any one.'

'I thought not; only if anything should pass, do turn her mind to us. It is not, of course, for the sake of the property, but if she just showed that sort of interest, it would give her weight with Adrian, and then if she suggests anything about the children he would be sure to attend. I can't say it, but you might.'

The motive was, after all, not so blameworthy; but before any answer could be given to this strange mixture of tokens of the long-dormant good seed, and the choking weeds of worldly care, the door was softly opened, a pretty glowing face peeped in, and was retreating with 'Oh! I didn't know,' but the morrow's bride might interrupt anything, and she was called back. 'Stella, my sweet Fair-Star, come in! Why, what have you got there? How it sparkles! What is it?'

'Eh!' exclaimed Alda, 'I declare it is a bouquet of diamond flowers and emerald leaves! I never saw anything more splendid. Where did it come from?'

'Out of Aladdin's cave? or is it dewdrops fixed by star-light?' said Felix, as the sparkles flashed on him. 'Stella, how did you come by it? It is not Audley family jewels, eh?'

'The Audleys never had—' but Alda checked what would have been spite, though Stella would not have minded it.

'Oh no,' she said. 'Cherry said you would guess.'

'Ferdinand Travis?' said Felix. 'Did he send it?'

'Charlie rowed him up in the skiff an hour ago, and ever since he has been showing us how to put it together, for it was all in separate velvet cases. It is all brooches and bracelets and necklaces, and a thing for one's head—a complete set really, you see,' said Stella, 'but it is just like a puzzle putting it up like this, and it is much prettier so.'

'Are you going to carry it as your bouquet to-morrow?'

'Oh no, that would never do!' interposed Alda.

'Oh no, I should not like that,' said Stella. 'Charlie has got me my bouquet, and that's best.'

'Much better taste,' said Alda; 'but this is truly magnificent. You will be prepared for the occasion, little Stella, even if you end as an ambassadress. The cost must have been enormous.' And she sighed.

'I am afraid so,' said Stella, a little oppressed; 'but Charlie is so pleased.'

'Yes, and Fernan can not only afford it, but must have thoroughly enjoyed doing it, my Star; so you need not scruple; he has robbed nothing he ought to benefit, you may be sure; so you may take lawful pleasure in it, little one, and "rejoice in your jewels as a bride doth."'

She smiled, but gravely. 'It is too beautiful,' she said. 'Isn't it a pomp?' she whispered into her brother's ear, as he turned the glittering thing about, enjoying the magic flashes of many-coloured rays.

'It might be,' he said, 'but it is not yet. It is the gift of a true and grateful spirit, and for itself—I never knew how beauteous these things were. Nay, Stella,' speaking low, as he laid a hand on her arm, and looked up into the sweet, thoughtful face, 'recollect that such are in the walls of the City above, and yet they are but the same stuff as earthly clay after all, showing us how dust can be sublimated. Look, the mysterious glory of those diamond lights may help us to dwell on the glories that eye hath not seen nor ear heard, and you know the rainbow round about the Throne is in sight like unto an emerald.'

'You've consecrated them, brother,' she said, with a sweet smile on her pensive face. 'When I think of that, it will keep them from being a temptation.'

He played silently with the flashing gleams a little longer, as if continuing the strain of thought, then said, 'Did you say he was here?'

'Yes; he only came back from Spain yesterday, and came down to bring this, though he did not know *it* was to be so soon.'

'Take your fairy bouquet, Princess Fair-Star, I'll come to him in a minute.'

'O yes, brother! There's the carriage coming down the drive!' and the voice was rather awe-struck.

'We will come too and help you through the introduction, little one,' said Felix, 'though I think you have self-possession to meet it.'

The little bride sprang away, and while Felix was slowly lifting himself up, he heard Alda murmur, 'Ferdinand Travis gave that! I wonder how many hundreds it cost.'

Certainly it was a contrast to the pinching and anxiety she had described. If she had but known, as Mrs. Underwood had said! Felix paused in the doubt whether to take any notice of the predicament, and said, 'He had gone to Barcelona, and I did not expect him to have returned by this time.'

'He has purchased a welcome,' said Alda, but her face glowed, and at the same moment the carriage crashed up to the door, containing the Audley party, who had all arrived at the Captain's the day before, except old Lady Margaret, who never left home.

'Thank you, Felix,' said Lady Vanderkist, as they repaired to the drawing-room in readiness for the reception. 'You have done me good.'

He could not quite see how, but no doubt there had been much in his look and manner of listening.

Sir Robert Audley was a pompous, formal old gentleman, tremendously condescending and courtly, and his first bow, his first tone showed Geraldine what a trial he must be to his sons—indeed the elder looked more bored than she had ever seen him.

'And where is the sweet young lady I am so soon to hail as my granddaughter?'

'Here she is, sir,' said Charlie, about to pull her forward, but she, by some intuition, advanced with a beautiful courtesy, perfect in grace but full of modesty and respect. Sir Robert was delighted, met her with a gracious gesture and kiss, and presented her to his daughter-in-law, Mrs. Somerville Audley—a dame stiff and fashionable-looking, and to Miss Audley, small, dark, and reminding Cherry of the old word 'modish.'

Alda was a great help, and so were the wedding presents. Ferdinand Travis had fled to Major Harewood's, but his bouquet evoked raptures from the ladies, though Cherry doubted whether the baronet were equally delighted that the Audley jewels he had produced for the bride of the heir presumptive should be eclipsed, for he kept on impressing on the young couple that these last were family relics, and must not be exposed to any risk, until Stella was ready to suggest that it would be wiser not to take them abroad, and was only withheld by the fear of seeming to slight them. Her habitual silence and observation had fostered a remarkable amount of simple tact, and this, together with her unusual loveliness, rendered her a great success; but the ceremonious speeches and grand politeness rendered the visit very fatiguing, and when the settlements had been duly signed, and the other high contracting power had bowed himself off, Felix looked so worn out that every one acquiesced in his shutting himself into his study. No one saw him again till the late dinner with which Sir Adrian must be regaled.

It was strictly a family party, and only the Harewoods, Vanderkists, and Mr. Travis, besides the whole eleven who still bore the name of Underwood, were assembled in the drawing-room. Marilda was there, hearty and good-natured as ever, but better looking at two-and-thirty than at two-and-twenty, for she had somewhat fined down, and actual work in business and charity had given meaning to her countenance, and energy instead of temper to her manner. She was assiduously courting little Gerald, and he backing out of her way into the more congenial society of Mary and Sophy Vanderkist. Cherry could not help thinking it an odd turn of the wheel of fortune that Alda should have so much nicer and better-regulated children than Wilmet. To be sure, Christopher and Edward were perfectly satisfactory to their parents, and obeyed them at a word, but the licence they enjoyed was a continual contrast to the strict rule Wilmet had maintained over her former charge, and did not render them agreeable company to their uncles and aunts. Moreover, the ruddy locks and freckles of the Harewoods had mastered the Underwood blonde complexion, while the two Vanderkists reproduced the elder twins at the same age, and were exemplary little maids, taught meekness by difficulties and yielding by seniority, grateful for notice from their uncles, and enchanted to find a boy so unlike their notions of the species. On the other hand, Gerald watched them like fairies, laid himself at their feet with precocious devotion, and mourned that he could not marry them both on the spot.

The grown-up party looked each other over rather as they had done on meeting fifteen years before at their mother's funeral—the years that had made their baby the fair little bride who was nestling as close as she could to her eldest brother that she might feel his hand on her shoulder. Those years had brought the 'little ones' of those days to be 'the tall ones' of the present, Bernard exceeding all the rest in stature, even Fulbert and Clement, with regular features, brilliant complexion, and glossy light-brown hair and moustache, but without as yet any particular expression except good-humoured complacency in his own appearance and deportment, being persuaded that Charlie would have to-morrow a true *best* man, unrivalled in looks and equipments; and without a regret, save that Felix was courteously deaf to all Sir Adrian's strictures on the scandalous state of his covers. Whatever those years had done for Bernard's outer man, his mind, or perhaps more properly his will, had not grown much older.

This could not be said of Angela, who sat so still and meek that Alda was meditating on transferring the governess proposal to her, but with a latent energy in the corner of the down-cast eye and firmly closed mouth, and the most anxious watchfulness of Felix's slightest movement. The change was comparatively small in sober Robina, whose steady equable nature had been early moulded, and who sat at the window curtain, with Will hovering over her, both trying not to contrast other people's love affairs with their own. The three brothers whose bickerings had then been so troublesome were now the most inseparable. If their paths had severed them, they liked each other better now, as they stood all in a row, with their backs against the mantel-piece, the big, bearded, sunburnt Australian, the close-shaven, alert clergyman, and the little bright-eyed, thin-faced, moustached tradesman, all eagerly talking in under tones of old Bexley pranks and comrades, laughing as they never did but in such a trio, and yet each bearing tokens of toil with the full might of vigorous manhood, unlike as was their work.

Geraldine's little bending figure had chiefly altered for the better. The mixture of arch lively grace and pathetic depth which gave her peculiar charm had increased rather than lessened, and though she had gained in dignity and confidence, anxieties and perplexities made her cheeks glow and her eyes wander restlessly as she tried to make talk for Sir Adrian.

The twin sisters were together on the sofa, both in black velvet. Wilmet had a bad cold, and indeed had never looked her best since the shock at Whitsuntide, so that Alda had regained the palm of beauty; but it was matronly content that had plumped the chiselled contour of feature, and if the colouring showed less clear and flower-like, it was by contrast with Alda's defined, over-transparent white and carnation, and the wasted look that threw out the perfection of the delicate moulding. One gave the notion of comfortable, peaceful motherliness, the other of constant anxious wear and tear; and the blue eye, so much larger and more hollow than the soft, calm one, rather weighed down by the cold, no doubt were rendered additionally restless by the presence of the man she had not seen since she had cast him off like a worn-out glove.

It was she who had married, but upon which had the impression lasted most painfully? There was a nervous quiver of her nostril, and a sullen scowl in her husband's eye, when, after the casual greeting, Ferdinand sat down among the children, took Gerald on his knee, and made friends with the little girls. He was indisputably the wealthiest man present, and the handsomest, except perhaps Bernard, whose good looks were merely the fair, scarcely developed graces of early youth, while his was the matured nobleness of countenance stamped on naturally fine outlines by a life of brave, unselfish activity and dutifulness. It was a calm, serious, dignified face, less melancholy than in his younger days, for the liquid wistfulness of the dark eyes had given place to vigilance and authority, and though there was still a want of susceptibility and animation, the dark colouring and statuesque outline did not need them.

'And he the chieftain of them all,' as Cherry liked to call her Squire—he was leaning back in the easy-chair by the fire, with a weary, placid smile on his face, and his fingers clasped lightly into one another, as his elbows rested on the arms of his chair. There was a strange monumental fixity of repose about him as if he were only half attending to the talk that passed by him, and cared more to gaze than to speak. However, on the announcement of dinner, he roused himself, gave his arm to Lady Vanderkist, and talked cheerily to her through the soup and fish, but while carving the turkey, he paused, a flush and then a whiteness came over his face, and saying to Alda, 'I'm afraid I must go, this is too much for me,' he rose, while Clement pushed back his chair and hastily followed.

Startled looks went round, and—'A tiring day'—'He has not done so much for a long time'—'That stuck-up old bore might *do* for anybody'—but in a few moments Clement came back, and said, while taking the seat at the bottom of the table, 'He is better now,' then tried to divert Alda's anxious inquiries whether using the arm had renewed the strain. Geraldine put on a defiant brightness, appealing to John whether Sir Robert were not enough to account for any fatigue, and with questionable taste in her excitement, giving Sir Adrian a sarcastic account of his compliments. Luckily, Stella was out of hearing, but John detected the ring of anxiety in every ironical word.

Knowing that a crowd coming after him was always oppressive to Felix, no one followed Wilmet when on leaving the drawing-room she went at once to the study door. She found Felix on the Squire's chair in its most couch-like form, looking even in the firelight exceedingly pale, but greeting her with a smile of welcome.

'Yes, I am better,' he said, in answer to her enquiry. 'I'll come into the drawing-room presently.'

'You had better not, you are overtired.'

'I like to look at them all,' was the answer.

They both sat silent awhile; there was something in the stillness that forbade Wilmet even to feel in her pocket for her tatting; but at last Felix surprised her by saying:

'I have been thinking about Jacob.'

'Jacob Lightfoot?'

'No, Israel. I think I enter a little into his surprise and gratitude. I look back—don't you, Wilmet?—to a shivering sense of loneliness and responsibility when we first realized the task before us.'

'I don't think I ever did,' said Wilmet; 'I never thought of mamma's not getting well, till I had grown quite used to it. It never occurred to me that our position was unusual till I heard people talking of it.'

'So much the better; but I recollect one cold winter day, soon after my father's death, reading Jacob's vow at Bethel to devote his best, if God would only give him bread to eat and raiment to wear, and longing for some assurance that we should have it—I felt so helpless, and the future so vague—and when I see how richly blessings and prosperity have flowed in on us, and look at those fine, happy, strong creatures, it seems to me like his return across the Jordan, or as if I could say, as he did at last, "The God that led me all my life through, the Angel that redeemed me from all evil, bless the lads."' And as the firelight shone upon his face, Wilmet recollected another saying about Jacob, and how the 'Angels of God met him,' but her answer sounded flat. 'Yes, it is a great comfort to see so many launched and doing well.'

'And, Wilmet, how much was owing to you! If you had not been the girl you were, we must have broken up; it could not have been done at all. Do you remember our councils over that spotted account book on Saturday nights, and our misery when Fulbert spoilt a new pair of boots in the river?'

'And your new coats! They used to weigh on my mind for months. I used to look at your elbows every evening, and reckon whether they would hold out till I had saved enough for the next.'

'Ah!' added Felix, laughing a little, 'do you remember my worst offence of all? No? My having my hair cut at Slater's—instead of letting you do it. I believe you had designs on the shilling, and that you thought me corrupted by the vanities of this world!'

'Yes, I was very hard and narrow then. John has shown it to me.'

'It could not be otherwise—you had to live in a continual state of resistance.'

'But how many mistakes we made!'

'It is those very mistakes that make me so thankful; that they should have been so many, and yet for the most part remedied, and that those boys and girls should have come out so sound-hearted, right-minded, and affectionate as all of them are, is to me as wonderful as it is merciful.'

'They could not well help it. John says it shows the force of example—that not one for whom you were responsible has gone wrong.'

'Of prayer—of being the children of the righteous, more likely,' said Felix; 'and there *is* a coming home, you know; I see the dawnings in Alda, poor child, though there is much to smother it. I am happier about her than ever before.'

'Poor Alda,' said Wilmet, 'I hope she will be happy in her children, though I should not like mine to be so stiff and prim, poor little dears!'

One by one Felix dwelt lovingly on the good points of each of the brothers and sisters on whom he had been gazing—speaking with an enjoyment that made Wilmet loth to leave him even for the sake of making the most of her brief time with her twin sister. When at last he recollected Alda and bade Wilmet return, blaming himself for having detained her so long, he said as she rose, 'Give me one kiss first, my Wilmet, for the sake of the old times when we worked and struggled together, and I think we tasted of the special promise to the fatherless.'

Wilmet, somewhat surprised, bent over him and gave the kiss. He held her a moment, saying, 'May God bless you, and return it into your bosom in your children.' The solemnity startled her, but the blessing was a joy to her for the rest of her life.

The sound of music drew him back to the drawing-room ere long. Alda had never heard Lance since his chorister's alto had passed from him, and everyone, even Fulbert, called for some old echo of the old times over the cracked piano. Sir Adrian had musical taste enough to be tamed and kept amiable by the domestic concert; and even Angela did her part, controlled by the resolution not to vex Felix. He indeed could take no share, except that of evident delight, and now and then his low voice chimed into one or other of his best loved choruses, but he told Alda when she regretted the lack of his tones, 'Lance was better worth hearing.'

'Let us have "Lead, kindly Light" again to-night, Clem,' said Felix, as they moved towards the Oratory. 'Little Stella will not think it a sad farewell.'

'No, indeed,' she said, holding his hand. 'I am sure we want the kindly Light; going so far away, and so young!'

The hymn sounded even more sweetly than on the first arrival, so sweet that Sir Adrian said to his wife, 'If all family prayers were like that, they would not be such a bore.'

Wilmet went home by the bridge in the carriage, taking Marilda with her, but Will and Ferdinand returned by boat. It was a splendid frosty night, and Felix came out with them as far as the terrace. Lance, who had gone down to the river, on returning found him still gazing at the glories of the stars—Sirius flashing with most dazzling brightness, and the Pleiades twinkling with their silvery mystery, and Aldebaran gazing down like a great eye.

'Still out, Fee; don't get a chill.'

'Everything is so goodly—so good—without and within doors,' he answered, 'that one hardly knows how to leave it. I wonder whether we shall recognise what our foretastes have been!'

Lance recollected how strangely that word 'foretaste' had fallen on his ear by Tranquillity Bridge as he sat in the solitude of his heavy trance of disappointment; and as his brother's face came again into the lights of the hall, something in it struck him with a sense that even then he had been far from knowing what sorrow could be.

Of course the wedding morning was a scramble, though no one beyond the family was invited, except that Dr. May brought his daughter Gertrude to act as bridesmaid. Felix, who had since the hospital meeting ceased to leave his room before breakfast, sent word that he should keep quiet till Stella was dressed, and then that she would find him in the study.

How lovely the little white Star looked may be imagined. She was quite calm and self-possessed, softly tender and loving, but too gravely serious to be excited or agitated as she went, in deep, trustful love, to meet the great unknown life, carrying about with her a certain hush of sweet gentle awe.

So in her snowy robe and veil and wreathed brow, with her modest head still bearing the long shining curls, she floated down the dark oak stair, and crossed the hall, without casting a look on those who were watching her, and knocked at the study door.

'Come in.' Felix rose to greet her, taking both her hands and kissing her through her veil. 'My Star of the East, my happy gift!' he said. 'Stella, eighteen years ago father put you two freshly christened babies into my arms. I gave dear little Theodore in his innocence back to him last Whitsuntide. I am thankful to be allowed to give you in your bridal white to the home that is to cherish you for the better Home.'

She looked up in his face, which a flush of rosy colour was restoring to something of its old self. 'Oh! brother,' she said, 'I am so glad you spoke of dear Theodore. Charlie says we may take him my flowers as soon as it is over. I wonder if he knows.'

'It may be, better than if he were here,' said Felix. 'Then it would have been a sad day for him.'

'I could not have done it,' said Stella, and lowering her voice, 'I don't know how I can have done it now. Oh, brother, nothing ever can be like you!'

'It is one of my great comforts that you have done it, my Star, my own especial child. I am glad you are the one I give away. Are they all ready?'

'I think so.' And just then Geraldine knocked to intimate that the Audley party were known to be arrived at the church, and that the clergy and choir were ready. So Stella took the arm, not clinging, lest she should hurt him, but lightly resting her fingers on it, and they came forth, he with that youthful flush of colour on his cheek, with all his scrupulous grace of attire, and with a white camellia in his coat, but with that far-away look in his eyes; and she with bent head, and deep concentrated spirit, never lifting her eyes from the ground. The bridesmaids fell in behind, first the three small nieces, Mary Harewood trotting between the other two, then the two sisters—Robina in her sedate reserve, and Angela, flushing, quivering and trembling, and never taking her eyes from Felix; and next the ill-matched pair Gertrude May and Margaret Audley, the former thrilling at the smile and clasp of the hand she had exchanged with Felix, the latter's little black eyes taking note of everything not accordant with Audley conventionalities.

Then came the rest in due order, Geraldine upon Ferdinand's arm, glad it was so strong and friendly; for this, the first home wedding, made her shiver with nervous excitement.

The elder Charles Audley, who had assisted in the twins' baptism by their dying father, and had stood as their sponsor, was standing robed at the inner archway of the tower, with Clement and William on either side, while behind were the choir, Lance leading them.

Of course the whole parish was in the seats, Miss Isabella herself, unable to help feeling that the marriage was infinitely more solemn, and full of real praise and prayer, than those whose 'simplicity' she had been wont to uphold.

No one ever forgot the quietly loving gesture with which the fatherly brother put his fair young sister into the hands of the Church to be 'given to this man,' and the movement after the trothplight up to the festally decked chancel was an exceedingly beautiful sight in itself. Mr. Audley took the licence of giving a short but beautiful address of his own on the significance and glory of holy wedlock, and then the union was crowned and sealed by the hallowed Feast; for it had not been thought fit to hurry it over out of sight beforehand, out of deference to the two baronets, who, like the children and idler gazers, left the church, and loitered outside, observing that 'this was too strong.'

After this, the signatures were to be made in the north transept that served as vestry, and it was while the movement in consequence was going on that Bernard felt a convulsive grasp on his arm, and the whispered words, 'Help me home,' were so full of suffering that he was not surprised to see his eldest brother's face deadly pale, and contracted by pain.

Ere they had moved five steps, Fulbert too was supporting Felix, and not without need, and Dr. May and Wilmet were following.

Consternation communicated itself to those around the little table. 'Felix ill!' The last Underwood that Stella Eudora ever signed herself showed her start of dismay, and Clement, who was presiding over the register book, turned pale, and gave a groan.

'God in His mercy help us! It is come!'

'I knew! I knew,' cried Angela—darting away.

'You apprehended'—began the amazed bridegroom.

'He was in some pain in the early part of the night, but slept towards morning, and was resolved to go through with it. Stay—you must write here while we know what we are about; this can't be left half done.'

The blow was known to all that sad wedding party as, instead of making a joyous procession to the great door, they found their way through the cloister to the house. The crisis that Felix had been led to expect would steal on him by slow degrees, and with full warning, had come suddenly on, accompanied with acute inflammation, producing pain so terrible to witness that the great strong Fulbert came downstairs sobbing like a child at the sight, and Geraldine was taken by both hands by Bernard and dragged away to the painting-room, with almost angry orders not to come near that door. The poor boy held her tight by her wrists, as if he feared she would disobey, reiterating, 'He said—he said you mustn't come.' Fain would John Harewood have used equally decisive measures with his wife; but neither he nor Dr. May could prevail on her to relinquish her place as foremost in the attempts at alleviation.

No one could be allowed to come even to the door who had not nerve to endure the sight of severer anguish than most of them had ever deemed possible. Clement and Angela were doing their utmost under Dr. May's directions, but Mr. Audley found himself less needed there than by poor Cherry, whom he let loose from Bernard's grip, and after sending the boy for a cordial for her, gave them both a clearer explanation of the state of the case than they had yet understood. At first she felt it hard to have been in ignorance all this time, but when Mr. Audley had helped them both to pray, she fastened upon the hope that the very suddenness and violence of the attack proved that the evil would the sooner be over and leave no ill effect.

A report was circulated that Dr. May had given some such hope, and therewith that there was some respite in the paroxysms of suffering. There was a little movement among the crushed and dismayed party who had at first straggled up to the hall and drawing-room, and sat, or stood about, as if a thunderbolt had descended among them.

Alda was the first to make any sort of move, impelled by the fear of her husband's impatience, and recollecting the guests. Sir Robert and his daughter-in-law were stiff and uncomfortable, wondering that things should have been allowed to go so far, and wishing themselves away. Alda looked about for her sisters, but could only find Robina, who assisted in proposing that the strangers should come and eat. Sir Robert, on this, uttered polite condolences, begging that his carriage might be sent for, but consenting to come into the dining-room.

Where were the bridal pair? Poor young things, they were found in one of the hall window seats, where they could catch sounds from the sick room, all crushed up together, his arms round her, and her head, with wreath and veil pushed aside, on his shoulder, as if she were passively submitting to such support as he strove to afford.

'My dear children,' began Sir Robert, as they stood up startled, 'it is indeed a mournful turn that this festive occasion has taken, but I am relieved to hear that the patient is somewhat relieved, and you will, as Lady Vanderkist suggests, assume your places at the table. Or perhaps our bride will first change her dress, as it may be better to hasten your departure.'

'I can't go away.'

But Sir Robert with his conventionalities, Mrs. Audley with her proprieties, nay the Captain with his morbid horror of everything painful, all came round, declaring that Charlie was bound to take his bride away; they need not go far; they might wait where their rooms were engaged, but go they must; and appeals were made to both Vanderkists on the necessity.

There however quiet, gentle Stella became wild, nay almost frantic. She broke away from her husband, whose 'You shall do exactly as you please' was drowned in the authoritative commands of his grandfather. 'No! No!' she cried,' I will not go! No one can take me, while my brother is so ill,' and she burst into an irrepressible passion of weeping, leaning against the tall post of balusters, and pushing Charlie away when he would have taken her hand. 'No, no, don't, I don't want any one. I won't go away from my brother,' and she flung her arm round the post as if she fancied she would be forcibly dragged away, and not so much as hearing, 'This is very amiable feeling,' from Sir Robert, or if she did, it distracted her the more, while Charlie stood in utter perplexity, for it was of no use to protest that he did not mean to take her away, when it only on the one side made his grandfather order him the more decidedly, and Stella cling the more desperately whenever he tried to approach, scarcely restraining her screams as her agitation became uncontrollable. 'No, no, let me alone, trouble only comes with me—I want no one but my brother!'

A step on the stairs startled her into breathless silence. It was Clement. 'Hush, Stella,' he said, sternly and shortly. 'Felix wants you and Charlie.'

'He heard,' some one said reproachfully.

'Yes. Don't detain her,' he added, as Alda would have modified her dishevelment by removing the wreath and veil. 'I don't know how long this interval may last.'

Stella, instantly controlled by the home voice, and ashamed and grieved at having disturbed her brother, made no resistance to Charlie's taking her trembling hand as Clement preceded them to the room, all silent now save for the constrained breathing which showed the interval to be far from painless. The ashy face of suppressed suffering recalled to Stella her watch by that same spot during the suspense about Theodore, and she dropped on her knees, trying to hide her tears and stifle her sobs in the bed-clothes. Felix after laying his hand on the poor little head held it out to Charlie, and evidently commanding his voice with great difficulty said, 'I did not think *this* would have come till you had her safe away, Charlie.'

'I am very sorry,' was all the poor bridegroom could say.

'I am very sorry,' repeated Felix, his hand resting on her hair again, 'but as it can't be helped, I think it will come harder to her if she is taken away just now. This can't go on long as it is now. Ask Dr. May. And when you see—'

He paused from inability to achieve a steady tone, and Charlie answered, 'I never meant to go. I'll stay till you are better, as long as ever she likes, indeed I will, my sweet—' but again she seemed to shiver away from him with a sort of repugnance, which Felix perceived. More faintly he said, 'You'll be his happy gift, my child, I'm so glad to leave you to—Oh! go now!'

The fingers grew rigid and seemed to push her away. Wilmet half lifted, half thrust her into Charlie's arms. He almost carried her, pressing her face against him that she might not catch a glimpse of those spasms and uncontrollable writhings of anguish that were returning. The door was shut, and the young creatures cowered in the gallery in one another's arms, catching the sad sounds that neither patience nor resolute will could prevent. Stella slid down on her knees, and Charlie was fain to do the same, thankful that she let him hold her in his arm instead of repelling him.

'There! it is all quiet. He must be better again,' he whispered after a time, and this was confirmed by Angela coming to send out a prescription of the doctor's. The chill look of her white dress suggested to Charlie to say, 'You will be as cold as ice in that whiteness, my

Star. Suppose you took it off, while I go and tell Sir Robert that nothing shall move us till he is all right again. You couldn't think me such a brute.'

Poor little Stella held up her tear-stained face for a kiss with a vague sense of having been naughty and wanting forgiveness.

'You'll come back to me when you have dressed! I'll come and wait up here again.'

'Do. I'll be quick. They can't send us away, can they?'

'I'll see them shot first,' then repenting the schoolboy defiance of the words: 'No, Stella, I'm your husband, you know, and can guard you. I had no intention of going, not a bit. Only they can't see when one is a man, and they frightened you with the noise, poor little thing! If I tell them *he* wishes it, no one can say a word. Don't be long.'

He nearly walked over a pair sitting on the stairs, too dejected to heed anything, namely, Lance and Gertrude, drawn together by the fellow feeling of being both too unhappy to speak or be spoken to, yet finding a sort of companionship in wretchedness as they listened and caught fragmentary tidings from above.

Charlie showed his manhood in quiet self-assertion. He told his grandfather that it would not be right to take his wife away, and that her brother wished them to stay; and though this was viewed as very ill-judged, there was no gainsaying it, especially as his uncle had come down decidedly of the same opinion.

Geraldine had likewise descended. The sanguine view she had contrived to take up had given her strength to take up her necessary part as mistress of the house making farewells and excuses. Marilda had, she found, swept off all the children to the Harewoods' house, including Gerald, who had allowed Ferdinand to carry him away, and in the present state of things she could only be thankful he was beyond hearing and questioning.

As the hours passed, and winter twilight gave way to early night, there was something of a lull. The alleviations had not been entirely without effect, and Dr. May felt obliged to go home, promising that he or his son, or both, would come early on the morrow. When Felix understood this, he asked whether Gertrude were still in the house, and hearing that she was, begged for her presence for a moment.

'Most certainly,' said her father. 'Where is she?'

'She has been sitting on the stairs all day with Lance,' Angela answered.

'With Lance?' Felix nearly smiled.

Dark as were the stairs, there they still were. Lance had executed numerous errands, and had made Gertrude swallow some tea, but they had not spoken ten words to one another. There Dr. May found his daughter, and, with a word or two of warning and preparation, led her in. She could not see much, for the light was shielded from the face, and only threw up the shadow of the cross and the angel's hovering wings on the ceiling above. The hand that lay on the sheet, curved, but not with repose, closed on hers with a '*krampfhaft*' pressure. 'You have been comforting Lance,' said Felix. 'Thank you.'

'I couldn't,' she faltered, more overcome by voice than look, it was so thin and weak.

'You prayed! You will pray! "Each on his cross still let us hang awhile." Pray that I may not let go. "Suffer us not at our last hour,"' his lips moved on—'Pray that for me.'

'Indeed! indeed I will!'

'Thank you; it will be your greatest kindness. And one day remember that wish—that one wish. I wanted to wish you good-bye. God bless you. Kiss me once, my *sister* Gertrude.'

She could not have staid a moment longer than to give and receive that kiss. She almost fled into the room where her wraps were, and there cried as if her heart would break, feeling scarcely able to bear it when Robina came to see whether she had warm things enough.

But Gertrude had a twelve miles' drive with her father, and in it she experienced as never before, the depths of his tenderness and delicacy of his sympathy, and he found what were his once wilful petted child's yearnings towards that lofty noble character just out of reach, yearnings by his own forbearance just not stirred into active conscious love, such as would have left her heart entirely widowed. For in reply to the questions she scarce durst utter, the Doctor declared plainly that his own hope was small, though there still remained the possibility of a turn for the better, and Tom's more modern science might have further resources.

This was what he had left with the family, and most of them turned 'not hopeless' into hopeful, more especially as the most distressing form of suffering had not recurred, though even now Felix begged that Cherry might not see him, and feebly tried to send Wilmet home, but nothing would induce her to leave him. Her whole self seemed bound up in the single thought of ministering to him, and she was almost incapable of attending to remonstrance from husband or doctor on the special risks in her case, as if her strong will had mastered her very understanding, and they feared that to insist might do her more harm than to let her have her way. Clement kept equally close at hand, resolved that she should never be alone with the patient to bear the first brunt of those appalling attacks of suffering, and Angela was never further off than the next room, with the door open.

Those downstairs achieved a conventional cheerfulness. Stella was there in her ordinary black dress, and it was not easy to realize that she was Mrs. Audley, while Charley hung over her, petting her, though very anxious to be useful.

The chief use to which Geraldine wanted to put him or any one else, was to entertain Adrian, who looked as if he thought the illness of the master of the house a special injury and act of inhospitality to himself, and was, besides, much disposed to be rude to Ferdinand.

'Can't you take him into the long room and play billiards?' she asked Bernard.

'You'd hear the balls up in Felix's room. I never saw such a selfish brute.'

Bernard had found his Helot at last. 'Best way would be to get Fulbert to take him somewhere to smoke. I don't suppose he'll go for me.'

The somewhere was Sibby's sitting-room, and when Sir Adrian was carried off, Alda, Geraldine, Ferdinand, and Marilda had rather a comfortable talk over old St Oswald's Buildings days, in which Mr. Audley presently joined them.

221

The calm lasted, so that every one except the three actual nurses went to bed peacefully; but before the morning broke there was worse distress than ever. The worst attacks there had been at all set in, lasting longer, and with far less power of mitigation from the remedial measures, which seemed to be losing more effect every time, till the watchers scarcely durst wish to see the sufferer begin to revive only to undergo fresh torture.

That terrible morning broke Wilmet down. She had gone through all with unremitting energy and unflinching courage, but when Professor May had arrived, and brought some new anæsthetic, so that there was some relief and the strain slackened, she just crept into the next room with Angela and fainted away, only reviving to swoon again as soon as she tried to move.

The doctors were unanimous in sending her away, even while scarcely yet conscious, to her own house, and she was too faint to make any resistance or remonstrance. About an hour later, Ferdinand and Marilda, who were waiting in the billiard-room for the report of Professor May's opinion, were auditors of the following conversation, evidently the end of something that had been going on all the way from Major Harewood's house:

'Adrian! it is absolute cruelty! Why cannot you go alone, and send home the children?'

'Oh I daresay, and leave you to sentiment with that nigger fellow.'

'You need not have insulted me;' and her silk rustled upstairs, his steps following.

Marilda's eyes flashed and gave utterance to a fierce whisper. 'The cowardly ruffian! Can't you horsewhip him?' clenching her fist as she spoke.

But Ferdinand's dark face had indeed reddened, and his nostrils quivered, though not at the personal offence, as he muttered under his breath: 'To shoot him were the only cure for her! God forgive me for the thought, but to think of any woman in such hands, and to be the person most entirely unable to defend her!'

'I forgot! Of course you could only make it worse, but poor dear Alda!—It drives one out of one's senses;' and tears of anger were in her eyes.

'It stirs the devil within, and makes me wish I had never forgiven him,' said Ferdinand between his teeth.

'You need not forgive him this! *I* don't.'

After a few moments' pause Fernan said, 'The only service I can do her is to go away. Would that make him consent to her remaining?'

'Oh! we can't spare you. What shall I do with Gerald without you or Mary Vanderkist? He is always whining for Cherry!'

'Of course I can't bear to be away, but if I excite this idiotical jealousy, what can I do but take myself off? I'll go to London, and you can telegraph every hour. Go up and tell Alda—Lady Vanderkist, I mean. Casually ask what I can do for her.'

'That would stir him up again. And I don't think it would be of any use. He doesn't want to stay here, and means spite.'

'Then she could insist on staying.'

'She would be afraid. You see when people have used one another as they used you, it can't help rankling.'

'I ought not to have come here, but of course I thought the whole thing as utterly gone by with them as with myself.'

Marilda looked up with a curious expression of blushing gladness that made him exclaim,' How like you are to what you were when first I saw you!'

She blushed still more.

'That time!' he said, musing. 'Did you ever think I used you wrongly?' he suddenly added.

'*I* never did. I knew the difference between myself and Alda.'

'Nay, let me tell you, I never should have seen how beautiful she was, unless—I suppose it wasn't true, now—'

'What wasn't true?'

'That you and Felix—'

'Felix! No indeed! He is far too independent and disinterested. Who could have told you? You won't say? Not Edgar?'

'No. It was that poor lady herself.'

'Well,' said Marilda, infinitely shocked, 'I do call that wicked!' and as her mind glanced back to all the pain of those two years, she added, 'What did she say? Don't mind telling me. I'm old enough now.'

'Are you?' he said, with a quick glance of his dark eyes that made her glow again, and he continued: 'She gave me to understand that there was an old inclination between you and him, and that your father had such a regard for him as to be likely to yield if nothing more advantageous came in his way.'

'If you had only asked poor Edgar! Well! perhaps she flattered herself it was so! Yet, what could have put it into her head.'

'You know the rest, and how I was dazzled both by her beauty and the charm of her connection, but for years past the sense of my huge mistake has been upon me; yet till Felix came into possession here, I still thought it was his punctilious feeling alone that kept you apart.'

'As if he had ever cared for me except in a cousinly, brotherly sort of way! Did you think that was what made me hush up poor Edgar's affair, though indeed I never felt so thankful to any one as to you for having saved that secret.'

'Do you know what your generosity made me wish, though I never durst speak it before? That you would forget all these mistakes and forgive me, and come back to what things were before that misunderstanding.'

'Oh!' cried Marilda, with a long breath, 'you can't really mean it.'

'What else should I mean? If you will only forgive and overlook.'

'Don't talk in that way,' cried Marilda. 'Why I never cared for anyone else, and always have—but'—breaking off in the midst—'hark, there are wheels. That poor thing will be gone.'

'You had better go up and tell her.'

'Not *this*—I can't. It would only make him more savage; besides at such a time.'

'True. No—only let them know I'll go. I'm gone. No, I can't leave the place till I've heard his opinion—but I'll go over to Ewmouth. I'll see you again and settle—only don't let her be dragged away.'

Marilda was obliged to go up, with the vaguest ideas as to what to say, in a case that even she felt to be delicate, but on coming to the scene of action, she found that the words she had overheard amounted to no more than an ebullition of temper. Sir Adrian did not wish to leave behind him a character for brutality, and since he could plead an appointment and escape from the house of mourning, he could endure leaving his wife to it; and an excuse for yielding was afforded by the maid who, coming up with the two little girls, brought word that Mrs. Harewood was asking for my Lady.

So Mary and Sophy were sent back to Ironbeam, their father went to meet his pheasants, and their mother hurried back to her twin, all that old tenderness reviving instinctively so as to render the sisterly contact the greatest comfort then possible to either. Ferdinand had taken care to inform the departing Sir Adrian that he was about to leave Vale Leston, and was in fact only waiting for the opinion of the London doctor who had seen Felix before, and for whom, with Tom May's sanction, he had telegraphed.

Gratitude to him for having devised this, and trust to further advice buoyed Cherry up, as she watched in the painting-room, giving orders, answering inquiries, and never swerving from hope and that intense prayer for her brother's restoration, which no one could discourage, nor even qualify in vehemence. Why should not a life so valuable be given back to her entreaties and those of many another suppliant? Yet Mr. Audley, going backwards and forwards between her and the patient, could not but be struck by observing that Felix himself rather allowed than demanded the supplications for recovery, and though extremity of pain often wrung from him cries for relief and sobs for mercy, yet in the calmer periods these became sighs for the power of enduring his cross better, and of not loosening his hold on his Saviour, and sometimes even the moan had more of praise than of plaint. He was still quite sensible, but the intervals between the paroxysms were so far from painless that he never showed any wish to see or speak to any but those immediately about him, namely, Clement and Angela, with Lance and Robina as supplementary helpers, and Mr. Audley, when he could bear it.

Tom May waited all day, doing his best till his London friend came, and could do nothing but confirm his treatment, and agree that the shadow of hope was not yet absolutely impossible, though human means were unavailing. However, between exhaustion and a fresh form of anodyne, a sort of stupor was induced towards the evening, and this was again a relief, at least to those who durst call it sleep.

Ferdinand profited by it to tear himself away according to his promise, and Marilda betook herself and her much aggrieved maid to the Rood, carrying the children with her, to spend the day, though there was no room to lodge them at night; poor Gerald submitting passively, as the fresh misfortune of losing both Fernan and Mary Vanderkist fell on him. Marilda's quarters were left to Sister Constance, who arrived at the appointed time, to find herself less needed at the Priory than the cottage, where the greeting she received from the sorrowful and anxious Lady Vanderkist was no small contrast to the manner in which Alda Underwood had requited her services.

The beneficent torpor lasted far into the night, and in some way or other all, save Clement and Angela, consented to take a certain amount of rest. Even Angela, though refusing to lie down, must have dozed in her chair by the fire, for as her perception gradually returned to her, she heard broken tones from Felix, and saw Clement standing over him. The first words that fully met her ear were the conclusion of what had gone before. 'There! stained, weak, failing, erring, more than I can say—more than I can recollect—I can only trust all to the washing in my Saviour's precious blood. Let me hear His message.'

The deep, thankful intensity of the gaze, looking far beyond Clement standing over him and pronouncing the Absolution, impressed Angela with strange awe.

> Full of the past, all shuddering twilight,
> Man waits his hour with upward eye,
> The golden keys in love are brought,
> That he may hold by them and die.

It was a face of love, eagerness, absorption, that no one could ever forget, as the voice of pardon was listened to with folded hands.

She dared not move till there was again need of her assistance. When she could utter a word to Clement, it was: 'Is not he better?' but Clement shook his head. Still the last doctor's advice had enabled the worst part of the suffering to be so far kept in abeyance, that before that morning's dawn the Feast could be held in the sick chamber, among those whom Clement ventured to call together for it. The greater calm much encouraged Cherry, and she went away cheered by the face that could still give her a smile, declaring that Felix did not look worse than when he was bloodless after the accident.

Both she and Bernard hugged their hope. Even when, before the day was out, all the family knew of Tom May's verdict that those symptoms had set in which extinguished all chance of recovery without a miracle; still those two upheld one another in shutting their eyes to the inference, and continued to rejoice in the comparative relief from the heartrending spasms of the previous days, while others knew but too well that this was only the token that the struggle of the constitution was over.

Other forms of suffering had set in, but attention was sometimes free. Ferdinand and Marilda, though ashamed of having fallen into their engagement at such a time, could not help believing that to him at least it would give pleasure, and it had been breathed into Mr. Audley's ear. In one of these pauses of tranquillity Felix was told of it, and said with a smile, 'That is well. God is giving me every wish of my heart—"Grant thee thy heart's desire—"'

For his words had a tendency to flow into psalms and prayers, which the others took up and finished; but he was generally quite sensible, though sometimes restless and sometimes torpid. He asked for Wilmet, and hearing she had gone home, and that Alda was with her, seemed satisfied. He murmured something about Sir Adrian, and on learning his departure, said, 'I meant to have spoken to him—I don't suppose I could—some one tell him—he must be kind to Alda and the little ones—poor Alda!'

The day passed in this manner, and when at its close the familiar sounds indicated shutting up for the night, he showed an expectation of good nights. Geraldine came, and was charmed with the calmed, soothed countenance; she kissed him and told him he was better, and would sleep. He answered, 'Thank God, yes; thank God for you, my Chérie.'

Clement was afraid to let her agitate herself or him, and led her away to her own door, appealing to him all the way whether the worst were not over. He trusted that it was.

To Stella Felix gave only a blessing and good-night, but he thanked Charlie again for letting her remain, and to Bernard he said what the lad at the moment thought wandering, 'You'll swim for yourself now your plank is gone.'

There were no such positive farewells to those immediately about him. He depended most for aid both bodily and spiritual on Clement, but he took the most notice of Angela, often thanking her, with some tender name, even while he seemed continually drifting further and further out of reach.

Life is strongly bound into a frame scarcely at the midway of age, and the change came so slowly that Cherry had begun to say that when the Epiphany was past, the day of his father's death, she was sure the corner would be turned. He was very weak, but he had been as weak before.

Weak? Yes. The mind was failing now, not the soul. The ears still opened to prayer, the lips joined in it, the speech was of another world. "The hours of the cross—when will it be over?" Or the wedding might guide the thought to "the Bride prepared." "The white array"—"the diamonds—the jewels He will make up—the emerald rainbow round about the Throne."

Falterings very feeble ensued, as if he were talking to his father: 'Indeed I tried. I think they are all coming. Father, may I come now? Isn't it done?'

That was the last word they caught distinctly, except fragments of prayer, before the long hour when he lay on Clement's breast, each long labouring breath heaving up as though the last. Lance had fetched Cherry, telling her Felix was going. He had had to change the word to dying, actually dying, before she could understand its force. Then she stood, gripping his arm, at the foot of the bed, while nothing was heard but those gasps, and the continued prayer of Mr. Audley, until the moment came when he bade the Christian soul depart into the hands of the Father of Spirits.

That was just as the winter night was darkening on the Saturday evening.

CHAPTER XLVIII.

SHATTERED PILLARS.

> 'The heart which like a staff was one,
> For mine to lean and rest upon,
> The strongest on the longest day,
> With steadfast love, is caught away,
> And yet my days go on, go on.'
> *E. Barrett Browning.*

In the darkness before the winter dawn, William slowly put the little skiff across the river, and went up to the Priory, where only one or two upper windows showed a pale light behind the blinds. All was intensely still, as the garden-door yielded to his hand, and he crossed the dark hall, then mounted the stairs, which creaked under his tread, and, pausing in the gallery, seemed drawn irresistibly to the door of the room which had been the centre of all their thoughts and cares.

His cautious touch of the lock was responded to from within. There was enough light in the room to show the carved Angel, and beneath it the silent face that seemed to be watching in hope for the trumpet.

Not much less white and set was Clement's face as, laying a cold set of fingers on William's arm, he drew him into his own room where they stood for some minutes, neither knowing how to speak, till the church clock striking broke the silence, and Will said:

'Clement, I have taken upon me to silence the knell—on Wilmet's account. John would not let you hear how alarmed we were last night, thinking you had gone through enough, but they say such a shock as that bell would be, might do all the harm imaginable. Sister Constance thinks she will pull through, but she has been fancying Felix was calling her, and poor John was quite overpowered.'

'Our other pillar!' said Clement, dreamily.

'She is better,' repeated Will. 'Sister Constance would not let her give way—told her not to fancy. She only wanted to prevent that sound.'

'Right,' murmured Clement in the same tone.

'And I will take the service.'

'Thank you, I am coming, but I don't know whether I have voice.'

'You ought to be in bed. Have you had any sleep?' For Clement had never attempted to rest from that Wednesday morning to Saturday night.

'I don't know,' he answered, passing his hand over his face. 'I've been a great many hours in bed, but there's no getting away from the sense for a moment,' said he, thawing under Will's sympathy, shown more in gesture than word. 'I don't seem able to care at this moment even for poor Wilmet and John. Everything seems swallowed up in this one. I've known these six months it was coming, and discussed it with himself, yet it comes to me as stupendous and appalling as if I had never thought of it before. The one that there was no doing, no living without! There seems no standing up against it.'

'You have stood more bravely than any, and you will.'

'I *must*,' said Clement. 'Of course it is faithless selfishness, and one cannot but rejoice that all that torture is over, and rest begun, but consternation and helplessness will come foremost, without him, brother, father, everything for all these eighteen years. Poor Cherry! what is to become of her!'

'How is she?'

'There it is! I don't know. I staid to help Sibby, and by that time I was so done up, that it seems a perfect blank. I must have frightened Sibby, for I remember her scared eyes, and then I fancy Fulbert and Lance were dosing me with soup, or wine, or something, and I went to bed; but what they said about any one, I can't recollect. I'll ask Lance.'

Lance sat up in bed, after a sleep he had fallen into towards the morning. Poor Cherry! he said, he had led her back to her room perfectly passive, and put her in her chair, but she seemed turned to stone. Mr. Audley had come and taken her hand, but it lay passively; she did not seem to hear his words, and her eyes had a stony mechanical glare like paralysis. The suddenness was practically as great to her as if Felix had been drowned at once. Mr. Audley had advised them to give her time to recover from her stunned condition, and she had been left to Stella, who had last reported that her stupefaction had passed into heavy slumber as soon as her head was on the pillow.

Robina had been entirely taken up with Angela, whose fatigue was almost as great as Clement's, and who had besides caught a bad cold and toothache on the wedding-day. Her prostration had taken the form of violent weeping, which Lance had heard half the night, and now, though all was quiet, the brothers durst not run the risk of waking her.

Indeed, when Mr. Page looked in with a somewhat more cheery account of Mrs. Harewood, he advised that no attempt should be made to disturb either sister, but that, in especial, Geraldine's room should be darkened, and she should be allowed to lie and doze, without being roused, under peril of mischief to brain or nerves.

As to Angela, she awoke soon enough, and then nothing would keep her from getting up and wandering about in restless misery and much bodily discomfort, almost engrossing Robina, while Stella guarded Cherry. Very thankful were all for the presence and aid of that little bride, whose names, the gift of her dying father, had never fitted her better, for she was the household star, the happy gift through those mournful hours. The loss to her was as of a parent, and no father could have been more beloved than her "Brother," but the change in her life had made it just not the utter desolation it was to the home sisters, and the strength of the new bond, and the soothing bliss of her husband's caresses, lifted her up enough to make her sympathy a support. She had never been a childish girl, and the last remnant of childishness seemed to have passed away in that struggle on the stairs. Her brightness had always been pensive and subdued, and in the time of distress there was a kind of lamp-light lustre in her looks, words, and ways that relieved dejection wherever she went, while either her powers were greatly developed or only had full scope when she and Robina had to share all the feminine cares of the stricken family.

That leaden state of Geraldine's continued the next morning, though she rang her bell mechanically for Sibby at her usual hour, came down, poured out breakfast, and ordered dinner as usual, then returned to her painting-room. If addressed, she gave a vacant look and a brief matter-of-fact reply, and volunteered nothing, nor attempted any employment. She seemed neither to care nor comprehend when told that Wilmet had had a quiet night, sat mazed and unhearing when Clement read, Angela roamed in and out like an unquiet spirit, as her brothers and sisters consulted in her presence, all feeling what it was to see her for the first time devoid of her own peculiar comforter.

Stella watched over her incessantly, and sat writing letters in the painting-room. Poor little bride—what letters they were to bear the date of her eighteenth birthday and her first Stella Eudora Audley's! About one o'clock, however, there was a shuffling sound of feet, a rattling of the lock, and little Gerald came breathlessly stumbling into the room, and in a moment was clasping his arms round Geraldine, 'Chérie, Chérie! you aren't gone too. Keep me, keep me!'

'My Gerald, my boy, my own!' He was on her lap, in her arms, and they were kissing each other with passionate fervour. 'Oh! Chérie, my back does ache so. I came all the way and up the stairs. Oh! my back.'

'My dear little man! There,' and Stella helped to place him on his couch, where she hung over him, the dumb spell broken by force of the little hands that clutched her fast.

'Don't let them have me again.'

'No, no, never, never,' cried Cherry, 'you are mine! my own all that is dearest, my boy, his boy.'

'Oh! please don't cry, Chérie, please,' and he stroked her face, while Stella was only too glad to see the tears. 'My back is better now, and I don't care, if you won't go away like my Daddy.'

'Not now, my child, don't be afraid.'

Then in an undertone 'Is *he*?' and at her look and gesture, he again clung to her, burying his face on her neck, 'O Chérie, Chérie, why do people die? I wish it had been Kester.'

'O hush, Gerry,' and just then manly steps came along the gallery, causing the child almost to choke her in his grasp, as trembling all over, he implored her not to let him be taken away.

'Is Gerald here?' asked Clement, opening the door, 'ah! yes, John, here he is!'

'No, no one is going to take you! Oh! Clem! John, is this a fit! my darling! Speak to him.'

'My dear,' said John, 'no one wants to take you away, I am only thankful you are here! Don't be afraid.'

The grasp, which had for a moment had something convulsive in it, slackened, but the poor child panted out 'Hold me! hold me, don't let me go.'

'No indeed, Gerald,' said Clement in his sweet voice, as he smoothed the tumbled hair, and as the boy did not recoil, took him on his strong arm and knee, 'no one can take you from us. You are our child, Chérie's and mine, the treasure trusted to us.'

Cherry looked up to her brother with an exquisite pathos of gratitude, and the child lay back, long shudderings still heaving up through his little frame, and drawing deep sobbing breaths, but his brown eyes showing his exceeding repose and confidence in his tall uncle's arms, and with Chérie's hand in his.

'I am most glad to have found him here,' said Major Harewood. 'Gerald, dear boy, I fear you have been very miserable. Marilda undertook the care of the children at the Rood, but she could not get on with them. Was that why you came home, Gerald?'

'It was all so horrible when Mary and Sophy were gone,' said Gerald.

'I am afraid Kester and Edward have been very naughty,' said John. 'Gerald, what have they been doing to you?'

The child hid his face on his uncle's breast. Timid and nervous as he was, he was precocious enough to be too honourable for personal accusations, and Major Harewood respected him. 'No, my dear, I will not vex you with questions. I am exceedingly grieved at the treatment you have had in my house. I must go, for there is much alarm.'

'Not Wilmet?'

'O no, poor dear, she takes their voices for those of her own little brothers, and asks them not to wake your father. Alda seems to have carried her back to her old days, but she is really better this morning and quite calm. I must hasten back.'

He was very pale and worn, but had a look of relief, as he wrung Cherry's hand without trusting himself to another word. Clement followed him to exchange a few more sentences on the blessing the child's return had been in rousing Cherry, but he was thoroughly angered and vexed at the usage his sons had evidently inflicted on their guest.

Poor child, he would have been far better off taking his chance amid all the home distress than dragged off to the tender mercies of his natural enemies. Marilda had received him as a sort of prey of her own, and resolved to win his heart while doing a real service by undertaking the care of the children, but the three boys were all of genera new to her. Kester openly defied her and led his little brother, and she grated on Gerald just as she had once grated on his aunt. As she had seized him officiously without asking counsel, she had not been cautioned on the peculiar treatment he required, and Ferdinand never thought of her not understanding it by sympathy like the aunts. However, as long as the kind almost motherly Mary Vanderkist was there, the child was tolerably happy, but when she was gone, and Fernan in his voluntary exile, he had no protector, and matters became far worse when Marilda had removed to the Rood, intending the children to spend the days there with her.

The first day had disgusted Kester and Edward with her parlour and her babyish games, and they refused to go thither again, or else rushed home as soon as her bonbons failed. Gerald could not walk so far, and no one remembered to take him, while Marilda, hurt at her ill success with the ungrateful boys, absorbed in tidings from the Priory, and in sending them on to her mother and Fernan, and provided with a very different object of life from the adoption of Edgar's boy, was more relieved than disappointed at their non-appearance. The cottage and nursery were disorganized by the mother's illness, and the two boys exercised unlimited tyranny over their victim. Kester, two years older than Gerald, and with twice his strength, could inflict all the cruelties by which the young male animal delights to test his power. The little wretch had Harewood wit enough for the invention of horrid bugbears, frightful to the nervous temperament he deemed cowardice. Between these, and the torment of being pushed, pinched, drummed, and hunted with ruthless violence, together with a mind confused as to whether all he loved, Felix, Chérie, Lance and all, had not vanished like his father, poor Gerald had come to such misery that, on being told that cousin Marilda had sent for a great new Locomotive, named Fiery Dragon, to carry him away right in the boiler, he could bear it no longer. He had certified himself from the window that the Priory at least still existed, had struggled down that giddy horror the stairs (where indeed Kester had once already goaded him down with a broomstick), and when once alone, awakening to his prairie resources, had made his way to the road, on seeing no means of passing the river to the garden, and had crept along, sitting down to rest, till seeing a carter boy with his sleek horses on the road, he had coaxed him to give him a ride on the broad back of one, and thus had arrived at the garden gate, made his way in, again achieved the staircase, and found his refuge at last in his Chérie's arms, not, however, till his system had received shocks enough to throw him sadly back. He was stiff in every limb, and wearied to excess, but slightly fevered, and haunted with terrors none the less miserable because imaginary. Nothing soothed him, but to have his aunt hanging over him caressing, talking, reading, nay even playing with him with a lump like lead in her heart, but her child's necessities preventing it from rising up to crush her.

Major Harewood might permit licence, but he was thoroughly master, and presently he brought up his culprits, shame-faced and tear-stained after their first castigation, and dictated their sobbing but sullen apology. The benefit to them, and to all whom they might have bullied in the future, might be great, but the scene was dreadful to the sufferer, who shook from head to foot, and when bidden to shake hands, held out his little white fingers with tremor that grieved more than it surprised the Major after the confession he had extorted, of hair pulled to make the scar bleed, of ambushes in dark corners, of the stimulus of the gig whip to quicken the steps.

He sent Mr. Page to inspect the victim, who was pronounced to be on the verge of nervous fever, so that Cherry and Lance had to devote their whole selves to him for the next few days, watching even when he dozed, since he would sometimes scream himself awake in a renewal of the real or imaginary horrors.

Was it a burthen? It might seem one, but such anxiety was the best distraction, the child's improvement the best earthly solace of which the sick and laden heart was susceptible.

The unmarried woman seldom escapes a widowhood of the spirit There is sure to be some one, parent, brother, sister, friend, more comfortable to her than the day, with whom her life is so entwined that the wrench of parting leaves a torn void never entirely healed or filled, and this is above all the case when the separation is untimely, and the desolation is where lifelong hopes and dependence have been gathered up.

Thus it was with Geraldine. Her brother had been the medium through which earth had love, joy, or interest for her. He was gone, and after her first annihilation, she mourned less externally than some of the others, because she knew she should mourn for life.

She did not weep nor bewail herself, but when not engrossed by her boy, she sat silent, inert, crushed. However she responded to all kindness, sadly but gratefully, and Mr. Audley soon found that the fittest way to cheer her was to lead her to the dear reminiscences of her brother's past life, of which happily Gerald was pleased to hear. He might not enter into all, but he would lie gazing with his soft dark eyes, and sleepily listening, soothed by the low calm voices in which the dear old days were called up, and Mr. Audley was told the details of Felix's doings and sayings in the years of his absence. And out of such memories seemed to rise upon the sister strength, serenity, and a sense of unbroken love, as though Felix were still her chief comforter, even as when he used to rock his baby. The sorrow was unappeasable, and external words even of the highest comfort fell cold on her ear, though she tried to accept them, but to recall the thoughts and promises through her brother's value for them gave them life, and quickened her into the endeavour to attend to all he would have wished to be done for the others.

Angela, unwell with a heavy feverish cold and pain in the face, could by no means be kept still, wandering about like a perturbed spirit, trying all sorts of occupations, but never pursuing them for five minutes together. When her Hepburn friends came to see her, she sent down for answer a fierce impatient 'I can't,' which Robina of course translated more civilly. The good ladies were greatly moved and full of sympathy, eager to tell of the exceeding sorrow of the whole parish, and in the midst, Angela, in her aimless changes of purpose, came into the room. Miss Isabella's kind arms were held out, but she backed out of them, and when after some more kind expressions the visitor added, 'certainly, whatever differences existed, we all feel that your dear brother was truly one of the elect,' Angela startled her with a sort of shriek—'Miss Isa, don't go on! I won't have it! You don't know what a ten thousand times better Christian than any of us you are patronizing. You and your—your—your (Robina was afraid she said cant) have gone and set up a barrier between me and the very dearest of brothers. Oh! my brother. Oh!'

She fled in a passion of tears, Miss Isabella looked inexpressibly shocked, and Robina tried to plead ungovernable grief that knew not what it uttered. The kind ladies excused readily, only begging to be sent for in case her mind should turn towards them, a contingency just now most unlikely; for of all names poor Angela seemed to loathe none so much as Hepburn, and she absolutely gave way to a fretful fit of scolding when Clement gratefully mentioned their consideration in undertaking some of the parish Christmas business.

For several days Sister Constance had never ventured to leave Wilmet, but on the last evening when it was possible to look on Felix's face, Major Harewood released her from the bedside, and bade his brother ferry her over to spend an hour at the Priory.

After a solemn interval spent in the infinite peace of the Oratory, William conducted her to the painting-room. It was twilight, Geraldine was sitting by the fire with little Gerald on her lap, murmuring some story to him, and Robina was stamping a pile of black-edged letters, while notes of the organ, Lance's chief solace, came ever and anon in from the church. As the Sister advanced something long and black reared itself out of a dark corner, and clasped her round the waist, crying out, 'Sister Constance! Sister, take me! Why was not I always with you! Oh! I must come.'

It was enough to startle any timid person, sobbed out as the words were. 'Gently, Angel, gently,' said Cherry, and Robina was prepared to unfasten her like a wild creature, but Sister Constance, tenderly kissing the hot forehead, said, 'Softly, my poor child, we will see about it.'

'Don't see about it!' cried Angela, in the childish phrase of impatience. 'It is my only refuge! I'm not fit to be in the world.'

'Let go, Angela,' said Robina, 'you don't know what you are doing!'

'Promise! promise!' repeated Angela, only the more passionately.

'I have no power to promise,' said the voice, so soothing in its authority. 'You know you have given up your claim.'

'Oh! I was misled! I was blind! I did not know! I was mad; but you'll forgive—you will let me come.'

'Only our Mother Superior and the chaplain can judge whether you can be taken back. Nothing can be done in this sudden way. We will talk it over quietly by-and-by. Now, my dear, let me speak to your sisters.'

Subdued by her tone, Angela stood aside, and after the greeting, Robina collected her letters and went away to her Willie.

Sister Constance was little changed since she had come in among the desolate children eighteen years ago. That which had taken away her youth and sunshine had been long previous, and there was little noticeable alteration except that each year which carried her further from the agitation of grief confirmed her habits, strengthened her hope, and added to her serenity and sweetness. As she sat down, Angela dropped on the floor, leaning against her black serge dress, while her gentle stroking hand on the coils of hair must have been almost magnetic, for it was long since the girl had spent so many minutes in tranquillity, as while the Sister and Cherry talked over her head.

First as to Wilmet, who was rallying the forces of her sound health and constitution. Throughout, Sister Constance said the presence of her twin sister had done more good than anything else. When nothing was so needed as quiet and sleep, Alda had lain down by her side and stroked and fondled her, and she had forgotten all that had passed since the two fair heads had last rested beside one another, laid the invincible weight of sorrow on her, to the account of the earliest sorrow of her life, and when disturbed by her boys' voices, called them by the names of her brothers, and yet she had never failed in recognition of her husband. She was now quite herself, only so weak that she shrank from thought or speech, and merely rested in Alda's presence. Cherry had hardly hitherto comprehended how nearly both their pillars of the house had gone together, and she could now feel thankful, though more for John's sake than with the sense that any loss could make much difference to herself, and much more did she care to hear Sister Constance express her admiration of the calm victorious beauty of the brow she had first seen on that dark confused winter evening when the task was just beginning which was at last laid down. She had been struck by the identity of the countenance. The man of four-and-thirty had lost none of the candour and purity of the boy; the lad of sixteen had already much of the grave steadfast sweetness of the man. She thought they would know him in the Resurrection by that look.

The talk came only too soon to an end. With the precision of a woman living under discipline, the Sister watched the clock, and rose up five minutes before it struck, saying that her time would be up by the time she was put across the river. Geraldine kissed her in acquiescence, but Angela pursued her into the gallery, and tried to drag her to her own room, 'I must talk to you, I want to tell you how I came to send back my medal!'

'My dear, I cannot stay. Major Harewood must be set free to go to his dinner.'

'Only five seconds, to beg you to manage! I must confess to Father Willoughby.'

'Angela, you know enough of us to know that it is not allowable to linger over an appointed time.'

'Oh! I know I am undisciplined.'

'Submit to discipline, then.'

'I wanted to explain,' following her downstairs.

'Hush!' said the Sister, gravely signing towards the curtains that hung over the archway leading to the long room and the oratory beyond. Awed by this ruthless silencing, she could only follow spaniel-like to the drawing-room, where William had told Sister Constance she would find him, and he was standing over the fire talking to Robina.

Allowing them a moment for their farewells, Sister Constance put her arm round Angela. 'Poor child,' she said, 'when I can, we will talk. Meantime this is the best I can say to you: "Commune with your own heart, and in your chamber, and be still."'

Poor Angel! The religion that had consisted partly in music, flowers, and excitement, and the rest in mechanical party-spirit, had been totally unreal and unpractical, though with a sound theology and fitful aspirations for better things when she should have had her swing.

When religion *such as she had made it* proved wholly inadequate to her need, her friend's influence led her to the central Verity where alone rest could be found. Then having brought herself to the sense of individual pardon through faith, she discarded all besides, hotly revenging herself on what she took for impediments, and striving to stir up that assurance of forgiveness which was all feeling by all external means. The discovery of the inconsistency of her guides, and the knowledge of Felix's condition had come upon her at the same time, and the latter had blotted out everything else. During the ensuing weeks everything was lost in the sight of her brother's fatal suffering, all through her own ungovernable levity. The sting she had smothered in the vague *en masse* repentance which made an unsorted heap of her sins, and lavished hard names on it, now came forth with a barb of poisoned acuteness. For those two months devoted attendance on her brother had been her whole religion, but there was that about him which always made the endeavour to please him no small training, how much more when he was on the verge of the River.

He did not preach or argue, he was simply himself, and the constant endeavour to ascertain his doings and understand his expression revealed to her much of his mind, all the more perhaps because she never spoke, she hardly thought, she only received impressions. And above all, that upward look with which he met that last full absolution, that expression of intense acceptance and gratitude of sight rather than faith, had dwelt on her ever since, not merely casting out the memory of the pain-wrung features, but even overmastering the image of the grand monumental placidity which had settled down on the countenance at rest from its labours.

That absolution! She had heard it before, perhaps too early, certainly too much as a matter of course, for actions whose faultiness was visible enough, but which involved no true contrition. So little had it touched her innermost soul, or so little innermost was there to be touched, that its familiarity had made her spurn it as an empty insufficient delusion in her despair in the summer, and catch at the notion which condemned its utterance by a mere man as vain and presumptuous. Her careless touch had turned the Golden Key to lead, and only when she saw it held to the faithful did the gold shine out once more.

There was no pause to think till the mortal struggle was over, but then came the revulsion, and the peace she had seen so real in her brother brought her back to the wildest longing to experience the same, through the same means, and yet the reluctance to turn to the ordinary helps before her still made her hang back from her brother Clement, or Mr. Fulmort. They would look, if not say, 'So here you are at last.' If their principles were right, as Felix's acceptance proved, of course it was their own fault that she had not been more good. They shared in her intolerable loathing for whatever was around her, her madness to be out of sight of everything and everybody, and wretched feeling of impatience. The sight of Sister Constance suddenly gave this longing an object. Her old love of St Faith's revived, and therewith the desire to find a spiritual healer in Mr. Willoughby, the chaplain, who was comparatively a stranger to her, though Mr. Audley had left Cherry under his care, and he had of late become a good deal noted as a director. This was what she wanted to say! Could she but have talked to Sister Constance, and shown the peculiarity of her case, the insufficiency of her guides, the really tragic nature of her troubles, she *must* have obtained the object she had become set upon in these few minutes, namely, leaving the dreariness of home by hurrying to St Faith's and Mr. Willoughby, when Lance should return to his business on Monday.

Cruel Sister, to have postponed such misery to John Harewood's dinner! 'Commune with your own heart.' A fine way of refusing confidence! Yet Angela was nurse enough to know the need of punctuality in relieving guard, and Sister Constance could not have been spared much longer. Wilmet knew it was Alda's last evening, and must not be allowed to dwell on the thought. For poor Alda durst not ask for a respite. She must go away with her husband as soon as the funeral was over, for she believed Ferdinand Travis was still at hand, and durst not inquire. She was still conscious. Nay, most poignant grief of all was the sense that the dark noble countenance was dearer to her than when she had raved about its beauty, and that it could still make her heart throb wildly. It was a humiliating, involuntary sin, the outcome of the voluntary sin of past years, of those blind heartless manoeuvres to which she looked back in amazement as she contrasted her actual life with that which she had thrown away, while watching unconscious manifestations of devoted conjugal affection, such as she had never before missed because she had never conceived them. Avoidance was all that was possible to her. Her little girls must be her refuge! Was not the man still single, and could she help feeling a certain satisfaction in the thought?

Poor Alda! She was up in her sister's room that afternoon when Marilda and Miss Martha Hepburn encountered one another on their daily visit of inquiry in the cottage drawing-room, and Miss Martha had ventured on congratulating Miss Underwood.

'Who told you?' bluntly exclaimed Marilda.

'I beg your pardon! Indeed—I thought—We heard it on good authority—Shall we contradict it?'

'Say nothing about it! We particularly wish it not to be mentioned,' almost growled the heiress, 'I would have given anything that it should not have been known at such a time.'

Miss Martha was dismayed, and retreated amid showers of promises of secrecy, but with the elation of having confirmed the fact.

Marilda exclaimed, 'How horrid! Who can have gossiped? Now, John, do me a kindness! You tell Alda! I can't!'

'I am afraid I must ask the other half——'

'Can't you tell? No wonder. He is so much too good for me.'

'That's uncle Bill,' broke out the unsuspected Eddie, with his mouth full of her chocolate creams. 'He's worth ever so much more than you.'

'I have a better guess,' said his father, unable to help laughing, 'Travis? I heartily congratulate you. Never was there a nobler fellow!'

'It ought not to have been *now*,' said Marilda, 'but we could not help it. It had all been one long, long misunderstanding, and it came right of itself as soon as we began to talk to one another. Fernan says poor Edgar wished it, and dear Felix knew it, and sent us a blessing through Mr. Audley, but we meant no one to know for a month, or till I had gone home. It seems so unfeeling.'

'I do not think it will seem so here,' said John. 'You know Charlie's proposal rose almost out of Stella's grief for Theodore,' and as Marilda was trying to guess who had spread the report, he added, 'Never mind. Of course we know such things are in the very air.'

'It is Alda that concerns me,' said she, her face on fire, 'I would not have her hear it indirectly.'

So John, who had first known Alda and Fernan as the senior lovers, while he was still in suspense, undertook the communication and made it when Alda was pouring out his tea that evening. Her hand was steady, but her lips drew together as she said, 'Riches to riches.'

'True, but hardly just.'

'No. *She* likes him,' and the emphasis was bitter. 'Can a woman be fair towards the man who once loved her?' thought John, but restrained his speech.

'How long has this been?' asked Alda, presently.

'I cannot tell. Quite recently, no doubt, but long enough to give pleasure to your dear brother.'

'Felix knew?'

'So she says.'

He did not understand her look of pain as she thought of Felix's cry of indignation on her light avowal of the insinuation which had parted those two, securing the one for herself and casting the other over to him, but her womanly instinct strove to hide the pang or excuse it with a half truth.

'I can't help thinking of my husband's disappointment. He reckoned on her as the benevolent genius of our family.'

'I have little faith in benevolent genii.'

'Not equal to three per cents, as he would say. You are wealthy enough to be shocked at the worldliness of those who have to live up to a position. However, there is no reason to regret it! They have more in common than appears at first sight.'

And she soon escaped. Three lines of truly kind congratulation lay on Marilda's toilette table the next morning. Alda attempted no more—hers was a grief that would not brook the light.

So morning dawned on the day when the Church was to give the brothers and sisters voice for their farewells to that beloved and honoured head of their orphaned home.

So far as depended on them, and by Felix's own express written desire, all was far plainer than in the case of their parents, when he had been in bondage to Thomas Underwood's views of propriety. Now—so far from the seventy-five yards of black cloth bedecking the church, it had not lost one holly wreath, one ivy streamer: the scarlet and white flowers were fresh, the star of Bethlehem in pale bright everlasting flowers still stood prominent, and in letters of golden straw the Epiphany promise:

'The sun shall no more be thy light by day,
Neither for brightness shall the moon give light unto thee,
But the Lord shall be unto thee an everlasting light,
And thy God thy glory.'

No pauper funeral there was simpler, for the same purple velvet pall with the red cross stretching its arms over the coffin in protection was used for the poorest; the plain oak only bore the name and date, and the brothers and friends bedizened themselves with no foolish gloomy streamers or scarfs, as they drew together to follow the farm-labourers who bore what remained of Felix from the steps of the hall door where, four years and a half before, he had spoken forth his purpose to live there to the glory of God and the good of his neighbour.

So he passed from the home he had never coveted, though he had loved it better than aught save the home beyond.

The Bishop of the diocese had desired to testify his esteem by welcoming him to the Rest of those who die in the Lord, and Clement was thus one of the eight brothers and sisters who followed first. The nearest of all was tacitly allowed to be Geraldine, upon his arm, while he led Gerald. Not only was the child his uncle's heir and head of the name, but Cherry and Lance found that to see and know all was best for him. Poor Edgar's wish that people could be sublimated away had been in a measure fulfilled in his case as regarded his little son, and the consequence had been a vague horror and mystery that had haunted him till he was led to gaze at and kiss his uncle's calm white face, and then, after long dreamy thought, he had said in a voice of comfort, 'Then Daddy was like that.' Kester was there, too, in his father's hand, awed but sharply observant. And besides these, and the nearest connections and friends, there was all the parish, farmers, tenants, labourers and all! Scarcely a cottage but rang with the lament, 'We, shall never have such another Squire;' almost every woman was sobbing with the infectious agitation of that class; the big lads, whom he had taught on many a Sunday and winter evening, were even more unrestrained in their grief, and many a rugged old labourer echoed the elegy, 'Well now I did reckon never to have seen the last of he, but the likes of him was too good for we. I never had a beast out of the ordinar but it was sure to go the first!'

Not only Vale Leston was there but almost all the gentry and fellow-magistrates, Sir Vesey Hammond's white head conspicuously, also a whole company of familiar Bexley faces. They had given no notice lest the family should put themselves to inconvenience, but there they all were, the Mayor, Mr. Bruce, Mr. Jones, Mr. Prothero, and many another also come with old Mr. Harewood and Ernest Lamb, who, poor fellow, looked as if the foundations of the earth had given way with him. The late Rector had written his excuses on the score of health, but Doctor Ryder was present, and Mr. Audley had been called out to speak to his old colleague Mowbray Smith, who had come many miles to testify his gratitude to 'the best friend and truest I ever met, though I was such a fool as not to know it at the time.' Of course the Vicar of St

Matthew's had come early enough to join the family in the morning Sacrifice of thanksgiving, and as Robina moved on in the confused maze of sorrowful faces, she recognised the familiar head of Lord Ernest. It was as if Felix had left such a mark on all who came in contact with him, that none could abstain from testifying honour and gratitude, and yet it had been a very simple life. As he had said himself, he had done nothing but what he felt obliged to do. There was nothing however to which he had set his hand that was not in a better state than when he had taken it up.

So 'his works did follow him,' so had he 'served God in his generation'—as happy a fate as man can have, and those who were older than the bereaved brothers and sisters had learnt that however sad it seems to be cut off in the prime of life, with schemes of good all unfulfilled, yet it is like a general dying in the moment of victory, with the cup of tedium, failure, disappointment, and decadence all untasted.

It was a long procession that was met by the Bishop and his clergy, with the present Rector of Bexley and Mr. Colman of Ewmouth, and not only the Vale Leston choir, but many of those from St Oswald's. Well might Felix thus be greeted. Very few were the Sundays, since his father first had robed him in his little surplice and told him of Samuel, that he had not sung his part, he had not even had any long interval of broken voice, and had been retained during that time for the sake of his influence. Like everything else, his musical talent had been used primarily for the glory of his Maker.

What with the sweet sounds, the evergreen wreaths, the festal colouring, and the flowery crosses and wreaths carried by so many, there was more of grave joy than of grief and wailing apparent after the service once began. Sorrow without hope it could not be, solemn as it was when, as Felix himself had bidden, looking up to his Angel with the trumpet, it was the awful *Dies Irae* that heralded his way to the open grave beside his little Theodore, under the leafless willow-tree, which recalled the effort that had cost them all so dear.

Yes, Felix had laid down his charge, and gone to rest from his labours, and as 'Safe home' finally closed the service, did not Geraldine think of her fleet of boats and long for safety in the haven, whither her flag-ship had now attained? Yearningly she bent forward, aided by Clement, for her last sight of the coffin and the dear name 'Felix Chester Underwood,' never again to be a household call. She hung so long over it that Clement would fain have drawn her back, and as she resisted, was trying to find voice to bid her remember that 'he is not here,' when little Gerald, struck perhaps by the words of the hymn, and connecting it with the earth he had seen and heard dropping in, reached out of Lance's arms, where he had been lifted, touched her and said, 'Was not that baptizing him again for the Resurrection of the dead?'

She heard, and her boy was her best comforter again, bringing back the trust to see 'that countenance pure again,' and to look up instead of down.

So her brothers led her away, but there was no quiet time yet The Bishop had considerately refused to come to the house, but Clement must of course go and speak to him, thank him, and bear the expression of his warm feeling for the family and reverence and gratitude to the man who had so changed his parish.

Geraldine had to go to the drawing-room with her sisters, Marilda, and Gertrude May, whose right to be present all had felt. Her eyes were dim, her colouring paled, she looked as if she had been weeping ever since they had last met, and she only tried to avoid obtruding her presence or her grief. Her father soon came for her. He took Cherry's hand, saying, 'My dear, trust an old man. You can't feel it now, but our jewels become dearer in the diadem, and when our hearts go after them, there is rest.'

Cherry tried to smile thanks but was too sad to take home the comfort. She wanted her jewel now!

Food must be eaten, for Marilda and the two married sisters were going away, but before the move to depart, Clement said, 'There are so many of us that we think all should hear about the property together before there is any break-up.'

So Major Harewood, with a draft of the will in his hand, explained. Land, house, furniture, everything at Vale Leston of course, descended to Gerald Felix Underwood under the trusteeship of Clement, John Harewood, and Ferdinand Travis. The personal guardianship was reserved to Geraldine with £500 a year until the heir should be of age. If he should die without children, the succession would of course go to Clement, and after him it was entailed on the brothers, or their heirs in due order. Besides this the estate was charged with £500 a year, as an income for each of the sisters who might remain single. On her marriage each would have £500 down, the annuity of the others remaining untouched, unless one entered a sisterhood, when £50 per annum should be paid for her. To Lancelot was left unreservedly the whole of the acquisitions at Bexley, house, shares in the business, stock, and Pursuivant. There was an annuity of £30 to Sybilla Macnamara, a legacy to Martha, and to the old foreman, and that was all. John and Lancelot were executors.

The first feeling was of surprise that Bernard was only mentioned as last in the entail. Cherry and Lance both turned to him. 'It shall be all the same, Bernard; he means us to do it.'

'No, he doesn't,' gruffly answered Bernard.

'Of course we can manage for you,' added Clement; 'as long as you work, there can be no difficulty.'

No thanks, no reply, indeed, followed, and Sir Adrian bade Alda hasten if she wished to take leave of her sister. Major Harewood would take her across at once, and she would be called for at the cottage on the way to the station. Wilmet was reported to have lain very still, shedding a good many soft tears, but not seeming the worse.

Alda held Geraldine closer than she had ever done before, and entreated, 'Write often, and let me know about you all. I wish we had been more together.'

Marilda was going to London with her, Sir Adrian was still in ignorance of the coming blow, and there was nothing in the farewell to Ferdinand to make him expect it, so his scowl at his wife's hand-shake was on the old score. Poor Alda, at least she had her children.

Their sweet Princess Fair Star! Yes, she must go! Captain Audley was waiting to drive the young couple to meet the express. They were to take a fortnight's quiet in the Isle of Wight, and then enter on their new world. It was time Charlie should have his wife to himself after all the patience, unselfishness, consideration, and helpfulness that had sealed him as a true brother, and endeared him the more from the contrast not only to Alda's husband but to his own father.

Clement had to be the parental brother to lead the bride to the carriage. He kissed and blessed her in the porch, saying, 'Little one, you have had a sad beginning, but I am glad you were still one with us. We know you all the more.'

'We are glad,' said Stella. 'This is worth more than weeks of happiness.'

'She is right,' said Charlie. 'We would not but have staid for worlds! We ought always to be the better for it. It has made the world look so different to us!'

'But that difference is not gloom,' said his uncle; and the 'Oh no' on his lips, and the bright crystal tears in Stella's eyes were no more gloomy than her diamonds when Felix was musing over them.

So the others turned back into the house that felt so large and empty, and they so few. Clement tendered an arm to help Geraldine upstairs. Somehow, long as it was since she had leant on Felix, this action brought a great sense of change. Clement's aid was the careful bending tenderness of a very tall man towards a small woman; Felix had been more nearly on her level; and merry old boasts on this score came piteously to the minds of both. The brother, who had borne up so strongly through all these days of sorrow and suffering, and months of pain and suspense, found his effort at cheering turn to a sob as he said, 'Ah, Cherry, you must make the best of me. I will try to be all I can, but never, never——'

'You are not your own self?' said Cherry, just then the braver. 'Have not we two always hung together, Clem?'

'You are very good to say so,' he faltered.

'Good! when I just feel it,' and she pulled his arm round her. 'Dear Clem, don't you remember the time when our pillars were away before, and all you did for me then, when I was cross and ill? He is only gone for a little time, you know, and he never did tell you and me to take care of each other, because he knew it would come naturally. Dear, dear Clem, if you weren't Clem already, should not I love you for having been so much the nearest and most helpful to him all this time?'

'The joy of my life!' murmured Clement in a choked voice, most unlike joy, as he leant against the door-post quite overcome.

'You'll tell me all in our long evenings. We will live with him a great deal still, and keep him before the eyes of our dear little boy—our charge.'

'Charge! Everything is a charge!' said Clement, wearily. 'How to act or decide without that clear, cool, wise head! To fill his place is impossible!' Then rousing himself, 'I beg your pardon, Cherry, I thought I was going to do something to comfort you, instead of making a fool of myself.'

'Making a fool of yourself makes you a great deal dearer and nicer than if you set up for comforting,' said Cherry. 'You know as well as I do that nobody can ever do that. Poor, dear old Clem, you are quite worn out, and no wonder, everything has come harder on you than on any one else. Sit down and rest;' and as she seated herself she tried to pull him down on the sofa beside her, but he resisted. 'I wish I could, Cherry,' he said wistfully, 'but I ought to go up to the Rood to thank the mayor and all the rest.'

'Kind friends!' said Cherry; 'but can't Lance do it, when he goes back?'

'Less gracious; and I sent word by Lamb I was coming. There's no good in shrinking!' said Clement, resolutely rearing himself up, but coming back to kneel on one knee, take another embrace, and say, 'O Cherry, I am so sorry for you, and you are so good to me!'

The humility touched her deeply. 'Not good,' she said; 'I want you, you are my own home brother,' and he allowed his wearied head to repose for a few moments on her shoulder as she threw her arm round him. 'Just tell me,' she said, as he stirred again, 'does Mr. Fulmort stay?'

'Yes, over Sunday.'

'That is well. I thought so,'

'Why?'

'Because you never dare to give way but when he is at hand. Dear Clem, I did not mean to vex you. Where should we have been if you had not been brave and strong?'

'I can't say much for that now, Cherry,' he said, 'I must not stay. I shall not be fit for what has still to be done.'

She heard him walk across to that untenanted room, and her love for him was quickened. Trust in his highly principled kindness she had always had, but to find him crushed, oppressed, overwhelmed, gave her a fellow-feeling for him as she felt him leaning on her; and this was not indeed consolation, but something not entirely removed from it.

His resolute, evenly-balanced manner, guarding jealously against whatever could unnerve him, had however been kept up all along to all the rest, as perhaps was needed by the exigencies of his situation, and perhaps it helped to actuate Robina in the conversation she was holding as she paced the cloister with William.

'Should you very much mind my not earning that last two hundred?'

'I? You speak as if I had ever asked you to earn anything.'

'For don't you think it seems my duty to stay and look after poor Cherry? If Stella were left I should not mind, but no one can tell whether Angel may not be worse than nobody; or she might yet go to St. Faith's.'

'The best place for her.'

'So I cannot bear to leave Cherry alone with Clement and the child. There will be Wilmet when she gets about again; but as long as her boys are such little ruffians——'

'Not worse than we used to be to the little trebles.'

'The little trebles were not like Gerald, I should hope, and Cherry must not have everything thrust on her at once—she who has been always petted and made *his* darling. Clement will be substantially kind, but he has no petting in him, and no mercy on his tools for parish work. He will be attentive, but all in a grand grave way, not spontaneously, because he can't help it, and she will pine. That she will do any way, poor dear, but it ought not to be without a sister.'

'Precisely. I am very glad.' Which he sincerely was to see affection triumph over prudence.

'So I think of writing to Lady de la Poer and telling her not to wait for me. Indeed, I know who would suit her. I can go and wish them all good-bye when Wilmet is better, but I must give notice; so of course I told you first, and I suppose I must speak to Clement.'

'He will be very thankful. He is very anxious and unhappy about Cherry.'

'And the unhappier he is, the sterner.'

'You hardly do Clement justice,' said William, gravely. 'Think of the knowledge he has silently borne these six months. Both as brother and as priest, he has gone further down with Felix into the valley of the shadow of death than any one else could do, and if the chill of it has stiffened him, it may be that only so could he serve as a support. I assure you, Robina, I watched and wondered all last long vacation. I saw he was unhappy and uneasy about your brother, but only now that I understand it all do I fully appreciate his self-control and energy through it all.'

'Self-control and energy,' said Robina. 'Yes that's just what I mean. Don't look at me so, Willie. He is a model clergyman, I know, but I fancy that very perfection hinders him from being the brother poor Cherry needs. There! we are not going, of all things in the world, to quarrel about Clement.'

'Certainly not,' said Will, smiling, 'especially as this conviction of yours leads you in the very direction I wish, and will cure itself.'

'I know him so little,' added Robina, in excuse for herself, as she saw how she had wounded Will's enthusiastic admiration of the very qualities in which he felt himself the most deficient. 'You know I have never spent three months together at home since I was seven years old, so it is full time I learnt home-life.'

'To be domesticated,' said Will; 'but look here—why should not I go in for the curacy, and then——'

'That's the way I am to devote myself to Cherry, eh? No, Bill, we must be all the more staunch. Mind, the question is not whether you and I can be content in poverty, but whether we will be a drag on our brothers, and you a less efficient clergyman. Recollect my father.'

'I only recollect worn-out Dons.'

'Dons minus brains! You always wanted to do it all, and now you have your way. Two years more, and I really think we shall do!' (For Robina kept the account of the investments.)

'You miser! At least I shall know you are safe here, and of that I am heartily glad. I never could forgive the Repworth folk for being your masters.'

'Very ungrateful!' said Robina. 'I don't know how to think of not going back to my dear little girls, and their mother!'—and tears came to her eyes, for she could not but feel that home had lost all its brightness and much of its sweetness.

'I think,' said Bill, musingly, 'it is wonderful how, with such a set of strong wills as you Underwoods have, you should have all preserved such perfect union.'

'Have we such strong wills?'

'Do you ask a poor victim like me, whose only chance is in some slight confusion on your part which your own Will may be? Look at Clement, like a piece of iron when his mind is made up; look at Wilmet; look at Angel; look at Lance. Why, his power of resistance had changed the whole tone of us choir boys before he was thirteen. In fact, I believe it is that strength of character that keeps you harmonious. You don't worry about straws, or clash, or pother, but know when and to whom to give way with a good grace.'

'We did,' sighed Robina. 'We could not help it then. Ah! here comes Clement. I had better have it out with him at once.'

She was touched, perceiving the tokens of tears, and still more by his gratitude when he learnt her intention. 'Thank you,' he warmly said. 'I durst not ask it of you, but it is an immense relief to me on our dear Cherry's account.'

'Have you been with her? How is she?'

'Braver and sweeter than I dared hope,' he said, his eyes filling again. 'Surely the Communion of saints is beginning to bring her refreshment and strength! She put me so much in mind of *him*—'

He passed on, for he was on his way to the Rood, but meant to calm himself by a few moments in the Church. There, however, he was surprised by a low sound of voices, and noiselessly following it up, he beheld, unseen himself, Mr. Fulmort and Angela in the Lady Chapel, and went on his way with a heart disburthened of one of its loads.

Yes. This had been the effect of Sister Constance's words: 'Commune with your own heart.' In the hope, nay, purpose, of at least going to Bexley with Lance on the Monday, and laying her case before Mr. Willoughby, Angela had gone to her room to prepare her confession, using the methods of self-examination taught her in old times, and in a mood to enhance rather than slur over anything she detected. Behold, as she tried herself by the questions so long laid aside, they assumed new force and meaning! The once blunted probes had acquired a sharpness they had never had before, and among her many discoveries was that her extreme dislike to having recourse to the Vicar of St Matthew's was, first, because it was Clement's desire, secondly, because, instead of an interesting penitent with a tragic crime on her hands, she should only come as the naughty girl he had known all her life; and thirdly, not because of his mismanagement, but because he understood her all too well, and had warned her of the very errors that had eaten into her life. It was only pride and love of excitement that impelled her to seek a fresh director; and it was the turning point of her life that when the conviction dawned on her she did not turn her back on it, but it so wrought with her as to take her to the Lady Chapel with her first and most parental spiritual guide on that winter afternoon of mourning.

At the end of the long interview, as the young moon shone into the twilight church, while Angela knelt on, humbled, softened, the turbid waters of her spirit quelled, and a more peaceful sorrow than she had ever known resting on her, there stole along the aisles the notes of—

> 'Comfort ye, comfort ye my people, saith your God.
> Speak ye comfortably to Jerusalem, and say unto her,
> That her warfare is accomplished,
> That her iniquity is pardoned.'

It was like a welcome from the heavenly choir to the one sinner that repenteth.

Of course it was Lance, after his duty by his fellow-mourners had been done, and he had seen them off to Bexley. He had no one to pace the cloister with, and the organ had been the chief solace and exponent of his sorrows and his yearnings. Poor Lance, who must henceforth work for himself instead of his brother, and turn out Pursuivants, for which at present he only cared because any deterioration therein would be treason to that Editor who had worked at them with loving conscientious might. The whole bequest, so justly earned as all felt it to be, was heartless and distasteful; he was disgusted to find himself a man of substance, and not only his fellow-citizens, but Fulbert had distressed him by congratulations. Fulbert had employed his time at Bexley in falling in love with Lizzie Bruce, and had therefore kept close to her father all this time, and finally driven him to the station in the dog-cart; and it was rather an effort to Lance to listen amiably to the raptures of prosperous love; above all, when he had just missed the glance, hand-pressure and farewell, which however mournful and indifferent this would have probably been, his heart and soul hungered and thirsted after. He had fancied Dr. May and his daughter would stay for luncheon, and had missed their departure by exhibiting little Gerald to some of Edgar's old friends, and the loss of the one moment he had anticipated with a throb of pleasure depressed him more than was reasonable. And yet!—There was nothing for it but to try to soothe his spirit with the harmonies that often seemed to him all he cared to live for, and fortunately there was a musical pupil teacher always looking about in the hope that Mr. Lancelot would want his services to blow for him.

He played till the bell began for even-song, and, one after another, an unusually full congregation began to drop in, including even two of the Miss Hepburns. The service was shared between old Mr. Harewood and Mr. Fulmort, only glad to relieve the three overwrought clergy who had borne the brunt of this Epiphany tide. Clement's paleness and depression were evident enough now, though still against his will.

'Angela, my dear,' he said, overtaking her in the hall, as she was going upstairs, 'Wilmet has asked for you to come and help Sister Constance in Alda's place. If you can fetch what you want at once, I will put you over.'

'O, thank you!' she cried, flushing with colour at the unexpected boon, as well as at the soft gentleness of his tone, which had of late in their hours of nursing been apt to be quick, stern, and decisive towards her, partly from his own repressed grief, partly from her habit of repelling his advances.

'You had better let me,' said Lance, as she ran upstairs. 'You are pretty well what Gerald calls used up.'

'Thank you, I wish to do this,' said Clement. 'O Lance, Dr. May and his daughter asked especially after you, and told me to give you their good-byes. And here,' lowering his voice, 'here is something I was bidden to give you.'

Lance looked at the address, and carried it quickly upstairs. It was one of Felix's neat envelopes with the crest and motto, and the address to L.O. Underwood Esq., in the familiar writing, just such as those which he had been wont to receive by hundreds. Within was a note with a still fragrant spray of dried myrtle. The contents were:

August 20th, 1872.
MY DEAREST LANCEY BOY,

I do not want to make the business a burthen and a tie to you. You have slaved enough at uncongenial and solitary drudgery for my sake. I would not ask you to go on with it on any account. I only beg you to wait one half year, and if by that time you see no prospect of what would sweeten your labours, then do as you judge best about disposing of it, and using the proceeds as you please. I know you will provide against my poor Pur falling into hands that might sully or pervert such testimony as it is able to bear. For the rest, let it be as your judgment and wishes guide you. But be patient and not discouraged. I have ascertained that there will be no opposition from the father, and I am mistaken if you do not succeed at last. I dare not pray for any earthly boon, the sense of ignorance in asking becomes so much deepened, but if I prayed for anything definite it would be for that reward for you. As it is, I venture only to ask that joys and blessings the highest and the sweetest may be showered on you, my very dear brother; you who came to help me in the time of greatest need, and whose whole life has been a continual sacrifice of taste, enterprise, and ambition for my sake. If Clement is my chief aid in this present pass, it is you to whom I have owed the most through life, and I cannot believe I shall ever become insensible to it. Perhaps there will be no leave-taking. If not, take this as mine, and believe, as I do, that we shall still join our voices with Angels and Archangels, and all the company of Heaven; and look on to the day when for the sake of the Lamb who was slain our praise may be perfected. God bless you, my dear Lance, and bring us both to meet in that everlasting Home where there is no parting.

My love to dear old Mrs. Froggatt.

Give your Daisy this myrtle spray when she is yours, and with it a brother's love from me.

Believe me ever
Your grateful and loving brother,
F.C. UNDERWOOD.

And while Lance stood in his room, drinking in with his eyes these words of affection, Angela upon the moonlit river was craving Clement's pardon for all her manifold transgressions against him.

'My dear,' he answered in a deep, sad, but sweet voice, 'I have quite as many errors against you for which to reproach myself.'

Then as they landed on the narrow sward, he put his arm round her and kissed her, and she found his tears raining on her face.

'My child, I have not done well by you,' he said, 'but I believe our dear brother has turned your face right again, and I am thankful for it. I think we shall begin a new life towards one another now. Good night, and may His blessing be with you.'

CHAPTER XLIX.

THE RIVAL OWLS.

'Save that from yonder ivy-mantled tower
The moping owl doth to the moon complain
Of such as, wandering near her haunted tower,
Molest her ancient solitary reign.'
Gray.

'Poor caterpillars, with our web broken, trying to gather it close round us,' said Geraldine, with a sort of playful melancholy, when old Squire Underwood's little table was produced, that so vast and sad a tract of table-cloth might not divide the four who met at meals.

For Sister Constance and Mr. Fulmort had won back for Angela permission to make a visit at St Faith's, certainly during Lent, and probably for a longer time, that she might be regularly instructed in nursing. The wild spirit craved for discipline as by a sort of instinct, and this the orphaned family had never been able to supply, and her affections had really been wounded enough to render nothing so welcome as shelter and protection against herself. Fulbert's English visit soon came to an end. Australia was his element, he was weary of the old country; declared there was no room to move, and having been refused by Lizzie Bruce, only wanted to get back as soon as he could. He looked Bernard all over, and pronounced that there were too many of his sort out there already, and he had rather help him to the University.

Bernard might in fact have been sent thither by subscription from the family, but he surprised them all by showing Cherry his letter to accept an under-clerkship in the house of Kedge and Underwood. It was the consequence of a consultation with Mr. Travis on means of living, though the lad had kept his own counsel till all was settled, and, he added, 'I know I've been an idle dog, but I do mean to work now;' the hitherto obstinately childish face showed manhood and self-reliance. Felix had done quite right to knock all his supports away, and that he knew it was shown by his acting at once instead of grumbling. The fate of many a comrade had taught him to rejoice that his post was not the prize of a competitive examination, and if his features and bearing perilously reminded Spooner of his brother Edgar, the absence of Edgar's tastes and talents exempted him from some of the same temptations; nor did Miss Underwood show any symptoms of spoiling him, only settling him in respectable lodgings, and making her house no more than a friendly cousinly resort. His public school-life had likewise given him a less dangerous set of acquaintance than Edgar's had been, and there were wholesome opportunities of gratifying his love of athletics. Lady Caergwent, too, on coming to town for the Session, did not forget the solitary Vale Lestonite, but requited his botanical exertions with friendly invitations for gay evenings and for quiet Sundays, both of which did much to keep up what was good, both outwardly and inwardly, in the youth.

'Kedge and Underwood' in all its branches was intensely elated at its approaching union with the great Mr. Travis of Peter Brown and Co., who was to take the style and arms of Underwood, well pleased to appropriate the rood, and bear the name of those whom he had always regarded with a true family love. The wedding was to be soon after Easter, and the pair were then to go out and make arrangements for the future welfare of the American property. Ferdinand had in jest asked Gerald if he would go back, and the child had drawn back into his aunt's arms, and answered, 'Not without Chérie.'

Wilmet had soon come downstairs again, but with the first visible signs of departing youth, the first dimming of the freshness of complexion, the first marring of the perfect oval contour of face, and with a heart heavy as much for the living sister as for the dead brother, and with the sad grieving which only mothers know for the babe whom she had never seen. John was anxious to take her from home. The last old Miss Oglandby had died suddenly during her recovery, and as all three had left him half their portions, he was now a man of considerable means, rather disproportioned to his cottage at Vale Leston. There however he meant to remain, for the sake of attending to the estate, but he hastened the preliminary business in order to proceed to that in Buckinghamshire, so soon as Wilmet should be capable of the journey. And he found the less to do, that never man had set his house in order more thoroughly than Felix. Every paper and letter was sorted, and so marked that there was not an instant's doubt whether it concerned the estate or the business; every account was clearly brought down to Christmas, and nothing left that could complicate or perplex: in many cases, especially with regard to the farms and Blackstone Gulley, there were notes of conversations, promises, or intentions. The executors had little but formal work to do.

Wilmet was only once able to come to the Priory before she left home, and she could hardly bear it, breaking down with showers of tears, as if the grief were fresh; while Geraldine went about, calm, dry-eyed, occupied, attending to Gerald, receiving callers, writing letters, and consulting with her brothers, or even helping Lance with work for the Pursuivant, but all as if the taste and flavour had gone out of her life, and nothing could interest her, except Gerald and one other employment.

She had copied her miniature of Felix for Stella, and the wistful admiration of some of the others had made her volunteer to give one to each of the family, and she spent many hours over the square open brow, clear, fearless, stedfast, well-opened grey eyes and firm sweet mouth. Wilmet, discovering what she was about, thought it so bad for her as to call for a scolding to Clement and Robina for having permitted her to undertake what must injure her eyes and feed her sorrow.

'No, don't stop me, Mettie,' said Cherry, 'I *can* do them now, perhaps I could not later.'

'You need not do them. Photographs would do quite as well, and save you.'

'I don't want to be saved. It is my great pleasure.'

'A morbid pleasure, I fear, my dear. At any rate I will not be the cause of your hurting yourself. I *will* have a photograph.'

'Don't take it now at least,' implored Cherry as the white resolute fingers closed on the original. 'Please! I cannot quite bear to let him go. Besides,' with a smile of entreaty, 'I don't think you perceive. It is not morbid. It does me good. It is like getting Clement to talk in the evening. I go over those dear lines and curves, and every touch brings back some look or word, so that it is living with him, and learning him over again, and I get to giving thanks for him best that way.'

'Well! I couldn't,' said Wilmet, not even able to look at the picture, and cautioning Robina to interfere at the first symptom of damage to eyes or spirits.

No one could be more tenderly cherished and watched over than Geraldine. Clement's devotion was more genuine and less dutiful, more loving and less compassionate than Robina had expected, for it had that essential though involuntary quality of dependence. Never before had his life given him the personal experience of affliction, and it had softened him into gentleness. He had almost erected Cherry into the place of Felix as well as her own, and leant on her for advice and sympathy. Whatever approaches to relaxation or amusement he allowed himself were to lure her to be pleased, and if she tried to be lured, it was only because she thought he needed the relief.

Robina meantime was highly effective. She took Gerald's lessons, made herself acceptable in cottages, worked hard at the schools, and got on well with Clan Hepburn, who were unusually conformable, and thoroughly considerate. Moreover, if Robin could not be the idol of the lads, she took in hand the farmers' daughters. She allured them with a German class, got up some Mission working parties—and great victory of all—persuaded a selection not only to teach in the Sunday School but to meet beforehand to have instruction for this purpose from the Rector, without imputing to them the full extent of their ignorance. Clement might well own that Lent that there were some things Robina did better than anyone else.

He had a very youthful Curate at last, lodged at the farm, and he was also assisted by Mr. Audley, who was still living with his brother, frequently going up to his oculist, but devoting himself chiefly to the care of his future district at East Ewmouth. He had accepted the offer of the incumbency willingly, for between his private income and the endowment he would be able to keep up such a staff of Curates as would compensate for his defect of eyesight, and the Mission work of the little post needed an experienced head more than good eyes.

After a few weeks it became known that on his refusal of the Bishopric of Albertstown, the offer had been transferred to the Vicar of St. Matthew's, Whittingtonia, probably at his suggestion, for he was very anxious for its acceptance, and Clement listened to him with a divided mind, for St Matthew's was still the young Rector's first love, and he loved it a good deal more than either settlers or black fellows at the antipodes. As he mournfully observed to Cherry, they would go and get some married man who would not live at the clergy-house, and would spoil the whole spirit of the place. It scarcely consoled him to be reminded that Mr. Fulmort having founded and endowed the living, had the patronage, and that being elected by the Synod in Australia, would not have to leave the appointment to the Crown.

'Ah! the Vicar!' he proclaimed as he unlocked the post-bag, and distributed the letters at the breakfast-table in the austere sunshine of March.

Next came a sort of gasping grunt.

'Well?' said Cherry.

No answer, but to lay down the letter and begin cutting bread, but in an absent way, going on as if instead of four he had the original number to cut for.

The sisters saw that no more questions were to be asked in the publicity of the breakfast-table, limited as it was. Self-contained man! Any one of his brothers would have had it out in that gasp. Robina, aware that the world consisted of herself and Gerald, would have removed it quickly, but that Gerald prolonged the consumption of his egg so unreasonably that his uncle had time to eat, drink, and look over the letter again, open the others, and even grow impatient enough to say, 'We can't wait for you all the morning, Gerald.' Then he said Grace, gave an arm to Cherry, with 'Can you spare me a few minutes?' and took her into the library.

'Does he go?'

'He says he hardly can, unless I will take St Matthew's.'

'You!'

'I can't understand it; but he says none of our old set are available. Don't be frightened, Cherry, I am not going to do anything to overthrow such comfort as is left you.'

'You can't mean that!'

'I do. This is not the kind of call that should disturb the claims of what is closest to me on earth. Nor have you been forgotten, as you will see,' as he gave her the letter.

The first thing she remarked was how differently the six years' priest was rated from the deacon who had been hunted down to the country parish. Mr. Fulmort reviewed the difficulty of finding a successor, for his most trustworthy *élèves* were all either engaged elsewhere, or else ineligible on account of health, voice, or families. Fred Somers was admirable as senior curate, but could not take the lead where both familiarity with the place was needed and experience of parsonic authority. Thus Clement Underwood, loving Whittingtonia and beloved there, full of ardour and devotion, gifted with a fine voice, facility of preaching, and musical talent, as well as a growing dignity of presence and address, together with a strong and resolute temper, powers of judgment trained under his brother, and a constitution matured in pure country air to a considerable capacity and aptitude for work, seemed to combine most of the requisites for a City parish. 'More especially,' wrote the Vicar, 'if your sister could be induced to come with you. Her quickness, ready judgment, and especially her sense of the absurd, are just what would be valuable. Mind, I don't think of her as a worker, only as an Egeria to the clergy-house, and I can even provide her with a grove, where my dear old friend Miss Charlecote, as you may remember, did the like for us.'

He explained that Miss Charlecote now entirely resided at Hiltonbury with his sister and her husband, and had made over her beautiful old house to his disposal, not to be sold or broken up, but used as a residence for some of the clergy or Church helpers. Was it possible that Miss Underwood would come and live there with her brother, while Fred Somers would act as prior to the clergy-house? Mr. Fulmort however was most guarded in not pressing his plan, and aware of the possibility of strong objections, marking his desire that Clement should not feel himself bound by what must only be considered as a feeler, since his work at Vale Leston was thoroughly valuable. Mr. Fulmort added that the endowment of St. Matthew's, with four curates and sixteen choir boys always in the clergy-house, was £600,[1] whereas the Rectory of Vale Leston, needing only one assistant at the utmost, was now reckoned as above £800.

'What do you wish, Clement?'

'Don't talk of what I wish.'

'Then what do you think right?'

'What is best for you and Gerald?' he answered, with the hardness of tone that was only pain; 'you are my trust.'

'Never so as to fetter a priest from higher duties,' said Cherry. 'Suppose this was Albertstown.'

Somehow her odd tone of consternation was a pleasure to Clement; he smiled and said, 'Never mind, that's not the question; though I suppose this is a more perplexing one, as it leaves a choice, or the semblance of one,' and he sighed.

'You know Dr. May said Gerald ought to have constant attention from a London surgeon. Would the house be healthy for him? Do you know it?'

'O yes! We choir boys used often to be entertained there. We could play at cricket in the garden, and thought it paradise. It is an island of the old London before the fire, in a quiet street all warehouses; nothing newer than Queen Anne's time; delightful to us, but I don't know how it would seem to you after this place.'

'This place! I liked it when *he* was here, but now it is only a vast desolation. Everything is that indeed; but you see, I never had roots here, like him. What should you do with it?'

'I don't see why Bill Harewood should not take the living. He is older than I was when first I came here; he makes good way with the people—better than I do with many—and he ought to have a parish that would leave him a margin of leisure—besides Robina.'

Cherry clapped her hands. 'Well done, Bobbie! She has actually earned her promotion. Even you, reluctantly as it came out, allow that she is cut out for a clergyman's wife.'

He smiled. 'Well, I allow that she is worth the most to the parish of all of you, and that it would be a cruel pity to take her away.'

'And Bill will be twice the man, and half the March hare, with her, instead of without her.'

'Yes. Granting married clergy, they are the very people for it.'

'That's right! Dear Bob! Good old Will! It is enough to decide us at once after all their patience! They would have the Rectory, but how about this house?'

'Probably John would rent it. What?'

'Only naughtiness! A little jealousy of Kester running rampant over poor Gerald's house as if he were master and more.'

'Gerald will find out who is master only too soon.'

'Ah! he sometimes asks who this and that belongs to, poor boy, and why they call him the young Squire. It may be well for him not to hear too much of that, or to begin to lord it.'

'Besides, you would bring him down in summer, and if he spends his holidays here, he would see as much of the place as boys ever do of home.'

'Ah!' cried Cherry eagerly. 'We can have poor Bear to live with us. How delightful!'

'A great consideration,' said Clement 'You really think you can stand the City?'

'As well as any place! Oh, Clem! as long as you don't want to leave us behind I am glad.'

'I was so much afraid of your sending me away alone that I begin to fear you are making home too dear.'

'Nay,' with a sobbing laugh, 'if your Vicar told you to bring me, you need not mind. I do believe those dingy streets are more to you than all that cloister and river.'

'I can't help it, Cherry. I came here solely because my brother wanted me, and am heartily thankful for it; but, as you say, I have not rooted. We could not have his love from old association, and comparatively only cared for it through him. No doubt there is much that I love and prize, and any cure of souls must be most important; but now that East Ewmouth is to be separated and Blackstone Gulley is in a manner tamed, I can't get rid of the sense that it is too highly paid and too easy a life for a strong man of thirty, good for nothing but sheer work. Nor would *he* think it desertion. He told me on that last day, when the Rectory was transferred, that the purpose was fulfilled, and I need not be hindered.'

'Too little work! Yet you are often on the point of being overdone.'

'I have been, but that was from East Ewmouth and other things that are over now. A curate there must be, because one can't be in two places at once, but except at special times of pressure, the work is hardly enough for two. It is just the thing for a man who has a brain and a pen like Will's. I never saw anything more telling than his pamphlet on godless education.'

'So we leave it to them.'

'Not so fast. I must be sure this consent is not the restlessness of grief, Cherry. Besides, we must ascertain that John approves on Gerald's account, and in the meantime, we had better say nothing to Robina.'

The proposal was too advantageous to his family for John not to look at it on all sides, indeed he would scarcely hear of it till he had met Clement and Mr. Fulmort in Whittingtonia, and looked over the house; but the inspection made him listen more favourably, and so did an interview with Gerald's doctor, and a correspondence with Cherry. Taking into account the child's incapacity for out-door sports, and Cherry's artistic and literary tastes, he saw advantages in the scheme. The Priory was too large for the reduced numbers, and all its interests and enjoyments had hinged on its loving master; but Cherry's London associations were disconnected from him, and the inducements to cultivate her art would save it from being dropped for want of the stimulus he had given; nor was the benefit of the family home for Bernard to be by any means forgotten. To be sure, Wilmet believed that Cherry could never be well or happy there, but then her rooms should be kept intact for her return when Clement might betake himself to his congeners in the clergy-house, and Wilmet was secular woman enough to think £800 a year wasted on him and his subscriptions, when it might be making Will and Robina happy.

So one spring afternoon, as Robina was trudging homewards, basket in hand, from a distant hamlet, pausing on the topmost point of the bridge to look at the swelling of the river, and the swirling eddies that rushed out of sight, she heard herself hailed, and on the Ewmouth road beheld a broad clerical undress hat, surmounting a black figure, with a bag over his shoulder. To run down the bridge and meet in the middle of a miry pool was the work of a very few seconds.

'Willie! How delightful! You're come for Easter?'

'I thought you were looking out for me.'

'Do you think I always am? for I didn't expect you. You said you were going home first.'

'So I thought till yesterday evening, but I thought—here, give me that.'

'You haven't a hand, unless you prefer it to me,' said Robina. 'No, you can't sling it up with your bag. You aren't to be trusted. There's a basin in it.'

'A regular goody basket. Eh, Bobbie, ain't you a born parson's wife? You've never asked what brought me.'

'You've not heard of a school.'

'No. What do you think of a living?'

'Oh, Willie! And is it enough?'

'That's as people may think.'

'How much is it?'

'Nearly £800.'

'Bill! You don't mean it. There must be some drawback. Who offers it?'

'Oh! just a friend.'

'A Christchurch friend? A pupil?'

'The reverse. He's a Cambridge man, and has rather been my master.'

'Your master? Not the Dean of Minsterham. Didn't I hear something about a chapter living?'

'Nothing that concerns us.'

'Do tell me, Will. You've got me on the tenterhooks. I'm sure there's something against it. It's not St Matthew's.'

'St. Matthew's! They would about as soon give it to the Walrus and the Carpenter.'

'I'm glad it is not that. What sort of a place is it? In the country?'

'Beautiful country, splendid church, freshly done up, tip-top schools and all the rest of it, that a lazy dog like me might never have hatched, but he may just manage to keep stirring.'

'Nonsense! you know better than that. What population?'

'Six hundred, or thereabouts.'

'Just the same as this. It is too good to be true. There must be some great drawback to come. Let me hear it.'

'Well, if you will have it,' said William, with appalling gravity, 'it is much the same drawback as exists in the Russian Church, where preferment goes by the petticoat. The fellow offers it to me on an understanding you mayn't approve.'

'What?'

'That I should marry his sister.'

'Oh!' with equal gravity, 'did he really make that stipulation?'

'Not in so many words, but there's such a thing as an honourable understanding.'

'And pray, what does the sister say?'

'That remains to be proved. What does she say? Come, darling Bird, had you really no notion?'

'I knew Mr. Fulmort wanted Clement to take St Matthew's, but I did not think he would.'

'He said he left me to tell you, but I did not think he could have kept it so entirely back.'

'But what is to become of Cherry?'

Will told her the designs as far as they had been unfolded to him, and her eyes glistened with tears.

'Dear Willie,' she said, 'it is not that I am not thankful and glad, but it comes so suddenly after all these long years, and it is so like turning them out.'

'Not if we set up in the Vicarage—Rectory—I beg its pardon. Besides, they'll be down here pretty often, and I shall never feel like anything but Clement's curate. It is the most wholesome thing for me, that his mode of coming up to breathe will be running down here to take note of my shortcomings.'

'As if you meant to short come.'

'I don't mean, but I shall—if ever man needed whipper-in. So you see I've taken care to provide myself. Seriously, I don't think I should ever have worked up this place as Clement has done, but having worked under him, and with you all about me, I trust not to let it down. It is too good for me, that's a fact; but then it is not too good for you.'

Robina was forced to hear, though she viewed her Will as far superior to Clement, as indeed he was in intellect and largeness of mind, though not in energy and power of work.

Earnestness and devotion were, as she well knew, deep and true in him, though native indolence and carelessness were at continual strife with them, and he was a man fitter for a small parish than a large one, since study was his happiness, and he could make the results beneficial to a wide circle, while Clement had no natural turn for books, or for anything but downright practical ministerial labour.

The change could not be made quickly, William could not resign his tutorship till the long vacation and Clement was to retain the incumbency till the new church at East Ewmouth was consecrated and the district separate, while an answer from Albertstown to Mr. Fulmort's acceptance of the diocese must precede his resignation of St Matthew's. So if restlessness had prompted Cherry's assent, she had time to find it out. The outlook however seemed to lessen her sense of dreariness, since it made her go through each sweet spring pleasure as if storing up precious memories of him who had prized them all, and as if this restored the power of feeling all things new. She talked freely and affectionately of Robina's prospects, encouraging the girl who felt her happiness rising out of the family sorrow, and grew quite shame-faced about taking the measurements of the Rectory, which she was to have the pleasure of furnishing out of her own savings. Little had been heard of Lance since he had seen Fulbert off on his second voyage. Postal cards and hurried notes kept up intercourse with Cherry and the Harewoods, but chiefly on the Pursuivant's behoof, and when he had met John in London, about the executorship, he was reported looking thin but well, and intensely busy.

In effect, he had set himself to master and estimate his business, sadly enough, but there had been hope in his brother's farewell letter, and to patient Lance a very small spark sufficed for a long time.

He found himself fully capable of maintaining the level of the Pursuivant. Not only did both Harewoods supply him with able writings, but payment and circulation were such as to attract and secure other contributors, and he, though he might not write fully up to the mark of his more scholarly and better-read brother, had all the requisites of an excellent editor, in trained facility, sagacity, common sense, humour and power of arrangement. The paper showed no tokens of declension, and the business flourished, Lance still spending part of the day in the shop, and enjoying the intercourse with his friendly customers all the more for the strong feeling they had shown for his brother. His place as gentleman had long been established, and he could always have had more society than he had time for. He was invited to fill his brother's place in almost all his capacities as citizen of Bexley, but to what could bind him permanently, he showed some doubt about immediately pledging himself. Moreover, Mrs. Froggatt was anxious to give up Marshlands to him 'whenever he should settle.'

By Lady-day he was able to make an estimate of his situation and prospects, and having done this, he wrote to Dr. May, laying the statement before him, and begging to be told whether there were any insuperable objection to his presuming to declare his attachment to Miss Gertrude May. The letter was just in the formal style for which Felix used to laugh at himself, but as the Doctor said, when showing it to Ethel, it was thoroughly manly and straightforward, without the least palaver about his position.

'No, I think he feels that his brother has ennobled it, so that he would be ashamed to apologize for it.'

'What will the child say? She has been drooping ever since poor Felix's death.'

'Long before! She flags the moment you are out of sight. I hate to see her without her little spirts of naughtiness, and my heart aches to think I ever wished to see her softened.'

'Poor Daisy-bud! It says much for her that her heart should have gone out to such a man as that. Heigh-ho! those were good old times, when one disposed of one's daughters without so much as saying, "by your leave, miss."'

'Should you ever have done it?'

'Well,' said the Doctor, not choosing to answer the question, 'you may tell him to come for Easter. I suppose that is his only time. He would have been wiser to wait a bit longer—may be till this foreign trip is over—that is if the child goes, and I don't believe she will.'

The Mays themselves had had a winter of sorrow. That living death—for it had long hardly been life—of poor little Margaret Rivers had come to an end in February. It was scarcely to be mourned. The poor girl had, since her conscience had awakened, grieved so bitterly over every outbreak of her own unhappy temper, and had suffered so sadly from depression of spirits, that the peace of her final decay had been an untold blessing. Even her mother, when she thought of the dreary lot of a sickly, suffering, almost deformed heiress, could not but resign herself to feel that 'it was well with the child.' Her father, however, who had been spared much realisation of the distress of body and mind, was restlessly unhappy at the loss, and fancied he should cure his wife's sore heart by taking her to Switzerland and the Tyrol; and Flora, in the desire to make the journey a pleasure to somebody, and noticing Gertrude's pale cheeks, proposed to take her. That whole last year, ever since her Christmas at Vale Leston, Gertrude's whole treatment of her poor little niece had been reversed; and she had changed from the somewhat hard deportment to which young aunts are prone, to a kindness which, being a late and unexpected boon, had been valued by poor capricious Margaret beyond all the steady tenderness of her grandfather and elder aunt. It had endeared Gertrude greatly to Flora, and the benefit to the girl's spirits influenced her quite as much as the advantage it would be to George to have some one to conduct to the sights, which for his own part he did not care for.

Daisy herself gave no consent. 'To be lionised by George! Rather worse than an excursion of Cook's,' she said; 'and fancy the evenings!'

'It would be a kindness to George and Flora,' said Ethel.

'You horrid creature! That's to set my conscience worrying.'

'At least, there would be the coming home again.'

'That's the way you look on travelling!' said Gertrude, laughing a little, but returning to her weary attitude, and Ethel abstained from persuasion. She had not sufficient experience of change of scene to believe greatly in its advantages, and though she was in favour of the project, it was rather with a view to the fresh start it would make for her sister at home than with the belief that either pictures or mountains could be enjoyed under George Rivers's lumbering escort. She expected that poor Lancelot Underwood's attempt would precipitate the decision, when, in answer to her brief note of invitation, he replied that he would arrive on Easter Eve.

'That's all right,' quoth the Doctor. 'He knows better than to come a-courting on Good Friday.'

The day was not, however, exempt from a visitor; Dr. and Mrs. Cheviot were away for the holidays, and the Mays were the more surprised to see Mr. Rupert Cheviot, with his dapper little umbrella, issue from the professor's door to join them on their way to church.

Except that they would have preferred not to talk at all on such a day, there was no fault to find with him; he was subdued and proper behaved, and had a good deal to say about Ammergau. He had not been so much at Stoneborough within the last few months, and Ethel suspected that he had been warned by Tom to give his sister time to recover from her winter's grief. To her, he was amusing, he was a candid, lively, pleasant person, and rated her more highly than she was used to from her sister's lovers, and seldom came in her way without holding a lively tournament in the language of jest, but with a good deal of earnest in it, and she saw enough stuff in him to make his self-complacency not so obnoxious to her as it was to her juniors. She was not sorry that Gertrude's aversion to him was so strong, but she thought it rather instinctive than reasonable. He was a man whose opinions and disposition would right themselves in process of time, but the having Daisy bound to him during the process was quite another thing.

So when Gertrude proposed walking to Abbotstoke Church in the afternoon she readily agreed, perceiving that it was far more because Cocksmoor was too obvious a resort than for the sake either of Flora, flowers for decoration, or even of Dickie, who could not be refused to his uncle for this sorrowful holiday.

And when George Rivers returned to the charge, and again promised to show the Alps through the Mont Cenis tunnel, Gertrude accepted—accepted definitively! Yes, she would go, and she talked fast and eagerly of the pleasures she anticipated.

But when walking home with Ethel, she did not utter one voluntary word.

'What time did you say young Underwood was coming?' asked the Doctor at breakfast next morning.

'He did not say the time,' said Ethel.

'Which?' asked Gertrude.

'Lancelot,' said Ethel, who had put off the announcement in hopes of doing it naturally till she had grown absolutely nervous about it.

'Not for advice?' in a startled voice.

'Can no one come here but for advice?'

'He was ill last year.'

'Aye,' muttered the Doctor, 'and got advice that he has taken pretty effectually.'

Whereupon Ethel, feeling horribly and ridiculously conscious, jumped up and talked of Cocksmoor decorations. Gertrude had insisted on making them up at Cocksmoor instead of at home. It would be a little further out of reach of 'the enemy,' and in the parsonage the sisters and Richard worked unmolested all the morning, but in the afternoon, while they were putting up their wreaths, there drove up to the lych-gate Mrs. Thomas May in her donkey chair, bringing her choice manufacture of crosses and devices, escorted by her sister Ella Ward and Rupert Cheviot. It was too cold and damp for her to venture into church, but Richard hastened out to beguile her into his parlour, and refresh her with tea, while Mr. Cheviot helped to carry in her contributions, the very crown and glory of the whole, looking about with the critical suggestive patronage of a man who had seen the world, and making recommendations which Ella eagerly seconded, and Ethel did not disapprove, but Gertrude combatted vehemently: 'It had never been so! Richard would not like it!' and out she hurried to appeal to him and call him to the rescue.

Rupert Cheviot moved to the door, perhaps in hopes of mitigating her, but as she reached the lych-gate, a young man in deep black came up on the other side, and their hands met with something in the manner that made Mr. Cheviot turn to Ella Ward and ask, 'Who is that fellow?'

'That? Oh! one of the Underwoods. The one in the business.'

'What business?'

'Oh! he's a printer, a bookseller rather. Those Underwoods pretend to be county people, but they are nothing *really* but tradesmen.'

'Mr. Cheviot is not so behindhand with the world as to think that a reproach,' said Ethel, as she caught the words, while coming forward, and over her spectacles she gave Ella one of the repressive glances which the young lady felt in her backbone. She was not at all a bad sort of girl, but the ingrain likeness to her brother Henry grew with her growth, and she had just come to the age when to get any sort of notice from any young gentleman was the prime object of her desires. Rupert Cheviot, of course, at Ethel's words went forward, and on being introduced to Mr. Lancelot Underwood, shook hands with him with rather unnecessary *empressement*.

Gertrude at once appealed to Lance's taste, 'Was it not *the thing* to have the festoons hanging loose and natural, not in stiff lines?'

'It is our way at St. Oswald's,' said Lance, 'but at Vale Leston Clement holds to following the architectural lines.'

'Ah! Vale Leston. Is not that a remarkable specimen of the later Early Pointed? I must run over some day and see it.'

'It is a very fine tower. Aren't there plenty of owls' nests in it?' said Gertrude, with a perfectly grave voice, but which brought an odd thrill of mingled amusement, pleasure, and pain, as the conviction crossed him that this was the rival owl of the academy, and he recognised the likeness to the photograph. Perhaps Gertrude was only too strongly reminded of Cherry's sketch of himself, for between grief, hard work, and anxiety, he was very thin-cheeked and large eyed, and she was by no means clear that he had not come to consult her father professionally, and that the odd answer she had received in the morning had not been an evasion.

Richard came in with a casting vote in favour of the architectural style, at which Gertrude shrugged her shoulders but submitted. Ere long a messenger appeared with the candlesticks adorned by Mrs. May, and a message that she could not stay later; and Richard, going to see after her, brought back her urgent desire that Gertrude would return at the same time. Tom said she had not been strong, and must not be out after sunset.

'O, I dare say,' said Gertrude.

'There's no more than I can easily finish alone,' said Richard.

'Indeed! Look at the font!'

'The wreaths are all ready. She really ought not to stay,' he added to Ethel; 'you know there is always a sudden chill when you come down the hill late, and as Ave says, the child is not in health to take liberties.'

Ethel went up to Gertrude and whispered, 'We must give in, Daisy, we shall have a fuss if we don't.'

She had almost said she did not care, but it was in church, and she abstained, only adding, 'You'll come too.'

Ethel assented, though it was the ruin of the quiet Easter Eventide walk her father must have meant them to have when he sent Lance to meet them there. All that could be done was to keep together. In general Rupert Cheviot was content to get up a discussion with the elder sister, but he must have scented a rival, for whether Gertrude walked fast or slow, she still found him by her side, preventing all the inquiries she was burning to make about Geraldine, and the reported changes, things that could not brook discussion before a stranger. She did manage, while Rupert was tucking in a loosened fold of Averil's cloak, to say, 'I suppose Geraldine has no picture for the exhibition this year. She has not finished her Academies.'

'No. They are nearly done, but she has not touched them for a long time now. There is a very pretty little group of some of the village children that she did last summer, but I don't think she will send it up.'

'What became of the Maid of Lorn?'

'Of course, Lady Caergwent bought it.'

There Rupert Cheviot swooped down. 'Are you any relation of Miss Underwood who painted that capital likeness of Lady Caergwent? Then I congratulate you. But is it not a great pity she does not paint in oils? There is so much more satisfaction in them.'

And no more was possible than walking five abreast, close in the rear of the donkey chair; a desultory, almost mechanical skirmish going on between Ethel and Rupert Cheviot, interspersed with occasional pert remarks from Ella and tart ones from Gertrude.

When presently Rupert began to talk of some lectures which were to be given in May, she made quick answer, 'I shan't be here. I am going abroad with the Riverses.'

This of course started the experienced vacation tourist, an Alpine clubbist, into all kinds of counsels and inquiries, evidently with a view to meeting the party on their route; but though Gertrude took care to assure him that she should be at home long before his free time, the tidings of her intended journey were, as Ethel could hear, in his very footsteps, reducing Lance to the brink of despair.

He had not recovered it when they came home, and was besides in the embarrassed state of a man who had made his purpose only too well known to the spectators; but that quality which had been audacity in his boyish days, enabled him to revive and return free and grateful answers to Dr. May's inquiries into the family plans and welfare.

But when the evening meals in the two houses were over there was nothing to prevent Tom May and his friend from strolling up the garden to the elder house, whence sounds of music were audible.

It was from the 'Messiah,' for Dr. May had asked for 'He was despised and rejected of men,' unwitting that a Sunday evening a year and a quarter ago it had rung on Gertrude's ears in a voice that, in such a passage as this, Lance's reproduced with startling, thrilling exactness.

Gertrude sat in a dark corner, with streaming eyes and heaving sobs. It was almost more than she could bear, till her tears were dried by vexation at hearing a connoisseur kind of compliment, while Dr. May observed, 'I did not know what an instrument it was you thought you were losing when you asked me about it, Lance.'

'I have seldom heard it surpassed, except by first professionals!' said Mr. Cheviot. 'May I ask what teaching you had?'

'I was a choir boy at Minsterham,' said Lance, in his straightforward way.

'Oh! I did not know cathedrals gave such advantages. Ah! I see you have "My Queen" here, Gertrude. May we not have it?'

It would have been an utter impossibility even if it had not been as the Doctor said, speaking up for her. 'We do not have that style of thing this week.'

'Quite right, sir; one forgets.'

What! was he going to patronise Dr. May? And then he began to talk of the choruses at Ammergau.

'I do believe,' exclaimed Gertrude, as she parted with her sister at night, 'that he has primed himself with it on purpose.'

'I think he was really impressed there, and that it has done him good.'

'I believe you have a turn for him! I should not mind if he would only not come here bothering poor Lance. How worn he looks! Mind, Ethel, you tell me if Papa says anything about him. I could not bear for poor Geraldine to have any more troubles.'

'Very well,' said Ethel, 'but I do not think there is anything amiss with his health.'

'He has with his spirits though, and spirits tell on health; his especially. Now, Ethel, I know Rupert Cheviot always was a hero of yours.'

'A most unjustifiable interpretation of my not hating the poor man as much as you do,' said Ethel, much amused.

'I will say for him you are the one person he never patronizes. But I want you to look at the contrast, Ethel, between the two owls—simplicity and self-complacency; and when *one* really has such a splendid talent.'

'Yes, a double first class man,' said Ethel, in wilful mischief, exceedingly tickled at Lance's unconscious auxiliary, though sorry for him.

'Who cares for a first class?' exclaimed contemptuous Daisy. 'It only makes people intolerable.'

Nevertheless Lance did not spend by any means the happy Easter Sunday he had figured to himself, and many times felt that he would have done better to have deferred the crisis of his hopes and anxieties till the great feast day was at an end. For the May family were beset by Rupert Cheviot from morning till night, and Lance was tormented at moments when he most desired to free himself from the whole subject, by instinctive perception of his rivalry, and sense of the small chance that he, the half-educated tradesman, could have beside the brilliant, successful scholar, in a gentleman's position, and rising fast.

That Gertrude was cross was plain enough, and much more so to the Owl of the Academy than to the Owl of the Church tower; but Lance was sufficiently aware of the wayward nature of the damsel to ascribe her contradictoriness to the rampant coyness of inclination, and her civility to himself to kindness to her father's guest, Felix's brother and a manifest inferior, like the chemist at Ewmouth. Then her foreign tour was so often mentioned that it seemed to him that her father must have intended it as a diversion after all the agitations she had undergone, and that his coming had only been encouraged in order to put an end to the whole affair, and dispose of him and his presumption as soon as possible. So that all the kindness he received from the Doctor and Ethel only went for compassion, and he tossed about all night—true owl as he was for sleeplessness—meditating on the coming death-blow to his hopes, and whether it would be better to resign them in a conference with her father, or to put his fate to the touch in person, since he had gone so far that he could not hang back and do nothing.

The wan heavy-eyed countenance that came down in the morning moved the Doctor to the observation to his elder daughter, 'Daisy has got a fellow there more finely strung than most men. I hope she will comport herself accordingly. Tantrums won't do with that sort of organization.'

Ethel most decidedly put herself out of the way that morning, resolved not to make the holiday serve as a plea from absenting herself from the Monday care she bestowed on sundry charities, and declining the aid Gertrude offered, as a refuge from possible inroads from the Cheviot.

'You had better not waste your opportunities,' said Ethel; 'I dare say Mr. Underwood would show you the way through that thing of Mozart's that you have been despairing over.'

'O no, Ethel,' with a glance at the pale face, but it suddenly grew vividly bright as Lance said, 'If you are so kind as to be thinking of my headache, I do assure you it is nothing at all—just what this would be the best cure for.'

'Are you sure?' asked Gertrude solicitously.

'Quite,' he said, smiling. 'I should make no difference at all at home. It is the sort that is defeated by taking no notice of them; and music, and with you——'

'Would drive such ears as yours distracted, I should think,' said Gertrude, nevertheless consenting. 'You see I have tried to follow your advice, but what I have never heard, and have no one to interpret, becomes a mere wilderness to me.'

Lance knew that in his native language of melody he should, birdlike, win courage, but hardly was his finger on the keys before Daisy leapt up in a kind of fury. 'There's that eternal Owl coming down the garden! Come this way,' and she rushed away, beckoning him to follow her into the schoolroom. 'There, the windows look out the other way! It is too intolerable to be taken in the rear! I'll not stand it any longer! The Moss troopers in the morning indeed!'

Both were full of that odd sort of exhilaration always inspired by hide and seek with a visitor, and Lance looked about and recognised the room. 'I have been here before,' he said, 'when you showed me your aquarium.'

'Ah! the Daisiana. You were the hero of that watery adventure, though we little thought that small boy Charlie was to come forth in such colours! What an age ago it seems! I should like to see the Kitten's tail again.'

'Should you? I am sure Cherry would manage it! It would be——'

'Only too full of recollections,' said Gertrude, with a little shudder. 'It was the first time I ever saw——'

Instead of answering, Lance took a miniature from his breast and put it into her hand. She drew in her breath with a gasp. 'How beautiful!' she said, and gazed on through one of the tear mists that can almost convert a portrait into a presence. It was a long time before she said, 'This is better than the first.'

'Each that Cherry has finished has brought out some fresh expression. You like it?'

'O, so much!'

'Will you keep it?'

'She was only to do one for each of you.'

'Don't you remember what *he* called you?'

Gertrude held the picture to her lips for a moment, wiped a tear from the glass and said, 'That dear Cherry hasn't been doing it for me.'

'N-no, not exactly.'

'Then it is yours! Oh! that is not right. Only let me have a photograph.'

'I had rather you kept this.'

'I could not! I must not! I ought not,' putting it from her like a temptation.

'Nay, it is yours by every right. By that which makes it unspeakably precious to me to give you my very best and dearest, and by a better right of your own, of affection,' he said, eagerly.

She gave a little cry.

'Don't start,' he said. 'Perhaps I ought not to have said so, but when one watches with feelings such as mine, one sees——.'

She leant back, hiding her face, and crying quietly but unreservedly.

'If he had been like most men,' said Lance, 'if he had not made his whole life a sacrifice and had ever let himself out, I fully believe he would have given you the right. I felt and knew he had never been so near caring for any one.'

She looked up with glowing face, and moist eyes, and tried to say something, but could only utter 'No! It would be too—too much to dare to think so.'

And as she thought of that interview, she wept more than before, though they were scarcely sad tears. Lance longed for the right to soothe her, but only durst lay his hand on the back of her chair. 'If anything could make you more dear to me,' he said, bending over her, 'it would be this! Nobody else so revered that great heart. I thought I knew him best, but every day at Bexley brings up so many tokens of what he was that I seem to have only known him by half.'

'Tell me.'

And Lance told many an instance of the doings of Felix's right hand unknown to his left, and she listened with all her soul. It was more than half an hour before she said, 'Then are you all alone?'

'With Mrs. Froggatt for the present, but I have decided on nothing permanently. My dear brother told me I need not hold on, nor do I think I can without a ray of hope.'

'What would you do?' she said, a thrill or two having half but indefinitely revealed to her his drift.

'I don't know yet! Nor care! Most likely, try what music in Germany or Italy would do for me.'

'O, don't go!' cried Gertrude, 'don't!'

'Do you tell me not?'

'I don't know, but oh! my heart has ached, ached, ached, all this time, and somehow it aches rather less when you are here!'

'Dearest!' he exclaimed.

'Stay,' she said, pushing back her hair, and looking scared. 'I don't think it fair. You know I never could, if—if——.'

'Of course not; I understand that,' said Lance; 'but is not that what I love you ten thousand times more for?'

'But I shall always care most for him!'

'Yes, yes, I know you must; but now I know that some day you may care a little for me, I can wait patiently, any time you please.'

'And not hate it all, nor go away?'

'Never, while you bid me stay.'

He broke off as steps came along the passage, and a maid's knock, and 'Mr. Rupert Cheviot is in the drawing-room, ma'am.'

'Miss May is *out*,' said Gertrude emphatically.

The maid had sentiment enough to abstain from saying he had asked for both sisters, but the next moment she returned to say he had asked for Miss Gertrude.

'Tell him I am particularly engaged,' she said, leaping up indignantly. 'Aye!' she exclaimed, 'I will be delivered from that prig of Tom's. He shall never pester me more.'

'There is an effectual way of preventing that,' said Lance, with a lurking smile.

'Well, I suppose it must come to that sooner or later, and I do trust you not to tease and bother.'

'I will strive to make your feeling the rule, not of mine, but of my demonstration of it,' said Lance, tingling all over with suppressed ecstasy; 'that is, as far as I can help.'

'I can't understand your liking it! An old, dry, used-up heart!'

'But on whom? I am but too content with——'

A rapid booted tread was at the door; it was hastily opened. 'Gertrude, what's the meaning?' said the professor. 'Oh! I beg your pardon, Mr. Underwood.' This with withering politeness, and the door was shut again.

'He is going to Papa,' Gertrude laughed, with her natural mischievous triumph; then, laying her hand on Lance's arm, she exclaimed, 'Now, whatever you do, promise me not to be bullied into giving up the shop;' then, lowering her tone to its former tenderness, 'What he could do is good enough for any one.'

'So I feel,' said Lance, 'though I could drop it, if you wished. My personal share in the retail trade I mean, of course, not the editorship, for that is my sheet-anchor.'

'The Pursuivant! I thought I never could touch it again.'

'His poor Pur,' repeated Lance. 'I must show you this note, though I am ashamed. And he bade me give you this;' as from the depths of a business-like pocket-book he extracted an envelope, and from it the note and dried piece of myrtle. She greeted it with a little cry, and fresh tears. 'Ah! he said you would remember,' said Lance.

'Remember! I should think I did! Didn't he tell you?'

'I know nothing but what he wrote here. He left this for me to have, after it was all over.'

'I see! I see! O, I am glad you did not give it me at first. Dear, dear thing! Now I know! That day when he came here he made me gather it for him, and told me he had one great wish, and I was to remember it when I saw this.'

'And that great wish?' It was an odd sort of wet-eyed smile of Lance's, but then she had rested her head against him. 'Did you know it?'

'I don't know. It was the day I was half wild with misery and a strange sort of gladness together, only one could not break out with his calm eye on one—the day he came here, and Papa told him what was the matter with him. Then he sat with me, and he said things to me that made me feel as I had never done before. He didn't mean it, I know, for it was all telling me how it was with him, and how, if he were well, he never could have thought in that way of any one. It just made me feel that his saying it to me showed——'

'Showed what might have been,' said Lance. 'Yes, it was more than direct words would have been from any one else.'

'And he kept on mixing in things about you, and what you had been to him, but I wouldn't see what he was driving at; for, Lance, I must tell you now it did make me feel to love—love him really—and not be ashamed; if he thought me worth telling *all that*—and it was so nice to be able, however it was to end, that I did not want to do anything else, and I couldn't bear the sound of your name then, though when I remember that look, and that wish, and see the spray of myrtle, Lance, I must have had you if you had been—as bad as Rupert Cheviot himself.'

But she actually did lift up her face with a look that allowed him to bend down and kiss it, as he said, 'See, he only told me to give it you, *when*—not on those terms. Though you are doubly precious, because I shall ever feel you to be his gift.'

She had certainly accepted infinitely more than he could have dared to anticipate from her outset, and now she was perhaps glad of the respite afforded by reading the letter that he had put into her hand, and which lasted till again came steps.

'Papa this time,' she whispered, as he opened the door, calling, 'Ethel, here's Tom in a—Hollo, I thought you were in the drawing-room.'

'Don't go,' they cried with one voice, and Gertrude, saying, 'May I? I must!' put Felix's letter into his hand.

He pushed up his spectacles to read it, but he could not do so dry-eyed, and Lance turned aside blushing and embarrassed.

'Dear fellow!' he exclaimed. 'Well—that's a pretty good testimonial to bring in your hand, Lance.'

'You must not believe half of that, sir,' said Lance huskily.

'Eh, Daisy, mus'n't I? And pray what am I to say to Tom about your shocking behaviour in denying yourself to Mary's brother-in-law? Music lessons have been dangerous things ever since the gamut of Hortensio.'

'May I? He knows!' was Lance's eager question to Gertrude, as he took her hand and looked up mutely, but with lustrous eyes, to the Doctor.

'So you have made it right, children. There, then, Lancelot Underwood, you have got my youngest darling, and I can tell you I never made one of them over with greater confidence and comfort. If we have spoilt our most motherless one, you know what that is, and there's good stuff in her too. Indeed, I never thought so well of the chit before.'

'I'm sure I didn't,' said the chit herself dreamily, causing them both to smile, and Lance to mutter something inarticulately foolish and happy, but the clang of the dinner-bell startled them, and they sprang away to their rooms during the five minutes' law; while Ethel, coming in from the street, met her father in the hall, smiling unutterable things. 'No!' she exclaimed. 'You don't mean it! I didn't think she could so soon!'

'I fancy Lance may thank Tom and his great Rupert for that.'

'He did worry her intolerably! Oh! papa, I trust it is no mistake.'

'I think not, Ethel. Once accepted, the warm living outcome of affection cannot fail to be infinitely better than the dream she has been brooding over so long, and as saint-worship it will hurt neither of them. Ah well! I should have liked the other to be one of us, but it was not to be. He was the making of our Daisy, and this one is his equal in all but what age only can give.'

'Ah! I always wished to see Daisy in love,' said Ethel, rather as if the wish had recoiled upon her.

'What's to be done now? There's the Grange carriage,' exclaimed the Doctor.

Yes, Flora, George, and Dickie, all had driven in to lunch at the early dinner, and to face those cheeks whose glow no cold water could moderate, those eyes that shone strangely under downcast lids.

In fact, Mr. Rivers had been so much pleased by Gertrude's consent to the Swiss expedition that he had given his wife no peace till she had come to arrange it. Gertrude was taken aback. 'Oh dear!' she exclaimed, 'I had forgotten all about it.'

'Forgotten!' Poor Mr. Rivers looked at her with all the amazement and reproach his lustreless black eyes could express.

'I remember now, George,' she faltered, colouring unreasonably; 'it was very kind.'

'But you promised, Daisy,'

'We will talk it over, George,' said her father, coming to her rescue, as in her increasing softness she looked down convicted. 'You see, *I* have not been consulted.'

George took this in earnest, and lumbered into an apology, while Dickie rather unrestrainedly laughed, and said, 'Grandpapa, when does Aunt Daisy consult you?'

'When she has made up her mind,' said the Doctor, with a glance at her.

But Daisy would at that moment have been thankful enough to consult him. True, the sentiment she had felt before had scarcely been love, so repressed and undeveloped had it been; and the flood of bliss, the wonderful sense of affection that had mastered her, was something entirely unlike the slow, measured way in which, even at the first moment of her half-consent, she had fancied yielding to Lance. In this one half-hour he had acquired a place with her so entirely independent of his being Felix's brother, nay, so substantially dearer than Felix himself, that she was half ashamed of her present self, half shocked at having called her former feelings by the name of love, and wholly and foolishly in despair at the notion of a six weeks' tour away from Lance.

Thus Ethel found her, when, on the break up of the dinner, she stole a few moments of consultation with the two young lovers before following her father and the Riverses to the drawing-room.

'Oh! Ethel, what shall I do?' Daisy was saying with tears in her eyes. 'Isn't it a judgment on me for ever saying I would go! I only did it because that Rupert baited me so, and I was so miserable I was ready to go anywhere out of his way.'

'But is it not a pity you should not go?' said Lance.

'What, you?'

'You know I cannot be much away from Bexley, so it would not make much difference that way,' he said, blushing; 'and I am afraid you will have to lead a very humdrum life; so had you not better see a little of the world?'

'I shall hate it all. Oh! Ethel, get me off! Things like this are acts of oblivion, you know.'

'I certainly would if it were for your pleasure,' said Ethel, thoughtfully; 'but you see this is the first thing that has seemed to do poor George Rivers any good.'

'And,' said Lance, affectionately, 'surely, dearest, it can do our happiness no harm to try to lend a little of it to others.'

'Ethel!' she cried out, 'I do believe he is going to make me good. There! I give in; I'll go, and not be more a victim than I can help.'

'Lance,' said Ethel, 'by-the-by, I've never congratulated you. Just tell me—suppose you were asked to go too, could you?'

He considered a moment, shutting his eyes as the brightened face looked up to him. 'I don't like to say no,' he answered; 'it is an immense temptation, but there is nobody to take my place on the spur of the moment, and at this time of year too. Indeed, if I went now, besides upsetting everything, it might hinder me from getting a holiday later, when we might want it more,' he added, crimsoning.

'I see,' said Ethel. 'Do you know, Daisy, I've a great mind to go instead of you.'

'O you old darling duck of an Ethel! I should as soon have thought of asking the gate-post. But if you would! Oh! wouldn't I take good care of Papa.'

'Yes, I think you would, Daisy, and it is my last chance, you see. I believe I shall do as well for George to lionize.'

'And be a dozen times better for Flora—and write such letters!'

'So here goes.'

'Now, Lancelot, if you don't delight in that Ethel of mine beyond every other creature—I suppose, for human nature's sake, I must let Cherry come first, but if I thought you would snub her like Charles, or patronise her like George, or even be hail fellow well met with her like Hector, I'd never let you into the family! Now—' as signs of clearing the dinner became evident—'I'll get my hat: there's no place to sit in in the house.'

Ethel's proposition was received with rapture.

George and Flora had just been informed by the Doctor how the case stood. They had been far too much absorbed in their own sorrows to mark the course of Daisy's feelings, but Flora had seen enough at luncheon to be prepared for the disclosure. Nobody could like his position, and she did not pretend to do so; but she saw it was of no use to expostulate, and abstained from letting her husband perceive, as she did, how entirely that of a tradesman it was.

'I am sorry it was not Rupert Cheviot,' was all she said, 'and very sorry not to take Daisy with us; but it is no use to coerce her, even if one could. She would be no good now.'

So Ethel was the more warmly accepted. Even the Doctor was happier that Flora should have her sister with her, and liked the notion of a *tête-à-tête* with his Daisy ere she was transplanted; and as to Flora, her gratitude on her own and her husband's account knew no bounds.

'Dear, dear old Ethel!' she said; 'such a life-long sister as you, bearing with one, and forgiving one through all, is as sweet and precious a relationship as almost any the world has to give!'

[1] To this it had been raised from the original 250*l.* partly by the Ecclesiastical Commissioners, and partly by Mr. Fulmort's brother and Miss Charlecote. (*author*)

CONCLUSION.

'Now for the double wedding!' said Mother Constance, as one September evening the Reverend Charles Audley entered the Superior's room in the temporary daughter-house at East Ewmouth.

'What should an old blind Australian know of gay weddings?'

'Don't you know that to hear of mundane festivities is the delight of convents?'

'The festivities were to no great extent.'

'Of course not, but you must begin at the beginning, for I lost all knowledge of everybody and thing that had not got small-pox.'

For the malady had been raging in a town at the other end of England, and the special hospital where she and her staff had done service had only just closed, and quarantine was over, so that she could return.

'Which is the beginning?'

'Mine are only confused lights since Lance brought his Daisy to see me on their way to the sands by St. Kitt's Head. What a fresh pleasant face it is! and with a spice of originality in it, too.'

'Commend me to the elder sister's. Leonard Ward had prepared me for it, when I met him circulating among the unhappy deported Melanesians in Queensland. I believe she was the making of him, and a noble work he is.'

'Come, I can't let you go back to the Antipodes. Miss May was abroad at that time, and plans were not in the least fixed, only that Lance should not give up the retail business.'

'No, he said very justly, that if he did so, Mrs. Lamb would never be contented without her husband doing the same, and that would be destruction. When I went down to the S.P.G. meeting at Bexley, I saw a good deal how the land lay, and found that all the neighbours were quite ready to visit Lance's wife, and she will live at Marshlands in a very different style from the old times we remember. I am afraid Mrs. Lamb will be a trial, but she is prepared for that.'

'It was an excellent plan to have the weddings together at Stoneborough. They could hardly have borne another here.'

'No. There was a proposal that Will and Robina should be married at Minsterham, but they rather shrank from that, and the De la Poers wrote urgently to persuade her to have the wedding at Repworth, but she saw he disliked it, and then Miss May came forward and undertook to manage it all, "being inured to such affairs," as she put it; but there was an old promise in an unguarded moment that all their young Ladyships should be bridesmaids, and they held to it: so Lord and Lady De la Poer brought a bevy of daughters to the Swan at Stoneborough, and you had better be prepared, for they are coming to see Vale Leston to-morrow, and probably will come on here. Nice people, exceedingly fond of Robina. I never saw such loads of wedding presents. Lady Caergwent gives a great Russian samovar, labelled for "school feasts."'

'I suppose Fernan—I beg his pardon, Mr. Travis Underwood—did not give another diamond bouquet.'

'No. The common sense keeping he has got into showed itself in the choice of all the household plate, just the same, for each of the couples.'

'And Angela was not there, I know. Our Mother wrote to me that the poor child was so distressed at the notion of going that as they did not make a point of it, she thought it better not to send her. I think she will soon be allowed to become a postulant. It seems evidently the life she needs. But who were Miss May's bridesmaids?'

'She set her face against any but her sister and Geraldine—would hear of no one else, though Cherry had always avoided it before. They called themselves the elderly bridesmaids. What! does the conventual mind require to know what they wore? Not the same as Robina's, who had white and blue ribbons; but they were in—what do you call it?—a Frenchified name for some kind of purple.'

'Mauve?'

'Yes, mauve with white fixings; very becoming to Cherry.'

'Who married them?'

'It was a joint performance of Mr. Wilmot, Richard May, and myself, but we had a characteristic hitch. They gave my couple the first turn, and when I held out the book for the ring, my bridegroom began fumbling in his pocket and reddening up to the roots of his red hair, while poor Robina's eyes grew rounder and rounder under her veil, and Clement rose taller and taller behind her, looking as if just cause or impediment had arisen, and he only wished he had not been commanded to hold his peace.'

'Did you marry them with the key of the door?'

'Not exactly—Lance's long hand came in between with the ring in his palm.'

'Only one between the two couples?'

'No, Bill had asked Lance to get both together, and had never claimed his own. It was a fine incident to tease him about, but he says he has his memory made fast to him now for ever. After all, Lance gave him the wrong one, and the brides had to change afterwards.'

'So they were married with each other's rings?'

'Yes, and I don't think they much regret it.'

'Where are they gone?'

'To see little Stella in her glory, and the other two are bound to a great Rhenish musical festival, and to hear the Freiburg and Lucerne organs. They went off together in the same railway carriage, and were only to part in London. The whole affair was as quiet as possible. I am glad it was at Stoneborough. Dr. May filled the place that neither Clement nor Harewood could have borne to take.'

'And you have not told me of Cherry or Clement.'

'You will see them to-morrow, and I think you will be satisfied about Cherry. The wrench last July was dreadful; both she and Clement say that they could never have made up their minds to it if they had known the grief it would cause in the village, and the partings they would undergo, but it has certainly been good for her. She looks well, and she says that though a little while ago she felt as if she had nothing to hope or fear, a month of Whittingtonia has shown her enough to engross a hundred lifetimes.'

'And little Gerald?'

'He walks better, and he is exceedingly happy at Stoneborough. Dickie May, the Archdeacon's son, you know, a fine fellow of fourteen, is so kind to him, teaches him to make models, and I fancy has secured that admiration little boys pay to big ones. They say the poor little fellow will probably outgrow his weakness and do well in the end, but that he must be kept at home for a good many years.'

'At which I suppose Cherry cannot repine.'

'No; he is her delight; and with Bernard to give the element of manhood and spirit, I don't think he will be spoilt, for Clement is sure to be strict enough. I never saw any one more improved than Bernard, by-the-by; he is grown into a reasonable being, and as devoted and attentive to Cherry as they all are. I am sure she is happier even now than she ever thought to be again! There was as much smile as tear when she told me that she was coming to see Felix and Theodore to-morrow, and to admire Wilmet in the Priory. She is carrying on a gleam from the past sunshine of her life.'

'She is learning to *pleurer son Albert gaîment*,' said Mother Constance. 'So we must when the pillars of our joy are taken from us here. And sooner or later we can do so, if we can believe of them that they have become pillars that shall never be removed, with the new Name written upon them, in the House of the Lord above.'

245

Made in the USA
Middletown, DE
29 June 2020